The Chocolate Maker's Wife

ALSO BY KAREN BROOKS

Fiction

The Brewer's Tale

The Locksmith's Daughter

The Curse of the Bond Riders trilogy:
Tallow
Votive
Illumination

Young Adult Fantasy

It's Time, Cassandra Klein

The Gaze of the Gorgon

The Book of Night

The Kurs of Atlantis

Rifts Through Quentaris

Nonfiction

Consuming Innocence

The Chocolate Maker's Wife

Karen Brooks

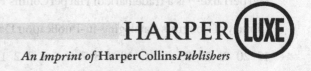

HARPER LUXE

An Imprint of HarperCollinsPublishers

Originally published in Australia by HQ Fiction in 2019.

HarperCollins books may be purchased for educational, business, or sales promotional use. For information, please e-mail the Special Markets Department at SPsales@harpercollins.com.

FIRST HARPERLUXE EDITION

ISBN: 978-0-06-291238-1

HarperLuxe™ is a trademark of HarperCollins Publishers.

Library of Congress Cataloging-in-Publication Data is available upon request.

19 20 21 22 23 LSC 10 9 8 7 6 5 4 3 2 1

This book is for two Stephens.
First, Stephen Bender: dearest of friends, and mentor.
It's also for Stephen Brooks, my love, my life.

It is interesting to consider that beverages like coffee, chocolate and even sherbet, seemingly innocuous to us (because they are non-alcoholic) began life in England as dangerous, expensive and exciting symbols of dissidence . . .

—Antonia Fraser, *King Charles II*

Revenge is a kind of wild justice; which the more man's nature runs to, the more ought law to weed it out . . . Certainly, in taking revenge, a man is but even with his enemy; but in passing it over, he is superior; for it is a prince's part to pardon . . .

Some, when they take revenge, are desirous the party should know whence it cometh. This is the more generous. For the delight seemeth to be not so much in doing the hurt, as in making the party repent.

—Francis Bacon, "On Revenge," 1625

Contents

PART ONE
May to September 1662

To conclude, if God give you success, use it humbly
and far from revenge. If He restore you upon hard
conditions, whatever you promise, keep.

—Charles I's final letter to his son, Charles,
Prince of Wales, 1649

'Twill make Old women Young and Fresh;
Create New-Motions of the Flesh,
And cause them long for you know what,
If they but Tast of Chocolate.

—*Chocolate: or, An Indian Drinke,*
translated by James Wadsworth, 1652

ONE
In which a young woman encounters four men and some horses

On the 29th of May, 1662, God Almighty and Ever-Punishing chose to make it bloody hot. At least that's what Rosamund heard Sissy Barnes say as she staggered into the kitchen with a pail of milk. The current of warm air she brought with her caused the other two scullions to moan and flap their aprons at their faces, earning a scolding from Dorcas, the housekeeper, who told them to stop making such a blasted fuss. Rosamund pressed her lips together lest she too be accused of making a blasted fuss and instead picked up the tray of bread, melting cheeses and coddled eggs to deliver to the sweltering guests waiting to break their fast in the taproom.

Tobacco smoke hung thick in the air, punctuated only by the chittering of the finely dressed women, who appeared to be competing with one another to see who could be the loudest. As Rosamund entered, one of them lamented in strident tones that the inn didn't provide coffee, a protest greeted with much head-shaking and tut-tutting. Rosamund didn't feel inclined to inform the heavily powdered woman, whose cheeks carried more patches than flesh, that they did indeed provide the bitter, silty beverage, but supplies had run out with the sudden influx of visitors. The women made a point of ignoring Rosamund, holding her responsible for their having to drink ale or sack like commoners instead of the fashionable new drink fast becoming the rage in London. Their male companions offered her sly smiles and surreptitious winks. One of the so-called gentlemen even leaned behind his lady to pat Rosamund on the bottom. Overlooking this liberty, as she did all others because her stepfather, Paul Ballister, said a man was within his rights to treat a woman any way he wanted (a view Rosamund silently maintained her grandmother, Lady Ellinor Tomkins, would have contested), she replaced the tray behind the counter and waited to see if her services would be further required. The men and women puffed on their pipes, sipped the liquids they claimed to despise, ate the tepid but tasty food placed in front of them and prattled emphatically—usually about whatever they were reading in the news sheets and pamphlets so many of them brought with them from the capital or purchased in town. She'd have to make sure to remove them when they'd finished lest Paul happen upon them. Poring over the discarded papers that he was too tight to buy himself, he would rail about the "rubbish royalist clap-trap" the "cunting correspondents" published, then take his anger out on all those around him—mostly, her. He never said anything negative about the King within earshot of the guests; he was too clever for that. Choosing to nod amiably as they recited snippets from the pages and praise His Majesty like the most prac-ticed sycophant, he presented a picture of affability.

Looks could be so deceiving.

Rosamund rubbed a streak of egg white from her bodice and frowned at the greasy mark it left on an otherwise reasonably clean gown. For the umpteenth time she wished she could read the news sheets too, especially since whatever was written seemed to incite such passionate conversations and aggravate Paul so very much. A contrary part of her had no doubt she'd like what he loathed, and that gave her a little warm feeling right between her breasts.

She examined her fingernails and resisted the urge to chew them. Her mother had warned her that her usual lackluster efforts at personal hygiene were unacceptable while there were so many guests, and insisted she wash her face and hands every night and morning. Pleased to obey her parent in this instance, knowing the additional patrons also meant Paul was kept occupied tending to them, Rosamund enjoyed feeling relatively clean, even if the condition was only temporary.

When she glanced at her reflection in the moldy mirror hanging behind the bar, she marveled at how pink her cheeks were when they weren't decorated with smut and mud, and how her brows formed neat arches without soot in them. Whereas no one would have given her a second look a week ago, it was remarkable what a little soap and water could do. Tucking a stray lock of hair back into her cap, she was trying to fathom how she could remove the egg stain when she caught a glimpse of her stepfather weaving his way among the tables, bowing in his fawning way to all and sundry. Before he could detain her, Rosamund ducked below the counter and slipped out of the room. Keen not to be accused of slovenliness, or anything else that might earn her stepfather's opprobrium, she grabbed the besom and some rags and swiftly ascended to the upper floors, wiping the bannister as she went, searching for the dust and dirt inevitably trailed inside from the road. The Maiden Voyage Inn might be on the verge of decrepitude, but there was no reason for the old place to be filthy as well.

Squeezing against the wall to allow some patrons passage, dropping a curtsey and murmuring a "God's good morning" as she did, Rosamund couldn't remember the place being so full. Why, if they'd been in Bethlehem and the blessed Joseph and Mary had asked for a room, they would have been turned away. As it was, anyone who was anyone (and quite a few with no claim even to that) had left London either to join the King in celebrating his bride's arrival in Portsmouth or simply to celebrate. Rumor had it the real festivities wouldn't commence until King Charles brought his Portuguese wife, Queen Catherine, back to Hampton Court, and would no doubt resume all over again when the court moved to Whitehall. Not that anyone seemed to care. Lords, ladies, courtiers, hangers-on, servants, messengers, actors, actresses (whores by any other name, according to Paul—which didn't stop him ogling each and every one), and canny vendors had spent the best part of the past month rushing from town to country and back again like bees in a summer field. They drank like thirsty dogs and, as she overheard Mr. Rohan, the night soil man, saying to Dorcas, rutted like "tiffanytraders persuaded they were bleeding rabbits," whatever that meant.

With all the extra guests came additional duties, and Rosamund didn't mind throwing on an apron and helping the servants they'd employed to assist with the rush—after all, they lightened her tasks considerably. With more hands, they could present the illusion of being accustomed to serving fine people and catering to their peculiar needs and tastes, never mind all the personal servants guests had at their beck and call. Beds for the extra men and girls had been made up in the stables, and two lads even dossed down in the kitchen. There was no doubt her stepfather and mother were enjoying the bounty these sorts of patrons and their coin provided. Her mother donned her best dress each day, fashioned her hair beneath a stylish bonnet (Rosamund was certain she'd seen it atop the head of an actress who'd stayed with them one night about three months ago) and, apart from ordering the staff around as if she were a queen in her own right, had arisen early today so she might escort a party of their guests to the river. From there, some would board craft to take them back to London, while others would watch the flotilla of caparisoned boats passing. Even Paul had made an extra effort with his brocaded Sunday jacket, fixing a smile beneath his finest periwig and visiting the barber for a shave. He'd ordered his sons from his first marriage, the twins Fear-God and Glory, to bathe, make sure their collars and cuffs were clean, and to assist the ostler they'd hired, an ex-sailor named Avery who'd joined the Navy years ago and fought under Cromwell and, after the Restoration, for King Charles too, in the hope it would make his fortune. Fighting for the Lord Protector, he'd enjoyed regular pay, but since the King returned, he hadn't seen a single penny, even though he'd been back from Guinea for months. He'd many a bitter word to say about His Majesty, who could spend a fucking fortune on his strumpet's jewelry but not see fit to pay good honest sailors who helped secure the throne as well as new territories for the crown.

Rosamund was actually grateful to the King—not for spending the money Parliament granted him on his latest fancy-woman, but because his marriage kept her stepfather from noticing her lapses of judgment or finding flaws in her work and using these as a pretext to give her one of his lessons. She tried so hard to be good and obedient as the catechism she recited for him every day demanded. While she didn't adhere to the rules around cleanliness as much as she probably should, she felt there were good reasons for that and God in His wisdom would understand. Mind you, spotless or dirty, well-behaved or disobedient, it didn't seem to matter, as Paul would always find reasons to punish her. Thus she'd developed the habit of keeping her ears and eyes tuned for his presence lest he order her into his study and close the door or find her alone in a corner of the inn or the stables and begin the lesson there. He could be quieter than a hungry cat stalking a mouse, looming out of the shadows and pouncing when she least expected it. However, as long as the inn was at capacity, she was relatively safe from Paul—and his sons, who were fast developing the unnatural tastes of their father—and could enjoy the pleasure of warm water and soap and more besides. If that meant the King deserved her gratitude, well, she wouldn't begrudge him a little. As far as Rosamund was concerned, even though these royal hangers-on treated her as if she were the ash in their hearths, she wished they'd never leave.

Rosamund wished for many things of late. It was nine years since her beloved grandmother Lady Ellinor Tomkins had died and she'd been rudely taken from the comfort of Bearwoode Manor. She might not have been a legitimate granddaughter—no one, not even the servants at Bearwoode, bothered to pretend that her father, the dashing Sir Jon Tomkins, had ever considered marrying her mother, a mere miller's daughter—but when Rosamund's mother left her newborn bastard on the doorstep of the Tomkins estate, Lady Ellinor had taken her in and cared for her as if she were a rightful scion. Her heart would not allow her to do otherwise, having lost her son to the first King Charles's cause, despite, or perhaps because of, those who held firm to the notion that in publicly acknowledging Rosamund her wits had deserted her. When Rosamund remembered those days, days when her laughter rang through the house and grounds at Bearwoode and her ready smile brought answering ones from everyone around her, she also recalled she'd never had cause to mourn her state as a bastard. On the contrary, she'd reveled in the firm love and many kindnesses proffered to her. Lady Ellinor might not have shown a lot of affection, but she took care to instill in her granddaughter good manners, an appreciation of her position and the rudiments of an education. Alas, this was short-lived as, upon Lady Ellinor's sudden death, the moorings securing Rosamund to her life at Bearwoode came adrift. The mother she knew only from dreams and had been forbidden to mention sailed into her life. Tilly Hobson, miller's daughter, had become Tilly Ballister of the Maiden Voyage Inn. Respectable, married and, after taking the payment promised her, prepared to be what she had once denied—a mother to Rosamund. Tilly and her husband, Paul, brought eight-year-old Rosamund south to Gravesend. And put her to work. Barely given time to draw breath, let alone become accustomed to her change of circumstance, Rosamund went from being waited on to doing the waiting. And wishing.

Sissy always reckoned wishing was a waste of time, but the cook, the Widow Cecily, told her to ignore Silly Sissy as it did no one harm and if it made you feel better, then wish away because you never knew when God was listening and would grant one. Figuring Widow Cecily might have cause to know, Rosamund kept wishing— often late at night when the rest of the inn was asleep and she could gaze at the stars without fear of interruption. They were the same ones she hoped the steward of Bearwoode, her much-loved Master Dunstan, was looking upon. She'd send her wishes heavenward where they'd be kept safe with her grandmother, her father and God Himself, and meted out when necessary. Somehow in her mind God, her father and her grandmother had become one and the same. Whenever Reverend Madoc delivered his Sunday sermons and spoke of the Lord, she'd imagine her dead relatives sitting either side of God, who was perched upon a grand golden throne. She felt certain they advised Him on whose prayers to heed and whose to ignore. She knew it was unfair she had such an advantage and figured that was probably why her prayers weren't answered. Her grandmother could never abide favoritism.

Sighing, Rosamund shook herself. Dwelling on the past did no good. It wasn't as if you could return there, was it? That's what her grandmother used to say, mostly when anyone expressed sorrow that her son had died so ignobly. From the face her grandmother would pull whenever this word was used (mostly by Puritan neighbors), she thought it must be a synonym for "painfully." Certainly, it was painful for Lady Ellinor to hear. So was thinking about the past, and when it was within one's compass to prevent pain, it made sense to do whatever it took to avoid it. Thus Rosamund tried, often unsuccessfully, not to think about her life before. The Maiden Voyage Inn was where she lived; that Paul and his sons happened to dwell there too was not something she could alter. She had to make the best of it; it was what her grandmother would expect of her, no matter how cruel the circumstances, how perverse the situation.

Rosamund paused in wiping the windows upon the upper floor, the rag unmoving against the thick glass. She pushed the window out and inhaled the sweet fragrance of hawthorn and the pungent odor of horses, and gazed upon the vista. It was a glorious blue-domed day without a cloud to be seen. A sultry breeze made the trees quiver and their leaves shake; the tendrils of hair that escaped Rosamund's coif lifted as if to wave back.

There was a whinny and the sound of hooves striking the ground, followed by gentle laughter. Avery's voice carried as he spoke to one of the guests. She heard mention of the unaccountable heat, the relatively good condition of the road now it was so dry, and then the river. Captured by the idea of the water, she stood on tiptoe so she might see it. On the other bank, she could just make out the dark stones of Tilbury Fort before her gaze returned to the fluid expanse. Sunlight struck the surface, disguising its usual muddy-green color and transforming it into a sparkling ribbon. Already the river traffic was thick: wherries, barges laden with brimming crates, overflowing barrels and bleating livestock; tilt boats as well as the occasional ketch moved both with and against the currents. Most of the pleasure craft carried people dressed in splendid clothes, some reclining languidly as if the warmth was already too much for them. Stuart colors abounded and Rosamund could just make out the faint strains of music; it might be early, but this was a time for festivities. It wasn't every day the King brought a bride home to London—and on both his birthday and the anniversary of his restoration two years earlier.

The river and its attractions were all well and good, but they wouldn't clean the inn, so Rosamund dismissed them and continued to dust, praying Paul would remain occupied below. He'd be pleased she was attending to the housework, something he considered within her ken. Never mind that Rosamund not only took charge of the presentation of the rooms, but it had been her idea to hire Widow Cecily to cook for them after her husband died a few years ago. Listening to idle gossip in town one day, Rosamund learned Cecily Brickstowe's husband had been so fat when he expired, she couldn't afford a coffin. It had taken six winding sheets to cover the body and eight men to carry him to the churchyard. Rosamund concluded you didn't get that size from want of food and decided the widow must be a very good cook. Her hunch was right and now the Maiden Voyage Inn, the first or last place one came to on arriving or departing Gravesend, was earning a reputation for fine fare. Not that you'd know it today, when, according to Widow Cecily, the heat ruined everything.

Paul had begrudgingly conceded that Rosamund, whom he first thought was touched in the head because of the way she constantly found reasons to smile and laugh when he could see none, had business sense. Why, she overheard him saying to Tilly one day—admittedly after he'd downed a few more ales than usual—the girl could barely read or write, but somehow, when it came to the inn, she had a head for knowing what worked and what didn't. She knew how to set things right, make disgruntled customers content and ensure that even in the lean season coin crossed their palms. She knew how to strike a bargain with suppliers and what to order in bulk. Messengers made a point of staying, even if the horses were better at the Cock and Bull or beds didn't have to be shared at the Privateer's Chest. Somehow, Rosamund remembered how the men preferred their ale, what their favorite food was and even to ask after their children, offer condolences if their wives had passed away or inquire whether they'd recovered from that wretched toothache.

If only her stepfather had asked, Rosamund could have explained how she came upon such knowledge: it was no trick. All it required was a set of ears, a willingness to listen and a good memory—all of which Rosamund possessed. Above all, Rosamund enjoyed people and, when they understood that this young woman really wanted answers to her questions and was genuinely interested, they indulged her. Who didn't like a sweet, albeit dirty, face and a set of ears in which to pour their stories? People spoke to and around her and, like the rags she used to wipe spillages, she absorbed all they said. She might not have a tutor like rich folk, her lessons in reading and writing being consigned to the past, or attend the Petty School as the twins once did, but she didn't need to when she had so many people from whom she could learn. What they shared also made Rosamund understand that while the burden she bore in private was great, there were those who carried greater. Most people delighted in talking with the unusual girl with huge, sad brown eyes and a lovely if fleeting smile. When they saw it, they felt as if the sun had peeped from behind the clouds just for them.

It was those brief smiles and daily interactions that allowed Rosamund to keep the joy that had burst forth the day she was born burning within her. Master Dunstan once told her (having heard it from one of the midwives present at her birth) that unlike most babes, who wailed upon leaving the womb, Rosamund had entered the world burbling with laughter. Her stepfather might have done all he could to douse her happiness, but she kept one tiny, belligerent spark alive. It was her single act of defiance, a keepsake from Bearwoode Manor and her grandmother that she refused to relinquish. One day, she promised herself, it would have cause to flare again . . . one day.

For now, she beat the dust out of the wall-hangings, which, despite having faded to the color of the river, hid some dire cracks, then swept the floors and polished the glass and sills, humming a ditty the sailors often sang. Passing by the open window again, she heard her name spoken. Startled, she fell silent.

"I said, have you seen Rosie?"

Rosamund gripped the sill.

"Not since the kitchen, Pa," said Fear-God.

"Want we should fetch her?" asked Glory.

"Aye, I do. Her mother's about to depart, it be a good time for a lesson. Bring her to my study. Don't let her sweet-talk her way out of it either."

"No, Pa," said the twins in unison.

Rosamund risked a look. Paul disappeared inside the front door while the twins ran around the back toward the kitchen. No doubt they'd split up as they had before to catch her on the landing. They knew she wouldn't dare make a noise and risk disturbing any of the guests still in their rooms. Shoving the broom and rags behind a tapestry, Rosamund did the only thing she could. Hoisting her skirts, she swung a leg over the sill and, bracing herself against the edge of the window, hurled herself at the nearest tree. Two nesting sparrows shrilled their protest and took wing in fright.

"Sorry," whispered Rosamund, clinging onto the branch. Praying her slippers would grip, she clambered down the tree. Above, she could hear her brothers calling, using their "mannered" voices, the ones their father knocked into them to deploy around the inn. Glancing up, she saw their hulking shadows as they moved along the corridor. She wished she'd thought to shut the window.

Once on the ground, she crouched so she wouldn't be seen and, bent double, scooted past the bewildered horses, who snickered quietly, and around the side of the building. Only then did she stand upright, dust off her hands and skirts and fix her coif; it wouldn't do to look like a fugitive if she encountered anyone. Her stepbrothers' voices were fainter now, but she knew they wouldn't stop looking. There was no hope for it, she simply couldn't abide the thought of another so-called lesson. She began to recite the catechism, as if to somehow compensate for her recalcitrance. "My duty is to love, honor and succor my father and mother; to honor and obey the King, and all that are put in authority under him; to submit myself to all my governors, teachers and spiritual pastors and masters; to order myself lowly and reverently to all my betters . . ."

But Paul was her *step*father, not her father, who, she was certain, would never have countenanced such instruction. As for her mother, why, she had no more cared what Paul did to her than she did about the hen whose neck she had ordered wrung last night. Whether it was the memories of childhood she'd stirred earlier, the day's dazzling sunshine or just some contrary part of her nature, Rosamund decided being obedient didn't prevent her being held unfairly to account. What would happen to her if she defied not only the catechism, but her stepfather for once? Surely it couldn't be worse than what she regularly endured. Paul flouted God's words daily; the same catechism told him he should "hurt no one by body or deed" and "do to all men as I would they should do unto me." He did not. Yet the Lord didn't smite him.

Walking past their old milk cow, Mabel, Rosamund patted the gentle creature before opening the rear gate and, keeping to the shadows offered by the stables, climbed up the hill and into the fields beyond before heading back down the slope to join the main road. As she did, the church bell struck ten of the clock. She'd managed the impossible—freedom was hers for a time. God knew what would happen to her for such willful disobedience.

She hadn't gone very far when she began to regret she didn't have her broad-brimmed bonnet, the sun was so intense. Her bodice stuck to her skin and her coif began to itch. Undoing her apron, she scrunched it into a ball, conscious how drab her clothes, how scuzzy her hands. Only her slippers hinted she was not what she appeared—a lowly servant on an errand. No, she was an errant princess, having escaped a wicked tyrant.

Of course, she knew this was pure fancy that belonged on a stage, not in real life. Yet, like the plays performed by traveling troupes at the Cock and Bull, real life did have monsters, monsters who wore a vizard before others, concealing their true selves.

She reached into her skirt, searching for coins so she could buy a drink and some nourishment, her fingers finding the cold hard comfort of a couple of pennies. As she waved at Farmer Blount, plowing his fallow field, the oxen in the shafts patiently plodding through the dirt, the sun beating on their pale, bony backs, she felt a spring in her step. When was the last time she'd done this? Fled the inn? Why, never. Something stirred within her, a peculiar sensation that both tickled and hurt. Her breath came fast; her skin felt clammy. Her eyes shone.

Rosamund crossed to the grassy verge opposite, enjoying a brief respite from the heat as she passed into the dappled shade of some mighty oaks, wiping her forehead and the back of her neck with a kerchief. All along the riverbank, the royal colors blazed in the bright sunlight, streamers and garlands hung from fenceposts and doorknockers and twisted around pylons and across wharves to show loyalty to a king who, though he might not pass this way, had courtiers who would no doubt report such deference.

While the town might have dressed in its best, as she approached Rosamund saw that the usual throng of people and carts was absent, apart from a few stalwarts, like the girl, Betty, who sold oranges, and old man Otway, who wheeled his oyster barrow along the docks. The streets were all but deserted. Dull hammering and other workday sounds emanated from nearby warehouses, a shanty was being sung upon a docked ship and wood and tobacco smoke emerged from a nearby tavern, competing with the odor of cooked meat and drying horse shit.

Uncertain, Rosamund lingered near the alehouse. Maybe she could watch the parade of boats awhile . . . or perhaps go to the baker's and visit Frances, the one friend she'd made in all the years she'd been here. Just as she was about to knock on the bakery door, she saw the sign. It was shut. Quashing her disappointment, she decided to find somewhere to sit on the riverbank, purchase a drink and pastry elsewhere and while away some time. Aye, she'd quite a hankering for one of Master Denis's pasties . . .

"God's good day to you, Rosie," panted a deep voice behind her.

"Fancy finding you 'ere and all," said another.

Standing on the high street were Fear-God and Glory. Stocky, with broad shoulders and thick arms, they were three years older than Rosamund and at least twice her size. They stood with their legs apart, arms folded, their faces red and sweaty, their chests heaving. A cat busy grooming itself in the shade of an awning froze and, fixing its golden eyes upon the brothers, bolted into a narrow lane. An old dog lying outside a suddenly silent alehouse whimpered and, its tail down, scraped at the door for admittance. Rosamund wished she could do the same. A window fell shut with a bang. A door quietly closed. Fear-God and Glory's reputation had grown of late; they were not to be countered—in anything or by anyone. Hidden eyes waited to see what would happen; concealed folk drew their collective breath.

"You be for it when Pa finds out you scarpered down here," growled Fear-God. "What with the inn full and all."

"I had to get supplies," said Rosamund calmly, holding up the coin as proof.

"Nah, you didn't," said Glory, adding, "Think we're stupid? It be the King's birthday; everyfing be shut. You buggered off, you did. And Pa don't like that, do he, Fear?"

"Nah, he don't, Glory. He'll teach you a lesson all right."

"Unless we teach ye first, Rosie." Glory licked his lips.

"It's Rosamund," said Rosamund, more from force of habit. She loathed that the twins and their father insisted on the diminutive. It wasn't that she disliked the name—on the contrary, one of the scullions was a Rosie, a lovely girl. It was just she never was and never would be a Rosie. Her grandmother had called her Rosamund and that's who she was.

"Gone all hoity-toity, you have, *Rosie,* since them fancy guests been hanging about," said Fear-God. He took a step toward her.

"Seems you've forgotten your kin," sneered Glory, emboldened by his brother.

"No," said Rosamund, taking a small step back. She measured the distance to the lane that ran behind the alehouse, which intersected with a veritable labyrinth of snickets and alleys. "I've not forgotten." An image of her grandmother appeared.

"Then, prove it," said Glory, coming closer, moving to cut off her escape.

"Give us a kiss," Fear-God said and lunged.

Rosamund threw the coppers, smacking him in the face. Then she flung her apron, which embraced his features and was repelled. Instead of turning, she ran straight at the men and squeezed past. Pausing briefly to kick off her slippers, she hoisted her skirts and bolted.

It was as if she were possessed by a demon. She flew along the road, attracting attention from the river, people watching her with open mouths, some crying out encouragement as bets were laid as to who would win the chase. She raced past Farmer Blount's lands, maintaining her pace as she drew level with the inn. Glancing back, she made a decision. The horses raised their heads, one whinnying as if to spur her on. Her feet were fleet, her arms pumped at her sides, her lungs filled, her hot cheeks were bellows.

Just beyond the inn was a crossroads. Without hesitating, she turned away from the water. Small stones and dried mud stuck to the soles of her feet; she stubbed her toe against a rock, dislodging it and almost tripping over. She ignored the pain in her foot and blossoming beneath her ribs. The dull thud of the twins' boots resounded in pursuit, their breathing hoarse as they tried to gain on her. When they understood she wasn't going to seek the shelter of the inn, their cruel laughter was like a punch to her stomach.

Still Rosamund ran. Her chest was burning, her face afire; her feet, numb. The sun's brutal beams began to take their toll.

Rounding the last corner before the long stretch of road took travelers south, Rosamund determined to duck into the woods and pray she had enough of a lead to hide beneath a fallen tree or skitch up a tall one. Using every last ounce of strength, she was about to leap off the road when a cry of alarm forced her head up. There was the discordant jangle of harnesses, dirt and pebbles flew in her face and the shocking screams of horses rang in her ears before a great force pushed her back.

She struck the ground hard, crying out as her punished bottom bore the brunt, then swiftly rolled and flung her arms above her head to protect her face. But the sun found it, the abominable sun that filled her eyes with tears, turning the world into a blur of dark spots and whirling shapes. A writhing mass of powerful legs circled above her. There were shod hooves, wild eyes and the dark wood of shafts before, incongruously, she saw a man's appalled countenance staring. His mouth was agape, his voice hoarse, but she couldn't make out what he was saying. She tried to squirm out of the way, then something struck her hard upon the temple and she knew no more.

TWO
In which Sir Everard Blithman finds a treasure

S ir Everard Blithman gazed in dismay at the girl lying askew in the dirt. If he hadn't been anxious to avoid the traffic cluttering up the Great London Road, never mind lurking highwaymen, he wouldn't have come this way or been so sorely inconvenienced.

The coachmen tried to calm the horses as they argued over who was at fault. Sir Everard shut out their noise and with some difficulty, using his walking stick for leverage, kneeled beside the unconscious girl. Pushing aside her hair, he felt for a pulse at her throat and saw her bosom rising and falling. A sleeve had ridden up her arm. He frowned and, reaching over, pulled up her other sleeve, before laying her hand upon her stomach. While her dress was crude, comprising a simple skirt, plain bodice and petticoats that had been mended numerous times and could do with a laundress's touch, her feet were not accustomed to being unshod. It was evident from the raw scrapes her toes had suffered in her dash upon this Godforsaken road. Yet there was no sign of shoes or stockings. Her skirt was torn and any cap or coif she had been wearing had blown away in the wind, which, even as he bent over her, was increasing in strength and heat. Her hair was so very long and unruly. Though it could do with a wash, the color was so eye-catching, so uncommon. It reminded him of . . .

Pulling a kerchief from his jacket, he wiped his brow, pushing it up under the band of his hat, which also served to hold his periwig tight to his scalp. Damn this heat. Damn his whim to take what was supposed to be a shortcut.

Whoever this young woman was, once you saw beyond the patina of dirt, she was really quite striking. Perhaps that was why the rogues were chasing her, for he'd no doubt that's what they'd interrupted: some country yokels seeking to make sport of a pretty maid. She didn't look like a servant, though her reddened hands bespoke labor, as did her clothes. There was a quality about her, even as she lay there with a nasty gash upon her temple, that suggested she was more than she seemed. Most likely it was the brave manner in which she'd stood before his frantic steeds, neither screaming nor fainting, but trying to work out how to rescue herself that appealed to him and set his mind racing. She was clearly possessed of both a stout character and courage—something lacking in so many of his acquaintances these days.

Then there was the uncanny resemblance. The more he stared, the more apparent it became.

Most extraordinary.

Who was she? Squinting, his faded blue eyes scanned the crossroads ahead and the river beyond before once more considering the girl at his feet. He let out an exasperated sigh. It was tempting to simply leave her. There was not a soul in sight, and no one would ever know he'd been there. Apart from the hired men, the only witnesses were two mangy-looking crows and a thin cow. The rogues who'd pursued her had made themselves scarce the moment she fell and were hardly going to admit to anything.

A gust threatened to snatch his hat away, forcing him to half rise and clutch it to his head. What if those same villains returned to finish what they started? What if news he'd effectively left an injured chit in the road reached London? There'd be hell to pay—something he could ill afford in light of recent developments. He couldn't risk it.

And there was the remarkable likeness. Was God having a lark or offering something else?

Mopping his forehead, he turned to the man waiting patiently behind him. "Jacopo." He gestured for him to come forward.

Jacopo gazed upon the woman before a hand swiftly covered his mouth. "*Mio Dio!*" he exclaimed. "She's very like the Lady Helene—"

"I noticed," said Sir Everard dryly.

Jacopo continued to stare. "*Lei è bella.* Like a painting, she's so perfect."

"Not quite perfect," Sir Everard said and, using his cane, pointed to her clothes then her head. "There's the matter of her state, never mind her injuries."

"*Allora*, quite," said Jacopo. "Should I fetch a *dottore?*"

"A doctor? Here, in this backwater?" Sir Everard shook his head. "I wouldn't inflict such a creature upon the poor child if we were in London. Not after what she's been through."

"'Twasn't your fault, *signore*, nor the coachmen's. She ran straight toward them. How she didn't hear—"

"I'm not referring to the damage we exacted and which, no doubt, was the final straw," said Sir Everard impatiently. "Look here." Bending down, he ran a light thumb over a livid purple bruise near her elbow.

Next to it, a series of mustard-colored marks the size of large fingers could be seen; closer to her wrist, red welts from some kind of binding.

The young man squatted beside him, his fingers unconsciously wrapping around his own wrist and rubbing a few times.

With a beringed finger Sir Everard pointed to a slight discoloration upon her cheekbone. "We'd naught to do with this. That is old. The girl has been manhandled and not just the once. God only knows what we cannot see." Heaving himself upright, he sighed. "If there's one thing I cannot abide, Jacopo, it's *unnecessary* cruelty."

Sir Everard deigned not to notice the expression on Jacopo's face. Instead, he stared in the direction the girl had come from, his eyes becoming harder than the steel poniard he wore at his hip.

"Well," he said, brushing the dust from his fine satin breeches and the jacquard of his coat. "As God is my witness, we've no choice. Pick her up, Jacopo, and place her in the carriage. I need to think."

Jacopo bowed. *"Si, signore."* As tenderly as he could, Jacopo lifted the young woman into his arms, screwing up his nose as he caught a whiff of her odor. Once his master was seated in the carriage, he hoisted the girl inside and placed her along the padded seat opposite, rearranging the cushions so her head was supported, and setting a pomander of rose petals and violet beside her.

As he slowly withdrew his hand from the back of her neck, brushing the marks on her wrist almost reverentially, the girl groaned and her eyelids flickered.

"*Signore*, she wakes."

The girl blinked, gasped and, with a strength no one expected, pushed Jacopo away and retreated into the cushions.

Jacopo raised his hands. "*Va tutto bene* . . . It's all right, *signorina*," he said quickly. "I mean no harm."

"For God's sake, Jacopo, move aside so the girl understands she's not been captured by an Ethiopian." With a sweep of his stick, Sir Everard shoved him against the carriage wall. "You may yet frighten her to death."

The girl said nothing, just stared first at him, then Jacopo, with huge dark eyes. Recognizing that if she wasn't treated with kid gloves she might bolt before he could be assured of her health, Sir Everard began speaking, all the while observing her carefully.

"Good morning, mistress. My name is Sir Everard Blithman of London. I'm sorry to say my horses struck you down, but I'm mightily relieved to see you're at least partly restored, despite the wound we've inflicted."

She raised her hand to the spot, drawing her fingers away and rubbing the blood across the tips. Gazing at them uncertainly, she neither swooned nor fell into hysterics as Sir Everard half anticipated. Why, she was a bold one indeed. A rare one. He wondered at the state of her clothes, her all but unwashed condition.

She took his proffered kerchief, wiped her fingers and cautiously touched her head. He waved toward a small chest at his feet. "Jacopo, give her some medick."

"*Signore.*" Jacopo opened the clasps, extracted a small bottle, popped the cork and offered it to the girl. "Venezia treacle," he said. "Good for all ailments."

Sir Everard bade her drink and watched as she first sniffed, then looked at Jacopo before her eyes alighted on him again. "Please," said Sir Everard. "I assure you, it's the best of physick—the King himself takes it."

Rosamund took a cautious sip, her eyes upon Jacopo, who urged her with a nod and a smile.

She used the kerchief to dab her mouth, a gesture that confirmed Sir Everard's suspicion she was of a better class than her clothes and musky scent indicated.

"If you please, mistress, what is your name?" asked Sir Everard.

The girl didn't answer immediately, folding the kerchief into a small square and glancing around as if to seek an exit. At first affronted, Sir Everard quickly saw the humor in the situation. Here he was, a renowned London merchant and knight, being assessed by a country lass who couldn't recognize a gentleman when she saw one and didn't have the sense to watch out for carriages on the one road that ran between her home and the city. If indeed Gravesend was her home. The longer she took to answer, the more humorous the moment became. Unable to help himself, a laugh exploded. Erupting from his very middle, it filled the carriage and was answered first by a horse's indignant bray, then a chuckle from Jacopo and finally by the girl, who joined in with a laugh so pure, so unutterably joyous, it quite took Sir Everard's breath away. Her face, already absurdly enchanting in an unorthodox way and not merely because of the sentiments her similarities aroused, was quite transformed. Her great brown eyes twinkled in pleasure, her teeth, a row of white pearls, were exposed as her exquisite pink lips parted. Taken aback, Sir Everard ceased to laugh and his heart all but seized.

Immediately, the girl's fingers flew to her lips and the delightful noise stopped. Sir Everard felt gloom descend and, in yet another attack of imagination (two this very hour), felt as if the sun had been wiped from the skies.

"I haven't done that in so long, I astonished myself." Her voice was curiously mellow for one so young. It reminded him of honey and the creamy top of fine beer. The way she enunciated the words suggested good breeding; good breeding overlaid by a veneer of ill.

She tried to sit up, flinging her arm out as she was momentarily overcome. Jacopo leaped forward. Raising her hands, she prevented him from touching her. Instead, both men watched as she rearranged the cushions to support her back.

"Please, forgive my rudeness," she said. "I blame the gash upon my head." She touched it gingerly. No blood stained the kerchief this time. "My name is Rosamund To— Ballister, and it's a pleasure to meet you, Sir Everard Blithman of London, and you too, sir, I'm sure." She bowed her head toward Jacopo. "I thank you for your timely appearance. While your horses and I . . . er . . . enjoyed a rendezvous, the one awaiting me had you failed to materialize would not have brought such delightful company into my orbit."

Jacopo gave a splutter. Sir Everard caught his eye. "This is Jacopo, my valet and factotum," he said. "He hails from faraway climes."

"I thought you must," said Rosamund. "I've only ever seen folk such as your good self at a distance, upon the ships that anchor at the docks in town. You're not as dark as some, but darker than most." She hesitated. "You speak with an accent. You're not a Hollander, perchance, are you?"

Jacopo glanced at his master in mock horror.

Sir Everard coughed into his fist. "He's no swag-bellied Hollander, so you needn't be alarmed; the language he spoke was Italian. He's from Venice."

Rosamund, whose color was just starting to return, fluttered her hands. "Aye, of course; I can hear it now. My humblest apologies for my ill manners, my boldness in asking. It's just, my stepfather doesn't approve of . . . Hollanders."

"He's not alone on that score." Sir Everard smiled. "Like the damn Frenchies and, with one or two exceptions, the Papist Spanish, they're not to be trusted."

"Whatever you are, whoever, it matters not as you've shown me such kindness. Much more than I deserve or that my state"—she grimaced at her dirty clothes—"demands." Nodding toward the bottle still in Jacopo's hand, she smiled. "That treacle was excellent." She smacked her lips together, the sound an angel exhaling. "I detect some honey, lavender, juniper and perhaps some St. John's wort?"

Sir Everard blinked. "You can taste those?"

"Aye, and many other ingredients besides, which,

sadly, I am unable to identify but which no doubt have contributed to my recovery."

Jacopo stared.

"My many thanks."

Outside, a flock of birds screeched. Restless now, the horses stamped their hooves and the low chatter of the coachmen carried.

Sir Everard exchanged a look with Jacopo which Rosamund intercepted. "Forgive me. I've inconvenienced you both. I feel much restored. I'll be on my way."

Sir Everard was not ready to let this young woman go. There was a reason God arranged this encounter—he simply had to fathom what it was. He placed his fingers on her forearm. She flinched and he quickly withdrew them.

"Soft. We're not going anywhere until we hear *your* story and can assure ourselves of your ongoing safety. There were two brawny lads chasing you. It would be remiss if we did not ascertain they no longer pose a threat."

Rosamund's eyes flew to the door and she plucked her lip. "You may rest assured. They do not."

"Are the scoundrels known to you?"

Raising her eyes, she took a deep breath. "Known to me? Aye. Those lads are my brothers. Well, stepbrothers, Fear-God and Glory Ballister."

Sir Everard prayed she didn't see him recoil at what the names signified. If there was another thing Sir Everard couldn't abide, it was Puritans. And where there were Puritans, there were Roundheads. Anger began to build. Jacopo wore a heavy frown.

"They're not like their names, good sir, Master Jacopo," she said swiftly. "They were bestowed at a different time and to signify an allegiance that's no longer binding. Their father, my *stepfather*, Paul Ballister, is an avowed royalist and loyal to the King. As indeed we all are."

But he wasn't always, thought Sir Everard. No doubt her stepfather had her recite such a response lest anyone make the obvious assumption. Like so many Englishmen before and after Cromwell, this Ballister was a despicable turncoat, a veritable poltroon with no convictions upon which to hang his hat.

"Your *brothers*, you say?" Sir Everard frowned.

"Aye."

"They saw the accident befall you and, instead of rendering aid, fled?"

Rosamund found her hands interesting. "Did they? Perhaps they've gone to report the . . . mishap. We only live around the corner."

Sir Everard's frown deepened. "There's a posting inn, isn't there?"

"The Maiden Voyage Inn," Jacopo replied.

"That's where I live," said Rosamund, in a voice that would have been appropriate at a funeral.

Sir Everard had never heard of this Maiden Voyage Inn, but then, he had very little cause to come to Gravesend, his interests being met in London, Deptford, Portsmouth, Dover and beyond.

"Well, I'd best get you home," he said.

"I didn't say it was my *home*," said Rosamund firmly, locking eyes with him. "I said it's where I live." And she let out such a wistful sigh it made Sir Everard shift in his seat, as if the cushions had become stones.

An uncomfortable silence descended. There was no help for it, he must return the girl to her family, home or no home, and be on his way no matter what his mind was whispering to him. He felt for his purse. He would give this stepfather a gold coin to compensate for her injuries, ensure she received some broth and the attention of a cursed physician if needed. He knew how tricky head injuries could be. He'd fought in enough battles, seen enough men succumb to the smallest blow to know the humors could be struck out of balance in an instant. His hand tightened on his stick. He was living proof. Still, her eyes were clear, and she made complete sense—well, to a point. To differentiate between a home and the place she lived . . .

"If you feel ready to travel, then," said Sir Everard jovially. He must be on his way; he had business in London, urgent correspondence to deal with, and he was now very late. "I'll ask my men to take us there."

Did he imagine it or did disappointment cross her face? No, he did not. Her joyous eyes dimmed, the corners of her mouth became downturned. Sir Everard felt as if he'd struck a puppy. Guilt rose within him. Such an unfamiliar emotion.

"It's not very far. I could walk the distance."

"I'll not hear of it," Sir Everard said and was rewarded with that smile. "Best tell the driver to take it easy, Jacopo. I don't want to risk our guest's health any further, no matter how close our destination."

Flashing one last grin at Rosamund, Jacopo leaped from the carriage and shut the door, the conveyance rocking slightly as he hoisted himself onto the driver's box.

The carriage lurched as the horses, with the encouraging cries of the men, walked forward, the wheels jerking over the ruts and potholes.

Sir Everard and Rosamund were thrown from side to side. Sir Ever-ard watched as the girl edged forward on the seat, one hand resting upon the window, which was left unsealed. As she peered out, her mouth was slightly open, her eyes round.

"You've never been in a carriage before?" he asked and was blessed with a quick laugh. Though abrupt, it was no less magical.

"There was a time I was no stranger to such transport." Her face clouded, and instead of asking the questions burning inside him, Sir Everard wasted the few precious minutes he had alone with her trying to think of something he could say, a witty observation, an inoffensive story, anything to recapture that smile, to hear that charming peal of mirth again. Its power was remarkable. Imagine what he could do if he could bottle such a thing, sell it. And when it came in such a package, one that with some tweaking bore such similitude. What an attraction; what a lure . . .

Before he could say anything, Rosamund sat back. "We're here."

Astonished, Sir Everard looked out just as the carriage rolled to a stop right outside a rather derelict inn with a faded sign that creaked as it blew back and forth. The carriage door opened, admitting a gust of searing air and a blast of earth stirred by the horses.

"*Signorina?*" coughed Jacopo, waving the dust away before offering his arm.

With a sweet smile at Sir Everard, Rosamund refused Jacopo's assistance, rising with an elegance that belied her appearance. She steadied herself and her features settled into what Sir Everard later would describe as a state of resignation and resilience. It was like curtains closing after a wonderful performance or the moonlight drowning in clouds. Her eyes lost their sparkle, the felicity she'd so readily expressed was all but gone. About to leave the carriage, she turned, her face close. "Thank you, Sir Everard, and you too, Master Jacopo, for rescuing me," she said. "From the road and . . . from any other misadventures that may have befallen me. I do ask God to bless you for your kindness; I'll not forget it. Good day, sirs."

Unable to summon a response, Sir Everard was imagining the effect she'd have upon others if she were washed and dressed in fine apparel. How no one would ever suspect someone who looked and sounded like that of ill will or malice. Knowing he should give Jacopo the coin to pass to the stepfather, he didn't move.

As Rosamund walked toward the pitted front door, the horses hitched to the railing raised their heads to regard her. She caressed a warm neck in passing, the beast shuddering beneath her gentle touch.

Why did he feel as if he'd found a treasure and now had to surrender it?

He gazed at the inn, taking note of its shabby exterior, the overgrown grass he could see in the yard behind it. Nevertheless, the glass in the windows was spotless, the curtains clean. An image of reddened hands, dirty knees and elbows, bruised wrists, sprang into his mind, along with those merry pipes. The inn was an unsightly shell housing a pearl . . . a hardworking pearl that by rights deserved a much finer setting. What he could do with such a prize; how it could work to serve his interests.

Good God, her misery was evident; she said it herself, this wasn't her home. She'd no allegiance here . . . Only a stepfather and a pair of footpads she called brothers who didn't understand the jewel in their midst.

This would not do; he hadn't made his fortune by ignoring his instincts. In his eagerness to stop Rosamund, he almost fell out of the carriage.

"Mistress Ballister!" he called, raising his stick.

Rosamund halted abruptly and with an apologetic look at Jacopo, whose arm she now held, spun around. "Milord?"

Sir Everard hobbled toward her, a preposterous idea growing in his head. He was about to speak when the door to the inn flew open and out stepped a tall man with a generous paunch. Dressed in an ornate jacket with a heavily frilled shirt, a dark horse-hair periwig and over-size hat, he paused in the shade offered by the huge trees growing near the front door, took in the scene before him, then, with a huge smile that revealed enormous sulfur-colored teeth, flung out his arms.

"Rosie, my dear child, where have you been?"

Before Rosamund could respond, the man snatched her off her feet, swinging her around, depositing a wet kiss upon both cheeks then setting her down.

"Why, when your brothers returned saying you'd set off down the southern road, I thought I'd have to raise a hue and cry. I sent them to fetch your mother. But look, here you are. Returned to us safely, and by such august personages." Keeping one arm draped across Rosamund's shoulders, the man lifted his rather fine hat and attempted a bow. "Paul Ballister at your service and in your debt. How can I ever thank you for returning my Rosie to me?"

Touching his hat, Sir Everard introduced himself and Jacopo and explained what brought them to the inn. His mind was galloping. So, this was the stepfather, the cowardly Roundhead who could look to the cleanliness of his own person and attire but allow his stepdaughter and the exterior of his premises to present in such a state. This was a man who could pretend affection, shower it upon a lass who neither invited it nor, by her distasteful expression, wished it, for the benefit of his own reputation. What was he hiding?

All these thoughts tumbled in Sir Everard's head as he spoke. He omitted the part about Rosamund being chased by her brothers. The entire time, Ballister never released hold of his stepdaughter, and made sounds that were no doubt meant to express shock and sympathy. When Sir Everard reached the part about the horses knocking Rosamund unconscious, Ballister took hold of both her shoulders, bent his knees so he might study her closely and, upon seeing the cut to her head, clasped her to his bosom.

Rosamund never uttered a word. Neither did she resist nor return the many affections this man bestowed upon her; not his kisses, embraces or chucking of her chin. She could have been a life-size puppet whose strings had been severed. Her mouth was immobile; her eyes hollow. Sir Everard wondered if her smile was something he'd invented, let alone her astonishing laughter, only he knew they weren't.

"Does it hurt, my little kinchin?" said Ballister in a voice reserved for a beloved pet, studying the recent injury closely and conveniently ignoring the others.

Sir Everard had to resist the urge to strike him.

Before Rosamund could answer, Ballister slapped his forehead. "What an addle-brained ruffler I am, keeping you standing out here in this heat. Please, please, come in, come in. After all, it's not every day a

London gent, a knight no less, brings my pretty heart, my sweet dimber panter back." He squeezed Rosamund against him. She was crushed to his side like an empty chaff bag.

"That won't be necessary," began Sir Everard. "I'm more than relieved to find your daughter unharmed by the sorry experience. Nevertheless, I think it appropriate I offer you compensation for damages done, then we'll be on our way."

Ballister's hand fell from the door as he turned around, relinquishing Rosamund at the same time. The relief on her face was palpable. She shuffled out of reach.

"Compensation, you said?" Ballister stroked his thin moustache, a feeble effort to disguise his Parliamentary propensities and mimic the King, as so many were wont to do.

Sir Everard cleared his throat. "I did."

Rosamund was forgotten. Jacopo went and stood next to her.

Rubbing his large hands together, Ballister sidled closer to Sir Everard. Ballister's features were strong, his brows heavy, but his eyes were too close together, which spoiled the effect. His pores were large and his swarthy skin bore the marks of the pox.

"I knew the moment I set my peepers upon you, my lord, that you were a generous cove, a man of high principles and sound sense." He smiled again, standing so close, Sir Everard caught a whiff of his sour breath. He was reminded of a riddle: *Why is it better to fall into the claws of crows and ravens than of flatterers? Because crows and ravens do but eat us when we are dead, but flatterers devour us alive.* Having encountered Ballister's kind before, he'd no intention of providing this particular man with a meal.

"Poor Rosamund." Ballister sighed, looking back to where she waited, pity etched upon his face. A frowsy smell arose from his wig. "What will her mother say when she spies her grievous hurts? Now I understand the dire extent of them, I doubt the lass'll be fit to do her duties for months. I can see something's not right with her. Look how close she's standing to that tawneymoor, unaware of the danger she's in." He waggled his head sorrowfully; Sir Everard put more distance between them, which Ballister swiftly closed. "So, what kind of compensation are we talking about, milord?" He lowered his voice. "I'll have you know, I'm no nizzie to be bought with a few coins."

Sir Everard stiffened. "And I am no cully to be gulled."

Ballister looked at him agog, then his smile returned. Sir Everard could see it didn't reach his eyes, which were of an indiscernible color and as cold as the Thames in winter.

"I didn't think you were for a moment, sir. Not you, a London gent"—there was a flicker of scorn as his eyes alighted on the walking stick—"with as fine a carriage and horseflesh as I've seen in these parts— even if they did mow down my little one and almost take her life."

A distant shout distracted them. A group of well-dressed people slowly approached, chattering and laughing, led by a woman with dark hair wearing a green dress and a large hat. Two robust young men walked on one side of her while a gentleman in a long periwig held her arm on the other.

"Why, it be my wife, Mistress Tilly, and my boys," said Ballister, his brow creasing. Their appearance didn't please him.

It didn't please Sir Everard either. Unable to bear a moment more of Ballister's company, let alone the rest of his kin, he felt anger rise within him. The girl was completely wasted here. This man and no doubt the entire family had no idea who and what they housed; look at the state of her, the way she tried to avoid her stepfather's consideration, how her mother's appearance made her more crestfallen.

Before he could change his mind, Sir Everard unhitched his purse from his belt, noting the widening of Ballister's eyes, the way his thick tongue sought his lips. "Listen here, Ballister. I'm only going to make this offer once, so think carefully."

With his eyes fixed on the purse, Ballister raised a brow. "And what might that offer be?"

"You acknowledge Miss Ballister won't be able to perform her duties for months?"

"Aye, at least. Could be years, for all we know. Head wounds are funny things; suffered a few myself during the war." He pushed aside his coarse wig to reveal a faint scar near his shaven hairline. It looked like the scratch a nail might leave.

"In that case, she'll be of very little use to you," said Sir Everard.

"No use at all," agreed Ballister. "She be damaged goods. Just another mouth to feed, as if times ain't tough enough."

"Well, allow me to relieve you of that burden." Trying not to show his distaste, Sir Everard held up the purse.

"Relieve me?"

"Aye. Since I've damaged your 'goods,' allow me to take her off your hands. What do you say?"

Sir Everard saw the look of incredulity cross Jacopo's face. Rosamund took a step forward, but whether in protest or approbation, he couldn't tell.

Ballister stared at Sir Everard, the dangling purse, then at his stepdaughter, who quickly lowered her head. "What do you mean?"

"I want to buy your daughter, Ballister. What do you say? Will you sell her to me?"

THREE

In which an unconventional deal is struck

N o!" came a shout.

Rosamund twisted at the sound, in time to see her mother, forgetting all propriety, break away from the group she was escorting and start running toward her. On her heels were Fear-God and Glory. Upon seeing Rosamund they slowed, confusion and guilt drawing them together. Glory had her slippers in his hands and quickly hid them behind his back.

"Ah, you must be Mistress Ballister," began Sir Everard, taking off his hat and bowing. "Allow me to introduce myself. I am—"

"I don't care who you are, sir." Tilly halted before him, huffing and puffing, perspiration running in rivulets down her face, taking the poorly applied powder and patches with it. Looking him up and down, she all but sneered. "My daughter can't be bought and sold like a slave at a market"—she glared in Jacopo's direction—"or a horse at a fair. How dare you. I'll have you know we be no pinchbecks." She marched over to Rosamund and pulled her close. Rosamund made an effort to free herself, then gave up. Tilly would not be gainsaid.

Joining his wife and stepdaughter in front of the inn, Paul smirked at Sir Everard. "Well, milord, you heard my wife. In fact, she took the words right out of my mouth. Rosie's not for sale." Inserting himself on Rosamund's other side, he placed an arm around her waist, his eyes on the purse in Sir Everard's fist. "Though an offer of compensation still be on the table."

By now the guests had caught up and stood in the shade of the trees, watching events unfold. The women made use of their ostrich-plume fans, waving them back and forth and whispering to one another behind them. One of the men lit a pipe.

Uncaring of the audience, Tilly continued. "If you want her so badly—" She slapped Paul's arm off her daughter and took Rosamund by the wrist, dragging her toward Sir Everard. "If you want her so badly you can bleeding well do the right thing. You can marry her."

There were gasps. One of the women tittered. Rosamund stared at her mother. The heat must have affected her. She'd taken leave of her senses.

"Don't appear so shocked, sir," cried Tilly. "What's a wife but the property of a husband? What's marriage but a business transaction? She's as good as a chattel, eh? Even if she be spoiled." She was referring to the mark on Rosamund's forehead, but the bitter look she cast was directed toward Paul.

When Sir Everard didn't answer immediately, Tilly came even closer, lowering her voice. "I haven't kept her beneath my roof this long to have her given over to some knave so he can have his way. I don't want her coming back 'ere with a belly full of sprog, leeching off me. You want 'er, you can buy 'er all right—as a bride. Otherwise, you'd best say good day, sir."

Rosamund knew Tilly was upset. She was dropping her haitches as well as her decorum.

"But, Tilly, wife . . ." Paul stumbled toward them, wringing his hands. "You don't mean that." Wearing a silly smile, he nodded toward the guests, half bowing toward Sir Everard.

Tilly's mouth twisted as she leered at him over her shoulder. "Don't I?" Her look was a shot from an arquebus. "I've never meant anythin' more in me life."

Ignoring her husband, she faced Sir Everard again. "What will it be? Will you make an 'onest woman of me daughter? I'll have you know, though 'er clothes 'ave seen better days and she could do with a wash, good blood flows in 'er veins. More than that, she be a boon to us 'ere and will be a sore loss. Why, if you be the canny merchant you appear, what better than a wife who can read, write and is possessed of as fine a business 'ead on those pretty shoulders as you'd find in the Royal Exchange?" She lowered her voice. "You'd not be shortchanged in this bargain, milord. Not on any count. Why, look at 'er." She stepped away from Rosamund, inviting his gaze.

Rosamund's cheeks grew hot. She wished the ground would open up and swallow her right there and then. Tilly was behaving like a street vendor selling hot pies, and she was telling pork ones as well—bold-faced and as loud and public as you like. Exaggerating her abilities, pretending she possessed skills she hadn't practiced in a long time, let alone mastered. She might understand and even have improved the running of the inn, but reading and writing fluently were beyond her. Knowing she should protest, Rosamund stayed mute. Aware of Jacopo's remarkable blue-green eyes upon her, she wanted to squirm with shame. Was it not a sin to lie? Yet she could not call a stop to this transaction.

She wanted to see where Tilly's sudden boldness led. Rosamund was filled to the brim with needlelike anticipation. It poked and prodded, making it difficult to stand still. Around the corner of the inn peered Widow Cecily, Sissy, Dorcas and Avery, their eyes wider than the skirts on the ladies' dresses.

Recognizing the deal was not yet dead, Tilly stood behind Rosamund, clasped the girl's shoulders and thrust her forward. "Just so you know what you be gettin', she might look like a dirty drab, but she be a Tomkins of Bearwoode Manor in Durham." Addressing Sir Everard over Rosamund's right shoulder, she continued. "Daughter of Sir Jon no less, she was raised by the Lady Ellinor herself—a proud royalist to the core, in case you're wonderin'—until such time as the old woman cark— I mean, passed into the Lord's arms. It's not like you'd be plighting your troth with common muck an' all."

It took all Rosamund's control not to let her mouth drop open. Not once had her mother ever acknowledged the relations whose blood, as she described it, flowed in her veins. The fact she was a bastard aside, here she was being forthcoming about them and in a voice that carried. It was as if she *wanted* Sir Everard to take her; Tilly, who'd never put herself out for anyone, least of all her daughter—not since she carried her away from Bearwoode that wretched, rain-filled day so many years ago.

Beyond Sir Everard, the women ceased waving their fans and appraised Rosamund, craning their necks to study her boldly. Aware of their scrutiny, Rosamund's chin lifted. Even the men straightened and cleared their throats noisily, one spitting, others averting their eyes as if to compensate for the manner in which they'd appreciated her assets that morning. Like she was common muck an' all.

Everyone waited with bated breath for Sir Everard to respond. First replacing his hat, he plucked a kerchief from his waistcoat and slowly dabbed his forehead.

"Bearwoode . . . a Tomkins . . ." he said quietly. He studied Tilly's apparel, her face, before his eyes slid to Rosamund. For the first time in months, Rosamund wished she'd washed that bit harder, spent more time scrubbing her neck and hands—only, any time she did, she paid a hefty price.

"When I suggested I . . . er . . . um . . . buy . . . your daughter," said Sir Everard, "I'm afraid you misunderstood my intentions. I sought no mistress nor a wife, but to take her under my wing, like she was my . . . my . . . my own daughter." He glanced toward Jacopo.

"Daughter? Ha! Think I haven't heard that kind of confeck before? I know what you're offerin' all too well," said Tilly, earning a snigger from Paul and some of the men.

Sir Everard ignored them. "I never meant to imply my offer was less than honorable—"

"Well," interrupted Tilly, waving a hand to silence him, "if that's the case, our business 'ere is concluded. We've nothing to discuss. You'll not be takin' 'er anywhere, 'onorable intentions or no. She's not for sale, not without surety, and, in this case, that be a ring and your name. Daughter my arse. She be *my* daughter and that be it. May God give you good day, sir. Come, Rosamund." Swinging Rosamund around, she tucked her arm through hers and pulled her away, head held high, her back straighter than the fine piece of wood upon which Sir Everard leaned.

Casting a smug look in Sir Everard's direction, Paul followed. "Quite right, dear," he said, catching up, patting his wife's forearm. "Rosamund's no dell to be bought with coin. She's a good, hardworking girl, beloved daugh—"

"Cease your prattle, husband," said Tilly, rounding on Paul, eyes blazing. They stood staring at each other, Paul's mouth opening and closing like a fish brought to land, his neck turning a deep shade of puce, his fists clenching. With an audience, he dare not act. Rosamund knew this and so did Tilly. Satisfied he'd nothing further to add, Tilly spun on her heel and, with Rosamund in tow, continued. Tilly paused briefly to beckon the guests, who'd long ceased to talk.

"Hope you enjoyed the little performance, done in honor of the King's special day: his nuptials and homecoming." This time, she stressed her haitches.

Paul was quick on the uptake, bowing and scraping. "Aye, aye. A mighty jest; has not the King bought himself a bride? Only his came with Bombay *and* Tangiers." Weak chuckles met his poor quip. "Now, if you'll just follow me to the taproom, we have some refreshments for you to enjoy." He jerked his head toward the twins, indicating they should run around the back and ensure what he promised was available.

Widow Cecily, Sissy, Dorcas and Avery made themselves scarce.

Tilly graciously accepted dubious congratulations for the dramatics, offered in a combination of falsetto and sardonic tones. From the looks exchanged as they entered the inn, few of the guests were gulled; nonetheless, they played along. Paul led them inside and could be heard directing them to sit and ordering the maids, Lucy and Rosie, to pour drinks. Much to Rosamund's chagrin, most sat in the front window, determined not to miss anything else that might unfold. She felt curious eyes upon her; no longer was she simply the serving wench or pitied daughter of the establishment, she was a Tomkins of Bearwoode. Landed gentry or the closest thing to it, according to Tilly, and that made her one of them or possibly even better. Unless of course it was all a delicious fiction.

As the last of the guests tried to linger, two women with large hats and fans obstructed the doorway, each refusing to concede to the other. Tilly pushed them through the door, ignoring their outraged squeals. Rosamund cast a despairing glance in Sir Everard's direction, and resisted her mother's efforts to squeeze her indoors one last time. Their eyes locked just as Tilly went to shut the door.

"Wait," called Sir Everard for the second time that day.

Taking a deep breath, Tilly slowly spun around. "Aye, milord?" She pulled Rosamund to her, shut the door and leaned against it.

Sir Everard was only a few paces away.

"You have something to say?" asked Tilly calmly. She reached for Rosamund's hand and gripped it tightly.

Sweating freely now, Sir Everard patted his forehead and upper lip with his damp kerchief before his hand dropped to his side. "I've something to ask."

"Go ahead," said Tilly.

"Is the girl legitimate?" asked Sir Everard.

Tilly opened her mouth.

"I want the truth."

She closed it again and shook her head.

"She can read?" he asked.

"Like a nun in a cell."

If anyone thought the allusion inappropriate, they didn't say.

"And write?"

"Better than a lawyer's scribe," said Tilly.

Rosamund couldn't help it, she laughed.

Sir Everard studied Rosamund for a full minute, then, taking a deep breath, made up his mind. "Very well. If that's what it takes to secure your daughter, then yes."

Jacopo made a strangled sound. Tilly inhaled sharply. "Beg pardon, milord?"

"I said"—Sir Everard stood as straight as his infirmity allowed—"I'll marry *your* daughter." His voice was clear this time, a clarion that shook the torpor of the day. He began to chuckle. "Why not." He flung out an arm. "I'll marry her and give her an opportunity like no other." He brought his hands together on his stick and looked at Rosamund directly; time stood still.

As his words sank in, a wave of warmth spread across Rosamund's breasts and up her neck before manifesting in a huge smile. Her eyes sparkled like uncut jewels. Another laugh escaped. Hers. It was a small bell: pure, sweet.

Sir Everard laughed harder. Tilly winced.

Jacopo gave a long exhalation and shook his head in what to Rosamund appeared to be sorrow. She wanted to reassure him, take him by the hands and dance across the yard. This was no time for sadness. Beside her, Tilly swallowed, her fingers tightening painfully upon Rosamund's.

There was a faint squeal before Rosamund became aware of a commotion at the taproom window. Faces were pressed to the glass; fingers pointed, mouths opened and closed as chatter flew thick and fast. They were a spectacle after all.

The door behind them flew open as Paul stumbled outside. "You can't," he cried. He looked in desperation at Tilly, then Rosamund.

"He be a gent," sniffed Tilly quietly. "He can do what he likes."

"She has no dowry," said Paul.

Sir Everard's eyes narrowed. "As you said yourself, Mr. Ballister, I'm an august personage. I've no need of a bride's dowry. On the contrary, I'm offering *you* coin, only this time it will be for Mistress Tom— Ballister's hand."

"You were right the first time, milord. Her name be Tomkins," said Tilly sharply. "Rosamund Tomkins, and don't you forget it. You neither, Rosamund." She turned to her daughter.

Rosamund had never noticed before how clear her mother's eyes could be. They were the color of a dove's wing.

"Now, girl," said Tilly, taking her hand. "Go to your room and gather your belongings, wash and dress in your finest. Sir Everard and I have a great deal to discuss. We'll talk while your stepfather here"—she remembered her haitches again—"fetches the reverend."

"I'll do no such thing," protested Paul. "This is madness. Surely you don't expect him to marry her *now*? Here?" His arm swept the inn.

"Why not?" She rounded on Sir Everard. "Do you object, milord?"

Sir Everard shrugged. "Waiting will make not a whit of difference to me; not once I've settled upon a plan."

"Then that confirms it," said Tilly, slapping her hands together. "He's not taking her nowhere without I know she's wed. A gentleman's word has as much value as a palliard's to me. A real gent's worth lies in his actions. No offense, milord."

"None taken," said Sir Everard.

Tilly nodded. "Husband, fetch the reverend." She pointed toward the church.

Paul looked from one to the other with growing dubiety. "Madoc'll never agree. What about the banns?"

Sir Everard flapped his hand. "A trifle. I know the bishop; he'll waive those for a fee. They needn't concern you."

Rosamund couldn't remember the last time she saw her mother really smile. Ever since she'd come to the Maiden Voyage Inn, she'd been so wrapped up in her own change of circumstance, her loss of happiness, she hadn't realized her mother might suffer from a dearth of it as well. Even with teeth missing, she looked quite lovely. It was clear Sir Everard thought so too, the slow way he returned a conspiratorial grin.

Paul hadn't moved but stood looking at them as if they'd transformed into the Hollanders he so despised. Trying to get their attention, he stamped a booted foot.

"This is nonsensical. I won't have it, you hear? This . . . this ancient cripple"—he gestured to the walking stick—"can't just appear and take away our Rosie."

Tilly's gaze would have turned the Medusa herself to stone. It unnerved her husband. "*Our* Rosie? I don't think so. She be all mine, Paul Ballister, as you've been swift to remind me on many an occasion. And, as mine, I say she is going with Sir Everard Blithman, ancient cripple or no—no offense, my lord—"

"None taken."

"—to be given the opportunity to become a lady, and nothing, especially not *you*, is going to stand in her way."

Rosamund wondered who this woman was with the strong voice and firm convictions who so readily defied her bully of a husband.

"This is outrageous—" Sweat poured from beneath Paul's hat and ran down his face.

"I'll tell you what's outrageous, Paul Ballister, and that's what you did during the wars. If you even try to prevent this, I'll tell . . ." Tilly stared at him. They regarded each other for a long moment before Paul's shoulders drooped and he turned away. With a desperate look at Rosamund and one filled with loathing and rage at Sir Everard, he kicked the door of the inn. There was a resounding crack, and a cry of both pain and impotence escaped.

"You'll regret this, wife. As God is my witness, you'll regret this." He shook his fist at her. "You too . . . *Rosamund*."

Tilly held her head higher. "Maybe. But not as much as if I don't ensure my Rosamund takes this chance."

Paul turned on his heel and stomped down the road. "Get the fuckin' reverend yourself." The chickens squawked and parted. He never looked back.

They watched him; the sun reflecting off the sheen of his coat, the dust from his boots raising small eddies that spiraled and dispersed. The breeze married the calls of gaiety from the river with the sound of a lute. It broke the trance.

"Rosamund," said Tilly, suddenly businesslike. "Go; ready yourself. There be a man of the cloth staying at the Cock and Bull. I'll send the twins to fetch 'im."

Afraid this was but a dream caused by the blow to her head, Rosamund gave a small curtsey and, casting Sir Everard and Jacopo a look of incredulity, obeyed. As she darted up the stairs, she saw no one, but hesitated at the door to her bedroom.

She could hear muffled voices from the taproom, ribaldry and the clank of tankards and goblets as if they'd already begun celebrating her marriage. *Her* marriage! The very idea. Earlier that day she'd been pondering His Majesty's nuptials and here she was, on the brink of her own. Marriage and, it seemed, depar-

ture. Once again she was to commence a new life with
strangers, only this time she would call one of them
husband. A real-life knight who was going to take her
to the city and a fresh beginning. Surely what lay ahead
couldn't be worse than what she was leaving? Only: Sir
Everard didn't understand that he was being cheated.
By mother. By me. If she were a decent girl, a good
girl, she would run straight back down those stairs and
tell Sir Everard the truth. Confess her weaknesses, how
soiled she was, expose her mother's forked tongue, and
allow him to ride away without the encumbrance of a
barely literate wife whose virtue was in tatters. Hesitating, she half turned toward the stairs.

She couldn't. Not when escape was being offered,
when she was being promised an opportunity "like no
other"—whatever that meant.

*Dear God in heaven, Grandmother, Father, may I
never disappoint him.*

She opened the door and gazed around her room,
expecting everything to have been transformed. But
no, there was her small pallet with its worn blankets,
the pillow still bearing the imprint of her head; here
the battered chest which held her Sunday best, some
shirts, bodices, collars and skirts as well as stockings
and coifs. Her one hat sat on the stool by the window.
She picked it up and glanced outside. Through the thick

glass she could just discern the outline of her mother and Sir Everard deep in conversation. As she watched, Sir Everard gestured for Jacopo to join them.

She opened the window slightly and could hear murmurs, but not what was being said. Sir Everard was listening intently to her mother, who was gesticulating and talking rapidly. Rosamund wondered what she was saying. What had possessed her to offer her daughter in marriage? What in God's good heaven had possessed the gentleman to agree? What manner of man was he that he could afford to disregard his reputation and take her to wife?

He even had a tawneyman. This Jacopo was more than a servant; Rosamund could see that. What had Sir Everard called him? A factotum. Was that a synonym for "slave" or "friend"? Perhaps both? Did the gentleman make a habit of buying creatures whose lives he pitied and putting them under his roof? For what purpose? Did he give them all opportunities? Or did he indeed intend to use her, even as a wife, in the manner Tilly first alluded to? Whatever his schemes, the very notion he was buying a bride was madness.

Utterly preposterous.

Rosamund sank down onto the stool and perched her hat on her head.

It was also bloody marvelous.

Closing her eyes, she sent another swift prayer to her grandmother, her father and God Almighty, thanking them for finally answering her prayers and making her wish come true. It might have taken almost ten years, but at last they found the means to rescue her from her stepfather, Paul Ballister, and she thanked them with all her beating heart.

And she thanked them for Sir Everard Blithman. Whoever and whatever he might be.

FOUR
In which a newcomer is made to feel most unwelcome

From the moment the carriage arrived in a flurry of dust and sweating horses in the courtyard of the large three-story house in Bishops-gate Street, and an aching and only half awake Rosamund (who, much to her disappointment, had slept the last part of the journey to London) alighted, nothing was as she expected. Not the orange smoke-filled air, the calamitous noise and pungent odors of the surrounding lanes, the tall, gloomy house, the assembled servants holding torches and lanthorns, nor her husband's behavior. She might as well have been a Hollander for all the welcome she received. While Rosamund wasn't entirely sure what she expected, it wasn't the suspicious looks, barely concealed hostility or shocked silence that greeted Sir Everard's announcement to the curious household: "This is your new mistress, Lady Rosamund Blithman."

Rosamund experienced a frisson of panic when she heard her title. The moment they left the inn, she had wanted nothing more than to ask Sir Everard what might be awaiting her once they reached the capital. But as the door of the carriage closed, before she could even formulate a question, Sir Everard propped first his stick, then himself in a corner of the carriage, tilted his hat over his eyes, folded his arms and, with a quiet chuckle, promptly fell asleep.

After she overcame her admiration for his ability to doze through the equivalent of being tossed about like hay at the end of a pitchfork, Rosamund wondered if he feigned slumber to avoid her company. Before they'd even left the shire she had convinced herself he already regretted his hasty decision. Who could blame him? There was no doubting he had struck a poor deal, yet everything about him, from his clothing to his manner and his men, suggested this was not someone accustomed to making bad decisions. Casting sidelong glances at her *husband* (the word was something she'd have to get used to, as one did a new pair of clogs), she was able to study him at her leisure. She noted the way the sunbeams roved over his rather solid form, revealing long-fingered hands which had slid from their initial position to relax across his lap. The fingernails were scrupulously clean and positively pink. The golden shafts made the bristles that limned his jowls glint. In repose, he had a strong face. The heavy brows and pouched, deep-set eyes, hidden now by the wide brim of his hat, were complemented by broad cheeks and a large chin. His legs, which were encased in fine hose, stretched out before him, showing no sign of the limp which disfigured his walk. She wondered what had caused it, and what he and her mother had so earnestly discussed. Even if he'd been inclined to conversation she doubted she'd have the courage to ask.

Contemplating her mother elicited a long, sad sigh. Was Tilly giving her daughter a second thought or was she, as Rosamund suspected, glad to be rid of the child she'd always regarded as a burden? Eager for Rosamund to leave the inn before Paul returned, Tilly had swept her and Sir Everard out of the taproom even as final blessings were being bestowed. Planting a kiss on her daughter's cheek, she whispered in her ear, then all but shoved her into the carriage before pulling Sir Everard aside and again speaking urgently. Rosamund tried but failed to hear what was being said. She did, however, see Sir Everard wave Jacopo over and deposit a heavy purse in Tilly's outstretched hands. Without hesitation, Tilly slid the money into her pocket. As they rolled away from the inn, Rosamund issued a small cry of protest. Tilly jumped to life and ran alongside the carriage, leaping every so often to catch a glimpse of her daughter.

"Don't forget what I said, Rosamund," she cried. "Don't forget!"

Reclining in her seat, she was relieved her new husband was already asleep; she didn't want to admit what her mother had said was, "Don't say I never do nothin' for you. Just don't you never come back, you hear?" It had been a stinging decree, but one Rosamund vowed to obey. She never wanted to be anywhere she wasn't wanted. Her eyes had slid toward Sir Everard . . . He wanted her. Not only had he paid a goodly sum to wed her, he'd promised her an "opportunity." The words lodged in her center as she wondered what they meant. Surely being the wife of so fine a man was opportunity enough?

As she gazed out the window, holding tight to the sill, the sky transformed from periwinkle to a deep violet, striated with bruised clouds. That's how she felt— bruised inside and out. It wasn't only her body that had received a pummeling, but her soul as well. Deep down she knew why her mother had acted the way she did: Tilly had asserted herself and told such dreadful lies to give her daughter a future. Having abandoned her once, Tilly had done so again. Long ago Rosamund had decided that this was what Tilly did best: distant devotion. She prayed this second effort would yield similar, if not better, results than the first. Surely that's what her callous words really meant.

Did it erase the years of neglect? The willful blindness to what was going on beneath her very roof? Rosamund waited for a sense of attachment toward her mother to descend like a cloak over her shoulders. Instead, she felt a combination of despair and a little nub of anger that her mother had waited all this time to defend her daughter and assert her rights. What she couldn't understand was why, if Tilly had cared so much, she had gone out of her way to appear so impervious for so long. From the moment she'd collected her from Bearwoode, it had been as if her daughter was the least of her concerns.

Paul had been the only one to give her any attention, and then in a manner she couldn't comprehend or change, no matter how often she pleaded or transformed her ways. It was as if her mere presence provoked something in him beyond reason.

But all that was in the past now as she stood in the dark courtyard and tried to shrug off the aftereffects of her exhausted slumber and take in her imposing surrounds. It wasn't until the housekeeper, a regal woman with bronze skin and a white cap over tightly coiled black hair, stepped forward that the silence was broken. Sweeping Rosamund from top to toe with flashing eyes, she dropped the slightest of curtseys and muttered what might have been "my lady" but sounded more like "malady."

Her action woke the other servants from their stupor and they bowed, curtseyed, scraped off caps and mumbled greetings as they shot Rosamund sidelong glances, taking her measure and behaving as if she were an infection, not a person. Not that Sir Everard noticed; he had turned aside to speak to another man who was quickly introduced as the steward, Wat Smithyman. Of middling age and slightly stooped, with a vivid scar cleaving his left cheek, he stepped briskly past her, swinging his arm so hard she felt the rush of air against her ear, and shouted above the ruckus of the horses, the church bells and the cries of the nightwatchmen beyond the gates. It wasn't until two young men shot out of the shadows that she understood what he was doing.

When the assorted trunks, barrels and sacks were unloaded from the carriage, including Rosamund's meager burlap, Wat directed the coachmen as they wrestled with the horses to turn the vehicle in the confined space. Finally, facing the street, the driver held the beasts until Wat gave him a purse. Cracking his whip, he rode off into the night, yelling at a poor vendor who trundled his cart past at the wrong moment, causing onions to scatter across the road. From nowhere, beggars and urchins appeared to scoop up what they could. Instead of helping him, Wat supervised the shutting of the gates, only turning away when the latch was finally lowered. Rosamund felt a twinge of pity for the poor vegetable seller.

Satisfied all was under control, Sir Everard waited for Wat to reach his side, then ordered him and Jacopo to follow, sweeping past Rosamund as if she too were simply something he'd purchased on his journey and was to be stored until required. With a wry smile at the truth of the thought, Rosamund watched as Sir Everard pulled the housekeeper to one side and muttered in a low voice. When the housekeeper turned toward her, eyes narrowed, a glint of what looked like triumph on her face, Rosamund knew she was the subject of the hurried conversation. Would Sir Everard ever admit how he met her and the bargain he'd struck with her mother? And, if he didn't, would Jacopo ever tell?

God forbid if the servants found out . . . She glanced at the housekeeper, who watched Sir Everard as he disappeared from sight, the lanthorn she held aloft shining in her face. Disapproval emanated from her like a strong perfume.

Sir Everard's voice carried from inside the house. "Any more letters arrive in my absence?"

Whatever Wat replied was indistinguishable. Soon, the only sounds were the grunts of the men stacking the barrels and sacks on the other side of the courtyard.

Rosamund longed to stretch, rub her hindquarters, examine this place to which she'd been brought and ask the thousands of questions fluttering around in her mind. Only, she didn't dare. Stifling a yawn, she waited.

The housekeeper gazed at her. Rosamund tolerated the brazen study, determined to neither move nor comment. Instinctively, she knew this was important. With a small harrumph, the woman finally lowered the light and gestured for Rosamund to precede her.

"The master is a busy man," she said. Her voice was lilting, deep and musical. "He's been gone for over three weeks. Much has happened in his absence and not only here, it seems."

So this was how it was to be. Rosamund was an event, unexpected and unwelcome. She took a deep breath and, though she tried to summon a smile and bring a lightness to her tone, found it difficult.

"Then," she began, pleased her voice was steady, "I am fortunate indeed in having so conscientious a husband." There, that little reminder wouldn't go astray. She faced the housekeeper and, tilting her head, looked straight into her face. In the shifting light, her features were patrician, the cheekbones high and wide, the unhappy mouth full. The contrast between the Puritan white of her collar and cuffs against her skin was striking. "And to have you to introduce me to my new abode. That is, if you would be so kind as to do so?" She smiled.

There was a moment's hesitation; the eyes flickered. "It would be my pleasure, my lady," said the housekeeper, her tone suggesting otherwise.

Rosamund swallowed her disquiet. "Then, since you are being so agreeable," she said, "could I also beg your name?"

"Bianca."

Rosamund ignored her failure to address her as "my lady" and wondered if this was a jest. Surely that could not be her name. There was a servant at Bearwoode who bore the same name, and she was certain her grandmother had said it was the Italian word for "white." Who would bestow such an appellation, a constant reminder of her difference?

"Bianca," she repeated. "Pleased to meet you. Shall we?" Rosamund indicated the door and, before Bianca could move, stepped over the threshold.

Her heart, already beating like a soldier's drum, flipped. She hadn't even entered the place and already she'd gone to war.

But at least she'd won the first skirmish.

FIVE
In which a new role
is bestowed

Rosamund's sense of victory was short-lived. It turned out that they had entered the house from the rear. Led along a dingy corridor, she caught glimpses of a large kitchen from which interesting smells emanated, passed what might have been the main entrance and went up a narrow staircase. She heard the murmur of male voices behind a closed door on the first floor and assumed that must be where Sir Everard, Wat and Jacopo were closeted. It was dark inside the house, the few candles in sconces casting faint light. She had an impression of many rooms, threadbare tapestries and a couple of portraits, though Rosamund couldn't discern the subjects. Her boots clanked on the wooden floors in contrast to the silent steps of Bianca, making her feel both clumsy and an intruder.

The house was clearly old; the wainscoting had seen better days, the bannister was scratched and the steps worn with the tread of many feet. Lemon and beeswax almost disguised the musty odor that grew as they climbed another cramped staircase. It wasn't anything a few flowers, a fresh coat of paint and some brighter wall-hangings wouldn't improve.

Bianca showed her into a room on the second floor, and before she could even remove her gloves, there was a knock and two drudges entered, one rolling a large tub, the other carrying two steaming buckets. They poured the water into the tub and made sure they took a good long look at Rosamund. Barely able to withhold their whispers until they'd left the room, they swiftly returned with more hot water, drying sheets and soap. Herbs and petals were scattered across the bath and a sweet perfume arose. Once the tub was filled, Bianca ordered more water on standby and then dismissed the women. They filed out, dropping curtseys and murmuring "madam" with barely concealed sneers. It took Rosamund a moment to understand the sneers weren't only directed at her.

She glanced at Bianca, who, busy opening the window and admitting some air, appeared not to notice. This was not a happy household. Rosamund's heart beat a little faster.

Uncertain what to do, Rosamund waited as Bianca lit more candles. Once that was accomplished and the room glowed, Bianca strode toward her and began unlacing Rosamund's bodice. Startled by the woman's temerity, Rosamund stepped back, gathering her clothes to her.

"Wait. What are you doing?"

With a thin smile, Bianca folded her arms. "Master's orders; he said you were to be bathed immediately and your clothes changed. He said you smelled like the Fleet . . ."

Rosamund gasped.

"In summer."

Heat rushed to Rosamund's face as shame filled her body. Even she knew about the Fleet River, how it was little more than a sewer, often choked with the corpses of dead dogs, shit and offal. How could he? How could Sir Everard say such a thing? And to someone who would have to take orders from her, the mistress? A mistress who smelled like the filthiest of waterways. It was too much. Horrified and embarrassed in equal measure, tears welled. But her humiliation was not yet complete.

Knocking Rosamund's fingers aside, Bianca quickly undid her laces and wrenched the bodice away, screwing up her nose in disgust. She pulled down Rosamund's skirts and then dragged the shift over her head, tossing the linen to one side as if it were fit only for the rag woman. Rosamund's cheeks flamed, but what could she say?

It simply wouldn't do. She had to assert her authority, claw back the ground she'd so recently gained.

About to protest her treatment, Rosamund glanced at her bodice and sleeves lying on the floor and saw the state of the cuffs, the ingrained dirt in the laces, the encrusted mud on the hem of her skirt—her Sunday best. Then, she caught the odor rising from her body. Dear God. Sir Everard was right. She stank. Even though she'd washed, it was only the parts of her the public saw. While she'd good reason not to attend to her ablutions, that was between her and God and no one else. It had served its purpose.

No more.

Naked now except for her boots, she saw herself through others' eyes. The runnels of filth sitting inside her elbows, the smudges between her full breasts and around her knees; the muck around her navel, the dirt she knew rested between her toes. Why, she was no lady, and certainly no fit mistress for this house or this majestic tawneymoor, who not only smelled of violets and wild roses but who wore clothes so clean a saint could have donned them. No wonder she turned up her nose, looked at her with such disdain and spoke with musical contempt.

How could Sir Everard have borne to share a carriage with her, let alone wed her? He'd slept to avoid not conversation but her scent.

Bianca gathered Rosamund's clothes into a bundle and tossed them toward the hearth. Rosamund was sure had a fire been lit, they would have been cast upon the flames. In an effort to wrest back some dignity, she took off her boots herself.

Without giving away what she thought of the scuffed and worn footwear, Bianca pushed them aside with a sweep of her ankle.

"Come," she said. "Let's sweeten you up."

Bianca held Rosamund's arm as she stepped over the rim of the tub, her thumb compressing a fresh bruise. Rosamund sucked in her breath and tried to extract herself from the firm hold. Bianca gripped tighter. Tears spilled and she stared in abjection at Bianca's dark fingers against her pale skin. Following the direction of her gaze, Bianca seemed to see not just Rosamund's arm, but her flesh for the first time. Eyes of a startling turquoise widened. Her grip loosened, and she slowly extended Rosamund's arm toward the light. Without saying a word, she lifted it higher, turning it slightly and studying the inside slowly. Standing in the tub, the water reaching her knees, Rosamund could hardly object as Bianca wordlessly circled her. With fingers as gentle as the first snowfall, she coolly touched each and every mark upon Rosamund's body. Some were old and faded, others newly wrought. Rosamund felt her skin begin to goose, her nipples firm.

She didn't say a word, but by the time Bianca had finished her examination, her features were cast more softly.

"My lady?" she whispered, gazing up at Rosamund with huge, all-knowing eyes. Why, her lashes were longer than Mabel the cow's and curled like Jacopo's. "Who would do such a thing to you?"

"The grazes upon my arms, the gash upon my forehead"—her fingers danced over it—"are the result of my carelessness."

"They are not what I am referring to, *signora*." Bianca frowned. "These"—she elevated Rosamund's arm higher, exposing bruises, a series of raw lines made by a switch, a bite mark upon her breast—"are no accident."

Rosamund's throat constricted. She swallowed and breathed slowly, forcing herself to calm as Bianca lowered her arm.

"It's all right, Bianca," said Rosamund quietly. "He . . . he can hurt me no more. My . . . my husband has seen to that."

"The *signore* does a good deed, then?" Bianca's slight inflection suggested surprise.

Their eyes met and for a second, something inside Rosamund unfurled and reached out. Bianca's lips parted and an odd look crossed her face before it just as swiftly vanished, replaced by a brittle, hard expression. Disappointment drowned the tentative connection, and Rosamund's eyes began to sting.

Before she could rub the feeling away, or even dare to try to recapture the moment, Bianca pushed Rosamund down into the water, dousing her thoroughly from a nearby pail. Spluttering as hair and water streamed into her eyes, Rosamund pushed the soaking strands from her face as Bianca attacked her with soap. Forgetting the bruises and scrapes she'd touched with such tenderness only moments before, she washed her mistress as if she were a piece of laundry, eliciting shrieks and objections. The louder Rosamund cried, the more vigorously Bianca scrubbed. Old wounds reopened and blood streamed into the water, staining it. Her bruised hind found no respite against the solid bottom of the tub.

Rosamund knew the woman took no pleasure from her ministrations yet could no more prevent her cries than she could the sadness and anxiety rising inside her as pain flared and her modesty and dignity were trampled.

Understanding her objections were falling on deaf ears, Rosamund forced her mouth shut lest she add to the rumors she'd no doubt were already flying about the house, or swallow more soapy water. As Bianca tended her, she began to forget the aches and enjoy the sensation of being clean; the sting of the cloth on her scrubbed flesh, the rawness of grazes exposed, the water lapping them, the aroma of roses and lavender. With each swipe of the cloth, every lathery cloud washed away, it was as if she was cleansed of the last nine years. She imagined every day at the Maiden Voyage Inn, nay, every moment spent with her stepfather and his brutal attentions being purged from her flesh. If only she could do this to her mind, she would achieve peace.

As the second lot was poured over her head, making Rosamund gasp and her eyes fly open, Bianca propped herself on the edge of the tub and began to carefully comb the lice out of her hair.

When she was finally dried, dressed in what Bianca called a "house-gown" (a flimsy, apricot gauze procured from God knew where), the housekeeper departed before Rosamund could thank her.

"The *signore* will join you in due course," she said in her lyrical accent and, without a curtsey or fare-thee-well, shut the door.

A knock followed shortly after and one of the maids entered, a pretty girl with a snub nose, freckles and dimples. Rosamund flashed a smile and scurried forward to help her. Carrying a tray laden with food, the girl shied away from Rosamund's outstretched arms, appalled. Understanding she'd made another error—the lady of the house did not aid a servant—Rosamund retreated to the cold hearth, watching while dishes and cups were arranged on a small table by the window. When the girl finished, Rosamund thanked her warmly and was rewarded by an astonished widening of the maid's eyes and the glimmer of a grin before two more maids were admitted, who quickly removed the buckets and tub, exiting swiftly along with the first.

Alone at last, Rosamund stood in the center of the room and let out a breath so long and deep it was as if she'd held it all the way from Gravesend. Oh dear God. How could she have thought this might be easy? That she was being rescued? While it was a relief to be free of the Ballisters, they were a known quantity. Surprises were few and far between; she was able to navigate her way through each day and had even accrued allies. Here, she was a stranger cast upon an unfamiliar shore. She didn't even speak the same language. Not only would she have to accustom herself once more to being served—rather than doing the serving—but

Sir Everard owned slaves. Rosamund had heard of the trade in human cargo, the stories of how some city merchants and nobles flaunted their newly acquired property, dressing their blackamoors in fine clothes and treating them much as they did their servants, only without the inconvenience of a wage. But she had never thought to see one, or to have one attend to her needs, however grudgingly. Yet, Jacopo didn't hail from the Africas but Venice. From her accent, Bianca did as well. Well-spoken, clean, and with some authority if their titles were anything to go by, they were not what Rosamund expected. Nothing was.

Taking in the huge old four-poster bed, the diaphanous curtains swathing it, the discolored blankets and pillows atop the coverlets, she did an inventory of the room, something practical, achievable, anything to ease the tumble of emotions inside. It was at least three times the size of her small one at the inn and though it was darker than her bedroom at Bearwoode, there was much to remind her of it—the decorative mantel, the deep hearth, the wooden armoire, the curtains billowing gently at the window and the landscapes hanging on the walls. It was akin to snatching a moment from her childhood. Her heart contracted. Then, she'd been loved. Then, she'd laughed—and often. Here? She gazed around. What would she do here?

Well, at least she was clean. Smoothing her hands over the gown, she admired her scrubbed skin, though it made her bruises stand out. Raising her hand to her nose, she inhaled deeply. Lifting the long, damp strands of her hair, she studied them. They no longer crawled with vermin and her scalp didn't itch. That was something to delight in. Spinning in a circle, her arms outstretched, she felt a laugh begin to build; then she remembered the horrified looks of the servants, Bianca's coldness and Sir Everard's words, "She stinks like the Fleet," and the laugh died. She ceased to turn. Crossing her arms, she bunched her fists in her armpits. Sadness welled.

This wouldn't do. Cursing her weakness, she resorted to pragmatism again.

Testing the mattress, she was pleased to note it was soft. She sank into the feathers and wondered who'd slept on it before. Was this Sir Everard's bedroom? There were two doors—the one she had entered by and another. Where did it lead? To Sir Everard's chamber? Any thoughts she had about opening it were quashed. Was she to share his bed this night? Her throat grew tight. As his wife, was that not his prerogative? She offered up a swift prayer to God (and to her grandmother) that, even though he was old, he would be gentle and courteous, like the knights in the stories her grandmother told her. That he wouldn't notice. That he'd be nothing like . . . nothing like . . .

Stop. She was cleansed now. She wouldn't sully that feeling by thinking of . . . the past.

The mouthwatering smell of roasted meat reached her, reminding her she was utterly famished. Uncertain whether she was meant to indulge in the repast spread across the table or wait for company, Rosamund decided the amount of pheasant, bread, cheese and fruits, and the brimming decanter of wine, must be meant for two. Still, as the melting candles and the rhythmic tick of a clock suggested, Sir Everard's "due course" was taking a very long time.

Resisting the cries of her stomach, she rose and went to the window and gazed out on the shadowy outlines of church spires and slate roofs, admiring the glow of distant bonfires and trying not to breathe in the thick smoke that hung in the air. Here was the city of which she'd dreamed, the city everyone spoke of—some reverently, in hushed tones; others more boldly, as if discussing a bear baiting; some spoke of it with such displeasure, it was as if they were describing Sodom and Gomorrah. In the distance she could hear the peal of a bell, the loud thump of a door, then a scream followed by coarse laughter and a volley of dog barks. London was wearing all its faces tonight. Turning away from the window, she continued her exploration of the room, opening empty drawers, running her hands over an assortment of glass ornaments, some with chips in them, picking up a fan, stroking a bedcover or chair. She was admiring a rich, if somewhat bedraggled tapestry hanging between the fireplace and the window when Sir Everard knocked and entered.

"The room is to your liking?" he asked, his arm describing an arc before he beheld her and froze. "My," he exhaled.

Reddening under his appraisal, Rosamund was quick to respond. "Oh, indeed, sir. It's . . . very nice."

Sir Everard returned to his senses. "I've been remiss in not saying it before, I do offer you welcome, Rosamund, and might I say, you look . . . well." He nodded. "I knew that with a bath and change of attire your loveliness would be evident." A look Rosamund was not unacquainted with appeared upon his face.

Unable to help herself, Rosamund gave a dry chortle. "I would have thought you might also note the alteration in my fragrance, sir, since you found it so offensive before."

Sir Everard's expression changed, his mouth opened and closed and he turned aside. "Ah . . . indeed. I see. Quite." His eyes fell upon the untouched food. "You haven't eaten anything. I assumed you would be all but prostrate with hunger. You barely ate a morsel at the inn."

Rosamund dropped another curtsey. "I was waiting for you, milord."

Taking her by the elbow, he led her to a chair, using his stick to push aside an errant cushion. "Well, I'm here now. Sit, eat. Take your time. I've ordered the servants not to disturb us."

That comment gave her pause, but she arranged the flimsy robe and watched as Sir Everard sat in the chair opposite. "Will you join me, sir?" she asked.

He flapped a hand. "I've already eaten. Please, don't stand on ceremony."

Repressing her shock that the meal was for her alone, and imagining how many customers such fare would feed (and the resultant profit), Rosamund began to pick at the meat, observing Sir Everard from beneath her lashes.

Conscious of his eyes upon her, she ate slowly, making sure to chew with her mouth closed and holding a napkin close by to remove any grease from her lips or fingers. As the minutes passed and still Sir Everard didn't say anything, Rosamund realized what a dullard she'd been.

"Allow me to pour you a drink, milord," she said quickly. Half standing, she splashed ruby liquid into the glasses, lifting one into Sir Everard's outstretched hand.

"May I propose a toast?" asked Sir Everard.

"Please."

"To my new wife."

Rosamund drank slowly. Summoning what little remained of her courage, she decided she'd nothing to lose and much to gain. While her mother thought knowledge overrated and questions intolerable, had not her grandmother said the ability to learn is man's greatest asset? And how did one acquire learning if not by asking questions? A talent at which blasted women excelled, according to Paul.

"Thank you, milord." Putting down her goblet, she began, "You referred to me as your new wife, which would imply there was an old one." She met his steady gaze.

Sir Everard's brow furrowed. "Indeed, there was. In fact, this was her room. I've not been in it since . . ." He didn't finish.

Despite the expression on his face, the fact he was forthcoming heartened Rosamund's resolve. Enjoying the mellow feel of the claret on her throat and the rich taste of pheasant, she leaned forward. "May I be so bold as to ask you a question?"

Sir Everard waved his permission.

"Why did you marry me? It's evident your servants were astonished." He didn't correct her. "While it's clear I've much to gain from this arrangement"—her nod encompassed the house—"I'm yet to understand how *you* benefit. What can you hope to gain from plighting your troth with me?"

Sir Everard drummed his fingers on the arm of the chair and took a long draft of his wine. "Why did I marry you?" he repeated slowly, staring at a point beyond Rosamund's shoulder. "It's not the first time I've been asked that question tonight. It will not be the last."

Snapping out of his reverie, Sir Everard regarded her solemnly. "I'm not surprised my behavior at the inn, offering to . . . errr . . ." He paused, flicked his hand toward her a few times. "Must be troubling you. What sort of a man does that on a whim?"

Rosamund nodded. She'd be lying if she didn't admit it caused her more than a little perturbation.

"You see, Rosamund, despite my impulsiveness, I married you with a particular purpose in mind. You're quite correct that marriage never entered my initial reckoning, but when your mother pointed out it's essentially a business transaction, I thought, damn it, she's right. After all, when I married Margery (my *old* wife), I gained useful family connections, some of whom you're bound to meet, and I'm afraid they must be endured, and her generous dowry. In return, she gained my name and a title, and later shared my growing wealth. Neither of us was too proud to turn to trade and improve our situation through hard work . . . unlike some. It was all that saved us during the Interregnum and Cromwell's rule. Our families invested in us and we invested in each other. Just like a business. We protected each other, profited from our relationship. That's what I'm doing now: in giving you the advancement that comes with my name, I'm investing in you with the intention to profit. It's evident your fortunes have undergone dramatic alteration, allowing me to find you in such reduced circumstances. Despite your father's name, marrying you was a risk; but something tells me"—he thumped his breastbone to indicate what that something was—"you'll be worth it." He leaned forward, his right hand curled upon his knee. "Understand this, Rosamund. I always expect good returns on my investments."

Taken aback, Rosamund waited.

"As my wife, even though you're a bastard—"

She winced.

"—you'll enjoy a certain degree of prestige . . . and notoriety." He sank back into the seat.

Rosamund worked to keep her face impassive as she wondered exactly what that meant.

"What of the house, milord? I've never been responsible for so large an establishment, for running it. As
your wife, I assume I—" How could she confess she'd
never been responsible for *any* establishment? Unless the Maiden Voyage Inn counted and then she was
hardly accountable—that particular pleasure had been
Paul's. Not that it prevented him apportioning blame
when things went wrong, and punishment when they
did . . . or didn't. She swallowed and looked around,
hoping her sense of being overwhelmed with responsibility wasn't apparent.

Sir Everard dismissed her anxieties. "Bianca is my
housekeeper and has done a fine job of taking care
of Blithe Manor since Margery's death. Until you're
ready to take on the various duties a wife would, she
will continue to manage." Leaning back in the chair,
he smiled. "You're not to concern yourself with such
trivialities yet. I've another task I want you to focus on.
My only expectation of you, Rosamund, is that you do
exactly as I ask."

Rosamund's mind was spinning. "What do you ask
of me, milord?"

Sir Everard adjusted his necktie, smoothed his hands
down the front of his waistcoat then rested them atop
his knees.

"Quite simply, what I require of you above and beyond anything else, is both loyalty and obedience."

Rosamund waited for him to say more, but he appeared to have finished. She could hardly believe her ears. Was this all Sir Everard wanted in return for not only providing her with the means to escape her previous life, but giving her his name and the benefits of his fortune? There had to be a catch. Surely no man could be so generous, so forthcoming. What had she, Rosamund Tomkins, done to deserve such a benefactor? Why, she was already loyal—how could she not be? As for obedience, was it not a woman's natural state?

Sitting very straight, her hands folded in her lap, Rosamund said, "I can be both those things, milord."

"I never doubted," said Sir Everard, smiling at her. She hadn't noticed before, but his teeth were quite crooked, like the tombstones in the churchyard at Gravesend. Whether it was a trick of the candles or not, there was something predatory about his expression. "I'm also pleased you're not one of those women who bombard men with questions. I don't like them."

Rosamund felt a rush of discomfort. Nevertheless, she took note. The last thing she wanted to do was displease him.

"There's something else you should know as well," said Sir Everard. "Something that will help you understand what I'm going to ask of you in the coming weeks—the task for which I want you to prepare."

Rosamund swallowed. Here it comes. "Oh?"

"You see, Rosamund, when you married me, you didn't just become Lady Blithman."

Unable to prevent it, the words tripped from her mouth. "What else did I become?" Her voice was barely a whisper as her heart tumbled in her chest.

"Today, my lady, you also became a chocolate maker's wife."

SIX

In which husband and new wife discourse about chocolate

C hocolate maker?" She swiftly adjusted her tone, turning her involuntary question into a statement. "You're a chocolate maker."

"Among other things, yes." He smiled at the expression on her face. "It's a . . . new venture of mine. One in which you will play an important role."

"Choc-o-late," she said again, lingering on every syllable, making it last longer.

"Yes," said Sir Everard, smiling. "Chocolate. I'm about to open a chocolate house here in London."

"A chocolate house?" She'd heard of coffee houses, but chocolate ones? Why, this was completely splendid.

"I've recently, er . . . acquired property in Birchin Lane, not far from here. It's being renovated to accommodate the new business. In a matter of weeks, we'll be open to the public. What say you to that, Rosamund?"

"I'm not certain what to say, sir. I'm . . . shocked, nay, delighted. This isn't what I expected at all."

Sir Everard smiled. "Have you ever tasted chocolate?"

Clearly the prohibition on questions didn't apply to him. "No, I . . ." She shook her head. "No." Paul had intended to purchase some to serve at the inn, but since the excise was twice that imposed on coffee, the cost had been prohibitive.

Sir Everard's eyes crinkled in anticipation. "Well, that's an oversight we'll remedy. Let me tell you, it's the wonder of our age." His head rested against the back of his chair and he shut his eyes. "I remember the first time I tried it. I was in Spain. I thought I'd entered the gates of paradise. I knew then, I was destined to introduce my countrymen"—his eyes flew open—"and women—to its joys." He frowned. "Even so, I'm not the first to bring the beverage to London. Already, there are booksellers offering the drink and extolling its medicinal value. They say it prolongs life." He made a disparaging noise. "There's Sury's near East Gate serving a dreadful version, and a man named Richard Mortimer has started making medicinal comfits in his shop in Sun Alley in East Smithfield. He calls them 'queen's *chocolatas*,' but they look more like tiny hedgehogs, smell as bad and have the consistency of nuts. They break teeth." He tapped his cheek. "Much is claimed for chocolate—from curing stomach complaints to coughs and other diseases, which is all very well and good, but that's not the most interesting thing about it. There's another advantage to the drink which will, if I do it right, set my chocolate house apart from any other establishment." He cocked a brow, daring Rosamund to ask.

Up for the dare, she did. "May I know the nature of this advantage, milord?"

"You may." Sir Everard lowered his voice. "I have it on the best authority that chocolate is the most marvelous aphrodisiac known to man." He grinned wryly. "It's an elixir that will increase a man's sap and incite love-passions in women. It rules *amour*, Rosamund, and in a kingdom that's controlled by love and lust, that has a king who holds his prick the way other rulers do their scepters, that makes it priceless." He studied her a moment, pleased he was spared the usual maidenly blushes at his vulgarity.

"It's this aspect of chocolate I believe will allow our establishment to cast others into the shade. In due course, naturally." He smiled. "While coffee clears the mind, facilitates conversation and allows insights,

chocolate is for those who seek pleasure. It's the ulti-
mate temptation: Eve's apple in this overgrown city
garden. I intend that every man and woman will desire
to bite into its flesh and drink its juices."

He reached for her hands, holding them tightly. His
skin was warm, his fingers soft. A gentleman's. Yet what
he was discussing wasn't very gentlemanly. It made her
feel hot and a little uncomfortable in a dreamy sort of
way. Shafts of quicksilver speared her chest, her loins,
made her flesh dance beneath her shift. She shivered.

"What say you to that, my Lady Rosamund?"

Rosamund stared at his white hands gently holding
hers. "I think it sounds . . . fascinating. Fascinating
and, if I may be so bold, sir, naughty."

Releasing her, Sir Everard guffawed. "Naughty.
Now, there's a word I haven't heard since my boys
were breeched." He wiped an imaginary tear from
his eye. "Naughty. I like that. Yes, I intend we'll be
very naughty indeed. More than you realize." His eyes
ceased to see her as he looked inward.

My boys. Rosamund stored that for later.

Rising, he began to pace again, his leg dragging
slightly. "In the Queenshead, a tavern at the end of this
very street, there's a Frenchman making and selling
chocolate. I've been watching him since he started; the
men working at the Royal Exchange go there in droves.

There's also Morat the Great in Exchange Alley; he offers drinks of it in his coffee house. Christopher Bowman purports to serve it at the Turk's Head, but those who've tasted the bona fide article know he's really selling coffee but charging for chocolate." He shook his head, but whether in dismay or admiration, Rosamund couldn't tell.

"The Frenchies love it, so do the Spaniards and God knows, there's plenty in this city who love *them* and ape their every fad and fashion. London is about to go wild for this West Indian drink—the *genuine* product—as word of its taste and the benefits that accrue from drinking it spreads." He paused in the middle of the room. "Especially its *naughty* benefits." He chuckled. So did Rosamund, pleased she'd delighted him so.

"Before any *more* competitors arise, I will open my dedicated house, where anyone and everyone can come and taste what's been described as sin in a bowl; where they can relax, converse and drink my specially prepared chocolate." He stopped and stared out the window. "It will be *my* house; *my* triumph."

"May I see it?" Rosamund thought a few more questions wouldn't hurt, especially when Sir Everard was being so loquacious.

He glanced over his shoulder. "Oh, my dear, you will do so much more than that." Before she could ask what he meant, he raised his glass. "To chocolate," he said.

"To chocolate," she replied and drank. Her head swam; her senses were afire. Unaccustomed to so much wine, so much physical comfort, she felt the urge to sleep begin to settle, and her head began to ache again.

"Tomorrow, I will take you to see the chocolate house and introduce you to its delights; I will have my man prepare for you the most delicious thing you've ever tasted."

"You don't prepare it, sir?"

"Me? No, my dear. I've contracted the services of the King of Spain's former chocolate maker—stole him, truth be told." He laughed. "A man named Filip de la Faya and his son, Solomon, make the chocolate for me. For us," he corrected quickly. "It's his chocolate you will drink. The Spaniards might be bloodsucking Papists, but they're the only ones who really know how to prepare it."

"I will look forward to that very much, sir," said Rosamund.

"Now that's settled," said Sir Everard, putting down his wine and reaching into his waistcoat. He pulled out a long-stemmed clay pipe and pouch. "Let's return to our earlier conversation."

Stifling a yawn, Rosamund did her best to appear alert.

Sir Everard tamped tobacco into the small bowl. "Allow me to tell you about my first wife, my family. I feel I owe you an explanation—"

Rosamund interrupted. "Sir, if any dues are owed, then I think it's me who has incurred the debt. But aye . . ." She twisted the ring on her finger, a gold band that Sir Everard had taken from his smallest one to place upon hers. It was a little big, but he'd promised her another as soon as possible. "I would be grateful for any understanding about your life—former and present—you might offer, thus ensuring my mistakes are few and far between." She thought of the servants, of Bianca.

Sir Everard grunted. "Very well." He sat back in his chair. After a time, he began to speak, his voice low and measured as if he was unaccustomed to the topic. "My wife, my *old*"—he winked at Rosamund—"nay, my *first* wife, was Margery Montagu—her uncle was the Earl of Sandwich."

Rosamund hoped she looked suitably impressed.

"We were married many years. Of all the children she birthed, there were two sons, Gregory and . . ." He hesitated. "Aubrey, and a beautiful daughter, Helene, who survived. In fact, you look uncannily like her; you may hear the servants who knew her say as much."

Rosamund tried not to appear astonished. Three children who lived—and one who resembled her. Resisting the urge to look around, as if the children would suddenly manifest from behind the tapestries or march through the doors, she dared more questions. "What . . . what happened to your wife, sir? Where are your children?"

"Sadly, Margery left us," said Sir Everard brusquely, his eyes flickering toward the bed. "She died more than two years ago."

Rosamund plucked at her robe as the understanding she'd been so eager to attain dawned. She was not only wearing a dead woman's clothes, she was about to sleep in her bed and walk in her shoes.

Lost in his own thoughts, Sir Everard failed to see her unease. He put the pipe in his mouth, struck a flint and lit it, drawing heavily. Smoke poured from the bowl and settled around his head. His eyes grew distant.

"The boys, well, where do I begin? When he came of age, I sent Gregory to take care of my interests in Africa. He was killed by savages."

Rosamund's hand flew to her mouth. "My lord. I'm . . . I'm so sorry."

"So was I, so was I." Sir Everard let out a deep sigh. "What about your other son, Aubrey?"

Sir Everard's eyes darkened and his entire body grew still. It was a while before he spoke again. "I encouraged him to settle in the New World."

Rosamund's ears pricked and, as she caught the expression on Sir Everard's face, the way he lingered on the word, she wondered what Aubrey had done to require "encouragement."

"But he too is dead." Sir Everard cleared his throat. Rosamund was lost for words.

"Margery found it . . . difficult. The loss of our boys was more than she could bear; Helene was all she lived for." Sir Everard's voice was tight, as if he was working to bury the pain. "She was all I lived for as well." He studied Rosamund, his mind working behind his eyes. As if he had reached a decision, he took a deep breath and sat up. "I was going to spare you the less savory parts of my story, but now that you're here . . . now that you're my *wife*, I feel you deserve to know them."

Rosamund waited.

"Just before Aubrey left for Virginia, an acquaintance of his, a man named Matthew Lovelace, son of a poet and with very modest means, began to pay court to Helene. Swept her off her feet." His eyes clouded. He rested the pipe on the edge of the table and picked up his drink. "I admit, I abetted him in his pursuit, blessed their union. I even brought him into my business, encouraged him to invest as I do in the Royal Adventurers into Africa. With the right investment, the right attitude, there's a great deal of money to be made."

"There is?" asked Rosamund.

"Indeed. I only learned later that Lovelace was not the man I thought. He disapproved. The man was in possession of a conscience." Sir Everard's mouth twisted; the quality an unforgivable flaw in his eyes. "Still, all was not lost. He'd caught wind of a new fad—chocolate—and recommended investing. After he and Helene wed, we even traveled together to learn what we could about the stuff, set up agents in Spain and the Americas so we could import the raw materials. In fact, the chocolate house was his idea." With a laugh that sounded like a howl of pain, he dashed the goblet upon the table so hard, what remained of the wine slopped over the lip. Rosamund jumped. "No sooner had we returned from that trip than he revealed himself for the rogue he was, the black-hearted knave."

He paused. Rosamund held her breath.

"He turned Helene against us, against me. If it hadn't been for Margery, I doubt I would ever have seen my daughter again. But she begged to see the baby . . ."

"There was a baby?"

"My grandson. I knew Helene was being coerced, forced against her will to deny me. How could she call the baby Everard, after her father, if she didn't love me?"

Rosamund shook her head.

"Yes, there was a child. But I only saw him once. Once! So did Margery, God bless her soul. You see, the very same night Margery held her little grandson, she passed into the Lord's arms."

"She was so ill?"

"Beyond physick. Her loss was . . . unexpected. I knew she wasn't well, but . . . You see, Rosamund, before Margery was even pronounced dead, Helene was gone. Helene, the babe and Lovelace." He growled at the memory. "He stole her from me, the last of my children, the last of my family. He took her away as if she was a common bawd and put her on a ship bound for the colonies. God damn his rotten soul." This time, he took a deep, shuddering breath. "Helene never made it."

Bands tightened around Rosamund's chest. "Oh, milord, you have my deepest sympathy." She wanted to reach out, but a little voice inside her head warned her to keep her hands in her lap. When he said nothing, she finally asked another question. "What happened?"

Sir Everard raised bleak eyes to hers. "The black-guard murdered them. Helene and the child. Lovelace killed the last of my kin."

Rosamund could scarce believe what she was hearing. Why, this Lovelace was a scoundrel of the worst kind. Far from being in possession of a conscience, he was unconscionable. Poor Sir Everard, poor Helene and her little boy. Poor Margery. She repressed a shudder, the urge to cast off the gown and slip her feet out of the satin pumps.

Wine forgotten, Sir Everard puffed silently on his pipe for a while. "That was over two long, wretched years ago. I just thank the good Lord Margery wasn't here. If she hadn't already gone to God, the knowledge that the last of her children was dead would have killed her. It near enough killed me."

This man had been visited by so much grief in such a short space of time. Sympathy welled within Rosamund as the smoke thickened, and she coughed into her fist.

"Forgive me, sir, but I must ask. What happened to Mr. Lovelace? Did the law catch him?"

Aware of the discomfort the tobacco was causing, Sir Everard rose and went to the window. "I prayed the poltroon was dead. Alas, my prayers weren't answered." His quiet words took wing into the night. "He stayed in the New World awhile, flitting from place to place, causing trouble, leaving misery and strife in his wake. As for the authorities? The law—well, sometimes you have to . . ." He waved a hand dismissively. "I've recently learned he's returned. His intention is to commence business here, in London."

"He would dare? After what he's done?"

"He exists merely to torment me. But not for much longer." His eyes met hers briefly before he returned to contemplating the view from the window.

Rosamund studied the set of Sir Everard's shoulders. How could he stand the weight of such grief? To know that the murderer of your child and grandchild walked God's good earth; the streets of this very city. No wonder Sir Everard rated loyalty so highly—and obedience.

"Still," he said, turning back toward her. "This is not the night to raise ugly specters, is it? I made myself a promise I wouldn't speak the knave's name again, and here I am . . ." He shrugged. "Now you're a Blithman, you must needs know who we call enemy as much as those we embrace as friends. And believe me when I say that Lovelace is my avowed enemy."

"Well, then he's mine too," said Rosamund swiftly. She meant it.

Sir Everard gave a wry smile. "Thank you, my

dear. Now, let us put the sorry past behind us; after all, we've much to celebrate." Limping back to his chair, he picked up his goblet, raised it toward her and drank. Smacking his lips together, he sat back down. "Which brings me to the other reason I wanted to talk to you tonight, to set your mind at rest regarding your other . . . how do I put it delicately . . . obligations as my wife."

Rosamund felt her heart grow cold and heavy. Her mother's words rang in her ears; dread filled her chest.

"Why do you think I married you?" he asked softly.

"I . . . I assume you wanted a wife—another one, that is—for the reason any man does . . . because . . . because you would like an heir . . . especially since . . ." She left the sentence unfinished, grimacing at how clumsy she was.

Sir Everard made a bitter, angry sound. Rosamund tried hard not to recoil. "Not this man." Composing himself, he sighed. "Anyhow, even if I wanted to father another child"—his mouth worked itself into a peculiar shape—"I cannot."

Oh, dear God, he was . . . What was the word she had heard Widow Cecily use to describe Reverend Madoc? That's right, a sodomite. A man who loved men. She tried to keep her expression neutral. Well, there were worse things.

Sir Everard looked her directly in the eye. "Don't misunderstand, Rosamund. I find women very attractive—"

Out went that notion.

"And you're a very beautiful young woman. Very. If circumstances were different, I would enjoy what's now rightfully mine." His eyes lingered on her and she shivered, resisting the urge to wrap the gown about her more tightly. "But you see, some years ago I was beset by an affliction which kept me abed for a long time. When I could finally rise, I had a most peculiar tremor in my hands." He held them out and for the first time Rosamund saw that they did indeed shake slightly. "It comes and goes. The worst thing was my sense of balance was disturbed. I took a tumble in the middle of Cheapside. Couldn't move. Had to be carried home and one of those bloodthirsty quacks examined me—he and his foppish cronies. Upshot was, they attributed it to an imbalance of the humors. They purged me, lanced my veins, stuck me with leeches, gave me emetics. Depending who it was, they all had a different solution. One of them swore I'd never walk again. Shouldn't have said that, should he?" His face grew grim. "No one tells me what I can and can't do. I took it as a challenge. With Margery, Helene, Jacopo and Wat's help and the aid of my stick"—he wrapped his hand around the gold-tipped head—"I was back on my feet. It was declared a miracle; I was the toast of the medical establishment, let me tell you. The Royal College of Surgeons came to examine me; doctors published pamphlets about my remarkable recovery."

Finally, his limp was explained.

"That's marvelous," said Rosamund, bringing her hands together beneath her chin.

"Marvelous?" Sir Everard blustered. "It was a bloody catastrophe."

"Oh, no." Her hands dropped.

"Oh, yes. While my legs worked, and the shakes that occasionally beset me became less frequent, there was a part of my anatomy that ceased to function."

Rosamund stared at him blankly.

Slowly, he spread his hands and lowered his gaze to his crotch.

Rosamund's cheeks flooded with color. "Oh."

"Indeed." Sir Everard wasn't laughing now. "My fleshy flute has fallen silent."

She looked away swiftly; anything she said would be wrong. How could you offer any reassurance about *that*?

"I've embarrassed you. I've grown used to my . . . my situation. Well, as accustomed as a man can. It's God's will, isn't that what they say? Either that, or punishment for my many sins. Likely for those I'm yet to commit as well." He chewed his lips for almost a full minute, as if trying to swallow something unpalatable. "Now I'm an old man. Margery is dead. Not being able is not as . . . hard for me as it once was." He gave a bark of laughter.

Why, this wasn't funny at all. She didn't think it was possible to grow any hotter, but she did. If she'd been in possession of a fan, she would have hidden her face behind it.

Sir Everard shifted in his seat. "I've given you cause to be further discomfited. My apologies."

"None necessary, my lord, I assure you. I'm sorry for your"—she glanced at the area between his legs before looking away quickly and, searching for a word, said the first one that popped into her head—"loss."

He snorted. "I didn't lose it, dear girl. It simply no longer works. For all the good it does me, I may as well be a blasted eunuch. I hope you don't feel cheated," he said. "Though, from the look in your eyes, I imagine you feel somewhat relieved." Now it was her turn to find the floor interesting. "But I'll not expect anything from you in that regard. Only, as I said, loyalty. Loyalty and obedience."

How did she articulate, without causing the utmost offense, that she felt nothing but joyous relief? To be spared the attentions of a man, even one who seemed as nice (if somewhat old and lame) as Sir Ever-ard, her husband by law and God. Why, she couldn't quite believe her luck. Not for the first time, she sent thanks to the twins for chasing her, the horses for running her down . . . Oh, and her grandmother, her father and God. Immediately, she felt bad that she was thanking them for another's ill fortune and tried to reverse her prayer.

She simply said, "You have them, milord."

A couple of minutes passed in silence. For all that Sir Everard appeared to have the world at his feet, with wealth, fine clothes, servants to attend his every need, slaves at his beck and call and a large if somewhat damp and ancient home, as well as a chocolate house, appearances didn't account for everything. He was like the portraits she had glimpsed in the corridor, or those that used to hang in her grandmother's hall and parlor; often she'd wondered what the subjects were thinking, how their lives were beyond the frame. She'd never have guessed that behind those searching eyes, the facade of success, was a man buried in grief with no family to support him, an enemy hovering, and a terrible affliction.

She poured more wine while Sir Everard repacked his pipe. "I'm told tobacco helps my condition, that it will keep the tremors and other symptoms at bay." She waited patiently for him to elucidate, but he did not.

"Well, my dear. There you have it. Do you have any more questions?" It was evident she'd extinguished the quota allowed.

Outside, bells began to toll, sonorous and hollow. It was later than Rosamund thought. They'd been talking for hours. The food was still largely untouched, but she felt as if she'd gorged. As for questions, oh, aye, she had many, but they could wait.

"No, no more questions, not tonight. Oh, forgive me. That's not true, I do. One."

Sir Everard arched a brow.

"Where does that door lead?"

Sir Everard followed the direction of her gaze. "That was Margery's closet—her equivalent of Tradescant's Ark—you know, the fabulous collection of objects the Tradescant family put together over years." He snorted. "I'm afraid it's not in their league even if it's where she kept her curios and useless flibbertigibbets. You're welcome to use it. Discard or keep what you find. I care not. I'll have Bianca find the key."

Rosamund wondered what flibbertigibbets were, and why they were useless; she also wondered how Sir Everard could be quite so dismissive of them. Uneasy that what was Margery's was now hers, including a defective husband, she refrained from asking.

"Very well," Sir Everard said and, with some difficulty, pulled himself out of the seat. Rosamund leaped up to assist him. He waved her away. "Please, do not fuss." Grabbing his stick, he slowly straightened his back, wincing. "Tomorrow we'll attend the chocolate house."

"That would be wonderful, milord."

"Call me Everard." He reached out and gently pushed a stray hair behind her ear. It had dried in the warm breeze drifting through the window. "Your hair is very long; long and untamed . . ."

Startled by his touch, Rosamund jerked away from him. Sir Everard frowned. "Forgive me, milord . . . I mean, Everard. I'm unaccustomed to . . ." She paused. How did she explain the kind of touch she was used to receiving? She could not. Once again, her cheeks grew red.

"You owe me no explanations, Rosamund." With another sigh, he headed toward the door. "One last thing." He stopped and looked over his shoulder. "Tomorrow Jacopo will bring some papers for you to sign. They're not important; they're to do with our nuptials." He turned around. "But you can read that for yourself." He smiled that odd smile again.

Rosamund felt her face burn. "Indeed." So much for loyalty. Just how long could she keep up a masquerade of being literate before her deceit was discovered?

His hand was on the door when he appeared to recall something. Gazing for a moment at his shoes, he took a deep breath and raised his head. "After my son . . . sons and daughter died and Margery too, and Lovelace roamed the earth able to spread his foulness, I believed God had deserted me. That was, until something miraculous occurred."

"What was that, milord?" asked Rosamund softly.

He turned and beheld her. "I met you."

SEVEN
In which a new wife begins a new life

Waking before the sun had quite risen, Rosamund was disorientated as her dreams melded
with reality. The strange blankets, the unfamiliar scent
of the pillows, the shift tangled around her legs, all
filled her with momentary panic. She sat bolt upright
and peered through the swags of sarcenet and heavier
fabrics surrounding the bed, seeing nothing until she
slowly recalled where she was and why. Gradually, her
breathing returned to normal, her heart steadied. She
twisted the little gold band about her finger, cast aside
the demons of the night, tossed back the covers and
bed-curtains and ran straight to the window.

Rooftops thatched and shingled and a forest of stee-
ples met her gaze, rising like a wave until they dipped at
the great stone wall encircling the city. Beyond the wall

lay ordered fields and what looked like a huge manor house in the distance. Lines of people—so many people, little more than dots on the landscape—moved steadily into the city through one of the great stone gates. In their wake came carts, animals, carriages, barrows and men and women laden with baskets, screeching, lowing, talking and shouting. A river of humanity, they surged into the streets, some peeling away from the principal stream to form narrower tributaries, the noise rising and falling. Above her, flocks of birds wheeled in the air, their songs simultaneously melodic and shrill. Wreathing all was heavy smoke that wove its miasma over those below. Rosamund longed to explore and hoped Sir Everard would be kind enough to allow her a tour. Though how could she expect to see the city when she'd not yet inspected the house?

Uncertain what to do, or wear, since Bianca had removed the clothes she had traveled in, she opened her burlap and began to pull out the few possessions inside. A silver hairbrush belonging to her grandmother, a spare pair of gloves (that had seen better days, she thought as her fingers breached the tips), two old shirts, some collars and cuffs, her everyday dress, which, she noted with disgust, was horribly discolored and stained. Lifting it to her nose, she quickly pushed it away. Hopefully, she could get her clothes laundered.

The last thing she wanted was to be accused of smelling like a jakes again. She placed the remainder of her paltry belongings on the mantel—a silver toothpick, her grandmother's copy of Descartes's *Meditationes de prima philosophia* (though she couldn't read it, nor could she bear to part with it), a cracked hand mirror, some ribbons her friend Frances had given her and a small bottle of perfume she'd bought from a pedlar. It wasn't much to show for seventeen years—well, almost eighteen—and two different homes. No. Only one was a home. The other was just a place. A place she wanted to forget and to which she had been forbidden to return.

Don't worry, she thought, *I won't.*

Dropping the ragged burlap and kicking it under the table, she wondered whether dressing herself was expected. Recalling the indignity of last night, bathing was clearly considered beyond her capabilities. The apricot ensemble was hardly suitable past the boudoir. Staring at her only dress, it was evident she possessed nothing worthy.

Instead of dwelling on what she lacked, she focused on what she'd gained, her eyes alighting on the other doorway. Margery's closet. It sounded tiny. Full of useless curios and flibbertigibbets. It also sounded very interesting. Expecting it to be locked, Rosamund was surprised when the door opened.

Beams of sunlight filtered through an oriel window revealing an appreciable space crammed with shelves filled with objects of all shapes and sizes. The first thing she noticed was how neglected everything looked. A shawl of cobwebs wrapped itself around two large shells and all but obscured a dull jug. There were ostrich feathers, a dried-up inkhorn, quills that appeared never to have been used but possessed beautifully engraved shafts. There was a small tarnished container that might have held toothpicks. Some books leaned casually against three folded fans, the titles eluding her. There were also gaps where books must once have stood, giving the shelf the look of a mouth with missing teeth. A much-loved hat with the brim almost detached hid a tiny round box studded with turquoise and painted with ruby swirls. There were ribbons, a baby's bonnet eaten by insects—and rat droppings everywhere, which accounted for the pungent smell. Dust lay thick upon everything. Rosamund dragged a finger along a shelf, creating a path that only ended when she reached a carved wooden box with an ornate key. Unable to resist, she turned the key, gratified when the lock clicked. The interior was filled with beads of all colors. Thrusting her hand inside, Rosamund delighted in the feel of the smooth baubles and wondered why Margery had collected them. What was their purpose apart from looking pretty? Then her fingers felt something buried beneath them: a wad of paper tied with string. Folded many times, it was yellow with age and slightly brittle. Rosamund sat on the window seat, raising more dust as she landed on the cushion, and untied the bundle. With great care she smoothed the pages out, anxious not to damage them. They appeared to be torn from a book. Unable to read them, she stared at the words, wondering why Margery had hidden the pages in the box. Who had written them? What did they say? What would possess someone to remove pages from a book? Or were they from a diary?

Before she could fathom an answer, she heard a noise in the bedroom. Swiftly she refolded the pages and shoved them and the string back under the beads in the box. She wiped her hands on her clothes as she exited the room, her face flushed. Why did she feel guilty?

As she shut the door to the closet, Bianca was closing the outer one, bearing garments and a pair of worn but serviceable shoes.

"God give you good morning, *signora*," she said, dropping the barest of curtseys and holding up one arm, over which a dress was draped. "I've had these modified for you to wear." Putting down a pair of jade-colored shoes and draping a clean silk shift over a chair,

Bianca shook out a pale green gown with long puffed sleeves and a cinched waist, heavily embroidered. It was also, Rosamund noted as she stroked the fabric, well loved, in truth quite shabby, even for a once-fine piece of apparel. A faded port-colored mark blossomed in the center of the skirt and the stitching around the neck was frayed. Even so, the dress was grander than anything she'd worn for a long time. The color was not what she would have chosen, but then, who was she to gripe?

She caught herself. She was the lady wife of Sir Everard Blithman; the chocolate maker's wife, no less. The thought made her smile. From the way Sir Everard spoke of his venture, how important it was to him and how he valued her participation in it, that must account for something as well. She noted the impatient look in Bianca's eyes. Fat lot of good those titles did her here.

"Why, thank you." She smiled. "It's quite lovely." She meant it, well loved or not, and held the dress against her. It was a bit long and quite wide. "I'm certain it will fit," she lied. "Can you thank the person who adjusted it for me? They must have stayed up all night."

"Only half, *signora*." Turning aside, Bianca began to pour water into the washbasin.

Rosamund tried hard not to sigh.

When she was washed and dressed and her hair styled, she was escorted to the withdrawing room. It was only as Bianca left, flashing a hesitant smile in response to Rosamund's thanks, that she'd felt something of the person beneath the housekeeper's cold exterior. The thought gave some comfort. It would be good if they could be allies. Better than good.

She sank into a chair, once again not knowing what to do. Two young men in blue livery entered, one carrying a tray of food, the other what appeared to be a pot of coffee. Rosamund's heart sank. She'd never developed a taste for the acidic, silty drink and avoided it wherever possible. Nevertheless, she greeted them with a "God's good day." They gave her the briefest of nods, their noses averted, as if she'd just carried in horses' ordure from the street. Rosamund felt her cheeks begin to color with a mixture of disappointment and embarrassment. What had she done to earn their contempt?

She had to admit, the conditions of her arrival and the way she'd looked . . . and smelled . . . she'd struggle to gain respect as well. Well, if she wasn't going to be given respect, she'd just bloody well earn it.

After depositing the tray and pouring a bowl of coffee, the footmen retreated to stand on either side of the hearth, their faces neutral as they stared toward a space in the middle of the room.

Waiting to see if they'd leave (and wishing they would), or if Sir Everard would join her, it was some time before Rosamund understood that she was on her own, or as alone as one could be with two other humans pretending to be furniture in the room. Marveling that their duty was simply to stand when such a large house needed tending, Rosamund tried not to be self-conscious in their presence. Accustomed to doing the watching, to fading into the background, she felt awkward in the lead role. Anything she did or said would surely become fodder for the servants to gossip over; after all, that had been the way at the inn. This natural state of affairs would only be magnified in such a grand house with so few interlopers to discuss. She sat demurely.

Outside, the cries of the ostlers rang, answered by the throaty neigh of horses and barking hounds; faint shouts came from vendors beseeching passersby to examine their wares, carriage and cart wheels ground on the streets and the ever-present clamor of bells interrupted the illusion of peace the room bestowed. Dear God, the city was a noisy place. With a small sigh, Rosamund raised the cup to her lips and took a sip.

Her memory served her well. The coffee was vile whether taken in the taproom at the Maiden Voyage Inn, her friend Frances's kitchen or in London. Not even the delicate porcelain bowl could disguise the taste. It was like drinking dirt, including the gritty aftertaste. Holding the cup to her mouth, she pretended to swallow a little more before exchanging the bowl for a piece of bread, and caught a look of sympathy from the taller of the footmen. She gave him a smile. Dear God, she prayed chocolate was more to her liking or every time she drank it she'd be conducting a performance that would do the actor Charles Hart proud.

She had time to finish a single slice of bread when, with nary a knock, Jacopo appeared, a folder of papers under one arm, bowing deferentially. The footmen's backs straightened.

"You slept well, madam?"

"Very, thank you, Jacopo." The falsehood tripped from her lips; she'd had a wretched night filled with dreams of Paul, of her mother screeching, "Don't you never come back," while the servants at the inn cheered. There were rearing horses and the milling, smiling, sweating faces of strangers urging her to kiss her husband, who, when she turned to him, was a vile old leper with no teeth who forced her to drink chocolate from his decaying mouth.

Jacopo laid out the documents on the table. "*Allora. Signore* wants you to read these carefully and then sign. He would have brought them himself, but he's currently indisposed."

"Indisposed?"

Jacopo grimaced. "The last few weeks have been most busy and yesterday . . ." He searched for the right words. ". . . was extraordinary to say the least. I'm afraid the *signore* is taking a little more time to rise from his bed."

Trying to ignore the twinge of regret that the trip to the chocolate house might be postponed, Rosamund made noises of sympathy and prayed it hadn't been revisiting the grief of the last few years or talk of that cur Matthew Lovelace that had upset Sir Everard.

"Please pass his lordship my good wishes." She wondered briefly as she shifted on her seat if his backside was also suffering from yesterday's coach ride.

"But," continued Jacopo, "he did ask me to inform you that he looks forward to escorting you to the chocolate house later in the morning." Rosamund's heart soared. "He asks that you remain here until then. He said to tell you that while you are to feel free to explore the house, he wants you to know his study is out of bounds." Jacopo paused for Rosamund to acknowledge this. "He also said to reassure you that he will refrain from announcing your nuptials as long as possible."

Rosamund glanced at Jacopo in surprise. "Announce? To whom?"

Jacopo shrugged. "It's what is expected. There are those among Sir Everard's business associates who would be most offended if they're not informed of his . . . change of circumstance."

"Oh."

"It's to the master's credit that he wants to ensure you're suitably . . . ah . . ." His gaze swept her clothes. ". . . . prepared before this happens, before any announcements are made."

"So I don't embarrass him," said Rosamund.

Jacopo took a step back. "I don't think you could embarrass anyone, *signora*." He regarded her solemnly. "No, I think the master does this so *you* might feel more comfortable."

So I don't embarrass myself, then . . . . Rosamund tried not to gather the gown about her gaping décolletage. The first Lady Blithman had been a buxom woman indeed. "That is most considerate of him."

Jacopo flashed a smile, his teeth so very white against his dark skin; his eyes twinkled. Rosamund could not help but return it. Jacopo was possessed of very long eyelashes. Perhaps all blackamoors had the good fortune to be so blessed? She considered him more closely.

"Jacopo, do you bear any relation to Bianca?"

Jacopo lowered his head. "I do indeed. She is my sister. Older by five years."

Rosamund was about to ask more when he leaned over and turned a page.

Understanding it was his way of prompting her, and that he was likely avoiding questions about his personal circumstances, she made a show of reading the papers, hoping and praying he could not tell she was struggling. Too ashamed to admit she could make out only a word here and there such as "of" and "it," she pretended to scan each page, nodding and making approving noises now and then, hoping Jacopo wouldn't fathom the extent of her ignorance. Her reading had never advanced since she was taken from Bearwoode. When she reached the final page, she dipped the quill and left her mark where Jacopo indicated. At least she could do that.

Jacopo sanded the ink, allowed it to dry, then shuffled the pages.

"Thank you, madam. I will tell Signor Everard you have no concerns or complaints about the agreement."

"None," said Rosamund lightly, trying not to consider what it was that she'd signed.

There was no point worrying about it, especially when she had a house to explore and chocolate to taste.

EIGHT
In which a wife indulges
in sin (in a bowl)

In order to compensate for what would have been a
short journey to the chocolate house, which was only
a few streets away, Sir Everard ordered the driver of the
hackney carriage to take a longer route so Rosamund
might see a little of the city. Filled with excitement at
the prospect and touched by her husband's consideration, she sat on the edge of her seat, leaning forward.

It was past midday, the heat growing as the small
conveyance maneuvered its way between slow drays,
ornate coaches, impatient horsemen, messengers and
tired vendors wheeling carts or carrying laden pan-
niers promising "sweet oranges," "fresh oysters" and
"oven-hot pies," uncaring their falsehoods were as apparent as the scorching sun.

The swell of people grew as they passed the grand Merchant Taylors' Hall before turning into Leadenhall Street and the markets. Some folk loitered around the buildings, others strode swiftly along the cluttered street, papers tucked under arms, or lugging baskets filled with purchases. Many strolled, stopping to examine the contents of a barrow or exchange a "God's good day."

The carriage made its way past wagons jammed so close together, Rosamund could have reached out and touched the sides as curses and greetings were offered in equal measure. Sometimes they were forced to a standstill as drivers argued for precedence based on the rank of the passengers they carried. Urchins took the opportunity to approach and beg coin or take some, darting dangerously between vehicles and hooves to escape, the shouts of their victims following them. The smell was pungent, a mixture of animal and human waste, unwashed bodies, flensed carcasses, cooked and rotting foodstuffs, all overlaid by various perfumes, most of them completely failing to mask the powerful combination of crowds and the reek of the nearby tanneries. Then there was the omnipresent smoke.

Rosamund was transfixed. She had never seen quite so many people in one place before. Sir Everard pressed a scented kerchief to his face while Rosamund inhaled and rejoiced in all she beheld that proved she was, indeed, in London.

"How long is this blasted trip going to take?" exclaimed Sir Ever-ard, beating his cane on the roof.

"Almost there, milord," cried Jacopo, who was atop with the driver, just as the carriage lunged forward.

Moments later the conveyance bounced to a halt amid shouts of protest that they were blocking the way.

Alighting carefully to avoid the dung, a hand on Sir Everard's arm, Rosamund looked around. They were at the crossroads of Birchin Lane and Lombard Street. The latter was a cobbled street filled with carts, horses and people. There was an array of businesses down both sides of it selling everything from toys to oils and buttons and offering the services of a notary and a barber. On one corner was a stationer's and across the road from him an insurance office. Inside narrow Birchin Lane she could see a crowded ordinary, a coffee house and at least two taverns before a bend obscured the rest. Above the businesses were residences and more offices with protruding upper stories, replete with crooked, belching chimneys, making the roadway much darker than it should be for that time of day.

Sir Everard led her down the cobbles into Birchin Lane and past the curious bystanders who gave her more than a cursory glance. It wasn't until they halted at a wooden door with a bell and a shiny doorknob, and a shingle swinging in the breeze above depicting a pair of crossed swords, the blades long and threatening, that Sir Everard smiled. Painted beneath the swords was, incongruously, an open book.

"This is the chocolate house."

"It is?"

Seeing her puzzlement, Sir Everard explained. "This used to be a blacksmith's premises, a long time ago. Now it's a bookshop—the Crossed Blades and Open Book—at least, downstairs. The chocolate house is above." He gestured toward the upper stories.

Rosamund studied the facade with great interest. The building was twice the size of its neighbors. There were three stories, the lower one with large glass windows. Above them was blackened stone and long casement windows with tessellated glass. Above this was a jettied wooden story with small dormers. The place was imposing. Directly opposite was the entrance to Exchange Alley, a tight covered walkway that broadened into what appeared to be a cruciform shape, exposed to the skies.

Sir Everard pushed open the door and bade Rosamund enter. A merry bell trilled her arrival.

She stepped into a room lined with shelves filled with

all manner of books. There were two large tables in the center, and a long counter occupied the far wall. Behind this was a rear door, which was ajar. On almost every surface were stacked books, folios, piles of news sheets and news books, almanacs and numerous pamphlets with prints of flowers, women, children and buildings upon them. There were posters and notices tacked to any available surface and scrolls tied with string in bundles on the counter. Candles burned in lamps, illuminating pockets of the shop, their greasy scent mixing with the more pleasant one of old paper. Quills and inks also occupied the counter as well as an open ledger beside which sat a lump of cheese and a tankard. There was a steep staircase to Rosamund's immediate left. Overhead was loud thumping, hammering and the guttural shouts of working men. The entire room was filled with what Rosamund first thought was smoke, but quickly realized was plaster dust when something heavy was dropped on the floor above, causing a cascade of white to rain upon them. The shafts of light, from both daylight beaming through the window and the candles burning within, created passages in which colonies of motes spiraled. Reaching for a kerchief, Rosamund sneezed three times in succession.

There was the scuffle of boots and a man rushed through the door behind the counter, positioning himself swiftly as he wiped stained hands on an old cloth tucked into his apron.

"Oh, it's you, Sir Everard," he said with relief. He was of medium height and sported a strangely colored periwig and frilled shirt, the latter all but hidden under a leather apron. He had the biggest nose Rosamund had ever seen, maybe because it was so very red and had a rather large wen in the corner. His eyes, which were bloodshot, appeared swollen.

"God's good day to you, sir." He smiled, flashing a mouth with as many spaces as teeth and doffing his cap. "I thought you were Muddiman or worse, L'Estrange, here for a reckoning."

"Ah, William," said Sir Everard amiably, touching the brim of his hat. "Still suffering the effects of the renovations, I see." He gestured to the man's clothes and face.

William rolled his eyes toward the ceiling. "Me and my goods. A bibliophile only likes dusty books when they're discovered in foreign monasteries or left in some benefactor's will. No one likes new items to be so afflicted, not even me," he said with a droll expression, beating his apron from which clouds of white chalk plumed. "It renders them old before their time."

And men. Rosamund noted the way the dust settled in the creases on his face, emphasizing them. His shirt was not gray, it was actually cream. Rosamund peered at the wig more closely.

"How much longer do you think they'll take, milord?" William swept his hand across the counter, revealing the chestnut wood beneath the dust. "It's affecting my business. If it weren't for the printing press out the back and my license, I'd be sore pressed to make a living." As he finished, there was a loud bang above, followed by another shower of plaster and laughter. Footsteps could be heard before hammering resumed.

Sir Everard made a click of exasperation and slapped the powder from his jacket. "The men are working as fast as they're able. Just be grateful I'm paying you for the inconvenience. That should more than compensate for any losses and enable you to meet your debts."

William muttered something under his breath. "Financial losses, maybe, but it's goodwill I can't account for, and it's not like there are no other bookstores customers can patronize, what with St. Paul's and those places in the Poultry. Even my regulars are choosing to buy their stationery from Watson's over there." He jerked his chin in the direction of the shop on the opposite corner. "Scot reckons his business has never been better since you bought into the Lane." He nodded toward the bookseller across the road. "And God knows how long my license will last with the mercurial L'Estrange about to be put in charge of printing. All it takes is one wrong word and he'd shut me down." Finally, he paused and noticed Rosamund.

"Forgive me. Here I am complaining and forgetting my manners. Who might I have the pleasure of addressing?" he asked, looking her up and down as he bowed, grinning broadly, the powder on his face settling into friendly creases. "Haven't we met before?"

"No, good sir. Of that I am certain." Rosamund dropped a curtsey. "I am—"

"My wife," finished Sir Everard, covering Rosamund's hand, which was still on his arm.

"Wife?" William gave an awkward bow. "Why, I didn't know you had another one, sir. I mean, I didn't know you'd re— I mean . . . ah . . . welcome to my humble shop, my lady. I must say, your resemblance to—"

"This is the Lady Rosamund," said Sir Everard brusquely. "She's a Tomkins of Durham and newly arrived from the country. I've brought her to London to teach her everything I can about the trade before we open." He pointed a finger upward.

"Hmmm, Tomkins, hey?" He looked at her with fresh appreciation. "Learning about the trade, you say—the chocolate house, no less." The way William said it, he might have been discussing a conventicle of Catholics. "Have you tried the stuff yet, milady?"

"No, Mr. . . . ?"

"Henderson, but you may call me William, or Will. Most do. Then I hope you like it better than I do. Not that I've had any from upstairs yet." He pulled a face. "Nasty foreign ooze if you ask me. Best left to the Spaniards and Catholics with their pleasure-loving ways and fancy notions, him above excepted." He pointed a finger toward the ceiling.

Startled, Rosamund wondered if he was referring to God.

"No one did ask you, Mr. Henderson," said Sir Everard, reminding the man of his position. "And I'd appreciate it if you kept your opinions to yourself."

"No, yes, well," said Mr. Henderson, understanding he'd overstepped the mark. "Don't let me hold you up. Pleasure to meet you, milady. If I can assist you with any titles you might like to read . . . ?" His arm swept the room, raining more flecks in its wake. "Or a news book or two?" He flicked a stack of papers on the bench.

"You too, sir," said Rosamund quickly, dismayed by his offer and wanting to quit his sight before he repeated it.

Leaving Mr. Henderson and the deluges of plaster behind, they climbed the stairs.

Whatever she had imagined when she tried to picture the chocolate house, it wasn't this disordered room filled with men in stained breeches and aprons, their sleeves rolled, bent over sawhorses, up ladders, hammering, painting and altogether appearing remarkably busy. There were dust sheets—for all the good they did—jumbles of chairs, pieces of broken wood, buckets filled with a noxious-smelling liquid, and windows so filthy there was little point to them. An astringent smell enveloped everything, underpinned by tobacco, sweat and another, richer, more earthy aroma.

Jacopo held the door open and Sir Everard tapped his cane hard against the floor. A man detached himself from a group. Doughty, with a stomach that arrived before he did, he doffed his cap to reveal a pate on which some strands of dark hair were buried beneath fine white specks. He gave a bow to Sir Everard, winked at Jacopo and flashed a wide, toothless grin at Rosamund that almost made his fleshy cheeks explode.

"Good afternoon, Sir Everard."

"Remney," said Sir Everard. "Rosamund, this is my builder, Mr. Remney." She waited for him to formally introduce her, but he continued on. "You received my note regarding the wood for the bar?" Sir Everard scanned the room.

"Aye, milord. This morning. The men have wasted no time removing it." Remney performed a flourish with his cap. "We've already reordered and will have its replacement built as soon as able."

Sir Everard nodded approval.

"Since your last visit," continued Mr. Remney, "that wall is complete"—he pointed toward a structure at the end of the room—"as is the kitchen, which pleased Señor Filip no end, let me tell you. We're in the process of building the three tables you requested, and after we've rebuilt the bar, we'll make the booths, fix the broken stools, paint the walls, hang the lights, bolt the last of the sconces, and then you can spruce the place up all nice." As he spoke, he regarded Rosamund with a very healthy curiosity. As did the other men, who, though they kept working, did so with one eye upon her.

Self-conscious under their scrutiny, Rosamund edged a little closer to Sir Everard. She was his wife, after all.

Preoccupied, Sir Everard released her and beckoned for Remney to follow him. Soon they were thick in conversation.

Rosamund wasn't sure what she was supposed to

do. The room was like the aftermath of a battlefield, strewn with the corpses of wood, paint and rags.

"*Signora*," said Jacopo. "While the *signore* inspects the works, would you like to meet the chocolate maker, Señor Filip?"

This must be the man Sir Everard claimed he stole from the King of Spain. She glanced at her husband, who was using his stick to lift a dust sheet. "I would, Jacopo. Very much."

Picking their way through the workmen and debris, Jacopo led her toward a heavy curtain at the back of the room. It reminded Rosamund of the one traveling players would erect upon their temporary stage at the Cock and Bull at Gravesend.

In an act of pure showmanship, Jacopo gripped the middle of the fabric and lifted it.

Ducking slightly, Rosamund went through, Jacopo so close behind her she could feel his warm breath on her neck. The curtain dropped, and she found herself in a long, narrow room that disappeared around a corner, filled with steam and gurgling noises.

"You must needs be more careful, sir!" cried a stern voice.

"My apologies, *señor*," called Jacopo, peering through the mist. "I bring you a guest—of Sir Everard's."

"Well, what are you waiting for? Bring her forward."

Jacopo steered Rosamund through the damp air, his hand at the small of her back.

It wasn't until they came closer to the two great bubbling cauldrons hanging over a huge hearth that Rosamund was able to see her surrounds more clearly. Not that she needed her eyes to tell her what was happening when her nose was already alert. The heady smell of spices and something she didn't recognize filled her nostrils, making her head spin and her senses reel.

It was warm this side of the curtain. Near the hearth was a smoke rack filled with small dark stone-like objects. Against one wall were shelves scattered with all manner of instruments. There were shiny pots, pans and any number of what looked like silver coffeepots, each with a slender wooden stick jutting from a hole in the middle of its lid and a long handle protruding at the back. There were lovely porcelain bowls and plates as well as ladles, spoons, copper jugs and jars of colorful spices. She could just discern cinnamon, anise seed and what looked like vanilla pods, along with pails of liquid. There was milk, water, one filled with petals, another with the peels of oranges and lemons. Curious, Rosamund would have moved closer, only Jacopo pulled her in another direction.

"Allow me to introduce you to our chocolate maker extraordinaire, Señor Filip de la Faya."

A compact man with a thick mop of graying hair—no cap or periwig for him—emerged from the steam on the other side of the hearth. His eyes, which were almond-shaped and alive with curiosity, were a vivid gray, startling against his swarthy complexion. Bowing low, the man smiled, revealing uneven teeth.

"May I welcome you, mistress? Madam?"

"*Señora* will do," said Jacopo. "This is *signore*'s wife, the Lady Rosamund. She's here to taste the chocolate."

"His wife?" Filip's eyebrows rose. Recovering, Filip's smile broadened to include Jacopo, who returned his grin warmly. "Welcome, my lady, to the chocolate kitchen, where we're perfecting the drink for English palates. I beg your forgiveness for the noise." He shook his head in disapproval toward the curtain, where the hammering and sawing continued. "And for the mess. *Querido Dios*," he exclaimed as a sneeze the other side of the curtain exploded. "And the dust. Most of which we manage to ensure remains out there." He looked pointedly at Jacopo before slapping him affectionately on the back.

Rosamund decided she liked this forthright man with the lilting voice, even if he was a Spaniard and likely a Papist with pleasure-loving ways and fancy notions. The dust he complained of was barely noticeable in this part of the room.

"Thank you, Señor de la Faya," she said and noticed

a rather sallow-skinned boy with unruly dark hair sticking out beneath his cap, who sat at a low table bearing a large stone. He moved a fat roller back and forth across the dense blackish substance splayed across the stone. Ignoring the strangers in the kitchen, the boy continued working, the tip of his tongue peeping from the corner of his mouth.

"This is my son, Solomon," said Filip, urging Rosamund closer and placing a hand on Solomon's shoulder. The boy ceased rolling and looked up. He had his father's eyes. Upon seeing Rosamund, his eyes widened and the color in his cheeks deepened.

"Hello, Solomon. That's a fine name you've been given." Rosamund smiled.

The boy bowed his head. "It's the name of a king in God's good book." His hand flashed across his chest before it froze then dropped into his lap. Despite His Majesty's calls for religious toleration, already the boy had learned to suppress the signs of his faith. Best in a country that, whatever King Charles said, regarded all Catholics as enemies. Rosamund prayed no one else had seen his action lest it bring trouble.

"It was his grandfather's name, and his before that." Filip's fingers dug into his son's shoulder, causing Solomon to wince. The action had been noted after all. "We come from a long tradition of proud Spaniards."

Determined to put father and son at ease, Rosamund said, "I have it on the best authority that Spaniards are the finest chocolate makers."

Filip gave her a startled look.

Nodding, Rosamund said, "I can think of no one better than you, Señor Filip, to tell me how the chocolate is made."

The wary expression on Filip's face altered immediately. "Is that so? Well . . ." Reaching into a sack sitting on the floor beside his son, he pulled out a round dark mass. "Let's start here, shall we? This is a chocolate cake."

He passed it to Rosamund, who first removed her gloves, and held it in her palm. Heavy, thick and sticky, it was nothing like the cakes she knew. She wondered how it was eaten.

"It's the basis of the chocolate drink—broken into pieces before boiling water is added. We're attempting to make our own cakes in the hope we do not have to import these from my homeland. This is what we've been doing since our arrival."

"You're not long in London?"

"About six weeks. The equipment only arrived two weeks ago, the raw materials a few days past, thanks to Sir Everard." He nodded toward what was in her hands. "That's made from crushed cacao beans."

"Cacao?"

"*Sí*, cacao." Filip strode to the fireplace and returned with some small dark-brown pods, the same kind Rosamund had seen on the smoke rack and thought to be stones. "These are taken from inside the fruit of the cacao tree—*Theobroma cacao*. It means 'food of the gods.'" He beamed. "*Sí, señora*"—he tipped the tiny pods into her other palm—"in your hand, you hold the equivalent of ambrosia. An ambrosia we turn into nectar."

"Food of the gods . . ." Rosamund stared at the seeds. They looked so ordinary, yet their name was so grand.

Filip continued, "They're roasted until the husks become brittle and we can peel them away. Then we grind the insides on a special stone called a *metate*—what my son is using. After any remaining grit is winnowed out, we're left with a paste. This is fashioned into cakes. This is what Solomon is making. Smell it." He lifted her hand with the cake toward her nose.

Rosamund inhaled. There was little scent, just faint hints of earthiness, of duskiness. Same with the pods. "I can't really smell—"

"There's not much odor. But once we add our flavorings . . ." He gestured to the jars on the shelves, the sacks on the floor and the pails of liquid and flowers.

"Then dissolve the cake in hot water, well . . ." Once again, his eyes sparkled. "You will see."

"Indeed, she will." Sir Everard let the curtain fall behind him and brushed bits of detritus from his jacket. "Prepare some chocolate for my wife, Filip. First, let her taste it in its natural state, then include those additives of which you spoke."

As Filip strode to the shelves to grab one of the silver pots, Sir Ever-ard began a running commentary.

"Did Filip explain about the cacao tree? He did. Good. Watch as he breaks off a piece of the cake and places it into the chocolate pot. Now he adds some boiling water, stirs vigorously to dissolve the cake, and *voilà*—you have a drink. After you've tried it, he'll add some sugar. Not all of us can drink it unadulterated like the Spaniards. It's, shall we say, an acquired taste." He reached down to tug Solomon's hair. "We English need sweetening, don't we, Thomas?"

The last comment was directed toward another lad who sat on the other side of the hearth, quiet and unobtrusive. Now he all but cringed and began to work a large bellows to keep the fire burning hot. Sweat dripped from his brow, and the front of his shirt, where it peeped above his apron, was wet. His hair, which was autumn brown, stuck to his moist forehead. He gave a quick nod.

"Yes, milord." His voice alternated from high to low.

"That is Filip's other apprentice," said Sir Everard quietly. "Thomas Tosier. I've only recently hired him. In time, we'll employ extra apprentices, more help. We also have Widow Ashe." As if on cue, a woman emerged from around the corner, a besom in one hand, a rag in the other. Dropping a curtsey, she could scarce look anyone in the eye; her cheeks were flushed, her face swollen, and she quickly disappeared to continue her duties. Sir Everard explained that her husband, one of Mr. Remney's men, had been killed when the cart delivering wood to the chocolate house had rolled back onto him. Rosamund bit back an exclamation. Why, the poor woman was not much older than her and already a widow. Since she had no family or friends to rely on in London, and had no desire to return to her native Berkshire, Sir Everard had told Mr. Remney to put her to work. Responsible for keeping the kitchen free of dust while the renovations were in progress and fetching fresh water from the conduit, she'd only been working two days. No wonder her face was etched by sorrow; it also explained how awkward she was around the men. As soon as she could, she had allowed the steam to swallow her.

Rosamund regarded Sir Everard with kindly eyes. Seemed she wasn't the only one to benefit from his largesse.

It was only when Thomas resumed breathing life into the fire that the spell cast by Widow Ashe lifted. Nevertheless, Rosamund found herself searching for her; aware of the scratching of her besom, her soft shuffle.

Encouraged by Sir Everard, Filip closed the lid on the unusual pot. Placing his hands on either side of the stick protruding from the hole in the lid, he began swiveling it back and forth between his palms.

"Agitating the chocolate is, along with choosing the right additives," explained Sir Everard, gaining Rosamund's full attention, "the most important part of preparing the drink. The stick, or *molinillo*, as the Spaniards call it, has ridges on the end." At a signal from Sir Ever-ard, Jacopo darted over to the shelves and extracted a stick from a pot to show Rosamund, who placed the chocolate cake and cacao seeds on a nearby table and took the stick in her fingers. Sir Everard explained, "It not only helps dissolve the cake and ensures the spices blend but creates the most delicious foam on top."

Filip ceased to work the drink and placed the pot on a tray with a beautifully patterned porcelain bowl. As he went to pour the chocolate, Sir Everard intervened.

"Allow me," he said. He took the silver pot and, holding it with one hand by the long handle at an angle above the bowl, while using his other to keep the lid shut, poured from a height. A stream of muddy liquid splashed into the dish. "Here." He passed it to Rosamund. "As promised. Your first taste of sin in a bowl."

Aware everyone in the room was watching as she raised it to her lips, she closed her eyes and drank. All at once, the sounds that formed a percussive backdrop died away as a warm ribbon of thick fluid flowed down her throat, coating her tongue and leaving a small residue on the back of her lips. Heat filled her mouth and lapped her teeth before cascading in a hot waterfall to sit in her very core. Initially heavy, that feeling dissolved to be replaced by something oily, sour and very gritty.

Unable to prevent it, she gagged. Resisting the urge to spit, she stared at Sir Everard and Filip in dismay. Only then did she see the grin on Filip's face and the barely contained glee in Sir Everard's. Even the boys turned their heads away lest she see their smiles. Jacopo simply shook his head. What tomfoolery was this? Why, no one would pay to drink this rubbish, unless it was a torturer in the Tower who could put the threat of such a drink to good use.

"It's completely horrible," said Rosamund, coughing and smacking her lips together as she looked around for something that would rid her mouth of the awful taste. She'd be better off drinking coffee mixed with refuse from the streets.

Sir Everard gave a long, loud laugh. "Without any additives, it is indeed a dreadful drink. My apologies, Rosamund, I'm deeply sorry. But you had to try it in its raw form to appreciate what comes next. You see, this is where Filip comes into his own. While the Spaniards can drink it untouched, emulating how the Mayans and Aztecs drank chocolate, they've also perfected what to add to transform it. Filip?"

Filip swiftly opened the lid of the pot and with a flourish added first a little milk, then sugar, a pinch of cinnamon, some red powder and other spices Rosamund didn't recognize. He agitated the liquid with the *molinillo* once more and poured the contents into a second bowl, which he offered to Rosamund.

She hesitated.

"Go on, my dear. Taste it. I promise, you won't regret it," said Sir Everard softly.

Taking the bowl from Filip, she gazed at the frothy contents. Sir Everard gently raised her hands toward her unwilling mouth. "What you drank before is how the other businesses serve their chocolate. This, this is how we will serve ours."

Shutting her eyes and praying she wouldn't embarrass herself by choking on the drink, Rosamund took a cautious sip.

All at once something light and wondrous wrapped itself around her tongue and traveled down her throat in a sweet river of molten marvel. Her eyes flew open, followed by her mouth. A long, sweet breath escaped and her lips curved into a beatific smile. Slowly she licked her lips, trying to recapture the taste and understand it. Colors leaped into her head. She thought of the deep purple of her mother's favorite hat, the soft velvet of the puppet show's curtains, the stars above Bearwoode sparkling as if just for her, winking and blinking against their onyx backdrop. She recalled birdsong, the hum of bees in summer, and, before she could prevent it, a burble of laughter escaped, rising from the same spot where the chocolate now pooled, lifting her heart and exploding like the tiny bubbles that sat atop the drink.

The contrast between this and her first sip could not have been greater. Her laughter grew, mingling with the bittersweet taste in her mouth, melding with the steam and honey glow of the candles and the hearth. The sound was so pure, so heart-achingly magical, that each person beside her would recall it later that night in their dreams.

For the first time in weeks, Filip would be able to reconcile his guilt over the circumstances in which he'd left his homeland. Solomon would clutch his pillow and see the face of the little girl in the barber's next door with the tumbling curls and toothy grin. Thomas would remember the newly born kittens being licked by their mother. For the first time since her Davey died, Ashe wouldn't weep herself to sleep. Sir Everard would be spared dreaded nocturnal memories of his wife and children, while Jacopo would wake with an erection so painful, he surprised his lover by thrusting into him without warning, delighting him with his sudden manliness and need.

As if waking from a dream herself, Rosamund gradually became aware of the men and the boys staring at her and Ashe, her broom still, observing her with undisguised envy. As her laughter eased, her delight was echoed back in their expressions.

"Why, milord," she said, composing herself, "if there is a way to find paradise on earth, then surely this is heaven."

At the end of the day, while fires were doused, stock set in order for the morrow's preparation and perfecting, Rosamund wandered around, a bowl of chocolate in her hand, noting the number of chocolate cakes being stored, the type and quality of the equipment.

She drifted toward a table hidden around a corner at the very back of the room, aware that wherever she wandered, Ashe hovered nearby, afraid to approach her but curious all the same. It reminded her of what she'd been like as a child at the inn, watching the guests, the servants too, longing to befriend them but knowing it was not her right. She made sure to smile warmly at the woman but was disappointed when she turned away. To Ashe, she was as remote as those at Gravesend had once been. The thought filled her with sadness—she was caught betwixt two worlds, belonging to neither.

The table before her was strewn with ledgers, paperwork and quills. Her hand alighted upon a sheaf of bound papers with a picture on the front she'd never seen before. It was a botanical of some sort, broken in half exposing tiny beans, much like the cacao ones she'd held earlier. Were these the chocolate pods of which Filip spoke? How fitting they were heart-shaped. For Rosamund knew, as sure as her eyes were brown and her hair pale gold, that Londoners would grow to love this enchanted substance—at least, they would the way Filip prepared it. Flicking through the pages, she was dismayed she could only admire rather than discern the content. Words such as "its," "with," "and" and "others" she could recognize and sound out, but these were merely words that fitted beside important ones. On their own they had little meaning. Defeated, she pushed the pages away.

"Wadsworth's translation," said a voice by her elbow.

She'd been so lost in studying the documents, she hadn't heard Sir Everard approach. "I haven't had time to read it yet, but I'm told if you want to understand chocolate, it's invaluable," he said. "Wads-worth was a captain, took it upon himself to translate a doctor named Antonio Colmenero de Ledesma's work on the drink. He had years of experience making chocolate, refined the process." Picking up the documents, he gave them to her. "Here. Take these home. I want you to read it; no, I want you to understand it."

Horrified, Rosamund quickly dissembled. "Thank you, sir." Tucking the pages under her arm, her heart sank into her too-large shoes. How was she to read it if she could only decipher a few words?

Suddenly, this delightful excursion became a reminder of all that was wrong with her sudden marriage—apart from the obvious. Here was Sir Everard, who had shown her nothing but kindness and understanding, who had given her the gift of his name, his wealth and her first taste of chocolate. No. That she wanted to forget. Given her a second taste of this nectar of the gods. All she'd done was be complicit in the illusion of her talents, the falsehoods her mother told in order to trap the man and which she'd made no effort to undo.

Torn by the desire the chocolate had aroused, Rosamund also wanted to flee and retreat to the sanctuary of her bedroom. There, she would pray to God and ask for his help in unraveling the dreadful knot of lies before they did any more damage. For a fleeting second, she was shocked to realize it was her room at the inn she pictured, not the one at Blithe Manor. Despondent, she thought of the closet and all the memories it contained.

Sensing the shift in her mood, Sir Everard tilted his head. "Forgive me, Rosamund," he said softly. "I was so determined to show you the chocolate house, to have you experience the drink, I forgot that yesterday you were not only ripped from your old life but were the victim of a harsh accident. How is your head?"

Grateful she had an excuse, Rosamund lifted a hand to where the hooves had struck. "I fear I have a megrim coming on, sir."

"Come, we'll get you home. The chocolate house will still be here. Remember, you may return whenever you wish. In fact, I insist you do. I want you to feel as at home here as at Blithe Manor."

Uncertain how to respond, Rosamund nodded and smiled.

It wasn't until they went to leave, and she said farewells to Filip, Solomon, Thomas and Widow Ashe, taking a last, lingering look at the chocolate beans, the elegant pots, the delicate serving bowls and the magical stick that worked such wonders upon the liquid, that she acknowledged that until she told her husband the truth about her so-called literacy, she could never allow herself to enjoy chocolate or the chocolate house again.

NINE
In which a husband hears a confession

There was not one part of Sir Everard's body that wasn't aching or beset by confounded shaking. His fingers quivered before his eyes as if possessed and his legs weren't cooperating either. With a click of annoyance, he forced his hands back under the coverlets. Sinking into the pillows, he tried to breathe deeply and allow the mulled wine he'd drunk as quickly as he was able to take effect. Jacopo fussed in the background, brushing his jacket, folding his clothes, his head turned aside discreetly so as not to see his master ailing. Sir Everard stared at the curtains as they billowed about the bed in the evening breeze. He detested being at the whim of others, blown in directions he'd no control over. Damned if he wasn't again now Lovelace had re-entered the picture.

Quashing the anger that thoughts of the murderous turncoat and his written demands engendered, he reflected upon the day and decided that, altogether, it had been most successful. Not only had the chit looked lovely clean, with her hair styled and a decent dress (even if it was out of fashion and swam on her), but she entranced everyone they encountered. Rosamund had not only played her part to perfection but she'd been seduced by the delicious temptation of chocolate. Chuckling inwardly, he recalled her face as she drank—her first predictable reaction and her second taste. How those long dark lashes swept her creamy cheeks, her full lips thinning in appreciation of what she held in her mouth; those sweet dimples forming. She put him in mind not only of his beloved daughter, but the King's sister Henriette-Anne, whose complexion had been likened to roses and jasmine. Had he been younger, more capable, he would have hardened at the sight. As it was, he knew Filip and Jacopo had visceral reactions, the young lads too. Widow Ashe had stared like a moonstruck loon.

News of her presence would be irresistible, even to one who thought himself beyond such temptations. Once he was enticed by the idea of her, there'd be no turning back.

His jaded heart quickened with excitement. That young woman was a prize; she would give him the advantage. With every breath he took, he knew she would be the instrument of his revenge.

A quiet drumming at the door ended his self-congratulation. Jacopo paused in combing Sir Everard's periwig.

As if conjured by his thoughts, the door slowly cracked open to reveal Rosamund.

"Milord," she said quietly. Gowned in the apricot gauze, with her long, shining curls tumbling down her shoulders to brush the tops of her thighs, she was like an angel fallen to earth. "I apologize for disturbing you, but I was wondering if I might have a word?"

Trying not to show his astonishment, or how his heart ached at the sight of her and the memories she conjured, Sir Everard sat up, once more cursing his frailty. "Of course, my dear, of course." He waved her toward the bed, touching his head to ensure his night-cap covered his barren scalp.

Jacopo closed the door behind Rosamund, found a stool upon which she could perch and tied back the filmy bed-curtains, raising his brows in an unspoken question.

Rosamund dragged the stool closer at her husband's urging, giving Sir Everard time to compose himself and cover his legs so his affliction would not be apparent.

"What brings you here at this time of night, my dear?"

Rosamund, who'd barely looked at him since she entered, raised her chin. Her face was pale, and she wore a deep frown that somehow managed to lend her sweetness an air of surprising gravity. Sir Everard found he wanted to wipe that frown away. Good God. He was getting sentimental in his dotage. It would simply not do.

"Good milord, I fear you might not like what I have to say."

"Then perhaps you might do best to hold your tongue."

Rosamund searched his face and Sir Everard thought how the likes of Charles Sedley or Alexander Brome would compose poems for her eyes alone. He marveled at their color. Helene's had been a pallid blue. While Rosamund's were the same almond shape, her eyes were unfathomable inky stains; at other times, when the light struck them, they were swirling pools of chestnut and amber, capable of twinkling with delight or darkening in fear and sadness. They were the latter tonight, and Sir Everard felt as if he'd been told to whip an already broken creature. He was unaccustomed to such a feeling and uncertain how to deal with it.

Taking a deep breath, Rosamund sat up straight. "My lord, I cannot—not any longer. It's my duty to inform you that you've plighted your troth under false pretenses with a miscreant of the worst kind."

Whatever Sir Everard had anticipated hearing, it wasn't this.

"My mother told you I am learned; that I can read and write. While I did indeed begin to acquire both these skills, I'm no more proficient than a babe, my education being . . . interrupted. I can scarce make out words on a document let alone craft them for myself."

"I see."

"Do you? In omitting to tell you the truth, milord, I fear I've already failed in both the obedience and loyalty you require." She stared at her interlocked fingers a moment, her mouth moving, but no sounds issuing. When she started speaking again, her voice was so quiet, Sir Everard was forced to lean forward to hear. "At first, I didn't think my ignorant state would matter. I know many wives of gentlemen who can scarce make their mark—which at least I can do—or read, but now I've seen the chocolate house, now you've given me those papers and tasked me with learning what's contained within them, I can hide the truth no longer. Sir Everard, I am not the boon my mother promised; I am nothing but an ignorant burden."

Sir Everard glanced at Jacopo, who had ceased to tidy and was listening to the conversation with great interest, his face betraying nothing.

"I see," Sir Everard said again.

"You do?"

"You're telling me you've been party to a falsehood that you believe renders our marriage null and void."

Rosamund let out a shuddering sigh. "Aye, that's exactly what I'm saying. You deserve better and I'm so sorry I was complicit in this deception. Having spent a mere day and night in your company, having met Señor Filip and his son and learned of your generosity to Widow Ashe, having seen for myself your intentions, I understand you have need of someone who grasps the complexities of your enterprises, someone who can offer you much more than I ever can. You require a helpmeet in both words and deed. So, sir, if you decide to . . . break our bond, I will quit your sight immediately and our vows will be as if they were never spoken. You will not hear from me again."

Sir Everard indicated that Jacopo was to pour some wine. Two goblets were brought over while Sir Everard pretended to consider her words.

Taking a long draft, he watched Rosamund over the rim of his vessel as she sipped her wine. "Yet you signed the papers I had Jacopo deliver this morning."

Rosamund shifted on the stool, the glass clasped firmly in her hands. "I did, sir. I was loath to reveal my ignorance." She lifted her chin slightly. "I've not done the wrong thing by signing, have I?" Her eyes were huge.

There was a crash as Jacopo knocked a candlestick over. The flame was snuffed out against the table and wax flowed over the wood. "My apologies, *signore*," he said, reaching for a rag to wipe up the mess.

Sir Everard smiled. "No, my dear. You've not done anything wrong." His mind worked as he finished his drink. How could he reassure this young woman, this precious resource, that the last thing he required of her was the ability to read and write in the manner her mother boasted of—and which he had known immediately was at best exaggerated if not an outright falsehood? In fact, he'd banked on it. He could not, not without revealing his hand. This was not the time.

"Rosamund," he said, his voice heavy.

"Sir?"

"While I'm deeply disappointed you didn't reveal this to me sooner, it doesn't change the nature of our marriage or my desire for it to remain intact. There's still much you can do for me without being literate."

Rosamund softly exhaled. "I would I could, though . . . considering my normal wifely . . . ah . . .

duties are"—she glanced toward Jacopo then dropped her voice—"not required, I feel I could offer you so much more than being a mere ornament; an ornament that does nothing but take. I would that I could give back to you, repay your generosity somehow."

A shaft of excitement lanced Sir Everard's side. "You will have ample opportunity to do exactly that."

"When?"

"Soon."

"I would it were sooner." Rosamund's disappointment descended like a soft winter mist. "In fact, if I may be so bold, sir, I have already been putting my mind to ways in which the chocolate house might be . . ." She hesitated.

"What?" encouraged Sir Everard.

"Improved."

"Oh?" said Sir Everard. Jacopo raised his head. It was all Sir Everard could do to maintain control. He could feel his heart beating rapidly; the tremor in his hands came back with renewed force. Who on earth did this chit think she was? *Your wife, dolt. It's you who raised her, you who have promised her entry into a new world of which she knows nothing. All she is doing is trying to please you. Remember what her mother said: she is built for pleasing; it's in her nature.*

Swallowing, he forced what he hoped was a smile to his mouth. It felt like it was cooperating. "And in what ways do you think the chocolate house might be *improved?*"

Unaware of the turmoil she'd created, Rosamund smiled. This time, he was pleased to discover, it had no effect upon him.

"Well, milord, while I think chocolate would have to be one of the most wonderful drinks I've ever had God's grace to try, I couldn't help but be concerned it might not be to everyone's taste. Take Mr. Henderson, for example. I found that even the finest wines, the most expertly prepared coffee—even a dish of coddled eggs—do not please everyone. We are all so different, and for that we should thank the good Lord."

Sir Everard's eyes narrowed. A tic in his cheek started and he could feel his left eye begin to twitch. "And why should these differences be a cause for concern?"

Proud of his restraint, as what he really wanted to say was "*your* concern."

Unaware of any tension, Rosamund's smile widened. "Many people simply expect you to meet their needs, regardless of how outrageous or even seasonal they might be. At the Maiden Voyage Inn, we tried to accommodate all our clients' beverage demands. It saves a great many complaints and, milord, it makes for tidy profits." She paused. Sir Everard stared at her. Jacopo moved to the other side of the room. "As your wife, I would help you profit in all ways possible—to run the best of chocolate houses and therefore dispatch any . . . er . . . competition."

Sir Everard nearly choked.

Waiting until he recovered, Rosamund continued. "I noticed there's a great deal of unused space in the kitchen. It's like a great storeroom and I thought that maybe, because you import so many other wonderful drinks—or at least that's what Jacopo and Filip told me"—she flashed Jacopo a smile—"we might consider also serving beer, different wines and even coffee. I know that's very popular. At the Maiden Voyage Inn, everyone asked for it, even if they didn't like it . . ."

When Sir Everard didn't respond, she sighed. "Please, sir, do not think I'm complaining. I know how fortunate I am, but I feel at a loss. I want very much to help in any way I can. I'm accustomed to being busy, to being . . . useful. My mother was persuaded I had a good head for business and I just thought—"

Sir Everard raised his hand. It took all his will-power not to order her from his sight. How dare she. How dare this . . . this grubby little doxy (albeit clean and sweet-smelling now) even think to lecture *him* on ways to improve business—especially the chocolate house. One person ordering him about was more than enough. For the time being the place existed to serve one purpose alone. How it functioned as a business he cared not—not until after. The girl had been in London, in the chocolate house, less time than a ripple on the Thames and she was seeing fit to advise him. *Him.* Where was the young woman built for pleasing? He did not like this assertive creature one little bit. Still, she had confessed her lack of literacy. She was honest. This too, this desire to advise, he supposed, was a product of her honesty. He must focus on that, accept her suggestions graciously, lest his temper reveal too much. After all, she knew naught of the letters, of Lovelace's outrageous demands regarding the chocolate house, his insistence he employ a crazed widow and an inexperienced apprentice. The terrible threats Lovelace made that forced his compliance.

Rosamund ceased talking. Jacopo no longer moved. Even the breeze had stilled; the only sounds were some distant revelers and the unholy screech of an owl.

"Child," said Sir Everard finally. "Listen to me."

Those eyes of hers were so damn trusting. God . . . was he wrong to marry her and make her an integral part of his plans? He must not think that. She was not

Helene, for all she looked like her. She was a bastard; a used and abused slattern accustomed to far worse who had crossed his path for a reason. He was doing this for his daughter, his family; for the Blithman name. Lovelace could not win. He would not, not now he had Rosamund.

"What do you think it is I do?"

"I . . . I . . . You are a merchant and a chocolate maker, sir."

"Among other things, yes, I am. This is very important, Rosamund. I want you to consider this carefully. At any time, have I told you I am opening a tavern?"

"N . . . no, sir."

"An alehouse?"

She gave a delightful giggle; she didn't understand how close she was sailing to the wind. Jacopo did, standing like a statue in the corner, watching, waiting.

"Have I told you I am opening a coffee house?"

"No, sir." Finally, realization dawned and her face began to color. The smile faded.

"Exactly. I am opening a *chocolate house*. I will serve *chocolate* and, for the time being"—he bowed his head as if acknowledging her suggestion—"that is *all* I will serve."

"But, sir—"

Jacopo drew his breath in sharply.

Sir Everard cast her a disbelieving look. "But?" He sat up straighter. "*But?*" Rosamund leaned away from the force of the word. "My dear"—the endearment was sour—"I don't care what my patrons' 'beverage demands' are."

Rosamund began to bite her lip and her eyes to fill.

"Or what you might have done at that . . . that inn. We will not consider serving anything. That is what *I* decide. Not Jacopo over there, not Filip, certainly not you, but *me.*" He settled back into his pillows. "And I say we serve chocolate. Am I clear?" He awaited an answer.

"Very, sir. I'm sorry if I have overstepped my . . . my role. But—"

He studied her a moment. Sarcasm wasn't within her ken and yet, from the play of emotions across her face, the way she willed those tears back as if she were a conduit, she wasn't pleased. So, when she managed a small smile, he was the one to look astonished.

"I would read those papers and learn all I can about chocolate and its making, to obey your command in that."

Sir Everard stared at her in disbelief and, if he was honest, some wonder. Already he regretted his outburst and what it might reveal. Time to make amends.

"You would?"

She nodded eagerly.

"In that case, how would you like to pick up your childhood lessons from where you left off?"

"Sir?" This time the shine returned to her eyes. "I would like that very much. My mother couldn't afford to continue my education. My stepfather didn't think it necessary."

Well, God bless them, thought Sir Everard, who found clever women both abhorrent and redundant. Women need only do three things: listen, obey their menfolk and breed fine sons. Rosamund would at least fulfill two of those requirements. Pity Margery had failed on that score. He clamped the thought down.

"I can see it's important to you, and there's no doubt, if you can master that translation I gave you, it will help you understand the chocolate."

"And would *that* be of use to you?" asked Rosamund eagerly.

"Of course," said Sir Everard, avoiding her eyes.

"You're not too cross at me for my falsehood?" Rosamund was on the edge of her seat.

He noted she made no mention of her suggestions to improve trade. Sir Everard dared to pull his hands from beneath the coverlets and lift Rosamund's from her lap. "I'm not . . . angry about that, child. In fact,

I'm relieved you came of your own volition to confess your deceit to me."

"Can you forgive me, sir?"

"I can. And," he added, a notion forming, "I hope you can forgive me my . . . assertion regarding the chocolate house. I can be very . . . proprietorial." *If only she knew.*

"Oh, I do, milord. You're right. I forget my place. I will try not to do so again." Her dimples were positively impish in the candlelight. Was she flirting with him?

Casting aside his doubts as to her sincerity—the chit didn't have a deceitful bone in her body—or so her mother said—he firmed his intentions. He didn't want her about the house, under his feet or sulking and wishing to be entertained. And what if she stumbled upon one of Margery's blasted notebooks? Or worse, came upon one of Lovelace's damn missives and uncovered the truth? Learned that all the wonderful ideas for the chocolate house, its interior, the design of the booths and bar, the changes he insisted on and which made him appear unable to make up his mind, were not his, but Lovelace's. Worse, that the generosity he showed to Ashe, his beneficence in employing Thomas Tosier, were forced by the same man and his bloody threats. He had to ensure she never did. One way of doing that was by meeting her desires. She wanted to be kept busy, well, he could assure she was.

"Tomorrow, your reading lessons will begin."

"Tomorrow?" Rosamund clapped her hands together in delight. "And who will be my teacher, my lord? You?"

Sir Everard quickly schooled his face, appalled at what being with her for hours on end would do to his business, his plans, his sanity. "No, not me. Jacopo will be your teacher."

Jacopo almost stumbled as he carried an armload of clean drying sheets to a chest.

By the time Rosamund swung around to regard him, he'd recovered.

Sir Everard tried hard not to laugh as his factotum struggled to maintain his composure and appear as if the notion of teaching Rosamund filled him with delight.

"*Signore,*" he said, his voice strained, his bow hiding his dismay.

"Yes," said Sir Everard, warming to the idea. "Jacopo will teach you the rudiments of reading. In no time at all, you'll be able to grasp the contents of Colmenero's translation and discuss them with Filip, who is already conversant, and share the essence of it with me."

Rosamund giggled. The sound was so sweet and pure, it quite took Sir Everard's breath away. It also gave him another idea.

"However, I don't want the household to see their lady being instructed by a . . . servant. Therefore, the lessons will take place at the chocolate house. That way, my dear, you can not only gain literacy but also learn how to prepare the chocolate the way Filip does. You will devote each morning to reading, while the afternoons can be spent putting into practice the knowledge you glean. How does that sound?"

Rosamund rose and dropped into a low curtsey. "It's so much more than I expected, than I deserve. Why, I'd already packed my burlap in the full expectation you would send me away. I'm beyond grateful to you, and Jacopo as well." She gestured to him as he closed the lid of the chest soundlessly.

"It will be my pleasure, *signora*," said Jacopo.

He was rewarded with one of Rosamund's dazzling smiles.

"I've no intention of sending you away, Rosamund," said Sir Ever-ard. "At least not before the chocolate house opens, before I've introduced you to my . . . acquaintances." Seeing her crestfallen face, he reached for her and drew her closer. "I jest. I've no intention of letting you go. Not when there's so much for us to accomplish together."

Rosamund flashed another smile. "And when will I meet your acquaintances, milord?"

"Ah, I have been giving that some thought. While I'll have to make a formal announcement regarding our marriage, I'm not yet ready to launch you upon the world; nor are you ready to enter it as Lady Blithman. I'll introduce you in my own time and when we're ready. Till then, only the household, Filip, and possibly a few others I can trust will know our little secret." He lifted his chin, his brows raised, waiting for her to agree.

"Until the chocolate house opens."

"Indeed. It won't be long now. I'm certain. Not now you're here."

Her equanimity restored, Rosamund stood and, hesitating for a moment, dropped a kiss upon Sir Everard's hand. "I thank you, my lord, from the bottom of my heart. You are my benefactor and friend. I do not know what I've done to deserve you, but God has seen fit to bless me and I thank Him for it."

Embarrassed, Sir Everard waved her words away.

"I promise to be the best of pupils," she added.

"I know you will be. I'm counting on it," said Sir Everard kindly. "Now, it's time for you to return to your room and sleep. You've a big day ahead tomorrow. You need to be sharp for your first lesson."

Curtseying again, Rosamund bestowed a final grin upon both men and left.

As the door closed, Jacopo spun toward his master. "How will you prevent her from learning the truth about the chocolate house if she can read, milord? By teaching her to read and write, are you not arming the enemy?"

Sir Everard shook his head so vigorously his nightcap almost slipped from his scalp. "Jacopo, Jacopo. She's not the enemy. Don't you forget that. She is the weapon we'll use to bring him down. When the time is right, I will use Lovelace's words, his unruly commands against him and, in doing so, recruit another ally to my cause."

"I understand, my lord. But if she can read, we will not always be able to censor the material and if she should intercept a letter . . ."

Sir Everard pointed at him. The trembling in his hands had all but ceased. "You are her teacher. It's up to you how much she learns and at what pace. *Capisci?*"

Jacopo lowered his gaze. *"Capisco,"* he said and collected up the goblets, then paused beside Sir Everard a moment.

"What? Out with it and be damned, boy," growled Sir Everard.

"If she was possessed of Catholic tendencies, she'd bless you as a saint and burn candles for you daily."

Sir Everard laughed. "She would. We did well finding her, didn't we, lad? We did well . . . What was that?" asked Sir Everard sharply.

"Nothing, *signore*. Merely agreeing." Jacopo returned the stool to where it belonged.

Grunting, Sir Everard glared at him a moment before rolling over. The boy was forgetting his place. Him and his damn sister. They were getting airs above their station, ideas that had no place in a tawneymoor's head, regardless of what their lineage might be.

"Draw the curtains before you leave. Oh, and Jacopo?"

"*Si, signore?*"

Settling into his pillow, Sir Everard could see Jacopo's outline beyond the curtain. He was lean, with strong shoulders. "If she ever finds out the truth . . . If she should thwart my purpose in any way, I'll hold you responsible. You and your sister. Remember that."

"She will never learn it from me," said Jacopo, rubbing the back of his neck reflexively as he left his master alone.

TEN
In which a Navy clerk responds to gossip

What Sir Everard hadn't accounted for as he lay in bed early the following morning, his leg refusing to bear weight and a megrim threatening to take his vision, was how, despite his determination to keep his nuptials in Gravesend a secret, the news would spread. The luxury of anonymity was not for the likes of him. In an uncharacteristic lack of judgment he had failed to consider those who had witnessed his marriage at the Maiden Voyage Inn.

Not only had most of the guests hailed from the city, but they had no reason to be discreet. What did discretion matter when there was such a tale to dine out upon? Why, the cachet and invitations which would come from relating a scene which included none other than Sir Everard Blithman, a man already at the center of an old scandal, could scarce be measured.

Mrs. Clementine Rochford—she of the broad-brimmed hat who'd been forced through the door of the inn by the mother of the bride—shared the delicious news over chocolate with her dear friend Mrs. Barbara Crew. The next morning Mrs. Crew told her husband, Mr. Reginald Crew, who upon hearing it went straight to his place of work, ignoring the beggars on Tower Street, the young woman offering to tell his future, even the smell of mutton pies, and all but ran to the Navy Office.

Reginald, being the porter, not only greeted everyone who entered and exited the building, but also related to them any little morsel of news he might have gleaned. Reginald was particularly thrilled when one of his favorite people, the earnest and hardworking Mr. Samuel Pepys, was among the first to arrive. Even though he'd left the office around midnight the night before, Mr. Pepys was back at his desk before the bells tolled eight. Well, what was Mr. Crew to do but reward the man by inviting him to sup at the gossip table.

What Mr. Crew didn't know was that Pepys, being a distant relative of the late Lady Margery Blithman, connected through the Montagu line, was shocked by what Reginald told him. Dissembling quickly, he nevertheless wasted no time and set foot into the offices simply to excuse himself. He hurried home and collected his wife, Elizabeth, their two servants and some victuals. Using the boat put aside for the Navy Office's use, Pepys ordered it rowed to Gravesend under the pretext of entering the waterways of the Hope and boarding the ship *Royal James*. What he learned while questioning folk at Gravesend excited him so greatly that, much to his wife's chagrin, he ordered them to turn back to London so he might see the evidence for himself.

But first he had to endure a meeting with an acquaintance, Mr. Shepley, and then invite the man to supper, a delay Pepys could barely tolerate. Somehow, amid the fluster of his thoughts and halfhearted responses, first to Shepley and later to Elizabeth, he promised to take his wife to Hampton Court on the morrow, when what he really intended was to visit his widower cousin. It was only when he finally fell into bed late that night and listened to Elizabeth's joy in their plans that he understood he would have to fulfill his hasty promise. Ever resourceful, Pepys decided it didn't mean he couldn't also get to the bottom of the rumors.

Rousing himself early the following morning, he ordered his servants to tell his wife he'd gone to the office and, without an invitation or warning, made his way to Bishopsgate Street, pausing only to down a dish of coffee in Mark Lane. Not even the other patrons' cries of "What news?" tempted him to reveal what he'd learned.

As a consequence, he arrived on the doorstep of Blithe Manor just as the gates were being opened so a sleepy drudge could find a maid from whom to purchase milk—all as the sun was just opening its igneous eyes.

Pepys's reserve counted for nothing in a city of gossips. Clementine Rochford, Reginald Crew, his wife and all those who entered and exited the Navy Office, fanning out into the streets, down to the docks and even as far as Whitehall, Moorfields and Deptford, had already done the damage. Before midday the day after the marriage, half of London knew what Sir Everard had done—Sir Everard Blithman, the man who'd bought his way back into the King's good graces in an effort to save his family name and mitigate the damage caused by his younger son's rumored treachery.

By midnight, the other half knew and by then the narrative had undergone dramatic changes: Sir Everard had kidnapped a bastard child and wed her; fought a duel, killed a man and was now responsible for his progeny; some claimed he'd rescued a noblewoman from a highwayman; married his mistress's daughter; snatched his niece from a fate most foul; committed no sin but kindly employed the widow of a worker; married his own daughter; and, most hilarious of all, that he'd bought a blowsy bride from a former Roundhead.

Samuel Pepys was, by his own admission, a highly regarded clerk at the Navy Office in Seething Lane, an honest and diligent justice of the peace, a beloved relative of Sir Everard and Lady Margery Blithman and an up-and-coming gentleman of London who could number among his acquaintances peers of the realm (the Duke of York; Sir William Batten; Sir William Penn; Sir George Downing; Sir Carteret and his own distant relations, Lord and Lady Sandwich, of course); and, he knew the King personally, having been aboard the very ship that returned His Majesty from exile. He had heard from the King's own mouth marvelous stories of his escape from England years earlier—including the miracle of Boscobel and the grand old oak in which His Majesty concealed himself from searching Roundheads.

On arriving at Blithe Manor at cock's crow, Sam was ordered peremptorily to remain in the hall like a common servant. But the man who knew the King refused to obey. When that curmudgeon Wat had gone to fetch his master, Sam swiftly followed him up the stairs and diverted down the corridor toward the withdrawing room his cousin (God bless her) used to enjoy. Sam reasoned if it was good enough for the first Lady Blithman to favor, then it was highly likely her replacement would also find it pleasant.

He was not mistaken.

Without knocking, Sam cautiously opened the door to find a young woman standing by the window, a book in her hand.

He saw the book was by Descartes and could not help but be impressed. As she was unaware of him, he made a leisurely study of her profile, noting a mark upon her forehead; a recent injury perhaps, but which brought to his mind thoughts of an angel's brand. Was this the woman who had caused London's tongues to wag so furiously? Pale golden hair fell in waves against her face before tumbling down her back. Her slim figure was topped by a generous bosom that even from the door he could see rising and falling, the exposed flesh glowing in the early morning sunlight streaming in the window. The way the ill-fitting gown nevertheless cinched her waist before falling to the floor failed to hide a bottom that was just begging to be pinched and all but made his mouth water. Her eyebrows and lashes deserved sonnets. Her mouth a melody. Good God, who was this ravishing creature? Surely she couldn't be the source of all these rumors, the inn sloven to whom Sir Everard had hitched himself? The highwayman's get? Or his mistress? Sam couldn't quite recall; not that it mattered. Whoever or whatever she was, whatever her origins, one could hardly blame Sir Everard. He'd paid his penance and deserved a reward. Why, if Sam wasn't encumbered with a pesky wife . . .

He was unaware he'd made a noise until the woman looked up, the book almost falling from her grasp. Sam swiftly swept off his hat, not so much because he suddenly remembered his manners, but to hide his rather prominent erection.

Stumbling forward, his other arm outstretched to suggest peace, he tried to speak, but as he drew closer and she turned in the light, he saw her face and stopped.

"How extraordinary," he blurted and wondered if, despite what he'd been told, perhaps the rumors of a niece were indeed true.

"What is?" said the young woman, unperturbed by his manner as she placed the book on a table.

"Why," said Sam, still staring at her face, "for a moment there, I was struck by your resemblance to Sir Everard's daughter, Helene."

Was the girl—no, woman—trying not to smile? Surely those lush, rose-petal lips were twitching; certainly, a pair of exquisite dimples impressed those porcelain cheeks.

"Ah," she sang. "Sir Everard has made mention of a likeness."

"Indeed. But upon closer inspection, I see your eyes are darker and not so near to each other; your face lacks the sharpness to which Helene's tended and your . . ." His own eyes locked onto the woman's bosom, before with flaming cheeks and much clearing of his throat, he tore them away. "You are taller and more . . . more . . ."

"More likely to ask who you might be, good sir?" the woman finished. This time, she was smiling.

Sam's breath caught; his heart stilled. Now he was only a matter of inches away, he could smell the perfume coming from her. His mind began to drift, his pulse to quicken. Forget Helene, this goddess eclipsed even the Lady Frances Stewart, the beauty who currently preoccupied the King—though why he bothered when he had the alluring Lady Barbara between his sheets was beyond Sam's ken.

"Forgive me, madam." Unable to help himself, Sam took the young woman by the shoulders and kissed her lingeringly on the lips. "I am your cousin, Samuel Pepys, at your service."

Releasing her with great regret, he ran his tongue over his mouth, hoping to recapture the taste of hers, to imprint it on his memory. Her lips were so soft, like pillows. Damn if the maypole in his pants wasn't stirring again. He willed himself to concentrate. Think of Elizabeth, his sister, the clotpole who opened the door to him . . .

The distaste that crossed her face was surely a trick of the morning shadows. She touched her fingertips to her lips (was she wiping them?) and the goddess's eyes twinkled. "Then it's a pleasure to meet you, sir. Will you please sit and I'll have one of the servants notify Sir Everard of your arrival."

Grateful to be asked, Sam wasted no time falling into a chair, his hat in his lap, and waved a hand at the door dismissively. "Do not trouble yourself on that account . . . Madam . . . er . . . Cousin . . . er . . . What do I call you?"

"My name is Rosamund . . . Just Rosamund."

Hardly just. As she seated herself across from him, the sunbeams struck eyes that a moment before were almost black, but now contained flecks of amber and honey and swirls of iridescent chestnut. He felt sure if he kept staring, he'd be mesmerized or, far worse, allow her access to the secrets in his soul and find himself confessing all his wicked thoughts about Lady

Barbara, his wife's maid Jane and his imbroglio with the delicious Betty Lane.

"Rosamund," he repeated. (*Rosamund, my sweet almond* . . . No. That would never do. *Rosamund, the flower of Eng-a-land* . . . *Rosamund, I do envy thy hus-a-band* . . .)

Aware she was speaking and he hadn't listened, Sam nodded but was devastated when she rose and went to the door. It was only when he heard her talking to someone (good God, even her voice was delightful, a dulcet siren's song to lure men to their ruin), asking for coffee and breakfast beer to be brought to the parlor, that he began to relax. He could savor her company longer.

When Sam first heard the news about Sir Everard, he thought the dreadful scandal of his son, followed by the terrible tragedies that had visited his cousin, had finally undone him. But now he'd met the woman—*Rosamund*, he sighed—he quite understood why Sir Everard had wed her. If, indeed, this vision *was* his wife. But who else could she be? Not even the descriptions the Gravesend locals had given yesterday prepared him. Oh, they'd prattled on about an unusual-looking chit, a good-natured, hardworking sort and her terrible parents and even worse bully-boy siblings. They'd spoken of her piety and goodness almost as if she were some Romish nun. But good God, "unusual," even "lovely," didn't begin to describe her. She was a beauty, and not the regular sort that was much admired like the sumptuous darkness of Barbara Castlemaine. Rosamund was both darkness and golden light. A striking and most disturbing combination. No wonder Sir Everard snatched her up. And curse his luck he found her in a backwater like Gravesend . . . or mayhap he knew she was there all along and had delayed until now to fetch her. Wait until the King saw her. Or, God forbid, Buckingham or Sedley. They wouldn't be able to keep their eyes—their hands—off her.

And she was clever too, he thought, glancing at the book. No woman of his acquaintance read Descartes first thing in the morning. No man either, for that matter.

Moments later Rosamund returned, shortly followed by servants carrying a tray filled with a steaming coffeepot, bowls and some warm bread. In no time at all, the drink was poured, the bread smeared with butter and the servants positioned by the hearth, unmoving, unseeing, all-hearing.

Damn their souls.

Now there were chaperones he would just have to make the best of it and find another opportunity to question the woman closely. Sam took the bowl and sipped, expressing surprise it wasn't chocolate. He leaned back and smiled.

"So, my dear cousin, for that is surely what you are. Tell me, what do you think of your husband's new venture with the West Indian drink? Have you tried it yet? You have? Someone, and I know not who, left a quantity for me at my house months ago. Is that not strange?"

"I would have said, most generous," replied Rosamund.

"Ah . . . yes. Of course. It was. Yes. Yes." Flustered, Sam forgot what they were discussing.

"You have tried chocolate, sir?"

Bless her for rescuing him. "Oh, many times now. The first was the day after the King's coronation. What a fine day—such pomp, such ceremony, and a banquet of many courses. When, after the King left the hall that evening, a mighty, tree-shredding storm broke, it was only matched by that in my head and stomach for, I confess, I was utterly foxed. The following day, I went to my very good friend Mr. Creed's house and, upon seeing the condition I was in, he offered me a bowl of *chocolata*, swearing it would soothe my wretched discomfort."

"And did it?"

Sam patted his rotund paunch. "Very nicely, though I recall a bitter aftertaste."

"Then you have not tasted Sir Everard's chocolate."

He grinned. "In that regard, you have the advantage of me. In fact, I've not seen my cousin—oh . . . for some time." He paused. Did she know the scandal that had attended her husband and all that he'd done to try to repair the damage? Clearly not. Best he not be the one to tell her. "Tell me, cousin, coming from Gravesend, what do you think of London so far?"

If Rosamund thought it odd that he knew her origins, she didn't remark on it. She broke off a piece of bread and chewed slowly, considering her words.

"Why, I have seen so little of it, I do not think I am fit to offer an opinion, Mr. Pepys."

"Come now," said Sam, daring to reach over and pat the back of her hand, a pat that quickly turned into strokes. "We are related. Call me Sam."

"Then Sam it is," said Rosamund, withdrawing her hand. She smiled to soften the gesture, then her mouth drooped.

"What is it?" he asked, tilting forward so hastily he almost spilled his coffee.

"Well, here I am, given the gift of a new relative and yet I know nothing of *you*. It would give me the greatest of pleasure if you would tell me about yourself, sir. About *your* life in London. Perhaps you can be the window through which I come to view this marvelous city," she said and bestowed upon him the most glorious of smiles.

Sam sat back. Could this woman be any more wondrous?

ELEVEN
In which Sir Everard recruits an ally

Forced out of bed earlier than planned because damn Sam Pepys had arrived unannounced like a recurrence of the French pox, Sir Everard was most vexed. Why, the man had not darkened his door since the business with Aubrey, and even then, despite repeated attempts to gain entry after Margery's death, he hadn't been admitted. And here was Everard thinking the fool had learned his presence wasn't wanted.

When he entered the parlor with Wat and Jacopo close behind him an hour after Sam burst in, it was to find his new wife looking glorious in one of the old gowns Bianca had the seamstress, Mrs. Wells, adjust. A pale blue–and–rose ensemble, it showed her coloring off to perfection. Calmly seated with the naval clerk by the window, pretending to drink a bowl of coffee (the servants had informed Jacopo she didn't seem to enjoy the beverage; Sir Everard kicked himself he hadn't thought to tell her to order chocolate), she was chatting to him as if they were old acquaintances. Through the window, the sky was a wash of coral and plum, the mellow light making Rosamund's hair glow like spun gold. The room, lit by burgeoning sunlight and smelling of leather and beeswax, looked tired. Fortunately, Rosamund did not.

Fixing a welcoming grimace, Sir Everard shook off Jacopo, nodded to Wat's unspoken question and with no small effort tapped his way toward the little tête-à-tête.

"Samuel Pepys. What a surprise. It's been too long. Too long."

Sam leaped to his feet, sweeping off his hat and bowing deferentially. "Why, cousin, your man over there told me you were indisposed." He flapped his hat toward Wat, who hid his expression as he left the room. "But instead, after all this time, I find you looking the picture of health. Now I know why . . ." He winked in Rosamund's direction. "You old dog."

"Don't stand on ceremony," said Sir Everard with more tolerance than he felt. "Sit, Sam, sit." While he might look the picture of health (something he very much doubted), Sam was wilting, in either the growing heat or, more likely, Rosamund's presence. His puffy face, usually ashen, was pink and shiny and his protuberant eyes gleamed with discovery. Signaling to one of the footmen, who, understanding the gesture, dashed through the doorway, Sir Everard flipped the tails of his housecoat and lowered himself into the chair Jacopo deposited by the table. He smiled at Rosamund, who returned his greeting cautiously.

"My lady," he said. "I trust you're well."

"Indeed, Sir Everard, most well." She gave a bell of laughter.

Staring with his mouth open, Sam reclaimed his seat along with his wits as Sir Everard and Rosamund exchanged pleasantries like a well-acquainted couple. His eyes flicked from one to the other as if he were watching the King play tennis. Sir Everard could see Rosamund was very amused. His rebuke the previous evening had not affected her.

"I hope I'm not interrupting anything?" Sir Everard asked and blessed Rosamund's astuteness that she knew exactly what he was asking.

"No, no, not all, sir. Mr. Pepys," she began, and Sam coughed. "I mean, *Sam*—" She flashed him a smile.

Good God, did Sam just groan? Sir Everard buried a smirk.

"—has been entertaining me with stories about his family and his work." Before Sam could protest she continued. "Did you know Mr.—*Sam* is responsible for victualing the King's entire fleet?" Without waiting for an answer, she went on. "And, as if that weren't enough, he's made it his business to learn how to draw the ships as well as read sea and tide charts. Why, your cousin, *my* cousin—"

Sam clutched his heart and Sir Everard thought the man was about to expire. Rosamund had Sam spellbound, clever minx. Why, she was masterful. As if she were born to it. Tilly Ballister had the right of it. This woman bewitched men.

Just so long as she bewitched one in particular . . .

"—is a man of many talents, sir." Rosamund leveled another charming smile at Sam. Sir Everard watched as she continued to extol the naval clerk's virtues, chuckling drolly sometimes, beaming at others and being altogether captivating. It took Sir Everard a moment to understand what Rosamund was about. She was reassuring him she hadn't yet revealed any details about their hasty nuptials; on the contrary, she'd made Sam the center of conversation and flattered him outrageously with numerous questions. He studied her with growing wonder and respect.

Sir Everard knew that although Sam was currently distracted, it wouldn't be long before he addressed the reason for his visit. He was right.

"So, cousin, how'd you do it?" asked Sam, edging forward on his seat and nudging Sir Everard with his elbow.

"Do what?" Sir Everard pretended not to understand.

"Come now." Sam laughed. "How'd you find such a one?" He made a flourish with his hand, encompassing Rosamund, who merely lowered her head modestly. "The ravishing Rosamund. News of your marriage is all over the coffee houses and discussed in the finest homes. No question, the Navy Office talks of nothing else, so just imagine court. Frankly, cousin—when I heard, I thought it too outrageous to be true. A posting inn? Gravesend? I decided I'd quash any rumors before they took flight—especially after . . . you know . . ."

Sir Everard bristled, but caught up in his mission, Sam failed to notice.

"—by discovering the truth for myself. I went to the source; I went to Gravesend."

"You *what*?" Sir Everard's voice could have cut glass. "Why didn't you come to me, you fool? *I'm* the source."

Sam gave a leery grin. "True. But since I've not been welcome here awhile, and as I was intending to go there anyhow, no inconvenience was involved. Along with Elizabeth, my clerk and maid, I went to see for myself."

"And what did you see?" asked Sir Everard, his mind afire, wondering how he could make this unexpected turn of events work in his favor.

"Apart from a posting inn which, I was reliably informed, was the scene of a lively wedding only the day previously, I'd a very interesting conversation with the owner."

"Paul Ballister?"

"Your stepfather, Rosamund?" Sam turned toward her.

Rosamund, who had blanched at the name, gazed toward the window, plotting her escape if the look on her face was anything to go by. Curse Sam Pepys and his propensity for facts.

Unabashed, Sam continued. "That would make him *your* father-in-law, Sir Everard, if I'm not mistaken?"

Sir Everard didn't answer. Sam was enjoying this a little too much.

"A greasy sort of fellow, wouldn't you say?" Sam added.

Recognizing that any attempt to control the news of his marriage was already beyond him, Sir Everard conceded defeat. He had to move swiftly to moderate the damage and turn things to his advantage. To do that, he had to work against his inclinations and trust his dead wife's idiot of a cousin to at least operate in his interests—and if not his, then maybe someone else's. Seeing how Sam was already enthralled by Ravishing Rosamund, there was only one way to do that.

"Rosamund," said Sir Everard with more sharpness than he intended. "I think it's time for you to attend to your duties. Those we spoke of last night." His eyes alighted meaningfully upon Descartes. "Jacopo will accompany you."

Sam stood. "Oh, please don't leave on my account . . ."

With a look, Sir Everard silenced Sam, who sank back into his seat. "I assure you, Sam, it *is* necessary. Anyhow, we've a great deal to catch up on, have we not?"

Rosamund put down her bowl of coffee eagerly and, after rearranging her skirts, picked up the book, curtseyed first to Sir Everard, then to Sam. Jacopo moved swiftly to her side, and Sir Everard heaved himself up and took her hand.

"I will try to call by later today and see how our . . . new venture is progressing." He squeezed her hand and felt her fingers tighten around his in response. Good chit. She understood.

"I shall look forward to that, milord," said Rosamund, curtseying again. She turned to Sam. "It's been a pleasure meeting you, cousin."

Sam stood and gave a formal bow. "Believe me when I say the pleasure has been all mine."

"Thus far, you've given me no cause to doubt you," said Rosamund straight-faced.

One of the footmen coughed.

Enjoying Sam's discomfort, Sir Everard burst out laughing, his eyes narrowing as he beheld his new wife.

Sam watched Rosamund and Jacopo depart, Wat on their heels, then swung toward his cousin.

"Please, Sir Everard, cease your chortling. There's much I wish to discuss with you now the lady has left." Dejected, Sam resumed his seat. "Dear God, but she is dazzling. A veritable Helen, no, a *Helene* in our midst. The resemblance is uncanny. Why, when I first opened the door, I thought the dead had arisen . . . Oh, that was imprudent. Forgive me."

"I do." Sir Everard barely heard. His mind was racing. Whereas he'd first begrudged his cousin's presence, he now recognized it, gauche comments aside, as a Godsend.

Sam blathered on. "She's also very like Frances Stewart, don't you think? Older, but not by too much.

I am sure the men of the court will note this and—are you listening to me, cousin?"

Sitting down, Sir Everard beckoned Sam closer. "No. I'm not. I've much on my mind."

A lascivious grin parted Sam's lips as he shifted in his chair. "I can only imagine . . ."

Feigning great reluctance, Sir Everard regarded his cousin earnestly. "Can I trust you, Sam?"

"Of course. We may not have seen each other since before the business with your son and Margery's death, that drunken card game aside, but are we not family?"

Sir Everard nodded sagely, as if he'd not thought the one benefit of the Aubrey affair (as he'd come to think of it) and Margery's death had been divesting himself of the likes of Pepys.

"Then, allow me to tell you the truth about Rosamund and the situation in which I found her; a situation made all the more abhorrent to me precisely because of the likeness she bears to my daughter . . ."

Slowly, Sir Everard outlined the facts: the horses, Rosamund's injury, the return to the inn; how he felt stirred to rescue her from the villain Ballister. Of his own intentions, he remained mute. Omitting the finer details of his "rescue," he paused only when goblets and a decanter were delivered and drinks poured.

As he listened, Sam's expression changed from one of triumph to pity, then simmering outrage. Observing his reaction, Sir Everard knew this was the version Sam would tell over and over. If the cat was out of the bag, well, let it wear a bell he'd fashioned. A version in which he was the hero, Ravishing Rosamund very much the victim and Lovelace not mentioned. Not yet.

By the time Sir Everard had finished, Sam was incredulous and indignant. "Well," he said, drawing himself up, his portly frame filling the chair, his chin tilted. "I say, cousin, while I found the swiftness of your nuptials somewhat troublesome and had cause to doubt your sanity—at least until I set eyes upon Rosamund—I was wrong. I did you a grave injustice. You've done a most noble thing. Rescued Rosamund from a veritable dragon. I just wish you'd slain the beast."

Sam's face softened as he gazed toward the door. "She's an absolute beauty. That hair. That figure. That *laugh*. I don't think I've seen her match." He sighed before his expression hardened. "Wait till His Majesty sets eyes upon her, let alone Buckingham or Bennet; they won't be able to resist. As for William Chiffinch, the royal procurer, he'll be keen to teach her the route to the King's chambers, mark my words. I don't envy you that moment, cousin. If I were you, I'd do everything in my power to keep those men away."

Pretending a calm he didn't feel, Sir Everard brushed the air with a lazy hand. "Once word gets around, I'm afraid that's all but an impossible task . . ." Rubbing his chin, he pretended to think. "And then there's the chocolate house . . ."

"What has that to do with Rosamund?"

Sir Everard steepled his fingers beneath his chin.

Outside, a bird began to trill. The day grew dim as a bank of clouds slowly swallowed the weak sun.

"Tell me, please."

Feigning reluctance, Sir Everard sighed. "As you have made clear, I can't prevent people from knowing about Rosamund or embellishing the circumstances surrounding our nuptials, no matter how deep my desire to protect her. I understand I was a numbskull to think I could." He gave Sam a warm smile of gratitude. "But, the more I consider it, the more I believe it's important folks' curiosity about Rosamund is, to a degree, sated." Sam nodded vigorously. "But I want their sympathy engaged. If they have her name upon their lips, I want it uttered kindly. I want descriptions of her loveliness and innocence to fly through the air and scatter in all directions, like perfumed flowers on a blustery day. I understand her resemblance to Helene will be impossible to deny—"

"It is."

"If everyone is going to talk about her——"

"They already are."

"I want to extend their conversation beyond any history involving *my* family. I want it to be as if the Blithmans have, with Rosamund, been born again. Do you understand?"

"I . . . I think so. Like the mythical phoenix?"

Sir Everard regarded him askance. "If you say so. Anyhow, I'm relying on your help. I want you to tell people there is no scandal, no wrongdoing—at least on my part—not that there ever was." He frowned. "There is just a guiltless young woman who was rescued from a dire future by a lonely old man who saw his daughter reborn in a hapless young chit. A chance to restore the Blithman name."

"But, cousin, I thought with the money you gave the King, you already had? Certainly, if ever he makes mention of you, it's with much favor." When Sir Everard didn't respond, Sam continued. "I'm not certain this desire to point out the likeness to Helene is wise. I mean, people might find such a comparison . . . How do I put it? Inappropriate? Monstrous even? After all, you *married* this likeness. They might traduce you, sir."

"Let them. My soul is untroubled. Rosamund is beyond reproach even if I am not."

"Of course, of course."

Sam's brows puckered. He went to speak, then changed his mind.

"Can I trust you with such a mission?" asked Sir Everard. "Trust you to help ease Rosamund's passage into this city of gossips? Navigate those who would sooner flense an ingenue, divest her of the innocence you sensed, suspect her of crimes she has in no way committed? I would protect her, Sam. I would that *we* protect her."

Sam's back straightened, his shoulders set. "It would be an honor to be entrusted with such a task." A thought crossed his mind. "But how long before others can bear witness to the delight that is your new wife?"

Sir Everard appeared to consider his answer. "If anyone wants an introduction to Rosamund, then they must wait."

"But . . . but . . . that's preposterous. You can't expect people to do that."

"Why not?"

"Because . . . because . . . it's not what's done."

"And since when have I followed rules, Sam— unspoken, written or otherwise? I would not be the success I am if I had. If anyone wants to meet Rosamund, then they can damn well wait until the chocolate house opens."

"What has the chocolate house got to do with Rosamund?"

Sir Everard smiled. "Everything, Sam. Everything."

Releasing a long sigh, Sam fell back in his seat, drink in hand. "I will not pretend to understand your purpose, cousin, but if you seek to safeguard Rosamund and her reputation, then putting her in the chocolate house, even as a means to shelter her, is not the way to do it."

"Why not? She's my wife. It's my right to control access to her."

"Perhaps, but women can't patronize those establishments—not the kind who will be her equal."

"But it's not women I want Rosamund to meet," said Sir Everard smoothly.

"Ah, you desire men to fall under her spell." Jealousy flashed across Sam's face. He was so transparent sometimes.

"You forget. I'm a businessman. I desire men to spend their coin at my chocolate house—and what better incentive than a lovely young woman?"

Sam frowned and shook his head. "Sir Everard, cousin, forgive me. But is this wise? For all you desire to insulate her, won't you be risking her reputation with such a strategy?"

Sir Everard bestowed a smile. "Wisdom has nothing to do with it. My primary intention is to attract those who have . . . avoided my company over the last couple of years and ensure they make a path to my door."

Sam studied Sir Everard. "Well, I for one am glad to hear this, cousin. Truth be told, I've been most anxious for your well-being. While I know you don't want to discuss that terrible business with Aubrey, facts are, it did untold damage to your name, until your efforts to mitigate it, of course." He hesitated. "It also hurt those associated with you—friends, family—"

Sir Everard knew then that Sam sought forgiveness for withdrawing from his company for so long. Who could blame him? Sam was right, the taint of traitor tarred all. Unlike those who avoided him when Margery and then Helene and the baby died, Sam had tried to reach out and offer solace. It was he who had refused his overtures. He felt a sudden rush of affection for the silly little man.

"Then, naturally, you were not yourself after Margery's death, and Helene and the babe. God knows," added Sam swiftly, "one could not expect you to be."

They sat quietly. Raised voices drifted up from the courtyard below as Wat directed some deliveries.

"Well," Sam said finally, slapping his thighs. "I'm most gratified to hear you talk in such terms, and if I had any concerns about your hasty nuptials to Rosamund, well, they've now been put to rest. But, cousin, if I may proffer a word of advice."

It was all Sir Everard could do to control the flare of anger that rose. There was nothing worse than unsolicited advice. "What might that be?"

"If you wish your wife to make a grand entrance upon the stage of the chocolate house, play her part, then I suggest you look to her costume."

Sir Everard appeared puzzled.

"It's not . . . seemly to dress her in another's clothes, no matter they are dear to you and conjure fond memories. There's no doubt that would set even male tongues wagging and, dare I say, most unkindly. Your sweet Rosamund deserves better."

How could Sir Everard explain that attiring Rosamund in Margery's clothes was not an oversight but a deliberate strategy? Neither did they conjure fond memories. On the contrary, like the portraits in the study, they kept him focused. Simple.

Sam gave a nervous giggle. "I am just relieved you haven't dressed her in Helene's wardrobe. Imagine what assumptions would be drawn then."

Sir Everard's eyes narrowed. "Helene's clothes? She took them with her when she . . . left." His mind began to tick. Images of Helene in her wedding gown, her favorite day dress of azure and silver, edged with black. In fact, so many of her gowns had been edged with ebony. Margery would oft castigate her and remind her black was for widow's weeds . . .

"Are you listening, cousin?" asked Sam in a tone that declared offense.

"Yes, yes," said Sir Everard, clearly lying. "You were discoursing on Helene's clothes, were you not?"

"No, not Helene's, my own wife's and that God-forsaken tailor of hers, Mr. Unthank. The . . ." har-rumphed Sam, halting as Sir Everard rose from his chair and moved behind him to grip his shoulder.

"You may regale me with that tale later." He tightened his hold. "For now, let's talk about my wife a little longer . . . What were you saying about her clothes?"

Sir Everard loosened his hold as Sam eagerly blathered on. Making his way back to his seat, he downed a cooling ale, his mind afire.

So long as Rosamund became the subject of the chatterers and correspondents on terms he set, he could focus on far more important matters.

TWELVE
In which a woman's worth is determined

For all that Jacopo's spoken English was a darn sight better than most in Gravesend, his vocabulary being vast and his accent lending a charming musicality to his words, when it came to teaching Rosamund how to read, she was forced to acknowledge he was completely hopeless.

They had made themselves comfortable at the table at the back of the kitchen, but before he'd even opened the chocolate treatise Jacopo had leaped to his feet twice to answer some imagined summons. Once he started reading, and had her repeat what he said, a finger under each word and sounding them out, he yawned prodigiously. He fiddled with the edges of the pages and at one stage, even as Rosamund said the words, began to tidy the desk. When he broke away to speak to Filip, presenting Rosamund with a bowl of chocolate upon his return, she began to suspect Jacopo was deliberately sabotaging his efforts and thus hers. Stifling her frustration, Rosamund kept her patience, asking him to please point to and reiterate words so she could lodge them in her mind. At her insistence, Jacopo painstakingly reread the first part of the work—for the third time—mispronouncing words he'd read correctly the first and second times.

Rosamund's suspicions were confirmed: Jacopo found his teaching duties an imposition and did not wish to be lumbered with his master's illiterate wife. Heat rose in her that had little to do with the trapped steam in the kitchen and everything to do with her shame and discomfort—she hated to think she was a burden. If she hadn't been determined to learn, she would have snatched the besom from Widow Ashe and swept the kitchen—at least she could do that.

She suggested a break so she might use the "house of office" and stretch her legs, and wasn't surprised when Jacopo eagerly agreed.

As she squatted inelegantly over the jordan, voluminous skirts gathered in her arms, Rosamund couldn't help but consider that if the morning was any indication of the type of lessons she'd receive, it would be impossible to learn a thing.

Rosamund wondered what to do. Dare she complain to Sir Ever-ard? What if Jacopo was rebuked? She could never forgive herself and, furthermore, bringing trouble upon Jacopo would hardly endear her to his sister, or indeed the other servants. She would think about other ways to make the time at the chocolate house beneficial. There was much she could grasp from observing Filip and the boys. As for reading, she *would* master it, despite Jacopo.

What she didn't admit to him was, with every line he read and she repeated, some of her early lessons were returning to her. The thrill of recognition, the blooming of understanding caused a frisson similar to encountering an old friend. No matter what it took, she would read Wadsworth's translation of Colmenero and learn all she could about chocolate.

She wished she'd been more tactful in presenting her ideas for the chocolate house to Sir Everard instead of blundering in. Had she learned nothing from her time at the Maiden Voyage Inn? It had taken her years to acquire and hone the skills that allowed Paul to believe her notions regarding the business were in fact mostly his. It was strange how women weren't supposed to have original opinions or contribute to business or, it seemed, society in any meaningful way. Not openly, anyhow. It was as if everything was invented by men—even when it wasn't. Women had to behave as if they hadn't a serious thought in their heads. Smiling, being ingratiating and deferential, that was the sensible path, even for smart women. It was something she'd learned from observing Tilly, Widow Cecily, Dorcas, even the serving girls when they flirted with male customers. And had adopted in her own interactions with her stepfather and the twins.

Believing Sir Everard was a different kind of man, more like Master Dunstan and what she imagined her father would have been like had he lived, she'd misstepped. He'd seemed so prepared to listen, to accede to others' suggestions, even a woman's (hadn't he listened to her mother when she'd said he should marry her?), that she'd misread him. It wouldn't happen again.

What was it Widow Cecily always said? Grin and endure. It was something she'd become proficient in, smiling as if her life depended on it.

She wasn't surprised to find Jacopo had vanished when she returned to the table. Rosamund pulled the treatise toward her, studying the paragraphs Jacopo had already read, trying to make sense of them, able to recall parts. She made a note to tell Sam that Dr. Colmenero found drinking chocolate "cured the stone." During their conversation that morning Sam had told her in considerable detail how, four years earlier, he'd seen a surgeon called Thomas Hollier, and had a stone the size of a tennis ball removed from his lower regions.

Such a peculiar man was Sam Pepys, but very nice all the same. Rosamund had enjoyed listening to him, even about his operation. She was left with the strong impression that he was oft underestimated due to his rather plain countenance and short stature. She smiled and hoped he was serious in his invitation, issued just before Sir Everard appeared, to take her to the theater. Appalled she'd never been to a proper playhouse, he'd immediately offered to escort her.

Delighted, Rosamund had clasped her hands. "That would be lovely. And I would get to meet your wife."

"Oh, her," said Sam, with a dismissive twist of his wrist. "Perhaps." The glow in his eyes dimmed.

Upon reflection, though Sam had spoken a great deal about himself and the important people he knew, he'd barely mentioned his wife. Rosamund couldn't even recall her name.

When Jacopo still didn't reappear, Rosamund waited a few more minutes then decided to go in search of him. She'd been so lost in revising, she'd failed to notice that not only were Filip and the boys gone, but the constant clamor of the workmen had ceased. Parting the curtain, she found the large room deserted. At that moment, bells began to toll. Why, it was midday.

Where was everyone?

"Widow Ashe, Ashe?" she called.

A timid face peeked around the corner. "Madam?" said a soft, high voice.

"Where are the men?"

"Gone to the ordinary down the road for vittles, madam," she said, jerking her thumb toward the street. "Said they'd bring us back som'in." Before Rosamund could ask another question, the woman slipped away.

Emboldened at being left alone, Rosamund stepped beyond the curtain, keen to inspect the chocolate house without having to endure the stares of the workers. As she wandered about, noting some fine new benches in need of sanding and the wooden bones of what would become a row of booths, all constructed since yesterday, she hoped Jacopo wouldn't be gone too long. She'd barely broken her fast that morning, she had been so taken up with Sam's arrival; she was quite famished.

Back in the kitchen, the vats bubbled, but the pans that held cacao beans had been removed from the heat and the *metate* upon which Solomon had rolled cakes was clean. She made her way out of the kitchen area toward a small window and pushed it open, inhaling the sultry air. Across from where she stood was the roof of the barber's, and beyond that, she could see shadows and the glow of candles in the rear windows of the offices along the street, but little else. The clop of hooves, the rumble of iron wheels, traders' shouts and even the faint clucking of chickens carried. Immediately below was a small yard with a ramshackle building that might have been stables. Feeling uncomfortably warm, and with Widow Ashe reluctant to keep her company, she decided to explore outside. Around the corner from the table, almost hidden by a cupboard, was a door. With some difficulty she opened it to reveal a dark, narrow staircase. Eschewing the lanthorn hanging from a hook, she descended carefully, hands pressed against the walls.

At the bottom she opened a door into the yard and blinked in the daylight. It was bound by side walls shared with the neighbors, and at the rear was a fence with a gate that led to a church which fronted Lombard Street. The yard was compact and very untidy. There was a strong smell of urine; urine and another, metallic smell. Empty barrels were stacked along a wall, some split from being left out in the elements. A pile of refuse had matured beside them and shuddered slightly as if rats burrowed within it. Trampled grass led to the old stables. The building was timber with double doors tightly closed, incongruously, by a shiny lock. If it wasn't for the fence on one side holding it up, a gust of wind might blow the building over.

The new lock intrigued her. Why bother securing such a ruin? Before she could reach the doors, the rear gate swung open and two men staggered in, clearly cupshotten. Their paint-spattered blue shirts and the sigil on their aprons identified them as Mr. Remney's apprentices. Rosamund stopped, uncertain what to do.

When they saw her, the men also halted.

"Hallo, what 'ave we here?" called out a thickset young man with a ruddy face, and nudged his companion hard in the ribs.

His friend swung around and hastily shut the gate. He grinned, revealing brown teeth. "Something sweet from the chocolate kitchen, if I'm not mistaken."

The greeting Rosamund prepared died on her lips. If she'd hoped they were somehow bonded because they worked in the same space, she understood how naive she was. She was a woman and as alien to these men as cats to canines. She noted how they quickly weighed up distances, saw she was alone. Thinking to tell them who she was, she remembered with dismay she hadn't been introduced. To the workmen she was but a navvy or servant—likely another Widow Ashe—and thus, in their eyes, fair game. Her ill-fitting gown, the dust covering her apron, the mud and bits of grass spattering her skirts simply confirmed it. Even if she announced her identity, she'd scarce be believed. Would it even matter? From the looks upon their faces, she feared not.

The men moved closer and she began to back away toward the house, her eyes flitting from one to the other. The man with brown teeth jerked his head in her direction, then spat. Following the unspoken command, the ruddy-faced one moved behind Rosamund, blocking her exit.

Rosamund tried not to let her growing panic show. Raising her chin, she nodded to both the men. "Gentlemen."

"Oh, you be mistaken, miss." Brown Teeth leered. "We be no gentlemen."

Ruddy Face lunged and grabbed her wrists from behind. Holding them tightly with one hand, he pulled her against his chest and covered her mouth with the other before she could cry out.

"And you," whispered Ruddy Face in her ear, "be no lady." His tongue swiped the side of her face. "Tasty morsel, she is."

There was a noise above and a pale face retreated with a cry. Widow Ashe. Would she raise the alarm?

Unaware they'd been seen, Brown Teeth began to loosen her hair, his filthy fingers twining through the tresses, raising them to his nose as he inhaled loudly. "Her 'air's so long, she be like Lady Godiva." She caught a whiff of beer, sweat and the rank odor of onions. "She needs be naked," he murmured and began to nuzzle the other side of her neck while his friend thrust his hips into her back.

Struggling against Ruddy Face's hold, unable to break it, Rosamund tried to appeal to Brown Teeth with her eyes. He simply laughed and, losing patience, tore away her apron before he reached into her bodice, exposing the shift beneath, pulling it away as if it were but thistledown so he could stare at her breasts.

"Cor, a dimber pair of paps I've not seen."

With a guffaw of delight, Brown Teeth began to squeeze her breasts and roll the nipples between fat, greasy fingers. Striking her legs hard to stop her kicking, he tugged at her skirts, lifting them, pawing her thighs. "We got ourselves a right rum mort here, Jed."

"Watch her stampers, Ben," mumbled Jed, dancing out of the way of Rosamund's shoes as he drove his hips into her, his breath hot and rancid against her neck. Keeping ahold of her wrists, he tried to lift her off her feet.

Pressed between two stinking chests, she could scarce move, let alone call out. And even if she could, then to whom? Cries might attract more who would view her as a recreation rather than a victim. The stench of the men's bodies, of their anticipation, swamped her.

She tried to bite the hand clamping her mouth, kick out at the one who held her skirts around her waist, but they were too strong.

Aware of a hard prick prodding her in the back and a capless head of bristly hair grazing her chin while wet lips sought her breasts, she shut her eyes. Had she not fought off Fear-God and Glory? Had she not resisted their attempts to "teach" her until they grew too big to repel? One of the ways she did that was by pretending acquiescence. Resisting every instinct shouting at her to fight with her last breath, she went completely limp.

The men's hold relaxed. It was enough. With a bray of rage, risking having the hair torn from her scalp, she lunged sideways as swiftly and forcefully as she could. She kicked Brown Teeth Ben in the shins and he fell to his knees in front of her with a loud *oof.* Spinning, she kneed Ruddy Face Jed in the cock. As he doubled over, she turned back to Ben and slammed her bent leg into his face. The resounding crack as she connected with his nose and the blood that spattered her stockings gave her nothing but satisfaction.

"You cuntin' whore," he screamed, his hand flying to his face. "You broke me nose."

A dull roar filled her ears. Her mind became a melange of images, smells and sounds. Her heart, a confusion. No longer was it a dirty, unshaven worker on his knees before her, but Paul Ballister. Out of the corner of her eyes, she saw the rear gate open and a shadowy figure step through. Another come to join the sport. Well, she'd not surrender willingly. Not this time.

Without hesitation, she began to kick Ben furiously, the pointed toe of her fine shoe striking his groin, then, when he bent over, his mouth, discolored teeth flying. She booted his cheek, his shoulders, his ribs. He fell backward, howling, hands raised to protect his face then dropping to cover his balls. He tried to roll away.

"Yer bitch," he said as blood flowed. "Leave off; we meant nothin'. Help! Help!"

Aware of muted cries and grunts coming from Jed behind her, she wondered why he didn't come to his friend's aid and pull her away. Why whoever had entered did not intervene.

Ben found his feet and staggered back, an arm raised in surrender. Frozen in place, she stared at him. His nose was flattened across his face, blood smeared his cheeks, his shirt, and flowed down his chin, his lips coated in rubicund liquid. She felt nothing. He hadn't listened to her pleas. He'd ignored her cries, her anguish; her terror.

It didn't matter what she promised, how good she

was, he never let her go . . . He never, ever stopped, however great the pain . . .

Calling on God to give her strength, she strode forward, fists raised above her head, when another pair of hands seized them.

With a cry of rage she twisted around to find herself held firmly by a stranger.

"Madam, it is over." The voice was calm, authoritative. "You are safe."

A huge gloved hand engulfed her wrists. She looked up into an unfamiliar face, aware of the blood pounding in her ears, the harshness of her breathing. This man's fingers were strong, his words firm, but his manner wasn't threatening. He was clean shaven, with thick arched black brows and a wide mouth, but it was his eyes that held her. They were the color of the evening sky upon twilight; a deep blue tinged with lilac. His lashes were long and inky, as if black lines had been drawn around his eyes.

While one hand captured both of hers above her head, his other held a sword which was pointed at Jed, who lay unconscious at his feet. She blinked.

"Who are you?" she asked breathlessly.

"A friend," said the man, slowly lowering her arms. "I'm going to release you." As he loosened his grip, his eyes never left her face and he continued speaking soothingly.

"They will not harm you, on that you have my word."

Standing perfectly still, she tried to concentrate on breathing. Her breasts, which she quickly covered, heaved. She was so very hot and yet cold at the same time. She shuddered.

"Are you hurt?" the man asked quietly.

Was she hurt? Not in the way one would expect. Apart from a torn shift, unpinned hair, a few bruises and a complete loss of dignity, she was, to all intents and purposes, unharmed. She'd experienced worse. Snatching up the apron from where it had been discarded, she clutched it to her chest to protect her modesty and shook her head.

"No. I am well."

There was a moan. "All right for some," said Ben. "I be in a right state thanks to this doxy." He found his knees and tried to stand.

Horrified by what she'd done, the fear and uncertainty on Ben's bruised and battered face as he regarded her, Rosamund stepped away. The man with the lovely eyes reached over and hauled Ben to his feet. The apprentice barely reached his chest.

"Thank the good Lord you came, mister," said Ben, one hand across his midriff, wiping his nose with his sleeve, wincing and smudging the blood on his cheek. "This vicious little kitchen bitch attacked me—" He glanced to where his friend lay. "Us."

The man raised a black brow, growled and brought his sword to bear upon Ben.

"Watch your language, scoundrel. I witnessed the attack and know it was not of the lady's instigation. This 'vicious little kitchen bitch' "—he flashed an apologetic look at Rosamund—"has your life and that of your friend in her hands."

"She did attack all right, sir. Why, if you hadn't come—"

"You two would have forced yourselves upon her, which is what I will tell the constable when he arrives."

"There's no need to call the constable, sir." Ben held up his hands in conciliation. "No need to involve the law. Why, we done nothin' wrong, me and Jed. She be no innocent either, she asked for it, she did. Beckoned us in here and—"

The man thrust his sword under Ben's chin, silencing him. "I've told you once, you ruffler, watch your tongue. If you cannot, I will take it." He flicked the sword. Ben screamed as blood poured from the scratch upon his neck.

"Forgive me, sir, forgive me," he whimpered, clutching the wound and scooting out of reach.

There was a muted groan and the apprentice called Jed stirred, rolling onto his back, one arm draped across his chest.

"Forgiveness is not mine to offer, but the lady's. If it were up to me, I'd serve justice and see you hanged this very moment, right here."

Dropping to his knees, Ben crawled toward the man and grabbed his coat. "Please, sir, I beg you, you too, missus, we meant no harm. 'Twas just a bit of rollick." He began to cry, great sniffles made worse by his ruined nose.

"What would you have me do, madam?" the man asked evenly, ignoring Ben's weeping. "Hang them or fetch the parish constable?"

Jed managed to sit up and, hearing the choices on offer, buried his head in his hands. "We be for it now, Ben," he murmured.

Rosamund regarded the youths who had attacked her. Now they were cowed, she could see they were really very young. Workers who knew little in their lives but beatings and harsh words. A part of her wished they *were* Fear-God and Glory and experiencing this man's wrath, feeling panic as his steel pressed against their flesh and the point of her shoes cracked their bones. Only, they weren't. They were two strange men, boys, really, employed to renovate the chocolate house. And what if they had fathers like Paul? Fathers who taught them women were theirs to command, to beat, to take pleasure from, to discipline using their cocks, fists and teeth? What if their mothers also believed this? What if they didn't know any different?

Ben raised his swollen, damp eyes to hers in a silent plea. Jed ceased to move. He was like a statue, waiting for sentence, his head lowered in preparation for the sword about to fall. For the first time in her life Rosamund was judge and executioner and she liked it not. Maybe if she showed clemency, then one day these boys might as well.

"I would let them go."

Ben's eyes widened. Jed began to raise his head.

"Are you sure, madam?" asked the man, glowering at the two rogues, who quickly looked away.

Rosamund nodded. "I would let them go so they might leave this place and never return, for if ever I see them again I will make certain justice is served."

Lowering his sword, the man stared at her as if, like a mythic maiden, she'd been transformed from alabaster into flesh. He gave a half bow.

"And I, madam, will serve it." Facing the two men, he flicked his weapon. "On your feet, rogues, the lady has spoken."

The two men struggled to stand, tucking in their shirts, searching for their caps.

"Be gone from here and don't ever set foot on this property, street or ward again. If I hear but a whisper of Jed or Ben, then you shall feel the weight of my anger and the wrath of my blade."

Ben glanced toward the first floor of the chocolate house and looked as if he might argue. Rosamund guessed he'd left tools as well as his reputation upstairs. She quickly damped a flare of sympathy for him. They no more deserved her compassion than they did her clemency, but they had both.

Without another word, the two workers were escorted to the gate by her unexpected ally. As they left, she fixed her dress, retied her apron and tried to tame her hair, her hands clumsy as shaking threatened to overtake her entire body. She was thirsty, tired and close to tears.

This wasn't meant to happen anymore, not here, not now. Not in London. She was married and respectable. Had not Sir Everard told her he wished her to be safe? Had he not sent her here today in the belief she would be so? Aye, and promised reading lessons, yet neither of his wishes had been met.

Holding open the gate, the man spoke harshly to the two boys. Their faces transformed from surly and regretful to terrorized. Casting looks of horror in Rosamund's direction, they pulled off their caps, bowed and stumbled over each other in their haste to escape.

The man waited, his back to Rosamund. He was broad-shouldered and his hair was long and very dark beneath his fine feathered hat. He'd no need of a periwig. His breeches and shoes were not those of a worker and his gloves were finely made. The shirt that rose high on his neck was made of quality material, as was his jacquard coat. Who was he and what had prompted him to enter the yard? Was he a parishioner? Had Widow Ashe summoned him?

Before she could assemble her thoughts, the man returned.

Maybe it was the dreadful kindness which set his eyes ablaze, or the smile he tried and failed to kindle and which was for her alone. Whatever it was, it was more than Rosamund could bear. She opened her mouth to thank him for his intervention, once, twice and then, much to her chagrin, began to cry.

THIRTEEN
In which Lady Harridan is introduced to Mr. Nessuno

U nlike most women of his acquaintance, who would have fallen into hysterics at such an assault, this woman had not only defended herself with a strength and will he'd not seen before, but now sought to hide her quiet tears.

He approached her cautiously (after all, he'd seen how she wielded her fists and feet), and before he could offer words of comfort, she held up a palm, shook her head and backed away.

Discommoded, the man stopped. "My lady, please, tell me what I can do to ease your evident distress."

"*Madam?*" The call from inside the building was faint but clear.

The woman's head jerked up as she surveyed the upper story. It was the first time he had seen her clearly.

Good God. Hailstones pummeled his body from within. Forgotten scenes rose to taunt him. The rumors were true. She was Helene reborn.

Only . . .

He took in the dark, swimming eyes, the concern clouding them as she stared aloft; the little frown puckering her brow . . . remembered the way she granted forgiveness . . .

She was not.

"Please," she sniffed in a most unladylike manner, swiping her sleeve across her nose. "They cannot find me—not like this." She pressed the heels of her hands into her eyes then looked down at the wreckage of her dress in dismay. Much to his surprise, her lips began to twitch. "They'll think I invited the attention." She gave a laugh. The bitterness forced him to take a step back.

His mind became as disordered as the leaves scattering in the rising wind.

"I will assure them you did not."

"No, no." She shook her head, resigned. "They cannot find you here . . . They mustn't."

On that score, she was right.

She grabbed him by the hand and began to lead him toward the gate.

"*Madam?*"

This time the voice was nearer; a head appeared at the window directly above. The woman flattened herself against the wall of the house, forcing him to do the same. To make matters worse, some coxcombs in the lane took up the cry, calling out, "Madam! Madam!" to raucous laughter.

The woman rested her head against the building and then whispered, "Is it always like this?"

"What?" The man was unable to tear his eyes from her face, her form—so familiar and yet so very different.

"London."

"Like what?"

"A hodgepodge of danger and drollery." She nodded in the direction of the cheeky cries. Dimples creased her cheeks and her eyes, shimmering with unshed tears, were large and molten, the lashes ridiculously long and wet.

Before he could find his voice, the one above called again. "Madam?" It was closer this time.

"Please," the woman beseeched. "I do not want them to know what happened." The man's eyebrows rose. "I'm all right now and I do thank you. Please, just go." She gave him a push.

"But I cannot leave you," he said, even though that was exactly what he must do. He could not risk being seen.

"Why not?" She was genuinely surprised.

Uncertain how to respond, he allowed himself to be encouraged toward the gate, torn between amusement and utter bemusement.

She paused as she was about to open the gate. "Forgive my rudeness, sir. I am ever so grateful. If you hadn't come, well, I don't know what would have happened . . ."

Something in her face told him she knew all too well. He would erase that expression from those features, return the spark that had fired her earlier. Such boldness; courage the like of which he'd rarely seen and never in a woman. A woman whose face brought back so many bitter memories, aroused feelings he'd thought forever banished.

Aware she was waiting for him to say something, he obliged. "Aye, if I hadn't appeared when I did, I fear those ruffians would be in a far worse state."

She blinked, taken aback.

"The moment I heard their cries, I knew I had to rescue them."

"I beg your pardon, sir?"

"From a kitchen doxy. Nay." He paused. "A veritable harridan." He performed a flourish, removing his hat, one leg bent.

The woman met his eyes and then she did the most surprising thing of all: she burst out laughing. Astonished, the man straightened and replaced his hat. As she continued to laugh, his eyes grew wide, his lips twitched and, before he knew it, he was doubled over, laughing with her. She rested a hand on his back to prevent herself from falling.

The clouds chose that moment to release their burden.

"Go, please, go," she said, removing her hand, composing herself swiftly. Though her eyes still twinkled. She fiddled with the latch, the rain making the metal slick.

He understood her haste, but he wouldn't let her have it all her way.

Removing her hand, he wrenched the gate open and stepped through. About to have it shut upon him, he stopped it with his boot. Reaching through the gap, ignoring the rain, he cupped the woman's face in his gloved palm. "I must have your name. A condition of my silence," he said.

"First, what is yours?" demanded the woman. Water trickled into her eyes.

"Nessuno," said the man. "I am Nessuno. Now you."

Pulling his hand away from her face, she dimpled. "Why, the Lady Harridan, of course."

There was a beat in which his foot slipped. Before he could prevent it, she shut the gate.

"Wait," he cried, hoping she was still on the other side. The rain soaked his hat, his jacket. He pressed his face against the wood. "Farewell, my Lady Harridan, and may God keep you."

He heard the latch fall into place followed by faint words as the rain grew harder and he too ran to seek shelter. He was certain he'd heard, "You too, Mr. Nessuno. My friend."

Upon discovering Rosamund idly leafing through the treatise on chocolate, absentmindedly brushing crumbs from her bodice, Jacopo and Filip's breathless concern at her absence and her explanation she'd simply wandered out into the back lane to get some fresh air, but was forced to shelter until the rain eased, quickly turned to mystification.

"But the gate was latched," said Jacopo, when Filip glared at him. "I went through the church to check it myself." The panting, red-faced boys behind him nodded.

Rosamund sent a swift prayer heavenward his search had not found her or Mr. Nessuno.

"It wasn't latched when I first went down," she said truthfully. "It opened easily. Someone must have latched it later." This, of course, was also the truth. "Perhaps it was Mr. Henderson?" she said sweetly.

"Perhaps . . ." said Filip, scratching his head, looking about. "If he's been in the stables using the press . . ." Ashe discreetly disappeared behind the shelves. Rosamund prayed he wouldn't ask Mr. Henderson.

"Sir Everard will not be happy," said Jacopo dolefully.

Rosamund paused in the act of turning a page. "I would not want to alarm him the way I inadvertently did you, Jacopo, Filip—and for that I'm so very sorry. You too, Solomon and Thomas. There's no need to raise the matter with him, is there?" She glanced up from the treatise and bestowed a wide smile. "After all, I'm here now, I've eaten—thank you for the pie, it was delicious—and no harm has befallen me." (That she kept a straight face when she said this owed much to her time at the Maiden Voyage Inn. *Aye*, thought Rosamund as she prattled away, she really should be on the stage.) "I think it's time we returned to our lessons, don't you, Jacopo?"

Referring to her lessons was exactly the diversion Rosamund hoped it would be.

Jacopo coughed into his fist. "As it happens, *signora*, while you were . . . in the lane"—doubt inflected his words—"I received a message. The *signore* is en route and desires to take you to his tailors, the Wellses—the same couple who looked to his first wife and daughter's needs in Foster Lane near St. Paul's."

"Sir Everard is coming here?"

"*Si*. At any moment," said Jacopo. "He's determined you're to receive a new wardrobe." He reached into a pocket to produce said message, then recalled she couldn't read and stopped.

Rosamund was filled first with consternation at her lack of reading skills, then joyous anticipation. If anything could have distracted her from thoughts of Mr. Nessuno and what had just happened, it was the notion she was to be given her own clothes—not ones her mother had worn and thrown in her direction, not those discarded at the inn and patched, or those the former Lady Blithman had once dressed in and which no adjustment could quite make fit—but her very own. Clothing that no man, no matter how sodden with beer, or unaware of her status, would dare rip from her body.

Not since she lived at Bearwoode had someone made her clothes. What a magnificent indulgence. She sent thoughts of gratitude winging to her husband before they were replaced with memories of a pair of mischievous eyes that gleamed as their owner called her a harridan. With a secret smile, she banished Mr. Nessuno from her mind.

"Well, this is good news indeed." Rising, she straightened her skirts, rubbed at a spot of blood she'd missed and found her gloves and hat.

"We'll await him downstairs," Jacopo said and stood aside so she might precede him.

She placed the treatise in the satchel Jacopo had given her so she could study it at leisure in her room later, though the futility of this didn't escape her. Rosamund could barely contain her excitement. Not only was she being endowed with new clothes, but she was going to see more of London. St. Paul's Cathedral! Foster Lane . . . well, that didn't sound quite so prepossessing, even if its inhabitants did (tailors!), but it was a novel destination.

With a warm goodbye to Filip and the boys and another apology for causing them anxiety, Rosamund rushed through the main part of the chocolate house. As she did so she heard Mr. Remney remonstrating with his workers as to the whereabouts of his apprentices Jed Franklin and Ben Miller.

Needless to say, she didn't enlighten him.

FOURTEEN
In which a wife befriends a correspondent

A few days later, as she exited the chocolate house, a figure detached itself from the shadows of Exchange Alley and dashed across the lane toward her. She barely managed to contain her astonishment as she recognized Mr. Nessuno. Sensing he'd been waiting for her to emerge without Jacopo, she tried to appear as if she were accustomed to well-dressed gentlemen accosting her on the street as he joined her beneath the bookshop shingle.

"What luck," he began, doffing his hat. "I was wondering how I might inquire after your health without arousing suspicion—and here you are. Are you well, my Lady Harridan?"

Rosamund nodded, flustered, simultaneously hoping that no one heard how he addressed her and that she had wiped the last chocolate she'd tasted from her mouth. She stared up at this man, whose presence was so unexpected yet so very welcome. He was just as noteworthy as she remembered.

He wore a dark blue jacket, a cream shirt with a flounced collar and a broad-brimmed hat sporting a splendid peacock feather. A satchel was slung across his shoulders and, as before, his hands were encased in fine gloves.

"Are you sure, my lady?" His deep voice purred as he regarded her. "Seems you're sorely afflicted, as you appear to have lost your voice. Should I fetch a physician? Just nod if it be necessary and I will attend to it at once."

Rosamund nodded, then quickly shook her head. "Aye. I mean, no." She began to chuckle and waved a hand to dismiss her words. "I can confirm I've no need of a doctor. I'm most well." She searched the street behind him for any sign of Jacopo, praying he wouldn't appear just yet.

"Are you sure?" he asked again, turning first one way, then the other in an effort to see what was distracting her. "Though, I confess to feeling reassured now your voice has indeed returned. I thought for a minute those rogues had stolen it. However, it seems you're unable to make up your mind; they didn't carry that away while my back was turned, did they?"

Rosamund frowned, then began to laugh. She had his full attention now. "No, sir, they did not. Though I admit, I cannot decide if you're phantom or real."

"Quite real," said Mr. Nessuno. "As is that smudge of chocolate you have just there . . ." He pointed to the corner of her mouth.

With a click of consternation, Rosamund dashed it away with her hand, annoyed to feel heat fly to her cheeks. "Is it still there?" she asked.

Smiling down at her, Mr. Nessuno shook his head. "You've vanquished the mark." His eyes twinkled. "I'm delighted those rascals have not erased your dimples or silenced your laughter. Such an act would be beyond redemption."

"Never fear," said Rosamund carelessly. "I've endured much worse than those villains, and my dimples and humor have not yet deserted me."

Mr. Nessuno's face darkened. "Worse?"

She could have kicked herself. Honestly, when this man was about, her body might be secure, but it seemed her tongue could not be trusted.

"My lady," he said, after studying her a few moments. "Such news strikes me to the core. Name the blackguards at once so I might smite them."

"Is that not the Lord's duty? To smite sinners?"

"If that were the case, my lady, I would be smitten where I stand."

Curious as to what sins he'd committed, Rosamund could not help but laugh again as he swept off his hat and bowed, but as she looked around to see if they were observed, she failed to see the expression that crossed his face.

"And what do you do with yourself, Mr. Nessuno, that you should be in these parts again?"

"Fie upon you, madam, is the desire to know your well-being not cause enough?"

She arched a brow.

With a grin he continued. "I am what's called a correspondent." He slapped the underside of the satchel. "I write for the news sheets. For a fellow named Henry Muddiman—have you heard of him?"

"You're a wordsmith." Her eyes widened. "What is it you write about?" she asked, praying he didn't suddenly produce a sample and ask for her opinion. "I think Mr. Henderson has made mention of a Mr. Muddiman."

A gleam of amusement flashed across his face, followed by something a little sinister. "Henry Muddiman is a most important person—he's a publisher. Even more importantly, he's *my* publisher. At least, for now. He keeps me solvent. Mr. Henderson, too." He cast his eyes toward the bookshop. "As for what I write, it's a range of things. I find there are many stories to be found in these parts, what with merchants, lawyers and all other kinds of rogues gadding about . . ." He nodded in the direction of the ordinary just down the road and the coffee shop further along before his eyes lifted to encompass the roof of the Royal Exchange with its gilded grasshopper weather vane. "That is, if one keeps eyes and ears open. Mind you, stories are everywhere if you know where to look."

And how to read them . . .

"No doubt your chocolate house will provide me a few more."

They both gazed up at the building.

"Ah, you know about the chocolate house?" asked Rosamund.

"I don't believe there's a soul in London who does not. But while I know about it, *you* remain a mystery. Pray, what is it you do here, apart from overcome rogues?"

"What do I do?" Rosamund hesitated. She couldn't very well confess that she was shuffled out of the house so the servants didn't see her learning to read. Not that she was doing much of that. She thought of what Filip was teaching her—about cacao and chocolate. It was almost better than learning to read. Almost.

"Why," she said, as Mr. Nessuno waited patiently for an answer, "I help my husband. He's a chocolate maker, you see—well, truth be told, it's his business. Another gentleman is responsible for making the chocolate. I'm learning all I can from him in the hope I'll be of use to my husband."

"Is that so?"

A rider clattered past, the horse's hooves throwing up some stones. Mr. Nessuno took her by the elbow and pulled her gently out of the way.

Understanding she'd revealed far too much, Rosamund sought to change the subject. "One day," she said, smiling her gratitude, "I would like very much to read what you write, sir." The longing in her words drew a look from Mr. Nessuno.

"Would you?" he asked. "Then I will have to remember to include something of interest to you. Perhaps a piece on pugilists? Or would fighting duels be more to your taste?" His eyes shimmered with amusement and she laughed again.

Before she could think of a retort, a hackney carriage pulled up on Lombard Street. Not wanting to explain to Jacopo or, indeed, her husband why she was discoursing with a strange man as she waited to be conveyed back to the tailors, she stepped around him, intending to swiftly excuse herself. Before she could, Mr. Nessuno replaced his hat and departed with a hurried "Till next we meet."

"So much for smiting blackguards," Rosamund muttered as he was swallowed by the press of people and horses in Birchin Lane.

At that moment Jacopo jumped from the cab, craning his neck and waving her to come forward. As they rode east along the cobbles toward Fenchurch Street, she searched the crowds for Mr. Nessuno, but there was no sign of him.

Nonetheless, he managed to occupy her thoughts for the entire distance to Foster Lane and throughout her fitting. While patient Mrs. Wells, the tailor's wife, measured her and held fabrics against her body, she thought about Mr. Nessuno and how he'd given her another reason to master reading. Fancy meeting a correspondent. Someone who made a living from words. Was Mr. Nessuno one of the sort Paul had detested? A "cunting" kind? She sincerely hoped so. Perhaps he wrote about the court, religion, the Hollanders and the French, or the type of things that set tongues wagging and pricked men's consciences. She could imagine he would do that sort of thing. A man who saw fit to offer aid and seek justice for a woman had to be a gentleman who also believed in things like toleration and fairness.

Inconveniently, Mr. Nessuno also managed to appear in her dreams that night, where he behaved in a most ungentlemanly manner, using his quill to write upon not paper but her flesh. His hands, encased in those soft gloves, trailed after every word he wrote, smudging the ink and making her skin burn.

The next morning Rosamund recalled the pressure of his nib as it traced words upon her—long elegant ones, causing shivers of pleasure from head to toe and in between. Especially in between.

And she a married woman. She should be ashamed of herself.

FIFTEEN
In which a friend fails
to live up to expectations

The bells were tolling ten of the clock when Filip asked Rosamund to take a hot drink down to Mr. Henderson.

"Once he tasted my chocolate, he ceased to object. Now I am making a point of ensuring he drinks a bowl or two each day," he explained. "After all, we will want to keep a steady supply of the news sheets and pamphlets he sells flowing through the rooms once we open." He finished agitating the *molinillo* and poured a thick, sweet bowl of chocolate. "It's very handy having his business beneath us and, hopefully, the chocolate sweetens the arrangement."

"How is it Mr. Henderson is able to print material as well as sell it?" asked Rosamund, thinking it was also wise to placate a man who thought Spaniards were all pleasure-seeking Papists.

"From what I understand, he's been granted one of the few licenses available to printers in this city. You English have very strict laws around publishing. I'm not sure I grasp them myself—you must ask him." He passed her a tray upon which she set the bowl and a jug of milk. "I also think it would do you good, as the *señor*'s lady wife, to get to know the man better. Offer him a pretty smile and a ready ear when you give him the chocolate. The man likes to talk."

Mr. Henderson was serving a customer when she came downstairs, so she waited until the gentleman had left before she approached the counter and deposited the tray.

"Good morning, Mr. Henderson." She curtseyed and dimpled. "Señor Filip asked me to bring you this."

"Ah," said Mr. Henderson, eyeing the bowl gratefully as he closed his tin of coins. "I confess . . . for all I resisted the chocolate at first, having tasted the muck being sold in the alley, Señor Filip's drink doesn't bear comparison. He certainly knows how to soften up an old bookseller, doesn't he?" The way he looked at her signaled he meant more than the drink.

Rosamund simply laughed. "I believe you're more

than a bookseller, sir. It's my understanding you print material here as well."

Taking a cautious sip then adding a little milk, Mr. Henderson nodded and wiped his mouth. "I do indeed. I have a printing press out the back. In the stables."

Ah, that explained the shiny lock.

"I'd very much like to see it, if I may."

Mr. Henderson stared at her in disbelief. "You would?"

"Of course, when it suits you. I understand you cannot simply leave your shop."

"Well, if you come downstairs after closing one day, I would be happy to show you around." Seeing the joy on her face, he drank some more chocolate and smiled warmly. "Sit down, sit down, lass—I mean, my lady. Unless you have cause to run back upstairs?"

"No. Not immediately," she said. Jacopo had been sent on an errand for Sir Everard, Filip and the boys were cleaning equipment, Widow Ashe was endlessly sweeping. The noise of hammers and the gruff voices of the builders carried. She climbed on a stool, narrowly avoiding a shower of descending dust.

Mr. Henderson grimaced and wiped the counter with a cloth that left as great a smear as the one it tried to remove.

"Señor Filip tells me you have a license . . . I'm not sure what that means. Where I come from, while news sheets, pamphlets and books were eagerly read, the niceties of printing were unknown."

Mr. Henderson drew up a stool and leaned his elbows on the counter. "Well, my lady, up until recently, there were numerous printers and publishers operating here in London, and down in Oxford, too. We would print the usual government-approved books, news sheets and newsletters, the latter two containing information about everything from trade embargoes to war, who'd been appointed to Parliament, marriages, thefts, what plays were being performed at the theaters and gossip about the actors and actresses and the goings-on at court. But lately it's all changed. You see . . ." He paused and looked beyond her into the shadows of the shop. Rosamund followed his gaze. There was no one there. Rising briefly, he shut the door behind him. "I'm not sure if I should be saying this. There are eyes and ears everywhere these days, ready to take down good men to serve their own purpose."

Rosamund sat up and drew in her breath. "I can assure you, Mr. Henderson, I've no such desire."

He regarded her. "I'm sure you do not. I just wish I could be as certain about others."

"I am not others, Mr. Henderson." She waited until he looked her in the eyes. "I respectfully assure you, whatever you tell me will go no further."

Mr. Henderson drained his chocolate and stared regretfully at the residue in the bottom of the bowl. "Goes without saying, if you're involved in a chocolate house, you'll need to be familiar with the rules around publishing—official and unofficial. After all, what's the point of a chocolate house, or a coffee one for that matter, if not to exchange news?"

Rosamund started. "I thought it was to enjoy a drink."

Mr. Henderson guffawed. "That's what the people who own them like the authorities to think. Trust me on this, my lady," he said, touching the wen on the side of his nose. "They're all about talking: reading, learning and sharing information, discovering what's going on and trying to be the first to benefit from any new knowledge. That's why these places"—he pointed to the ceiling as another shower of dust fell—"are where you'll find correspondents and government agents lurking. They're everywhere these days—forget coin, news is the greatest currency. The more you're in possession of, the wealthier you be."

An image of Mr. Nessuno appeared before her.

"Reporters and spies hang about, ears waggling, quills at the ready to write down whatever they hear and then send it to their publisher, who decides what to use—and who to use it against."

"If they merely overhear it, how do they know it's true?"

"A fair and important question, my lady." Mr. Henderson regarded her approvingly. "Good correspondents will check the veracity of what they learn. Many, however, are neither good nor particularly honest and do not. All they care about is whether they're paid; all the publisher cares about is whether the public will pay for the information—information that appears in the news sheets and news books that the likes of me are licensed to print. Of course, I only print what's recorded in the Stationer's Company register. Everything I do bears my name and that of the author—as required by the Licensing Act."

Rosamund nodded. "You said there used to be many printers?"

"There were. According to the authorities most of 'em were printing rubbish—lies, dissenting material, things that undermined the King's authority and those he'd placed in power. While there are many who contest the notion it was lies and believe dissenting's a good thing because it keeps the nobles and their lackeys on their toes, the government and the King did not. As a consequence, they clamped down on publishers *and* printers. Officially, there be only two publishers now and a new Act that insists the writer puts his name to his words. Easier to write inflammatory ones when they're anonymous, isn't it? Hence these laws."

A frisson of fear lanced Rosamund, and she found her own eyes darting toward the darker corners of the shop.

"Rumor has it, one Roger L'Estrange, currently acting Surveyor of the Presses, is soon to be confirmed in his appointment. Once he is, he'll ferret out anyone who writes, prints or distributes dissenting information, news that might have His Majesty's subjects questioning royal decisions or indeed those made by Parliament." He grunted. "God forbid that should happen."

Rosamund looked askance at Mr. Henderson, uncertain whether he was being sarcastic.

"Anyhow, this L'Estrange has given authorization to twenty printers. Twenty! For an entire city. God was on my side the day he came here and gave one of those precious things to me. I'm licensed to print whatever L'Estrange and the other publisher on the scene, Henry Muddiman, give me. That is, once it's approved by the Stationer's Company and the court."

Henry Muddiman. That was the man Mr. Nessuno worked for. Rosamund's heart quickened. Then something occurred to her. "But, if you can only print what the King and government say, how do we know it's true?"

Mr. Henderson cocked his head to one side. "We don't. Much like what's overheard, hey? There's many believe that if L'Estrange and the court have their way, all we'll ever read is bloody propaganda. Oh, forgive me, my lady."

Rosamund bowed her head. Bloody propaganda indeed. Was that why Paul decried correspondents as "cunting"? Because they were reproducing information they were told to? Inventing "news" to make the King and Parliament appear in a good light? Writing what they thought people should read instead of what they needed to?

Dragging a sheet of paper off a pile near his elbow, Mr. Henderson slid it in front of her. "Where there's a will, there's a way. And while the law is starting to deal harshly with dissenters and those who print and distribute their words, there are those who have found a way to bypass it. See here?" His finger stabbed a word at the top of the sheet. Below it were lines of very neat handwritten script. They danced before Rosamund, and she prayed he wouldn't ask her what they said.

"This is Muddiman's answer to some of the tripe that appears in his news sheets, the *Kingdomes Intelligencer*, which he publishes each Monday, and the *Mercurius Publicus*, which appears on Thursdays. Both of which are licensed news—published with government approval. But . . . look—he produces this as well. This newsletter is different. For a start, it's written by hand. And see here at the top? It says Whitehall—makes it look official. He sends these handwritten pieces out to his subscribers, who pay a monthly fee, from his office at the Seven Stars in the Strand—over by the New Exchange."

"I see," said Rosamund, even though she did not.

"That's where he's been so clever. He's able to avoid the rules that apply to printers like me by keeping these little newsletters handwritten and keeping the numbers he produces to a minimum. Despite what's sometimes in them, the government thinks it all a relatively harmless exercise. Muddiman employs a raft of scribes who, using whatever he's gleaned from his army of correspondents—many anonymous—put this together and distribute it. He's been doing this for over thirty years and makes a tidy profit, let me tell you. I never used to think too much about them, not until the government began treating the presses this way. Now I think Muddiman's handwritten newsletter is all we have to sort the wheat from the chaff, if you understand my meaning, my lady."

Uncertain she did, Rosamund simply nodded.

Mr. Henderson lowered his voice. "I hear tell Muddiman opens the mail delivered to the King's secretaries and reports on the contents."

Rosamund gasped. "But isn't that asking for trouble?"

Mr. Henderson grinned. "It would be if he printed it. I think because this"—he tapped the newsletter—"is handwritten, he avoids the government's scrutiny. But I've no doubt L'Estrange will take a good hard look at what Muddiman's doing once his role's made official next year. The time for caution is upon us. I've no desire to spend time in Newgate or the Tower. Or worse."

In answer to the quizzical look Rosamund threw him, Mr. Henderson made a slicing gesture across his wrists followed by his neck. "A person caught printing information, let alone writing anything, that offends the King or government can lose not only his hands, but his head."

Rosamund gulped and stared at Muddiman's newsletter with respect and not a little fear.

"This writing and printing business, this sharing of news is dangerous, Mr. Henderson."

Mr. Henderson nodded. "That it is, like any worthy enterprise. Take heed, my lady, for what your husband intends to create up there"—he raised his eyes to the ceiling—"a place where all and sundry will come to read the news—whether it's Muddiman's, L'Estrange's or anyone else's—and discuss it, could bring a world of trouble upon us all if he's not careful."

The chocolate house was far more naughty than Rosamund had first realized.

Gazing back at Muddiman's newsletter, she had a thought. "Mr. Henderson, do you have any writings by Mr. Nessuno?"

"Ah, Nessuno? You've met him?"

She nodded.

"A fine gentleman," said Mr. Henderson. "Why you'd want to read the rubbish he writes defeats me. Though I guess, being a woman, it would be more in line with your fragile sensibilities."

Rosamund tried not to take umbrage but couldn't help feeling peeved by this assumption. On the contrary, Mr. Henderson's warnings excited her. They made her keener than ever to master reading. It wasn't just the treatise on chocolate she wanted to read, but Muddiman's handwritten newsletters, the official and unofficial news sheets, bills, pamphlets, letters and books. She wanted to be part of the daily conversations that happened in coffee houses (and, hopefully, their chocolate house) and on the streets, and the grand, eternal conversations that had been going on since Adam and Eve were in the Garden.

Mr. Henderson rummaged through a pile of old papers on the counter. "I've some here I can show you if you like."

"I would . . . But why do you say his work is rubbish?" Associating that word with Mr. Nessuno seemed impossible.

"Here," said Mr. Henderson, producing not one, but two newsletters with a flourish. "Read them for yourself, my lady, and you'll see. Gossip about the King, whose horse won what race at Newmarket, which lord was found blathered from drink in Milk Lane and so on. Why a man with a mind like his wastes his time with such frivolities is beyond me. Look, don't get me wrong. He has a lovely turn of phrase— No, take those, with my compliments. I'll see if I can find some more if you're interested."

"I am, Mr. Henderson, and in any other material you can spare. I'm very interested in learning about these laws you mention, and about religious toleration, and what the Hollanders and Spaniards are up to. Anything . . . and everything."

Mr. Henderson scratched his head and regarded her with astonishment. "You are? Forgive me, my lady, I thought Mr. Nessuno's work would be far more to your taste. How wrong can an old man be?"

Rosamund's laughter built at the incredulous expression on his face.

The shop bell tinkled and two men thick in conversation spilled through the door. Mr. Henderson slid off his stool.

"Speak of the devil. Mr. Nessuno," he called out and waved. "We were just talking about you."

Rosamund spun around and saw not only Mr. Nessuno but Jacopo. Her cheeks flooded with color.

Upon seeing her, Mr. Nessuno whipped off his hat and bowed. Jacopo followed suit, a peculiar expression on his face, like a child caught stealing an extra jellied fruit.

"My lady," said Mr. Nessuno cheerily. "What a pleasant surprise." He navigated his way among the tables to the counter. Jacopo remained near the foot of the stairs, watching. "And what is it you have there?"

Reeling that the very man she was discussing had suddenly appeared, and with Jacopo in tow, Rosamund took a moment to find her composure.

"Why," she said, holding up the newsletters, "some of your work. It's not every day you meet a correspondent, and I thought I should acquaint myself with your writing." She flashed a pointed look at Jacopo.

Mr. Nessuno pulled a face.

"I did warn her." Mr. Henderson chuckled.

"My lady," said Mr. Nessuno, holding up his hands. "I pray you do not judge me by what is written there . . ."

Rosamund glanced down at the papers in her hands. "But if a man cannot be judged by his words, good sir, then pray, how does one judge him?"

Mr. Nessuno stepped closer, his cerulean eyes capturing hers. "By his deeds, my lady, by his deeds."

The sincerity of the statement made her catch her breath. She laughed to cover how very disconcerting she found his nearness. The smell of him reminded her of the chocolate kitchen, the headiness and rich spice. She stepped back and struck him lightly with the pages.

"That is true, sir, unless, I assume, one is a correspondent. Then, surely, words—the weapon he wields—maketh the man?"

Before he could reply, she swept past him and Jacopo, keen all of a sudden to return to the kitchen. Mr. Henderson's voice followed her.

"If you still want to see my printing press, my lady, just let me know."

"I will, Mr. Henderson. Thank you," she replied, and resisted the urge to run up the steps. It was a moment before Jacopo followed. Folding the newsletters, she shoved them in her placket. She might not be able to read them yet, her lessons with Jacopo being little more than a waste of time, but there were other ways of learning and other things to learn—and who better to teach her all about chocolate than Filip? After what Mr. Henderson had told her, she determined to master this new environment through actions *and* words.

"How do you know Mr. Nessuno, Jacopo?" asked Rosamund as they climbed the stairs.

Jacopo paused, gripping the railing. "We spoke briefly outside," he replied, gesturing for her to continue.

She wondered why he avoided answering her question. With an internal shrug, she realized she'd been so keen to remove herself from Mr. Nessuno's company she'd forgotten to bring the tray back up with her. Never mind, she could fetch it later. She'd wait until Mr. Nessuno, the man Mr. Henderson claimed wrote rubbish, had left.

Loitering by Filip's elbow as he explained the art of additives, she allowed her mind to wander. If writing and publishing and now the chocolate house proved so perilous, she could hardly blame Mr. Nessuno for sticking to gossip. So why did she feel a wave of disappointment wash over her that the man who had come to her rescue, who showed such wit and kindness on the street, lacked the courage of the convictions she was certain he possessed?

As Filip passed her a bowl of anise seed and asked her what quantity the drink required, she wondered if she'd ever have the opportunity, or indeed the courage, to ask him.

SIXTEEN
In which plans
are gently foiled

It was a dreary summer's night about three weeks later and Rosamund sat in her bedroom succumbing to an uncharacteristic bout of self-pity. Learning his wife had arrived home after a long day at the chocolate house, Sir Everard had swiftly left the manor, claiming he'd business requiring his attention—business being another word for wine and gambling. On the table before her was the treatise on chocolate, and a crumpled pile of the newsletters Mr. Henderson had given her. Slowly she turned the pages, as if simply gazing at them would reveal their secrets.

Carrying a glass of the malmsey she knew Rosamund had grown fond of, Bianca knocked quietly and stepped into the room. Busy repeating the words she could identify over and over, Rosamund failed to hear her until the door shut and the key turned. She quickly swiped at her wet cheeks with her sleeve, sniffing and blinking, trying to smile.

"*Signora*," said Bianca. "Forgive me, but I cannot bear to see you in such a state. Night after night, you sit before those papers, those news sheets, and sigh like your heart will break. I've heard you parroting words and phrases; I've heard your gentle curses."

A strange sound came from Rosamund. "And some not so gentle, no doubt."

Bianca gave a small dip of her head. "You wish to read so badly?" she asked, crossing the room and placing the wine before her mistress.

Rosamund stared at her, noting a change in those startling eyes, in her entire demeanor; a sudden resolve.

"More than anything, Bianca . . . I want to know." She smoothed a hand over the paper. "I have to—for consolation, inspiration, and above all, so I might shuck off my ignorance."

Bianca locked eyes with her, then bowed her head slightly before holding out her hand. A slow, brilliant smile infused with such warmth transformed her face. It caused Rosamund's heart to expand. "Then, madam," she said, "please. It would be my privilege to help you."

"You can read?"

"*Sì, signora.* In English and other tongues. And I would that you could as well."

Bianca drew up a chair. Rosamund passed the treatise over and watched with wide eyes as Bianca, aware she had the best and most earnest of pupils, began to read, her finger under every word.

Jacopo might have been forbidden to teach the master's new wife to read, but no such prohibition applied to his sister. If Bianca dwelled on the consequences should Sir Everard find out, she didn't show it. And Rosamund resolved that she would never divulge the identity of her new tutor; her new friend and ally in the enterprise of learning.

At the completion of their third evening together, after they'd frozen at each footfall in the hallway outside the bedroom and every rattle of the window, Bianca suggested they move their lessons to the closet. Not only did it reduce the risk of discovery, but it meant they wouldn't have to hide the evidence of their activities from the other servants lest they talk. Armed with boxes and cloths, they packed up all Lady Margery's objects. It was like Ali Baba's cave—at least, that's what Bianca called it as they folded the purple curtains away then rehung the tapestry with the pink-cheeked putti frolicking. When Rosamund asked her what an

Ali Baba's cave was, Bianca explained it was an old Maronite story she'd heard from sailors who, in turn, heard it in the city of Aleppo. It was about a poor man who found a treasure trove belonging to thieves and gained access to and finally ownership of it, transforming his life. The tale so thrilled Rosamund, she decided she too wanted a cave, only she would fill it with words and ideas, not only things like the Tradescant's Ark, and these would work to alter her life as well.

After they'd removed all of Lady Margery's possessions—with the exception of an assortment of old pamphlets, books and almanacs, and the elegantly carved wooden box with the lock and those beads—they gave the shelves, table, cushions and window seat a good clean.

Not sure why, Rosamund kept the presence of the box with the ripped pages she'd found to herself, slipping it behind the books, determined that one day soon she would read what had been carefully hidden underneath all the pretty baubles.

In the garret upstairs, they found a disused table and two chairs. The chocolate treatise took pride of place on the shelves, alongside the newsletters Mr. Henderson had given Rosamund, which included Mr. Nessuno's writings, an almanac for the current year, as well as, in a fit of optimism, a sheaf of paper, quills, an inkhorn and knife. Since Rosamund couldn't yet write to her friend Frances, she would ask Bianca to scribe for her. The closet would be bitter when winter came, but the room could easily be warmed with a small brazier or, if she left the door open, the bedroom hearth should suffice. The space was cozy and the oriel window admitted much-needed light and air as well as not-so-welcome drafts.

As they progressed through Colmenero's treatise over the following weeks, and Rosamund learned about the various additives that could be put in chocolate, she began to think of how she could use the drink to benefit others. She persuaded Bianca to accompany her to purchase some herbs from the apothecary in White Lyon Yard, and asked that a pot of chocolate be brought to her room each night. Once she was safely in the closet, she would break the chocolate cake into pieces and add the steaming water before agitating the *molinillo* and pouring the mix into the bowl. She would toss in everything from mint, which signified virtue, to honeysuckle for love, fennel for strength (it was very strong in taste) and peppermint for warmth of feeling. Mint also helped settle upset stomachs and the apothecary told Rosamund fennel would ease flatulence, which made her chuckle. She would be sure to add some to Sam's chocolate. Hyssop and anise seed, she knew from Widow Cecily back at Gravesend, would help with a cold, as would marshmallow and orange or lemon juice. Other herbs, depending on the strength, became purgatives, an effect Rosamund was grateful she discovered before offering any to Bianca or Jacopo or experimenting on the workers at the chocolate house.

Keeping little jars of dried herbs, plants and some spices on her shelves, Rosamund felt a little bit like the natural philosophers she had heard about who met regularly at Gresham College to present their findings to one another and, occasionally, the public. She knew it was immodest of her and very unfeminine to contemplate such a comparison, and begged God's forgiveness for such vanity. Slowly, she began to understand not only what to put in the chocolate to achieve a particular result, but also how much so it wouldn't be detected. As a consequence, she began to put a tiny sprinkling of gladwin root in Sir Everard's bowl in order to ease his shakes. Sometimes she added celandine as well, so that his eyes might be opened to the joy she hoped to bring him. When his manner toward her didn't change, she was forced to concede that maybe the chocolate killed its efficacious properties. Keen to share her discoveries with Filip, she nevertheless bided her time. She didn't want to alienate the man who was fast becoming her mentor. For the moment, she kept what she was doing a secret.

Within the confines of the closet, and as a reward for her efforts, at the close of each lesson Bianca would read to her. Usually, it was from a discarded news sheet or handwritten pamphlet she'd brought up from Sir Everard's study. From these, Rosamund began to learn not only about the state of the country and those powers who sought alliances or to make war upon it, but also about the various religious and other tensions within London and beyond. She learned about the Act of Uniformity, which demanded that all ministers be ordained by a bishop and subscribe to the new Anglican prayer book and the 39 Articles of Faith or quit their living by the 24th of August, St. Bartholomew's Day—a matter of weeks away. The religious toleration King Charles had promised when he took the throne was hollow. Any who refused to accept the Anglican form of service were labeled dissenters and thrown in jail.

A religious group called Quakers were particularly targeted, and many were being arrested and flung into prison.

One night, after they had read a harrowing account

suggesting over fifteen thousand Quakers had been imprisoned and that hundreds had died, Rosamund asked, "What are Quakers?"

Bianca grew very still, the pamphlet she had been reading (which Rosamund suspected came from an illegal press, as it was very critical of the government) open on her lap.

"From what I understand, *signora,* the Quakers, who are also known as Friends, are a small group of devout people who worship in silence, believing no one person can interpret the word of the Lord but all have the Light of God in them. When it shines, whoever feels it may address others—the Friends—who gather for meetings. They believe that under the loving eyes of God the Father, all men and women are equal."

"Equal? Men and women?" Rosamund could scarce believe it.

"Men and women, the nobles and the poor, the gentry and the servants—even those with dusky skins or cream. All are the same."

"And they worship in silence? How?"

"By communing with God in their own way."

Rosamund regarded Bianca carefully. "How do you know so much about them?"

Bianca gave a ghost of a smile. "I do not know much, but what I do know mainly comes from reading the thoughts of their leader, a man called George Fox."

Keeping her suspicions to herself, but glad beyond measure that Bianca, and no doubt Jacopo, were able to worship among similarly inclined folk without judgment, Rosamund nodded.

"You read to me about him the other night. He was the one who's been arrested many times and yet still had the audacity to write to the King from his cell, advising him how to govern." She laughed.

"You were listening," said Bianca, flashing her rare smile, a proper one this time. "*Si*. George Fox believes that all outward strife and wars are against the will of God and urges that Friends take no part in them. It's called his Testimony to Peace. He has written to the King many times, asking that the persecution of those who would never offer harm but seek only to worship God in their own way be put aside and that they be left to practice their faith."

"I might have been listening, but I don't think the King is," said Rosamund quietly.

"Like all those he has thrown in prison, I know he is not," agreed Bianca.

"Bianca," said Rosamund carefully, "if one day you

should happen to meet with these Friends . . . I think I would like to meet them too."

Bianca regarded her quietly. "If one day I do . . . and it is safe . . . you will."

They shared a conspiratorial smile.

Rosamund also learned about the regicides—those responsible for the beheading of the King's father—who were being ruthlessly hunted down and put to death. For all that King Charles was criticized as being too merry and concerned only with pleasure, his reign was also marked by dissidence, religious discord and blood-shed. So much bloodshed.

Keen to discover whatever she could, Rosamund was forced to concede Mr. Henderson had been correct when Bianca finally read a selection of Mr. Nessuno's writings to her. They were, if not exactly rubbish, cer-tainly trivial. Unless one was interested in the King's favorite mistress (who, according to Mr. Nessuno, was as beautiful as she was vulgar) or how often her cousin, George Villiers, was to be found drunk at a tavern, which horse had won at Newmarket, who was seen leaving Lady Frances Stewart's bedchamber late at night or who had broken the King's laws and fought a duel, his work was scurrilous and shallow.

Disappointment threatened to swamp her. How could she have been so wrong? Was it because, like a hero from a folktale, he'd come to her rescue and she'd endowed him with qualities he simply didn't possess? She might have been turned by his sapphire eyes and warm gleaming smile, but she knew kindness when she saw it, didn't she? She knew a good heart and mind?

For some reason, thoughts of Sir Everard intruded and doubt bit at her confidence. Hadn't she once thought Paul the answer to her prayers? That a step-father would be a wonderful acquisition?

Maybe, when it came to men, she didn't know anything.

Pushing aside her grim thoughts, she begged Bianca to read her more—not from Mr. Nessuno's works, but from Muddiman's other correspondents, the news sheets and, of course, the books Bianca brought from the library and which, as summer continued, she slowly began to master.

Together they read plays and poems by William Shakespeare and Thomas Hobbes's *Leviathan*, and Bianca translated some of Ovid's poetry for her as well as parts of Homer's great works. They relished the poems of Andrew Marvell, John Dryden and John Milton. They read excerpts from the King James Bible, as well as passages from books of history, gardening, medicine and more.

The closet wasn't much, but it was Rosamund's, especially now it bore no resemblance to its former owner. It was her cave in which, like Ali Baba, she kept her trove of treasured ideas and growing knowledge, but could open and close it at will with the key hanging around her neck. It was in this room that Rosamund finally started to feel a sense of belonging.

SEVENTEEN

In which the many benefits of chocolate are explained

C hocolate dominated Rosamund's increasingly busy days and sleepless nights. Every morning, she traveled to the chocolate house with Jacopo and saw the progress of the renovations, inhaled the robust, malty odor of the chocolate and drank the liquid velvet, the taste becoming as familiar to her as the ill-fitting garb she was still forced to wear. At her husband's insistence, her new clothes were to be kept until the opening of the chocolate house. All the while she maintained the illusion of her lessons with Jacopo. No mention was ever made of her evenings with Bianca.

Whenever she left the house, whether it was to go to Birchin Lane, the tailors in Foster Lane, or a quick visit to the shops at the Royal Exchange and the markets in Cornhill Street, or even to examine the Blithman warehouses by the Thames, whispers and stares attended her. They were particularly prevalent by the river—an area at once crowded, pungent and carrying with it both an air of promise and an overarching sense of menace.

The contents of her husband's warehouses brought the wonder of a wider, exotic world to her doorstep—the hogsheads of wine from Bordeaux, the Rhine, the Canary Islands, Tuscany and La Ribera; the pyramids of intoxicating spices and colorful bolts of silks and other rich fabrics for dresses, coats and upholstery. But it was the sacks of hardened cacao beans and the carefully packed porcelain bowls and plates from China that most interested her. She could only imagine what his other warehouses along the English coast held, not to mention those she knew he leased in other countries.

Lost in the quantity and unfamiliarity of the goods her husband imported, she wasn't at first aware of the attention she attracted, as if she too were a peculiar consignment. Some folk were open and curious, others guarded and hostile. Occasionally, words carried, and at first Rosamund thought she'd misheard "slattern," "strumpet," and "harlot" until she'd recognized the accompanying glare and understood she had not. It also happened on her first visit to Westminster Hall (where she saw the rotting heads of Oliver Cromwell, John Bradshaw and Henry Ireton—the three men considered most responsible for the execution of the King's father), and again later at St. Paul's, accompanied by the words "chocolate house," muttered in a tone that brooked no misunderstanding. These experiences went some way to explaining why, while there'd been a flurry of invitations for her to dine with respectable people when she first arrived at Blithe Manor, these had eventually dried up. No one, it seemed, wanted to share a table, or even a cup of chocolate, with a woman learning to make it. Neither her married name nor her family one could protect her from malicious gossip.

She had learned that Sam had been tasked with modifying the rumors that spread in the wake of her nuptials, but it appeared his efforts had simply fueled more. After all, why let the truth spoil a juicier tale? Understanding she could not change the way people saw her, Rosamund buried how much it hurt and pretended to see the funny side. Each night, she would regale Bianca with the latest version of her history as told by Mrs. So-and-So to Mistress Whoever who then whispered it to Mr. Prepared-to-Listen-and-Repeat before, like a will-o'-the-wisp, it broke apart and scattered in all directions, bearing no resemblance to its source. Sometimes, as Rosamund had learned from long experience, if you laughed often enough, the pain dissipated, even if only briefly.

If Sir Everard knew what was being said about her, he never mentioned it. Not that they encountered each other anymore.

Being left to her own devices at the chocolate house and Blithe Manor suited Rosamund. She was keen to learn all she could from Filip. Over the summer she worked hard to master the art of chocolate making. She sampled each additive he used and noted the changes it made to the drink. Rosamund questioned him thoroughly about his choices. It wasn't long before he invited Rosamund to select a spice or floral supplement. Drawing on her own experiments, which she kept to herself, her options proved irresistible according to Thomas, Solomon and their enthusiastic tasting recruit, Ashe. Delighted with his talented protégée, Filip encouraged her to develop flavors they might serve when the chocolate house opened.

The more she read of the treatise, the more she learned about the variety of additives at her disposal beyond those she'd already tried. Some were not only tasty, but beneficial for particular ailments or complaints—whether something as troublesome as a hacking cough or a dolorous mood.

Giving thought to what to mix, such as an extra pinch of black pepper or the red root Filip asked Sir Everard to acquire called *Tauasco*, she included a little when she noted Thomas complaining of a sore throat. Not only were these ingredients medicinal, they altered the flavor, giving the chocolate a sharpness that took one's breath away and made the tongue tingle. While not everyone would find this pleasant, it could be offset by adding more sugar or cinnamon. According to Colmenero that particular spice stopped urine, while anise seed helped colds (she added that to Thomas's next drink as well). Colmenero also referred to the work of a man called Galen, who, she discovered, was a doctor in ancient Greece, a disciple of a man called Hippocrates.

As she gained confidence, she brought some of her little pouches of herbs from home and mixed her own concoctions for Filip. He thoroughly enjoyed the mint and fennel she included but felt the gladwin root was bitter and that the hyssop didn't combine well with the chocolate. After referring to the treatise, the next day she persuaded a reluctant Filip to include ground hazelnut to thicken the drink, which added a nutty, wholesome flavor they agreed was very palatable. When some hours passed before Rosamund desired another bowl, she made a note to herself that hazelnut might not be good for profits. One didn't want patrons to be satisfied with merely one drink, not when they could linger beneath the roof for hours, as she'd been told they often did in the increasingly popular coffee houses sprouting about the city.

Hazelnut might not have found favor with her, but orange-flower water did, proving a better addition than orange juice, allowing the drink to acquire subtle floral notes. Each time she added something Filip hadn't tried before, she explained what she'd learned to him—not only from the apothecary whose premises she was frequenting, but from her own observations. Cloves sweetened the breath and stoppered up the bowel. A drop of musk or ambergris was likely to inspire passions by firing the lower regions. Rosamund was a little hesitant with these last two lest she unleash something beyond anyone's control. Filip had chuckled when she confessed her fears to him and threatened to advertise these when the place opened.

The varieties of what could be added were endless, as was the transformation even a small sprinkle of something like vanilla or milk could lend the dark fluid. It changed from being a little bitter to luscious. Likewise, a few extra twists with the *molinillo* and the consistency altered from gritty to frothy, to smooth as silk, leaving a fine coating on the tongue and throat that could be revisited for hours after. Including a small quantity of chilli made the drink hot and spicy; cinnamon made it sweet and even heady. Each night, Rosamund would lie awake, deliberating what she would combine the following day, what sensation she sought to achieve, what mood to alter, cure to facilitate. She and Bianca had recently read the pamphlet *The Indian Nectar, or, a Discourse Concerning Chocolata* by a doctor named Henry Stubbe, which suggested adding milk *and* eggs. She began to think of other types of accompaniments.

It was from Filip she first learned that, just as supplements could be added to enhance the flavor and be a physick for a person, so too additives that were not beneficial could be included.

"What do you mean?" she asked him as he patiently taught her to master the action of the *molinillo*.

"I am referring to poison," said Filip.

Rosamund stopped agitating the *molinillo* and stared at him in horror.

Filip quickly tried to reassure her. "Not that we'd ever stoop to such methods, but there are many who have and in Spain, it's almost a pastime." Taking the *molinillo* from her hands, he rolled it in his palms with practiced ease.

"Have you heard the story about the women of Chiapa Real? A town in the South Americas?"

Rosamund shook her head. Out of the corner of her eye, she noted Ashe had drifted closer, sweeping the same spot on the floor over and over.

"I'm astonished Señor Everard hasn't told you. It's a tale he likes to recount often." He smiled and shook his head.

How did Rosamund explain her husband barely exchanged a word with her, far less shared a favorite story? The only task she performed for him was to blend his chocolate each morning before she left for Birchin Lane. Even then, she never saw him, but simply left the tray with the prepared chocolate pot and empty bowl for Wat to collect. Her secret hope was that, by learning to read and thus vicariously experiencing, through words and ideas, the circles in which her husband moved, she would one day delight him and his acquaintances—who she prayed would accept her once the business opened—with all her newly acquired knowledge.

She fixed a smile on her face. "I would love to hear it from your lips, *señor*."

With a pleased half bow, Filip obliged. "According to Thomas Gage—a man of God who wrote a book about his travels through the New World—the white women of this town were incensed by their bishop, who, believing the ladies were so addicted to chocolate it was causing them to turn from God, forbade them from consuming the drink during his services (a habit to which they'd grown accustomed). In revenge, they slipped some poison into his chocolate. It took him eight terrible days to die."

"Oh, my."

"Indeed. As a consequence, there's a saying, 'Be careful with the chocolate of the Chiapas.'"

"I imagine, then," said Rosamund, amazed the drink she was growing to love could also become deadly when prepared with nefarious intentions, "it wouldn't be a far stretch to consider adding elements to make people sick—not unto death," she added swiftly, lest Filip believe her a monster. "But to render them poorly for a time; to make them bilious, purge their stomach, slumber heavily or act as a costive."

Filip conceded this was not only possible but had been done. "Any decent apothecary would know what to add."

Rosamund became thoughtful. What would one have to add to make a person content? She glanced at Widow Ashe. To ease grief or allow them to open their heart to love—if not for the first time, then again? Was there a substance able to do that? What about to induce forgetfulness? A picture of Paul loomed large. She shuddered. How marvelous it would be if there was and they could mix it into the drinks.

Regarding her kindly as he whisked the chocolate, Filip continued to tell her about the history of chocolate. How, when the Spanish found the New World and began trading with the Mayan, Aztec and Olmec peoples, they discovered chocolate (the beans even being used as currency), and shared chocolate drinks with the leaders as part of their rituals. The priests and monks who remained in the Americas to try to convert the natives to Christianity grew accustomed to the spicy, bitter drink. While some credited the explorer Cortez with sending the recipe for chocolate home to Spain along with cacao beans so their King and his court might enjoy the ceremonial beverage, the truth was that some Dominican friars took a contingent of Mayan nobles to Spain to visit King Philip and brought the drink with them.

"And so, what started on the other side of the world, before moving into the Spanish, Italian, then French courts as drink for the nobles and the rich, is now available to anyone with the money to buy it here in London. Even so, there are those who refuse to imbibe, believing it a Papist drink that leads one to sin. Those who prepare it, *señora*, are oft tarred with the same brush."

"Is that so?" said Rosamund, her heart sinking. A Papist brush was even worse than a whore's . . .

"And, because it is so expensive compared to coffee and ale, it's still quite exclusive," finished Filip, pouring her a foaming bowl.

"Unless one is fortunate enough to work in a chocolate house," said Ashe.

They turned toward Ashe in astonishment. She was usually so reticent.

"*Sí, señora,*" said Filip, sharing an amused look with Rosamund before pouring Ashe a bowl as well. She took it gladly.

"But still, the notion of ritual remains," said Rosamund, watching the way Filip poured, his face solemn, the height from spout to bowl just so, the way the molten chocolate flowed, a river of delicious goodness.

"Indeed, it does," said Filip, casting her a look akin to pride.

"I think this is something the chocolate house should promote," said Rosamund. "The idea of ritual. Of pleasure in that . . . and other things." She recalled her conversation with Sir Everard that first night at Blithe Manor. How he chuckled when she said the idea of chocolate seemed "naughty." If naughty brought the patrons through the doors, and not merely for the news sheets they'd provide . . . then so be it. People already believed her worse than naughty. Why not embrace it?

Filip nodded slowly. "I agree, *señora*."

"If chocolate is, indeed, naughty . . ." She took a sip. ". . . then let us call it a heavenly sin." She swallowed and beamed angelically, raising her eyes skyward.

They all laughed.

Rosamund touched Filip's arm gratefully. She was learning so much, and about her coworkers as well. Filip had revealed some of his own story to her. When Sir Everard had approached him in Spain to come to England, he'd been in negotiations to work for someone else. Though the chocolate house wasn't open for business yet, Sir Everard had been determined to employ a man known to be both knowledgeable and adept, even if that meant paying a high wage to lure him and his apprentice son. Filip had finally been persuaded. When Rosamund asked Filip if he regretted leaving his home, especially since the opening of the house was still weeks away, Filip considered his response.

"Not that. It's the manner of my appointment I regret." Much to Rosamund's frustration, he wouldn't elaborate, though she assumed it had something to do with the other gentleman for whom he had considered working. She thought about asking Solomon, but decided against it. If Filip wanted her to know, he would tell her; the last thing she wanted was to break the trust growing between them.

Filip understood that in Rosamund he'd found someone who not only enjoyed the taste of chocolate but had a genuine passion for it and a yearning to learn its mysteries. As the weeks went by and her understanding grew, so did her talent for making it.

When Rosamund wasn't mixing additives into the chocolate or mastering the action of the *molinillo* so as to produce a thick, creamy foam on top, she wasn't above supervising the roasting of the beans in the large pans with small holes drilled into the bottoms, pushing up her sleeves and crushing the cacao husks to extract the seeds, sieving and later rolling them upon the stone slab, the *metate*, and then shaping the dense, sticky substance into chocolate cakes alongside Solomon. These were passed to Thomas, who wrapped them between pieces of waxed paper and stored them in boxes or sacks to dry. Sir Everard was determined they would have plenty of stock so that the mob of gentlemen he was expecting to descend upon the place could drink to their hearts' content and even take away cakes to be dissolved and made into chocolate drinks at home.

Noting Ashe's fascination with all things chocolate, Rosamund asked Filip if there was something Ashe could do so she too could be part of the process and partake in their conversations more. Happy to comply, Filip gave her the loaves of sugar to grind in the large mortar. Ashe thrived in her additional duty. Sitting alongside Thomas and Solomon, she would pound away at the crystals, sieve them, then grind them again. Often she would catch Rosamund's eye and offer her a shy smile, aware who it was that ensured she was included. Excellent at this task, she was soon given others—from supervising the roasting of the beans, washing the precious utensils and replacing them on the shelves, to keeping the fires stoked, the latter freeing Thomas so he too might learn more about chocolate. All the while she kept the kitchen dust free and the working areas spotless.

Sometimes as they were working, one of them would wonder aloud when the chocolate house might open and they'd set to guessing, their hearts leaping, their grins broadening as they longed to share the delicious substance with patrons and watch the transformation its taste wrought. More and more coffee houses were opening around the city, some serving chocolate; all, according to Mr. Henderson, devouring Muddiman's news sheets and handwritten newsletters as well as what L'Estrange was publishing. Filip became increasingly anxious lest they miss their opportunity. Work on the main room was progressing. A huge mirror had been hung upon the wall above the bar, creating the illusion of even more space, and the windows had been measured and curtain rods nailed into position. The small group in the kitchen, wrapped in a cocoon of cacao and spices, felt the day must, at the very least, be drawing near.

EIGHTEEN
In which a troubled conscience is pricked

It was a long, soggy summer, the endless rain turning the streets into rivers of mud as the capital was deluged and damp claimed every nook and cranny outside and in. Mostly oblivious to the effects of the weather, Rosamund threw herself into chocolate making by day and her reading lessons with Bianca by night, improving her skills in both.

Colmenero's work on chocolate was all but known to her. Alas, while it was filled with interesting information, it was also quite dry. There was only so much about the "complexion of cacao" one could read.

The only interruption to her otherwise routine days was the unexpected (but no less welcome for that) presence of Mr. Nessuno, who had taken to visiting the bookshop on a regular basis. First believing his lunchtime visits to be a happy accident, she started to wonder, in a most immodest fashion, when they became a regular occurrence, whether it was Mr. Henderson's company or hers Mr. Nessuno sought. The very idea that a gentleman like Mr. Nessuno, a correspondent, might seek her conversation, made her feel warm, as if furry little caterpillars were inching their way around her body, tickling her flesh.

Nevertheless, she had to remind herself that while the man himself was so impressive and his conversation remarkable, what he wrote in the newsletters was less than edifying. While some correspondents risked all by supporting dissenters or calling for religious toleration, what Mr. Nessuno wrote mostly made her blush or gasp in dismay.

One wet day when the rain fell in never-ending sheets that emptied the streets of all but the most stubborn couriers and vendors, Mr. Henderson finally fulfilled his promise to take Rosamund to see his printing machine.

Together they ran through the rain to the old stables in the backyard and Mr. Henderson quickly undid the lock, wrenched open the door and Rosamund squeezed through. It was dark inside, and she waited while he lit a lanthorn and a few candles, bringing the dank, metallic-smelling interior to life.

In the middle of the room stood a tall wooden contraption with levers, a flat tray and a series of knobs and ropes. On a table near it were boxes filled with letters and whole words made from lead. She picked up a couple, delighted she knew exactly what they were. Buckets of dark, oily liquid sat beneath them. She saw with dismay the stains on her fingers from handling the small letters and, indicating the buckets, she asked, "Ink?" She sniffed her fingertips, capturing the odor of almond oil, turpentine and something smoky.

"Yes." Mr. Henderson smiled and handed her a cloth.

Wiping her hands, she noted shelves of books, stacks of paper, pamphlets, newsletters and news sheets. "How does it all work?" she asked in wonder, amazed such a drab space could contain such a fortune of ideas and knowledge.

For the next little while as the rain hammered the roof, she was lost in a world of paper and ink and typesetting blocks, including joined letters like "ae," which were called ligatures, and punctuation marks. Mr. Henderson explained that once the leaden letters were set and the ink soaked into them, a roller worked to impress them onto paper.

Under Mr. Henderson's supervision, Rosamund set a page and was about to have a turn printing it when the door was shoved open and Mr. Nessuno burst in. "There you are, Will. Oh, my lady," he said, swiftly doffing his hat, spraying an arc of water. "What on earth are you doing here?" He brushed excess water off his arms.

"I was showing her my printing press."

Mr. Nessuno's brows shot up. "Well, I've been looking all over for you. You've customers."

"I have?" Swiftly cleaning his hands, Mr. Henderson threw the cloth aside and undid the leather apron he'd donned. "Forgive me, my lady. Must attend to any mad bastards who'd brave such weather. If you could escort Lady Rosamund back, Nessuno?"

"Gladly," said Mr. Nessuno.

Glancing dolefully skyward, Mr. Henderson hesitated a second before ducking out into the rain.

When he heard the shop door slam, Mr. Nessuno turned to Rosamund. "Fascinating, isn't it? The process."

"Indeed, it is. I had no idea." Rosamund regretfully put away the paper she'd been ready to print and wiped her hands, glancing at a box of paper. The title on the top sheet read *Preface to the Book of Common Prayer*. Mr. Henderson was printing the approved text.

"Most don't. I too was ignorant until Will showed me how it was done." Mr. Nessuno began to fiddle with the printing press.

"He doesn't do this by himself, does he?" asked Rosamund, joining him.

"He has a couple of apprentices who generally work here, but I guess the rain kept them away today. I've helped him on a few occasions."

Wondering what to say next and sincerely hoping he didn't ask for her opinion of his writings, Rosamund was relieved when Mr. Nessuno pulled a pamphlet out of a box. "Ha! Will has a copy of 'Character of Coffee and Coffee-Houses.' Have you read it?"

"No. I haven't, but it sounds like something I should."

Mr. Nessuno passed it her. "Here. Take it. I'm sure Will won't mind. And if he does, then it's a loan." He grinned at her.

She took it from him and smiled back. As she glanced down at the pages, she wondered if what she read was in fact what was written. "Listen to this," she said. " 'The other Sex hath just cause to curse the day in which it was brought into England' . . . I gather it's referring to coffee?"

Mr. Nessuno nodded.

She continued, becoming more confident. " 'Had Women any sense or spirit, they would remonstrate to his Majestie, that Men in former times were more able, than now, They had stronger Backs, and were more

Benevolent, so that Hercules in one night got fifty Women with Child, and a Prince of Spain was forc'd to make an Edict, that the Men should not repeat the act of Coition above nine times in a night' . . ." She stopped. Her face grew hot.

"Pray," said Mr. Nessuno, folding his arms, "do continue."

She cleared her throat and, throwing him a look, did so. " '. . . for before that Edict, belike Men did exceed that proportion; That in this Age, Men drink so many Spirits and Essences, so much Strong-water, so many several sorts of Wine, such abundance of Tobacco, and (now at last) pernicious Coffee, that they are grown as impotent as Age, as dry and as unfruitful, as the Descrts of Africk. Having remonstrated this, they then would (were they wise) petition his Majesty to forbid Men the drinking of effeminating Coffee, and to command them instead thereof to drink delicious Chocolate.'" Rosamund stared. "Oh."

"Oh, indeed." Mr. Nessuno laughed. "My intention was not to embarrass you by having you read on, but reach the point where chocolate is praised."

"And here I was believing chocolate to be naughty when this person . . ." She flipped to the face page. "An MP by the name of John Starkey believes it to be the panacea for coffee-induced . . . ah . . . impotence." She paused. "He rather does the impossible, doesn't he? Transforms naughty into nice."

They both laughed.

"And what do you think, Lady Rosamund?"

"I think chocolate is whatever you want it to be—nice and beneficial or beneficially naughty." She dimpled.

"And what about you?" asked Mr. Nessuno suddenly, closing the distance between them. "What are you?"

He stood so near, she could feel the damp heat of him, see how wide and dark his pupils were in his azure eyes, eyes which gazed solemnly into hers. Resisting the urge to touch him, to answer the molten melt in her veins, the quickening of her heart, she inhaled and took a step back. "My grandmother always said I was 'mostly good.'"

She prayed he would not venture any closer. If he did, she feared that mostly good would transform into something mostly sinful. Struggling to regain control of her senses, she began to recall what he'd written, her overwhelming disappointment at his words.

"Mostly good?" He chuckled quietly. "I too had a grandmother who was, how do I say it, reluctant to praise. She would oft say I was *mostly* clever."

"And when you weren't mostly?"

"Then, I was an addle-witted loon."

Rosamund flashed a grin. "My grandmother raised me for a number of years."

"Mine too. My father . . . well, let's just say he didn't have much to do with me."

"What about your mother?"

A shadow crossed his face. "She died when I was born."

"Ah. I'm sorry."

"And you? What's your story?"

Sir Everard had instructed her not to tell anyone too much, but Rosamund decided sharing childhoods was harmless. Anyhow, wasn't it what friends did? And wasn't Mr. Nessuno a friend? While she couldn't admire his writing, there was much about the man she could. Aye, a very great deal, she thought as she took in his frame against the small window, the way he waited patiently for her to answer.

"Mine is very like yours, sir, except it was my father who died—fighting for the current King's father against Cromwell during the Civil Wars—and my mother who . . . didn't have much to do with me. Not at first." She grew quiet.

Sensing her discomfort, Mr. Nessuno moved away to scrabble in another box, lifting pages out, giving them a cursory glance and replacing them.

"I adored my grandmother," said Mr. Nessuno, filling the silence. "It was she who first taught me to believe in the power of words—how, when used the right way, they could be harbingers of change." He made a dry sound. "She didn't suffer fools—and she thought my father one and was determined I would not be—but she was kind. At least to me. What about yours?"

Grateful he didn't pursue the subject of her mother, Rosamund could not help but wonder what his grandmother would think of the words he wrote now. "My grandmother was . . ." Had she been she kind? Rosamund recalled the way Lady Ellinor would sit quietly in a room as her granddaughter practiced her scales, as she tried to read, stumbling over words and letters, as she unpicked a sampler . . . all the time insisting she try harder. She was firm, refusing to comfort Rosamund when she became frustrated, or to make light of disappointments. She rarely scolded, but never offered solace—except by her silent presence. She was always there, while appearing never to be, whether Rosamund needed her or not—watching from a chair, a window, the end of the garden. Often Rosamund didn't know till afterward. In hindsight, her grandmother wasn't unkind. Rosamund always knew she was loved. It was more complex than that. Her grandmother was strong. A strong woman who thrived in a man's world and desired that her granddaughter, regardless of her inauspicious beginnings, would as well. She also didn't suffer fools, or those who bemoaned God's will or fate. She believed in being a survivor, no matter what was meted out. The way to do that was by cultivating inner strength. That was what she tried to instill in her granddaughter. Mayhap she had. She prayed it was so; determined it would be.

"My grandmother was noble—" began Rosamund. "Not in the sense of gentility, though she was that. I mean, noble in that she believed in matters of honor—personal, social. She believed in the truth."

Mr. Nessuno dropped the pages he was holding. "And what about you, Lady Rosamund? Do you believe in the truth?"

Rosamund considered, understanding that somehow this was very important. She locked eyes with him. "Aye, Mr. Nessuno. I do. I believe that being true is the only way to be."

Before she could protest, he came closer, the look on his face unmistakable, the answer to the question her body was posing with every breath, every heartbeat. Dear God, was she the trull some whispered? What was this feeling flooding her veins, making her lose all sense? Was this truth? If so, she was certain it wasn't one her grandmother would approve of, but try as she could, she couldn't prevent her body from calling out to his, just as he answered her unspoken summons.

"So!" Mr. Henderson stumbled through the doors, stopping in the small space between them. The rain had disguised his approach. At once Rosamund swung toward the press, as if it had kept her attention the entire time. Mr. Nessuno returned to the box and flicked some papers.

Mr. Henderson looked from one to the other. "What have I missed?"

In the bookshop a short while later, Rosamund listened as Mr. Nessuno and Mr. Henderson discussed first the Licensing Act and how it prohibited the importation or printing of any material that questioned Church or State, and then the Act of Uniformity, which would evict many clergy from their livelihoods and even their homes.

"How are people supposed to swallow these measures?" Mr. Henderson growled. "And let's not mention the blasted Hearth Tax. Since when are people charged for their chimneys? If it's not more money the King's after, it's our faith. He can't ask for both and not expect a reaction." He put his head in his hands and groaned. "They talk of little else in Elford's Coffee House."

"What? The unjustness of the laws? Or ways to fight them?"

"Both."

"It's the same in the Rainbow," said Mr. Nessuno. "These new laws have men a-fired and not in a way that would please His Majesty. It's a sorry state of affairs." He picked up a quill and began to twirl it in his fingers. "Already, hundreds of clergy are being forced to quit their parishes. They won't even be allowed to teach. Whoever this latest act is designed to harm, it's not just the Quakers, Anabaptists and Papists who will be hit, but all of us. What affects one affects all, if only the authorities could see that." He made a bitter sound. "There's already been riots." He nodded at Rosamund's gasp. "A few have been killed; many have been imprisoned. They intend to transport the Quakers. I've even heard of folk stockpiling gunpowder and arms lest war break out."

"But that's terrible," said Rosamund.

"Beyond terrible," agreed Mr. Nessuno.

Mr. Henderson raised weary eyes. "Please God, it won't come to that again, will it? Riots? Bloodshed? Turning on our own? Civil war? Regardless of spiritual differences, aren't we all English?"

Mr. Nessuno bit back a wry laugh. "There are those in power and those who listen to them who refuse to see what unites us and focus instead on what divides. But when you take a man's livelihood, make him quit his parish, his community, just because you don't like the way he worships the same God, and demand people take oaths they cannot in all conscience make, let alone keep, then trouble *will* follow. One has only to look to the past to know this."

Mr. Henderson nodded gravely.

Listening to Mr. Nessuno, Rosamund marveled. Here was a man who thought Lady Castlemaine's bosoms worthy of words, but not those things he felt so passionate about. She could no longer keep silent.

She touched his arm. "Forgive me, sir, but if you are so concerned about these important issues, why do you only write about ridiculous happenings in the court? Seems to me you have an eye and ear for real news, for matters that mean something to people. Why are you not devoting your energies to them?"

Mr. Henderson pretended to find his ledger very interesting.

Mr. Nessuno's face reddened slightly. "You think what I write about is ridiculous?"

"Don't you?"

He didn't reply.

Uncertain how to continue, but knowing she had to—after all, she'd insulted the man—she sighed. "I fail to understand how you can discourse so emphatically and eloquently about the rights of people, about religious toleration, and then report on—oh, let me think—the King and Queen going for a ride in the gondolas the Venetian Senate gave them. Or the King's bastard son, James Croft, arriving any day. You have such a gift, such a mind, yet, to my way of thinking, you don't use it."

"I'm flattered you think so, madam." His tone suggested she choose her next words carefully.

She did not.

"Well, you shouldn't be. Frankly, sir, you should be ashamed. If I had your gift, your ability"—she flicked the stack of newsletters on the counter—"I wouldn't waste my time or my readers' on such nonsense, but instead seek to jab their consciences about vital matters. Seek to make real and lasting change by arguing on behalf of those who cannot argue for themselves."

"And what makes you think the people you wish to champion cannot?"

She took a deep breath and drew herself up. "Because, as a woman, I am one of them. I know what it is to have no voice, to not be heard."

"You seem to have no trouble finding it now," he countered, his eyes flashing.

Rosamund swallowed a little flare of annoyance. "That's true. Your conversation inspired me—me, a mere woman. Imagine what your written words, focused on such matters, might do for others?"

Dragging his eyes away from her, Mr. Nessuno studied the counter. "You don't understand, it's not that simple. I cannot."

"Cannot or will not?" asked Rosamund.

"Both. There are crucial matters that need all my attention."

Rosamund shook her head. "I fail to see what's more important than championing the rights of others, putting authority on notice."

"Even if it brings the authorities down on you? Runs the risk of prison, transportation or worse?"

Rosamund recalled how Paul changed from a Puritan to a royalist and would pretend to be whatever anyone wished—including righteous and godly. Weak, he had no courage, no convictions, and she loathed him for it. Give her a man of sound principles, even those she disagreed with, any day.

"Aye, even then. Sometimes, one has to make a stand. Fight for what one believes in, what is right."

"They may not always be the same thing."

"That's true; nonetheless, I think a time comes when one must say enough is enough."

"And you would do that?" There was an edge of mockery in his words.

Affronted, Rosamund put her hands on her hips. "If I had your abilities, the means at my disposal, then I like to think I would. Someone has to. To say nothing is to do nothing. It's to *be* nothing."

Mr. Nessuno made a noise of exasperation. "Then, madam, clearly you are a better person than I am. You're right, someone has to, but that person will not be me." He began to gather the pile of newsletters in front of him. "I too say enough is enough—enough of your righteous ignorance. No matter how passionate one's beliefs or ability to express them, the current laws don't allow for that; the authorities do not. A dead correspondent is no good to anyone. Now, if you have no further insults to level or reproachful suggestions to offer, I'll be on my way. I must needs find something . . . How did you put it? Ah, yes, ridiculous to write about and thus earn my keep for the next few weeks." His look dared her to say more.

She pressed her lips together and turned aside. An uncomfortable heat traveled her body. Tears gathered behind her eyes.

Mr. Nessuno pushed some coins toward Mr. Henderson and shoved the newsletters into his satchel. "I will see this *nonsense* gets to Muddiman so his men can distribute them," he said, glowering. Flinging his satchel back over his shoulder, he doffed his hat and gave Rosamund a deep bow. "My lady. I'm so sorry I prove to be a disappointment. How fortunate it is that you can console yourself with the likes of your husband and his chocolate house."

Rosamund was already regretting she'd said anything. "You're wrong, Mr. Nessuno," she said, her voice small. "I do not find you a disappointment. On the contrary . . . Merely your words." She slipped off the stool and tipped her chin so she could look in his face. "Much as your grandmother would, I suspect."

Each stared at the other.

Before she could say anything more, he was gone. The shop bell's merry tinkle a contrast to the heaviness of his departure.

"Oh, dear," said Rosamund, slumping onto the stool. "I made a mess of that, didn't I?"

Mr. Henderson patted her hand. "Not at all. I think you said exactly what that man needed to hear."

"I did?"

"For too long Mr. Nessuno has been resting on his laurels, taking the easy way, avoiding risk. He holds you in high esteem, my lady, so you may have pierced his armor, wounded him right where it's needed."

"Where's that?"

"Right where you said: his conscience. If your disapproval wasn't the prick the man needed to stop wasting his life on those inane scribblings of his and do something worthy with those words and ideas that tumble around in his head, then I don't know what will. If I had your gumption, I would have told him the moment I met him."

"I hope you're right, Mr. Henderson. If you're not, then I fear I may have lost the only friend I have here in London."

Lifting her hand into his, Mr. Henderson gave it a squeeze. "Not the only one, my dear. Not by a long way."

It was a remorseful Rosamund who dragged her feet up the stairs, her mind buzzing, the empty bowl of chocolate in her hand.

Words were just like chocolate, able to provide pleasure, but when used a certain way, they could provoke pain as well. Words could be weapons. That's what the King's enemies, as well as those seeking justice, were doing with their pamphlets and newsletters. Only the King and his government were conflating the two, making those who pointed out injustice into enemies. Yet they were not the same.

If the chocolate house was to become a place where words were shared, discussed and fought over, Rosamund would need to be well armed whichever way she chose to fight. She made up her mind then and there to redouble her reading efforts.

NINETEEN
In which Sir Everard stipulates the impossible is possible

The following day the weather turned unexpectedly cold. In the chocolate house kitchen, with its constant heat and steam, the workers were oblivious to the frigid gusts of wind blowing hats from gentlemen's heads and sprinting up maidens' skirts. Likewise, they were spared the splash of icy puddles as horsemen rode through the streets, ducking beneath low-hanging shingles, narrowly avoiding the barrow-boys and the stalls that lined the lanes more by accident than design. Lost in the world of *chocolata*, Rosamund sat beside Thomas, taking her turn on the *metate*, listening to Filip tell Solomon about the time he prepared drinks for the French ambassador to Spain who, like Solomon, had been complaining about the cool weather. Thinking it would alleviate the man's suffering, Filip was ordered by the King to prepare him an extra spicy chocolate.

"It wasn't until tears sprang into the man's eyes," said Filip, making an explosive motion with his fingers, "that I realized I'd inadvertently added far too much chilli."

There were gasps and chuckles.

"What did the ambassador do, Papa?" asked Solomon.

"What could he do? To not drink or to spit it out would have offended the King. He drank and his face turned the most incredible shade I've ever seen. He neither coughed nor spluttered but drained his bowl soundlessly. From that day forward, I've had great admiration for the French constitution."

Solomon chuckled. Thomas too. Widow Ashe shook her head. She'd no love of the spice.

"At least he wasn't chilly anymore," quipped Rosamund.

Filip burst out laughing and Thomas joined in. Even Widow Ashe giggled. Solomon stared at them blankly. Homophones always stumped him.

Their amusement was cut short by raised voices on the other side of the curtain, followed by a crash. Everyone stopped what they were doing.

Swallowing the anxiety that anger in others usually presaged, Rosamund leaped to her feet. She recognized at least one of the voices. "Excuse me," she murmured, sliding past Thomas and brushing him on the shoulder reassuringly.

Filip grabbed hold of her skirt as she passed. "*Señora* . . . I don't think you —"

Squeezing his arm briefly, Rosamund gave a tight smile. "It's all right, Filip." Taking a deep breath, she parted the curtain and stepped into the main room.

Her husband and Mr. Remney stood facing each other like combatants. Mr. Remney was shouting with uncharacteristic vehemence. Sir Everard had his back to her but was bellowing much like Mabel when she birthed two calves three long summers ago as he tried to be heard over him. Mr. Remney's face was contorted with rage and his eyes were flashing; a nearby bench had been knocked over. It was evident how it had happened as his arms wheeled about, and for a moment Rosamund thought he might strike Sir Everard.

Glancing in her direction as the curtain fell into place, Mr. Remney turned his attention back to the object of his anger, who, much to Rosamund's horror, began poking the portly man in the belly with his stick.

How could she distract them and put a stop to their dispute?

"You assured me it would be finished in time," yelled Sir Everard. "We have a contract."

"And it would be honored if you'd but given me notice—a date, a time, sir," bayed Mr. Remney. In an act of defiance, he took a step toward his employer, the stick burying itself in his girth, forcing Sir Everard to back away.

Where was Jacopo?

"I'm giving you both now," growled Sir Everard, lowering his stick and lurching forward once more. He wasn't going to be intimidated. "You must be finished by Monday morning at the very latest."

This time, Mr. Remney backed off. "I need more notice than three bloody days."

Raising his stick again, Sir Everard stabbed Mr. Remney in the shoulder. "You've had months."

Batting the wood away, Mr. Remney thrust his face into Sir Ever-ard's. "And I've not wasted a day of it. Every last thing you've asked for has been done, and then some." His burly arms swept the room. "If you hadn't kept changing your mind—"

"It wasn't *my* mind kept changing," bellowed Sir Everard, then clamped his mouth shut, breathing heavily.

Mr. Remney shrugged.

Whatever did her husband mean? Why, she'd heard him herself, demanding something be built or demolished one day only to send a note two days later countermanding his previous instructions. How Mr. Remney and his men achieved anything was miraculous. Yet they had.

In the weeks Rosamund had been coming to the chocolate house, it had been transformed. Gone were the dust sheets, sawhorses, tools and most of the men. In their stead were long, beautifully polished tables, benches, a line of booths with padded seats, a shiny bar that also divided the main room from the kitchen, elegant chandeliers, clean, bright walls and a wooden floor with the most wonderful sheen. All that remained to be done were the finishing touches—the gilt, the repair of plasterwork damaged while the tables were being built, a last dab of paint on the walls, hanging more paintings as well as the curtains and cleaning. A great deal of cleaning.

Mr. Remney oft reiterated the last twenty percent of a job always took eighty percent of the time; aside from the fact that Sir Everard continuously demanded additions or alterations for no sound reason. No wonder the builder was so upset.

Sir Everard studied his surroundings, a grim expression on his face. The set of his shoulders broadcast his unhappiness.

"It has to be ready. I will brook no argument."

Mr. Remney made a choking noise.

"If you cannot have this place finished, ready to be opened by Monday," growled Sir Everard, "I'll find someone who can." He swung away. "Ah, Rosamund." His face underwent a transformation. The unforgiving glower was replaced by a smile. A smile that failed to reach his eyes. The scorching tone became unctuous. He began to weave his way toward her. She dropped a curtsey, flashing a concerned look at Mr. Remney. Embarrassed at being caught losing his temper, the builder removed his cap and proceeded to strangle it. His two workers were frozen—one perched on scaffolding where he'd been painting the architraves gold, the other patching the wall where water had seeped in during the heavy rains. They did not dare to defend their beloved employer against Sir Everard, and the effort their restraint cost them was writ on their faces.

"Forgive the disturbance," said Sir Everard, coming to her side, taking her hand and bowing over it. "I was just in the process of firing Mr. Remney."

"Now wait a minute," said Mr. Remney, righting the toppled bench as he barged toward Sir Everard like an angry bullock loosed from its yoke. "You can't just dismiss me like that. We have an agreement."

"Oh, but I can," said Sir Everard. "If you cannot do the work, then I am within my rights. Speak to my lawyer if you doubt me."

Whether it was because of Sir Everard's threat or Rosamund's presence, Mr. Remney's anger deflated faster than a becalmed sail. "I didn't say we *couldn't* do the work, milord. I said we don't have enough time."

Flapping a frilled wrist, Sir Everard turned his face away. "And I told you I don't care. I will find someone who thinks the time more than adequate."

"The chocolate house is to open?" asked Rosamund, finding her voice. A draft behind her told her the curtain had been parted.

"Yes," said Sir Everard, his equanimity seemingly restored. Rosamund could see the white line around his mouth, the effort it took to control his wrath. Gesturing to the curtain, which admitted Filip, Solomon, Thomas and Ashe, he continued, "I came here to inform you all. We open on Monday, the 15th of September—at midday."

There were intakes of breath followed by fervent whispers.

"But that's only three days away. Isn't this rather

sudden?" asked Rosamund, immediately regretting it when Mr. Remney flung his arms wide.

"That's what I've been saying, my lady. Maybe you can talk reason into your husband."

There was silence. Sir Everard turned to regard his wife. "Well, my dear," he said, in a voice so quiet and deadly it turned Rosamund's blood to ice. His lips curled to reveal the sharp edges of his teeth. "Do *you* wish to talk reason into *me*?"

Before she could respond, there was a clatter of boots upon the stairs and Jacopo burst into the room.

Sir Everard pushed Rosamund aside. "What's their answer?" he asked, moving swiftly despite his impediment.

Jacopo bowed, a hand touching his hat when he saw Rosamund. "They say it's not possible, *signore*. The fastest they can make that curtain"—he pointed toward the long red velvet drape that separated the kitchen from the chocolate house—"fit those"—he gestured toward the windows—"is five days. But they would have to come and take measurements and there is no one free to do that until the morrow . . ." He would have continued, but whether driven by frustration that his plans were being thwarted, or wanting an easier target than Mr. Remney, Sir Everard raised his stick and brought it down hard across Jacopo's shoulders.

"No one?" he blared.

Rosamund let out a cry. If Filip hadn't prevented her, she would have flown to Jacopo's side.

The young man fell to his knees with a groan.

Sir Everard bent over him. "I. Told. You. I. Wouldn't. Accept. Anything. Less. Than. Three. Days." Every word was punctuated with a strike of the cane.

"*Signore!* Milord!" cried Jacopo, one arm above his head to stave off any more blows. "They're sorry, they cannot—"

With a roar, Sir Everard raised his stick again and again. There were gasps, a small scream, noises of protest. It took Rosamund a moment to understand most of them came from her. Wrenching herself from Filip's grasp, before she could think about what she was doing, she ran and seized Sir Everard's arm. Holding it aloft with two hands, she was shocked to see the blood blooming on Jacopo's cheek; his split lip. It was so red, so vivid against his torn skin.

"Please," she implored. "Please, stop."

Sir Everard threw her off him so hard she fell against a booth and tumbled to the floor. With a look of contempt, he slowly turned and began to strike Jacopo harder, grunting with effort.

Curled in a ball, his hands covering his head, the factotum whimpered as his master beat him repeatedly.

Gentle hands helped Rosamund to her feet.

They watched in silence. Only the swish of the cane, the dull thud as it struck clothes, the wet slap as it broke skin, and Sir Everard's strepitous exhalations, could be heard. Jacopo had ceased to make a sound.

Outside, the sun shone, the wind blew and people went about their day as if a man was not being beaten bloody by his master.

Finally, when Jacopo's coat was rent, when blood stained the fabric, coated his chin and cheeks, trickled into his swollen eyes and his body was still, Sir Everard's anger was spent.

Panting, he turned around. His eyes were glazed, his mouth open. His shoulders heaved. His periwig sat slightly askew, sweat beaded his forehead, his upper lip. He glared at Mr. Remney, who was holding Rosamund, then at Filip, who stood beside her, his face contorted by rage and sympathy. A weeping Widow Ashe, pale-faced Thomas and inscrutable Solomon were not spared as he lifted his chin and dared them to defy him. Mr. Remney's two workers looked on, stunned.

"There's reason for you," he said. Spittle collected in the corners of his mouth. He spat on the floor.

Warmth traveled down Rosamund's cheeks. Whether her tears were for Jacopo or herself, she couldn't tell. Looking at Sir Everard standing there, flecked with

Jacopo's blood, his ruddy cheeks and those cold, cold eyes, she wondered who it was she'd married. Where was the marvelous knight who had swept her from a life of misery to hope? Where was the man who was so forgiving of her flaws, who sought to repair them?

Who was this man?

Face the truth, Rosamund. He cares nothing for people; only profit. He didn't care for Jacopo, for the workers here or for her. He didn't even care for the chocolate house except for the money it could make him.

Wiping her tears away, she stood tall, watching her husband the way a rat does a hunting dog.

Sir Everard pulled a kerchief from his waistcoat and slowly mopped his forehead, his face, his mouth. On the floor behind him, Jacopo remained in a tight ball. Only the rise and fall of his back indicated he was still breathing.

Sir Everard met Rosamund's gaze. Perhaps seeing the judgment in its depths, he coughed and looked away.

"You have till Monday, Remney," he said evenly. "Hire as many as you need, but get the job done, do you understand?"

"Milord," said Mr. Remney tonelessly.

Letting his used kerchief drop on Jacopo, Sir Everard pushed aside a bench with his stick and headed for the stairs. "Clean yourself up, boy," he called over his shoulder. "I've need of you on the morrow." Once he reached the door, he paused. "Rosamund, see to it the Wellses know I'm most displeased. Tell them they too have until Monday. I'll brook no excuses. Make them aware they do not want my displeasure."

Was that what he called it? thought Rosamund. "Milord," she said, curtseying. The quivering beginning to overtake her body hadn't yet reached her voice.

"And hire extra hands. We'll need chocolate drawers, messengers. They'll need uniforms, and to be trained. Filip can see to the latter. I'll have Wat organize the designs for the uniforms be sent to the Wellses—make sure to tell them."

"Milord," said Rosamund, her mind awhirl, her heart sickened.

Once she heard the bell of the shop door downstairs, Rosamund flew to Jacopo and dropped to her knees beside him. "Oh, Jacopo." Filip joined her, murmuring words of comfort in his own language.

Lifting the kerchief from where it rested on his back, she and Filip placed tender arms about Jacopo and helped him sit. Rosamund tried to assess the damage as Filip took the kerchief and began to softly daub Jacopo's face. Blood flowed from the wound on his cheek, from his broken nose and lip. When Filip pressed the kerchief to his nostrils, Jacopo winced.

"Ashe," said Rosamund. "Bring water. Filip?" She touched him to gain his attention. When he gazed at her with unseeing eyes, she saw they were filled with tears. Her heart lurched. "Fix him a chocolate drink. Add whatever you think is necessary, though some St. John's wort would be excellent. Do we have some left? We do. Good."

With great reluctance, Filip heaved himself from Jacopo's side, cupping his face and whispering to him. Jacopo tried to smile, but failed.

"Thomas, Solomon," continued Rosamund. "I need you to go to the apothecary and get some lavender and feverfew—ask him to double my order for valerian. For a salve as well. Explain there's been an . . . accident." She wanted the boys distracted, given duties so they didn't dwell upon what they'd just witnessed. Best they were out, away from the building.

"What can I do, madam?" asked Mr. Remney.

Astonished, Rosamund gazed at the large man with swimming eyes. Not only had the others done her bidding, but Mr. Remney and his two workers were also looking to her for instruction, caps in hand. About to protest she didn't know what he could do, she paused. The clatter of pots carried, the murmur of voices grateful to feel useful. She'd done that. Was she not the Lady Rosamund? Was she not the chocolate maker's wife? Of course they looked to her for direction—who else? It was easy to forget that for all they embraced her as one of their own, she was still viewed as their mistress, Lady Blithman. It was time she deployed her authority—the authority they were willing her to wield. It was the least she owed them after her husband's appalling display. Ashamed and confused by the rapid alteration to his character when his plans were challenged, she pushed her feelings aside to be examined later. These people needed her. God, she thought, looking at Jacopo, they needed her. She would be their champion. Their lady. Their knight. Wiping her eyes again, Rosamund said clearly, "You must do whatever it takes to make my husband's demands possible, Mr. Remney."

"But, my lady, what he asks is impossible." Mr. Remney sank onto a bench, head bowed, shoulders drooping.

Filip brought the chocolate drink and insisted on feeding it to Jacopo himself. She was pleased to see he'd cooled it with extra milk. As he spooned it into Jacopo's torn mouth, she could smell the cinnamon, the musk and the chilli. She prayed Filip had not been heavy-handed with it this time. Flecks of brown and green herbs swam beneath the surface. There was egg and ground almonds as well. After a few mouthfuls, Filip began to help Jacopo out of his jacket.

When Jacopo had taken more sips, she took the kerchief and wiped his mouth. Inhaling sharply, he soon had his jacket off. Blood stained the white of his shirt. The flesh below would be a welter of bruises and cuts. Leaning forward, she caught her own breath. Her ribs burned from her fall. She too would bear the marks of her husband's loss of composure.

"Grazie mille, bello, signora," whispered Jacopo after he'd taken another cautious taste of the chocolate. *"Allora,* do not look so sad, both of you. I've suffered much worse."

Rosamund's eyes flashed to Filip, who nodded gravely. "Your husband, the *señor,* he often takes his . . . disappointments out on Jacopo."

Rosamund tried not to let either of them see how much those words, the very notion, stung. Sir Everard was meant to be a good man, a kindly master if a strict one. Not the monster unleashed before her eyes. She tried to return Jacopo's reassuring smile. Dear God. Jacopo bore no grudge. It was as if he expected such treatment. But no one should expect that, least of all a loyal servant. Only to Sir Everard he wasn't a servant, was he? He was a slave. A possession.

Determined to return Jacopo's courageous attempt at a smile, she fought to put one on her own face. Wavering at first, it grew steadily broader and she found herself feeling better, stronger for the attempt.

Rising to her feet, she looked at Jacopo leaning against Filip, at Mr. Remney and his workers, their forlorn expressions. She gazed at the pale faces of Thomas and Widow Ashe, the resigned ones of Filip and Solomon. They were all watching her, waiting.

"Mr. Remney, you say what Sir Everard"—she could not call him "husband"—"asks is impossible. I say that we—you, Mr. Remney, Filip, Thomas, everyone . . ." she said, her voice becoming firmer, as did her resolve, "together, we must make the impossible, possible." She began to chuckle at the absurdity of their situation. "As ridiculous as it sounds, if we work together, we will achieve all Sir Everard asks and more." Ignoring the pain shooting through her shoulder and side, she began to laugh, afraid if she didn't, she too would cry. Sir Everard might have beaten Jacopo, but she could not, would not, let him beat her resolve to succeed.

The power of her forced joy, the hope she infused it with and her determination to unite them, infected them all. As her laughter built like a peal of silver bells ringing for them alone and her tears retreated, shy grins were exchanged, nods, then slow chortles which built to defiant mirth. There were sympathetic glances toward Jacopo, who held his bowl of chocolate and managed a nod as they laughed. Together. Jacopo smiled, then spat a glob of blood onto the floor. A brazen chortle escaped him as his carmine spit sat upon the streaked wood, next to Sir Everard's phlegm.

Mr. Remney's laugh quickly died as he stared at the globule of blood. He was not persuaded.

"How?" he asked. "I've only two men. The rest of my workers are committed to other projects; they can't simply leave them because a roaring boy cracks his stick upon an innocent." Aware of what he'd just said, he shook his head. "Sorry, madam, I've no right to say such things. But I need many more people. Sir Everard doesn't realize what he's asking. There is much yet to do. It's not just your husband's reputation at stake here . . ."

What's left of it, thought Rosamund.

". . . but mine as well. How do you propose we make milord's unreasonable demands workable?"

They all waited for her to respond. Widow Ashe brought over a bowl of hot water and some clean cloths. Rosamund could smell the rose petals, the infusion of oranges and lemons. Widow Ashe kneeled beside Jacopo and turned her thin face toward Rosamund.

"Like this," Rosamund said and, gathering everyone around her while she and Filip tended Jacopo, outlined her plan.

TWENTY
In which the Lady Rosamund is declared fit for Bedlam

By afternoon, the chocolate house was crawling with people. Mr. Remney's two workers (his journeyman, Ralph, and older apprentice, Jerome) were sent to other sites he oversaw, and had managed to find three more men. When Thomas and Solomon returned from the apothecary, Rosamund sent them off to find the children who drifted up and down the lanes causing so much trouble. Perhaps if they were given something to do, they'd forget their mischief. "Tell them there's a shilling each in it for those who do the work. Make sure to add that Mr. Remney won't tolerate any devilment."

Having encountered Mr. Remney when they'd tried to break into the chocolate house and having received a good beating for their efforts, they knew and respected the builder.

With his wounds now salved and bound, and having consumed the herbal infusion Rosamund had prepared for him, Jacopo joined Filip to express his horror that she'd even consider bringing such rascals into the building, let alone paying them to do some work. The two of them tried to talk Rosamund out of it, but she would not be moved. The dozen extra pairs of hands—well, almost a dozen, as one poor child who turned up had only one hand, but more than made up for it in enthusiasm, the enticement of a shilling instilling good behavior in a way that no amount of threats and curses could—plus all the kitchen staff, meant the required tasks could be tackled with ease. While the experienced builders tended to the plastering and intricate painting, the rest of them mainly cleaned.

When he heard the noise and saw all sorts of vagabonds and rascals (his words) mounting the stairs, Mr. Henderson appeared and, learning what was going on, closed his shop and pitched in as well. It was all Rosamund could do not to throw her arms around him—more than once. She half expected Mr. Nessuno to appear as well.

Truth was, she more than half hoped he would.

Alas, he chose not to come this day. Nor the next three. The offense she had given was so great, it seemed her fears had been confirmed: she'd lost a friend. But, she thought, Mr. Henderson had been right—she had more friends than she ever knew. For what were Filip, Jacopo, Ashe, Thomas, Solomon and Messrs. Henderson and Remney if not friends? She sent a swift prayer of thanks to God for them.

Content Mr. Remney had the room under control, and everyone had a job to do, Rosamund made two bowls of chocolate and joined Jacopo where he was propped at the table out the back. The grayish cast to his skin had disappeared, though the cut on his cheek was swollen, one eye partly closed, and his lip was angry. Rosamund found it hard to look at him without feeling physical pain.

She placed a bowl in front of him and sank into the chair beside his. "Are you grievously hurt?"

"Not grievously." He tried to smile, then grimaced as the skin pulled.

His understatement tore at her heart. She wanted to ask him how often Sir Everard beat him, but having suffered someone else's mercurial whims, she knew the telling often caused as much torment as the acts themselves. Instead, she stuck to her plans.

"I wouldn't ask if this wasn't important, Jacopo, but I need you to write a letter for me. Do you think you can manage?"

Jacopo flexed his fingers. "They still work, *signora*. I can write whatever you want."

"And your eye? You can see well enough? Excellent. I need you to take down a letter for Mrs. Wells, the tailor's wife, and another to be delivered to a periwig shop. The drawers will be in need of hairpieces fine enough to impress gentlemen. I'll ask one of the boys to deliver the notes."

As the church bells sounded two of the clock, letters were carried through the streets—one addressed to Mrs. Wells. When the good lady saw who it was from, and read her most urgent and yet charming request, she swept into the workers' room and announced that all orders were to be suspended until the curtains and uniforms for Lady Rosamund Blithman's chocolate house were measured and made.

"You mean, Sir Everard's chocolate house," corrected Mr. Wells, pulling a pipe out of his mouth and blinking rapidly, nonplussed as his wife undermined his authority in his own establishment. Had he not told Blithman's blackamoor the work could not be done?

Before he could say anything else, Mrs. Wells said sharply, "I mean what I said." Her spaniel Charles barked, his little nose in the air, adding force to her statement.

And so it was that at three of the clock sharp, Mrs. Wells and three of her girls arrived at the chocolate house with string, pins, paper, scissors, designs for new uniforms (which arrived as they were leaving), samples of fabric and all sorts of accoutrements to measure windows and people.

Upon Mrs. Wells's arrival, Rosamund greeted her warmly and, to Mrs. Wells's utter delight, embraced her. But her appearance also revealed to Rosamund the flaw in her plan.

Concerned to have enough workers to finish the chocolate house, she hadn't yet turned her attention to hiring the chocolate drawers and messengers her husband had instructed her to employ. Mrs. Wells might be in possession of a pattern for the uniforms and know which colors they were to be, but if there were no people to measure, what was the point?

She frowned, gazing about.

It was just as well she'd been keeping a sharp eye on the children and the work Mr. Remney gave them. While they might have been intent on creating havoc in the streets, in the chocolate house, surrounded by other adults and children all working together toward a common goal, most of them were useful, polite and good at their tasks. Admittedly, bringing them bowls of choco-late encouraged their cooperative spirit enormously. Those who weren't as helpful or keen she noted and would be certain not to hire them again—in any capac-ity. Gazing at the remainder thoughtfully, she began to imagine what they could do if they were clean, clothed differently, taught some manners and other skills and, above all, trusted. It didn't bear considering. Or did it?

Excusing herself from Mrs. Wells, she whispered instructions to Widow Ashe, who stared at her as if an extra eye had sprouted in the middle of her forehead, then returned to Jacopo and asked if she might beg his assistance in another important matter—but only if he was up to it.

"For you, *signora*, I would douse the sun."

Rosamund laughed. "I would not ask that of you. Come with me. I have an idea but need you to tell me if I belong in Bedlam."

Lined up in the kitchen, with Widow Ashe's firm eye upon them, were the street children. Some were sniff-ing, others were shouldering one another and giggling. All looked a little afraid and a little defiant. Rosamund could scarce tell them apart—with the exception of the only girl, because she had freckles. They exuded same-ness in the way the same fruit grown from different trees does. With caps screwed into their mostly grimy fists, they bowed, wiped their running noses on their patched sleeves, shivered in their thin garments and eyed the blazing fire with envy.

"You are most certainly a loon, *signora*," said Jacopo softly, smiling warmly at her at the same time.

"Good," said Rosamund. "I just wanted to be sure. Now sit down and help me choose."

Moving along the line, she asked each child a series of questions, which many made sincere efforts to answer. With each response, she turned to Jacopo, who raised a brow, gave a slight shake of his head or nod. What she found, apart from Jacopo being in complete accord with her, was that the dirtier the boy and more inclined to spit, the more in need of work and thus a wage he appeared to be—and the more inclined she was to provide it. There was young Harry, with a mop of chestnut hair and a huge gap between his large front teeth, who was all his ailing mother had. Rosamund didn't care that his shoes were worn, his neck filthy and that he spat at least three times while she was talking to him, narrowly avoiding Thomas, who'd come in to grab something. He'd never even heard of a chocolate house (he wasn't alone there). If the kind lady didn't give him a chance (and a clean set of clothes), then who would? No mention was made of his missing hand. If Harry didn't regard it as a cause for concern, why should she?

Jacopo gave him a nod.

Then there was skinny little Robin. With a shock of hair the color of the ginger tom that prowled outside the ordinary, he had no front teeth and possessed knees and elbows so knobbly they were more like growths than parts of his limbs. Cock-eyed Lewis and his brother, the bow-legged Silvester, were only eliminated because Widow Ashe found chocolate cakes stuck to the insides of their pockets. After a lecture on stealing and a sound beating from Mr. Remney, they were ordered to leave immediately.

There seemed no end of them: Conrad, Owen, Wolstan, Hilary and two whose names she didn't hear aright, not that it mattered. The way those two looked at her and eyed the chocolate house and the serving pots and bowls as a fence might his goods, allowed her to dismiss them with a clear conscience and Jacopo's endorsement. They were given the promised shilling for work done. Tolerance and Zeal she chose not to hire because their Puritan names put her in mind of the twins and she could not bear the thought of being reminded of them here.

Finally, along with Harry, she chose Hodge, Art, Kit, Wolstan, Owen and Robin to serve at the front of the house. She hired the young girl, Cara, to help Ashe with the dishes and general duties. Trying not to feel guilty as the rejected trudged back to Mr. Remney, she hoped the coin and additional bowl of chocolate they'd all been given appeased their disappointment and rewarded the fortunate.

Late that afternoon, the new staff were rounded up by Mrs. Wells and measured for their uniforms, but not before Jacopo told them in a tone no one dared counter, that if they wanted to wear their new clothes it was to be on clean flesh. Ordered to wash or be washed—and before everyone in the chocolate kitchen—they swore to do so, goggle-eyed at the tall tawneymoor who'd clearly been in a mighty scuffle and lived to tell the tale. He also had the respect of Mr. Remney, never mind Señor Filip, who made the chocolate, and the kind and oh-so-pretty Lady Blithman, whose smile, when it was bestowed, made them forget the cold and their hunger, so much so they each secretly wished they could bask in its glow forever more.

TWENTY-ONE
In which a chocolate house is opened Monday, the 15th of September, 1662

If the paintwork on the architraves wasn't completely dry, nor some of the plaster, and a few of the candles were tallow instead of beeswax, no one except Rosamund noticed. If Sir Everard observed that Wolstan currently wore his own, albeit tidy, clothes, while Owen's new ones were held together by pins as much as stitches, or that Cara was dressed in a shift that had once belonged to Bianca and was tied about her waist so she didn't trip, he never mentioned it.

Though the impossible deadline he'd set was on the cusp of being met due to the extraordinary diligence and efforts of his servants, workers new and old, the Wellses and their team of seamstresses, the beneficence of the men at the nearby periwig shop, and his wife, they received no thanks nor praise. Sir Everard was in a right dudgeon and made a point of ignoring everyone—especially Rosamund.

He'd arrived midmorning and, after casting a critical eye over the chocolate house, demanded a bowl of the drink, which Rosamund alone had to prepare, and then retreated to one of the booths. While he drank and smoked his pipe, he checked the advertisement placed in the *Kingdomes Intelligencer* (another one was to appear in the *Mercurius Publicus* when it was published on Thursday) and in Muddiman's handwritten newsletters. On Saturday, he'd even placed an order with Mr. Henderson to print a couple of hundred handbills advertising the place. That was how Rosamund discovered the name Sir Everard had bestowed upon the chocolate house. It hadn't occurred to her it would require christening, but of course, it couldn't simply be known as "The Chocolate House." Being a creature of habit and wanting to thank Mr. Henderson again for his aid the day before, she'd hurried down to the bookshop on Saturday morning with a bowl of chocolate and seen the draft for the advertisement on the counter.

There it was, at the top of the handbill, bold as you like: "Helene's Chocolate House."

Alternately surprised and dismayed, she wished Sir Everard had prepared her. Prior to Friday, she might have thought it touching that her husband saw fit to call his chocolate house after his beloved daughter, a sort of living memorial to her name. In light of Jacopo's beating and her husband's preposterous demands upon Mr. Remney—and that he'd offered neither apology nor explanation for his behavior and had neglected to seek her out these last three days—she could only see the name as a riposte of the worst kind. Was not Helene also Matthew Lovelace's wife? Was he not using the name of his dead child to provoke his nemesis? A kind of revenge from beyond the grave?

She prayed Lovelace, wherever he was, would never know.

Her gaze could not help returning to Sir Everard as he hunkered against the wall. He'd visibly aged since last Friday. Gone was the older gentleman, and in his place was a bitter-faced, pouch-eyed curmudgeon, bowed by time, bewildered by the youth about him and determined to assert his authority through his presence alone. God knew, it was enough.

Thankfully, late morning Jacopo arrived with two footmen bearing welcome packages. Though his bruises were still evident, Jacopo was walking without a limp. Only Rosamund and Bianca, who'd come to help with the opening, saw him grimace as his jacket pulled too tight across his shoulders when he bent over, or when Filip unthinkingly hugged him fiercely. Now he ordered the footmen who'd accompanied him to hand out the remainder of the uniforms; the boys took the parcels almost reverentially, disappearing into different parts of the kitchen to dress. Bianca followed, needle and thread in hand.

Jacopo and Filip had dedicated a couple of hours the past two afternoons to teaching the boys how to serve, take orders and pour the chocolate. They had to learn to navigate the tables and benches first with empty trays, then with trays filled with old bowls and pots of water to accustom them to the weight and balance required. Finally, they were each given responsibility for a certain section of the room. Estimating the chocolate house would comfortably accommodate fifty men, Mr. Henderson warned them they could expect many more to come to sate their curiosity in the first days after opening—if not about Blithman's chocolate then—he shot an apologetic glance in Rosamund's direction—about Blithman's wife.

The boys took their work seriously and were instructed to report to either Jacopo or Filip if they were sent outside with a message. Only one bowl was broken, two trays and a chocolate pot dented. All in all, it was regarded as a successful training session.

"I wish we had more time," said Jacopo quietly to Rosamund as the boys dressed hurriedly. He sank gratefully onto a seat, his gaze traveling to rest upon Sir Everard, who ignored him.

"Alas, we don't," said Rosamund just as Harry appeared, bowing before her with a grand flourish of his hand.

"We be right, milady," said the lad and proceeded to parade before her, his chest puffed out, his wig making his head appear larger, his scarf sitting so high on his neck, it forced his chin back. "Once them coves set their glaziers on this"—his thumb indicated his clothes then encompassed the room—"or you"—he nodded appreciably toward her—"they'll be right keen on the place."

Before she could prevent it, Art emerged in his uniform, reached over and boxed his ears. "That be Lady Rosamund to you, you nizzie."

About to strike back, Harry became aware of Sir Everard approaching. "Yeah, right. Sorry, missus—I mean, my lady."

"That's quite all right, Harry."

"And I be no nizzie—" He swung to Art. "I be a drawer. A chocolate drawer, no less." He struck his thin chest.

"Who might this be?" asked Sir Everard, jabbing his cane toward Harry, looking him up and down.

"Harry Cooper, milord," said the lad, bending from

the waist. His elegant bow also drew attention to the fact he had only one hand.

Sir Everard's eyes widened and his cheeks began to redden. "Surely you don't expect this cripple to serve chocolate?" His voice grew louder with each word.

Flashing an uncertain look at Rosamund, Harry waved his stump up and down. "It . . . it b-b-be no h-hin . . . hindrance, milord," he stammered.

Rosamund gave him a warning shake of her head. The boy pressed his mouth shut.

Now Sir Everard was closer, Rosamund could smell the wine on his breath that her chocolate had failed to disguise and see the tremor in his hands. Not wanting to aggravate him further, she indicated the boys should retire to the kitchen. Once they had shuffled out of sight, she faced Sir Everard.

"I can assure you, my lord," she said carefully, "many cripples function as well as if not better than those with all limbs working." She tried very hard not to glance at his leg or his shaking hands.

Sir Everard gave her a long, studied look. "If he spills a drop, breaks anything, he's gone from here." He jabbed the floor with his cane.

Rosamund curtseyed, making up her mind there and then that if Harry should suffer a misfortune, she could obey her husband by limiting him to kitchen duties.

Thus, she was able to counter Sir Everard's suspicious glance with a beaming smile. It seemed to work. With a huff, he began to roam, his interest in the chocolate house rekindled.

Pleased he was taking a positive interest, Rosamund untied her apron and smoothed her skirts. Well, he might be interested in the premises, but still not his wife. Considering what had happened the last time he noticed her, she was relieved but also piqued that, unlike Harry, he'd made no reference to her attire. Gone were Lady Margery's hand-me-downs, replaced by the most resplendent dress she'd ever seen. The Wellses had outdone themselves. Bianca, too, having spent close to an hour before dawn first dressing her in the stiff canvas corset, helping her step into her skirts, lacing the bodice and, as she fixed the lower part of the dress to the tabs, ensuring the pointed waist sat flat at the front and center and exposed the elaborate underskirt—all without a word. In fact, Bianca had been unusually reticent and refused to meet her eyes, even when dressing her hair. Overall, she'd been swift in her ministrations, moving her fingers as if the fabric burned them. Made of cloth of gold with black velvet and lace trim, the gown shimmered whenever she moved. It caught the eye and, unfortunately, as Rosamund discovered when she entered the chocolate house, most surfaces in the kitchen.

Disappointed that Bianca had not offered her any reassurances about her appearance, Rosamund prayed she did the fine dress justice. Her fears were quashed by the reaction of the chocolate house staff. Upon her arrival just after dawn, the boys' mouths had fallen open and their eyes goggled. Ashe and Cara had curtseyed deeply, showing a respect her other clothes had never earned. Filip had stared and shook his head. *"Eres la criatura más hermosa que he visto."* He sighed and there were tears in his eyes. "And to think the chocolate is in such hands."

Who would have thought the grubby slattern from Gravesend Sir Everard had scooped off the road all those months ago would ever be wearing silk, damask and cloth of gold, let alone smelling of roses, musk and chocolate? If only Grandmother could see her now—though a chocolate house might not be the setting her grandmother would wish.

Regardless, as the bells began to sound midday, it was time for all their hard work to be put to the test. It was also time for the new Lady Blithman to step out in public.

Heart pounding, she stood next to Sir Everard and her eyes swept the room. It really looked very good. While fifty men might be a bit of a crush, the boys were resplendent in their new uniforms of brown, gold and umber and the smells wafting on clouds of steam from the kitchen were irresistible.

Before the bells ceased to toll, voices and heavy footsteps carried up the stairs. Taking a deep breath, Rosamund flashed a nervous smile at Jacopo and Bianca, who stood on the opposite side of the room behind the bar; she responded to Harry's cheeky wink with one of her own.

The voices drew nearer; the footsteps louder. What if Sam Pepys was right and a chocolate house was not the place for a lady to be introduced to society? Would the patrons misconstrue her role? Sir Everard had dismissed Sam's concerns with a careless "Women tread the boards in the theater, why not those in a chocolate house?" The matter had not been raised again.

It was too late to be concerned about that now, she thought, as the first customer entered the room. Pausing on the threshold, he drank in the surroundings before catching sight of Rosamund. With a wide, eager smile, he all but ran between the tables and stopped before her.

"Ah," he began with a swirl of his arm, doffing his feathered hat. "You must be the chocolate maker's wife. Allow me to introduce myself . . ."

TWENTY-TWO
In which the present is clothed as the past

I t was four in the afternoon before Sam Pepys discovered the handbill announcing the opening of the
chocolate house that very day. Why hadn't his cousin
mentioned this auspicious event to him? Where was his
invitation as a family member? And what on earth was
Everard thinking, calling it Helene's? *Oh, Rosamund,
how are you faring?*

Arriving in Birchin Lane minutes later, Sam found
the usually busy street mostly deserted. Assuming the
crowds must be enjoying themselves upstairs in the
chocolate house and concerned that he, a relative no less,
was missing out, he paid his fare to the coach driver and
all but ran down the cobbles. Wrenching open the door
to the bookshop, he ignored Mr. Henderson's greeting
and the customer loitering by the counter and took the

stairs two at a time. The roar of voices from upstairs was so thick, it was like a barrier.

He paused in the doorway, panting and sweating. The combination of smoke and steam swirling about the tables created the illusion of a fog-bound street in winter. Nonetheless, it wasn't so dense he couldn't see the dozens of bodies crammed on benches, elbows on tables, bowls and pots before them. They were squeezed into the booths down one side, all of which, apart from some spilled chocolate and sprinklings of ash, looked mighty fine. Chandeliers blazed from the ceiling. The mirror above the bar was a large gilded affair that served the purpose of not only throwing light back into the room but doubling its size. The windows facing the street gleamed and filled the room with gray light, piercing the smoke and steam roiling above patrons' heads.

Wondering whether or not he had to deposit a coin given his familial connections, he saw, much to his astonishment, a one-handed boy navigating his way toward him, an empty tray held above his periwigged head.

"That be four pence there, my good sir," said the boy in a much deeper voice than his height would have suggested.

Instead of arguing, Sam fished about in his purse and dropped his coins onto the growing cairn. Around him, conversation and laughter flowed. There was the pleasant chink of bowls meeting tables, the slurp of chocolate being drunk and the hum of appreciation as the taste was savored: *beyond delicious* and *nothing like the chalky, sooty rubbish others serve.*

Sam craned his neck and tried to search the crowd. Where was Sir Everard? He expected him to be strutting about like a cock in a henhouse. Was not this his day of triumph? His return to society? And where was Rosamund? Chocolate aside, was she not the star attraction? This room was her stage.

"Are you right there, sir? Wanna seat and a bowl of our finest?" asked the one-handed lad loudly as he peered up at Sam. He wore a smart brown waistcoat and breeches, trimmed with gold, and an umber shirt and hose. "I would guess you're a sweet tooth, so sugar with maybe a hint of ninamon?"

"Ninamon?" Sam stared at him and blinked. "What are you prattling about? Oh, I see, cinnamon. Yes. Yes. I am partial. But forget that. Where is your master? Where is your mistress?"

The boy turned aside and blew his nose onto the floor. Sam stepped back and swallowed. "They be out the back. The master, I don't think he be very well and the mistress insisted he sit awhile—out of the ruckus and smoke."

"I see," said Sam. "Take me to them. I'll not stand for an argument. I am their cousin."

With a shrug that said the boy cared neither about his relationship to the Blithmans nor whether there was to be an argument, he beckoned him forward, collecting empty bowls as he went and placing them on the tray with an adeptness that surprised Sam. The seated men barely looked up, too busy drinking and debating. Only one face was familiar: Mr. Wright, formerly a publisher until L'Estrange shut him down. He nodded gravely in Sam's direction.

"My lady," called the lad when they were closer to the bar. "Be a gent to see you. Claims he be a cousin."

Bristling at "claims," Sam pressed his lips into a thin line and removed his hat and fanned his face. Dear God, it was warm. The bar was cluttered with dirty bowls, chocolate pots galore and a tray of little dishes filled with colorful spices and other additives. Rosamund would be in her element here . . . but how did the men feel being served, not so much by a woman, something they'd be accustomed to from the many alehouses, taverns, inns and ordinaries, but by a lady? A Blithman? A name that once bore the blemish of traitor. Still, Sir Everard had greased many palms and been generous with loans and gifts to ensure he was at least accorded the semblance of respect. But what of his young second wife? Sam leaned on his elbow and turned to survey the room. Certainly the place was popular. But these were early days and all it took was a hint of scandal and, depending on the type, the place would either be bursting with bodies or emptier than a pauper's purse . . .

"Cousin?" said a voice that sent shivers down Sam's spine. He spun around quickly.

Ready to exclaim what a vision she was, even though she appeared quite downhearted, Sam dropped the arms he had raised in greeting as Rosamund stepped out from behind the bar.

"What is it?" She quickly scanned her skirts, patted her hair and brushed her cheeks. "What's wrong, Sam?"

"Why are you wearing Helene's wedding gown?"

"Helene's?" Rosamund gasped in horror. "What do you mean?" She became very still. "Her *wedding* gown?"

Clutching at the nearest object, which happened to be Sam, Rosamund managed to steady herself.

"Helene's wedding gown?" she gasped again as her light-headedness passed. She considered the dress in dismay. Only hours earlier she'd thought it the most beautiful garment she'd ever seen, even though, of all the clothes made for her, she couldn't recall being fitted for it. Nor could she remember it arriving or being stowed in the armoire. Bianca had been so quiet when she brought it to her room that morning and dressed her. Now she knew why.

"This—" She held the skirt away from her as if it were contaminated. "This was Helene's?"

"Maybe not the one she wore," said Sam, releasing her. "But it's identical in every way. I know—I was at the wedding."

Immediately, she wished she could rip it from her body. How could Sir Everard do this to her? To what end? Why hadn't Bianca warned her? Over Sam's shoulder, she spied Hodge ushering in a group of gentlemen. Sam continued talking to her, his words evaporating into the thickening smoke as she willed him gone so she might collect her thoughts, her very wits. She was grateful when Harry appeared and tugged Sam's sleeve.

"Master's this way, sir." For once Sam didn't protest as he was led away. He did, however, make many disapproving clicking noises and shake his head.

Rosamund inhaled sharply, smoothed the skirts and looked around. Fortunately, very few of their patrons would know the significance of the dress. Dear God. Why dress her in his dead daughter's wedding gown? Why name the chocolate house after her? Was it a macabre obsession or something more?

If only she could make some chocolate, she'd be able to push aside the terrible presentiments these questions aroused. Alas, that comfort was denied to her as Hodge ran past flashing her an apologetic look and went into the kitchen to fetch Filip. Once more the newcomers, while happy to set eyes upon her, thus giving them the authority to confirm or deny rumors, didn't want her to serve them. She tried to persuade herself it was their loss.

Hoping to convince the next lot of customers that her chocolate-making skills were at least equal to Filip's, she was about to return to her position by the door with a smile fixed to her face when another figure entered.

The day may have been overcast, but sunshine expanded her ribs, filled her heart. Thoughts of the dress were swept aside as she watched Mr. Nessuno add his coin and slowly take in the room. He'd come. He was no longer angry with her.

Even so, there was a strange expression on his face, as if he were seeing the chocolate house for the first time, though she knew that wasn't the case: he'd admitted to climbing the stairs with Mr. Henderson on more than one occasion to see how the work was progressing. He looked earnest, and also—what was it? Triumphant? Atrabilious? Like a soldier returned from battle. Or, perhaps, seeking one. Did he think to continue their discussion? His satchel was draped across his chest.

Filled with an emotion she refused to identify, she was about to go and greet him and ask forgiveness for words she didn't regret but wished she'd chosen more carefully, when a voice halted her.

"Rosamund." It was Sir Everard. Flushed and sweaty, he wore a too-broad smile as he held out a shaky hand in the manner of an apology. Sam had evidently wasted no time in raising the matter of the wedding dress. She hesitated, but nevertheless wanted to hear Sir Everard's rationale for outfitting her like Helene. She was not his daughter. God help her, she was barely his wife.

Ready to demand answers, she was stopped by the expression upon her husband's face as he gazed over her shoulder.

"What is it, my lord?" she asked, her stomacher suddenly tighter.

Sir Everard let out a long, hissing sigh of satisfaction, as if he'd held it within for years.

"It's none other than Matthew Lovelace," he purred with a predatory smile. "At long last."

TWENTY-THREE
In which Nobody
is actually Somebody

*L*ovelace? Fear traveled her spine and gripped the back of Rosamund's neck as she searched among the men. Her ears rang. "Where, milord?" she asked, her gaze alighting on the group who'd entered earlier, trying to match a face to the one she'd oft pictured.

Sir Everard pulled her closer and whispered, "Quick, quick, find Filip and fetch the tray I prepared for our special guest. Bring it to"—he surveyed the room—"that booth over there." He pointed to one in the center. She wondered how he could possibly squeeze anyone else into the booth, which was filled with patrons enveloped in smoke and engaged in raucous conversation. "I want you to mix a drink at the table, for him."

"For Matthew Lovelace? At the booth? Are you certain, milord?"

Gripping her arm, he shook her. "I said, prepare it before me and my guest. I want him to see you make it with your own hands. Is that clear?"

Speechless, Rosamund looked from the booth to her husband and back again. *Matthew Lovelace is his guest?*

"Are you deaf?" he said firmly, one hand upon the small of her back. "Do as I bid." He tightened his hold on her arm, squeezing so hard her breath caught. "I will brook no questions, no resistance. You would do well to remember what you promised—loyalty and obedience. Now is the time to exercise both. Go, do as I have instructed." He shoved her toward the kitchen.

Without waiting to see if she complied, he gestured to a man who carried documents under one arm lurking near the windows. The man raised a hand in acknowledgment and began to approach. She then heard Sir Everard call out, "Lovelace," in a bright, jovial tone. What was going on?

There were too many men in the way to see who responded to his hail. She would find out soon enough. Curious and yet also fearful, Rosamund disappeared into the kitchen. Best do what she'd been told. Loyalty and obedience.

"*Señora*. Are you well?" asked Filip, the *molinillo* temporarily still in his hand. Hodge loitered impatiently, waiting to put the steaming chocolate pot Filip was working onto his tray. Filip had been so busy making chocolate, the plan to have him and Rosamund prepare drinks at the bar so patrons might enjoy the ritual of the process had been abandoned. Rosamund remained behind the bar, smiling, nodding, her skills barely employed. She was treated as something to be admired, as one might a fine painting. Filip had thus retreated to the kitchen, where the ingredients could be swiftly assembled, and how the mixing was done was not important.

Rosamund gave Filip a sad smile. Even when he was so busy, he cared about her well-being. "I am, I think." She tried not to dwell on what she was wearing or Sir Everard's tone and his cruel grip as he issued his orders, or what they portended. She refused to think about Matthew Lovelace being among the men in the main room and the fact Sir Everard went to greet an avowed enemy like a long-lost friend. And who was the straight-backed man with the moustache he hailed—and what were those documents? How would Lovelace react when he saw her in his dead wife's wedding gown?

Her temples began to pound. Her mouth grew dry.

"Apparently there's a tray I'm to retrieve?" she said, clearing her throat. "Sir Everard said he prepared it himself." This very personal service had been thrust upon her, a surprise. Rosamund had learned over the years at the Maiden Voyage Inn to distrust surprises.

"Ah." Passing the *molinillo* to Solomon, who resumed the action, Filip nodded. "*Sí. Sí.* Here, *señora.* Everything awaits you." He indicated a tray laden with a large silver chocolate pot with the obligatory *molinillo* sticking out of the hole in the lid, a drinking bowl, and six small dishes filled with spices and two small jugs—one containing milk, the other beaten eggs. "The *señor* arranged this himself. He wants you to add a little of everything." He frowned. "He has chosen the ingredients. He must know this man very well."

"I see," said Rosamund even though she did not. Since when did Sir Everard care what went into someone's drink, let alone Matthew Lovelace's? Glancing at the dishes, she could see at least they contained no revelations. There was cinnamon, anise seed, some vanilla seeds, chilli, pepper and sugar. Standard additives.

"Thomas, fetch some boiling water. Solomon, carry the tray for the *señora*," commanded Filip, already crumbling chocolate cakes into the bottoms of empty pots.

"Don't bother, Thomas," said Rosamund quickly. She'd already wasted enough time. "If it is all right with you, Filip, I'll take this pot, the one you've already worked on?" She indicated the pot that Solomon was agitating.

Filip shrugged. "Of course. At least you know the cake is dissolved."

Swapping the chocolate pots over, Solomon picked up the tray, nodding for Rosamund to lead the way.

Sir Everard had managed to clear his chosen booth. As she wove her way past the crammed benches and tables, Rosamund could see the shoulders, back and hat of a tall, dark-haired man and another slightly shorter one beside him. As she moved through the crowded room, she was aware of many sets of eyes following her and the whispers of "common whore," "lovely trull," "lucky ruffin," said so only she could hear them. Some men took liberties, stroking her hip, pinching her bottom, one even brushing against her breasts. She ignored their unwelcome attentions and kept her eyes fixed on her husband. He was listening intently to the dark-haired man opposite him. Standing next to the booth, at Sir Everard's side, was Document Man.

Wishing her heart would stop its ridiculous tumbling and that her stomach didn't feel as if someone had reached inside and was squeezing it, Rosamund halted at the end of the table.

"Ah, Rosamund," said Sir Everard, not bothering to stand. "May I introduce you to, first, my lawyer, Mr. Stephen Bender." He waved toward the man standing at his shoulder. "And this is Mr. Isaac Roberts." The shorter man further in the booth half stood and doffed his cap. "He's a lawyer and gentleman."

"Madam," said Mr. Bender and Mr. Roberts in unison.

"And I know you've been eager to meet someone you've heard much about. This, Rosamund, is my son-in-law, Mr. Matthew Lovelace. Lovelace, this is my wife, the Lady Rosamund Blithman."

One is never really aware of the world turning. Not until it suddenly stops. Then you forget to breathe, fall to the earth and grip for dear life else you career right over the edge into a great void. That was what happened to Rosamund the moment Matthew Lovelace raised his twilight eyes to hers and ever so slowly rose to his feet.

"My Lady Rosamund," he said in a deep, controlled voice, bowing slightly.

Where the devil should have been standing was none other than Mr. Nessuno. The man she called her friend.

"*You* are Matthew Lovelace?" she said. Around her the room contracted; the noise became a roaring that drowned out everything but the pounding of her heart. The swirling smoke became a veil between reality and this . . . this nightmare.

Oh dear God. No.

Memories of their first meeting, their second, and all the rest flew into her mind and merged. The way he'd come to her rescue, allowed her to judge the fate of those rascals, Ben and Jed. How she'd invited him to call her Lady Harridan; how concerned he'd been for her well-being. She thought about his silly scribblings, the way she'd confronted him. He'd discussed politics, religion and so much more with her in Mr. Henderson's shop, happenstance bringing them there at the same time on too many occasions. Only, it wasn't happenstance at all, was it? Their meetings had been contrived. She recalled the times she'd spoken of her husband, of the chocolate house. Oh, how Lovelace must have enjoyed that. Siphoning information from her the way an apple press did cider. And it had flowed from her without pause. Like the country lackwit she was, she'd believed (hoped!) it was because he was interested in her; that for the first time in her life, she was being treated as a thinking, feeling being, not a man's plaything. Nor as a reminder of the past or a harbinger of vengeance.

And what about Jacopo? He must have known who Mr. Nessuno was and yet said nothing. And what of Bianca? Mr. Henderson? Suddenly, the friends she thought she had were revealed to be something else entirely.

How wrong she'd been. About Mr. Nessuno most of all.

Mr. Nessuno—no, *Lovelace*—was just like all the others. No, he was worse, for he pretended to be something he was not. At least, for all his faults, Sir Everard didn't do that, did he?

Her eyes slid to him and then back to Mr. Nessuno . . . Mr. Matthew Lovelace.

Awareness of how poorly she'd been used transformed into smoldering embers in her very middle. Images crackled, words danced, conversations flamed, looks burned, all feeding the spark of her indignation, until they came together in one great conflagration. At its searing heart was the man standing before her. The man with eventide eyes who looked at her now with a mixture of pity, sorrow and, as he observed her costume, distaste. His lips thinned and he cast a guarded look of contempt at Sir Everard.

Rosamund could forgive that—but not much else.

The man who had fooled her into believing he was a correspondent for Henry Muddiman and her friend.

Here he stood, taller than she remembered, his mien more diabolical, Sir Everard's greatest enemy—the man her husband blamed for the death of his daughter and grandchild. The man upon whom he swore to have revenge.

Sir Everard's eyes narrowed. "I believe you two have met." He waggled a finger at Lovelace as if he were nothing but a naughty child.

"Aye, milord," said Rosamund, finding the voice she believed had deserted her. "Only I know him as Mr. Nessuno."

"Rosamund—" began Matthew Lovelace. The lawyer, Mr. Bender, a man of military bearing possessing a thin moustache, gave a warning cough.

Lovelace sat down.

Looking from Rosamund to Lovelace and back again, Sir Everard grinned. "You know, my dear, Lovelace here was having a great jest with you—with us all. You see, 'nessuno' is Italian for 'nobody.'"

"Nobody?" repeated Rosamund in a small voice. Hadn't Sir Ever-ard once told her he was determined to grind Matthew Lovelace into insignificance, make him a nothing, a nobody? "I did not know that." She kept her face averted. Another mark against Jacopo, Bianca.

Unaware his wife was enduring her own epiphany, Sir Everard patted her hand in comfort. "Well, you do now." It was like being stung. "Imagine, here I was taking all sorts of measures to ensure you didn't meet just anyone." He gave a dry laugh. "And behind my back, you met nobody. There's a strange justice in that, don't you think?" Sir Everard made space on the table and gestured for Solomon to set the tray down.

Rosamund was left with the impression that her husband had known all along who Mr. Nessuno really was and how she'd oft spoken with him. The look of triumph on his face confirmed it. Of course, Jacopo would have told him. A great jest indeed, and at her expense.

Solomon slid the tray between the two men and sprinted back to the kitchen, where no doubt everyone would be told what was happening.

Rosamund wondered how these men could sit and exchange pleasantries as if they were old acquaintances. In a peculiar fashion, that's exactly what they were. Acquaintances who could barely stand to breathe the same air, let alone share an intimate booth.

"Now, my dear." Sir Everard turned his attention back to her. "While Lovelace, Roberts, Bender and I attend to business, why don't you mix my guest one of your magical chocolate drinks. I tell you, Lovelace, nobody"—he chuckled at his little joke—"prepares the chocolate quite like my wife." He raised his voice slightly in rebuke to the men nearby who'd refused to have her serve them. Some turned back to their news sheets and debates. Most did not. "I thought it fitting she mix a drink especially for you." The few men Rosamund had served raised their bowls to Sir Everard in congratulations and called out that Lovelace wouldn't be disappointed.

"You'll enjoy the ceremony," added Sir Everard, barely able to hide his smirk.

Uneasy and aware of the many eyes upon her, Rosamund turned the porcelain bowl over, ready to receive the spices and chocolate.

"Be careful not to damage that dress, won't you, dear?" said Sir Ev-erard. "It's been kept as pristine as the last time it was worn. As it happens, for a different kind of ceremony. Do you remember, Lovelace?"

Sam was wrong: it *was* the same dress Helene had worn.

"I seem to recall you admiring it greatly one time. Admittedly, the woman wearing it is not the same, but you have to confess, they do share a striking resemblance. Who wore it better, do you think? My wife or yours?"

There was a wave of chatter followed by a few guffaws. A white line appeared around Lovelace's lips. Rosamund's face burned. She wished to be anywhere but here as she threw a pinch of cinnamon into the bowl, followed by some anise seed.

Barely pausing, Sir Everard continued. "Rosamund has a real talent for making chocolate drinks." He smiled at the room. "They're singing her praises here—at least, they will, once they overcome their reluctance to be served by a lady, a Blithman, no less. She will be a great loss to you, Lovelace. An establishment like this could do wonders with someone like Rosamund at the helm. What a pity, heh?"

What did her husband mean? What business was it of Lovelace's if or where she worked?

As she scraped vanilla seeds into the bowl with the tip of her finger, she forced herself to focus on what she was doing. A touch of pepper, a fine dusting of chilli. Not since the first night she came to London had she heard her husband being quite so loquacious, so at ease. It utterly unnerved her. Her fingers trembled; the quantities were not quite right. She added a tiny bit more cinnamon. Why didn't Mr. Ness— Lovelace say something? She wished she could. Ask questions, express her fury at being hoodwinked, but also to apologize for her costume—for that's what it was. The chocolate house was like a playhouse and she was an actor who'd failed to con her lines.

What role was her husband playing? And Lovelace?

"Do you have the deeds?" asked Lovelace finally. He was not enjoying this performance any more than she was and certainly far less than her husband seemed to be.

"My man here has brought them." Sir Everard nodded to Mr. Bender, who was watching what Rosamund was doing with great interest, as were a number of people in the neighboring booths. Kneeling on their seats, they craned their necks.

Mr. Bender handed over a thick, folded document. Sir Everard rolled out a piece of parchment with a row of heavy wax seals along the bottom. They made dull thuds as they struck the table. He turned it around and slid it toward Lovelace. "Everything is in order. My signature is already appended, and Bender here"—he gestured to him—"has borne witness."

Matthew Lovelace and Mr. Roberts bent to examine it.

Rosamund finished adding the dry ingredients and began agitating the *molinillo* in preparation for pouring. Unable to resist, she glanced at the document. What she saw made her gasp.

"Are those for the chocolate house?"

Sir Everard's eyes snapped to hers. "What makes you ask that?"

"The address," admitted Rosamund. "And your name as well as his." She bobbed her head toward

Lovelace. Realization dawned. The *molinillo* fell from her fingers. "You're signing the chocolate house over to him, aren't you?"

Everything began to fall into place. The sudden urgency to complete the building. The initial indifference followed by intense demands. The hasty alterations to the plans. The letters arriving at the house at odd times which would inflame Sir Everard's temper. His whispered meetings with Wat. The anger, the moodiness. Jacopo's beating. Even the manner of Filip's recruitment, which he was reluctant to speak of. But why was Sir Everard signing the business he'd created over to the man who'd killed his kin? What bargain had he struck with this devil?

"You can read." Sir Everard's cheeks reddened as anger coursed its way through his body.

She was beyond caring. "I've been diligent in my lessons, sir," she said.

The pure fury lodging in her husband's eyes told her the real reason Jacopo had been lax. He'd been ordered. Which just raised more questions. Why was she to remain ignorant? Because of this? Had her husband also threatened Jacopo and Bianca to keep silent over Lovelace? Over Mr. Nessuno? The answer was clear.

She prayed she'd have time to warn them both when this was all over—whatever "this" was.

There was a cry from the kitchen, raised voices, a muffled shout followed by a series of thuds. None of the patrons seated near the bar appeared perturbed. Mayhap it was nothing. Trying to concentrate on preparing the chocolate, she finished whisking, satisfied the scum would be light and foamy, especially since Filip had already worked it. She tipped some milk and eggs into the bowl and mixed them together with the spices.

Lovelace completed reading the document and eased himself back into his seat with a sigh. "Everything appears to be in order, Blithman." He took the quill from his lawyer's hand and dipped it in the inkhorn set upon the table.

"Ah," said Sir Everard, his hand coming between the quill and the parchment. "Before you sign, you must honor your side of the agreement. I want the letters." He held his hand out.

Letters?

Matthew Lovelace looked at Mr. Roberts, who shrugged. "Very well," he said. Putting down the quill, Lovelace hefted the satchel onto his lap and opened the flap. From within, he pulled out dozens of letters, many blackened at the edges, tied together with a yellow ribbon. He threw them down. "There. As promised."

"Is that all of them?" asked Sir Everard. He weighed them in his hand.

"In my possession, yes."

Sir Everard's eyes narrowed. He nodded, placed the bundle back on the table and indicated for Rosamund to pour. "Let's have a toast, shall we? To business concluded. I tell you, Lovelace, you won't taste anything like my wife's chocolate ever again."

Rosamund lifted the spout above the bowl, embarrassed there was only one and she could not offer a drink to Mr. Bender or Mr. Roberts. She tilted the pot and watched as the rich stream curled into the bowl and slowly, unctuously, ribboned its way to the brim.

Fragrant steam rose as she gave the bowl a brief stir, then slid it over to Matthew Lovelace, doing her utmost not to look at him, though she was more than aware of his eyes upon her.

"Drink, Lovelace, drink," urged Sir Everard, standing and grabbing a bowl from Hodge as he passed. He raised it. "Here's to reconciling the past and to a bright new future; here's to *Helene's* Chocolate House."

Reluctantly, Matthew Lovelace and Mr. Roberts rose.

"To the future," said Matthew Lovelace. As he brought the bowl to his lips, Sir Everard inclined toward him, as if he were trapped in Lovelace's orbit. Just as he was about to take a sip, there was a scream, followed by a wail then a crash. Sam Pepys came hurtling out of the kitchen, waving his arms and shouting, "Stop! Don't drink!"

Matthew Lovelace put his bowl down, splashing the contents onto the table.

With a grunt of fury, Sir Everard pushed his way out of the booth just as Mr. Roberts and Mr. Bender, who was forced to leap up, moved the documents, inkhorn and letters out of the way. "What's the meaning of this? What's going on?" He waded past tables and people toward the kitchen.

Sam staggered forward, shoving men aside, his eyes bulging, his mouth trembling. Behind him were Jacopo and Thomas, their faces pale, their brows drawn in distress.

Customers followed in Sam's wild wake, desperate to hear what had happened.

"It's the boy," panted Sam, stopping in front of Sir Everard.

Rosamund pushed through the men who'd gathered about Sam and Sir Everard. She was followed by Matthew Lovelace and Mr. Bender.

"Boy?" Sir Everard's voice was strangled with anger.

"The young one with the hair," said Sam, as Sir Everard shrugged indifferently. "You know—" His hand pumped on and off his crown.

"Robin . . ." said Rosamund. No one heard. She looked toward the kitchen.

"What about him?" said Sir Everard.

Sam gulped. "He drank some chocolate and now he's dead."

There was a collective gasp followed by a wave of voices rising and falling as men staggered back trying to make room, as if Sam carried plague. Behind the bar, a small flame-haired boy limp in his arms, stood Filip. Tears flowed down his sallow cheeks. He caught Rosamund's eyes and shook his head in sorrow.

Rosamund's heart was ripped from her chest. "Dear God, no," she whimpered.

Sam spun to face the crowd, raising his arms above his head. "Don't drink the chocolate!" he cried.

Bowls shattered upon the floor and spilled onto tables, transforming the wood into liquid mahogany as the chocolate oozed across it. Men spat the drink onto the floor, onto the furniture, onto one another. They used their shirts to wipe their mouths and trampled one another, the broken crockery, the news sheets and handbills as they fled, keen to wash out their mouths and purge their stomachs. Among them were also those eager to tell Muddiman and L'Estrange what had transpired. They could see the headlines now, feel the cool coins in their hot palms. Death in Blithman's chocolate house. How deliciously terrible. They knew a lady serving would spell trouble; this was no place for a woman.

Rosamund stood her ground in the midst of the melee, her eyes fixed on the little boy in Filip's embrace; the boy who had been so happy to have employ, a wage. She recalled him standing by Filip as she went to fetch the tray, scratching his ill-fitting periwig, licking his lips, eager to serve but also to have his own bowl. Slowly she turned to regard the chocolate pot from which she'd just poured a drink. The chocolate pot she'd innocently swapped with the one left in the kitchen. The one her husband had placed on a tray with strict instructions for her to collect for his special guest. She looked at Matthew Lovelace, who followed her gaze, then looked back at her. Knowledge altered both their faces.

Matthew Lovelace returned to the booth and scooped up the letters. Shaking moisture from the deed, he folded it and put it, and the letters, in his satchel.

Fury bloomed on Sir Everard's face as he witnessed this. "What are you doing, cur? We have a deal." Shoving Sam out of the way, he used his stick to scythe a path through the departing patrons and back to the booth.

"Not anymore we don't," said Matthew Lovelace. "You've forfeited. Yet again, through deceit and treachery, you lose what you most value. The chocolate house is now mine, *and* I get to keep the incriminating letters."

Sir Everard released a string of expletives. "Jacopo! Don't let him leave. Wat? Where are you?"

Mr. Roberts gestured for Matthew Lovelace to precede him to the door.

The new owner of the chocolate house paused next to Rosamund. "I'm so sorry . . . about the boy as well," he said, and joined the crush heading for the stairs.

Sir Everard stood, his chest heaving, his face florid, an island in the maelstrom, before his face twisted.

"*You.*" He pointed a shaking finger at Rosamund. "This . . . this disaster is your fault." He tried to reach her; he was a man possessed. "I never should have tr . . . trust . . . trusted a woman." He shoved her, and she staggered into a table. A bench toppled. "You . . . y . . . you . . . stupid li . . . li . . . little doxy. You filthy, useless chit. After all I've done for you. After all I've given you." He grabbed a sleeve of her dress and tore it, flinging the fabric to the ground. "You are not fit to wear this gown, nor my wife's." He slashed at the skirt and the fabric came away in his hands. Rosamund grasped at the material, tried to preserve her modesty. "I give you one simple in . . . ins . . . instruction . . . one t . . . t . . . task, and you fuc . . . fucki . . ." His face underwent a change. One side began to collapse, as if it were formed from wet sand. His lips could no longer make words. Nonsense spewed forth.

Rosamund could hear every ragged breath. Trapped against a table, she was unable to do much more than raise a protective arm as a torrent of spit and gibberish rained upon her. Sir Everard lunged, ripped her other sleeve away and tore her bodice. Not one man came forward to aid her.

That wasn't quite true. There was one, but the patrons, halting their initial exodus, were keen to enjoy the show and wouldn't allow him passage: Lovelace couldn't reach her.

Refusing to cry out, to quiver beneath her husband's fury and beg for mercy, she thought of Paul and stood straight. With a yowl of sheer impotence and rage at her willfulness, Sir Everard raised his cane above his head and brought it down.

"No," screamed Rosamund and with a strength she didn't know she possessed, caught the wood in the palm of her hand and wrenched it from him, tossing it aside. It clattered and rolled under a table.

Sir Everard stared at her in shock and emitted a peculiar choking sound. He reeled and clutched the air, his fingers claws. His face, already red, turned vermillion, and his eyes, horribly bloodshot, protruded as he tried to speak. Rosamund stepped aside as he began an inexorable slide to his knees.

Jacopo caught him before he fell and lowered him to the floor. There were more cries, a babble of voices, calls for help.

Rosamund watched in disbelief and sank to her knees beside her husband. His limbs spasmed, jerking uncontrollably. He gasped and fought for air. She loosened his collar, feeling his throat hard at work. Jacopo caught a flailing hand and tried to straighten the bent fingers. Sir Everard kept glaring at them and trying to speak. His breath was raspy, short. "He . . . He . . . Hel . . ." His neck was twisted, his other hand rising and falling as if he were marching, striking the floor over and over.

A dark patch flowered around his groin. A sweet, sickly smell followed as his bowels opened too. "Fetch a physician," cried Rosamund.

The command was echoed. Men broke away.

There was a draft of air followed by a shadow. Matthew Lovelace kneeled opposite her and began to rub Sir Everard's arms. "Come on, old man. You can't expire on me now. We've unfinished business, you and I."

Astonished he didn't flee in triumph the moment they were all distracted, Rosamund regarded him.

"You have to believe me, my lady," he said, his eyes locking onto hers, "I never intended this to happen. If I'd known . . ."

Known what? He'd have . . . what? Never darkened the chocolate house door? Never agreed to whatever devil-sent exchange they were engaging in? Never pretended to be her friend? She wanted to believe him. Oh, dear sweet Lord forgive her, she wanted to . . .

Her treacherous mind whispered, *Why did it have to be you?* as her husband's terrible pallor and blue lips filled her vision.

Sir Everard's mouth worked urgently again, issuing primitive sounds. "Ma . . . Marg . . . Helene . . . Aubrey . . . Aub . . ."

His face twisted in a rictus. With hooked fingers he reached out toward Matthew Lovelace. Then his body gave one last great shudder and his arm dropped.

Rosamund gave a cry. Jacopo released his hand. The spectators drew back. Matthew Lovelace pressed his ear against Sir Everard's chest.

Outside, the clop of hooves, the clatter of carts and the calls of vendors intruded. Somewhere a dog howled. Inside there were whispers, cleared throats and discreet coughs; downstairs the shop bell rang over and over and footsteps resounded on the stairs. An errant sunbeam stole in the window to fall across Sir Everard's face—a face forever frozen in wide-eyed fury.

Full of disbelief and something else, Matthew Lovelace's eyes composed their own words, even as his lips formed others.

"I'm sorry to tell you, my lady," he said, shaking his head. "But Sir Everard Blithman is dead."

PART TWO

Autumn 1662 to Spring 1665

I love the old way best, the simple way
Of poison, where we too are strong as men.

—Euripides, *Medea* (translated by Gilbert Murray)

The great Use of *Chocolate* in Venery, and for
Supplying the Testicles with a Balsam, or a Sap,
is so ingeniously made out by one of our learned
countrymen, that I dare not presume to add any
Thing after so accomplished a Pen; though I am of
Opinion, that I might treat of the Subject without
any Immodesty, or Offence . . .

—Henry Stubbe, *The Indian Nectar, or, a Discourse
Concerning Chocolata, etc.*, 1662, 1682

TWENTY-FOUR
In which a chocolate house is mourned

It was hard to believe it was almost three months since Sir Everard died. He had been like a comet flashing through Rosamund's life and wreaking great change—though not in the way he intended. So much had happened, there were still moments when she had to reassure herself it wasn't all a dream.

There had been so much to do in the immediate aftermath of Sir Everard's and Robin's terrible deaths. The coroner's report had found Robin's to be the consequence of poison, administered via chocolate by perpetrators unknown, and Sir Everard's from apoplexy—though rumors of poison attended his demise as well. One question she had been determined to resolve, even while in mourning, was why Jacopo and

Bianca had withheld Matthew Lovelace's identity from her. What had motivated them to keep silent?

Once they confessed that Sir Everard had sworn them to secrecy on pain of punishment, Rosamund couldn't remain angry or blame them for obeying their master. Wasn't obedience what Sir Everard required from all who served him? Including his wife. And having seen his attack on Jacopo, the reality of what they would have faced had either of them broken their word did not need to be spelled out. Rosamund forgave them as soon as they asked it of her—after all, if anyone understood how coercion and fear forced even good people into behaviors they wouldn't otherwise countenance, it was her. Equanimity in the household was swiftly restored.

One consequence of Sir Everard's death was that she was no longer bound by the promises she'd made to him. Nor were Jacopo and Bianca. Rather than being pleased at this sudden liberty, they had all gone about their tasks as if little had changed.

But it had: Rosamund no longer had a chocolate house to visit each day. Was she so very wicked that she grieved more for that than the loss of her husband? Aye, she was wickedness personified.

After the initial outpouring of sympathy from Mr. Bender, Mr. Henderson, Mr. Remney and even a few of the patrons who ignored the salacious rumors, Rosamund was, with the exception of Sam, Bianca and Jacopo, left to herself. She might be a titled widow, but it was a dubious status—and everyone knew it. And she was a Blithman, a name that, wealth aside, still carried a taint. All of this might have been tolerated had she not sullied herself by embracing work. There was not a lady in town who would offer friendship to such a one.

Bianca tried to engage Rosamund by continuing their reading lessons and even introducing her to the practicalities of running a household. While Rosamund cooperated, her heart wasn't in it—it had been lost to the chocolate.

She kept thinking of what happened that day, of Matthew Lovelace, wondering how he was faring now the chocolate house was his—the cheating, lying blackmailer. Yet even those words took on a softer, less potent meaning, unlike the names gossips attributed to her in the wake of such scurrilous and tragic events.

She drifted about the manor in her widow's garb, unwilling yet to venture beyond its four walls, though no one prevented her, not anymore. Church was an exception, and there was a great fuss when she arrived the first Sunday following Sir Everard's death. There, the reverend, a portly man of middling years with a strapping Dutch wife (a cheese muncher, someone said unkindly and loudly enough for the poor woman to hear), offered his sincere condolences and to attend Blithe Manor so they might pray together for Sir Everard's soul. While she graciously accepted the first suggestion, Rosamund was appalled at the idea he might actually follow through upon the second. She'd no inclination to entertain anyone and no idea what was expected of her. Furthermore, she wasn't convinced Sir Everard's soul could be saved—after all, he'd not only plotted to kill but was responsible for Robin's death. Something she also blamed herself for . . . If only she hadn't switched the pots. But then Matthew Lovelace would be the one interred in the ground. Why did the notion seize her heart and make her vision blurry? Thoughts whirled in her head like autumn leaves along the riverbanks.

Sam, who'd abandoned his regular parish service so he might escort her to this one, saved her from having to respond to the reverend and whisked her home before the man of God could secure arrangements.

Most afternoons Sam made a point of calling. Appreciative of his concern, she nevertheless came to view his visits, accompanied as they were with his endless prating about naval matters, his house renovations and even the various ships he oversaw, with despair. Greatly excited about a play he'd seen on Michaelmas at the King's Theater, *A Midsummer Night's Dream,* he once spent an entire afternoon describing it in detail, oblivious to her mood. It didn't matter that she pleaded with him to allow her time to grow accustomed to her new status and what that entailed, Sam insisted on entertaining her—and lecturing her on the unhealthy state of widowhood.

Rosamund barely listened as he prattled, stroking her hand or arm as he did so. Once he even rested his fingers above her knee, his large eyes gazing at her, puppy-like, until she pried his fingers off none too gently. Unabashed, he saw the liberties he took about her person—including a lingering kiss on her lips whenever he entered or left the manor—as his right as her cousin. Indeed, as his right with any eligible woman, regardless of his marital state. The very thought of his wandering hands and where they might go, or his wet mouth, were enough to turn her not-so-delicate stomach.

After persevering for a few weeks, Rosamund told Bianca to inform Mr. Pepys when he next came to call that she was indisposed, and she was thus for three days in a row. Showing uncharacteristic insight, he ceased to call so frequently.

Every day she sent Jacopo to the chocolate house to inquire after Filip and to see how Widow Ashe, Cara, Solomon, Thomas and the others were faring, sending her best wishes and hoping that Robin's death had not affected them too badly. She prayed they thought kindly of her, despite her husband being responsible for so much heartache.

Jacopo would return with news they missed her presence greatly, they were all well, though having been closed for a month out of respect for Sir Everard and Robin, and only recently reopened, custom at the chocolate house (it was no longer called Helene's and was yet to be christened) had suffered.

She never asked openly about Matthew Lovelace, though no small part of her longed to. Jacopo occasionally mentioned him, and Rosamund would find her heart leaping and questions forming on her lips. Questions she swiftly swallowed.

As expected, news of the deaths spread—by word of mouth then in the news sheets. At first, they were attributed to the chocolate, but as the weeks went by after the place reopened and no more brave folk succumbed, and Rosamund remained out of the public eye, other rumors spread. Everything from a Papist conspiracy to plague to a rival business in St. Michael's Alley were held accountable for poisoning Sir Everard (Robin was mostly forgotten). Rosamund was mentioned in most of the reports—some described her as the injured party and a winsome widow who had a genuine flair for chocolate and whose talents would be sorely missed.

The word "talents" was underlined, which Rosamund knew indicated less flattering connotations. Others brazenly attributed the deaths to her—the boy having died from want of the lady, the husband from a surfeit.

"Oh, to die that way," muttered the men who'd spied her.

Few of the reports mentioned that Lovelace had taken over the business. No one made a fuss. After all, wasn't he related to the Blithmans by marriage? Anyway, no one in their right mind would give it to a woman to run, not when there was a perfectly healthy male member of the family to do so. Any history between Sir Everard and Matthew Lovelace was quickly rewritten to suit the outcome. Just as well Sir Everard had signed the deeds over before expiring . . . Clearly, the new wife and business had been far too much for the old man.

Rosamund was pleased to note that none of the scuttlebutt was written by Mr. Nessuno.

Nevertheless, many who had been present at the infamous opening returned to the chocolate house in the hope of seeing Ravishing Rosamund, the Winsome Widow. Learning she was no longer on the premises, despite being family, many took their custom elsewhere. In doing so, they could not help but note that no other place served chocolate quite like that prepared by the Spaniard or Lady Blithman—dangerous, delicious slut that she was.

Not even Sam relayed this information to his cousin. Some news was too sordid, even for a delicious slut to hear.

Rosamund was uncertain what she hoped to achieve by going to Sir Everard's study one evening weeks after his death. The only time she'd been there before was to view his body. As when she had gone to see Robin's corpse in the crypt at St. Helen's, she'd barely paid attention to her surroundings, drawn by the pale, bloodless form on display. Whereas Robin's slight frame lay on the stone floor, and she'd kneeled and stroked his thick, spiky hair, as soft in death as in life, and spilled tears over his skinny little limbs, twisted mouth and half-open cloudy eyes, bemoaning the waste of a precious life, she'd felt no emotion when she saw Sir Everard. Accompanied by Bianca and Jacopo, she'd stared at the large, blue-lipped man with the silver hair, his cane and sword laid diagonally across his broad chest, and spied a stranger. Touching his cold hand, she said a quick prayer and left the room.

Did she hope to understand why her husband had handed over the chocolate house? Why he'd succumbed to blackmail? The nature of it? To discover the contents of those letters that he'd been prepared to sacrifice the chocolate house to possess? Gah! She had to stop thinking about it. The chocolate house was no longer her concern. Only she couldn't stop caring.

Chocolate had seeped into her blood.

First she lit some candles and a small fire to keep winter's creeping chill at bay. Outside, thunder growled and lightning split the sky. Rosamund lowered herself into the chair behind the desk, her hands splayed across the surface, and, like a king atop a castle, surveyed the room. Twin turrets of correspondence sat either side of her. Since Sir Everard died, Jacopo had been dealing with all matters pertaining to his business. Mr. Bender had said that until the executor of her husband's will was located or proved dead, there could be no formal reading of the will or disposal of property. Who this was he did not reveal, and Rosamund did not have the energy to ask. Reassured it was business as usual (whatever that was), until such time as the will could be executed, she was to continue as she had—which meant, with Wat suddenly gone, Jacopo took on his responsibilities as well.

Wat. Wat Smithyman. Sir Everard's loyal steward, who disappeared two days after his master died (along with some household silver). There'd been no word from him since. Rosamund could only be glad. It made living at Blithe Manor far more bearable. Certainly, the servants seemed brighter for his absence. Jacopo said Wat had rifled through the study drawers, but if he had taken anything, they were none the wiser.

Dark wainscoting lined the walls, glowing gold and amber in the light cast by the flames. Altogether, the room was quite comfortable if somewhat smelly. Though it was weeks since Sir Everard had last used it, the odor of stale pipe tobacco, the acrid smell of coal burned over many winters, moldy paper, sweat and neglected food and wine perfumed the room as it had her mother's bedroom at the inn. A sword hung on one wall, a coat of arms beside it. Rosamund recognized the Blithman sigil—a large badger upright in a boat, adrift upon rough seas. Sir Everard had explained what it meant months ago. The badger signified independence and tenacity, focus and strategy; the seas were the forces of nature and God that, together, might rock the boat, but the badger would survive no matter what. The coat of arms appeared throughout the house.

And then there were the paintings. She had barely registered them when Sir Everard lay dead before them, and she was not yet ready to face them. Instead, she perused the desk further. There were two inkwells, quills, a knife for sharpening them, a handful of spare candles and some tapers, as well as a decanter of wine.

Bless Jacopo. Pouring herself a glass, she shuffled through the papers. There were what appeared to be letters from Sir Everard's secretaries in Holland, Venice and the New World. The words "tobacco" and "cacao" were oft repeated. There were what she guessed must be the names of ships as well: *Helene* (of course), *Lady Margery*, *Blithman's Badger* and *Gregory*. She wondered briefly what cargo they carried and was reminded of the well-stocked warehouses on the river. Beneath the pile of documents on her right was a fat ledger. Wat had not seen fit to take that. It was filled with neat entries and figures. She would have to become familiar with the contents, or at least have Jacopo explain them to her if she was to manage the Blithman estate.

Estate. Never in her wildest dreams would she have connected such a grand word and all it portended in terms of material possessions with her name. But here she was, the widow of Sir Everard Blithman and, according to what Widow Ashe whispered to her at the graveside, and Mr. Bender intimated, since her husband had no surviving progeny, she was entitled to a portion of her husband's wealth, or would be once the damn executor was found. Not that she felt either entitled or wealthy. Instead, she felt an acute sense of loss.

She wiped a hand across her brow and slowly drank her wine. It wasn't Sir Everard she missed, unnatural churl that she was, but someone with whom she could share her turn of fortune. She didn't want to think of it as "good"; how could it be "good" when it arose from such misery? Helene and her brothers' deaths, the loss of the little grandson, sweet Robin and Sir Everard himself. The latter embroiled in secrets, plots, blackmail and murder. It hardly bore consideration, yet wouldn't leave her mind.

The one thing that really mattered to her was the chocolate house. Her secret hope, which she'd foolishly revealed to Sam in a moment of weakness, was that one day, when the will was settled and the mourning period was over, she would be able to purchase it back from Matthew Lovelace. Sam scoffed and told her she'd best forget the place altogether. Her duty was to shop. When she regarded him askance, he explained that was what widows did: they shopped—for a husband. Mayhap that was why she felt empty. The thought of losing the chocolate house, of never again being able to work beside Filip, Thomas, Solomon, the drawers and the girls, to fulfill her aspirations for what she knew the place could be, filled her with despair. Now that Lovelace had it, what was she to do? She'd no desire to be an idle woman on the prowl for a man. She didn't want to be a merchant in the sense Sir Everard had been. Perhaps she could sell the ships? Or lease them?

That was something she had to ask Mr. Bender, discuss with Jacopo and Bianca. A little seed of determination took root; a sense of purpose unfurled.

Her hand brushed against a pile of notes, almost scattering them. Glancing at the topmost one, she frowned. She'd almost forgotten the lubricious invitations from gentlemen, noblemen, businessmen—even the King's procurer, William Chiffinch—all hastily scrawled and delivered to the house. They were very much the same. The men sought to either bed or wed her—though mostly, she thought wryly, the former. The notes had arrived daily since Sir Everard died, and she'd ignored each and every one. Rosamund had no regrets on that score, though she was puzzled that the higher the rank of the suitor, the more lascivious his suggestions. One even went so far as to describe Sir Everard's death as a "delightful convenience." At first she laughed them off, but they soon aroused nothing but sadness that men could be so lacking in respect for the deceased, for her mourning, that they saw her widowhood as an opportunity and sought to take advantage of it.

Maybe Sam was right. If nothing else, a man, a husband, would protect her from such unwelcome advances.

Pushing the notes aside, she scoffed at herself. She didn't need protection, not when, as a widow, she had autonomy for the first time in her life. As a widow, she had freedoms, limited as they were, that a single woman—a *feme sole*—or a married one could only dream about, including refusing unsubtle requests to "play at heave-and-shove." How often had her grandmother, for all the love she bore her husband, thanked God for her widowed state and the power it bestowed? No, Rosamund would not be in a hurry to seek out someone to wed, however much Sam and these so-called gentlemen might pressure her to do so. Still, it would be nice to share all this with someone.

Now that she didn't have a husband to dictate what she could and couldn't do, she could go to the theater, attend a lecture at Gresham College, go to St. James's Park, travel by river . . . All the things Sam had invited her to do and which Sir Everard had postponed. He'd wanted to keep her strong resemblance to his daughter as secret as possible until he was ready to reveal it.

But did she really bear such a likeness to Helene? Her gaze drifted toward the series of portraits on the wall to her left.

She rose and went to examine the faces of those whose estate, through sheer tragedy, had come to her. The thought made her stumble. She'd never asked or expected it, please God.

She gazed up at a much younger Sir Everard, who stood in front of a mighty oak dressed as a cavalier with a feathered bonnet tipped at a jaunty angle, a frilled collar framing his face and a sword with a shining quillon upon his hip. He stared out boldly, almost arrogantly. There was a time when arrogant was never a word she'd have used to describe her husband—not at first—yet here he appeared to personify it. How had she not seen it? Discomfited, she moved away. The next painting was of a woman—Lady Margery; Rosamund recognized the dress.

Rather buxom, with dark hair, thick brows and deeply hooded eyes that suggested secrets, she looked down a rather large nose. The artist had tried to soften her face by putting roses in her cheeks, but the high color succeeded in making her look angry. Rosamund wondered what had provoked it. Emboldened now, she moved to the next picture. It depicted a rather dashing young man dressed in the colors of his regiment. His eyes twinkled and seemed to follow her. He had his mother's dark hair and brows and his father's sky-blue eyes, but without the boldness. Gregory? Or Aubrey?

It was the final painting she was most curious about. As she stood before it, Rosamund's breath caught in her throat. Fair curls cascaded over one shoulder. Dark brows and lashes framed eyes the same color as her father's and brother's, only closer together. Her nose was long and narrow. Not as well endowed as her mother, but possessed of a fine figure nonetheless, the young woman chose not to smile, but instead to gaze earnestly upon the world with deep, deep sadness. Her mouth was downturned, her chin too, and one hand yearned for something beyond the frame, forever out of reach. What was it? Rosamund thought of the woman's dead brothers, her mother, her grieving father . . . and the poor baby forever lost. A lump filled her throat, her chest grew tight as she willed herself not to shed tears.

So this was Helene. The unfortunate, lovely Helene whose husband was Sir Everard's mortal enemy. Rosamund could see a likeness, of sorts. They were both fair and dark, neither tall nor short, skinny nor fat. Their hair was long, palest gold and unruly. But there, surely, the resemblance ended. Why, this woman was so miserable, Rosamund was surprised the picture hadn't fallen from the wall with the weight of her sorrow. It flowed out from the painting, swamping Rosamund. She reached out and gently touched the picture.

"I'm so sorry for what you suffered, for your terrible losses. I'm sorry you were wed to one such as he. I too know the levels to which men can stoop. What they can do to us. I pray that you are with God now, you and your little boy." She shook herself at her flight of fancy (her grandmother would not have approved) and, composing herself with no small difficulty, continued to examine the room. The only other portrait was a small one featuring King Charles and his Queen Catherine. The other paintings were pastorals or battle scenes. There was no sign of the other son. She glanced at the pictures again. The young man must be Gregory. There was something about the way Sir Everard had spoken of Aubrey which suggested he'd not found favor with his father. It would explain why his portrait wasn't hung with the rest of the family.

Aubrey . . . Had Sir Everard been calling for him in his last moments? Aubrey, Helene and Margery. She gave a shudder as she recalled his face, his lips twisting as he tried to speak, crying out to the dead.

Before returning to the desk, she paused before Sir Everard's portrait. "Did you see them beckoning in your last moments? I pray you are all together, united in death as you were not in life," she whispered, thinking how tragic it was that all three children had lost their lives so far from home, and before their father. "May you all find peace with God, milord."

She waited. Sir Everard ignored her, much as he had in life. Either that, or heaven wasn't where he was resting. Chastising herself for the uncharitable thought, she went back to the desk, this time approaching from the other side. As she did, she noticed a large object shoved between the cabinet and the wall. Putting down her glass, she slid it out with some difficulty and drew away the fabric covering it. The material caught briefly on a gilt frame before revealing another portrait of the same dimensions as the others. She propped it against the desk, stood back and gave a small cry. The canvas was slashed in three places, violent rents through the middle. Above the first of these was a young man's face. A very handsome one at that.

Laughing, he stood with one foot in front of the other, his arms folded across a broad chest. His hair was fair, thick and long and sat in waves beneath a fine feathered cap. His jacket was pinked and made of blue velvet, which served to enhance the light, periwinkle eyes. His brows were arched, his chin tilted upward. It would have been a joyous painting except for his mouth. The lips were thin, cruel almost, and the way they curled slightly to the right made his grin a sneer. Shivering, she wondered why the portrait had not only been savagely cut, but hidden away. This must be Aubrey: the family resemblance was obvious. Clearly, his misdeeds had been so very great he was shunned even unto death.

Instead of covering it again, she hefted it to a spot near the cabinet and leaned it against the wall. She owed her new comforts to all the family—including Aubrey. The slashes in the canvas were unnerving—a draft lifted them, giving the painting the illusion of being animated, as if Aubrey were about to step toward her and speak. Unable to tolerate it any longer, she rose and rearranged the fabric and stored the painting away again. Satisfied he was hidden, she was about to sit back down when there was a knock at the door.

It took her a moment to understand that whoever was on the other side was waiting for permission to enter. Her position was remarkably altered.

"Come in," she said loudly and strove to appear businesslike behind the desk.

The door opened a crack and Jacopo poked his head in.

"Jacopo," said Rosamund, placated. "I thought you were still at the chocolate house—come in. I need your hel—"

"You have a visitor, *signora*." He opened the door wider.

Before Rosamund could ask who would be calling at such a time on such a wretched day, in strode none other than Matthew Lovelace.

TWENTY-FIVE
In which the devil reveals a conscience

Rosamund felt as if she had lost possession of her body; if she hadn't been leaning on the desk, she would have fallen.

Unaware of her shock, Matthew Lovelace approached, whipping off his hat and executing a most elegant bow. Dressed in black with a violet trim, he appeared tired and worn. The lines around his eyes were deep crevices, his cheeks hollow. Rosamund could feel the painted face of the young Sir Everard glowering at the intruder—and at her—while Helene radiated more of her ever-present sadness.

While his actions were not tentative, his words were. "Forgive my calling at such a late hour, my lady," he said, as if it were his habit to visit the house. "Or perhaps I should simply ask you to forgive me."

A movement caught her eye. Ah, Jacopo remained by the door. Her breathing eased, though her heart beat fit to play at a royal procession.

Rosamund resisted the urge to ask after his health, and struggled to find not merely her voice, but the right words. Did she bid him sit as she should any guest? Did she curse and demand him gone? Did she ask why he looked as if the hounds of hell bayed throughout the night, chasing away the solace of sleep and comfort of dreams? Why did he look as if he grieved when she did not? What could she say? What could she do? Good God, what was Jacopo doing admitting him after everything they'd endured? She glanced at the paintings as if to find inspiration. They remained mute; haughty, but mute.

Matthew Lovelace was also looking at them— specifically, at the portrait of Helene. Was that regret upon his face? Or guilt? For all the man wore two faces, deployed two names (that she knew of), she did not want to believe him guilty of the crimes Sir Everard laid at his feet. Now he stood before her and she wanted to hear what he had to say.

"Is that why you seek me out at such a late hour, sir?" she asked, finding her voice at last.

With a sad smile, Matthew Lovelace replaced his hat. "I could leave it no longer. May I?" he asked, indicating the chair.

Rosamund's hand swept toward it. She sat as well, unable to trust her legs, they were shaking so badly. From fear, uncertainty and something else.

"First of all," began Matthew Lovelace, "let me reiterate how sorry I am for your loss, my lady. I knew Sir Everard was unwell, but I didn't know his palsy had weakened him so."

"The doctor said he died from apoplexy."

"I heard." He paused and studied his hands, still encased in gloves. She wondered why he always wore them. It was quite warm in the study. "I feel more than a little responsible for what happened . . . If I had not insisted upon redress; if the exchange of documents had not taken place in such a public manner . . ." He hesitated.

Rosamund pressed her lips together. The same thoughts had occurred to her. The doctor, a Spanish physician whom Solomon had found, later told Rosamund he suspected Sir Everard hadn't been long for this world. His coloring, the way in which she described his choking, sweating and shortness of breath, in addition to his slurred words in the lead-up to his collapse, all pointed toward him being gravely ill. While she had wanted to deposit more blame at Matthew Lovelace's door, she was strangely relieved she didn't have to, and accepted the doctor's diagnosis with grace.

Aware she wasn't going to make this easy for him, Matthew Lovelace continued. "I'm here not only to offer my sincere condolences, Lady Rosamund, I'm here to offer you an explanation for what you witnessed at the chocolate house so I might solicit not only *your* forgiveness, which is of the utmost importance to me, but also, as strange as it sounds, proffer a proposal."

For one mad moment, Rosamund thought he meant a marriage proposal. A bolt of lightning jolted her spine and a look of distaste briefly altered her features.

"While I welcome an explanation, anything to help me make sense of what has happened, what makes you think, Mr. Lovelace . . . or is it Nessuno . . ." She dealt the names like unlucky cards. ". . . that I would be interested in offering dispensation, let alone listening to any proposal you have to make? All that mattered to me in this world, you have taken."

Too late she realized it sounded as if she meant the chocolate house when she was referring to her husband . . . wasn't she?

Matthew Lovelace shifted in his seat and nodded. "When I embarked upon this course and entered into an agreement with Sir Everard, it was never with the intention to deprive you. You were not within my compass when this was started. My understanding is you were not in Sir Everard's, either. In all fairness, your union was still fresh . . . barely months old. If I'd been aware of you then . . ." He hesitated, looked across at the portraits. "I can only imagine what you've heard about me. However," he said, turning back toward her and raising a finger, "it's only one side of the story. As someone who I know believes at least in those whose voices are clamoring to be heard, in the truth—or a version of it—you might wish to hear mine. That is all I ask of you—for the moment. I ask that you lend me your ears."

Rosamund sniffed, her indignation growing. "My ears? Are you Mark Antony now?" She sent a silent thanks to Bianca for reading her *Julius Caesar.* "You wish to tell your side of the story? This is no fairy tale, sir; nor are you Shakespeare."

"No, it is not. And I certainly make no claim to be a bard, let alone *the* bard. But it is a tragedy borne of revenge. I think you would want to hear where it began. How it began."

"You thought wrong, sir." Oh, no he didn't, but she would not give him that satisfaction. Not in Sir Everard's study. Not before his portrait or Helene's. It didn't seem right. "And I'm afraid I've had cause to observe your intentions firsthand. You cannot deny you were blackmailing my husband."

"I do not. I was. Over many months, I sent him numerous letters outlining instructions for the chocolate house, its specific design, materials to be used, changes I wanted, the workers' conditions, uniforms, even who was to be employed—Filip, Solomon, Thomas and Widow Ashe. Finally, I dictated when the place was to open. When Sir Everard stalled in the last regard, I . . . let's say, used additional leverage to ensure he adhered to my command. I cannot begin to express the remorse I feel about that. For what occurred as a consequence." He turned toward Jacopo. "My apologies are not enough." Jacopo lowered his head. "But I'm afraid they're all I have." He threw up his hands. "Why do I seek to mitigate my behavior? Facts are, I made demands and threatened him if these were not met. I do not pretend otherwise, milady."

"Oh," said Rosamund, uncertain what to make of this confession. Could this be true? That Mr. Lovelace was responsible not only for the interior of the chocolate house, the uniforms, but for the people who worked there as well—even the marvelous talent of Filip? Was nothing the work of her husband, the man who styled himself the chocolate maker? Were even the acts of kindness she'd credited to him, such as giving Ashe work, because of this man before her? And his threats and blackmail?

No . . . this was too much. It was a fabrication, surely. This man—an accomplished wordsmith no less—was not to be trusted.

As if reading her mind, Matthew Lovelace canted toward her. "My threats were made with good reason. Even in your grief, you must realize there had to be sound motivation for my behavior?" When she didn't respond, he appeared resigned. He started to stand. "I'll not dally, then, but leave you to your—" His eyes fell upon a batch of letters. "You've read my letters to your husband."

Afraid to speak lest she utter words she might later regret, she followed his gaze. She hadn't even begun to explore the documents on the desk, locating the importuning notes had been enough to distract her, those and the portraits. Making a negative motion with her head, she decided that as soon as Mr. Lovelace departed, she would digest the contents thoroughly.

"Then," he said, "I beg of you, allow me to offer my side of this sorry story, and give you some insight into why I was so unyielding. If, at the end of it, you wish me gone, I will depart immediately and you need never endure my company again."

Rosamund's heart quickened. Never was a long time. She cocked her head, thinking. What he asked was not unreasonable. Didn't he deserve a hearing at the least? He looked so . . . what was it? Crumpled, like a letter squeezed in an angry fist.

"What have you to lose . . . my Lady Harridan?" he asked softly.

The armor of her icy resolve began to melt. That was what she was afraid of: that she would collapse into a puddle in the heat of his presence.

"Very well," Rosamund said as coldly as she was able. "Tell me."

Releasing a long sigh, Matthew Lovelace settled in the chair, his back to the portrait of his wife, who towered over him. He looked longingly at the wine.

Unable to help herself, her grandmother having instilled manners, Rosamund found a glass and poured him a drink and topped up her own.

Matthew Lovelace lifted his glass to her in salute, took a long draft and began. "As you are aware, I was briefly married to Sir Everard's only daughter, Helene. I wish to relate how this came about and what occurred after we were wed so you might understand how all the subsequent calamities arose."

Rosamund stayed very still. Her gaze remained locked on Matthew Lovelace's haunted face and those ardent sapphire eyes as his tale surged out of him . . .

"**I was** first introduced to Helene by her brother Aubrey." He paused. "I'd been ordered to keep an eye on him as he was suspected of running weapons and selling state secrets to the Dutch. Since we were both students at Gray's Inn, it wasn't difficult to befriend him."

Rosamund's eyes were upon his face, her body leaned toward him as she absorbed every word. Dear God, he prayed he could do this—give her the truth he felt she was owed. As much as he was able.

"Who ordered you?" asked Rosamund quietly.

Matthew shifted in his seat. "The Lord Chancellor, Edward Hyde."

The widening of her eyes indicated she understood the significance of the name.

"Since Sir Everard was known to be both sympathetic to the King and wealthy, before the fledgling government returned from exile, they wanted to see if there was any truth to the rumors of treason attending one Aubrey Blithman. After all, why cut off a generous benefactor by seizing his son if there was no sound reason, no proof?"

"Was there? Proof?"

How did he explain that, contrary to expectations, Aubrey was an affable sort; the kind of gentleman whose company was easy to keep. Not only was it hard to credit he would engage in such nefarious activities, within a short period Matthew found he did not want to—because of Helene.

"There were claims he was running guns for the Dutch, carrying them in the holds of his ships as well as selling state secrets—so there was suspicion. Whether it was justified?" He shrugged. "After I met Helene my—let's say, enthusiasm for finding evidence faded somewhat. It's not something I'm proud of."

Rosamund regarded him steadily. Unable to hold her gaze, he studied his glass.

"I oft wondered if Aubrey deliberately put Helene in my path to distract me. Whatever his intentions, it worked."

Rosamund glanced at the portrait behind him.

"Helene was . . . How do I describe her? Lovely to look at, that was undeniable, but it was more than that." He hesitated. Helene had been unlike any woman of his acquaintance. Cool and assured toward him, yet so loving and deferential toward her brother and father, she was an irresistible challenge.

He forced himself to continue. "She held me at arm's length, almost mocking my efforts, which were fueled by her apparent indifference. It wasn't until after I casually mentioned to Sir Everard that Aubrey was being watched by the government that everything changed. Not only did Sir Everard embrace my wooing of his daughter, but she capitulated to me in a way that was breathtaking.

"When Sir Everard insisted on our immediate marriage after only a few weeks of courtship, I was torn. If I married into the Blithman family, then where did my loyalties lie? I'd been hired to investigate Aubrey—quietly, surreptitiously. Telling Sir Everard of my suspicions was a ploy to ferret out the degree to which he was involved, and to force Aubrey to reveal his hand—if there was a hand to be revealed. To answer your earlier question, I was never certain if the reasons I was given to look into Aubrey's affairs were sound. The evidence, if you could call it that, was shaky at best. At least, that's what I told myself once I understood Helene was to be my bride." He gave a self-conscious laugh and reached for his wine.

"I still remember Sir Everard welcoming me into this very room and reassuring me that even if Aubrey was indulging in such reckless and foolish schemes (which he very much doubted), these would not only cease forthwith, but Aubrey would be dispatched to the colonies after my marriage, so any rumors surrounding these baseless accusations could die off. There was no need for me to take these nasty rumors further, was there? Helene awaited. If that wasn't enough to tempt me, he added that I would become the son he'd always wanted . . . someone to share in not only the Blithman wealth but in expanding it." Matthew knocked back the last of his wine and, without asking, poured himself more.

"In marrying Helene, I sold my soul."

It was a while before Matthew spoke again. "Our marriage was not what I hoped. Helene would oft take to her bed for days, pleading megrims, weeping for hours, but refusing to reveal the source of her grief, which I came to assume was me. Everything became worse after Aubrey, just as his father promised, departed for the New World.

"At first I was annoyed, believing I'd married someone who would use the misery of tempests and dazzle of sunshine to force her way. It wasn't until she shared the news of a child that I understood the source of her ambivalence, and God knows, I reveled in the notion of a babe. Though Helene sought to deny her family this joyous news, I could not. It was then Sir Everard tempted me once more: this time, with a chocolate house."

He couldn't help but smile when Rosamund gasped. "Yes. He wished us to be partners in the enterprise of chocolate. In order for this to happen, I had to learn what I could, source materials, find the right man to make the drink for us. That meant traveling. The last thing I wanted to do was leave Helene's side, but Sir Everard insisted.

"More than ever, I had to look to the future. I had a burgeoning family to support. Reluctantly, I traveled with Sir Everard to Spain. While there, we contracted the services of a fine chocolate maker before sailing on to Venice to make more purchases for the business."

Smoothing his hand over his mouth and chin, he thought about his next words. "Much to my gratification, on my return to England, I found my wife swollen like the globe I'd sailed: she was now, I told myself, my new world." He ran a finger around the rim of his glass. "I indulged her, loving her round form. Was it not our creation she carried? I introduced her to chocolate, purchased sweetmeats and other delicacies to spoil her."

He paused for a long moment. "I'd only been home a few weeks when news reached London that Aubrey had died. I was shocked. Helene was inconsolable. Aubrey's death was too much for her, having lost one brother already. Not even the knowledge that, with his death, the family's reputation as loyal subjects could be restored offered any consolation. Only the prospect of relocating to the place where Aubrey died gave her solace. She could not release the notion; would not. Night after night, she would whisper her longing to me. As if she'd already departed these shores, she turned completely from her mother and father, refused their efforts to comfort her. She would not tolerate their presence.

"It was as if with Aubrey's death, she renounced all those she could call family—myself included." He pulled a sour face.

"It wasn't long before the New World began to appeal more than the Old, especially if the Old meant megrims, wailing, sulks, vast silences, whispers of treachery and bribes, denial of intimacy. I felt like a sheep without a flock. Suddenly, London seemed as lonely as my wife claimed. I began to reconsider her proposition. The moment I did, her entire demeanor toward me changed.

"Over and over Helene made me promise that as soon as the child was born, we would leave and start a new life. As soon as I raised an obstacle, she would become hysterical. I was afraid for her health and that of my unborn child. Despite the promise of a chocolate house and my good relations with Sir Everard, in the end, I agreed. I felt I'd no choice. Helene was transformed. She began to make plans. Afeared her father would foil them, she begged me not to breathe a word; it was to be our secret, our adventure. Seeing the changes in her, in her affection toward me, my misgivings fled and I abided by her demands."

He lowered his head, shaking it slowly. His throat grew tight. Clearing it, he raised his chin.

"According to the midwife, the baby was early. When he was three weeks old he was taken to the parish church for christening and then, finally, to Blithe Manor. Poor Lady Margery had been unwell and unable to leave her rooms. It was only after I threatened to reveal our intentions that Helene agreed to bring little Everard to her.

"When Lady Margery took the babe in her arms and pulled aside his swaddling, there was a fraught whispered exchange. Helene's face hardened while her mother's melted into tears. The way Helene was regarding her mother and, in turn, the manner in which Lady Margery was staring at her, I was uncertain what exactly transpired. Before I could interrupt, Helene whipped the child out of her mother's arms and left the room without another word. I was dumbfounded. Apologizing to Lady Margery, explaining Helene was too soon out of childbed, I bade her farewell and swiftly followed my wife.

"She was with her father in the corridor. Helene was greatly distressed. Everard offered to arrange for us to be taken home. Helene almost spat at him and said something which struck me as most peculiar. She said: "You of all people, Father, should know I have no home. You made certain of that."

"Sir Everard stared at her with what I can only describe as loving revulsion. At a signal from him, I led her away. I began to believe Helene was right; there was nothing for us here anymore.

"That very night, we boarded a Blithman ship and, when the tide turned, we were sailing for the colonies."

Matthew stood and began to pace. He stopped by the hearth and picked up the poker. As he prodded the coals, sparks rained upon his boots.

Replacing the poker carefully, he continued. "Once we reached the Slave Coast, we took on something I should have anticipated—human cargo." He looked toward Jacopo. "Slaves."

Rosamund's lips thinned as her eyes also sought Jacopo's.

"There were over five hundred of the poor souls, chained and crammed into the hold. If . . . if I'd known . . . but I was unable to alter the route let alone the spoils of the voyage. The ship was not mine to command." He sighed and rubbed his temples.

Rosamund opened her mouth to speak but stopped. Matthew merely nodded, grateful for her silence, her lack of judgment. With a slight nod, Jacopo urged him to continue.

"While on the Slave Coast, we also received our first news from England. Turns out, the very night we snuck away on board the ship, Lady Margery passed into the Lord's arms."

"No!" Rosamund exclaimed.

Taking her shock as a cue, Matthew resumed his seat, all without glancing once at Helene's portrait. "Yes. Although she had been bedridden when we saw her, her death was unexpected. I chose then and there not to tell Helene—at least, not yet. She'd borne enough. I didn't want to add guilt to what I believed would yet become a heavier burden." He gave a cynical twist of his lips. "As it was, I never had a chance.

"There was a mutiny. Erupting from the hold, the slaves sought their freedom. I didn't blame them. Scared for Helene and the baby's safety, I did the only thing I could think of—I put them aboard a sturdy rowboat attached to the ship and lowered it into the water. The seas were high, but it was less dangerous than being among the murderers and cutthroats on deck—and by that I do not only mean the slaves. The crew were fearsome and bloodthirsty. Cruel. They didn't much care who they stabbed or disemboweled. Who they ran through with a sword or tossed overboard." He paused to drink. Rosamund didn't move.

"It didn't take long for the rebellion to be quelled. The fires that had been started were doused; the ringleaders were dispatched, their bodies thrown over the sides, their followers tamed with more lashes.

"It was dark by the time it was safe for Helene and baby to return to the ship. The seas were quieter now, and I sought the help of one of the crew to haul the tiny vessel back in. When we did, it was to find the rope had been cut—tellingly, at the boat end."

"Matthew . . ." Rosamund began to reach for him, but then withdrew her arm.

Matthew met her eyes. "There's no doubt in my mind, Helene severed it. Even so, I shouted until I was hoarse. Along with the crew, I threw torches into the ocean. But the seas were empty, the arcs of brief light revealed nothing but the bodies of the slaves. Only the swell of the waves, the peaceful growl of the ocean and the plash of water against the hull answered my cries.

"I don't remember when I returned to the cabin; I was exhausted and in such a state of despair. But there was one more surprise awaiting me: a small fire had been started in the cabin—upon a table against the wall, but it hadn't quite taken. In its center were dozens and dozens of letters. At first, I ignored them and sat by the small window and waited for the sun to rise, breathing in lungfuls of fresh air, allowing the stench of smoke and charcoaled paper to disperse. I could barely think, let alone move. Grief was an anchor that weighed me down. I barely recall the hours passing, only that they did. As soon as dawn splintered the horizon, I returned to the deck and scanned the ocean. After a few hours, the boat was found—adrift and empty. There was no sign of life. It was as if Helene and the baby had vanished.

"I fell into what I can only describe as a paroxysm of guilt and despair. I blamed myself. If only I'd hardened myself against Helene's entreaties, never agreed to leave England, if only I'd turned to Sir Everard for help, if only I'd sought the services of a physician. If only, if only . . ." He hesitated. "Instead, I sought the comfort of the bottle. Locked in the tiny cabin, I refused any company except the misery of my own thoughts. I didn't shed a tear, but drank myself into blessed oblivion, Helene's dresses draped across my lap, the babe's blankets over my heart.

"Lost in a fug of wine, brandy and whatever rotgut the captain left outside my cabin, it wasn't until the ship drew close to land that I remembered the letters.

"Barely able to gather my thoughts, let alone consider what they might mean, I nonetheless read them. Only a couple were burned beyond saving. The rest were perfectly legible. I hoped they would allow me to understand this mercurial, difficult woman I'd briefly loved."

He'd promised Rosamund the truth; what he didn't expect was that it would surprise him. Over the years, he'd tried to convince himself he hadn't loved Helene, that it had been an infatuation. Perhaps that's all it had been. Perhaps what he'd loved was the idea of her . . .

Rosamund was staring at her lap. He willed her to look at him again.

"You know what was contained in those missives?"

At his question, Rosamund lifted her enormous brown eyes to him, impossible to read in the flickering light.

He took a deep breath. "They were filled with declarations of undying love for Helene. They were not mine, you understand, but her lover's."

Rosamund's mouth formed a perfect O.

"Dating back to long before I ever entered Helene's life, they also revealed something I'd begun to suspect." He paused. "You see, the baby, the little boy Helene had named Everard, was not mine."

Rosamund released a small cry, her fingers to her mouth.

"I always wondered why you referred to him as the 'babe' . . ."

"Now you know." He frowned. "Just when I thought I could not be cut any deeper, feel more like a cuck-old and a fool, I learned that Sir Everard had known. Worse, he had conspired with both Helene and Aubrey to find her a husband so the child would not be born a bastard and her reputation and the Blithman name would not suffer." He shrugged helplessly.

"Here I was thinking I was being clever confessing to Sir Everard that Aubrey might be in serious trouble, that his business dealings were believed to be treason-ous, when I was the one being outplayed all along. In revealing my heart, I became the perfect candidate. Gulled on two counts, they used the promise of Helene to secure my loyalty and silence and to give the child legitimacy."

This time he laughed. It was long and bitter. "Ulti-mately it wasn't about me saving the Blithman name, but the Blithmans tarnishing that of Lovelace."

"What did you do?" asked Rosamund quietly.

"Do?" He leaned forward, his forearms resting on the desk. "Once I understood the content of the letters, I relit the fire Helene had started and tossed the pages one by one into the flames before, in a fit of fury, I threw in the whole damn lot. As they began to burn, I realized my error. I sought to extinguish the flames. Problem was, I'd drunk all the wine the captain had left, my jordan was empty and fetching water would take too long. I'd no choice. I reached into the flames with my bare hands—not once, but over and over. I rescued the only proof I had of Helene's infidelity and Sir Everard's and Aubrey's complicity in a plot to deceive me.

"Did I mention I was drunk? Yes, well. In saving the letters, I ruined my hands." He held them aloft, the kid gloves taking on a suddenly sinister meaning.

Before Rosamund could form a question, he continued. "I left the ship on the James River in Virginia. I carried wounds both physical and much, much deeper. They didn't prevent me writing at once to Sir Everard and telling him about Helene and the baby—I owed him that. But I also told him what I'd gleaned from the letters. I said I needed time to recover, to explore any opportunities the colonies offered. In time, I would return to London and, as originally intended, resume my stake in the chocolate house, which I trusted Sir Everard to keep for me.

"What did my . . . Sir Everard reply?"

"He didn't. At least, not in words. No, what he did was to seek to destroy me—the one man who knew the truth about his daughter and what her family had done."

"What do you mean?"

Matthew threw himself back in the chair. "This. Late one night outside a tavern in Jamestown, I was beaten to within an inch of my life and warned that if I ever revealed what I knew about the Blithmans, I would be killed. You do not look surprised, my lady."

Rosamund shrugged. "I wish I were . . ."

Matthew replenished his drink and Rosamund's. "It was only the letters and the fact I'd sent them to my lawyer in England, Mr. Isaac Roberts, for safekeeping that guaranteed my life. Not that this stopped Sir Everard trying to ruin me in other ways. Mysteriously, I would find my negotiations with the colonists ended before they began, my reputation, fresh in these parts, sullied beyond measure; any loans I managed to secure were withdrawn without explanation. I was outwitted, outbid and continuously threatened. Any ideas I had about beginning again were cruelly quashed. My only chance to salvage something of my life lay in returning to my old one. I decided to come back to the last place I wanted to be: London. With a pen name, a new identity and vengeance raging in my heart."

TWENTY-SIX
In which a widow
is propositioned

"And so," said Matthew, "before I left Jamestown, I wrote to Blithman, outlining a series of demands. If he would not allow me to enjoy my share of the chocolate house honestly, then I would come to it by other means. This time, I would deprive him of his share—I would have it *all* in my possession." He swirled the ruby liquid in his glass, watching as it caught the light, making eddies of carmine and gold. He rested his head on the back of the chair and stared at the ceiling. "I'm not proud of what I did." He lowered his chin and regarded Rosamund solemnly. "I hope you believe me when I say that. I had no other recourse."

Rosamund did believe him in regard to Sir Everard. After all, was he not talking about the same man who would have happily seen his wife charged with murder? It was time she faced that truth as well. Dear God. By simply surviving the attempt to kill him, Matthew Lovelace acquitted her of any crime. In a peculiar sense, she owed him. Shocked and sickened by what he'd revealed, she also felt a profound sorrow. How people could behave in such a way confounded her; to practice treason, deceit, lies, as if they were some art form to be mastered. *We are on earth by God's good grace for such a brief time; surely it is better to work together than against one another? Help one another, rather than to seek to fool, bribe and blackmail?*

Her eyes drifted to the portrait of her husband and the one of his daughter. Helene's misery suddenly took on an altogether different and sinister meaning.

And what of Sir Everard? What he did in gulling Mr. Lovelace was wrong; the manner in which he ensured her complicity was wicked, but wasn't he doing it because he loved his daughter? His son? Wasn't he doing it to protect his family? Maybe there was no other choice for him either.

But there had been . . . He didn't have to involve her. He could have encouraged Helene's lover to marry her. He could have stopped his son.

And what of Matthew? Was he really as innocent as he claimed? By his own admission he had turned a blind eye to suspected treason for personal gain. Had he really felt such passion for Helene that he would first burn then rescue the missives she had kept? Or was that a fabrication designed to arouse sympathy? Her eyes went to Matthew's gloved hands.

Without warning, he pulled off first one glove then the other. He held both hands up, turning them about.

Rosamund stared in horror. This was no fiction. The flesh was unnaturally pink, twisted, burned into knots and runnels, taut across his palms.

He flexed his fingers slowly. "It has taken me years to be able to do that. I thought my foolish impulse would mean I could never hold a sword again, much less a quill. Fortunately, I was wrong."

Before she could pass comment, he replaced the gloves.

"I'm . . . I'm so sorry," said Rosamund softly.

"So am I. I was a gudgeon to thrust my hands into flames and not expect consequences. Still, if I had not . . ."

Rosamund absorbed this. At least now she knew what the "other matters" were that distracted him from writing on the issues that meant so much to him.

"Why didn't Sir Everard force the rogue at the center of all this to marry Helene?"

Matthew Lovelace stared at his gloved hands. "Because he could not. The church would not have permitted such a union."

"He was a Papist?"

Matthew Lovelace took a moment to answer. "There was another impediment."

"Oh . . ." She wondered quickly if the man was low-born but couldn't imagine Helene mixing in such company in the first place. Then it dawned on her. "Was he already married?"

"Promised, aye," said Matthew Lovelace.

Rosamund sat back and silently twirled the stem of her glass, thinking.

"Thank you, madam," said Matthew Lovelace eventually. "The story is not easy to tell."

"It's not easy to hear, either."

Matthew grimaced. "I feared it would not be, but in light of what I wish to ask you, I thought it important you know the truth. I remember you telling me how important it was to you. If you knew then how much that disturbed me . . ."

She almost burst out laughing. Truth? What was that? Did she even know anymore? Sir Everard had chosen to believe that Matthew Lovelace killed his daughter and grandchild and allowed others, like her, to believe the same. For a time, it had been her truth.

While Matthew Lovelace had indeed placed his wife and child in the boat, if what he said was true, he wasn't responsible for what happened afterward. The rope had been cut. Could Helene really have done that and consigned herself and her child to a watery doom? Or was she trying desperately to reach somewhere? Someone? The narrow-eyed visage that gazed from the frame suggested anything was possible.

As for Aubrey, well, Sir Everard had omitted any mention of his perfidy, preferring to maintain a fabrication. Perhaps that was the only way he could deal with the truth.

But wasn't it also true that Matthew Lovelace had resorted to blackmail to get his own way? What sort of man did that?

"What do you intend to do with the letters now?" she asked.

Matthew sat on the edge of his seat. "I have thought long and hard about this. You see, while I wanted nothing more than revenge on Sir Everard for what he did, I understand he too sought vengeance for what he perceived as hurts *I* inflicted. What both of us failed to understand was that first Aubrey, then Helene, duped us both. They kept secrets from me *and* their father, used us both to pursue their own ends. If only we'd all been more honest with one another . . ."

"Would you have married her knowing she carried another man's child?"

Matthew Lovelace gave a huff of air. "I've asked myself the same question. Truth is, most likely. There was a time I would have done anything for that woman."

A peculiar ache throbbed beneath Rosamund's breasts; the air grew thick.

"I thought I wanted vengeance," said Matthew quietly. "I thought the chocolate house would serve as compensation for what he"—he jerked his chin toward the painting of Everard—"and his daughter had put me through. If he would just cede his half to me, all would be right. It was never my intention that Sir Everard would die—yet his death has made me see how empty my goal has been. How futile. All I wanted, or thought I wanted, was for him to pay for what he did to me. Literally. I wanted something in return for what I had lost—not Helene or the babe so much"—he gave a sour laugh—"they were never mine. But the trust I held them in, the faith I had in others. *My* reputation. That has all but gone. The Blithmans have ruined it. Had ruined it," he added softly.

Rosamund was about to protest that reputations were not for others to make or break, but oneself, but stopped herself. Now was not the time.

"I wanted to make the chocolate house a viable concern on my own. He would have hated that; being forced to surrender his portion, being outwitted in business. It would have hurt his pride. Only, he never intended to surrender it, did he? He sought to have me killed."

Rosamund couldn't meet his eyes. "I'm so sorry. I had no idea——"

"Oh, you owe me no apologies, Lady Rosamund. I know you were ignorant of the role he intended you to play." His eyes narrowed as he considered the portrait. "I never realized the extent to which he'd go to silence me and ensure his name was protected. I'm not referring to trying to dispatch me. On that count, he tried and failed a few times." He chuckled. "I'm not easy to be rid of—am I, old man?"

That he could say such things without so much as blinking astonished Rosamund, especially when her innards turned to ice at the very notion.

"My greatest regret is that he embroiled you in his schemes, my lady. Schemes that, had they borne fruit, would have seen you irreparably damaged." He leaned forward. "I knew him to be capable of much that was treacherous, but to find and marry you, to allow you to learn to make chocolate, to frequent the chocolate house, to dress you in his former wife's clothes and then Helene's wedding gown—"

"Not just the wedding gown," interrupted Rosamund. "There were other dresses he had made for me that were the same as Helene's. I asked Bianca, and Mrs. Wells confirmed it." She hesitated. Sickened by the knowledge her husband had planned to dress her like his dead daughter, she'd also tried to make sense of it. With Matthew's revelations, she felt she finally could. "I think his intention was to relive his victory over you every time he set eyes on me."

It was a moment before Matthew spoke, and then it was a whisper. "Before you embark on a journey of revenge, dig two graves." In response to Rosamund's quizzical look, he shrugged. "A saying I once heard." He studied his hands briefly. "You know," he continued, "it wasn't until I saw you in Helene's wedding dress that I understood just how far he was prepared to go to take revenge. When young Robin died, drinking what was evidently meant for me and which you were to serve, well, Sir Everard exceeded even my low opinion."

And mine, thought Rosamund bitterly. "I don't know how to express . . ." she began.

"My dear lady, I cannot repeat it enough. None of this is your fault. Blame lies firmly at Sir Everard's feet and, I'm ashamed to say, mine." He bowed his head. "I drove him to such measures."

"Maybe. But it was his choice to enact them."

They sat quietly. The fire glowed; the candles sputtered. Jacopo stood unmoving in the corner, his eyes drifting from her to Matthew Lovelace. She was beginning to understand why Jacopo and Bianca had kept his identity a secret from her. It wasn't only that Sir Everard had ordered them to, they did it to protect Matthew Lovelace; the man inspired devotion.

"And now that you have the chocolate house?" asked Rosamund finally.

He began to laugh. It was not a pretty sound. "It too is an empty victory—not because I don't want it anymore. On the contrary, I feel I owe it to myself to make it work. If I don't, all has been for nothing." He sighed. "I really believe it could be a fine business. Currently, because of what happened and the rumors attending it, it's been emptied of custom." He waved a hand. "'Tis but a temporary thing."

It pained her to hear that. She imagined Filip, Solomon, Thomas, Widow Ashe and the others sitting in the steamy kitchen, inhaling the rich aromas and having no one to serve. The anticipation which drove their early endeavors buried with Robin and Sir Everard.

"Aye," she agreed. "I think it would not take much to have the men return. For the few short hours I was there after it opened, the chocolate was much esteemed, the building, the entire enterprise. All it needs is a tweak here and there."

There was a long roll of thunder followed by a flash of lightning. The threatened rain began to fall, lazily at first, then loudly drumming against the window. Matthew Lovelace tilted the decanter over his glass. A mere few drops remained. Jacopo excused himself and left to get more wine. Rosamund sent a silent thanks after him.

"The other reason I desired to see you, my lady," said Matthew Lovelace, leaning forward over the desk lest the open door allow his voice to carry, "is because of the chocolate house."

Rosamund's chest contracted. "Oh?"

"I want to beg a boon of you."

"Of me?"

"Yes."

"A Blithman?"

"Like me, you're only part of that family through marriage." For some reason, Rosamund felt relief.

"True."

"But what you also became through marriage, and

how Sir Everard chose to identify you, was not just as his wife, but as the chocolate maker's wife."

Rosamund's burgeoning smile faded. Her attachment to that title was unnatural for such a short acquaintance, yet she'd cherished it. She hadn't known how much until she heard it again.

"Alas," she said, "that role was as false as the stories Sir Everard fed me. It was never mine to fulfill. It was the part Helene should have played—as your wife in the New World."

Matthew Lovelace shook his head. "Helene would never have been a chocolate maker's wife. Something I discovered too late. Anyway, she was too proud to ever don an apron."

Heat flew to Rosamund's cheeks. Matthew shook himself. "Oh, my lady, I speak recklessly. Forgive me, I didn't mean to imply that you lack pride or shouldn't feel it in such an establishment."

Unable to allow him to continue, Rosamund began to laugh. The sound was as cheerful as it was unexpected. "Cease, sir, cease. I do indeed have pride, but, unlike your former lady wife, it's provoked by being at the chocolate house."

"Ah, that is what I hoped you would say," he said, and relaxed once more. "You see, as I mentioned earlier, I have a proposal to put to you." His eyes sparkled with hidden depths and the beginning of a smile tugged his lips as he rested his hands on the edge of the desk. "How would you feel about becoming the chocolate maker's wife once again?"

For the second time that evening, Rosamund wondered if the man was going to offer marriage. "You jest, sir."

"No. I do not. I am quite serious. You see, while I was furious at you for what you said to me the last time we met in the bookshop—I understood I was only roused to anger because what you said was accurate."

Rosamund's cheeks began to suffuse with color. "I was most presumptuous . . ."

"No, madam, you were not—well, perhaps a little." He flashed a smile. "In fact, you have given me good cause to reconsider my work—indeed, my life. I'm pleased to say that I've made the decision to write about exactly the kinds of things I should have been writing about all along, but lacked . . . not courage, but the motivation to do so."

"You don't any longer?"

Matthew's eyes crinkled. "Being reminded by a beautiful woman that one's work should be honorable and not the work of a poltroon is marvelous motivation."

Rosamund lowered her eyes.

"In order to do this, to spend time seeking out injustice and writing under my own name in a manner that pleases the authorities and anonymously in a manner that does not, I need time and space. I cannot run the chocolate house and devote the attention required to my other employers at the same time—both suffer. The chocolate house needs someone who can dedicate themselves to the business in order to make it work. Furthermore, having spent some time in it these last weeks, I understand how ignorant I am. According to Filip and Thomas, I lack your zeal." He smiled. "I believe in the chocolate. I believe in Filip de la Faya and, Lady Rosamund, he believes in you."

"Filip?"

Jacopo chose that moment to return with a brimming decanter. On his heels was Bianca, carrying a tray with soft cheeses, some fruit, cold pigeon and a manchet, which she set down on the desk, casting an expectant look in Rosamund's direction.

"Mr. Lovelace, I believe you know Bianca."

Rising to his feet, Matthew Lovelace bowed. Rosamund could not help but be impressed, not merely by his manners but that he offered such courtesy to a servant.

"I have had the pleasure. Signorina Bianca," he said, "it is good to see you again. Properly."

Curtseying, Bianca bestowed one of her rare smiles. "Signor Lovelace. It is good to see you too. It has been a while."

"Too long, Bianca. Too long." Releasing her hand, Matthew sat back down.

"Sit, Bianca, Jacopo," said Rosamund. "But not before you've refreshed all our glasses." She found another for Bianca. "Whatever you have to say to me, Mr. Lovelace, can be said before these two."

Once Jacopo and Bianca were seated and had drinks, Matthew continued. "Filip tells me you are extraordinarily gifted when it comes to the chocolate. That somehow you infuse it with a quality that makes it taste like no one else's. Having had the privilege of drinking what you made while I was Nobody, I can only agree."

"He is too kind." Rosamund felt warm. "As are you."

"He speaks the truth," said Jacopo. "If I may, sir?"

Matthew waved a hand in permission.

"The *signora* is what they call in Spain an *aficionado*—she is someone with both passion and ability. Rare in a person, let alone a woman, but Filip, who has worked with *chocolata* his entire life, says he has never seen the like."

"Filip is the expert, not me," said Rosamund, shaking her head.

"Ah, he didn't say you were an expert, *signora*, but an *aficionado*—they are different. An *aficionado* is a devotee, someone with a natural gift for understanding and sharing the essence of something. Through the eyes of the *aficionado*, others come to appreciate and experience the joys and divine mysteries of a thing. An expert is someone with great knowledge, but who is not always able to persuade others to share it. Where one includes all who come in their compass, the other excludes. You, Lady Rosamund, are the former."

Rosamund didn't know what to say. Acutely embarrassed but also proud (she immediately asked her grandmother for forgiveness; Lady Ellinor could not tolerate pride), she gave what she hoped was a modest smile.

"It's true I do love the chocolate. And not the way one does a favorite dress or ribbon. But as a friend, a grandmother or, perhaps, a lover." She stared at Matthew in dismay—what had made her say *that*?

Matthew held up a hand, a grin transforming his face. "I understand. It is a true love, a love that acknowledges blemishes and foibles and seeks to make them part of the whole, not excise them as flaws."

"That is exactly what I meant."

They shared a slow smile.

Bianca and Jacopo tried hard not to look at each other.

"The *signora* has also dedicated weeks to experiments—with flavors and additives," said Bianca quickly, earning a wide-eyed look from Rosamund. Was this a conspiracy?

Matthew offered Bianca an encouraging smile. "Appreciating your unusual relationship with the chocolate and knowing how much the rooms benefited from your presence, as did the workers, I would ask, my lady, if you'd be prepared to manage the chocolate house. No." He held up his hand. " 'Manage' is the wrong word."

"Excuse me?" asked Rosamund, not daring to believe she'd heard him aright.

"I propose, my lady, that *you* take out a lease on the chocolate house from me. We can work out the period between ourselves."

"You would lease the business to a woman?"

Matthew Lovelace bit back a laugh. "Not any woman. I would lease to *you*. As I said, Filip tells me your understanding of chocolate and the English palate is unsurpassed. Jacopo tells me your business instincts are like a man's—"

"You would discuss me with my . . . ." She was about to say "servants," but stopped. Filip was no servant . . . . He was her mentor, her master. She looked at Jacopo. For all his failings as a teacher, she had learned from Jacopo too—things a slave had no business teaching their so-called betters. Likewise, Bianca. Things about resilience, loyalty, courage. Yet they'd kept secrets from her, albeit with good reason. "My friends," she finished.

"Friends?" He glanced over his shoulder at Jacopo then back at her. Both Bianca and Jacopo offered her shy smiles, Bianca going so far as to give a slight nod, as if in response to the question she'd not yet asked: *You may believe his word.*

"Yes, madam, I would—with Jacopo at least, I did. Forgive me, forgive *him.* He tells me I'd be an *idiota* not to let you continue to operate the chocolate house. Only if I do, it must be on *your* terms."

"My terms? I see. With you as my landlord."

"Yes." He flashed his teeth at her. Confound the man, but he had an infectious smile. "But I promise not to interfere . . . too much. I will continue to write—as I said—I will have to travel sometimes. In all but name, the chocolate house would be yours."

Men were such strange creatures. Did he make her such an offer out of pity for her widowhood or sentimentality that she reminded him of his late wife? Or was it guilt at his role in what had happened to Sir Everard and how narrowly she'd avoided being accused of a terrible crime? Surely now he'd explained everything to her, he owed the Blithmans nothing . . . on the contrary. Oh, perhaps that was it. He felt *she* owed *him*.

"But, sir, you know nothing of me or my capabilities . . ."

"Do I not? I know you do not take kindly to roaring boys and thugs. I know you to be brave, kind and curious, that you delight an old bookseller with your intelligence, that you give even street urchins and ragamuffins a chance. I know you to see good in those others refuse to, and to be accomplished with the chocolate. Why, even your late husband said an establishment like the chocolate house would do wonders with someone like you at the helm . . . remember?"

She did.

"You're also liked very well by those who would work with you—above all, you believe in the truth. And, my lady, you believe in me. At least, you did."

They stared at each other. Rosamund was the first to look away.

"Also," he added, "I like your laugh. Anyway"—he eased back into his chair—"it's my building, my decision."

"And if I say no?"

Matthew shrugged. "Then I will send Filip and Solomon back to Spain and lease the building to someone else."

"Send them back?"

"They've no desire to work with anyone else but you . . . and me."

Rosamund glanced toward Bianca and Jacopo—both were watching Matthew Lovelace closely. "But . . . but . . . this is tantamount to blackmail."

"In an excellent cause," he said. His eyes glinted, his mouth a work of mischief. "My Lady Harridan, I once told you I was a friend. For a while I feared you were the enemy—"

"I was," said Rosamund. "Or, at least, I believed I should be. I also believed you were mine. I was persuaded you were the devil made flesh."

Matthew nodded. "I would be your friend again, Lady Rosamund. I would, if it's at all possible, you be mine—without blackmail."

What an upset this was—a Blithman and Lovelace friends. Could she trust him? Filip seemed to, Jacopo and Bianca as well—and she trusted them. He clearly did as well, and that was important to her. Her eyes drifted toward Sir Everard's portrait. Rage emanated from the painting like an aura. She could imagine his reaction to the request, how he would use his stick, shout, level accusations and insults, demand justice. Only, his idea of justice was to beat people, to use poison—and have her unwittingly administer it. Perhaps *this* was justice? A unity of purpose in two people hurt by those closest to them.

For that was her truth, painful as it was to own: Sir Everard might have been her husband, but he was no friend.

Responding to Matthew Lovelace's tentative smile, she returned a warm one. "I am sorely in need of a friend, so thank you."

She'd believed that Sir Everard's death meant she'd have to forget about the chocolate house, become the grieving widow locked in this dark, drab house waiting until her husband's will was sorted out and she knew her real financial status. Sam had already made it clear that her best option was to wait until the mourning period was over and then search for another husband. Another? Why, she'd barely had her first. Then there were those who propositioned her repeatedly—for her hand, for sex. She had even wondered if she should go back to Gravesend. She'd written and told her mother and Frances what had happened. Frances had replied immediately. From her mother, she'd heard nothing. Returning didn't bear thinking about. But here was this man, this mysterious man who inspired such enmity and such devotion, who'd endured incredible heartache and narrowly avoided death, throwing her a lifeline. Offering her what Sir Everard had promised but never delivered—an opportunity. A real one. A proposition that involved neither marriage nor genteel whoredom.

Did she dare seize it? What would people say?

Sam would rail at her and tell her how much her reputation would suffer, how she would be viewed if she ran such an establishment without Sir Everard to protect her. Why, she'd be a pariah, constantly ogled and ill used in ways women of her station should never be.

What if she, already seen by some as a Jezebel of the highest order, accepted Matthew Lovelace's offer? An offer from the man once accused of murdering her husband's daughter and grandson?

"Can you imagine what people would say?" she asked.

"Oh, yes, my Lady Harridan, I can," said Matthew, his eyes gleaming diabolically. "Can you?"

"It can be no worse than what they already claim for me," said Rosamund with a shrug. Could she really dismiss those harsh words so readily? Aye, she must.

"And no worse than what they say of me."

She couldn't help it, she laughed. After a beat, he joined in. So did Jacopo, then Bianca.

As the laughter died and fresh drinks were poured, coal settled in the hearth, sending golden motes up the chimney and a large puff of smoke into the room, wreathing Matthew Lovelace in an opaque curtain. Aye, that was him in a nutshell, veiled in secrets and stories, dark smuts that would either stick or be cleaned away. In the semidarkness, he was more shadow than person, more darkness than light. The devil *was* incarnate, sitting opposite, making secret pacts with her, asking her to sign over her soul. Even so, he wasn't nearly as frightening as she'd believed. Truth be told, she trusted him just enough to perhaps say yes . . .

The rain beat a steady tattoo on the glass; the thunder now a distant purr, a large contented cat prowling over the land.

Before she could change her mind, allow the tiny warning voice tolling in her head to govern, Rosamund pushed back her chair and came around the desk. Matthew put down his glass and scrambled to his feet. Craning her neck to look up at him, she bobbed a curtsey. "I accept your proposition, Mr. Lovelace."

Bowing low, Matthew Lovelace took her hand in his gloved one. She remembered the first time he had held it, preventing her from beating Jed—or was it Ben?

"Thank you, Lady Rosamund." He squeezed her hand then reluctantly let it go. "I'll have Mr. Roberts draw up an agreement and send it over for you and Mr. Bender to consider tomorrow." He swept off his hat again, taking in the surrounds. The clang of church bells could just be heard above the rain, long, sonorous peals that marked the midnight hour. "Is that the time? Forgive me for keeping you from your rest, my lady. My business here is concluded." He returned his hat to his head. The feather made him appear quite rakish. "I'll bid you good evening, my lady, Jacopo, Bianca. And thank you—from the bottom of my black, cold heart. Thank you."

Despite all he'd suffered, Rosamund could not conceive of his heart being either black or cold. "Good evening, Mr. Ness— Lovelace," she swiftly corrected. "And, I never thought I'd be saying this, but thank *you*." A thrill like mercury sped through her veins. As he reached the door, she added, "You won't be sorry."

He glanced over his shoulder. "My only hope is that you are not." With a brief nod and smile, he left.

Aye, well. That was her hope too.

Jacopo gave her the broadest of grins and, closing the door, followed him. Their voices were low and deep in the corridor.

Rosamund sank into the seat Matthew Lovelace had just vacated. The chair was still warm. Sliding her hands over the armrests, she stared at the fire, ignoring the accusing eyes in the portrait above it.

"What have I done?" she whispered.

"What you must do," said Bianca, placing a hand over hers. "Put the past behind you—yours and the master's—and go on as the chocolate maker's wife. Though, truly, you will be the chocolate maker's widow."

Capturing Bianca's fingers, Rosamund raised their intertwined hands, bronze and cream. She glanced up at Sir Everard's portrait. "*His* widow . . . That must be why a small part of me feels as if I've just made a deal with the devil . . ."

TWENTY-SEVEN
In which a Navy clerk contemplates the passage of time

For all Sam Pepys had doubted Rosamund's sanity when she agreed to lease the chocolate house nearly two years ago from that scoundrel Matthew Lovelace—who, if he hadn't killed Sir Everard, had certainly contributed to the man's sudden death—after some months, he had to admit the wench was doing an admirable job.

In the early days after its reopening, there were those who avoided the Phoenix, as it was eventually renamed, either because the Angel of Death had swung his scythe through the rooms or they couldn't stomach the notion of a woman in charge. But when Christopher Bowman, the owner of the Turk's Head in St. Michael's Alley, died and his wife, Mrs. Bowman, took over its running, the regular patrons there remained loyal, which made those more inclined toward the chocolate house relax their stubbornness. It didn't hurt that Rosamund was a splendid sight to behold, unlike the homely Mrs. Bowman. Furthermore, she didn't assert herself in the manner of women inclined to intrude where females were not welcome—like Lady Barbara Castlemaine, they'd mutter wryly. Nor did it hurt that very soon after taking over the running of the place, Lady Rosamund saw to it that beverages other than chocolate were served and a variety of other pleasing distractions were made available.

The moment she signed the lease granting her twelve months (with the potential to extend it a further twelve) at a reasonable rate and allowing Lovelace thirty percent of the profits, Rosamund purchased ale from a local brewery. The brewer, Mr. Brogan, delighted to count a real lady among his customers, began telling all and sundry where his beer was now being served. Rosamund also asked Jacopo to ensure some of the coffee beans her husband's ships imported made their way to the Phoenix, along with a ready supply of canary, sack and a fine majorca. Coffee serving implements were bought and Filip trained Solomon and Widow Ashe in the making of it. Much of the process mimicked the preparation of chocolate, so it wasn't difficult to master.

It wasn't only the range of beverages Rosamund improved. Whereas on opening day the news sheets and books had been sadly out of date, they were now current. Rosamund ensured that L'Estrange's the *Intelligencer: Published for the Satisfaction of the People*, an eight-page news book, was readily available and, a few months later, the *Newes* as well. Now L'Estrange had been confirmed as surveyor of the presses, Muddiman had lost his license. Nevertheless, he continued to provide his handwritten news sheets, and Rosamund subscribed to these. Sam knew she also kept a supply of illegally printed news sheets and pamphlets (who didn't?), but made sure he never asked to see one lest a government spy be at his elbow. Talk at the Phoenix indicated that even if the men weren't reading the latest from Muddiman or those anonymous correspondents who dared to put their dissenting thoughts in print, other critics of the King and Council were making their opinions known. Debate was robust and oft times resulted in a gentleman storming out, or even, on two occasions that he'd witnessed, bowls of coffee and chocolate being upended on periwigs, much to the amusement of all and sundry.

Books were also available for reading, stacked in newly built shelves above the booths—another of Rosamund's innovations. Pamphlets about the latest quack medicines and horse sales were liberally distributed, including those advertising forthcoming plays in the King's and Duke's theaters, and lectures at Gresham College. One could stand at St. Paul's Cross in the cold and rain or the blasted heat of summer and listen to the criers delivering the latest information, or retreat to the comfort of the Phoenix, be served a fine beverage, gaze upon the Winsome Widow and read the very same. Those with time and money chose the latter option. Packs of cards and counters were there for those inclined to a hand of ruff and trump, gleek or piquet, and ticktack and chess boards were also available. Discounts were offered to any musicians who played while they drank, and when members of the Royal Society decided to regularly patronize a booth, they too were given a small discount, providing they welcomed strangers to the table to hear their latest findings. Candle auctions were held once a week with merchants from the Exchange, selling everything from ships to plots of land, wool, coal, tin, timber and hemp. The shouts of the men determined to secure their bids just as a candle expired made a deafening roar.

Less benevolent Londoners refused to believe anything good of a woman in business—especially a chocolate house. Claiming one could call that kind of place whatever they wanted, whether it be for the drink it served or the mythical bird that arose from the ashes, they knew what it was and, more importantly, what *she* was: once a trull, always a trull. Pretty dresses, a dimpled smile and a laugh that sounded like a chorus of angels didn't change facts. Everyone knew what chocolate facilitated (did they not enjoy a bowl or two daily?) and the effect it had on all who consumed it. Rumor said that was how the Lady Castlemaine kept the King panting after her, even though she'd borne him more children than a broodmare and lost much of her youthful appeal. Chocolate was an aphrodisiac—a Papist invention brought to English shores to corrupt the souls of good British Protestants. It might put sap in a man's hairy cullions, allow access to a woman's bowers of bliss, but it was devil's work all the same. As God Himself knew, that Lady Blithman let Sir Everard plow her. How else did she persuade him to marry her? Or that dashing correspondent, Lovelace, to hand over his newly acquired enterprise? While she called herself a businesswoman, they knew what she traded in—Cupid's warehouse: the heavenly cleft where men stored their seed.

One had only to look to Gravesend to know the truth of that. Forget those tales about her being related to the Tomkins. What was a member of a decent northern family doing at an inn, let alone with chocolate beneath her nails, smeared on her mouth, an apron over her admittedly silken dresses and parading about town with a pair of blackamoors by her side? Like they were equals! The woman had no class, just arse, and that's all there was to it.

Now Rosamund had been running the Phoenix for a couple of years, Sam had grown accustomed to seeing her at work and quite enjoyed the spectacle. Leaning back in a booth on this cold winter's day, he watched her standing behind the bar, her face a picture of sweet concentration as she mixed drinks for the patrons, her slender fingers hovering above a bowl here, agitating a chocolate pot there, moving around and beside that Spaniard, Señor Filip, as if they were dancing, and nodding as she listened to that rogue, the Duke of Buckingham, opining about his latest ailment. Sam noted the sympathy in her eyes was not forced, nor was the laughter that rang out when that impish Scot Robert Gilligan, with his dark eyes and voice like a gargling seal, leaned over and whispered something in her perfect ear.

Sipping his chocolate and marveling at the way it coated the roof of his mouth, a syrupy thickness that slid down his throat and made his loins stir, Sam studied Rosamund and couldn't help but reflect upon what had passed since he'd first met her.

Rosamund had altered greatly from the young woman he had encountered that memorable morning at Blithe Manor. Gone was the uncertain yet gentle deference, replaced by a confident modesty that greatly endeared her to all who came within her compass. Choosing discretion over flaunting her widowhood, she was rarely found outside the manor or the chocolate house. If women could attend the chocolate house, Sam thought, they would see that the only threat Rosamund posed was to men's dreams.

He sat up abruptly and shook his head. What was he thinking? Thank God and all the saints in heaven above the fairer sex were discouraged from entering. His eyes slid to the door to confirm it was so. The thought of anyone other than Rosamund and that doxy who worked in the kitchen sharing this space was *almost* enough to put him off his chocolate. The other one who used to work here had been delivered to Blithe Manor and given the role of housekeeper. When Rosamund had first told Sam what she proposed, to offer such a position to someone with no credentials other than loyalty, Sam nearly choked on his sack. Ignoring his entreaties, Rosamund did what she always did of late: exactly what she wanted. Installing Widow Ashe as housekeeper, she then elevated that Amazon tawneymoor, Bianca, to the role of companion. If running a business hadn't been enough to set tongues wagging, giving a slave such a position—as if she were a gentlewoman come by hard times and not a savage lucky to be living under the same roof—did the trick.

Draining his second bowl and smacking his lips in appreciation, Sam thought about calling over Harry for another. Good Lord, the lad had grown tall but not, sadly, another hand; though he appeared not to need one when he was so adept with that odd little stump of his. On second thought, he might sidle over to the bar and have Rosamund make him a drink while he waited. She was developing quite the reputation for soothing fractious spirits and helping with digestive problems, as well as other, less obvious maladies.

On third thought, given who had just monopolized her attention, maybe not.

Sir Henry Bennet had snuck in while Sam was distracted, his elbow resting on the wood of the bar, his entire body tilted toward Rosamund. The former Keeper of the Privy Purse, now Secretary of State and spymaster of the King, was like a raven all in black with that ridiculous plaster across the bridge of his nose. What kind of wound suppurated so long it required a fresh plaster each day? There were men who lost entire limbs during the Civil War and they didn't make a show of it. He was making Rosamund laugh, no doubt describing something to her in one of the five languages he spoke, gesturing with his elegant beringed hands. There was a time when Sam would have been jealous of the attention courtiers poured upon his cousin, and which she seemed to enjoy. Likewise, the flattery that idiot Charles Sedley, "Little Sid," bestowed, a man whose only claim to fame, apart from his wit, was strutting naked with Sir Thomas Ogle at the Cock Inn in Bow Street. Though any number of louche gentry had adopted the Phoenix as their own and would no doubt have taken Rosamund under more than their wings if she'd been willing, Sam found it no longer bothered him.

Well, perhaps a little.

Ipso facto, more than a little. Rosamund had not only resisted *his* attempts to get to know her better—oh, all right, seduce her—but had kept even her most ardent admirers (and there were many) at arm's length—including the King himself. That, decided Sam, deserved admiration, not disapprobation, at least from him. The day King Charles graced these rooms was, though she was reluctant to admit it, the making of Rosamund. It wasn't so much that Charles, dressed in what he thought were ordinary clothes (an outfit that Sam would have been proud to strut about in), had come to the Phoenix and was clearly smitten with Rosamund that surprised people, it was that Lady Castlemaine arrived not long after him. Seeing the King astride a stool before the bar, his deep hooded eyes fixed upon Rosamund as she mixed a drink for him, she'd let out a yowl akin to a breeding cat. Ignoring the looks of shock and disapproval around her, she strode through the room and shot Rosamund a venomous stare, upended the prepared bowl of chocolate upon the bar and took the King's arm.

"Do you not know this place, this Lucrezia, has a reputation that would make a Borgia blush?"

The King had barely formed a protest before she dragged him away, unaware His Majesty bestowed a weary smile and a cheeky wink upon Rosamund as she did.

No, it wasn't the King's patronage that shored up Rosamund's reputation, but Barbara Castlemaine's furious displeasure.

Not that this prevented the King from returning, albeit in his usual disguise as a regular gentleman about town, answering only to "Old Rowley." It always amused Sam that His Majesty thought by donning a dun-colored jacket and some worsted linen and pulling a cap low over his head, he was unrecognizable. He was well over six feet, a giant among men. Possessed of the swarthiest of complexions and lugubrious eyes, he turned heads no matter where he went—taking his morning stroll in the park, enjoying the horse races, or boating on the Thames. What was a chocolate house a few miles from Whitehall to him? Especially when it housed such forbidden fruit. Anyone who knew the King knew that was his favorite kind, and if the Lady Barbara had her wits about her, she would have urged him to attend to Rosamund rather than disallowing him. So, Old Rowley returned to the chocolate house occasionally to flirt with Rosamund, and even tried to bestow gifts upon her. All were exquisitely rejected. It didn't matter that he wore a crown—she refused all who sought her favors.

The only exception was Matthew Lovelace. Whatever that man had done to earn Rosamund's trust confounded Sam, but it seemed he had, and she in turn had earned his. So much so that the man oft gallivanted around the globe—ostensibly to uncover stories for L'Estrange or Muddiman, though Sam suspected there was more to it than that, especially if the occasional shared drink and unhurried conversation he had with Bennet alone in one of the booths was anything to go by. Curious as to Lovelace's whereabouts and wanting to confirm his suspicions, Sam had taken to reading every news sheet, searching for his byline to provide a clue.

No longer Nessuno, the name he had adopted to conceal his whereabouts (unsuccessfully, as it turned out) from Sir Everard, Lovelace now wrote for the official news sheets under his own moniker. Sam was unsure that was wise, as he'd dramatically altered the tone and style of his pieces and walked a fine line between comment and dissent. He needed to watch his back lest he draw down the wrath of the authorities.

At least with Lovelace absent, Sam could enjoy Rosamund without him overseeing their interactions. No longer wishing to bed her (quite so often) didn't mean he couldn't appreciate Rosamund. And he did. Almost daily. She was like a habit he didn't want to break.

He let out a great sigh, spinning the bowl on the table with a finger, watching the particles clinging to the sides. Sam had to acknowledge the man knew what he was doing when he asked Rosamund to manage the place.

The Phoenix was the place to go both to learn the news and to forget for a time the war against the Dutch and the plague said to be tearing through Belgium, Holland and Germany—topics that preoccupied those sitting in the booth beside him. Agog at the comet seen in northern skies a few days ago, the men were prognosticating about its significance. Sam heard references to famine, floods (no, he wanted to tell them, they occurred last year when all Whitehall was drowned), plague and fire. Next they'd be declaring the four horsemen had been spied on Fish Street. Sam had wondered about the comet himself, seeing it arc across the skies, a flash of silver that made him think of sylvan sprites. For all its majestic beauty there was no doubt it augured something terrible—every comet did. What was it to be this time? They were already at war and foiling Papist plots everywhere. There was that cluster of odd deaths in Yarmouth to consider as well—sailors, or at the least, travelers who sickened and died the moment they set foot on English soil. Covered in strange boils and spots, they had died swiftly.

A voice rose from the neighboring booth. "What does a comet portend if not doom?"

Sam repressed a shudder and pushed such bleak thoughts aside, focusing again on his cousin. Bennet sat back and took a deep swallow of warm, velvety goodness, his eyes screwing up tight, his tongue capturing residue from his rather sensual mouth. Rosamund smiled at him. She had a knack of appearing to concentrate solely on whomever she was serving, as if they and they alone eclipsed all others. She also had a damn fine memory, able to recollect insignificant details about her customers and to ask about them the next time she saw them.

Sam trotted to the bar and, acknowledging Bennet briefly, leaned over the counter to farewell Rosamund, who was holding her own court. He made sure to plant a wet kiss upon her pillow lips—the privilege of cousinage—and was gratified to earn the envious glances of all who loitered nearby.

Tugging his forelock to the Duke of Buckingham and the gentlemen forecasting the future, Sam left the chocolate house with a spring in his step. Life continued, comets and dire predictions aside. Christmas was almost upon them and then a new year: 1665. What would it bring? As he entered Birchin Lane, shivering in the sudden cold, he prayed fervently it was Rosamund to his bed.

Hope, like his prick, sprang eternal.

TWENTY-EIGHT
In which restoration
and anticipation rule

Rosamund folded Matthew's letter carefully and laid it upon the table in her closet, then poured two bowls of chocolate—one for her and one for Bianca, who sat quietly reading. It never ceased to amaze her, God's good earth. Here was Matthew, on the other side of the ocean, and he'd also witnessed the blazing star that had left its majestic trail across the firmament for weeks, causing all who viewed it to gasp in fear and wonder.

To think, Matthew had been watching the very same celestial object and recording what he saw for her benefit (and no doubt, the *Newes*). A wave of contentment swept over her, followed by a rush of warmth that reddened her cheeks and filled her chest. She opened his letter again. It had been sent weeks ago from Boston. Not only did he write about the comet, but other words she hadn't known she'd long to read. She began to fizz with happiness, like that peculiar sherbet drink Constantine the Greek sold in Threadneedle Street.

She found it difficult to imagine Matthew writing the letter, what his surroundings were like, how he was feeling. Her heart ached for him, knowing he was both dreading what he had to do yet driven to accomplish the task he'd set himself.

When he first told her that he planned to cross the world and deliver the letters he'd once intended to give to Sir Everard, she thought him mad.

"Why?" she asked, as they sat in their regular booth in the chocolate house drinking wine after closing one evening. It had been a cold day, and only the warmth of the bubbling vats, combined with the crackling fire in the main room that Wolstan maintained, managed to hold it at bay. Nevertheless, when Matthew announced he was sailing to the New World, Rosamund found herself shivering. It was those damn letters he continued to carry in his satchel. The ones that ensured that even when he was smiling or laughing, a tiny mote of shadow encroached upon his joy.

Matthew took a deep breath, set down his glass and looked her in the eyes. The candle burning between them made his own into inky pools, his face an alien map of smooth planes and craggy peaks. Soft chatter from the kitchen reminded them they were not really alone—they never were, the workers as well as Bianca and Jacopo always aware of preserving her fragile reputation. She waited for him to speak, wanting to hold on to this instant, knowing that when it ended, so did the intimacy of their stolen moment. The past would once again intrude and disrupt all they'd managed to build.

"I have decided that I must try to find Helene's lover and deliver the letters to him."

Rosamund released a long sigh. A part of her had always known this moment would come.

"You *must*? Why? If the man ever cared about them, cared about Helene, surely he would have sought them out for himself? Sought you out? It is he who owes you, not the other way around. If he's done nothing about them, or you, then why do you feel you must?"

Matthew's lips curled. "It's not for him I do it, Rosamund . . ." He paused, refusing to meet her eyes. "But for myself."

The hands she'd allowed to creep toward his on the table retreated. Dear God, he still needed to confront the man who'd cuckolded him. Had Helene meant that much? She'd hoped that over the past year and a half she'd helped him forget; that the chocolate house and all they'd accomplished, his writings and the debates they'd stirred, the praise he'd drawn (even if many still didn't know who the author of the more controversial pieces was), had helped him to put that part of his life in perspective. As her grandmother always said, you cannot alter the past, only the present and thus the future.

She didn't realize she'd said the last part aloud until Matthew responded.

"That's exactly why I am doing it. I realize that if I don't release this burden, or at least make an effort to, then I, and perhaps even others, am forever bound to it—to a past that will not cease to intrude. I'm unable to move into the future while I carry these." He slapped the satchel which lay on the bench beside him. "Not only in there, but in my heart."

Rosamund shook her head. Sadness overtook her. It wasn't until she became aware of Matthew's intense gaze, his hands palm up on the table waiting to receive hers, that she dared raise her chin.

"You see, Rosamund," he said, his voice barely a whisper, "until I rid myself of what they signify, of the man that I was and who I became, confront the cur behind all this, then I fear there's no room for anything . . . or anyone . . . else."

Ever so slowly, Rosamund placed her hands in Matthew's gloved ones. He stared at them before wrapping his long fingers gently around them. His grip tightened. "For a time, he called the New World home. So it's there I must go if I'm to learn anything of his whereabouts, much as the very notion of leaving for such a stretch pains me."

Unable to tell him it pained her too, she simply held his hands.

How long they sat there, she was uncertain. All she knew was that when they left that night, she with Jacopo and Bianca for the manor, Matthew for his lodgings, he had, if not her blessing, then her understanding. It was all she could give.

That had been nearly five months ago. According to Matthew's latest letter, whether or not he was successful, he was briefly extending his travels, journeying from Boston to secure business interests and, if she'd understood what he implied correctly, to report on rumors of Dutch uprisings for Sir Henry Bennet, and then returning via Spain and Holland. Calculating the number of days since the letter had been sent and how long he'd estimated his travels would take, Rosamund tried to work out when she might see him again. It was already February . . . February! And a new year at that. Where had the time gone? Before they'd even inhaled the last of the frosts, it would be March and spring. Ah, spring. Her smile broadened.

Melting snows, budding vines, barren trees welcoming suits of green, renewal, rebirth and, God willing, Matthew's return.

His return. What a welcome notion. She was too afraid to imagine beyond that lest she destroy the hope just thinking about it gave her.

Now, all the major players in this sorry saga had left the stage: Aubrey, Helene, the baby, Sir Everard, his first wife. The only ones left were her, Matthew and the lover. She wondered who he was. Jacopo said he didn't know and she believed him. Bianca was unusually evasive on the subject and seeing how uncomfortable it made her, she let it be.

After all, it wouldn't change anything.

Never mind, she would try to elicit the information from Matthew when she saw him. If it even mattered by then.

"What does he say, Signora Rosamund?" asked Bianca softly, interrupting her reverie.

"Oh. Well." How did she explain that it wasn't what he said so much as the fact he'd written. His reasons for doing so might be as simple as feeling obligated since they were, essentially, tied together by the chocolate house. All she knew was that his letters were welcome. More than welcome. They meant a great deal and demonstrated he respected her enough to keep her abreast of his movements. Gifted, and with a keen eye and a poetic turn of phrase, he described everything from the wonder of sunrise over the still waters of the Atlantic to storm-tossed seas along the coast of Guinea, torn sails and dolphins frolicking. With every word, the world contracted for Rosamund and she saw it through his eyes, as she knew he intended. In writing about the comet, he knew she too would have seen its journey and marveled; it was a wonder that bridged the immense distance between them.

"He describes the comet." Rosamund glanced toward the window as if it might manifest right there and then. "Imagine, Bianca, even though he is so far away, he saw it too. He writes that the Earl of Sandwich has kept a most detailed account of its passage for His Majesty. No doubt L'Estrange will publish parts of it. We should try to read that if we can." She imagined discussing it with Matthew and her heart quickened.

"And when he has completed his task, how do you feel about his return?"

Not much escaped Bianca, thought Rosamund. "Feel?" She gave a brittle laugh. "Why, relief the man will finally be here to help me with the chocolate house."

Bianca stared at her a tad longer than was necessary. "What? What am I supposed to feel?"

"It's not for me to say, *signora*, only I cannot imagine why you would want him to help when you've done so well on your own and it gives you so much contentment. He's been glad to let you manage the place whether he was in London or not. Unless, of course, the real reason is so you may dedicate your time as Signor Pepys thinks you should."

Rosamund pulled a face. "Finding another husband."

Bianca's eyes twinkled. "You are the weaker vessel, remember? And, what else is it Mr. Pepys warns? That having been 'framed to the conditions of a man' you must find it hard to forgo the marriage bed." Bianca wore an expression close to a smirk.

"Aye, well. Sam doesn't know what he's saying. My marriage to Sir Everard, as you know, was not . . . conventional. Anyhow, one has to look to find, does one not? I am not looking. Not for a husband."

"Because you've already found one?"

Rosamund spluttered, almost spraying chocolate back into her bowl. "You're very amusing tonight, Bianca."

"*Sì*. Always glad to be of service." Bianca returned to her reading.

Rosamund watched as her companion focused on Muddiman's latest private newsletter. Ever since Sir

Everard's death, she'd grown closer to Bianca than she thought possible—Jacopo too.

It had taken some time before they divulged their history to her, and then only parts. Evidently, speaking of it pained them, and while she was grateful for what she did learn, she would spare them. She gleaned that their mother was a slave, forced from her homeland and taken by ship to Venice, where she was bought by a cardinal. When he tired of her, he gave her to a house of ill repute. There, as a beautiful blackamoor, she was saved for only the richest clients. One of these insisted she be reserved for his pleasure, bestowing a comfortable amount upon her (and the bordello) to ensure his demands were met. When their mother fell pregnant, he moved her into her own quarters, and this altered her life significantly. She used the opportunity to educate herself and, subsequently, her children. Neither Bianca nor Jacopo mentioned the name of their father, only that, when their mother died, he kept his promise and ensured they were looked after.

Recalling the beating Jacopo had received at Sir Everard's hands, Rosamund wondered how their mother and this mysterious father would feel about their children being brought into the Blithman fold—or, more accurately, bought. Yet, for all that they were born slaves, Sir Everard had given them authority and treated them much like the other servants in his employ. Rosamund sensed no resentment regarding their station despite their evident learning, poise and decency. When she asked about this, Bianca simply replied, "We had a good life, in Venice; that is, compared to others in our situation—as the progeny of a black woman and a white man." Shadows flitted across her face, an array of painful memories, suggesting her "good life" was far from perfect. "Signor Blithman . . . well, it could have been so much worse." Their equanimity made her love them all the more and, when she thought about the events that brought them into her sphere, despair as well. She would do all in her power to shield them from further ill use.

Rosamund settled into the chair and took in what she now thought of as *her* surroundings, astonished, as she oft was, that such good fortune had fallen upon her and wondering for the umpteenth time what she'd done to deserve it.

Ever since she and Matthew had made their agreement, so much had happened—not merely at Blithe Manor and the Phoenix, but within her.

There had been a period of adjustment where she tried to grow accustomed to the fact Blithe Manor was, to all and intents and purposes, hers. At least until the will could be formally read and the contents made public. A jointure from the estate ensured her basic needs were met, and Mr. Bender released funds for everyday expenses. The only niggle of doubt she had about the process (never having been privy to the vagaries of wills before) was to do with the papers Jacopo had her sign that very first morning in Blithe Manor—the ones she'd been unable to read. It turned out she'd agreed to cede to the executor in all matters pertaining to the will and the arrangements therein. She also acknowledged Sir Everard's rightful heirs above her own claims. Puzzled by this, considering all his heirs were dead, she'd left the entire matter for Mr. Bender to sort out. When she happened to mention the circumstances of the will to Matthew, he'd become very quiet and then questioned her closely. Lacking any further details to give him, she'd promptly dismissed the matter from her mind.

Funny, she hadn't thought about that in ages. She'd no need. The servants were paid and Sir Everard's fleet continued to sail and trade. Notwithstanding port restrictions because of the Dutch War, or those blasted pirates that insisted on raiding ships, under Jacopo's experienced hand the Blithman business continued. This all allowed Rosamund to focus on the activities which, as Bianca reminded her, afforded her great pleasure and a sense of worth, something she was determined to impart to all those who helped her whenever possible.

After all, good fortune came about as a consequence of others' work, support and goodwill, and should be held in common.

She had devoted time to improving her reading and was now more than proficient. The shelf she'd first cleared with Bianca overflowed with tales of King Arthur and his knights, Ovid's poetry, plays by Sophocles, Aristotle and Aeschylus, Apuleius, names she loved repeating in her mind because the mere sound of them conjured the drama, pageantry, passion, transformations and suffering of their heroes and heroines. One of her favorite writers was Geoffrey Chaucer—his poems of pilgrims exchanging stories as they traveled to a shrine in Canterbury were both heartaching and often sidesplittingly funny. Admittedly, one of the reasons she loved Chaucer was because she could read him for herself. It was the same reason she picked up Shakespeare over and over, and the works of Margaret Cavendish, the Duchess of Newcastle upon Tyne. They all wrote in English. Regarded as quite the eccentric, the duchess was a woman of learning who, like Rosamund, was self-taught. Her autobiography, *A True Relation of My Birth, Breeding and Life*, a gift from Mr. Henderson, gave Rosamund a model to emulate. Here was a woman who dared to consider not only philosophy, science, astronomy and romance, but to write about her reflections and discoveries in insightful ways. Defying her critics, she determined that women were men's intellectual equal, possessed of as quick a wit and as many subtleties if only given the means to express themselves—in other words, access to education. This could be demonstrated over and over. One day in the chocolate house Rosamund heard John Evelyn refer to Margaret Cavendish as a "pretender to learning, poetry and philosophy." Rosamund didn't care; she gorged upon the pretender's writings, allowing them to saturate her senses and feed her hopes. Bianca enjoyed them too and the pair would debate the duchess's ideas. She could not help thinking her grandmother would be pleased.

The poetry of Richard Lovelace, Matthew's father, was also favored—and not merely because of the relationship. The way Lovelace's poems mingled politics, war, the vagaries of love—its passion and pain—with fighting for what was desired, was something she could relate to.

Of all the books, news sheets and letters she'd secreted away in her closet, the most important were stacked upon the table: Matthew's correspondence sat in a neat pile, ordered by date. Read and reread, as was any pamphlet or news book containing one of his reports, they remained where she could easily find them.

It didn't matter which one she selected, she knew the contents of each and where it had been written, what had struck him as important, what the weather was like, the landscape, the ocean swells and the scents he inhaled.

Through all her reading, Rosamund learned her place in the world: who she was—more importantly, who she wanted to be. She came to understand that being a bastard, and even fatherless, wasn't so very terrible. Suffering, joy, sorrow, happiness—the realm of human experience was not exclusive to the rich or poor. There were those who rose above adversity and triumphed. Those who defied God's will or embraced it. What it came down to were choices.

Her mother had made a choice when she abandoned her babe. Her grandmother made one when she kept her. Tilly made another when she took her back. Paul made his choices. Sir Everard made one when he married her. All around her, every day, people defined their lives through choices—good and bad.

Until she chose to lease the chocolate house from Matthew, choices had been made for her, and she'd suffered for it. This was something the tales she devoured taught her. They also enabled her to make another choice: never again would she allow someone else to determine her future. Never.

If only the men at the chocolate house knew what went on inside that golden head. Because she was a woman, and a beautiful one, they spoke of things in front of her they never would have thought to discuss in front of their wives, sisters, daughters, mothers. Working might not have given Rosamund respectability, but it did give her a degree of invisibility. She was a woman in a man's world—an ornament for them to appreciate and whose appearance reflected upon them in the way the furnishings in a fine establishment reflect the worth of the patrons. With the exception of Filip, Mr. Henderson, Jacopo and the boys, and even the most fearsome of their patrons, Henry Bennet, no one credited her with the capacity to understand, let alone seriously reflect upon what she heard. Except Matthew, of course. Privy to many conversations, ideas and opinions that might see some of the men locked up as dissenters, Rosamund stored the details away. To her, they were like the tales in the books in her closet, to be kept safe, secure, treasured.

She'd also mastered the art of writing. While her hand was not nearly as fine as Bianca's, she was able to pen the occasional letter to Frances and even to her mother. Any letters she sent in reply to Matthew's she dictated to Bianca. Her mother never responded to her notes, not even through the services of a scribe or notary. It was from Frances she learned that the inn had fallen into such a state of disrepair no builder could fix it. Likewise, Tilly and Paul, who, if Rosamund read aright, had grown fonder of the bottle than coin, cared not a whit for their business or each other. At first, the regular customers had tried to overlook the shortcomings of the Maiden Voyage Inn and its hosts, but gradually they stayed away. Widow Cecily had gone to work at the Cock and Bull. Sissy had been forced to leave when it became apparent she was with child. Who the father was, she never said. By far the biggest news was that the twins had been press-ganged into the Navy. At least, that's what everyone assumed. One day they were in town, bullying and demanding, the next they were gone. Someone claimed to have seen sailors in the area who were known to entrap any healthy men of age—and some who were not. Rosamund had read about impressment; even merchant sailors were not immune from being forcibly recruited. Once war with the Dutch was imminent, the King had been desperate to man his ships, and the only way to do that was by virtually kidnapping crews—even pressing those not accustomed to the sea. Rosamund couldn't be sorry, except for the captain the twins served. Nevertheless, she sent a prayer to God that He keep them safe. Not even Fear-God and Glory deserved a sailor's death. For weeks after learning their fate, she would drift down toward the Thames and stare at the forest of masts upon the river, watching the swirl of currents as the water raced east toward the sea and wondering about not only the twins, but another soul adrift upon the waves . . .

As she reminisced, Rosamund couldn't help but note how lovely Bianca looked. Upon discovering her newly made wardrobe was not original but a copy, she'd ordered Mrs. Wells to refashion every single dress to make new ones—not only for herself, but for Bianca and Widow Ashe as well—with additional fabric, lace and ribbons, and even using Margery's old gowns. Pleased and proud, Rosamund no longer wore what she'd come to think of as shrouds, but her very own clothes.

With new dresses to wear and shucking off Sir Everard's version of who she was, Rosamund also began to notice the interior of the manor more. While the chocolate house had undergone slight transformations once she took it over, Blithe Manor remained unchanged. It was dingy, dank and filled with unhappy memories. Rosamund determined to strip the darkness away.

With profits from the Phoenix accruing, even after Matthew took his share, Rosamund invested much of them back in the manor. Employing the services of Mr. Remney to oversee work, she had the curtains replaced, walls painted, fireplaces scrubbed, floors polished and the paintings in the study shifted to other parts of the house. The slashed portrait of Aubrey was repaired and then hung beside the rest of the family in Sir Everard's old bedroom. Bedding was aired and linen bought afresh. New furniture was acquired. At Mr. Remney's urging, and accompanied by Jacopo, Bianca and Mr. Remney's journeyman, Ralph, Rosamund paid a visit to the warehouses along the Thames and purchased some extraordinary pieces brought back from Venice, the Levant and the south of France. Rugs from Turkey were laid across the floors, tapestries from the mountainous regions of the Dalmatian Coast hung on the walls and the windows and chimneys were cleaned.

Just as Charles had been restored to his throne, so too Blithe Manor was restored, if not to its former glory, to glory nonetheless. Passersby would linger to see what the workers were up to on their scaffolding as damaged shingles were replaced on the roof, or tried to see the colors of the paints being lugged indoors and peer through the curtainless windows on the ground floor. Above the noise of traffic, whistling and singing could be heard echoing in the once-silent rooms of the manor. Even the most jaundiced Londoners attributed this to the joyous presence of the Lady Rosamund.

"Y'know," they'd say, nudging each other with a wink and brush of the tips of their cold noses, "this be the house of that widow, she who runs that chocolate house over by the Exchange and loves the blackamoors. They say she's cast a spell over the men who go there with her drinks and her person. They can't get enough of her."

Others would mutter, "They say the chocolate's magic."

Some would reply, their voices low and infected with wonder, "It ain't the *chocolata*, but the lady herself . . ."

TWENTY-NINE
In which there is a surprising homecoming

Rosamund firmly believed Matthew's homecoming was imminent now spring was here. The Thames had begun its slow, sinuous flow again after being frozen for weeks, and her growing excitement manifested as impatience—something those around her were unaccustomed to seeing. The result was, as days went by with no sign of him, she became distracted and clumsy, even when preparing drinks for regular customers.

After she'd inadvertently added two pinches of valerian to John Evelyn's chocolate instead of his usual one, rendering the poor man unable to write let alone think for a few hours, and tipped far too much rosewater into William Chiffinch's bowl, and Robert Boyle's was knocked over by her errant elbow before he could drink it, Filip suggested that Rosamund and her customers might be better served if she went home.

"You've been here since dawn and haven't stopped looking at the doorway. I fear the time for his arrival—at least at the chocolate house—has passed. The tides have retreated and no more ships will drop anchor till the morrow. Go home, *querida señora*, and save . . ." He hesitated, biting his lip.

"The reputation of our chocolate?" finished Rosamund, looking in dismay as yet another customer coughed while he drank and then flapped a hand before his mouth.

"Chilli," said Filip and Rosamund in unison. There was no need to add "too much."

They both laughed.

"I was going to say, *your enthusiasm* for another day." Filip chuckled.

"Aye, you're right." Rosamund sighed. Filip didn't even need to say whose arrival. He knew. They all knew. Was she so transparent? Apparently. Last month she'd received a missive from Matthew informing her he'd failed in his personal quest and was heading home. Alternately delighted she would see him sooner than she hoped and despondent that his intentions had been thwarted and what that meant, she could scarcely sleep, let alone make chocolate, for thinking about him.

"I just thought . . ." She gazed wistfully toward the doorway. ". . . he might be back today."

Or the day before, or the one before that . . .

"So did I," said Filip and placed a hand on her shoulder. "Perhaps he's yet making his way and will find you at Blithe Manor."

Her face brightened. "Do you think so?"

"Think, *sí*. Know, no. Now go. We will manage. You work far too hard, *señora*. Go and enjoy the snow while it still lasts."

They both glanced wryly toward the windows. Despite spring's arrival, snowflakes twirled and kissed the glass, dropping to form a white blanket upon the ground. It had been a long, cold winter replete with dangerous black frosts that brought with them a number of terrible accidents and deaths. There were many who complained they couldn't recall such a bitter freeze.

No one in their right mind enjoyed the snow, not when it was so relentless, the cold so piercing. Where were the spring rains? It hadn't rained since last October, when the new Lord Mayor, Sir John Lawrence, was installed and he and Their Majesties were drenched.

"Art has gone to fetch a carriage for you," said Filip. "Bianca is warming your coat by the fire." He nodded toward the kitchen. "I suggest you leave by the back door so the Unwise Men"—they both looked toward the booth nearest the counter—"won't be tempted to burden you with their feelings. Again."

Rosamund murmured her gratitude for the suggestion. There were three young men who had turned out to be among Rosamund's most ardent admirers. Rarely a day went by without one, if not all of them, patronizing the Phoenix. Once seated with a cup of chocolate, they would cast longing looks at Rosamund, brightening visibly when she deigned to notice them, adopting hangdog expressions when she did not. When they finally left the premises, doffing their hats, tugging their forelocks toward her, having exchanged nary a word, she would find little notes and poems left for her on the table. On the rare occasion she left before them, they would leap to their feet and press pieces of paper into her hand, averting their red faces, mumbling their apologies and begging her to take them. As if she could not.

Obliged to at least cast a cursory look at what they'd composed, Rosamund felt sorry for them. Nowhere in Matthew's league, their writing was execrable even if the sentiments were heartfelt. They were students at Middle Temple, and until she discovered they were all from wealthy families, Rosamund would oft wonder how they would ever pass their studies if they continued to haunt the Phoenix instead of attending classes.

"They've decided you're the only object worth studying, *señora*," said Filip one day. "They would be experts in all things Rosamund."

"Better they spend time on other projects," she muttered, stealing a glance in their direction. "Something laudable upon which to bestow their inheritances."

"They're noblemen's sons," Filip replied. "They've no need of those things ordinary people require to elevate or enlighten them. You're the sun around which they orbit."

"Then they'd best beware lest they get burned."

In an effort to spare them future hurt, Rosamund had tried to warn them they were wasting their time. It only fueled their ardor. To make matters worse, one day Charles Sedley and the Duke of Buckingham found their notes. After that, they composed mock replies to the men and satires to Rosamund, reading them aloud to anyone in the chocolate house who would listen—which was, of course, everyone. Rosamund was horrified and quickly put a stop to it.

Instead of gaining her affection, the young men became objects of scorn and ridicule, earning the sobriquet "the Three Unwise Men" or, more cruelly, "The Tomfool Trio."

Still they came . . . and wrote.

With one last, lingering look at the doorway, careful to avoid glancing at the hapless threesome, Rosamund undid her apron and complied. Filip was right. She was too distracted to be of any use today. Fortunately, the customers were more than forgiving even if, along with the Tomfools, they cast long faces in her direction once they understood she was departing. Already, Hodge had lit some candles; the day was darkening as gray clouds lowered. Soon the patrons would seek their own hearths. Time she went to hers. Bidding the men adieu, smiling sweetly at their protests, she waited until Thomas replaced her at the bar, then found Bianca, donned her coat and said goodbyes to the workers. Leaving by the back stairs, they slipped out the gate and into the carriage.

Less than twenty minutes later they arrived at Blithe Manor to find the withdrawing room fire crackling, the smoke all but dispersed, and the candles glowing. The newly painted walls gleamed as did the furniture, the scents of beeswax, lemon and honey filling the air. Rosamund passed her coat to one of the maids as Ashe took Bianca's from her—a small gesture that still had the power to make Bianca stiffen with discomfort. Ignoring her reaction, Ashe smiled at Rosamund, who stood with her back to the fire, holding her bare hands behind her, as if to catch the heat.

"I've taken the liberty of ordering some warmed wine, madam, and some supper. Jacopo arrived home earlier—and no, he has no news."

Rosamund's face fell. Under the pretext of checking inventory at the warehouse, she'd taken to sending him to the river daily to see which ships had arrived and to glean information from the sailors.

"He said to let you know he'll join you as soon as he's finished his paperwork."

"Thank you, Ashe." She looked at the pile of correspondence awaiting her attention. Two invitations sat atop the few letters—bills from tradespeople, by the look of them. "Anything else I should know about?"

Ashe shook her head. With a curtsey and warm smile to Bianca which was returned, she left, the maid in her wake. Ashe was a changed woman. No longer prone to hiding in the shadows, she had taken to managing the manor with the same pragmatism and pride with which she'd tended the chocolate house. Somehow Rosamund had sensed the woman's abilities, even if she hadn't realized them herself.

At that moment, Jacopo returned. Rosamund looked at him expectantly.

"No news, *signora*—of Mr. Lovelace or his ship. All talk was of the war between the Hollanders and Portugal and warnings about the Dutch plague. Despite precautions, it's spreading faster than anyone believed."

"Do you think it will come here?" asked Rosamund.

"Let's pray not," said Jacopo.

"There are some believe the second comet, especially arriving so fast on the tail of the first, portends death," said Rosamund quietly. Pedlars of all descriptions had come out in force selling philters, charms and amulets to protect against the disease, and depriving the superstitious (of which there were many) of their coin. One had even tried to enter the chocolate house, but Filip and a number of the gentlemen had sent him on his way. It was hard not to be concerned—not so much by the comet, but the reports of plague, despite being far away. Even one-eyed William Lilly had predicted in his *Astrological Judgments* for 1665 that the country would suffer a "Plague, or Pestilence . . . a World of Miserable People perishing therein."

According to Mr. Lilly, it wouldn't strike until June, so they had almost three months to make the best of it. Picking up the first of the invitations awaiting her decision, Rosamund tried to distract herself. It was from the Earl of Bedford to view his house in Covent

Garden and his splendid grounds. Rosamund knew what that meant. The second was from John Wilmot, the Earl of Rochester, to visit the wild animals in the Tower. Funny, she was certain the earl was presently confined there.

Throwing them aside, she stared at the window. What was wrong with her? She was giddy as a girl on May Day. Deciding the invitations could be declined later, she passed them to Bianca. The bills (from a wine merchant, a cordwainer and the candle maker) she gave to Jacopo with an apologetic smile. "More paperwork." The rest she bundled. She was not in the right frame of mind to deal with them. Pretend all she liked, but her mind was upon Matthew.

A tray was delivered, along with some wine. Bianca and Jacopo happily ate while Rosamund picked at the pigeon, pulled apart a piece of bread and nibbled some cheese, a faraway look upon her face. The brother and sister smiled softly at each other. Aware she was providing entertainment, Rosamund cared not. Soon, Matthew would be home.

The words they'd exchanged over the past few months would be spoken to each other . . . in person.

Just over an hour later, there was a rapping at the front door followed by the sound of hurried footsteps.

Rosamund turned from the window where she'd been gazing out through the curtains. Outside, it was dark, the snow still falling through the thick, choking smoke belching from surrounding chimneys. But she was looking inward, at her own thoughts and feelings—feelings she'd allowed to lie buried since Sir Everard died . . .

These thoughts were tossed aside as the heavy tramp of boots came up the stairs. Jacopo was wrong; Filip too. He was here. He was come. She quickly checked her hair, wiped her face and looked to Bianca for reassurance. Bianca pushed an errant lock of golden hair back into its pin and smiled, cupping her cheek softly.

"*Bella*," she whispered and resumed her seat.

There was a knock on the door.

"Enter," said Rosamund, pleased her voice didn't reveal her excitement. She slowly stood, her shaking hands pressed against her hips, her eyes flashing, her lips quivering with impatience. She prayed she wouldn't burst out laughing the moment he stepped into the room, such was her anticipated happiness at this reunion.

Ashe appeared, holding the door open, a warning look upon her face. Before Rosamund could ask what was wrong, a stocky, handsome man strode into the room. Dressed in dark green velvet, with a cream and black jacquard coat and buff lace at his throat, he was quite the dandy. Ignoring her, he gazed about with a proprietorial air, hands on hips.

Rosamund stared in disbelief.

Matthew Lovelace hadn't come back.

Instead, standing in the withdrawing room, larger than life, was the man from the ruined portrait.

Sir Everard's younger son, Aubrey Blithman, had returned from the dead.

PART THREE
Spring 1665

I having stayed in the city till above 7400 died in one week, and of them above 6000 of the plague, and little noise heard day nor night but tolling bells; till I could walk Lombard Street and not meet twenty persons from one end to the other, and not fifty upon the Exchange; till whole families (ten and twelve together) have been swept away; till my very physician, Dr. Burnet, who undertook to secure me against any infection . . . died himself of the plague; till the nights (though much lengthened) are grown too short to conceal the burials of those that died the day before, people being thereby constrained to borrow daylight for that service. Lastly, till I could find neither meat nor drink safe, the butcheries being everywhere visited, my brewer's house shut up, and my baker and his whole family dead of the plague. Yet (Madam), through God's blessing and

the good humors begot in my attendance upon
our late Amours, your poor servant is in a perfect
state of health . . .

—Letter from Samuel Pepys to Lady Carteret,
the 4th of September, 1665

THIRTY
In which the past returns with a vengeance

"**D**ear God!" Aubrey Blithman exclaimed. "I've had a devil of a time getting here."

Finding the voice that deserted her the moment she realized he wasn't Matthew Lovelace, praying the shock coursing through her body would rapidly subside, Rosamund stepped forward and gave a small curtsey, relieved she didn't stumble. "You're Aubrey?" she asked, though she had no doubts.

As he turned to meet her, the man swept her coldly from top to toe. She'd almost forgotten what it was like to be cheapened with a glance. Lifting her chin, she returned exactly the same regard, her heart drumming, her throat aching as she tried to swallow.

Aubrey bloody Blithman.

The man staggered. His eyes widened; his mouth formed an O.

Before Rosamund could prevent it, he lunged and grasped her hand, pulling her toward him.

Unyielding, she kept her fingers curled until he squeezed so hard she was forced to loosen them. "And you must be Lady Rosamund Blithman."

"Indeed." She bowed her head. Aubrey Blithman was dead. Sir Everard had said so. No one had contradicted this—not even Jacopo and Bianca, and, from the look on their faces, they were equally stunned. Yet, here he was, holding her hand, crushing it, a younger, slightly taller version of his father, the signs of dissipation upon his cheeks, around his nose and in his bloodshot eyes. He smelled of wine, smoke and sweat.

Suddenly, the documents she had signed for Sir Everard made sense: she agreed to acknowledge his heirs above her own claims. It had seemed simply an oversight, something left over from when the poor man still had children to inherit. On the contrary, he'd known this son was alive. As he had in so many other ways, Sir Everard had duped her.

Had Matthew known Aubrey lived? If so, what reason could he possibly have for keeping such information from her? No. No. It made no sense. He must also be ignorant.

"Father wrote that the resemblance was uncanny," said Aubrey with a whistle, still appraising her. An expression of delight and wonder arched his brows. "Apart from a few minor differences, it really is extraordinary. It's as if . . ." His voice trailed off. "How odd he married you." His features quickly rearranged themselves into a frown. "He told me he had. Did he?"

A fleeting doubt scratched at Rosamund. "Aye, sir. In Gravesend and before witnesses. Jacopo was one." She nodded toward him.

"Jacopo." Scowling, Aubrey stared at Jacopo before his scrutiny found Bianca. "Bianca. You're still about. What in God's name are you two doing, sitting in here as if you've a right?"

There was a sharp intake of breath. Rosamund's repressed anger made her sharp. "They have every right, sir. One I bestowed."

Aubrey raised a brow. "*You* bestowed it, did you?"

Widow Ashe remained by the door, her face a picture of confusion.

"Fetch some more wine, please, Ashe," said Bianca softly.

Rosamund smiled in gratitude.

"You don't give orders in my house," snapped Aubrey, releasing Rosamund as his finger became a weapon pointing at Bianca's chest.

"*Your* house?" The words were out before Rosamund could prevent them.

Bianca flapped at Ashe to make herself scarce. She didn't need to be told twice.

Aubrey lowered his arm and began to chuckle as he roamed the room, touching the curtains, stroking the walls, picking up the objects along the mantel and replacing them none too gently. Rosamund didn't move. Neither did Jacopo nor Bianca, though their eyes were locked on his every gesture.

"Yes, milady. Or, should that be Mother?" He glanced at her over his shoulder. "Mother. Fancy. Aye, *Mother,* you heard aright. *My* house. From what I understand, but will confirm as soon as I speak to Bender, Father left it to me." He muttered something inaudible. "A stepmother that looks like my sister." He sniffed a small porcelain statue and put it down.

Rosamund thought of the comets, of all those who believed they were forerunners of doom. Had she tempted fate by laughing at them? It certainly felt that way now. *Oh, please God, help me.*

"Did you know Father left the house to me? Is that why you've looked after it so well, like a wondrous caretaker? For certain, it has been transformed. I don't recall it ever looking so . . . jolly." He paused beneath a small tapestry displaying the Blithman coat of arms.

"Or did you think it was yours? I would have, had I been you; well, maybe. With the will not executed, everything was in limbo, like a lost Catholic soul. But you knew that, didn't you? Bender would have explained."

"Mr. Bender simply told me I have a jointure. That, until the will was settled, I could remain here . . ." She gazed around helplessly, her stomach churning.

Aubrey nursed his chin between two fingers. "I see. And, when I took so long to return, you began to think of it as yours."

"No, sir. I did not. You see, I thought you were dead."

"Dead?" He gave a hollow laugh. "Yes, well, that was Father's idea. It wasn't difficult. I assume you know the story—how Lovelace accused me of carrying arms for England's enemies?" When she didn't respond, he waved a careless hand. "Arrant nonsense, the lot of it. Still, declaring me dead was a way to ensure my safety—stop would-be assassins from hunting me down. It worked, for, as you observe, I'm very much alive. Once in the colonies, I simply styled myself as my father's nephew (which accounted for the familial resemblance); even called myself Everard. No one questioned the arrival of a wealthy relative keen to do business. Why should they, especially one so ready with coin?" He moved to the window and pulled aside a curtain, taking stock of the view. Dropping the fabric, he spun on his heel.

"Sorry for the inconvenience. No wonder you all look as if you've seen a ghost. No, I was only dead to my father." He laughed harder at his joke. "Now he's shuffled off this mortal coil and my name has been cleared, I'm able to return and claim what's rightfully mine." Pausing in his examination of the room, he gave Rosamund a pointed look. "It's kind of amusing, don't you think, to consider that you remaining here is now contingent on my goodwill?" He slapped his chest. "Mine."

Rosamund labored to remain calm. She wanted nothing more than to shut her eyes and unsee this man, pretend he didn't exist. Only, he did. And if what he said was true, then the life she'd relished and worked so hard for since Sir Everard died was about to crumble before her eyes.

Voices rose from the hall below. There were great thumps, followed by the bark of orders. Another familiar voice. Rosamund shot a look toward Jacopo. He looked gray, his mouth drawn; Bianca, the same.

Before she could ask Ashe to see what was happening, Aubrey sat in her chair, finished her glass of wine and poured himself another. They all watched him helping himself, putting his legs on the table, taking ownership.

"That would be my man looking to the luggage. Brought a bit with me. You can imagine, I've accumulated a great deal over the years—how many is it? Four? Five? But," he said, raising his glass toward Rosamund, "not as much baggage as my father." He tossed back the wine in two gulps. "Dear God"—he regarded her strangely, shaking his head—"I'm not the only revenant in the room." He poured himself some more.

There was a sharp rap on the door.

"What is it?" asked Aubrey. "Ah, come in, man, come in. I believe you know Wat?"

Dismay made Rosamund's shoulders slump as Wat Smithyman entered the room. With a sly smile and a half bow, he acknowledged her and ignored Jacopo and Bianca.

"Milord," said Wat. "Do you want me to organize your things be taken to your old room?"

"My old room?" asked Aubrey, patting his pockets. He pulled out a pipe and a pouch of tobacco. "I don't think so, do you? The lord of the manor should sleep in the finest room." He glanced at Rosamund, leering. "Put me in that one, would you, Wat?"

"With pleasure, sir." Wat bowed and left with one last triumphant look at Rosamund.

"No objections?" asked Aubrey.

"Objections? Why would I object?" Rosamund moved closer to Bianca. "This is your house, after all."

"I would have thought you would insist on keeping your bedroom. Though you'll hear no complaint from me should you wish to share it."

Rosamund had to work hard not to recoil. "The best room is Sir Everard's. With a couple of exceptions, it remains as it was when he occupied it."

"You didn't take it for yourself?"

"I prefer my *own* room."

Aubrey stared at her for a few seconds then began to laugh. It was bitter, forced. "Beautiful and willful. I can half see why Father wed you. He always liked to tame bitches."

Bianca stiffened. Jacopo opened and closed his fists.

Breathe. Breathe and smile, Rosamund told herself.

Taking a few puffs of his pipe so the tobacco took, Aubrey studied the platter of food, shoving the meat and bread aside with a finger, searching for choice bits. Finding one to his satisfaction, he picked it up and, tipping his head, dropped it in his mouth. The way he masticated, his tongue searching his lips and teeth for anything he might have missed, reminded Rosamund of the wild cats Sam had taken her to see at the docks.

Bianca's face wore an expression of utter desolation. Rosamund's heart cracked. She knew that look: the unraveling of dreams. Unless she was very careful, they were about to lose everything they'd worked so hard to achieve—together.

Aubrey flicked his fingers toward Bianca, a piece of meat landing on the new rug. "You still here? Surely, Bianca, you know your place by now? You too, Jacopo. While your mistress may have indulged some primitive fantasy, it has no place beneath my roof. Off with both of you until I call. And I will call." He bent over the tray.

"Bianca. Jacopo." Rosamund was not going to allow this. He could speak to her how he wished, look at her as if she were something dredged from the bottom of the Thames, but she wouldn't allow him to address her friends, her family in such a manner. "Stay where you are."

Aubrey's hand froze over a morsel. Sensing he was about to let forth, Rosamund quickly took the chair opposite him. "Here," she said. "Allow me." Moving his hand out of the way, she waited until he shifted his feet then deftly found a plate and sorted some of the choicer bits of meat and carved a piece of bread from the middle of the loaf for him, prattling all the while. She told him how hard it had been for her since Sir Everard died, how if not for the wisdom and experience of Jacopo and Bianca she would have been lost. Peppering her conversation with smiles and a few laughs (forced from some reservoir she'd forgotten she possessed), she didn't allow him time to think, let alone speak. All the while, he watched her, his eyes upon her face, openly appraising her décolletage, her hands, her mouth. She bestowed a huge smile upon him as she passed him the plate.

"Enough," he said finally, smacking the plate out of her hands. It clattered as food struck the floor, the walls, the chair. "Enough of your mindless chitter. Good God. Do you think I give God's good damn about you or how you *feel*? I'd sooner have a tooth extracted by a barber-surgeon than listen to any more of this . . . this blither. As for them"—he jerked his chin toward Bianca and Jacopo—"if they don't get out of here now, I'll call for Wat to have them taken away. And I don't mean to their rooms; I mean to where they belong."

"They belong here, with me—" began Rosamund, half rising. She felt Bianca's hand on her shoulder, pressing her back into the chair.

"They belong in the hold of a ship; they belong on a plantation and—get your hand off her—" he said to Bianca. The hand was slowly withdrawn. "And, if they don't quit my sight immediately, that's where I'll ensure they go." He didn't shout; he barely raised his voice, but each word was laden with deadly portent. He meant what he said and wanted Rosamund to know that.

"Very well," said Rosamund, standing slowly. "But I ask one boon."

"What?"

"I ask that Bianca be allowed to fetch me some chocolate. It's a well-known restive that your father and I were in the habit of drinking before bed. It's a ritual I've maintained. If you like, I can mix you a drink." She lowered her chin in obeisance. No doubt he would prefer her this way.

Aubrey tilted his head to one side. "I've heard about you and your chocolate. Unnatural, you working there, making drinks for gentlemen. He never would have tolerated Helene doing such a menial thing. Still, if it's good enough for the old master, then it's good enough for the new one. At least in fetching and carrying, she's"—he glanced at Bianca—"doing what God put her kind on this earth to do."

Rosamund felt Bianca touch her back. "Bianca." She didn't look at her but kept her eyes on Aubrey. "If you could also bring some of that herb Mr. Evelyn swears by and which the master so enjoyed as well, I would be grateful."

"*Signora,*" said Bianca and with a curtsey followed a silent Jacopo out of the room.

Once they'd shut the door, Aubrey began to eat again. Keeping her face neutral, Rosamund's mind raced. Aubrey Blithman was alive. The house was his. What did that mean for her, for the household?

"You're prettier than she was."

She didn't need to ask who "she" was.

"The men used to fall over her, you know. They must barely be able to stand in your presence. On their legs, at any rate." He chuckled, food spraying his chest.

Rosamund sat straight, hands clenched in her lap, and ignored his crudeness.

"Oh, come now. You work in a chocolate house; don't pretend a virtue I know you don't possess. My father married you. It's obvious why." He shook his head. "And he had the gall to question my tastes, my sanity."

Rosamund prayed this man liked to talk about himself. So far it seemed he was keen to bring almost every other topic back to his desires. "Forgive my surprise at your arrival, Aubrey. May I call you that? As I said, your father told me you were deceased."

He gave a bark of laughter. "The last time we spoke, he told me he would excise me from his life. I didn't realize the old fool meant it. I thought it merely a threat. Still, at least he remembered me when it was important."

"In his will."

Aubrey slowly relaxed into the seat. "Imagine my surprise when first Wat turns up and then these letters from Father's lawyer, inviting me to claim my inheritance. Took their blasted time finding me, I can tell you. But at least they did." He glanced at her. "Guess I must be a shock, then. Spoiled your plans. Not only am I like Christ, resurrected, but akin to some benighted thief: I snatch your wealth away when you least expect it."

"I'd no expectations, sir. The will was yet to be read."

"I know. It was waiting for me. I'm the executor. Father was thorough if nothing else. Fair, not so much."

Swallowing her astonishment, Rosamund remained silent.

"But you must be disappointed, surely?" he asked. "It's only natural." He heaved himself out of the chair and began to pace. He walked with a funny, rolling gait. Rosamund had seen it on the sailors who disembarked at Gravesend after years at sea. The man really had made his way straight from a ship. "After all, for over two years you've been ensconced in my house, believing all this was yours to enjoy. And you have." He turned and waggled a finger at her. "You've been spending my money."

Rosamund stood. "No, sir. I spent my own. Your father bestowed a jointure upon me, and I have the money *my* business made."

"Is that right?" He sounded disappointed. "Well, don't think I'm compensating you. I never asked you to undertake improvements."

Unable to think up a suitable retort, Rosamund was relieved when Bianca and Jacopo returned with the tray and some tiny bowls of additives. Until she saw the anger transform Aubrey's face.

"That will be all, Bianca, thank you," she said, moving between her friend and Aubrey. "Just leave the tray. Perfect. If you could draw a bath for me, per-haps ask Jacopo to help you—the tub is so heavy—I'd be grateful. I shan't be long." She prayed that Bianca would understand.

"*Signora.*"

"No." Aubrey slammed a hand down on the table in front of him, mak-ing Rosamund jump. "I'll not have that cursed language spoken here. English, do you hear me? You speak the King's English or I'll cut your tongue out. That goes for both of you." He glared at Jacopo and Bianca.

Rosamund tried not to let her fury show.

"Sir." Bianca rolled the r. "Madam." Curtseying most obsequiously, she swiftly left the room followed by Jacopo.

When the door was shut, Rosamund began to put a little cinnamon, a bit of sugar into a bowl. She expected Aubrey to come and watch and wasn't disappointed.

"What's that you're doing?" he asked curiously. His manner changed as quickly as the winds, blowing hot one moment, temperate the next.

"I'm mixing our most popular additives into the drink I'm preparing for you."

"Good. The Spaniard's version tastes like tar. Thick and bitter."

Never having drunk tar, Rosamund couldn't say. "I'm making it the way your father liked it—sweet, a little spicy."

"What's that?" he asked, pointing at the anise seed.

Relief swept Rosamund. Bianca had understood her message. Mixed in with the anise seed was a hefty quantity of valerian. "This is a special root that also gives the chocolate a slightly fruity taste."

"Give me plenty. I've a desire for something fruity." He cast her a look that made her stomach slide into her boots.

"Plenty it is." Throwing caution to the wind, she upended the entire contents into the bowl, quickly tipping in the milk. Little flecks of black, green and violet spun in the whirlpool her spoon created.

"Now I add the chocolate."

Knowing Bianca would have already agitated the *molinillo*, she gave it a further stir in the hope she'd increase the quantity of froth and hide the number of herbs. Pouring a stream of luscious chocolate into the bowl, she gave it a final blend and passed it to Aubrey.

Covering her hand with his, he took it from her slowly. He had peculiar eyes, the palest blue with very large pupils. One eye had a blot of brown disrupting the surface, making his gaze seem awry.

She allowed him to stroke her fingers, resisting the urge to pull away. His smile pulled back his lips, revealing crooked teeth.

"Ah, even before I left the New World, I'd heard talk of your chocolate. Don't look so surprised. I kept abreast of what was happening here. Everything except my father's death. For some reason, that bypassed me." He blinked and stared into space.

Rosamund moved back to her seat and gestured for him to sit opposite. "Please, sir. Enjoy your chocolate. And, if you would be so kind, tell me of your life in the New World."

Aubrey sat, holding the bowl to his mouth, his head slightly bent, and studied her above the rim. "You really are absurdly lovely," he said, moving the bowl away. "Even I have to admit, you eclipse Helene."

Rosamund forced her hands to be still. She wanted to lift the bowl to his mouth, pry his lips open and pour the contents down his gullet.

Taking a great gulp of chocolate, he smacked his lips together. "Why, madam. Tales of your magic are not exaggerated. This is wonderful stuff." He took another swallow.

Much to Rosamund's relief, Aubrey drank the chocolate, smoked his pipe and downed two glasses of malmsey while he regaled her with tales of Virginia and its sweeping coastal plains, glorious snowcapped mountains and verdant valleys. How he'd purchased land there and, with the labor of slaves, planted tobacco and cotton and, when he left nigh on three months ago, had just sown indigo. He spoke of how he'd increased business by advising other landholders to purchase slaves from him. Rosamund could barely keep a straight face as she recalled Matthew's recent writings about the conditions of the slaves upon the ships and in the brutal hands of English colonists in Virginia, Maryland and Carolina. Given how Aubrey spoke to Bianca and Jacopo, it wasn't hard to imagine how he treated those who worked his land. He told her about the Virginia Indians, the "savages," as he called them, with names like Cherokee, Iroquois, Algonquin and those belonging to what he called the Powhatan Confederacy. Contempt and what she thought might be fear dripped from him. Gradually, his words slowed and his eyes began to grow heavy.

"You should see 'em, Helene. So tall, proud. With their feathers and markings . . . like paintings. Like those ones you loved . . ."

For just a moment, she worried she'd added too much valerian. Poor Mr. Evelyn had still been asleep when she left the chocolate house, curled up in a booth as a result of her heavy-handedness. Rosamund determined he wouldn't pay for his chocolate on his next few visits—it was the least she could do.

Aubrey murmured Helene's name a few more times, then slid down in the chair. His pipe fell from his fingers, his head dropped onto his chest. Before long, he was snoring worse than Paul ever had.

She picked up his pipe, placed it on the table and stood back to study him. Her stepson by marriage. Even in repose he looked angry and spoiled. Yet it was clear he still mourned his sister. Did he despise his father? Or was he simply afraid of him? There was no indication he was grateful to him. Seeing her had sparked bitter, sorrowful memories. Aubrey not only blamed Matthew for his exile, but declared the accusations against him were untrue; she knew whom she believed. But that still didn't explain why, even two years after his son had gone to the New World, Sir Everard had maintained the ruse. Didn't Matthew say that Sir Everard had paid a huge sum of money to have Aubrey's name cleared? It must have worked or Aubrey wouldn't dare show his face now. What else had Aubrey done to make Sir Everard keep him away? To excise him from his life? What had sparked the rage that caused his portrait to be slashed and hidden from view?

Such peculiar men, the Blithmans. Dangerous ones, too. She recalled Aubrey's face as he barked orders at Bianca and Jacopo—oh, she saw his father in him then. But Sir Everard, thank God, never looked at her the way Aubrey had when he held her hand and caressed her fingers, remarking over and over how like his sister she was. They weren't the absent strokes of a bereft man, but more like those of a child whose favorite toy had been stolen and replaced. The shivering that racked her body was fierce.

What was she to do about him? Just as she'd begun to make real plans, they were dashed. If only it had been Matthew who'd come to the door. Where was he?

It didn't matter. She had to work fast to protect those she loved. Throwing open the door, she called, not for Widow Ashe, but for Wat.

On the third call, she heard the stirring of someone on the floor below and then shoes dragging on the stairs.

"What?" asked Wat rudely, running his hands through his hair as he reached the last step and spied her in the shadows near the door. "Whatcha want?"

"What I want, Wat, is for you to take your master to bed. He's quite exhausted." She stepped aside and gestured to Aubrey's recumbent body. He'd slipped further down the chair. His knees pressed against the table, the only thing stopping him becoming a human puddle on the rug.

"Whatcha do to him?" asked Wat, striding over to his master, shaking him. When there was no response, he turned to her and snarled. "If I find out you've done anything . . ."

"You'll do what? Tell me," said Rosamund, smiling sweetly. "Complain I didn't press charges after you stole those candlesticks from your master, or the silver urn?"

"I didn't steal them from my master—he was dead."

"Oh, I wasn't referring to Sir Everard—" Rosamund gave a pointed look at Aubrey. "According to your new master, this is his house. His property. And that includes everything within its walls."

Understanding he'd just admitted to the crime, Wat ceased to challenge her and, with a groan, heaved Aubrey up under the arms and managed to throw him across his shoulders.

"I think your master needs a good rest," said Rosamund, following him from the room.

Flashing her a look of pure resentment, Wat knew better than to argue this time. The young woman he'd left to fend for herself was not the same one he faced now.

Once he rounded the corner and she heard a door open then shut, Rosamund flew to her room. As she'd hoped, Bianca, Jacopo and Widow Ashe were waiting.

"Right," she said, closing the door. "We've no time to lose. All of you must gather your things and be gone this night." She raced to a small box on the mantelpiece, pulled out a purse of coins and counted some out. "I want you to take these and go to the Phoenix. Explain to Filip what has happened. You're to stay there until we sort this out." She prized open Jacopo's fingers and put the coins in the palm of his hand. "What are you looking at me like that for? Go. Now. You can't stay here." She spun toward the housekeeper. "Ashe, I am afraid for you as well. That man means to wipe out all traces of me and impose his own authority upon the house. You must go."

When they didn't move, she went on. "I saw the way he looked at you—" She grabbed first Bianca's hand, then Jacopo's. "He will do what he threatens."

"*Si, bella,*" said Bianca softly, lifting their joined hands to her lips. "And we saw the way he looked at *you.*"

Rosamund pulled out of her grip. Jacopo let her go. "I don't care. I will use the fact I look like his sister; I will use the chocolate if I have to. I can control him. What I can't control is what he does to you. Please, please, for my sake, leave and be safe."

Jacopo looked to Bianca. "You don't understand, *signora.* We're not free to leave. We're naught but property, slaves bound to the master of Blithe Manor. It seems the master is now Aubrey. If we leave, then we'll be fugitives. A price will be put on our heads. We'll be imprisoned and then deported, just as he wishes."

Rosamund sank onto the bed. "Is this true?" When they nodded, she put her head in her hands. "Let me think. Let me think."

They stood in silence watching her, the only sounds the snapping of the fire and the steady thrum of snow on the windows.

Finally, Rosamund raised her head. A smile broke, beaming to warm them all. "I have it. The will hasn't been read yet. Therefore, we don't know its exact contents, despite what Aubrey has said. First thing, I will seek out Mr. Bender and learn what I can and ask his advice on how best to deal with . . . with Aubrey. With you both. Can you trust me to do this? To look to your best interests?"

"When have you not done so, *signora*?" asked Bianca softly.

Jacopo let out a long sigh and reached for his sister's hand. "Very well. We will go and wait to hear from you, but only if Ashe stays. We cannot leave you alone with that man."

"I can manage him too, madam," said Ashe quickly. "If I can handle Mr. Remney's men, I can handle an upstart lord."

Rosamund began to pull at her lip. If only that were true.

Filled with gratitude and warmth, she drew Bianca then Jacopo into a long embrace. "I know there's no point arguing when you are united in your purpose."

"*Allora,*" said Jacopo. "None whatsoever."

Rosamund made a sound that could have been a laugh but was suspiciously like a sob. "Whatever happens, we'll do this together, all right?"

Three sets of eyes regarded her doubtfully.

Rosamund tried to smile, threw out her arms. "We made the impossible possible once—we'll do it again."

"*Si*. But then we worked together to save a chocolate house—" began Jacopo.

"And we did," said Rosamund. "Only this time the stakes are higher. We work to save ourselves."

THIRTY-ONE
In which Lady Rosamund becomes a woman of property

Well before dawn, Rosamund rose and left the house, taking a young, sleepy-eyed maid with her (Ashe would not allow her to depart otherwise). She ordered the hackney carriage to take her straight to Mr. Bender's at Gray's Inn.

Lanthorns swung from the walls of houses, casting crazed light about the dark streets in the predawn gusts of wind. The horses' hooves were a steady, empty crunch, interrupted only by the driver's hacking cough. Snow had fallen again overnight, but not enough to coat the streets, which were crusted with black ice. The pervasive smell of damp and mold barely disguised the other odors of urine, shit, tallow and stale beer. A dead cat had been trampled beneath carriage wheels. Rosamund turned away in despair, but not before she'd seen some crows pecking at the flesh, and large rats scurrying along the walls of the buildings, slipping between holes in the plaster, straw and wood, their night foraging complete.

Further on, shopkeepers were opening for trade, pushing snow off their stoops, opening their creaking shutters, slapping their hands and stamping their feet to restore warmth to their limbs. The markets were assembling, carts and barrows pushed into position, weary vendors setting out their produce, some even beginning to call, their cries piercing the air. Servants leaned from windows as the city woke, emptying chamber pots and other vessels into the street, uncaring who might be trudging below. More servants scurried through the city gates, heads down, strides wide as they passed the carriage, determined to claim the freshest and finest produce.

The closer to Gray's Inn they came, the more people they saw, and the roads started to become congested. At one junction there was even a great spit with pig on it, the fire and the smell attracting a small crowd.

Eventually, the carriage pulled up outside an expanse of frost-covered grass surrounded by hedges. Walkways led to a vast group of stone buildings four stories high. All but a few of the windows were dark. Rosamund asked the coachman to wait and, leaving the maid in the relative warmth of the carriage, begged the young doorman to wake Mr. Bender, slipping a few coins into his gloved hands. When it was clear who had come to visit, she was swiftly taken to the lawyer's rooms. While his servant lit candles and poured coffee, Mr. Bender rubbed his eyes and tried to look official in his thick emerald house robe. Rosamund swiftly outlined the events of the previous evening: Aubrey's return and his claim, not only on the house and the estate of Sir Everard, but upon Jacopo and Bianca.

"So," said Mr. Bender, stifling a yawn and reclining into his seat, his hands wrapped around the bowl of coffee, "Aubrey lives. I always wondered if Sir Everard was merely indulging in a guilty fancy, wishing a lost child back from the dead when he made out the will and named Aubrey executor, let alone heir. I'd heard rumors of a nephew doing well in the colonies, thus I wrote to inform him of what had happened, but didn't consider for a moment the living relative was, in fact, the dead son. You have to believe me, my lady."

"I do, Mr. Bender. But Aubrey Blithman is very much alive and, from what I understand, his father knew this. Together, they conspired to hide his existence." Rosamund tried not to think of those odd eyes, the moist fingers, the way Aubrey smelled. "He's been living these last years in Virginia mainly, managing his father's lands, making money by selling slaves to the plantation owners. I gather he's done quite well . . . ." Did she resent that he was able to take all that she'd come to think of as hers? Perhaps a little, may God forgive her. At least he couldn't touch the chocolate house.

Unable to sleep the night before, she'd given much thought to what Aubrey had revealed, especially the way he behaved toward Jacopo and Bianca. He'd created a problem she must solve. During the early hours of the morning, she'd snuck into Sir Everard's study in the hope of finding a document to provide guidance, if not answers. To no avail. Rosamund had sorted through Sir Everard's papers long ago, and there'd been nothing of a personal nature. Aside from Matthew's letters to him, everything related to the business. No letters to or from his wife when he traveled, or to or from his sons. Nothing. It was as if Sir Everard either had no sentimental attachments or kept such things elsewhere—though if he did, she'd never found them.

As she sat opposite Mr. Bender in his snug rooms, inhaling the mixture of beeswax, coal, brandy and burned chestnuts and watching the light creep up the stained walls as day broke, she outlined her plan for how she might alter the situation in which she found herself.

"As we know, Mr. Bender, my late husband left me a jointure." She held her bowl of coffee tightly, but mostly to keep her hands warm.

"He did. Not a very generous one, but then I guess you hadn't been married for very long. I believed it was temporary and that once Aubrey's death was proven—by this false nephew no less—you would be entitled to at least a third of the estate; more if we appealed to the Chancery Court. I must say—" He put down his coffee and rose to prod the coals in the hearth. His man darted forward and refilled his bowl, offering more coffee to Rosamund, who politely declined. It was hard enough swallowing Aubrey's presence; she didn't need more bitterness. "I thought the point moot. I really believed the boy dead. I don't understand why he didn't write and inform me."

"He's no boy, sir," said Rosamund, "but a grown man desiring to take up his rights and reestablish his name, as one would expect. As for not corresponding . . ." She shrugged. "I believe he came home as soon as he learned of his father's death."

Mr. Bender sat back down. "What would you have me do, my lady? With Aubrey alive, executor and in London, I doubt we can extract more from Sir Everard's estate than has already been granted. You did sign those papers, after all. Not even the most understanding of judges or sympathetic of lawyers can undo that—not an agreement between husband and wife, especially not a literate one such as yourself. Ah, yes, madam, I am aware your literacy is relatively recent, but persuading a judge this is the case would be beyond even my powers." He smiled sadly. "I wish I'd known better what Everard was about when he asked me to draw them up. At that stage, I hadn't met you . . . I had no idea—"

Rosamund waved a hand. "Please, Mr. Bender. Do not chastise yourself. I do not want any more."

"Then, my lady, what is it you *do* want?"

Rosamund took a deep breath. "What I want is to negotiate with Aubrey Blithman."

"You do? I'm afraid I don't understand."

Rosamund put down her bowl carefully and leaned forward. "First, I need to know where the law stands with regard to the rights and liberties of Bianca and Jacopo Abbandonato. I want to negotiate for their freedom."

If Rosamund had declared she wished to be treated as a horse from here on, Mr. Bender could not have been more surprised. "I see." His hair, which was shaved close to his scalp, glinted silver in the candlelight. "The laws around slaves are murky, but what is clear is they have no rights and certainly no liberties except those granted by their masters. They're regarded as goods when it comes to the distribution of an estate. They're like horses or cattle—ownership is transferred. They belong to Aubrey Blithman for him to do with as he wishes." The words were as distasteful for the man to say as they were for Rosamund to hear. She liked him better for it.

"Transferred." Rosamund stared at the fire, thinking. For something crackling so fiercely, it provided little warmth, and she felt cold and uncertain. Finally, she said, "In that case, he has it within his power to transfer their ownership, does he not? To sell or exchange them?"

"Ah . . . I think I understand what you're trying to accomplish, madam."

Rosamund took a deep breath. "You do? Good. I have a proposition I want you to put to Aubrey Blithman. It's my understanding that he's coming to see you later today to discuss the terms of the will."

"Is that right? Nice of him to inform me. Glad I'll be prepared." He tugged his robe over his legs. "What is it you wish me to put before him, my lady?"

As she outlined her plan, Mr. Bender began to shake his head but, as she continued, eloquently and sensibly, he stilled. He signaled to his servant for paper and quill and began to make a few notes.

"What you're asking for," he said when she had finished, "it's not impossible, though it will depend very much on Aubrey—what he wishes to do with his inheritance, how inclined he is to be agreeable. The degree of attachment he feels to the Blithman estate here in London. His attachment to the Abbandonato siblings."

"That's the sticking point. Though, when he is set to gain so much, I hardly think he'll object."

Mr. Bender gave a slight shrug. "If he's like his father, I fear he might consider this an imposition, a diminishing of his rights as property owner. Nor would he welcome what he would regard as interference in matters that are his to decide."

Rosamund's heart fell. "Well, then, Mr. Bender, it's up to you to put my bargain in terms he will understand."

"What might those be?"

She recalled Aubrey's face as he boasted of his acquisitions, the lands and businesses he had accrued. Her proposal needed to be put in a language he'd comprehend. She searched her mind for the right words. A smile brightened her face.

"I know," she said, and patted Mr. Bender on the knee. "Tell Aubrey he's so inspired me with his business success that I too desire to become a woman of property."

Swallows circled, greeting the gray morn as Rosamund arrived at the chocolate house. With a quick "God's good day" to Mr. Henderson, she snuck up the back stairs. From the kitchen she could hear a great ruckus coming from the main room. The place was full. Men from all walks of life—earls with their stars and garters, fops in their pretentious wigs exuding cloying perfumes, clergymen in cassocks and bands—were crammed into benches and in booths. There were black-robed lawyers, merchants and tradespeople; the poet John Dryden held court in one corner; Sir Henry Bennet and the Duke of Buckingham talked animatedly at the bar—evidently they were yet to go to bed. Smoke swirled beneath the ceiling and the windows were frosted from the hot air inside and the freezing gusts outside. Something had caused the men to bury their heads in news sheets and argue vehemently.

Was it news of Aubrey Blithman's return? Certainly, it had caused Rosamund's world to erupt.

Filip was deep in conversation with the courtiers propped at the bar. Bianca took trays laden with empty bowls from Jacopo, who was, in turn, trying to send orders out with the drawers. Behind her, Thomas and Solomon worked quickly to ensure chocolate and coffee went to the floor.

She should help. And she would, once she discovered what had caused the place to fill so early and the men to be so agitated. As she tried to puzzle the reason, the Unwise Men tripped in, adding their arguments to those already circulating.

"*Signora*," said Bianca with relief as she swept into the kitchen. "You're here."

"I am. What's happened? I don't think I've ever heard such a racket. But first, are you well? Is Jacopo?"

Bianca deposited the tray of empty dishes on a table so Cara might wash them. In her working dress and apron, she looked as pristine and well rested as she always did, despite fleeing the manor late last night.

"We are well, *signora*. Filip found us beds. It's not uncomfortable upstairs." She glanced at the ceiling. "The fires of the day keep the rooms warm throughout most of the night. But you? Were you disturbed?"

"Only by thoughts of Aubrey and what he revealed. The valerian did its work. I do thank you for that."

A swell of voices caused them to turn toward the noise.

"What has the men so unsettled?" asked Rosamund. "Has the King made a proclamation? Have we won the war?"

"No. That continues. What has happened will affect it, though. According to reports, the mighty frigate *London* exploded while sailing along the Medway toward the Nore."

Rosamund gasped. The *London* was meant to be the pride of the fleet, a great warship with which to defeat the enemy. "Was it the Dutch?"

Bianca shook her head. "They're saying it was an accident. I overheard some men blaming the gunners who were packing the cartridges; others said it was the way the gunpowder was stored. Over three hundred men and some women and children have died."

"Women and children? What were they doing aboard a ship bound for war?"

"Bidding their men farewell."

"Oh dear God." Rosamund fell back on a stool. "How terrible."

"Your cousin Mr. Pepys arrived some time ago and shared the dreadful news. Since then, more have come, adding their tidings of woe to this sorry tale. There are those out there"—Bianca jerked her head toward the main room—"claiming this is yet another portent. First the comets, now this. They say some great disaster looms."

"As if the *London* isn't enough," whispered Rosamund. Here she was worrying about Aubrey Blithman while hundreds of souls had suffered a horrible death. "There are those who would see doom in a drop of water." She looked toward the main room. "Is he still here? Sam?"

"*Sì*. But he's not well. He complains of a pain in his— What did he call them? Cullies?" Bianca shrugged.

"Ah, his testicles."

"Why did he not say so?"

Why indeed. Rosamund's mouth twitched. Sam had no decorum when it came to discussing his ailments. But, if he was in pain, she had just the thing. She rose, determined to speak with him—not only to learn more about this latest disaster, but, if the plan she had put to Mr. Bender was to work, she needed all the allies she could get. Also, as his cousin, Sam needed to know that Aubrey had returned and the Blithman estate had a new master.

"I'll make him a special drink to help with the stones, for that's what ails the poor man."

A few minutes later, Thomas, who was growing into a strapping lad, led the way through the throng with her tray. Sam was delighted not only to have his cousin's company, but to be seen to be chosen over men of greater rank and authority. Sam quickly made room in the booth for her and made a great show of leaning over and planting a kiss on her mouth, then looking around to ensure the gesture was seen. It was.

"How goes it, cuz?" he asked. "You heard about the

London? Frightful. Simply frightful." He shook his head in sorrow.

His face was pale, his mouth pulled and though the room was warm and the fire blazing, it wasn't so hot as to warrant the beads of sweat upon his brow. The poor man suffered, but not enough to forgo sharing tragic tidings at the Phoenix.

"I have heard. May God bless their poor souls. If not for such news, I would be well. Better than you, I fear, dear Sam. Here, drink this." She quickly added some herbs to a bowl, poured and pushed the cup toward him. "Bianca made mention"—she cleared her throat—"of your troubles."

"Oh, excellent," said Sam and took the drink gratefully. "Thank you."

She waited until he'd enjoyed a few sips and the men around them had returned to their conversations, then asked him to tell her exactly what he knew about the *London*.

He told her how the ship had been completely destroyed, with only twenty-four souls saved. When he finished, they sat quietly for a moment, listening to the chatter around them. Bianca was right. There were those blaming the Dutch, others claiming it was a sign of worse to come.

Finally, she tapped Sam on the arm and leaned over.

"I have some news to share as well. Do not look so concerned; it's far better than that you carried here." She quietly explained about Aubrey.

Sam's eyes almost started from his head. "Aubrey? *Alive?*" He choked on the chocolate, and Rosamund was forced to slap his back a few times. Wiping away tears, he shook his head. "When I was told he'd died, I never doubted Everard for a moment; I was overcome with sympathy. I thought all his children lost to him. But . . . how? Why? Why would a father disown a son in such a manner?"

Rosamund shrugged. "I know not, Sam. I hoped you might."

"Believe me, Rosamund, I would tell you if I knew." He shifted slightly on his seat as pain pierced his body. He let out a deep breath and flashed her an apologetic look before continuing. "There were rumors around the time Aubrey left—was sent to the New World."

"Such as?"

"Oh, that he'd conducted himself in a most unbecoming manner. There was mention of treachery, of deals being struck with Hollanders and such. But I always felt there was something else . . . I do know he and his father argued a great deal. There was not the accord between them that Everard had enjoyed with his eldest son." He tipped his head in thought. "I don't know. You've got to remember, it all happened when the King was set to be restored to the throne. Negotiations were under way. Preparations were being made. There was little else the city was talking about—"

Which meant there was nothing else Sam had been interested in discussing.

"All I recall is one minute Aubrey was here, next he was gone. Monies were paid to the privy purse, his name was cleared and then, a few weeks later, he was pronounced dead. Everard never spoke of him again."

"Not so dead; he has come back."

"Are you sure it's him?"

"If his portrait is anything to judge by—" *And his manner*, thought Rosamund.

"I'll know the moment I clap eyes on him. Where is he?" he asked and craned his neck as if expecting to see him among the patrons.

Rosamund had the grace to look guilty. "At Blithe Manor. He was . . . very tired."

"He's staying there? With you?"

"Where else would he stay?"

"But . . . but . . . it's not proper."

"But it is, Sam. We are family. I am his stepmother, remember."

A reluctant smile tugged his mouth. "I suppose you are, the lucky cur. Fancy, a stepmother younger than him and by some years. Even younger than his sister. You might be related—by marriage—but all the same, I don't like the idea of you alone there with him . . ."

"It doesn't seem right, does it?" agreed Rosamund, thankful Sam had taken the conversation in the direction she hoped. "And with my reputation already so . . . precarious."

"Only to those who don't know you."

She shot him a grateful smile. Really, he could be charming when he wished. And when he was suffering so. "You see, the potential impropriety of him and I sharing a roof is easily remedied. Well, maybe 'easily' is too strong a word. It can be fixed. I even spoke to my lawyer, Mr. Bender, about a related matter this morning."

"You did? What matter?"

"Ah, that is what I wanted to share with you. I may need your help," said Rosamund, and quietly outlined not only her reason for visiting Mr. Bender, but her solution to a very vexing problem.

Naturally, Sam protested—it was all quite unorthodox—but she managed to allay his fears and persuade him to support her. As she returned to the kitchen, her passage was slow, the men seeking her company, pouring out their views about the dreadful explosion, the loss of life, how they were inviting trouble allowing women on board in the first place, as well as suspicions a Dutch spy had blown the frigate up.

From Sir Henry, she learned of a British ship capturing French sailors and torturing them by burning their feet. "The foolish captain was determined to have them say their cargo was for the Hollanders," said Sir Henry, rubbing the dark plaster on his nose for the umpteenth time. "But they were innocent. The King is furious and intends to flog the captain and crew as soon as they make land."

Rosamund could not help but pity the misguided men. Feelings were running so high against the Dutch, inflamed by reports in the press and innate prejudices, it was no wonder men imposed their own justice on anyone suspected of aiding the enemy, hoping to insert themselves into His Majesty's good graces. She'd heard of the members of the Dutch church being threatened, beaten and stoned wherever they walked about the city. Neighbors were turning on neighbors. The flimsiest excuse was regarded as justification for violence. Foreign folk were scared to leave their houses. Known Papists and Quakers too. Businesses had been boycotted and people were suffering as a consequence.

War didn't just worsen prejudices, it legitimated them.

Those who didn't want to talk about the *London* or the Dutch wanted to know about Aubrey. Nothing stayed a secret at the Phoenix. Some uttered his name with distaste, some with surprise, some with caution. Looks of pity and, occasionally, calculation were cast in Rosamund's direction as the men weighed up what the consequences of his return might be. Some offered Rosamund a consoling pat on the arm, others even offered her a place to stay, the shrewd look in their eyes indicating the price of their generosity. Rosamund hoped she wouldn't have to stoop to that, but thinking about alternative accommodation might not be such a bad idea.

Pretending an indifference she most certainly didn't feel, and dismissing the less-than-honorable offers with a laugh, Rosamund kept her emotions close, even as her heart pounded. In the relative sanctuary of the kitchen, she collapsed onto a stool, her mind abuzz with what she'd heard. She smiled gratefully at Solomon when he brought over a steaming bowl of chocolate.

"Have you eaten, *signora*?" asked Bianca, sinking into the seat next to hers, wiping her hands and face upon the apron.

"This will do nicely. I've no appetite for food."

They both gazed toward the main room, watching Filip's and Thomas's backs as they worked hard to agitate and pour pot after pot of chocolate and coffee, while the drawers ran to and fro fetching jugs of beer, bottles of wine, cups of China tea and whatever else the customers desired.

"You know we can't stay here, don't you?" said Bianca quietly. "We'll have to return to Blithe Manor. If we don't, he can have us arrested. He's our master now."

"I know you'll have to return," said Rosamund. "But when you do, it will be on my terms."

"Your terms?" Bianca twisted in her seat. "*Allora*. I know that tone. What have you done?"

Before Rosamund could answer, who should step into the kitchen but Aubrey Blithman; Mr. Bender, Jacopo and Sam on his shiny heels.

Pouches cupped Aubrey's deep-set eyes, and his face was gray. He needed a good shave and his periwig sat askew. His clothes had been nicely brushed and the scent in which he was liberally doused almost succeeded in covering the odor of unwashed flesh. Almost.

"My Lady Rosamund," he said, opening his arms to appraise what stood between them. "You are full of surprises, are you not? Here you are, manager of this fine establishment"—he turned back to the main room—"filled to the brim with court and country, cowering in the kitchen with the menials." He dropped into an exaggerated bow beside her stool and pulled off his hat. "Still, I understand someone wanting to keep an eye on their investments—of all kinds. Maybe I can make a businesswoman of you yet?"

At his entry, Bianca had leaped to her feet. Cara, the kitchen hand, ceased what she was doing and faced the intruders, her eyes sliding toward Rosamund, uncertain and a little frightened. It wasn't every day the gentry tripped into this part of the chocolate house. Likewise, Thomas and Solomon regarded the newcomers curiously. Jacopo moved to stand with Bianca.

Rosamund rose slowly. She'd learned to respect the authority her title gave her, no more so than here, in her territory. She might be working in the kitchen with "the menials," but it was her kitchen and these were her people. Strictly speaking, they were Matthew's, and this was his business, but she wasn't going to let those details destroy her little claim on power.

Aubrey's last words caused a stir in her chest. What did he mean, keep an eye on investments? She glanced at Mr. Bender, who offered the slightest of nods. Sam made a positive sign with his fingers. She bit back a smile. Seemed her stepson had accepted her offer after all. She'd been right assuming money was more important to him than people.

"Ah, well," she said with a deep curtsey, sweetening her tone. "I'd be foolish not to ensure I was striking a fair bargain, would I not?" Praying Bianca and Jacopo would forgive her next words, she continued. "You said yourself an owner must wrest every last ounce from their slaves. You were right. Hence, I thought to test their value by putting them to work here as well as at the manor."

Beside her, Bianca grew very still. Jacopo made a noise that might have been a groan or a growl, she couldn't tell. She wished she could reassure them. She prayed with all her soul they understood her purpose.

"Indeed, one must give them as much work as one can. An idle savage is a dangerous one. Work them until they can no longer stand, so their minds do not stray to matters that are not within their compass to understand." Aubrey strode toward Jacopo and Bianca, stopping inches from them, examining them as if they were cattle about to be auctioned. *Mayhap,* thought Rosamund, *to him they were.* "Clearly, you aren't working this pair hard enough. Father never did. He allowed them to develop airs and ideas that have no right in a tawneymoor's head." He tapped Jacopo hard upon the skull.

To his credit, the man didn't flinch.

"That's why I was hesitant to concede to your wishes, Lady Rosamund—or may I call you Rosamund? After all, we're family, are we not?"

"Indeed, we are, Aubrey," said Rosamund.

He gave her a smile, his eyes crinkling in the corners, though there was no joy behind them, just pure calculation. "Excellent. Well, Rosamund, if you will but take my guidance on how to deal with your slaves, I will be happy to provide it. With correct handling, you can gain much from this pair—they're literate and, in the right conditions, they'll work hard and may even be a boon to you. In fact, that's how Mr. Bender persuaded me to agree to your terms. He reminded me that as an ignorant woman, you will look to a man for example. With Father being dead, I am now the example from which you will learn. The notion gives me great pleasure." He smiled again and gave a half bow.

Rosamund dipped her head. "And me too, Aubrey. I thank you. So am I to understand you have signed the relevant papers transferring ownership of Bianca and Jacopo to me?"

Cara dropped a bowl. It clanged as it struck the tub before breaking into shards on the floor. Red-faced, she muttered apologies and, with Thomas's help, quickly began to pick up the pieces.

"I have." Aubrey gestured to Mr. Bender, who passed a roll of documents to Rosamund. "They are all yours. I just hope, Rosamund, that what I saw last night, the liberties being taken, will not happen again. Not under my roof." He tugged at Bianca's apron. "You have given them ideas beyond their station. A respect they don't warrant. Time to end this. They are slaves. Your slaves. Your property."

"To do with as I wish," said Rosamund, an edge of sharpness creeping into her tone.

Mr. Bender gave the slightest shake of his head.

Sam cleared his throat as if about to speak.

Rosamund continued swiftly. "I assure you, sir, I will employ Jacopo and Bianca as you advise and in a manner suited to their birth." She smiled graciously.

"Their birth?" said Aubrey, his face growing red. If Rosamund thought to appease him, to reinforce their low status, she was wrong. He glared. "Do not speak to me of their birth. They're slaves. No more and no less on God's good earth and in His eyes. Remember that." He glowered. "You do but show your good Christian charity in thinking otherwise, madam." His frown transformed into a wide smile, revealing all that remained of his teeth. He was as mercurial as a summer storm. "And now, my lady mother, they're yours. Do not make me regret this."

"Of that you can be certain, Aubrey." Rosamund didn't dare look at either Bianca or Jacopo. What must they be thinking?

Mr. Bender sought to clarify matters. "You understand, Lady Rosamund, that from this day forth, in exchange for the slaves, you'll not receive another cent from the Blithman estate?"

"I do," said Rosamund.

Sam gave her a look that might have been approval but also could have been disappointment. She'd been less than open about this part of the transaction.

"Of course, as my stepmother, you will continue to live beneath my roof," said Aubrey suddenly. "In fact, I'm hoping we'll get to know each other better and, in time, very well." The way he regarded her with his asymmetrical eyes and thin, mobile mouth made Rosamund's skin goose. She swallowed.

"I would like that." She prayed she sounded sincere.

"Very well, then. I will retire to the main room and join the conversation. Appears the Dutch have been at it again. I look forward very much to trying more of your chocolate, Rosamund."

Rosamund curtseyed, keeping her head bowed. "And I look forward to preparing more for you, Aubrey. I will send out a bowl shortly."

Aubrey took her hand and helped her rise, then brought her fingers to his lips. At the last minute, he turned over her hand and impressed a kiss in the palm. His mouth was dry, hot. Unlike his tongue, which was slick and thick. A shudder passed through her, which Aubrey caught and read a particular way. His eyes gleamed.

"It's not just me who's been resurrected, Rosamund, but in your face, your presence, your status as a Blithman, my beloved sister too. Just as we looked to each other's well-being, loved each other as family should while she was alive, I hope and pray we can do the same."

With a final squeeze of her fingers, he released her. Before Sam could escape, Aubrey threw an arm around his shoulders and strode from the kitchen, laughing and nudging him when he didn't share his humor.

Mr. Bender went to speak, then shut his mouth. With a bow and a lingering look at Rosamund, he too left. Rosamund would be sure to thank him later, when she knew Aubrey was out of earshot.

It was some time before Thomas and Solomon started working their *molinillos* again. Some burned cacao beans had to be tossed into the rubbish and new ones set to roast over the coals. Cara returned to the dishes, casting furtive glances over her shoulder to make sure that man didn't enter again.

Aware something had happened, but unable to leave the bar, Filip sent querying looks toward Rosamund. She signaled she would explain everything later.

She sank onto her stool, the documents held fast in her fist. Aubrey had agreed to her bargain. She had the papers to prove it. In exchange for her jointure, calculated over a period of forty years (presuming she lived to such a ripe old age), he'd sold Jacopo and Bianca to her. They were hers. Could Jacopo and Bianca ever forgive her for dealing with them in such a manner? For not asking their approval? For owning them as one did a herd of sheep or a block of land?

Ready to face their accusations and their hurt, she rose as they approached, their faces unreadable. Before she could explain, Bianca kissed her soundly on the forehead and cheeks and pulled her into a strong embrace. Jacopo wrapped his arms about them both and held them tight.

"*Grazie mille, signora bella,*" murmured Bianca. Was that a quaver in her voice?

"*Grazie mille, grazie mille,*" repeated Jacopo over and over.

Closing her eyes, Rosamund lost herself in the wonder of two sets of arms enfolding her in gratitude and—dare she think it?—affection.

How strange that when she was certain she'd be showered with opprobrium, two of the people she cared for most felt nothing but gratitude. Yet, what she'd done was treat them like a commodity to be bought and sold. Aye, she'd bought them. Argued a price, bargained for their lives. The irony was not lost on her that this was exactly what Sir Everard had tried to do with her before Tilly had turned it into a transaction of a different kind.

The apologies she'd prepared weren't needed. Just as she didn't need a piece of paper to know Jacopo and Bianca were hers, they knew that she was theirs. The important thing was to ensure Aubrey never saw the depth of their feelings for one another.

Was it not a sin to covet possessions? Well, God forgive her, she cherished her two newest ones. With all her damned heart.

THIRTY-TWO
In which old wounds are made afresh

Despite being away so long, Matthew's first impressions were that nothing appeared to have changed in the river city. Better than anyone, he knew how looks could be deceiving, and even if London seemed to be operating under the principle of business as usual, it *had* changed—the last two hours he'd spent at Whitehall delivering his report on the situation in Holland to His Majesty and Sir Henry Bennet and his sidekick, Joseph Williamson, were enough to alert him to that. But it was what he saw and heard for himself as he strode the halls of the palace, the taut anxiety beneath the whispers, the false bravado—not about the worsening hostilities as he'd anticipated, but about the pestilence—that gave him cause for alarm.

Pushing aside thoughts of sickness, grateful to have executed his duty to King and country, Matthew gazed around, drinking in the sights from his vantage point upon a wherry. The sky was a cloudless blue, the church spires, which looked more like scaffolding designed to keep the heavens aloft, shone in the sun's glorious rays. The mud-brown river was filled with craft determined to make the best of the weather, though, according to the boatman, ever since spring took hold the sun had been a regular companion.

"So," Matthew said to his one-eyed boatman, an old sailor by the look of the many scars that bit into the flesh of his arms and neck, "what have you heard of this pestilence?"

The boatman gave him a grim look. "I hear it has taken some forty lives thus far, sir. All but one being outside London's walls, in St. Giles in the Field, St. Clement Danes and the like. No one credits 'em much, neither the dead nor their parishes, and by no one, I mean them rich coves what you be talking to back at Whitehall. The likes of them never does 'less they be afflicted, does they?"

In the main, the boatman had the right of it, Matthew thought. Providing the plague stayed among the poor, it was unlikely too much would be done. There were even those among the Council who regarded the pestilence as a way of controlling the underclass. He'd heard them with his own ears. He might yet write about such a cruel and ungodly notion.

"What's the cause of all the smoke?" asked Matthew, nodding toward great gray pillars rising around the city and soaring into the heavens.

The boatman followed the direction of his gaze. "Bonfires. Lit by order of the Lord Mayor. He insisted they be struck and the streets kept clean. Until the King moves court, we don't 'ave much to worry about. Once His Majesty goes, I'll reconsider my view. If there's one thing we all know, it's that fuckin' royalty are like rats—they'll desert a sinkin' ship."

Maneuvering the wherry as close to the riverbank as he could, the boatman rested the prow on the moss-covered stairs with his oar. "Still, doesn't hurt to be cautious, does it? Go with God, sir, and avoid crowds, that's my advice." He held up a jar with a few inches of grubby-looking liquid in it and indicated Matthew was to put his payment inside. As he dropped in the coins, the tang of vinegar was evident. Already such precautions were deemed necessary.

Matthew knew he should go to his lodgings and wash, erase some of the travels from his clothes and body, but he had only one thought, and that was the

Phoenix. Convincing himself it was because he'd been too long away from his business and that he needed to be there in case the precious cargoes he'd sent back from Jamaica and Spain were delivered, he refused to contemplate that a pair of brown eyes and sweet dimples also called to him.

It was midday before Matthew entered the familiar stones of Birchin Lane. Rather than increasing his pace now his goal was near, he slowed and thought about his ship, the *Odyssey*, anchored midriver near Gravesend as officialdom dealt with crew and cargo. He hoped the sailors would soon be allowed ashore and that the younger of the men heeded Captain Browning's warning about press-gangs. That was a subject upon which he intended to write again—the misery of impressment. He'd encountered too many broken boys and men on his ventures, snatched from their lives and forced onto ships and into battle before they'd time to catch their breath.

The bell over the door of the bookshop rang prettily as he entered, and he was grateful for the respite from the heat. He could hear Will talking with some customers. Matthew climbed the stairs, then hesitated on the threshold of the chocolate house and took a deep breath.

The bowl of coins was in its usual position. The room was a cacophony of voices and song. A recitation was occurring to his right. Near the window to his left, a game of cards was in progress. Laughter rang out and then a shout as a candle auction finished. God, he'd not seen one of those in an age. Cheers erupted and men stood, clapping one another soundly on the back. There was a call for drinks.

A few at the nearest booth looked up and saw him. "What news?" cried one, ever quick to be the first.

Before he could respond, another voice rose above the others.

"Matthew?" Pure, sweet and with a joyous inflection that rang with disbelief and hope all at once, it floated above all other sounds.

His eyes slid from the men waiting to hear his news to search for the lips bearing his name.

In all his imaginings, he hadn't pictured her like this. A lush, pearly-haired goddess with rosy cheeks, vibrant, flashing eyes and laughing mouth made her way toward him, acknowledging those who would detain her, including some young rakes who reached out in yearning. She smiled them aside and with a mere touch of her slender fingers parted shoulders the way God did oceans. Her forest-green dress made her look like a sylvan goddess come to play among the mortals.

Speechless, he watched her draw closer, seeming to float toward him, her skirts flowing, her smile radiant.

All that lay between them was a few feet of wooden floor. Smoke swirled and teased.

His voice was trapped in his throat. The remnants of his broken heart rode a tide of such longing, they stole his welcome. Instead, he held out his arms and, with a cry of wonder and delight, Rosamund Blithman, once the wife of his mortal enemy, flew into them.

At least, that was how their reunion played out in his imagination. The reality was, she stopped a few feet short of him, the expression on her face altering from joy to remembrance to distaste. The arms he'd started to raise dropped to his sides.

Curtseying before him, she said, "May God give you good day, sir," as if he were a stranger.

He bowed, remembering at the last moment to sweep off his hat, a lance of hurt slicing his chest. "And you too, my lady."

They stared at each other awkwardly. Her mouth moved. His too, but neither spoke.

"Welcome back," she said finally, looking uncertain.

Before he could reply, Filip came and slapped him on the back, embracing him as he wished other arms had, and planting kisses on both his cheeks and firing questions at him. Jacopo appeared, as did Harry. Hodge and the other boys hung off his arms, all talking at once and bumping his wretched satchel. Desperate to ask Rosamund what was wrong, he did not have the chance as he was swiftly escorted through the chocolate house and hailed by familiar faces.

All too soon he was sat in his favorite booth, surrounded by those eager to hear his stories.

Oh, he was back all right, he thought, as he nodded to all and sundry. But, as he began to tell of his adventures, his eyes strayed toward Rosamund behind the bar, her anxious face appraising him. Was he really welcome?

THIRTY-THREE
In which death rides
a pale horse

It took all her willpower, all the little tricks she'd learned presiding over the Phoenix and feigning interest she didn't always feel, *not* to stare. Here was Matthew, after all this time, safe and sound, returned to her chocolate house. *His* chocolate house.

Had she imagined the happiness she felt radiating from him when he'd stepped through the door? She knew she hadn't invented the emotions sweeping through her when she caught sight of him. Lord knew, her feet took on a life of their own, running toward him before she had a chance to think.

She wanted to laugh, weep, hold him, stroke his cheek, bombard him with questions just as the boys were doing, order the patrons out and lock the doors so she might have him all to herself. Mostly, she wanted to hold his hand lest he vanish like the smoke floating about the ceiling. For so long she'd envisaged just this moment, yet it was even better than her wildest conjurings—well, almost. In her wildest, they hadn't used words to welcome each other . . .

Stop that. Just as Matthew seemed reticent to show his pleasure at seeing her again, amid all her joy, she too felt an unpleasant tug, as if she'd repressed something that only he could liberate.

Then she realized. Of late two men had come back from their respective journeys and in doing so altered her circumstances. With the lease up for renewal soon, there was a chance Matthew might take over the running of the chocolate house himself; then where would she be? Never mind Aubrey bursting onto the scene and demanding his inheritance.

The peace of mind and autonomy her widowhood had brought were ending. As she stayed her impulse to run into his arms and held her emotions in check as a lady should, she remembered Aubrey Blithman and worked to keep the displeasure from her face. She had to tell Matthew he was back from the dead. They might have once been related through marriage, but there was no doubt in her mind Aubrey felt only enmity toward Matthew. The very idea stopped her in her tracks. Made the bile rise in her throat. Poor Matthew. She couldn't bear to give him such tidings—not yet. Better to keep her distance and tell him after he had time to settle. When they were, please God, alone.

Their reunion lacked the warmth she felt and which she hoped and prayed he shared. Before she could whisper that she would talk properly to him later, he was whisked from her side.

Surreptitiously watching him from the bar as he was surrounded by welcoming faces, she ceded other patrons to Solomon and Thomas and prepared Matthew a bowl of chocolate. If she couldn't express how she felt with words, she would do it with the drink.

She added everything she knew he enjoyed and carried the tray herself with a fine silver chocolate pot and a new porcelain bowl. The crowd around Matthew melted away as she approached.

Aware of his eyes upon her, she slowly poured the thick chocolate into the prepared bowl and passed it to him carefully.

Their eyes met through the steam and his hands enveloped hers as he took the vessel from her, sending a hot river of longing flowing down her arms, into her middle and infusing her every extremity with fire. All the words of welcome she'd been unable to say rushed out in a laugh of sheer happiness.

Much to her relief, his eyes widened and he too began to laugh, their initial discomfort forgotten. His eyes creased, his hands lingered over hers, and the noise of the room, the press of bodies and the chatter of those around them, faded away. All she knew was a pair of midnight eyes, warm hands, her heated body and their silent conversation.

When he finally took the bowl and blew across the surface, she slid into the booth and sat opposite him. From there she could see that beneath the weariness, the sheer exhaustion of traveling so far for so long, there was also great sadness. Was it because he had failed to deliver the letters? Or something else? Would he tell her? She prayed she was not the cause; while the prospect of his return had stirred a veritable storm of emotions within her, they were nothing compared to how she felt now he was really, truly there. Feelings that the chocolate and her laugh had, devil take them, revealed. It was as if someone had picked her up by the feet and shaken her so all her insides were in confusion.

Meanwhile Matthew recounted the final stages of his journey, how difficult it had been to leave The Hague given the suspicion surrounding English ships with the outbreak of war. It wasn't until he was vouched for by an Englishman living there, the son of a regicide no less, that he was allowed to leave. (Matthew would later tell Rosamund that though the gentleman, William Scott, was meant to be one of Sir Henry Bennet's spies, he believed he might be a double agent.)

"It took weeks to reassure them. I wrote I'd be here sooner—"

Rosamund rewarded him with a small smile.

"—but I hadn't anticipated war being declared. I'm sorry," he said. "Not for the war, you understand." He flashed a grin. "That was inevitable. But being so misguided in my timing."

"Don't be," said Rosamund. "All that matters is that you're back now; you're safe."

With that, she left him and returned to her neglected customers. The new ones were curious about the rather disheveled man who had drawn their Rosamund from behind the bar and into a booth, and wished they possessed the power to do the same. The regulars acknowledged Matthew with a glum nod, understanding that he took precedence in Rosamund's attentions.

It wasn't until the last customers had departed and the doors had been shut, that Matthew and Rosamund were able to speak. From the kitchen the clatter of washing and cleaning issued, along with chuckles and shrieks as the drawers and Cara prepared for the morrow, supervised by Filip, Solomon and Thomas.

Over a glass of Rhenish, Rosamund was able to tell Matthew what had happened since she last wrote.

When she reached the part about Aubrey's return, Matthew almost dropped his glass. "Aubrey Blithman? He's here?" He swung toward Jacopo and Bianca, who were hovering nearby, polishing pots and spoons. They both nodded solemnly.

It was only much later that Rosamund would reflect that Matthew didn't comment on the extraordinary fact of him being alive.

Matthew placed his hands on the table and stared at them. "Aubrey Blithman is *here*," he repeated slowly, as if by saying the words once more he might believe them. "In London."

"Aye, he is," said Rosamund carefully. "He's only been here a few days. He's taken up residence in Blithe Manor. I can still scarce believe it—"

"Truth, Rosamund, I can scarce believe it myself." Matthew's face took on a faraway look, as if his mind had departed his body and was traveling through darker reaches.

When he didn't speak, Rosamund continued. "He walked into the withdrawing room as if he'd never left."

Matthew returned to the moment. "And saw you," he said quietly.

Rosamund nodded.

Matthew began to drum his fingers against the table; a tic in his cheek worked frantically. Rosamund was uncertain what to say. She glanced toward Bianca, who found the chocolate pot she was shining very interesting.

Just when Rosamund thought she must break the silence between them, he began to chuckle. There was no humor in it. "Well, I'll be Satan's dalcop . . ." he said.

Rosamund picked up the tale. "He came with Sir Everard's steward Wat Smithyman in tow. He now serves Aubrey. I believe he was the first to deliver news of his father's death."

"I see. Wat . . ." Matthew shook his head in disbelief. "I confess, I hadn't expected this." He made a fist and rested it on the table, clenching and unclenching it. "It's not every day one returns from the dead."

Rosamund couldn't help but think how people had an uncanny way of reappearing in her life when she least expected it—look at Tilly and now Aubrey. Why, Matthew had been a revelation in more ways than one.

"I would like very much to see this miracle for myself," said Matthew and, finishing his wine, slapped his thighs and rose to his feet.

Rosamund leaped to hers in a rush of disappointment that he would consider leaving so soon. "You're going?"

"Only to my lodgings, my lady. I mean, you have everything under control and, frankly, I could do with a bath, perhaps even a brief rest. It's been a long day . . . a long . . . ." He didn't finish.

"Of course," said Rosamund swiftly, wringing her hands. "Forgive me. I just hoped we might . . . ." She stopped, unable to meet his eyes. What did she hope?

He rescued her. "I thought I might call upon you at Blithe Manor later tonight, if that would be suitable? Not only will I get to extend my greetings and express my delight at his resurrection to Aubrey, but perhaps you and I can find some time to discuss the chocolate house."

Rosamund, who'd been expanding inside with every word, almost deflated at the last two. As much as she loved the Phoenix and saw it as an extension of herself, surely they had more to talk about than that, even if it was the bridge that connected them. One bridge.

"That would be . . . most convenient," said Rosamund, trying not to show the disappointment she felt. "I will tell Aubrey to expect you when I get back to the manor."

Matthew began to say his farewells. Her spirits soared to think she would see him tonight and again the following day—and, God be praised, every day thereafter. Yet for all the pleasure he expressed at returning, she couldn't shake the feeling that somehow Matthew was disenchanted.

It couldn't be with the Phoenix, surely. Why, when he arrived it was filled to the brim and abuzz with men and conversation like bees in St. James's Park. Something else was bothering him, leaving him downhearted and restless.

Until she mentioned Aubrey Blithman. Then his entire demeanor had undergone a shift, and an expression crossed his face that even now she found puzzling. What was it? A slight widening of his eyes, followed by a furrow of his brow. The bitter laugh. A thinning of his lips and a tic in those fine cheeks. It wasn't disenchantment; it was resignation. As if he was about to face defeat at the hands of his enemy.

Upon her return to the manor that evening, Rosamund was met with a house in chaos. The hall was filled with chests, sacks of food from the larder and crates of wine. Maids and footmen ran to and fro throwing armfuls of clothes and linens into an open box here, pushing a wedge of cheese into a straw-filled crate there. In the midst of the mayhem Wat shouted orders to one poor wench, demanding a barrel of beer be brought from the cellar before swinging around to cuff a young footman and then bellowing for Widow Ashe. A slight girl appeared with a brace of stinking pigeons. Wat told her to take it straight out to the coach. Coach?

"What's going on?" asked Rosamund finally.

"Madam, you're back," said Wat.

"I am indeed." She peered about in amazement. Jacopo lifted a jug of cider from a crate and put it down. Bianca peered into an open chest.

"Leave those," snapped Wat.

"Please, Wat. What's all this about?"

"It's Mr. Aubrey, madam—he's ordered us to pack up the house. We're leaving."

"We? Leaving? But why? What has prompted this?" She swung toward Bianca and Jacopo and back again. "Where's Ashe?"

Before Wat could answer, there was a cry from the top of the stairs. Much to her astonishment, it was Sam Pepys. "Rosamund! At last. You're very late. Aubrey was about to send for you."

"Send for me?"

Before Sam could descend the stairs, Rosamund began to climb them, throwing herself against the rail as two footmen hurtled down carrying what appeared to be some ledgers from Sir Everard's—Aubrey's—study.

At the top, she tolerated Sam's usual kiss before sweeping him aside. "Where's Aubrey?"

"In the study, sorting whatever bookwork he needs to take with him."

"Take with him?" Dear God, she was like one of those colorful parrots in the market, repeating everything. For a brief moment, she wondered if Aubrey had decided to return to the New World and was astonished at the wave of relief that swept over her.

Sam stared. "You didn't know?"

"Know what?"

With a sigh of exasperation, Sam beckoned for her to follow him into the withdrawing room. She'd have preferred to go to the study and confront Aubrey then and there, but nevertheless complied, gesturing for Bianca and Jacopo to follow.

Before Jacopo had even shut the door, Sam began. "I fear this is my fault."

"What is?" asked Rosamund, moving to the window and glancing out, half expecting to see an exodus of people in the street below.

"Aubrey's plans," said Sam. "You see, I came here with the express intention to share with you my sadness at Lady Sandwich's intended departure from the city. While I think she may be a bit precipitous, when I called at the coffee house on my way—"

Rosamund could have screamed. Sam took forever to get to the point, and asking him to hurry only made things worse. Surrendering to his tale, she threw herself into a chair, nodding toward Jacopo, who held a jug of wine and glasses aloft. She pulled off her hat and gloves and listened.

Sam continued without a pause as he sank into the seat opposite. "I found the place agog with news. Not only were the men prating on about the Dutch movements at sea, but about the plague and all the varying remedies being proposed. You should hear what some are suggesting, Rosamund." He rolled his eyes. "Purges, balms, balsams, cordials, amulets—as if the blasted smoke from the Lord Mayor's fires isn't enough. There are those set to make a fortune from others' misfortune, you mark my words."

"I do, Sam, I do." Rosamund tried hard to keep the exasperation out of her tone. "Which is why I need you to tell me what Aubrey is planning. He's only just returned, after all. He has a manor to manage, staff to care for, his business . . ."

Sam's big round eyes blinked. "But I *am* telling. You see, when I told the Lady Sandwich the latest figures from the Bills of Mortality, she made up her mind there and then to leave the city. When I told Aubrey of her intentions, along with what I overheard in the coffee house, well, he made the decision he would not remain in London a moment longer."

"Surely he can't expect everyone to up and leave without warning. Where is he going?"

At that moment, the door flung open. Aubrey appeared, red-faced, his eyes bleary and his entire body reeking of wine. "Anywhere there isn't plague," he announced. "Which, I am reliably informed"—he gestured in Sam's direction and would have fallen had Jacopo not grabbed his arm—"is Oxford."

"Oxford." Rosamund started to stand. Had the plague suddenly swept down upon them while they were busy welcoming Matthew back? The Bills were published weekly and available for all who could to read. The last ones she'd seen hadn't given cause for too much alarm.

"Yes. Oxford," said Aubrey, snatching his arm from Jacopo. "I have it on good authority—not yours this time, Sam—that when the court defects, which will no doubt be any moment, it will be to Oxford. I want us outside the city gates before they shut." He flapped his arms. "Hurry, hurry. Go and change and pack whatever you deem essential for a long stay. I'll not set foot in London again until this dreaded visitation has well and truly passed." He burped. "I didn't survive the threat of assassins, numerous ocean voyages, the presence of New World savages, let alone reports of my demise, to be beaten by a disease."

Rosamund stared at Aubrey and Sam in disbelief. "But . . . but . . . what about the house? The servants?"

Aubrey blinked. "What about them? One will care for the other. Now, go to. I am not a patient man."

Rosamund gazed helplessly at Bianca and Jacopo. Dear God. This was madness. She couldn't just up and leave. Aubrey had only recently acquired his father's empire, but she had people who relied on her, a business to run, a household to oversee. What did he mean, one will care for the other? Could he be so indifferent in the face of something he so evidently feared? She wanted to protest, appeal to his better self, but the words became knotted. At last, something wriggled free.

"You cannot depart. Mr. Lovelace intends to call," she sputtered. Even to her ears, that sounded lame.

Wat chose that moment to enter the room. "Ah, there you are, sir. I need—"

"Lovelace?" interrupted Aubrey, holding up his hand to prevent Wat from continuing. "Coming *here?*" He gripped the mantel. "*Matthew Lovelace?* I thought he'd left these shores for good."

"Not for good. But for a purpose," said Rosamund. "He's back and intends to call upon you this evening."

Aubrey shot a look at Wat, who arched a brow.

"Well then, all the more reason to go," he said and pushed himself away from the mantel. "Immediately. I've no desire to see the man responsible for the death of my father."

He began to pace, his voice growing more forceful with every step. "I don't know what you're thinking, Rosamund. First you work for the man and now you have the gall to invite him to *my* house. I might be forced to tolerate this chocolate house and your unhealthy obsession with the drink, but I'll not tolerate his presence—certainly not under my roof." He swung toward her, shouting, "Do you hear me?" Aubrey's chest heaved; his eyes started from his head.

Sam gazed at him in astonishment.

Rosamund lowered her chin.

"Sir," began Wat, "the coach is ready. The horses too."

"Yes. Yes," said Aubrey, panting. "I know." He took a deep breath and held out a hand in a conciliatory gesture. "Come. We've wasted enough time. We must be going."

Rosamund looked from his hand to his face. "I would not wish to affect your plans, sir. I am grateful for the offer to accompany you, but I decline. I will await Mr. Lovelace in your absence."

"What?" roared Aubrey, slamming his fist upon the mantelpiece. "No. No. No. No. What do you think this is? An excursion to the country?" Wat tried to steady him, but Aubrey shook him off. "Who gives a damn about Lovelace? This is a matter of life and death."

"I well understand that, sir. My life, my death and those I am responsible for." She gestured to Bianca, Jacopo and Ashe.

Aubrey's face turned a peculiar shade of vermillion and his eyes narrowed. He pointed at Bianca then Jacopo. "This isn't about Lovelace at all, is it? You'll not leave *them*." Spittle flew. "Have you forgotten who you are? My father may have raised you out of the gutter, but you're a Blithman now, *Lady* Blithman." His voice rose an octave. "You're still under my control and you'll do as you're damn well told. Go and gather your things. If you don't, then you'll just have to make do with what you're wearing. I care not."

Shrinking the distance between them, Rosamund stood before him. Uncertain where her courage came from, she didn't question it but used it to fire her words.

"You're mistaken, Aubrey. Your father didn't raise me out of the gutter but lifted me off a road. A road

I chose of my own volition, taking my own path." He didn't need to know the details, and Rosamund was certain Jacopo wasn't about to enlighten him. Drawing herself up, her chocolate eyes flashed. "And yes, I *am* Lady Blithman and as such, I take my responsibilities to the name, and my staff and my friends, very seriously. You're right. This is nothing to do with Mr. Lovelace, and everything to do with my duty to those who need me. You go if you wish, but I intend to remain."

For just a fraction of a moment, a cat's whisker of time, Rosamund thought Aubrey might strike her. Perhaps he intended to, but with Sam present, he wisely changed his mind. His features rearranged themselves from incandescent rage to iron control as her refusal sank in. The color left his cheeks; the fury in his eyes dimmed. He glanced at Jacopo and Bianca with resentment and disgust before his gaze returned to Rosamund. He appeared to vacillate.

"Sir," said Wat, plucking at his sleeve. "If we don't leave soon, the gates'll be closing." He shuffled closer. "There are four parishes within the walls affected now. Remember what Mr. Pepys told us: he saw some houses shut up on the way here—with his own peepers."

"Only one or two," added Sam meekly.

Disbelief at Rosamund's decision transformed to fear. Self-preservation won. Rosamund didn't move.

With a roar, Aubrey dashed his glass at the hearth, narrowly missing Sam. It shattered, a musical rain as it struck the metal grate. "Very well, you little fool. Have it your own way. Stay. Stay and risk being condemned by your own stubbornness." He began to stamp out of the room, an overindulged child whose wishes had been thwarted. At the last moment he swung around and wagged a finger at her.

"Don't you forget, when you're ravaged by sickness, when you're crying out for a friend, that I could have saved you. That I would have spared you . . ."

"I won't," said Rosamund.

"I will look to her, Aubrey," said Sam gallantly.

His eyes flicked toward the naval clerk then fixed on Bianca and Jacopo.

"If the pestilence doesn't kill you," he said between clenched teeth, "I want you gone by the time I return, do you hear? I don't care that you belong to her, I don't care what she fills your barbarian heads with, she chose *you* above sense, above family. Therefore, you're no longer welcome in this house, in my presence. Understood?"

With an elegance Aubrey and his fiery, cruel words didn't deserve, Jacopo bowed and Bianca curtseyed. "Yes, my lord," they said in unison, their accents flattened into the broad syllables of English.

"Look after the damn house, then," he said to Rosamund.

Despite the heat of the moment, Rosamund felt a laugh mixed with tears start to build.

Aubrey stormed from the room and down the stairs, followed by Wat. The others stood in silence listening to Aubrey shouting orders as doors crashed, servants grunted as they hoisted the last of whatever he demanded into the conveyance he'd hired. Jacopo poured them each a wine, then carefully picked up the broken glass. Drifting to the window, Rosamund saw the moment the carriage took off down the street, its roof laden with boxes, the curtains and shutters drawn. Wat sat up beside the driver. Aubrey rode alongside it on a fine pale horse with a tidy mane and a high step. People moved out of its way and Aubrey used his crop to discourage their proximity, urging the beast to a speed that had no place on such a crowded street.

Soon he was out of sight.

Once again, the manor was hers, the manor and responsibility for all who dwelled beneath its roof. And who'd have thought Sam would be so principled? She felt a rush of warmth toward him. Not only had he stood by her but he had offered to watch over her in Aubrey's absence. It was more than her stepson had been prepared to do. Not that she could really blame him. When plague threatened, no one in their right mind would remain if they had the option to flee.

Why, she must be quite mad, then. Mad enough to stay, mad enough to choose to align herself with those who'd done nothing but cleave to her side these past years. She could no more leave them than ask for her head to depart her shoulders.

When Ashe found them shortly after, they invited her to join them as they sat around the table, sharing shy, knowing looks. Moonlight pierced the curtains, mellowing the room. Outside, the evening bells tolled nine of the clock and a flock of pigeons settled in the eaves across the road, their cooing an adieu to the day.

"Well," said Rosamund as the house slowly returned to normal, the scurrying of the maids and footmen ceasing. Doors shut without being slammed and windows were opened and curtains pulled back to allow the cool evening breezes (and the ever-present smoke) to enter. "If I'd known the lengths Aubrey would go to in order to avoid seeing Mr. Lovelace, I would never have invited him over."

There was a beat, then first Bianca, then Jacopo and Rosamund burst out laughing. Ashe smiled and buried her head. Sam was not quite sure what was so funny, as Mr. Lovelace's return was no cause for humor to him, but nevertheless he couldn't help joining in, the laughter was so infectious.

That was how Matthew found them only minutes later, bent over in gales of helpless mirth, tears streaming down their cheeks as beams of silvery light struck them, making them appear both lunatic and slightly ephemeral at the same time. As if the Holy Spirit had already claimed them.

THIRTY-FOUR
In which the bells were hoarse with tolling

The city was a furnace, a burning hellhole. Not even the cool interior of Will's bookshop or the cellars at Blithe Manor provided respite. The Phoenix, such a toasty escape in the colder months, became a hothouse where the inhabitants mostly wilted as the smoke and steam seemed to wrap opaque fingers around each and every person. Was not the pestilence caused by miasmas? The pamphlets recommended tobacco as a prophylactic against plague, so the men would puff away and regard the dusky clouds sprouting from their pipes with squinting satisfaction.

Outside, heat haze shimmered above the cobbles and barefoot urchins danced from shadow to shadow. Sweat dripped from the coach drivers, horses shone with perspiration and women forced to endure the outdoors fanned themselves, the effort required to arouse a breeze raising a greater sheen than enduring it. Flower beds and herbs shrank and curled into fragile brown skeletons; the ground their roots clung to cracked into crazed shapes. Beyond London's walls, the once green fields lay scorched and brittle, the cattle and sheep searching for sustenance.

The animals suffered and so did their humans, who were not only suffocating in the torrid heat but drowning in a well of fear as day by day the number of those infected by plague grew. At first, the pestilence appeared to be mostly contained outside the city walls, but like a greedy thief, it crept inside and swallowed life after life.

When Sam came to the chocolate house and told Rosamund and Matthew he'd seen the first house in Drury Lane marked with a crude red cross—the sign of plague—it had well and truly breached the walls.

"To think, I was only at the theater there a few nights ago. Hundreds of others were there as well . . . What if they're infected? What if . . ." Stroking his chest thoughtfully, he didn't need to complete the sentence; he shuddered and avoided their eyes lest he see in them an echo of his own terror, before finding himself a seat away from other patrons and ordering from a subdued Harry.

"They've closed the theaters now. What will be next? I wonder." Rosamund joined Matthew in his usual booth and filled the bowl at his elbow with chocolate.

Matthew put down his quill and watched the chocolate undulate from the spout. "Anywhere that people gather is potentially dangerous. The Inns of Court have been let go, and there's talk of schools and the like shutting." He flicked the news sheet next to him.

Rosamund pulled it toward her and digested the contents, then slowly looked about. The Phoenix was a place where people gathered—to read, talk, exchange information, be reassured, share their troubles, learn and be entertained. How was it different from the theaters? The Inns of Court? Half the time lawyers and students filled the booths discussing cases and points of law. Actors from both the King's Theater and the Duke's Company oft did readings at the tables.

"Do you think we might have to close?"

"Who knows?" Matthew followed her gaze as she stared at the patrons around her.

"Do you think we should?" She passed the news sheet back.

Matthew took her hands in his. He continued to wear his gloves. She wondered briefly what his tortured skin would feel like. When he'd shown his hands to her, they looked like rough shells or melted wax, with ribbons, craters and bridges of shiny skin. "Not yet. I think people need some normality at a time like this. It's the least we can offer."

"And chocolate," she said softly, smiling at him.

They locked eyes, liquid mahogany and shining cobalt.

"And chocolate," he repeated, staring at her lips as if he would drink from them.

She gently extracted her hands, gave a solemn nod and returned to the bar. How could she be so . . . wanton, when they'd been discussing such a serious matter? She thought about what Matthew had said. It was important to present at least a semblance of normality, even if beneath the veneer they were all at sea with their own anxieties. It was hard not to think about the plague. It was no longer a matter of if they'd be affected, but when.

News from the provinces indicated some of the towns outside London were afflicted. Sam arrived at the manor flustered one Saturday evening after taking a hackney coach to Holborn. The driver seemed fine at first, but after a while the coach drew to halt and the driver dismounted. Hardly able to stand, he staggered about the roadway. Sam stepped down to see what was wrong. The coachman complained he was very sick and unable to see, then collapsed. Sam didn't know what to do. Afeared and deeply saddened, he hailed another conveyance and left. He was certain the driver had been struck with plague. Rosamund gave him wine and chocolate to help soothe his troubled conscience.

In accordance with the plague orders, Matthew and Rosamund instructed the staff to sit patrons apart as much as possible and to keep the chocolate house extra clean. Each evening the floors were scrubbed, the bowls and pots thoroughly washed and the tables and bench tops wiped with a mixture of lemon juice and vinegar. Matthew also insisted the drawers wash their faces, hands and necks each morning and that their collars and cuffs be refreshed as often as possible. If they didn't arrive clean enough to pass his and Bianca's inspection, he threatened to march them down to the yard and strip and wash them himself. He also told the boys that if they developed a cough, fever, chills or headache, or signs of any spots or boils on their bodies—or indeed on the body of anyone in their household—they weren't to come to work, but send a message.

The boys and Cara exchanged frightened looks; they knew what that meant.

At Blithe Manor, Rosamund instigated identical practices. She asked Ashe to ensure all deliveries were left just inside the gate so only the servants carried them through the door. Instead of sending the laundry out and risking her dresses, sheets and other household linens coming into contact with potentially infected clothes or people, it was all done at home. Floors, cutlery and crockery were all to be washed daily. Cleaning cloths were to be either washed or burned. The maids didn't even complain. They understood these measures were to protect them.

When summer arrived in a blaze of heat, Matthew abandoned his lodgings in Beer Lane and moved into the Phoenix. He had already reassured Rosamund he wanted her to continue to run the business as per the lease they had signed; now she was able to see even more of him and observe the way he interacted with the customers as well as the staff. Only when it was essential did he serve or help out in the kitchen. His priority was continuing to write for Muddiman and L'Estrange, utilizing all he heard and saw at the chocolate house as the foundation of many of his articles. Inspired by what he'd learned on his travels, he began to take greater risks with some of his other work as well.

He began to write more tracts that could only be published anonymously for fear of the authorities. He wrote about how the court didn't care for the people but only their own necks, fleeing London when it most needed leadership. He began to record the names of all those in authority who had abandoned the capital, their businesses and professions. There were many, and not just nobles: physicians, lawyers, members of Parliament, constables, costermongers, coopers and men of God all fled. Determined to help, Rosamund persuaded Mr. Henderson to print Matthew's writings at night, when his apprentices had gone home.

When the Phoenix was quiet, she would send Wolstan, Hodge and whoever else she could spare to St. Paul's Cross or the Exchange to distribute the pieces, warning them to keep their caps down and their faces hidden. Leaving their uniforms behind at the chocolate house, the boys were grateful for the extra coin they'd earn. They also took pleasure in naming and shaming the "cowardly prigs" who had deserted their fellow Londoners at such a time.

In his efforts to uncover the author of the seditious tracts, L'Estrange sent men to investigate. Two came to the chocolate house. Far from subtle in their questioning, they leered at everyone and quizzed them where they sat, their purpose obvious in their dress and burly manner. This gave Matthew, Hodge, Art and Jacopo time to alert Mr. Henderson and swiftly remove any evidence—not that there was much. They were always careful. Rosamund worked hard to distract the two men, addressing them in a manner befitting their self-importance and inviting them to sit at the counter while she worked. She asked them about their jobs and homes and as they drank first one, then two more bowls of chocolate (on the house), they confided their fears for the future and the spread of the plague. They fell so completely under Rosamund's sympathetic spell, they left the premises persuaded only the best and most loyal of the King's supporters worked there—including Mr. Henderson, whose press, when they gave it a cursory glance, showed no evidence of having been used to print anything other than authorized material.

Matthew also wrote under his own name, emphasizing the plague orders and reminding people not to eat or sell rotten food, to be cautious when buying secondhand clothes and above all to remain clean. He also advised those who could afford it to seek the services of a reliable doctor, though God knew it was becoming harder to find someone to provide medick, let alone vittles, as bakers, butchers and other trades began to leave as well. The number of patrons coming to the Phoenix slowly reduced, which was just as well as it was becoming increasingly difficult to stock the chocolate house, and even Blithe Manor.

When the order came to cull all dogs and cats, they were rounded up and slaughtered by the thousands. The stench of their decaying corpses added to the horror crouching over the city. Rosamund could have sworn the rats celebrated now their predators were no longer there to reduce their population; every day she saw more evidence of them as the bolder ones crept along the sides of houses, crawled up drainpipes and even scavenged in the ditches. Cara said two had burrowed into a sack of flour that had been delivered. Rosamund told her not to worry, she was sure they hadn't eaten much.

When the old dog curled in the shade of the stoop opposite was there one day and gone the next, Rosamund had no desire to learn whether he'd been taken by a dogcatcher or spirited away overnight. She couldn't bear that innocent creatures were being sacrificed to the plague as well. It wasn't just dogs and cats either—rabbits, pigs, pigeons—none were spared. All were seen as potential carriers of disease and death. Mayhap they were, but if so, why was it that the more that were killed, the more humans died?

Rosamund could make no sense of it. God was not listening to her prayers—nor, it seemed, were her father and grandmother—much less the prayers of the entire city.

When Sam told them his doctor, Alexander Burnet, had succumbed to plague and his house had been shut up, Rosamund wondered what hope anyone had if even those who were experts in the disease were not spared.

The following day, Matthew accompanied Rosamund to church. As she stood in the warm interior of St. Helen's Bishopsgate, Rosamund was aware of the press of Matthew's hip against hers and the irony that, while gatherings of people were being discouraged, when it came to church services, all sense was forgotten. Or perhaps God would protect the righteous after all. Somehow, deep in her soul, Rosamund doubted it; if He did, He would have preserved Dr. Burnet and the little children in St. Giles. Perhaps he would have spared all the dogs and cats as well.

The reverend, emboldened now the King and court had fled, droned on about Sodom and Gomorrah and how a sinful city ruled by a lustful, hedonistic monarch should expect to feel God's wrath. The analogy was all too obvious and yet another indication of the low esteem in which His Majesty was held, even as prayers of thanks were offered for the safe return of his brother, the Duke, and the other naval commanders from the terrible battle against the Dutch at Lowestoft. Rosamund fanned herself with the old Bill of Mortality she'd found under the seat in front. Dated the week beginning the twentieth of June, it recorded one hundred and sixty-eight deaths, a marked increase on the week before.

For all the crush, the church was still emptier than it had been the previous Sunday. This wasn't so much because parishioners had fallen to the disease as it was a measure of how many had left the city. Once the King and court had retreated to Oxford, the wealthier citizens followed. All week, carts and carriages laden with families and supplies had rolled out the city gates and into the countryside.

Rosamund was surprised to find herself wondering how Aubrey fared. Tilly, too. Had the plague reached Oxford or Gravesend? She'd been remiss in writing to Frances and resolved that as soon as she returned home she would set aside time.

Bianca and Jacopo stood with the other servants at the back of the church. Rosamund found it difficult to reconcile the God she came to worship with the one who would shunt those who lived in her household to the back of His house. It had been the same at Graves-end. Tilly, Paul, the twins, Rosamund and the other merchants and innkeepers had always relinquished the prime seats to the gentry. Now Rosamund was gentry she didn't enjoy the privileges that came with her title when they caused a division she didn't permit in her daily life. She longed to sit with those she was familiar with and who, in such perilous times, she knew were not infected.

She looked over her shoulder and caught Bianca's eye. They exchanged a fleeting smile. Bianca didn't always attend church—at least, not St. Helen's. Not long after Sir Everard died, both Bianca and Jacopo explained to Rosamund what she'd long suspected—they were Quakers. At Rosamund's behest, Bianca introduced her to the writings of George Fox and James Nayler, two of the founders of Quakerism. Rosamund wasn't nearly as alarmed by their admission as she might have been; she'd secretly known Jacopo's occasional evenings off were for more than sport with a pretty maid. Though some Quakers made a show of resisting the various acts enforced by Parliament and were imprisoned and even transported, Bianca and Jacopo and the Friends they associated with weren't dissenters, no matter what the news sheets said or what the Earl of Clarendon and his cronies in Council bleated.

How she felt about them going to their meetings now the plague had crossed the walls had nothing to do with their faith and everything to do with contagion. Pulling at her lip, she knew she'd have to raise the matter with them. They were expected to attend church and thus far were safe. Rosamund couldn't be so certain about the Quakers and wanted to mitigate the risks to their health. God would understand, surely? One couldn't be too careful, not anymore.

"Are you well, my lady?" whispered Matthew.

When she cocked a brow, he pulled at his own lip and shrugged. He even knew her idiosyncrasies.

"As well as one can be when held accountable for the sins of mankind," she said, tilting her chin toward the pulpit.

The minister stopped his sermon and glared. Rosamund flashed him an apologetic look and felt her cheeks burn. Aye, being one of the gentry also meant sitting directly under the eyes and ears of the reverend. The worst part was feigning interest. Reverend Madoc's sermons in Gravesend had never been so dull. Maybe contracting the pestilence wouldn't be so bad if it meant she didn't have to sit through . . . *Stop it.* Her lips began to twitch as her notions grew more irreverent.

When the bells tolled midday they piled out of church, forgoing the usual greetings on the doorstep and hurrying home. Rosamund was glad. Together they walked swiftly back to Blithe Manor—gone were the days of strolling. Rosamund invited Matthew to dine with them.

As they entered the hall, Rosamund found that dinner was not the only thing awaiting her.

A flushed Widow Ashe whispered to her as she took her gloves and hat.

"Men? Upstairs?" asked Rosamund.

Widow Ashe nodded.

Matthew, who'd paused to hand his sword to a footman, grew very still.

"Who?" A prickle of unease galloped along Rosamund's spine. What men? It couldn't be Aubrey; Ashe would say.

"They said they be family, madam."

Rosamund's heart skipped; her skin grew clammy. She had no family, no men to call by that name, unless . . .

A noise at the top of the stairs drew her gaze. Her head spun; her vision blurred. Dear God in heaven. Leering down at her from the landing were none other than Fear-God and Glory Ballister.

"Told ya she wouldn't be long, Fear."

"You did indeed, Glory. Forgive me for doubting ya."

As the twins clattered down the steps, each holding a glass of claret that they paused to guzzle, Rosamund felt the room spin. Bianca took her elbow. The grip gave her strength. Jacopo came to her other side. Drawing herself up, pushing down the familiar fears the twins aroused, she tried to reconcile the collision of past and present here in Blithe Manor.

They seemed taller than she remembered, thinner. Their faces were weathered but not wise. Instead, they were hardened, furtive. They grinned at her with rotting teeth, and she noted how they catalogued objects and paintings as they descended.

Fixing a smile to her face, she was grateful yet again that she'd learned to dissemble.

"Fear-God, Glory, what a surprise." Over her shoulder, she was aware of Matthew partly hidden by an arras.

Swaggering toward her, Fear-God looked her up and down. "Gawd, you're even better in the flesh than I remember, ain't she, Glory?"

Glory sidled up beside his brother. "Smells better too, don't she, Fear?"

Their broad forms towered over her. They had changed in many ways yet in others were the same as they had been the last time she saw them outside the Maiden Voyage Inn. Cunning as foxes and as dangerous, until they were cornered, then they were deadly.

Tolerating their wet kisses upon her cheeks, kisses they tried to leave upon her evasive lips, she held her breath. Dear God, they stank worse than . . . worse than the Fleet in summer, she thought. Unable to help herself, she glanced at Bianca and saw her observation reflected in her wrinkled nose.

Following the direction of her gaze, the twins appraised Bianca boldly. "And who might this be?" asked Glory. "A beauteous blackamoor. Cor, what we could do with one of these, hey, Fear?"

With a wicked laugh, Fear-God lunged, but before he could touch Bianca, Matthew came forward, his sword, which he'd retrieved, drawn.

Fear-God yelped in fright.

Throwing a dagger to Jacopo, who caught it deftly, Matthew raised his blade, the point resting against Fear-God's chest.

Fear-God raised his hands and licked his lips, looking from Rosamund to Matthew and back again. Glory stepped back, his face bloodless, his shifty eyes wide.

"Unexpected visitors, Rosamund?" Matthew asked loudly. "Family, no less. Didn't know you had any in London, nor that they were so . . ." Moving his sword slightly, he slowly examined Fear-God and Glory from the toes of their scuffed boots to the tops of their greasy caps. He regarded them as if they were something a horse had just dropped.

Whether it was Matthew's demeanor, a recognition of their peril or the drawn weapons, the twins adjusted their manner immediately, slipping off their hats, lowering their chins.

"Coarse," Matthew finished.

"Matthew," said Rosamund, clearing her throat, "may I introduce to you Fear-God and Glory Ballister." Her face flamed with fury, shame and a strong desire to inflict injury. What were they doing here?

"Ballister?" said Matthew. "And what might Ballisters be doing here, so free and easy in their conduct?"

At the looks upon Fear-God and Glory's faces, Rosamund wanted to laugh. She wasn't sure if they were more astonished by Matthew's fearless swagger or his insults. "They are my stepbrothers."

"They are also deserters, from the look of their uniforms," added Matthew.

"We be no deserters, milord," said Glory.

Milord . . . How Matthew must love that, she thought.

"We've been given leave by our cap'n," added Fear-God.

"Really?" asked Matthew. "For what purpose? Other than to be rogues who've the manners of gutter rats and no idea how to treat ladies, let alone family?"

Fear-God and Glory glanced at each other. Unaccustomed to meeting the likes of Matthew, they didn't know how to respond. Certainly, the wind had blown out of their bravado and left them in the doldrums.

"We're assigned to the *Black Eagle*," said Fear-God.

"Given permission to deliver tidings to Rosie." He twisted his cap.

"It's Rosamund," said Rosamund automatically.

"Actually, it's Lady Blithman, family or no," said Matthew. "Surely your captain taught you how to address your betters, even if your father failed."

Fear-God muttered something under his breath.

"What was that?" asked Matthew, cupping a hand behind his ear. "I'm afraid you'll have to speak up."

Fear-God's cheeks grew mottled, and the muscle in his cheek began to spasm. His fist opened and closed against his thigh. Rosamund knew the signs, and her ribs became metal bands.

"What tidings have you brought?" she asked. "Tell me."

"And then begone," added Matthew grimly.

Fear-God shot him a look of such hate, Rosamund sucked in her breath. His mouth twisted into a leer. Leaning toward her, he said hoarsely, "Come to tell ye, your mother be dead."

"Tilly?" said Rosamund. A great wave crashed against her, throwing up all the detritus of the years and almost sweeping her feet out from under her. If Matthew hadn't taken her arm, she would have sagged against the balustrade.

Tilly. Her mother. Dead.

Her world went black before a small spot of light appeared, expanding with astonishing swiftness, illuminating the past.

From the moment Tilly stepped into Bearwoode Manor that cold, rainy day and stared at her eight-year-old daughter, appalled by her sweet peals of laughter, her giddy delight at discovering she had a mother, she'd been little more than a dark presence, an indifferent parent. Memories flashed by before focusing on an ill-favored few. Her mother's shrill voice condemning her, slurring drunkenly as she admonished her. She saw the set of Tilly's shoulders as she marched down the corridors of the inn, away from where Paul stood, his hand on Rosamund's shoulder before he led her into the office and closed the door. How she pushed Rosamund away when, at the age of ten, she came to her mother, blood on her thighs, cuts on her back and in her secret regions, pain in her belly and heart, wanting to be soothed, wanting to be told she was no sinner but sinned against. All the times her mother turned her back, stoppered her ears, refused to see what was happening, until Rosamund ceased to weep, refused to utter a word about it—even to God—and retreated into a place of darkness so great, it was a chasm that led beyond hell. Tilly, whose dove-gray eyes were layered with her own crushed hopes and broken dreams. Tilly, whose only acts of love were to abandon her daughter not once but twice, was dead.

Rosamund blinked, unseeing, unhearing.

"She's dead?" asked Rosamund of no one in particular.

"That's what he said, innit?" snarled Glory, darting behind his brother when Matthew tweaked his blade.

"Watch your mouth, knave." Matthew drew Rosamund closer, sharing a look of concern with Jacopo and Bianca.

Rosamund surfaced briefly. "How? How did she die?"

Fear-God shot his brother a look. "Broke her neck. Fell near the river."

"Was she cupshotten?" Rosamund could not utter the word "plague."

"She was never sober, not no more," said Glory.

Matthew went to bark something at him, only Rosamund wrapped her fingers around his arm. "He only speaks the truth. My mother was not . . . a well woman." But now she was a dead one. Dear God in heaven. Grandmother. Father . . .

Traveling down the rivers of abject hurt, confusion and hope until she reached her heart, she examined it. Held it up to the knowledge she'd just been given.

Truth be told, she felt relieved.

"And Paul? Your father?" Not that she cared, but it felt polite.

The twins again shared a look, then shrugged. "Dunno. Not since he ran off weeks ago."

Their indifference to their father's fate was as astonishing as the delivery. They really didn't care.

Rosamund sat upon the bottommost step, her head in her hands. Matthew stood over her.

"Well, you've delivered your news," he said. "Go, and allow the lady to think upon such sorrowful words."

Oh, if only he knew.

For a moment Fear-God and Glory looked as if they might challenge him, but then thought the better of it.

"Very well, but we'll be back, Rosie," said Fear-God, throwing his cap on his head and giving it a defiant tug. "After all, you're the only family we got." He stared about the hall, lingering on the silver, the fine artworks, the coat of arms.

"Be nice to get to know ya again, if ya know what we mean," added Glory with a sneer.

With a growl, Matthew strode toward them, sword raised. "Begone, you rascals, before I run you through." Jacopo joined him, his knife thrust forward. Two of the young footmen raised their fists.

"All right, all right, no need to get all glimflashy. We be goin'." Fear-God trotted quickly toward the door and one of the footmen opened it.

"If I catch sight of either of you again," said Matthew through gritted teeth, "I won't hesitate to do what I should have done this time." He held up the glinting weapon to make his point.

The twins were escorted to the gate by the footmen, casting resentful looks over their shoulders the entire way. Matthew waited until they were out of sight before sheathing his sword and turning to Rosamund, who sat almost doubled over. Matthew kneeled beside her and spoke softly.

"I'm so sorry, my lady. Sorry for the burden of the terrible news and for those who were chosen to deliver it. That you call those ruffians family tells me more about what you must have endured growing up than I ever imagined." He paused. Rosamund didn't move or speak. His understanding was far more than she deserved.

When she didn't respond, he continued. "I'm so sorry about your mother . . ."

"Are you?" asked Rosamund, raising her head. "Because I'm not sure that I am and"—she looked from Matthew to Bianca then Jacopo—"I fear that makes me the most terrible person, unworthy of God's love, let alone a mother's." She began to laugh, a dreadful, haunted sound before, with a strange hiccough, she burst into tears.

Matthew squeezed in beside her on the stair and, with a look of anguish and longing, took her into his arms.

THIRTY-FIVE
In which the chocolate maker's widow provides hope in a bowl

Not a day passed without rumors reaching them of more deaths, more houses being marked and their inhabitants quarantined. Each Tuesday, when the Bills of Mortality were published, they'd scan them anxiously to find out where the pestilence had spread. Throughout July the number of dead grew and the bells, which rang for each one, never ceased their tolling. What had once marked the passage of time became a continuous dirge, matched only by the carters' cries of "bring out your dead" as they moved through the streets. A pall of gloom and terror hunched over the city.

It didn't matter how warm it was, Rosamund felt a chill run through her every time those words carried up to the chocolate house or penetrated the walls of Blithe Manor.

So far, God be praised, they'd been spared the illness. Still following the plague orders, she moved between the chocolate house and Bishopsgate Street with relative ease. The once-crowded streets had grown quiet apart from the rumble of the dead carts and the murmurs of watchmen. The familiar sounds of the barrow-boys and milkmaids crying their wares were gone. No dogs barked their greetings; cats no longer prowled. Hackney carriages, sedan chairs and other conveyances ceased to roll along the cobbles, which sprouted grass and weeds.

Each day Jacopo, Bianca and Rosamund rose before dawn and went to the Phoenix, only going home once night had fallen. Neither the dark of evening nor the muted light of predawn could disguise the stench of sickness, or the sight of the watery red crosses painted on so many doors.

The chains across quarantined houses glimmered warnings, as did the pikes of the guards securing them, who cast steely looks at those passing by. The wails of those trapped inside were heart-wrenching as they mourned their dead and anticipated their own likely fates. They would lean from upper windows and shout to God, or to the few passersby, begging for release, succor, even forgiveness. Some spat vitriol. Others just spat. Once divided by wealth and birth, the city was now cleft by whether a person was healthy or ill. Homes became tombs. It was almost more than Rosamund could bear, but she had to stay brave and true. She had to.

Oft times Matthew would accompany them home, trying to entertain them with tales from his voyages. Sticking to the middle of the road, they steered well clear of doorways, the thresholds any contamination might cross. Once at Blithe Manor, they would retreat to the withdrawing room with a decanter of sack (recommended as a preventative) and discuss the day, how many customers they'd had, who'd fled the city, who remained and who they feared might be struck down next. It was on these occasions that Rosamund gradually drew from Matthew the story of his childhood and his family.

Born a gentleman from a long line of knights, he had a stipend provided by an uncle, a resident of the colony of New York who had the favor of the royal family, and rents from lands he inherited in Kent. She already knew his father was a poet, but what she didn't know was that Matthew had trained as a lawyer and had disappointed his family by not being called to the bar. Prior to meeting the Blithmans, he'd dabbled in trade via the East India Company, but mainly as a cover for the work he did spying for the King while he was in exile—a role that continued once His Majesty was restored. Initially, his job as a correspondent had served the same purpose, as he coded messages for the government into his reports. He was intending to reduce his spying work and write in earnest for Muddiman when, as a consequence of a commission he was given by the Lord Chancellor, he crossed paths with the Blithmans.

Matthew asked Rosamund about her life before London. While she was most forthcoming about her early life at Bearwoode with her grandmother, the steward Master Dunstan and the jolly if strict servants, she was reluctant to share much about her years at the Maiden Voyage Inn. Matthew didn't press her, changing the subject when she grew quiet.

If there was one topic which obsessed everyone, it was the pestilence. People pored over the news sheets and Bills of Mortality to see if their parish was under threat; many resorted to what Filip called "quack" cures to protect them. Every day Rosamund heard conflicting advice: burning juniper, purging, drinking urine and eating excrement or rancid meat, taking regular doses of London Elixir, keeping a gold coin in the mouth—preferably from Elizabeth's reign—or wearing a quill filled with quicksilver around the neck. Sam chewed tobacco; other men did all they could to contract the pox, also believed a preventative, bedding as many trulls as possible. While other businesses suffered, the oldest profession thrived.

Mr. Henderson wryly noted that while in the official news sheets L'Estrange downplayed the plague, he also sold advertising for curatives.

The practice of quarantining the healthy with the sick was widely condemned. One pamphlet, *The Shutting Up of Infected Houses, as it is Practised in England, soberly debated,* circulated in the chocolate house. It referred to "this dismal likeness of Hell, contrived by the College of Physicians" and railed against a barbarism that did more to increase the number of dead than protect the living. Matthew didn't put his name to it, and though his words provoked great discussion and much sympathy, nothing changed.

Rosamund marveled at Matthew's commitment, his need to challenge ineffectual authority that was more concerned with protecting those who could already protect themselves. Gone was the man who once noted all things trivial, replaced by someone determined to seek justice for those who could not do it for themselves. Knowing she was partly to blame for the risks he was taking, she did what she could to help him.

For all the chocolate house was a dreaded meeting place, it appeared to be one the men were prepared to tolerate, even if they did carry pomanders stuffed with aromatic herbs. Since the beginning of July, health certificates attesting one was not infected had been issued by the hundreds from the Lord Mayor's office so folk might leave London; these now also became essential to gain entry to the Phoenix. Rosamund had expected objections, but instead the patrons were grateful for the care being exercised to safeguard them and showed their appreciation by bringing friends who had also obtained certificates.

That gave Rosamund food for thought. If the men were healthy now, perhaps there were other measures she could take to ensure they stayed that way.

Rereading Colmenero's treatise on chocolate, and the work of Henry Stubbe, she extracted any information from them regarding both preventatives and restoratives. From one of the patrons, she heard of an apothecary named William Boghurst, who, despite going into houses and treating the suffering, survived to tell his tales. Located at the White Hart alehouse in Drury Lane, he swore by nutmeg, an additive Dr. Nathaniel Hodges also used to great effect. Rosamund ordered some from her apothecary immediately.

Along with extra sugar, vanilla and even some ground fennel, which gave strength, Rosamund put pinches of wood sorrel for joy, mugwort for happiness and celandine for joy to come, as well as the all-important nutmeg, in every single bowl of chocolate they served. No one noticed her little inclusions, so subtle were they—no one except Matthew and Filip. Yet after the patrons downed a drink, they certainly seemed less worried than when they arrived. Their friends wondered how they could be so calm in the face of the calamity all around them, especially as the bells rang and rang and the starving begged upon the streets. Customers would mention the chocolate they'd drunk at the Phoenix and how well it made them feel. Rumors began of an elixir made of chocolate prepared by a smiling angel that could not only chase away sorrow and fear, but possibly the plague as well.

For a time, they were inundated with new customers and orders for deliveries of chocolate cakes. They rose to meet the challenge, grateful for anything that could keep their own growing despair at bay, anything that could help ease distress.

August came, and with it the numbers of dead and dying became so great neither the bells nor the grave-yards could keep up. Huge pits were dug outside the city walls and cartloads of corpses flung into them and sprinkled with lime.

The air was thick with the sickly sweet odor of necrosis; flies multiplied as did the worms crawling through the rotting corpses.

Sometimes when she walked home Rosamund would see the bodies of the afflicted collapsed in the street. The dead had a strange gray tinge to their flesh, broken by the huge, suppurating mulberry and onyx tokens on their necks. The stench of unwashed, decaying bodies attracted swarms of flies and crows. Some swelled and burst in the heat, their entrails spread about them like a putrid skirt. Some were still alive, too ill to move or call out for aid. Rosamund would mutter prayers for their swift release and divert her eyes and stopper up her tears. She'd already shed so many. There were even those who ran, shucking off their clothes as they passed, hollering and dancing. Shouting to God or whoever would listen, they were oddly joyous in their abandon but deadly in their potential to infect. Everyone gave these folk a wide berth.

As if despair over the pestilence itself wasn't enough, rumors soon spread about the plague nurses and the searchers, many of them old women admitted to houses to confirm a diagnosis and, later, a death for parish records. Some not only stole from the dead, but on occasion ended a life so they might take something of value. There was a story of a young gentlewoman being smothered, another of a man having his nose and mouth held till he passed away. A few women were caught and whipped, but most were not. After all, they were doing a job no one else was prepared to do. Along with the animal catchers, mortuary cart drivers, gravediggers and watchmen, they prospered from the misery. Few begrudged them that—not then.

Believing the plague to be a manifestation of divine displeasure, people were encouraged, against all good sense and warnings against crowds, to continue going to church. But the greater the numbers in the churches, the more people contracted the sickness.

Rosamund had given up going to church and freed the household from any obligation to do so, promising to pay their fines when the outbreak passed—if it ever would. There were days where she felt as if she'd woken into an apocalyptic nightmare from which there was no escape. Yet within Blithe Manor it was easy to feel as if everything were normal. Apart from a scarcity of certain foods, there was an order to the mornings and evenings that was interrupted only by the hours she spent at the Phoenix. But even that became a matter of routine.

Sam, who would call by as often as his work allowed, treated the disease as an inconvenience to be tolerated. In his hard-heartedness he was reassuringly unaffected by events—happy even. He appeared oddly content, boasting of his new appointments—treasurer to the Tangier Committee and surveyor-general of the victualing of the Navy. When he was admitted to the Royal Society, he celebrated by purchasing a twelve-foot telescope. He even went to Moorfields to see the plague pits for himself, as one might attend the theater. His ghoulish descriptions allowed him to hold court at the Phoenix, and he relished the attention.

However, when he finally moved his household to Woolwich to keep them safe while remaining in the capital himself, Rosamund wondered at the wisdom of keeping the chocolate house open.

Every day she and Matthew reassessed their decision. The arguments were always the same: If they shut, what would happen to Wolstan, Harry, Owen, Art, Kit and Cara? They didn't have the resources to look after themselves and their families without the wages they drew. The number of customers had gradually declined, but there were still those who made a point of attending once a day, drinking their chocolate, sharing news, including the brave (some said foolhardy) Dr. Nathaniel Hodges; the nonconformist rector Thomas Vincent; John Allin and two of the Three Unwise Men (the eldest, young Sir Roger Catesby, having fled in the first week—not even Rosamund was enough to keep him in London); a Highlander, Grant McSearle, who picked the wrong time to come to the city, adopted the Phoenix, along with the jovial clerk Peter Goddard. Kit's and Owen's fathers would also attend.

Thomas Bloodworth, who, it was rumored, would be the next mayor, oft made an appearance along with Sir Henry Bennet, who made the odd discreet trip from Oxford. After reassuring himself as to Rosamund's well-being, he would find Matthew and disappear with him into a booth, where they would discourse in low tones. And then there was Mr. Henderson. And Sam. What Matthew and Rosamund silently conceded was that they needed the Phoenix to remain open as much as anyone else.

With anxiety gnawing their stomachs, they fiercely checked certificates of health, praying that the bearers were still pestilence-free and refusing to admit those in possession of obvious forgeries.

A slight cough, a complaint about a megrim or the heat, would give them all pause. A strange new etiquette developed where the drawers would leave the bowls and pots on the edge of the tables instead of placing them in front of customers, for fear they might breathe on them. The cost of admission was no longer thrown into a bowl, but a large jar of vinegar. No one objected.

Mid-August, Sam brought news that the Navy Office was moving to Greenwich. Along with the Treasury and other government organizations, they sought the safety of distance. The impact was felt directly by the Phoenix—some days they were lucky to have a dozen patrons come through the door. Not even Sir Henry visited anymore. Still they remained open and stubbornly adhered to routines, celebrated the small things and tried to make sure the plague didn't cross their threshold.

So when Wolstan didn't show up for work one day, they made excuses for his absence. When a scruffy young fellow gave Mr. Henderson a note to take upstairs for "the lady" midafternoon, claiming it was from Wolstan's mother, the workers gathered around Rosamund as she read it.

She raised her eyes from the hastily scrawled note, the color fleeing from her face as she passed it to Matthew, who'd followed Mr. Henderson into the kitchen.

"I'm afraid Wolstan is sick," she said.

Cara gasped and covered her mouth. Art, Kit, Harry, Owen and Thomas all moved apart and began surreptitious examinations of one another. Solomon looked at his father, who reached over and placed a reassuring hand on his shoulder.

Rosamund quickly thought about the last time she had really paid attention to Wolstan. He'd seemed fine yesterday, perhaps a little distracted, but weren't they all? He'd served the few who entered along with Kit, and she recalled he'd played a game of cards with Art and Mr. Henderson. She looked toward them—Art was staring at his hands, frowning. Mr. Henderson was shaking his head. She wondered who else among them had worked closely with him, if they'd shared a bowl, a cloth, anything other than cards. As she looked around, it was clear they were all doing the same thing, trying to recall their interactions.

"We must go to him," said Rosamund, pushing away her misgivings. What's done cannot be undone, wasn't that what Lady Macbeth said to her husband? She'd been terrified this day would come, and now it had.

Gathering some cakes of chocolate, she searched desperately for a cloth to wrap them in and a basket, anything to keep her mind off what Wolstan's illness signified.

"We'll take him food, drinks, medick." She whirled around helplessly. "He has a mother, siblings. His father is at sea, so he'll be fine—"

"Rosamund," said Matthew, forcing her to stop. She stared but didn't really see him. Dear God, Wolstan.

Matthew spoke softly. "We will ensure he has whatever nourishment and potions he needs—he and his family—but you'll not be delivering the necessities to him. I don't want you going anywhere near his house."

"I cannot ask anyone else to do it on my behalf, Matthew," she argued, pushing a stray lock of hair back under her cap.

"You don't have to. I intend to make the delivery."

"You? But . . ."

"Pack what you think they might need," he said before she could protest further, "and I will deliver it. He lives in the parish of St. Stephen Coleman Street, does he not?" There was not a spark of fear in those jeweled eyes, no indication the thought of entering one of the most afflicted parishes in London chilled him.

Standing straighter, she decided she would not show fear either, however much it gnawed away at her insides. "Aye, not too far from the church—next door to the sign of the bull and hen."

"I will go with you," said Jacopo, glancing at Bianca, who nodded her approval.

"Me too," said Mr. Henderson. "Why not?" he replied to Rosamund's unasked question. "Even books are considered carriers these days. No one enters my shop anymore. I may as well make myself useful. Anyway, he's a good lad. Beat me at Primo often enough."

With Cara's and Bianca's help, Rosamund quickly packed a basket with bread, cheese, eggs and some cold eel pie. Alongside the already wrapped cakes of chocolate she also ensured there was nutmeg, mugwort and other herbs she prayed would be efficacious. "Here," she said, passing it to Matthew. "Make sure you tell him, or his mother, to put a pinch of all the herbs into the drinks."

"I will."

"Oh, and tell them to burn juniper and whatever else they have at hand. Smoke is meant to repel the disease."

"I will tell them that and more," reassured Matthew, bestowing a smile filled with kindness, patience and something that made her think of fresh blooms opening even as death knocked at the door.

Though they all walked abroad every day to and from the chocolate house, the fact Matthew was willing to enter an infected area to offer succor filled her with a mixture of trepidation and pride.

"Go with God," she said, her words including Jacopo and Mr. Henderson as well. "And hurry back as if the devil is snapping at your heels."

Much to her astonishment, Matthew drew nearer and tilted forward. One moment there was three feet between them, the next, his mouth rushed toward her.

A delicious wave of heat rolled over her, banishing her unease and stirring parts of her body as if the *molinillo* were twisting them one way then the other. Caught unawares, she braced herself. But he never did reach her lips, only whispered against her ear, "You be careful too, my lady. Now more than ever." And moved away.

Bereft, pink-cheeked and grateful that Matthew, for all his fine qualities, was not a mind reader, she cleared her throat and, not trusting herself to speak, flapped her apron to send him on his way. The expression in his eyes as he drew back confused her, as did her own response to what she had thought—prayed, in her secret heart—was about to happen, and the wave of disappointment when it did not.

For the rest of the afternoon, though her mind was focused on Wolstan, Matthew, Jacopo and Mr. Henderson, she continued to prepare chocolate, occasionally revisiting the sensations a mere gesture had ignited. How was it possible to feel such . . . such pleasure? As if someone had poured chocolate into her bloodstream, filling her with such delicious anticipation. How was this possible when calamity was all about her? Matthew had never intended to kiss her. It would have been foolish in the extreme when contagion raged around them. And yet, what if he never did? She froze. What if the opportunity never arrived? The very idea left her more disconsolate than she had a right to be.

Puzzled at her reaction and forcing herself to send prayers that Wolstan would survive, she was utterly distracted. Not even the customers with whom she politely discoursed, or the clumsy lines two of the remaining Unwise Men left, were enough to break her reverie.

A few hours later, there was still no word. The chocolate house had been empty awhile. The workers sat about reading old news sheets, flipping through books, whispering together. The cards Wolstan had dealt the day before sat in a neglected pile. Restless, Rosamund went to the windows.

Immediately, she spied Matthew and Jacopo, running as if the devil were indeed snapping at their heels.

"They're coming," she said, a foul taste flooding her mouth.

It was only as she heard the chime of the doorbell below that it occurred to her there'd been no sign of Mr. Henderson. Before she could ponder what that meant, there were boots on the stairs.

Matthew burst through the door, his face shiny and red, his hair stuck to his forehead. Rivulets of sweat ran down Jacopo's face as he bent over and clutched his knees, breathing heavily.

Rosamund slowed then stopped as Matthew held out a warning hand. "No further, please."

Cold gripped Rosamund followed by a rush of virulent heat. She peered over his shoulder at the empty doorway. "Where's Mr. Henderson?"

The others waited a safe distance away.

Matthew shook his head. "I'm afraid I bear more bad tidings, my lady."

Rosamund swallowed. Her face was warm, her heart was beating a tattoo. "Go on." Her voice was unrecognizable.

"Wolstan is dead." There were gasps. Rosamund's hand flew to her mouth. Cara wailed and sat down heavily on a bench, her face in her hands as her shoulders began to shake. Matthew shot her a look of sorrow. "I'm so sorry. We were too late. He died before we could get there. The nurse had already been and gone. The house . . . is secured. But there's worse." Jacopo found a seat, staring blankly at the floor, ignoring the sweat dripping from his face to fall between his boots.

"Where's Mr. Henderson?" repeated Rosamund quietly.

Matthew grimaced. "That's what I am loath to tell you. As we returned from Wolstan's, he took ill. One moment, he seemed fine, then he became dizzy, unable to walk. We, that is, Jacopo and I, delivered him to his house, saw him to bed, gave him what comforts we could and notified the authorities—"

Bianca gasped and reached for Rosamund. Jacopo raised his head and stared at his sister before his eyes slid to Filip. There was a low moan. Filip stepped forward; Bianca stopped him.

"We left the basket with him, Rosamund. Wolstan's family—" Despair cast a shadow across his face. "They were beyond help."

Rosamund and Matthew gazed at each other in a silence that spoke volumes. Rosamund drew a long, shuddering breath. Mr. Henderson. So suddenly . . . just like the coach driver Sam had encountered.

"What do we do?" she asked finally.

"We?" Matthew gave a dry laugh. "We do nothing. What I want *you* to do is take Bianca, Filip, Thomas and Solomon"—he pointed to them in turn—"and leave. Cara, Harry, Owen, Kit and Art, you're to take what you need along with enough wages to last a few weeks and get away from here as fast as you can."

They all stared at one another in wide-eyed shock.

"I've no choice. We . . ." He gave that half laugh once more. "That is, Jacopo and I, we held Mr. Henderson, assisted him. We entered his dwelling, breathed the very same air. Do you know what that means?"

They did. "But, Matthew," protested Rosamund, her heart sinking. "We're all at risk. Wolstan, Mr. Henderson—they worked beside us; they were among us."

Cara cried harder. Rosamund returned the pressure of Bianca's hand. They were hurting each other in their desperation to remain upright, to not fall and fail now.

Matthew nodded gravely. "They were. But Wolstan looks to have caught the disease at home. Mr. Henderson, well, apart from playing cards with Wolstan yesterday"—he didn't mention Art—"had the bar or a table between himself and the rest of you. Jacopo and I discussed this all the way from his house. We can do one of two things: alert the authorities and be shut in here even though no one has sickened at the Phoenix, or go to our homes and wait to see if the disease manifests. If you go, then maybe, God willing, you have a chance. If we keep away from you, maybe we all do."

Rosamund shook her head.

"I won't risk you." His eyes locked on Rosamund. "Any of you," he said, looking at each in turn. "Not if I can help it. I won't risk anyone anymore. Lest this place be responsible, I'm closing the chocolate house. I think you'll agree, Rosamund, I—that is, we—have no choice."

Once more, he sought to include her—Jacopo too—in his decision-making. It was right that he should not bear the weight of this alone.

Her mind was afire. She looked about the room and took in the wisps of smoke and steam curling around one another in an unhealthy courante, like doomed lovers. The empty tables seemed desolate; the well-thumbed news sheets and the curling edges of the Bills of Mortality glared at her accusingly.

"We have no choice," she said.

Matthew flashed her a sad smile.

"What about you?" she asked finally. "You . . . and Jacopo?" Bianca inhaled sharply. "What will you do?"

Matthew and Jacopo looked grim. "We will stay here." Upending the jar of coin, uncaring as vinegar pooled across the table and dribbled onto the floor, he cast it to one side. What did anything matter now? "Take what you need from here." He gestured to the drawers and Cara. "Rosamund, can you see they do not go short?"

Shaking herself out of the heaviness that weighted her limbs to the spot, and slowly releasing Bianca, she went to gather foodstuffs, herbs and chocolate cakes to wrap in cloths for everyone. Bianca and Filip helped. Bianca pressed her lips together, her eyes suspiciously moist, as she worked. Filip looked broken. Leaving them to finish, Rosamund sourced additional coins.

Cara wiped away tears as Bianca gave her a wrapped cake and Rosamund passed over extra money. "Oh, my lady, Bianca, sir." She bit back a sob and swung toward Matthew. "How . . . how will we know when it's all right to come back?"

Matthew thought for a moment. "When the door downstairs is open again. While it remains shut, you're to keep your distance—all of you. Look to your own. Do you understand? What's important now is you keep clear of anyone you suspect might be infected." He paused. "I pray you will be safe. With all my heart I do."

Glances were exchanged. Harry brushed his forearm across his face. Rosamund wanted nothing more than to ruffle his hair, yet dared not.

Fearful and sad all at once, the boys and Cara took the coin from the table and, with plaintive farewells and anguished looks toward Rosamund, Filip, Solomon, Thomas, Bianca, Jacopo and Matthew, clattered down the stairs. She could hear their subdued farewells to one another and the tinkle of the doorbell as they left.

Rosamund knew she must take the others to safety, yet also wished she could remain. If her final days were near, she wanted to be here. But she was Lady Blithman and had to do what was best for everyone.

If it *was* best.

"Come along then," she said with forced brightness, clapping her hands and fooling no one. "Let's be moving too."

Matthew flashed her a look of gratitude.

As she turned to collect her hat from Bianca, she was astonished to see Jacopo and Filip silently weeping as they faced each other. The look of yearning upon their faces, and the way Solomon and Thomas turned aside, told her something she had been blind to for years.

"May God be with you," whispered Filip, his words an endearment that squeezed the breath from her body. He raised his hands before letting them fall, empty, to his side.

Jacopo bit back a sob. "And you too, *bello*." He tried to smile and failed. "Solomon." He cleared his throat. His voice was stronger this time. "Promise me you'll look after your father for me."

Solomon raised his head and nodded. "I will, Jacopo—you can count on me."

"And you can count on me, Filip," replied Matthew to his unasked question, moving closer to Jacopo. "You too, Bianca."

Bianca said something in her native tongue to which Jacopo replied in kind, their words lingering. With one last desperate look at her brother, Bianca gathered

Solomon and Thomas and shepherded them out. With red, blinking eyes, Filip followed.

Jacopo faced Rosamund. "I know you'll watch over her, *signora*."

Rosamund was afraid her voice would betray her. Eventually, she found the words. "I'll look to them both, Jacopo. I promise." She turned to Matthew.

She dared to take a step toward him but kept a table between them. "Matthew," she began.

He waited.

"I thought . . . I hoped . . ." She stopped, swallowing sorrow. "I wanted to . . ." She placed one quivering hand on the table. Tears filled her eyes. She blinked them away furiously.

"And I," he said, putting out his hand so it was mere inches from hers. They looked at their hands, reaching but not touching, so close and yet . . . "I will pray for that with all my heart."

Their eyes met. In his, Rosamund saw the stars writ large. Her heart expanded, and her soul filled with blazing light that swiftly dimmed.

"And I."

THIRTY-SIX
In which death enters unbidden

Rosamund was relieved to find the hall of Blithe Manor empty and called for Ashe. She'd already determined that Filip and Solomon could have her husband's old room, the one Aubrey had claimed but had no present use for. Thomas could have Helene's. She would ask Ashe to see to it the beds were made, the rooms aired—though, at present, that term took on a whole new meaning.

"Ashe?" she called again, before remembering her manners and welcoming Filip, Solomon and Thomas. The two boys stared at their surroundings, reminders that for all her hard work and lack of formality, Rosamund was a bona fide lady.

"Wait here," she said to them and signaled to Bianca. Where was everyone? The corridor to the kitchen was dark and cool. At any time of day there were usually the sounds of chopping and bubbling pots, and the voices of the maids, footmen and certainly the cook could be heard. All was quiet. As Rosamund peered into the kitchen she could see the fire was lit, a pot sat over the hearth and evidence of activity was scattered all over the table—flour, half-peeled turnips, chopped carrots, a skinned coney as well as half-drunk bowls of chocolate and coffee and empty glasses. Rosamund picked one up and smelled it. Who would drink the cellared wine at this time of day down here? What was going on? Rosamund's stomach fluttered. She liked this not.

Calling again, there was still no answer. She looked at Bianca, who shrugged. "Shall we try upstairs?"

Filip insisted on ascending first. The boys waited at the base of the stairs, their faces anxious. Certain they could all hear her heart beating, Rosamund used the bannister to propel herself forward as all her instincts shouted at her to retreat. A trickle of sweat slithered between her shoulder blades.

"Ashe?" she called again. *Oh, thank the Lord!* There was a response. It came from the withdrawing room.

With more confidence than she felt, Rosamund smiled at the others as Filip reached past her and opened the door.

With a cry, Bianca and Filip staggered backward. Rosamund pushed into the room, not quite believing what she saw.

Food was scattered across the floor. A jug of wine had been spilled on the rug. Empty glasses rolled nearby. But that wasn't the worst. Slumped in the chairs by the window, eyes shut, mouths fallen open, were Fear-God and Glory.

Within three steps, she struck a wall of stench. She pressed her nose and mouth into the crook of her elbow. Wine, piss, vomit—a veritable soup lay spread across Glory's lap—sweat and the unmistakable odor of sickness permeated the room the further she went in. Unable to help herself, she gagged and drew closer. Livid purple tokens were scattered across their cheeks and cascaded down their necks like a hell-spawned rash. Their half-undone shirts revealed it sprayed across their midriffs. Their legs were wide apart, as if some force didn't allow them to close anymore. They were filthy.

They were infected.

She began to cough, the reek making her eyes water.

Fear-God jerked and opened his eyes. Rosamund let out a small scream. They were the color of claret.

"Rosie," he croaked, trying to sit upright. "Ah, wondered where ye were. Sorry 'bout the mess. Said we'd be back. Only, before we could take shore leave, we were left to guard those bloody Quakers who'd been sat in the hull for weeks—fuckin' bastards. Half the Godforsaken wretches were infected." He spat. There was blood and a thick mucus.

Rosamund recoiled.

"Once we realized, we ran. Been hiding a few days. Be damned if we were getting back on board, 'specially since the cap'n's been arrested. They have to find us 'fore they can hang us, innit that right?" He took a jagged breath. "Never find us here, in Lady Blithman's fancy digs." He struggled to sit up, close his legs. "Help us, Rosie, won't ya?" he asked plaintively, hauling himself up, swaying a few times before stumbling toward her, arms outstretched. "Don't feel so good. Not even yer wine helped . . ."

With a whimper, Rosamund turned and ran. She felt Fear-God grab hold of her collar; his strength hadn't failed him. She swiftly undid the lace, and it came off in his hand. She fell forward. Filip caught her and swung her off her feet through the door. Bianca slammed it shut, and they leaned against it as she locked it with shaking hands.

"Rosie." Fear-God's muted voice was cracked, hoarse. "Rosie!" His hands pummeled the wood. "Help us."

Rosamund fell to her knees and stared at Filip and Bianca.

Bianca slid down beside her. "What do we do now?"

Unable to trust the lock, Filip held the door; his eyes were wide with fear, his usually sallow cheeks leeched of color.

Rosamund leaned her head against the wood as bitter tears stung her eyes and her heart deflated. The dull thud of Fear-God's fists tolled in her brain.

"Do?" She wanted to scream. Why did she have to be the one to decide? But she must. Matthew would expect it of her. Dear God, she expected it of herself.

She took a deep breath and said, "What we must." She peeled herself away from the door. "We cannot leave and risk others. Anyway, the servants will have notified the authorities."

"We'll be quarantined," whispered Filip, glancing down the stairs to where the boys waited. "Forty days."

"With them." Bianca's terror made her accent thick.

Rosamund saw her own fear echoed in their eyes and reached once more for the comfort of Bianca's fingers, twining them through her own. It was too late to worry about contact. The infection had already entered the house.

"Only if we last that long," she said.

THIRTY-SEVEN
In which the Lord
has mercy upon us

Thirty-one days," murmured Matthew, adding another mark to the piece of paper in front of him. He rested the quill in the inkhorn and rubbed his beard thoughtfully. Opposite him, Jacopo sighed and they both stared out the window.

The street below was empty; the grass was all that thrived in the heat and dust and even that was suffering. Late rains had allowed it to flourish temporarily before the hot weather returned with a vengeance. No cool moderating breezes blew; there was just the smoldering sunshine and searing gusts of wind that carried the stench of death. Rubbish tumbled along the street. A trio of large brown rats scurried along a wall, disappearing inside a hole in the plaster. They seemed to be the only creatures left alive in the street. Though when night fell, candles formed halos in windows, their gentle glow welcome signs of human habitation; for all their enforced isolation, they weren't alone. Not yet.

While he knew he should be grateful he was still alive, all Matthew could think about was the latest Bill of Mortality. Before he left to attend the Duke of Albemarle in Lambeth, Sam had slipped one under the bookshop door together with a variety of bills, pamphlets and news sheets. The rancor he once felt toward Matthew appeared to have dissolved into something akin to pity mixed with admiration for his stance over the chocolate house. Six hundred more people had died this week than last, taking the death total to well over seven thousand since the outbreak began. But as Jacopo pointed out, that didn't account for any nonconformists like Quakers and Anabaptists, let alone Catholics and Jews. God Himself knew the real toll.

Around him were reminders of better days. Cruel sunbeams danced their way through the windows, highlighting the emptiness of the place. The hollowness of his dreams. Pages of notes sat at his elbow, half-written pieces, thoughts on events, on what he saw as he stared outside with glazed eyes and heard through the windows. Ripostes to the writings of L'Estrange which not only appeared in the *Intelligencer*, but were repeated in his other news sheet, the *Newes*; remonstrations against

His Majesty, who had left his ravaged poor to starve, and the other professionals who looked to save their own fat skins first. That was before he set to against those who profited from selling false hope in the form of magical potions and cures. A pox on them all.

Rail all he liked, none of it would ever be published. He hadn't the heart since Will Henderson's death.

Without customers to serve, a chocolate house to run—without, let's be honest, vengeance to fire his soul and letters to deliver, except to Rosamund, and they were but brief notes each day—he'd had plenty of time to burn his anger through his quill and reflect upon his life and a future that might never eventuate. He cursed himself for wasting more than two years chasing atonement, and for the years before, when his need for revenge had taken over. Now he feared he'd lost his chance.

The marks on the page indicated how much time had passed since he had sent Rosamund and the others into the arms of death. Once more he asked God to keep her just a little longer. Please. So far, according to the news whispered through the doors of Blithe Manor, shouted from its windows, and the letters passed between the cracks in its gate which the watchmen allowed to change hands, he knew that Rosamund endured. She, Bianca, Filip and the boys had, thus far, survived.

Nine more days. Just nine more days.

Folding his arms, he stretched out his legs and buried his chin in his chest, feeling his bristles scratching through the fabric of his shirt. Without a decent bath, he itched all over. Not even a fresh shirt could quite disguise the stale odor of his body. He sniffed and pulled a face.

A noise from the kitchen told him Ashe had arisen. She must be feeling better. She'd been afflicted by a slight megrim and gone to lie down some time ago. No doubt she was seeing to coffee. God knew, ever since Rosamund had left, he'd no desire for chocolate. It simply reminded him of her.

The day he'd forced everyone to leave, effectively quarantining himself and Jacopo in order to save them, the last thing he expected was for Ashe to arrive less than two hours later, flushed, distressed beyond measure and demanding he return to Blithe Manor with her. When he learned what had prompted her to come to the Phoenix, banging on the entrance until her fists were torn, he felt paralyzed.

That evening Ashe and most of the staff had been finishing their dinner in the kitchen at Blithe Manor before preparing the mistress's supper when Rosamund's stepbrothers burst in. Unable to see them properly at first with the light at their backs and the darkened kitchen failing to reveal their features, they'd thought them simply cupshotten, boorish soldiers as they staggered about, their speech slurred, picking up a jug of wine and downing it, thrusting food into their mouths before spitting it back onto the table. It wasn't until the one called Glory fell to the floor, laughing like a lackwit, that they saw his face and understood with icy clarity what had entered their home.

Trying not to surrender to panic, Ashe had ushered all the servants out of the kitchen and through the front door, ordering them to wait for her at the church. Then, with great courage, she'd returned to the kitchen and coaxed the men to the withdrawing room with the promise of as much wine and food as they could consume.

She managed to shut them in, but in her haste forgot to lock the door before seeing to the servants waiting in the churchyard. Those who were able, she told to go to their homes, the others were to remain with the vicar until she could receive instructions from the mistress. Then Ashe had bolted to the chocolate house. When she discovered the door locked and the mistress gone, she'd become hysterical.

Immediately, Matthew and Jacopo set out with her for Blithe Manor. By then, some hours had passed and the sun was setting, the scorching air replaced by welcome cooler breezes. They'd arrived at Bishopsgate

Street to find watchmen already in place, a fresh red cross splashed upon the door and the rear gate chained to prevent anyone entering or leaving.

Matthew felt as if he had been punched in the stomach. What had he done?

It wasn't until he felt Jacopo's long fingers on his back that he straightened and, following the direction of his gaze, saw a sweet face pressed to a window. Rosamund leaned out. She tried to speak a few times, but tears rolled down her cheeks and fell upon the sill. Holding the window frame like a staff, she took a deep breath and tried once more.

"Matthew, it's here. The pl . . . pl . . ."

It was another punch. But this time he received it without flinching. "I know," he said. "Ashe told me."

Bianca appeared, then Filip, and they stood together, a forlorn tableau—the men and Ashe looking up, the women and Filip peering down.

"You need to move on, sir," said one of the watchmen. When Matthew didn't respond, he continued, "Please, sir, it does no good to loiter about lest you breathe in the foul miasmas and become infected yourselves." He lowered his voice. "If you bring supplies and the like, we'll make sure she gets 'em . . ." He held out his palm before rubbing his fingers together. "If you make it worth our while."

Matthew continued to stare up at the window. "Rosamund," he called. "Fear not, we will look to you and the others. Bianca, Filip, stay strong. Pray for your deliverance, as will we. Believe that we will do everything in our power to aid you however we can."

He could see the tears on Rosamund's cheeks, a rivulet of diamonds glinting in the gloaming.

It was Filip who answered. "*Gracias,* Matthew. *Gracias.* All we ask is that you look to each other."

"Look after Ashe as well," called out Bianca.

Quite forgetting the young woman, Matthew turned. Courageous, she too had faced the afflicted and risked herself for others. "You will come with us, back to the chocolate house." It was not a request.

"But, sir," she began. "I . . . I have touched them." She glanced up at the window. "The men . . . Lady Rosamund's brothers."

"Stepbrothers," said Matthew, as if it made a difference. "We will return to Birchin Lane together and live in self-imposed quarantine, leaving only to get supplies and share what we have with those here. These gentlemen"—the sweep of his arm took in the guards—"assure me they will see provisions and notes are handed over." He reached into his purse and deposited some coins in the eagerly awaiting hand. The man spat on one before secreting it about his person and handing over what remained to his partner. Matthew tried not to recoil. Gazing back at the house, he raised his voice.

"Did you hear that, Rosamund?"

"I did. You have my thanks, good sirs."

The men lifted their caps.

"I will come every day. I will write." Matthew's words were a vow.

That was over a month ago. Since then, many notes had been exchanged. The irony of being reduced to communicating through the written word when they were less than a bell toll away did not escape him. He glanced down at his papers, his eyes alighting on the other writing he'd done.

In the thirty-one days they'd been apart, there'd been so many deaths. He'd kept a list of those they knew: there were twenty names in all—so far. First upon the list were Wolstan and the rest of his family—seven in total. The father had gone to sea to support kin who no longer lived, poor man. May God bless him. Then there was Will Henderson, who had lasted two days after he collapsed in the street. Fear-God and Glory Ballister died the night they entered Blithe Manor. Matthew could hardly think of them as a loss. His fury that they'd brought plague to Rosamund, that God could be so cruel as to put her at risk, overcame all other emotions. He'd learned more about Rosamund from Jacopo—including the condition in which she was found by Sir Everard, which explained how she had come to be married to the man in the first place. Anger toward Paul Ballister grew and simmered; he understood now why Rosamund had been so ambivalent about the news of her mother's death. Between them, he and Jacopo had pieced together Sir Everard's intentions. His loathing of the Blithmans, which had been briefly dulled, burned afresh. It made him think of Aubrey, who'd so readily avoided an encounter with him, the poltroon. He pleaded with God to let the man survive so he might say his piece. Some things should not be denied.

Cheeky Harry and his four siblings had also died—only their grief-stricken mother lived. She was still shut away in their tiny house off Beer Lane; Matthew didn't know whether to pray for her death or endurance. Kind, gentle Cara had also passed away—not from plague but some other disease. It was easy to forget as the pestilence ravaged the city that there were still other illnesses capable of carrying away dear ones. Mr. Remney had been brought down with a terrible fever but recovered. The owner of the ordinary that supplied the chocolate house with food died, along with his wife, and the stationer across the street and his elderly sister. Art, Kit and Owen were alive, but of Mr. Remney's other workers, he knew not.

Matthew wiped his hands over his face and wondered if he shouldn't go down into the bookshop and select some reading material. God bless Will, he wouldn't mind. Not anymore. Fear of infection had been overcome by the necessity to amuse and distract themselves, and he and Jacopo had taken to treating the bookshop like a giant library, borrowing and returning books and reading to each other. Jacopo had also decided to teach Ashe to read.

"I'm atoning," he explained when Matthew queried him.

They were long, long days of waiting, dreading and hoping, devouring any morsel of fresh news. God knew, they were hungry for it.

"Would you like some coffee?" Matthew asked as Jacopo mounted the stairs from the bookshop.

Jacopo didn't hear him at first. He looked pale in the silver-gray light, and there were shadows forming beneath his eyes. No wonder. None of them were sleeping well. He stared at a note in his hand.

"What is it, Jacopo? News?"

Jacopo raised stricken eyes to his. "It's Bianca," he said hoarsely.

Matthew gripped the edges of a table. "Rosa-mund . . . ?"

Jacopo shook his head. "No, no. She's the author of the note, not the subject. My sister is infected. She has the pestilence."

Matthew froze as the enormity of this struck him; sorrow followed by, God forgive him, relief it wasn't Rosamund . . . yet.

"I . . . I must go to her," said Jacopo.

Matthew knew there was no point arguing. "Of course. I will come with you."

"You're not going anywhere," said Ashe, appearing from the kitchen, wiping her hands on her grubby apron. "Not until I've packed some spices and herbs. Milady would never forgive me if we arrived without the right ingredients or some extra cakes of chocolate."

"And some medick," added Matthew. "Leave that to me."

Sending thanks to God for Ashe, Matthew sent extra prayers for Bianca, and for Rosamund. She'd survived one bout of plague beneath her roof . . . Would the Almighty see fit to grant her another reprieve?

THIRTY-EIGHT
In which the calamity is inexpressible

Disturbed by movement rather than noise, Rosamund opened her eyes. She had fallen asleep in Bianca's room, and it took her a moment to orient herself. When she did, she was shocked at what she saw.

Lowering himself onto Bianca's bed was Jacopo.

"Jacopo!" exclaimed Rosamund, suddenly wideawake. She sat up and watched as he leaned over and stroked his sister's gray face. "How did you get in here?"

Bianca groaned.

"Jacopo—" began Rosamund. "You shouldn't be here. The risk is too great—"

"*Allora*, please, Rosamund. Do not waste your breath. I will not heed your warnings—not when it comes to Bianca. She's my sister."

Rosamund stood and stretched, brushing her skirts. Tears trailed down Jacopo's cheeks as he gazed upon Bianca. The love and utter devastation in his face took Rosamund's breath away. She wrapped an arm about his shoulders and pulled him to her. Still holding Bianca's hand, he resisted at first, then pressed his face into Rosamund's bosom and wept. Kissing the top of his head, she prayed he wouldn't feel her scalding tears.

She whispered comfort and held him as he held Bianca, who opened her eyes. "I . . . I thought I was dreaming," she said faintly.

Jacopo composed himself and smiled at her. "*No, bella.* I am here. I'm not leaving you again. When we came to this city, we promised never to be apart. It was the one thing the master allowed us—to be together."

Bianca smiled. Her lips were dry, and the action caused her to wince. "*Sì,* that's true. But even so, you will leave if I say so, *mio fratello.*"

Jacopo pressed his forehead against hers. "I won't."

"You're a fool." Bianca gave a laugh that became a cough.

Jacopo quickly tried to help her into a sitting position as Rosamund plumped the pillows behind her.

"Stay, Jacopo," said Rosamund. "I will fetch water to bathe her face and something to drink. I'll let the others know you're here." Opening the door, she paused. "How did you get in? There were watchmen on the gates, were there not?"

"*Sì*, but I didn't live here for years without learning how to enter and leave without the master knowing." He gave her a cheeky wink. "How do you think we went to the Friends meetings? How do you think I saw Filip?" He tilted his head. "You will tell him I am here?" he asked softly.

"I will, and you must tell me how you did so." She paused. "And what of Matthew? Is he with you?"

Jacopo frowned. "He has gone to seek medick. He may be a while."

Shutting her eyes briefly, she thought of him roaming the infected streets, risking himself for their sakes. She almost laughed. Here she was concerned lest he expose himself to the contagion when they were all in danger no matter where they were.

Touching Jacopo lightly on the shoulder, she whispered, "We will use what we have till Matthew arrives." She went to fetch all she thought Jacopo would need for Bianca.

Filip found her as she was carrying a bucket of scalding water upstairs. "How goes the patient?" he asked. His eyes were pouched with tiredness and an oily sheen on his cheeks reflected the dawn light.

Rosamund passed the bucket to Filip gratefully. "There's something I must tell you." She quickly relayed what had happened.

Filip almost dropped the bucket. Tears sprang into his eyes. "He's here?"

"Aye, but he's with Bianca. He is . . . You must understand, he's not keeping a distance."

"Of course he's not." There was pride in his voice. "And neither are you. You never have, Rosamund. We've been through too much together to consider keeping distant. What are families for if not to provide comfort and hope when others cannot? Are we not family?"

He smiled and ran a finger down her cheek, catching a tear she didn't know had escaped. He held it up to the light, where it sparkled like a jewel. Filip was right. It was easy to be a friend when times were good. It was in hard times that true friends revealed themselves. Their friendship had been forged in the hottest of fires and fused them into family.

"Come," she said, wrapping a hand around one handle of the bucket as Filip took the other. "Let's offer more comfort and hope."

In his wisdom, God saw fit to dole out comfort and hope in small but even measures. Where he gave to one, he took from another and so kept the scales in some kind of divine balance. As Bianca miraculously recovered, Jacopo fell ill.

The moment he did, they moved another bed into Bianca's chamber, placing brother and sister side by side. While Bianca looked pale and weakened by her ordeal, her body ravaged and the tokens still stark even upon her dark flesh, it was evident from her brighter eyes and husky voice that she was recovering.

As she grew stronger with each breath, Jacopo weakened. It was almost as if he were surrendering his life force to his sister. Bianca railed against what was happening, crying out to God in all the many tongues she knew, turning to Jacopo to whisper his favorite tales of heroes so he might carry the spirit of these mighty beings into his soul or, as he grew sicker, into the ears of God in heaven above.

Unable to leave his side, Filip had done what he could, forbidding Solomon and Thomas from entering the room, but asking them to fetch and carry clothes, water, medick. Between them, he and Rosamund cared for Jacopo and Bianca, hauling them out of bed when they needed to relieve themselves, changing and washing the bedding when they were not quick enough, spooning broth or chocolate into their mouths. Trying to adhere to the tenets of cleanliness, it was difficult.

The room stank, and Rosamund's clothes were stained with bodily fluids and foodstuffs, but she didn't care; she didn't want to waste a minute worrying about anything beyond Jacopo and Bianca and their recovery. But she was bone-weary and aching. Her head hurt.

When Matthew entered the room on the second day after Jacopo fell ill, supplies in hand, she thought he was simply a wraith from her dreams. She'd nodded off thinking about him, wondering how he was faring, and here he was. She smiled at him, but it wasn't until he kneeled by her side and took her hand in his and she smelled the blowsy odor of him that she knew he was real.

"Dear God," she choked. "You're really here."

"I am," he said and pressed her fingers to his lips. She began to cry. He put her palm upon his cheek.

A sound from Jacopo's bed interrupted them. "Matteo," he whispered.

"I'm here, my friend," said Matthew and, lowering himself carefully, took Jacopo's hand in his own. "I thought I was bringing physick for Bianca alone, but you're ever determined to share your sister's lot, aren't you?" He tried to smile, but his lips wouldn't cooperate.

Where he failed, Jacopo succeeded. "The eternal demand of the younger sibling." Jacopo shut his eyes.

The tokens on his neck were huge and weeping. His tongue was swollen, his breath rancid, yet the proud, beautiful man who'd endured beatings from Sir Everard without a whimper was still evident. The young man who'd been so torn by his master's order not to teach Rosamund to read he'd told his sister, who gave Rosamund what she craved so deeply. Jacopo, who'd protected her when she didn't know it, who'd hovered like a guardian angel, keeping secrets no one should be asked to keep, ensuring that after Sir Everard died, the businesses kept running. It was Jacopo and his sister who had told her to trust Matthew. To deal with the man she'd been led to believe was the devil.

The devil sat on the bed holding Jacopo's hand, gazing with sympathy at Bianca and Filip. Filip was just a shell, a scarecrow without his stuffing. How could she not have seen how Jacopo felt about him, how they felt about each other? Such love, such affection could not be unnatural, could it? Couldn't be a sin in God's eyes.

The acrid smell of death filled her nostrils. Love and death were both here, only death was winning this night.

In a daring gesture, she placed her hands on Matthew's shoulders, and shut her eyes in relief and pleasure when one of his gloved hands closed over hers.

"Your family is here, Jacopo," she said.

Jacopo's eyelids flickered. "More than you know," he said.

Bianca gave a dry laugh.

"What does he mean?" Rosamund turned to Bianca.

Jacopo signaled for a kerchief, which Filip passed. He spat into it and lay back again. "Bianca, please; it's time we tell her."

Bianca frowned. "Time for me to do as you tell me, *mio fratello*?"

Jacopo nodded and tried to summon a grin, but his swollen mouth wouldn't allow it; his expression was more a grimace. "*Sì*," he murmured.

"What he means, Rosamund," said Bianca, rolling on her side, "is this: just as you're a Blithman, just as Matthew married one and is thus connected, so are we—me and Jacopo."

Matthew's hand tightened over Rosamund's. Did he know what she was about to hear?

"I . . . I'm not sure I understand."

Jacopo's lustrous blue-green eyes were latched onto her.

"Me and Jacopo, we're Sir Everard's *piccoli bastardi neri*—his little black bastards," said Bianca. "At least, that's what he used to call us—his dirty by-blows—

and that's what Gregory, Helene and Aubrey called us too. We are Blithman spawn just as surely as his other children."

Her words took a moment to register, then Rosamund gasped. She looked anew at their coloring, their magnificent bright eyes. Of course.

"Sir Everard was the lover who paid your mother to remain his?"

"*Sì*. He would always promise that if anything happened to her, he would take care of us." She made a disparaging noise. "In that regard, he didn't lie. He took us away to England and, in his own way, cared."

Rosamund recalled the number of times she saw Jacopo limping, bruised; the beating he had received at the chocolate house that day. She thought about the way in which they would both accept and even protect Sir Everard and his secrets—from the other servants, from gossip, from her . . . even when he was at his worst. They were his children. His flesh and blood. Blithmans.

Her hands dropped from Matthew's shoulders and went to her cheeks. "Why did you keep this from me? I mean, I understand while Sir Everard was alive you probably had to . . ." Bianca nodded. "But after he died . . . why? Why not tell me?"

"We did discuss it, Jacopo and I." Bianca flashed him a look of love. "But we decided against it. You'd already endured so much. And would it have made a difference? You already gave us what no one, apart from our mother, had—love, the freedom to be. We could not ask for more; we could not burden you with the truth. Not then. Now? What difference does it make?"

What difference did it make? Rosamund knew that she could not love them more if they were—*oh dear God*, if they were Sir Everard's children, that meant she was their stepmother. The wickedness of Sir Everard's denial of his paternity, that he could treat them as he did, astounded her. They might have been slaves, but they were his in more ways than one.

And now they were hers.

"When you gave up your jointure so you might own us," said Bianca, "we knew then it didn't matter anymore. You gave us what he took from us—what he took from us all."

As Bianca spoke, Filip captured Jacopo's hand and held it to his heart. Jacopo's eyes found Rosamund. "You didn't need to buy us, Rosamund," he croaked.

"No," said Bianca. "We were already yours; you were already ours. A piece of paper makes no difference."

Jacopo gave a dry cough; his eyes were fevered, bright. "You are our family too." He searched for Rosamund's fingers. "And I do love you with all my heart."

Rosamund couldn't speak. She nodded and, taking Jacopo's other hand, pressed it to her bosom. Bianca reached and found her.

"We've all been touched by the Blithmans, for better or worse," said Matthew calmly. "For all they destroyed so much, they cannot destroy this."

Rosamund knew from the tone of his voice that he'd known who Bianca and Jacopo were all along. Just as they'd protected Sir Everard, they'd also protected Matthew from his wrath, revealing enough of Sir Everard's intentions to him to keep him safe. One had been served through obligation and filial duty, the other through love and respect.

Just as they protected her.

She didn't realize she'd said this aloud, releasing Jacopo's hand in her passion, until Matthew stood and pulled her into an embrace. Filip joined them and held them both to his chest. Bianca leaned across her bed and demanded to be included as well. Ever so gently, they all hugged Jacopo, uncaring of his tokens and the infection that with every passing minute was claiming his life force. They'd been careful for so long, and that hadn't helped. Why deny one another—why deny Jacopo—the comfort of human touch and the love that flowed from each of them when it was most needed?

And so as Jacopo passed into the Lord's ever-open arms, he was surrounded by his extraordinary family and enveloped in the deepest mutual affection.

PART FOUR

January 1666 to September 1666

Here is wisdom. Let him that hath understanding
count the number of the beast: for it is the number
of a man; and his number is Six hundred
threescore and six.

—Holy Bible, King James Version, Revelations 13:18

Kind Friends I am resolved to discover a thing
Which of late was invented by Foes to our King
A Phanaticall Pamphlet was printed of late
To fill honest-hearted Affection with Hate

—Thomason Coll, *The Phanatick's Plot Discovered*

THIRTY-NINE
In which voluntary exiles make their return

As the bells tolled throughout January 1666, Rosamund couldn't help but shudder. While they now rang for the reasons they had of old, to call people to service on Sundays, to chime the hour and to celebrate marriages and baptisms as well as deaths, for her they'd always carry the memory of pestilence and horror.

Carriages churned through the snow-covered streets, riders wove their way around the throng of conveyances and pedestrians. The new year had brought with it a dramatic drop in loss of life, and all manner of professions returned to the capital. A sense of renewal and fresh beginnings enveloped the city, despite the season. Shops reopened, vendors reappeared, markets thrived. The link-boys with their burning torches and lanthorns did their duty by folk at night, and the watchmen patrolled, shouting out the time and reports about the weather. It was a change from the cries that echoed in Rosamund's nightmares. Dogs and cats sprouted like seasonal plants, bakers stoked their ovens, butchers honed their knives and, once more, all was well. The dreadful visitation had passed.

The chocolate house had reopened just before Christmas, but they were yet to welcome back many of their patrons, and supplies were still low. Matthew had heard from his captain that the quarantine embargoes placed upon his ship were soon to be lifted and they could soon expect fresh stocks (the war notwithstanding) of cacao, sugar, vanilla and spices. Each day, the trickle of men coming through their doors grew thicker and stayed longer. Familiar faces reappeared—Thomas Bloodworth, the new mayor; John Allin, John Evelyn, Sir Henry Bennet, the Duke of Buckingham, Charles Sedley and, of course, Sam. Sadly, the Three Unwise Men had been reduced to one—Sir Roger being the only one to survive the pestilence. As if to honor his friends, he tripled his efforts, penning even more poems and notes for Rosamund. Not even Charles Sedley had the heart to torment him.

Patrons returned to the bookshop as well. Unexpectedly, Mr. Henderson had left his house to Matthew and the bookshop jointly to Matthew and Rosamund, doubling their businesses.

Rosamund was overwhelmed by her friend's generosity and found it hard to credit that she who'd been illiterate was now the owner of a bookstore. The very notion filled her with a combination of joy and great sorrow. It seemed wrong to prosper from a friend's death, yet, as Matthew said, it had only come to her—to both of them—because it was what Mr. Henderson wished. When Mr. Bender explained the conditions of Mr. Henderson's will, which included the printing license, Rosamund had wept for a great gift for which she could never thank him.

Between them they decided that Rosamund would continue to run the chocolate house with Filip's help, while Matthew would take care of downstairs as well as manage stock and figures for the Phoenix. Rosamund noted that he seemed keen to put physical distance between them. As soon as the forty days of quarantine at Blithe Manor had ended, he'd moved into Mr. Henderson's house around the corner from the bookshop in Lombard Street. She persuaded herself it was because he was keen to avail himself of the printing press in the stables and prayed he would be cautious. L'Estrange's news sheets had ceased publication and Henry Muddiman's new *Oxford Gazette* (another tissue of propaganda, according to Matthew) made him even more determined to offer alternative viewpoints to those endorsed by the crown.

Much was being written about how shutting up houses had not only increased the death toll in the city, but contributed to the spread of infection throughout the provinces, as those who were ill fled rather than be entombed in their homes. The war against the Dutch still continued and with the French entering as their allies just last week, there was much to report. Illegal presses were being rooted out and their operators severely punished lest they publish news counter to what was officially sanctioned. The names of Giles Calvert, Simon Dover, Thomas Brewster and the unfortunate printer John Twyn, who was hanged, drawn and quartered, were on everyone's lips—a warning to those who dared dissent. Not that it stopped Calvert's and Brewster's brave widows from continuing their husbands' work. Quakers too refused to be cowed, risking prison and death. Matthew's newly inherited press might not be illegal—Mr. Henderson's will and a word in Sir Henry Bennet's ear had seen to that—but much of the material he intended to print was. Perhaps he maintained his distance to protect her should he be discovered. Whatever his reasons, she wished he would not be so aloof, but was uncertain how to raise something that could simply be the product of her imagination.

Throughout January the apparatus of government slowly returned. The Exchequer came back to Whitehall; the Navy Board, much to Sam's relief, to Seething Lane. Having ordered the city cleaned and fumigated, the Lord Mayor hoped the last of London's citizens (and by that he meant the gentry and nobles) would hasten back. Whitehall and Covent Garden remained all but empty, though rumor had it the King and the Duke, as well as a goodly portion of the court, would leave Oxford and arrive at Hampton Court by the end of the month before proceeding to Whitehall. Everyone was returning to the city.

And so, it seemed, would Aubrey.

Rosamund received a hastily scrawled note from Aubrey announcing his return—a note with a shocking addendum.

She knew she'd have to raise his imminent return with Matthew, and soon. The question was how to do this without him mistaking it as a request for his intervention. Especially when what she really wanted was more of his company. At odd moments she found herself recalling Matthew's arms about her the night Jacopo died, the comfort and strength he had shared.

And then there was the way he would sometimes, even now, catch her eye and earnestly discuss an issue, whether it was cacao, books, customers or additives. The thoughts snagged her heart and made her soul ache. Pushing them aside, her priority must be how to deal with Aubrey and his unexpected proposal.

When she'd broken the news of his return to the servants at Blithe Manor last night, there'd been a mixed reaction. The new staff didn't know him and so simply accepted that a different master would soon arrive, failing to understand the impact it would have on them. The older staff—those who'd survived—mumbled dourly and set about their tasks halfheartedly. Rosamund could scarce blame them.

Retiring with Bianca to the closet, she'd pondered a solution to the dilemma Aubrey posed.

The thought of him coming back filled her with foreboding, though she was in a better position this time than on his first appearance. She knew not only that he was coming, but who her friends were. She had resources to draw upon which she'd lacked previously. Naturally, the news of Aubrey's imminent return had reached the chocolate house, and some of the regulars, knowing the type of man he was, or feeling the need to shepherd her, once again offered Rosamund rooms, houses—even an estate outside London. Most came with a now-familiar caveat and had little appeal, especially as she had the means to rent premises herself. Nevertheless, she knew there were those she could rely upon to help her find accommodation for her household if needed.

She hoped she would not have to take that option. Blithe Manor might not be hers in name, but she'd come to think of it that way. Filled with bittersweet memories, it was also the place where Jacopo had died, and to cede it to Aubrey without a whimper didn't seem right.

Studying Bianca, she wondered if Aubrey would tolerate her beneath his roof now her brother was dead. He'd made it clear he wanted both siblings gone before he returned, but didn't Jacopo's death change things? Bianca was his half sister, after all. A Blithman. The knowledge hadn't spared Bianca and Jacopo pain; on the contrary—their father subjected them to outbursts of cruelty, his other children harbored deep-seated resentment of them and, according to Bianca, Lady Margery had been much the same.

"She knew you were Sir Everard's children?" Rosamund asked one day.

"*Si.* And it made not a whit of difference to her. To the Blithmans we were slaves—human possessions— no more, no less. Our parentage did not affect their attitudes—except to sharpen them." Bianca's eyes filled with torment and betrayal.

Rosamund made her decision then: if Aubrey did not accept Bianca, neither of them would remain a moment longer in his presence.

The sound of coins clattering into the bowl and cries of "what news?" broke Rosamund's reverie. Fixing a smile to her face, she moved from the window and greeted the gentlemen, allocating drawers to take their orders while she slipped behind the bar. The new boys, Timothy, Adam and Hugh, circulated about the room; their uniforms—sewn by the Wellses—were still a little stiff, but she was pleased to see how well the boys had adapted.

It was hard to suppress the pain in her chest as the ghostly shadows of Wolstan, Harry and Owen (who died a week before they reopened) seemed to follow them. Filip, devastated by the loss of Jacopo, nonetheless determined to continue and to help Rosamund in whatever way he could. Having recently rediscovered his smile, she could nonetheless see the toll it took to use it. His determination not to let grief affect his workmanship defined the jut of his chin. Solomon was extra solicitous of his father, and Thomas too helped Filip and his friend. Between the four of them, they managed very well. They'd also hired a new girl, Grace, to help Bianca in the kitchen. With an unflappable disposition that not even the plague had quashed, she was a much-needed boon. Art and Kit came back, as irrepressible as ever.

Mr. Remney had found them a rather large gentleman, a former soldier with only one eye, named Mr. Nick, whom they hired to wander around the tables and make his presence known. Matthew was concerned about leaving Rosamund upstairs without a male chaperone other than Filip. Mr. Nick had only to fold his burly arms or cock a brow to curb any poor behavior.

Not that it was a problem. That the chocolate house had remained open through most of the plague and only finally closed to prevent becoming a source of contagion had done much to endear the widow, as they still called Rosamund, to the gentlemen of London. Matthew as well. Their names were mentioned in the same breath as others who'd earned the gratitude of the city, such as Lord Craven, General Monck, the former Lord Mayor, Matron Margaret Blague and the few physicians who'd braved the pestilence. Rosamund, Matthew and the Phoenix were much admired.

Sir Everard would have hated the names of Blithman and Lovelace being linked in such a manner. How would Aubrey feel?

On the first day of February 1666, the court and Aubrey returned to their respective abodes: King Charles to Whitehall and Aubrey to Blithe Manor. Bonfires and bells greeted the King's return, but Aubrey, looking about the capital as he and Wat rode through the cheering crowds that had braved the snow and cold, liked to think they were for him.

He paused briefly at his warehouses and was perturbed by the low quantities of stock. Like many merchants, his ships had been quarantined in the ports of Venice, Calais, Amsterdam and the Black Sea, unable to either deliver or receive goods, and he'd suffered heavy losses. Reassured by the lifting of restrictions—at least with countries not affected by the war—so trade could resume again, he signed various purchase orders and said he'd send further instructions the following day.

It wasn't until he arrived at Blithe Manor and saw the new faces awaiting him in the courtyard, the gauntness of the familiar servants and the lack of supplies in the cellars, that the alterations the plague had effected literally came home. Riding through London earlier, it had been hard to credit the stories of death and misery that had entertained him and those he'd kept company with in Oxford for so many months. All about, the streets were jammed with vendors, carriages and folk burdened with shopping baskets. Thick smoke chugged into the sky and the tang of tanneries and coal fires burned his nostrils, just as he remembered. Nothing seemed to have changed.

Only, it had.

When he first sighted Rosamund that evening, he was appalled. It was as if a paler, thinner imitation of a cherished memory had entered the withdrawing room and dropped a curtsey. The blasted blackamoor, who also looked worse for wear, followed close on her heels. Rosamund politely inquired after his health and asked him to describe his time away. Happy to oblige as his mind worked to reconcile reality and dream, he was barely able to recall what he said. Transfixed by the large-eyed, hollow-cheeked woman before him, he marveled that he ever likened this . . . this drab to his beloved Helene. Her skin was dry, her hair no longer shone and sadness was a perfume in which she liberally doused herself. The blackamoor was not much better, standing behind her mistress's shoulder, offering her profile. He'd heard her brother had died and good riddance. According to gossip, so had most of the drawers at the chocolate house. Maybe now Rosamund would come to her senses and abandon her designs on the place; maybe now she wasn't quite the beauty she'd been, she would see the sense in the proposal he'd added to his note. He'd demand a response from her shortly.

As he answered her query about the plague in Oxford (as far as he knew, there had only been a couple of deaths and those among the poor—though there was mention of one of the King's servants dying), he felt there was something almost ethereal about her, the way she listened so earnestly to his responses. There was a fragility that awoke a protective streak in him he'd thought long extinguished. Dressed in pale pink that captured the faint color in her cheeks, she made an effort to flash that lovely smile, even if it didn't reach her eyes. On second thought, though she looked different, there was a sense in which she was even more beautiful. Weak. Vulnerable.

Sitting up straighter, he cast aside the blasé tone he'd picked up from the other courtiers and described the journey back to London in a manner more becoming someone who'd survived.

Just as Rosamund had.

He supposed he'd have to ask her about that—and console her over the losses she'd endured, only he detested the thought of Lovelace's name upon her lips. It had been hard enough tolerating it from Helene, yet he supposed he must. Damn the fellow. He was a blight in every regard. In his mind, the plague and Lovelace arrived simultaneously—if only others would see it that way then he'd be rid of the man for good. How could he avoid him now he was here in London, working at the same premises where Rosamund dirtied her hands? He looked at her hands now, so reddened, so worn. Like a servant's. Indignation and anger flared. How could she do that to him? How could she do that to the family name, sully it in such a manner? Not only serving in a chocolate house, of all places, but by working with his father's mortal enemy.

His mortal enemy, too.

His heart began to thunder. He put a hand against his shirt and could feel its vibrations. It seemed so loud he wondered if anyone else could hear it. Damn his father for failing to rid them of the Lovelace curse once and for all. For leaving it to him. He'd no stomach for such matters. As far as he was concerned, the best revenge he could have upon Lovelace was to win Rosamund to his side; win her heart. He'd half expected to come home and find that she and Lovelace had made a promise to each other. Maybe Lovelace wasn't interested? He found it hard to believe, considering he'd been so infatuated with Helene. But maybe that was the point; the thought of a woman who would remind him of his dead wife was too much. For Aubrey, the resemblance only added to her attraction. Even if Rosamund no longer looked quite how he remembered, once she was fed and had slept well, it would be an altogether different prospect.

She dimpled at a memory, before her great eyes filled. Dear God, he wanted nothing more than to reach out and take her in his arms, sop up her misery with his lips. Damnation if his gospel pipe wasn't vibrating in his trousers. He shifted in his seat, becoming aware as he did so of the blackamoor watching him. He stared back, his eyes narrowing. She looked away, her full lips curved. He'd wipe that sneer off her face with the back of his hand given half a chance. Only, that wasn't the way to Rosamund's heart—or, if not her heart, her capitulation. He could be stubborn and persistent, and if he didn't have Lovelace to contend with in this race, he could well be the victor.

In fact, regarding Rosamund objectively, now was the time to strike. Maybe she wouldn't be so cocky having borne witness to death; maybe she'd view him and his suit favorably. Maybe, now Rosamund knew what awaited a woman alone in the world, she would be eager to marry again. She might be damaged goods, but she was still his—moreso than ever. This plague had done him a mighty favor.

He leaned forward eagerly and begged her to tell him what had happened while he was away: all that had been talked about in Oxford was the Bills of Mortality and they were impossible to give credence to—over two thousand deaths in a single week! He'd seen the mass burial pits outside the city, but they were covered in charming hillocks of snow and surely could not be evidence of such a calamity. And he was keen to discover what had happened at the manor while he was gone.

Rosamund looked at him in a manner he wasn't accustomed to: almost as if he were a stain upon a rug. Though perhaps he'd imagined it, for the expression disappeared, replaced by a flicker of something—her old self? She flashed him what he thought was a smile.

Knocking back a glass of sack like one of her patrons and ordering another to be poured, she quietly told him about the losses that had occurred—not only of beloved servants, but all her acquaintances. He was on the cusp of telling her that he didn't care about her drawers or the owner of the blasted bookshop when he recalled his new tactics: listen, be sympathetic, pander to her. At least give the appearance of concern. Absorbed in these reflections he only caught the end of her saying the white cross upon their door was harder to remove than the red. White cross? Red? Was not one the marker of infection within and the other a sign it had passed? Who had marked the door of Blithe Manor? Why?

Looking about, his skin began to goose, and not because he was cold. The fire in the hearth threw out a goodly heat and thick curtains were drawn across the windows to keep the frosty night at bay. He found his ears were pricked just as his stomach began to sink.

"Did I hear you aright, my lady? This very house was afflicted?"

Rosamund steadily told him how her brothers, the twins, not only had the audacity to intrude and bring infection into his home but Bianca had fallen victim as well.

The blackamoor? He recoiled as she outlined all that followed.

Opening and closing his fists, swallowing thickly, Aubrey longed to jump to his feet and run from the house. Why had no one told him of this? Why had that widow—what was her name? Ashe. Why had she not mentioned that the plague had invaded his home? Why had none of his friends?

Because you chose not to correspond lest you catch the pestilence, and all your so-called friends were in Oxford with you.

Unable to remain still as Rosamund described how, after her brothers died, among them she, Bianca and that Papist Filip had wrapped their bodies and dragged them down the stairs, he stood abruptly. How could he enjoy the comfort of his seat knowing some low-born cove had perished suppurating among its cushions? He signaled for the footman to fill his glass. Where was Wat? He should be here by now.

He began to pace up and down the room. As he paused by the window and pulled aside the curtains, Rosamund calmly told him how Jacopo had met his end.

"He died here?" choked Aubrey, dropping the curtains and spinning around. "In this house?"

"What choice did he have, sir?" asked Rosamund. Was she mocking him?

He repressed a shudder and brought the glass to his lips, but did not drink—what if an infected person had drunk from the very same vessel? Aubrey studied her anew.

"And you? Did you fall foul of the pestilence, madam?"

Rosamund considered his words and as she did, his heart dropped into his boots. "Aye, I fell foul of it," she said quietly, her head bowed.

"But you recovered?" Aubrey put down his glass and stepped away.

"Recovered?" Rosamund glanced up at Bianca, who met her eyes then looked away. "No, sir, I'm afraid I am not recovered."

Aubrey stared at her, his eyes growing wide, his cheeks pale. Suddenly, the dry hair, the pale skin, the merest hint of roses in the cheeks took on a whole new and sinister meaning. He bolted to the door and flung it open, shouting for Wat.

Aubrey turned back to face her. "Forgive me, madam, but I recall I have some very important business to attend to in town."

Rising, Rosamund brushed her skirts carefully. "I am sorry to hear that, sir. Shall I ask Ashe to see that your bed is prepared? It hasn't been used since . . . Who was it last slept in Aubrey's bed, Bianca?"

Bianca tilted her head and frowned. "I cannot remember, madam. It might have been Jacopo, or perhaps someone else . . ."

Horrified, Aubrey yelled for Wat again and, with a barely polite bow, rushed from the room.

Once they heard him stomping about in the hall, ordering his bags and chest to be loaded onto a conveyance, Bianca nodded for the footman to shut the door.

Sinking into the seat he'd so recently vacated, Bianca grinned. "You're a wicked woman, Rosamund Blithman."

"I didn't say I *had* the plague," said Rosamund, a whisper of a smile on her lips, "that would have been a lie. But did I recover from it? In answering him, I only told the truth. None of us have." A parade of bloated, swollen faces dying in agony tramped through her mind. "Anyhow"—she sighed as they heard Wat's voice—"he won't stay away long. I've merely bought us a few weeks, if we're lucky."

"A few weeks for what, may I ask?"

"To prepare for my future."

"Future?" asked Bianca, pouring herself a drink and refilling Rosamund's glass as she held it out to her. "But, *bella*, you have a future, don't you?"

"Didn't I tell you? I've been offered another. When Aubrey wrote to announce his return, he also formally asked for my hand in marriage."

Bianca almost dropped the jug. "I would remember if you made mention of *that*."

"Oh, how forgetful of me."

"But he cannot—in the eyes of God, surely, he cannot marry his father's wife."

Rosamund released a long sigh. "Apparently, if the marriage was never consummated, he can. And, as you know, Bianca—and it turns out Aubrey knew as well— his father, while a capable man in many areas, was not in that regard."

"*Allora*. He has thought of everything."

"His father did. Aubrey wrote he has proof of his

father's . . . incapacity. A doctor's note, no less. Keeps it with him at all times. Sir Everard wrote it as a precaution: to be used if ever I thought to contest the will or, I imagine, those papers I signed."

Bianca waited. When Rosamund said nothing, she cleared her throat. "You're not seriously considering marrying him, are you?"

Rosamund stared into her glass. "Considering, aye. Seriously? No . . . not yet. But there may come a time when I have to . . . seriously consider it, I mean. If my marriage to Sir Everard is to be annulled, as Aubrey suggests, then I lose my widow status, my title, this . . ." She looked about the room. "I become nothing but a single woman with, how did Aubrey put it? Ah, no prospects."

"Flatterer," said Bianca wryly.

"And I know what else you would say, Bianca, and it isn't anything I haven't already considered. I will do all I can to keep Aubrey, and his demands for an answer, at arm's length and have him believe his cause is not lost. I will play on his fears of contagion and suggest he fumigate the house, repaint each and every room and replace all the linens before he moves home. I will persuade him it is the safest thing to do and that I am the best person to oversee this. I will ensure it takes time. A great deal of time . . ."

"I see. And once he's back here and realizes his cause *is* lost?"

Rosamund made a bitter sound. "I think Aubrey thwarted will be much more dangerous than Aubrey courting. I need to be prepared."

Nodding solemnly, Bianca raised her glass. "To the future."

"To my widowhood, long may we enjoy it."

FORTY
In which the end of days draws nigh

Mr. Remney commenced the work on Blithe Manor a few days later. In the meantime, Rosamund continued to work at the Phoenix, looking after her patrons and finding excuses to interact with Matthew.

He was like the sun, drawing her into his orbit; the more she resisted him, the more she found herself compelled to seek him out, even if it was just to ask for the latest edition of what was now the *London Gazette* (it had moved from Oxford and out of Muddiman's hands; Sir Henry's secretary, Joseph Williamson, had taken over as editor, and Thomas Newcombe in Thames Street published it) or any new bills or pamphlets she might distribute among the patrons. Always friendly, always ready to talk with her about what she read and to share snippets of news, or surreptitiously pass her his latest tract for the drawers to distribute, he appeared content to remain the friend he declared himself so long ago. Whereas once she would've been overjoyed with that, in the secret recesses of her soul she longed for more, though exactly what "more" entailed, she wouldn't examine.

Sometimes she'd catch him in an unguarded moment and she would see possibilities she'd thought extinguished the moment Aubrey Blithman returned. But as soon as he was aware of being watched, his expression would alter. Other times, when he'd shut the shop downstairs and come to sit in a booth and scribble thoughts or simply listen to the men gossiping, she'd bring him a chocolate and slide onto the bench opposite. They would sit in companionable silence as nearby conversations washed over them about the King's many bastards, the resumption of trade, rumors the queen was pregnant and fear of what the continuing war with the Dutch signaled. Occasionally, they'd share a smile at some overheard absurdity. Then she would lose herself in those azure eyes and the laughter she feared had been stamped out would kindle once more—though not enough to give it expression.

But she could hope.

If only she could see into his head—into his heart. But Matthew wasn't going to grant her admission to that.

Preparations for yet another sea battle proceeded apace, especially since an attempt to sue for peace with the Dutch had failed. London was abuzz with news. Much to Sam's chagrin, his great patron Lord Sandwich was displaced as Admiral of the Navy by General George Monck. Monck and Prince Rupert, the King's cousin, were to lead the newly assembled fleet. Seamen were ordered to return to their ships, promises of overdue pay dangled before them like ripe fruit. Rosamund thought of Avery at Gravesend and wondered if he too was summoned to duty. Was the risk of death at sea worth not having to "fuckin' wait" for his pay anymore?

The plague had struck Gravesend with a vengeance. Even if her mother had still been alive, Rosamund believed she wouldn't have survived the pestilence. Part of her prayed Paul hadn't, but it didn't seem right to be so uncharitable. According to Frances, who had endured, the Maiden Voyage Inn had been taken over by a family from the country whose village had been all but wiped out. Frances had lost her mother to the contagion, and in her last letter she told Rosamund she and her father were moving north, away from shipping lanes and rivers and anywhere they might have contact with outsiders, in an effort to keep themselves safe. Although saddened by her friend's departure, she understood. London's streets were filled with those displaced by the plague and ready to fill positions left abandoned.

There was something to be said for beginning again, and if it wasn't for the chocolate house, Rosamund knew she would have been tempted to do the same. In a sense that's exactly what they were all doing: making a fresh start in a new year.

In fact, the year 1666 was a cause of great perturbation—both at the Phoenix and in the news sheets—with many writing about what the triple six portended.

Only last week, Sam showed her a book he'd purchased from Matthew called *An Interpretation of the Number 666* by Francis Potter. It discussed how such a number signified the end of days and related to the beast or the devil. Like many others, Sam was convinced a great doom awaited them, something Matthew scoffed at.

"As if the plague were not enough."

Rosamund was inclined to agree. Nonetheless, she was fascinated by how the number and what it portended preoccupied folk. When Matthew found an old copy of William Lilly's *Monarchy or No Monarchy* (a pamphlet that would have had Matthew thrown in the Tower had one of Henry Bennet's other spies seen it) and pointed out the part where he prophesized a period where England would battle disease then fire, she wanted to dismiss it with him. After all, as Matthew rightly said, it didn't take a seer to make such a pronouncement, not with diseases always afflicting the capital and fire a continual risk.

"It's akin to saying Tuesday follows Monday or it might rain in winter," said Matthew. They then spent far too much time laughing and thinking of other analogies. Rosamund relished those moments. Matthew dropped his guard and entered into discussion with fervor, treating her as both confidante and partner.

Rumors of a Jewish Messiah dominated the chocolate house for days. Even Sam had something to say about it, bowling in one Monday agog with the news he'd heard at his booksellers about a man all the princes of the East were accepting as the King of the World.

"Much like we do His Majesty, the King of England," said Sam, lest Rosamund failed to comprehend his meaning. "They're saying this one's the true Messiah."

Rosamund finished agitating a pot of chocolate, placed it on a tray and nodded to Adam to take it to the customer. "Is it not blasphemous to say such things, Sam?"

Sam glanced around and saw Sir Henry Bennet sitting a mere two benches away, the black plaster on his nose identifying him immediately. He hunched his shoulders and lowered his voice. "Only if they're not true," he whispered.

"What makes you so sure they are?"

"What makes you so sure they are not, hmmm? Surely it's better to have a foot in both camps, hedge your bets, don't you think?"

Rosamund felt laugher bubble. Good God, she loved this strange little man who could make her forget her woes. "Likely you're right, Sam, but I don't think your reverend or mine would be pleased to hear you say such things."

"I suspect you're right, Rosamund, so we'll just keep it to ourselves, shall we?" He paused and looked at the little bowls filled with an assortment of spices and other additives lined up on the bar. He indicated the ones he wanted in his drink and settled back on his stool.

"Mind you," he continued as Rosamund prepared his chocolate, "my dear friend Sir George Carteret is so perplexed by what he's hearing about the Jews being on the march across the Continent and in Persia, he's decided we're all about to face some great catastrophe. He's quite beside himself with melancholy."

Before Rosamund could make an appropriate noise of sympathy, Sam appeared to forget all about his friend and hopped off his stool and rested the back of his elbows on the counter, surveying the room and touching his hat to Sir Henry, who nodded gravely.

"Blithman not here?" he asked, swinging back to her.

"Aubrey does not come to the chocolate house," said Rosamund. "It's beneath him."

Sam turned slowly. "Ah, you mean Matthew Lovelace is beneath him, for I will not countenance for a moment that you are."

In that regard, Sam was right. Aubrey took the role of suitor very seriously, sending her tokens of his affection and, as if to make up for the fact he didn't write one missive the entire time he was in Oxford, scribbling something to her every other day, forcing Wat to deliver his notes. In different circumstances Rosamund might have been amused by his ramblings. As it was, she cast a cursory eye over them before sending a careless line or two in response.

"You're encouraging him," Bianca would warn.

"That's the point," Rosamund would reply.

She sighed as she passed Sam his chocolate.

"How go your preparations for his return to the manor?" he asked.

Was there anything this man did not know? "They progress . . . slowly."

Sam took a sip of his drink, let out an exhalation of appreciation and nodded sagely. "I've heard he's fallen in with John Wilmot, the Earl of Rochester."

"Is that a bad thing?" Rosamund continued to mix drinks.

"Only for those upon whom he turns his formidable wit. I hear the King intends to make Rochester a Gentleman of the Bedchamber. Never fear, Rosamund, the young earl will keep Aubrey occupied." Before she could respond, Sam saw someone he knew and, picking up his bowl, hurried off.

"A groat for your thoughts," Matthew said, slipping onto the stool Sam had vacated.

"I can assure you, sir, they're worth a great deal more than that." With a smile, she quickly threw ingredients into a bowl—sugar, musk, vanilla and a pinch of chilli—and poured him a chocolate. With a flourish, she slid the steaming bowl over.

His eyes twinkled. "Is that so? Well, next time, I'll fatten my purse before I come." He looked over his shoulder at the men bent over their news sheets, their voices rising and falling, smoke and steam swirling about their heads. "Custom seems good." He took an appreciative sip.

"Aye, it is," said Rosamund, as Hugh and Timothy ran over with more orders. They greeted Matthew before racing away to attend the tables. "Picking up every day. If it wasn't for the faces we no longer see, it would be hard to credit the plague ever happened." Her voice broke. Matthew placed a hand over hers.

"I know what you mean." He left his hand on hers a moment. The warmth of his fingers through the glove, their shared memories of Jacopo, Mr. Henderson and the others washed over them.

"Anything or anyone of interest?" asked Matthew, removing his hand and turning sideways to watch the room as she prepared more chocolate. Rosamund knew his question really meant: was there anything worthy of being written about?

Further down the bar, just out of earshot, Solomon made chocolate as well while Bianca mixed the coffee. In the kitchen, Thomas was supervising Grace using the *metate*, his voice authoritative as he gave directions. Matthew would later ask them the same question. It was surprising what could be gleaned moving between tables, serving and appearing not to listen. To many of the men, the drawers, Bianca and even Rosamund were simply there to serve them, and many were careless with their words. Considering they were at war and spies were being ferreted out everywhere, Rosamund found this casual approach to sensitive information appalling and fascinating in equal parts. News was currency—the more you had, the greater esteem in which you were held, and where better to flaunt your wealth than a chocolate or coffee house?

"Only the usual," said Rosamund. "Many are still talking about the Jewish Messiah; others grumble about how the King's many infidelities set a bad example. There are those"—she gave the barest of nods toward a group of men by the windows—"who bemoan the vice of the court and claim the King is ruled by his prick and not his head."

"Well, they wouldn't be the first to make that claim. Nor would they be wrong."

"True. But there's a viciousness in their words that wasn't there previously. Some mention the old ways."

Matthew cocked his head. "The old ways? Is that so? Do they mean the Catholic days or the Parliamentary? I wonder."

Rosamund gave a slight shrug. "They're openly referring to Lady Castlemaine as a whore and the Duchess of York as a slut." She winced as she said the words and wondered what was said about her.

As if reading her mind, Matthew closed his hand

over hers. "They could never call you anything but what you are, Rosamund."

Her eyes dropped to where his hand covered hers for the second time in a few minutes. "And what might that be?" she asked softly. Her heart tumbled at her daring, inviting him to reveal his feelings.

He didn't respond but tightened his hand over hers. Breathing hard, he stared at her, his blue eyes like a storm-tossed sea. Her mouth opened and his eyes dropped to her lips.

"What else," he said hoarsely, "but the manager of a fine establishment?" He withdrew his hand.

Rosamund's lungs deflated. "What else?" she said lightly and turned aside before he read her disappointment.

Sensing he was about to leave but not yet ready to let him go, she gave a weary sigh. "There is one other thing I must tell you."

He sank back onto the stool. "What is it? If it's that the queen's mother is sick, I know."

She placed her hands either side of the tray she'd just prepared and studied him. Whether or not he'd already heard, she knew the news needed to come from her.

"It's not that. It's something far closer to home—well, to the manor, really."

Matthew raised his brows.

"Aubrey is back from Oxford."

Did she imagine it or did Matthew's eyes narrow? She was certain color fled from his face before it returned, heightened, pronounced.

"I see," he said. "Thank you for letting me know. May I ask, for how long has he been back?"

"In London, or at Blithe Manor?"

"Either. Both."

Already, Matthew appeared to be planning some crusade. She could see it in his face, in the way his hands moved.

"He came back to London a short time ago. I probably should have told you, but it didn't seem . . . important."

"Important?" Matthew gave a dry laugh. "No. Not important."

"That's not what I meant." She sighed in frustration. "Truth is, I deliberately withheld the news as I feared it would upset you."

"In that regard, you'd be right. As it is, I'd heard rumors but awaited confirmation. Now I have it, I must make certain to welcome him back . . . this time."

Rosamund hesitated, then feeling guilty she'd not mentioned Aubrey sooner, capitulated. "I believe he has taken lodgings in Thames Street."

"He's not staying at the manor?"

"Ah . . ." Rosamund had the grace to look discomfited. "He was under the impression the premises needed to be fumigated before he took up residence again."

Bianca snorted. So much for believing she couldn't be heard. She had Matthew's attention now.

"And who," said Matthew, "gave him that impression?"

"I cannot think, sir."

Matthew gave a bark of laughter. It was so loud, the people at the nearest table swung around to look. They waved and turned back to their drinks.

"How goes it with you, Rosamund?" he asked. "With him, I mean. It can't be easy knowing he's returned. He does not . . . bother you?"

Surprised and secretly delighted he would think to ask, Rosamund hesitated. Should she mention the proposal? Mayhap that would be too forward. Anyway, what would it serve?

"Bother me? Not exactly, but I confess, it's easier with him absent." Did she reveal how Aubrey made her feel? The way he looked at her like a hungry beast?

Matthew's eyes narrowed and he considered her response carefully. "Do you know exactly where in Thames Street his lodgings are? I should pay my respects, offer my long-overdue condolences, especially considering the last time I tried, I was deprived of the opportunity."

Because Aubrey had fled as if the hounds of hell were on his heels.

"Bear with me," said Rosamund and searched her placket. She still had the last note he sent stuffed in there. "Here," she said, pulling it out and unfolding it.

"He writes to you?"

"Only every other day," said Rosamund smoothing out the paper. "He doesn't feel safe coming to the house—yet." She pointed to the address in the corner. "He's at the Dragon and Unicorn Inn, next to the sign of the spindle."

"You have my thanks, my lady."

"Shall I tell him you're coming, sir?"

Matthew shook his head. "I want to surprise him." From the look on his face, he wanted to ensure Aubrey had no chance to avoid him; it was a look that said if Aubrey had any sense, he would hightail it out of there.

FORTY-ONE
In which a threat is vanquished

Nice room, Aubrey," said Matthew, barging past Wat and sauntering over to the window as if he were a welcome visitor, not an intruder.

When Aubrey didn't reply, Matthew tore himself away from the vista to regard him. Aubrey sat, a glass of claret in one hand, a pipe in the other, his mouth still open at the sight of Matthew. The color had fled his usually ruddy cheeks, and his eyes were bloodshot. The smell of stale wine rose from him like heat off cobbles at high summer.

Unperturbed, Matthew dragged over a stool, removed the satchel from across his shoulders and, placing it by his feet, picked up the brimming jug and poured himself some wine.

"You don't mind, do you?" he asked as it splashed into the glass. "You look like you've seen a ghost." He gave a laugh and then drank.

Aubrey put down his pipe and took a hefty swallow of his wine without speaking. His eyes were wary and he kept shooting glances at Wat, who remained at the ready by the door.

Ignoring the exchanges between Aubrey and his steward, Matthew continued as if they were old friends. "Which is ironic, considering you're the one back from the dead. Speaking of which, that's what I'm here to discuss. The dead . . . and the living."

Aubrey indicated Wat should retire to the other room.

"I will remain in here should you have need of me, sir," said Wat, casting a cautious glance in Matthew's direction as he shut the door.

Knowing Wat's ear would be pressed to the wood, Matthew nudged his seat closer. "It's been a while, Aubrey. I have to say, I could scarce believe my ears when I heard you were not only alive but here in London."

The red stains that marked a heavy drinker slowly returned to Aubrey's cheeks. Putting down his glass, he sat back in his chair, resting his elbows on the arms and locking his fingers together over his lap. The appearance of nonchalance might have worked had his hands not been shaking. A tic pulsed in his jaw.

"Wh . . . what do you want?" he asked, his voice low.

"What do you think?"

"Truth be told, I do not know." His eyes met Matthew's before sliding away again. "I do not think we've anything to say to each other."

Matthew chortled. "You might not, but I've plenty to say to you."

Aubrey gripped the arms of his chair and pulled himself straighter, as if trying to gain higher ground. "If that is so, I do not want to hear it."

"Maybe not, but you will all the same." Matthew paused and took his time studying Aubrey. "But first, indulge me. I need to know. How did you do it?"

"What?"

"Avoid detection."

A sly look crossed Aubrey's face. "Why should I tell you?"

Matthew sighed. "I searched, you know—Africa, the New World—but everyone told me you were dead. I began to persuade myself that perhaps you were, after all. Yet here you are, larger than life."

A slow, smug smile transformed Aubrey's face. He waggled a finger at Matthew. "If Father and I learned anything from you, Lovelace, it was how to dissemble.

The moment I left these shores, Aubrey Blithman disappeared to be replaced by none other than Everard Blithman, nephew to his namesake, tasked with managing the business interests of his uncle." He laughed. "Preposterous, isn't it? So simple and yet so perfect. Making my new self younger by some years, all I had to do was steer close to the truth while at the same time never quite revealing it. Were you not a master of that? A lovelorn writer who was really a spy? Or was it the role of husband you never quite mastered?"

Matthew didn't bite.

"No one questioned who I was, my relationship; after all, poor Sir Everard had lost both his sons, hadn't he? It made sense that his closest living relative would look to his business interests." He cackled. "Whenever I was asked about the Aubrey Blithman business— and I oft was in the beginning—I was overcome with shame and grief. Once I established my reputation, and it didn't take long, people ceased to question me and prevented others from mentioning the name Aubrey in my presence. Before long, they were asking what they could do for me." He stared into his glass, a twisted smile upon his lips. "All I had to do was avoid those who had known me in London. It wasn't as difficult as you'd expect. I managed to avoid you, after all. When I couldn't? Well, wasn't hard to put about that the resemblance between cousins was striking." He smirked. "You'd be astonished what people will believe. All it took was a different name, a believable story and, of course, the occasional bribe."

It required all Matthew's willpower not to show his surprise at Aubrey's admission. He'd underestimated him. Oh, he'd heard of this nephew and even made efforts to contact him, to no avail. Now he knew why. That stung.

"There's no doubt, it was an adroit ruse," Matthew began. "But before you bask in any more complacency, may I remind you what works in the colonies will not work here. London has a long memory."

Aubrey reached over and brought his drink to his mouth. "Not so long it cannot forgive a man who contributes generously to the privy purse. Suddenly, my . . . how do I put it . . . colorful past has been painted in more attractive hues; my reputation is rakish rather than ruined."

"Maybe so, but never again will those in the colonies trust you, not now the vizard has been cast aside."

Aubrey inhaled, then flapped a hand in irritation. "Enough of this nonsense. Say what you've come to say, then leave. I've no desire to spend a moment more in your company than I have to."

"On that at least, we're agreed," said Matthew. It was hard not to grab Aubrey by the shirt and shake him. No, forget shake, he wanted to punch that arrogant face, wipe the smirk off that supercilious mouth, even if it was worn to disguise fear. How he could ever have thought this man a friend, been persuaded by his lies, his insistence he would be a great match for his sister, a marvelous brother-in-law . . . Truth was, he didn't want to be in the same room. The man repulsed him.

"I am here to tell you to leave Rosamund alone." Matthew's voice was firm.

"Beg your pardon?" said Aubrey incredulously.

"You heard me. I want you to stay away from Rosamund. I don't care what excuses you come up with, what reasons you give her, but you are to maintain a distance. A long one."

Aubrey's eyes started and then he sat back heavily and forced a laugh. "You've no right to tell me who I can and cannot see, no right to tell me to stay away from anyone, let alone Rosamund. Particularly when she's living in my house."

"Oh, I think I do—"

"Well," said Aubrey, heaving himself out of the chair in one motion. "You think wrong. I've great plans for

Rosamund. For me, us. Plans that do not concern you, Lovelace." He looked down at Matthew.

"You can forget your plans, Aubrey. Just as you can forget Rosamund."

Aubrey burst into shrill laughter. "Forget her? What? So you can swoop in and claim her? Ah, you think I don't know what you're about? Obviously, you're besotted with her. Think you can replace Helene with her likeness?"

"She is nothing like Helene—" began Matthew.

"Isn't she?" Aubrey began to pace. "You took my sister and now you seek to take Rosamund. I know what you're about, Lovelace, and you can bluster and threaten all you like, but I'll not listen, just as I won't be held to account for your misfortunes."

"My misfortunes? That's an odd way of describing the loss of your sister, your—"

Aubrey spun to face Matthew. "Don't you dare talk about their deaths. Don't you dare. You may not have dealt the killing blow, but I hold you responsible all the same, you cur. You still haven't answered for what you did—"

"What *I* did? Oh, that's rich coming from you, Aubrey. The man who was supposed to be my friend. I compromised my integrity for you. I risked a great deal to warn you that the authorities were casting an eye over your business—and only because I believed they were mistaken." He gave a bark of bitter laughter. "And how do you reward me?"

"I *was* your friend, damn it. But how can I be friends with the man who allowed Helene and the babe to die? Who was responsible for the death of my father? I cannot."

Matthew stared at him in disbelief. "You know I neither 'allowed' their deaths, nor was I responsible for Sir Everard's. You *know* that. Though I'm sorry, more than I can say, for all of them. Regardless of what happened, their deaths weigh heavily upon me."

Their eyes met. Aubrey's were watery, his cheeks blotched. Matthew's eyes were calm, his face cool.

"Get out," said Aubrey quietly. "And don't ever come back."

"Not before you give me your word you will stay away from Rosamund."

Aubrey threw back his head and laughed hard. "Are you mad? As if I am going to agree to something like that. Do you not understand? That woman is everything I ever wanted. She is my future. I have asked her to marry me."

"*Marry you?*" Matthew shook his head in bewilderment. "Good God. You really don't have a conscience, do you? No sense of remorse or guilt. No, Aubrey. She's not your future. She certainly isn't your past. I tell you now, you will cease your suit, swear to stay away from her, or else—"

"Or else what?" Aubrey downed his drink swiftly.

Reaching into his satchel, Matthew drew out a pile of bound letters. About to lay them on the table, he changed his mind and kept hold of them.

"Do you know what these are?" He held them up.

Aubrey squinted then blanched, staggering and clutching the back of his chair. "I thought . . . I was led to believe Father had taken care of those."

"Then you believed wrongly. I was going to give them to your father, but circumstances changed—and for that, as I said, I'm deeply sorry." He paused. "I thought of handing them to you, but now I see that would have been most foolish. God was on my side when I failed to locate your whereabouts. Now, having endured your bombast, heard your preposterous desires, know this: I intend to keep these letters and thus ensure you do exactly as I say. For, Aubrey, let me make this clear: if you do not find a reason to stay away from Rosamund and withdraw your proposal immediately, I will see to it that all of London learns the contents of these." He flourished the bundle.

Aubrey began to shake as rage swamped his frame. "You wouldn't dare."

It was Matthew's turn to laugh. "Wouldn't I? I think you know me better than that." Tucking the letters back into his satchel, he stood, draping the strap over his shoulder. "Imagine if these were published? Doors now open would slam in your face. The Blithman name would become a byword, whether you pose as Aubrey or a nephew, whether you prance about London or the New World. Your new friend Rochester would scorn you; the King and court repel you. The fine people of Virginia, New York and North Carolina would close their doors to you." Matthew lowered his voice. "Your man in there"—he jerked his chin in the direction of the room where Wat lurked—"do you think he'd be so loyal if the truth was out? Ha. People would spit in your face sooner than look at it. That is what your father feared, and that is what will happen should these letters fall into the wrong hands."

"Please," said Aubrey, putting down his glass, reaching, imploring. "You don't have to do this."

"I thought that once too. Rosamund changes everything. For her sake, I do, Aubrey. I have to protect her and I will. I believed myself done with blackmail, but it seems to be the only language you Blithmans understand." Finishing what remained in his glass, he returned it to the table. "So, do we have an agreement? You will stay away from Rosamund."

Aubrey fell into his chair and folded his arms. "As if I have a choice."

"Exactly. You do not." Glancing around the room, his eyes lingered upon the door to the adjoining room. "I include him in this, Aubrey. Do you hear me, Wat?" There was a dull scrambling. "You stay away from her too—no notes, no attempts to suborn her."

Matthew stood, brushing his breeches. "You will write to her this very morning and not only withdraw your suit but tell her she may remain in the manor for as long as she requires."

"What reason do I give? She'll hardly credit it when I have been so . . . ardent."

Matthew's eyes narrowed. "Ardent? Is that what you call unwelcome persistence?" He snorted. "I care not, Aubrey. I simply insist you take care of this immediately. Or else . . ." He patted the satchel.

Aubrey's shoulders slumped. "I understand." His hand cut the air. "It shall be as you say. Just promise me one thing."

"You have no right to extract a promise from me."

"Maybe not," said Aubrey reluctantly. "But I would beg it all the same."

"What?"

"I want your solemn oath that if I agree to your conditions, you will never tell Rosamund what's in those letters. Nor anyone else, for that matter."

Matthew locked eyes with him. Aubrey was the first to look away. "You have my solemn oath," said Matthew. "But I give it not to protect you, but to protect Rosamund and the innocent souls caught up in this sordid mess."

Aubrey nodded then sighed, his earlier bullishness gone. "Good. Good. Then you have no further reason to be here. Go. Take your threats and those damn letters and get out."

Taking a step toward him, Matthew pointed toward where Wat waited behind the door. "And don't even think to set your man upon me or attempt to steal the letters. If I but catch a glimpse of him lurking, or anyone suspicious for that matter, I will make the letters public."

The crooked leer on Aubrey's lips vanished. Matthew knew then he had guessed aright.

Releasing a long sigh, Matthew shook his head in disappointment. "Ask yourself this, Aubrey: Is it really worth the risk? Lest you've forgotten, I have a printing press at my disposal."

Aubrey didn't respond.

Adjusting his sword, Matthew tilted his hat. "If I

have my way, and I think I will, we won't meet again, Aubrey."

"I pray we do not." Aubrey strode to the window, refusing to face him.

"My sentiments exactly." With one last look at the man he was once foolish enough to deem a friend, Matthew went to the door.

Aubrey's voice stopped him. "You'll never have her either, you know."

His hand on the latch, Matthew froze.

"I may no longer be able to see her even though she dwells under my roof, or have her for wife, but she's still a Blithman, Lovelace. A Blithman. Just like Helene . . . and she didn't want you either. Whether you like it or not, whether I never see her again, she's still mine. Always will be."

Anger boiled in Matthew's veins. His vision was shot with scarlet and black. It took all his willpower to open the door and not look back; he knew if he did, he would draw his sword and run the prigging bastard through.

Back in Thames Street, the smell of the river caught him—brine, old fish and leather mixed with human feculence. Nonetheless, he had to stop, take a few deep breaths and clear his head. Dockers on the wharf before him were unloading cargo from a ship, their sea shanty giving a rhythm to their actions as they tossed bales and wound winches.

It was more difficult seeing Aubrey again than he had thought. Older, more lined than he remembered, the man he once called friend retained some aspects he remembered—the charming smile, the peculiar eyes, the way he carried himself. But all that was overshadowed by the truth, the truth he now realized he must carry for the rest of his life.

Whereas once he believed the burden too great, in the end it had served him well. Thank God Aubrey had evaded his hunt. If he had found him and relinquished the letters, where would they be now? Where would Rosamund be? In an ironic twist of fate, they allowed him to safeguard the woman he had come to care for in a manner he'd never thought possible, the woman he prayed with all his mighty heart might harbor feelings for him.

As he moved down the street, he found his chest freed of the steel that had girded it for years. Even his satchel was no longer a weight, but a guarantee. It allowed him to cast a protective net over the future.

Picking up the dockers' song, with a merry whistle he set off up the hill, back toward the chocolate house.

FORTY-TWO
In which a proposal is made

Matthew happened to overhear Robert Boyle and George Villiers, the Duke of Buckingham, talking about Rosamund the following day as they descended into the bookshop, and was struck by the nature of their discussions. It was not unusual for the patrons to speak of their hostess—usually about her striking beauty and the wondrous taste of the drink she served, a taste they could recall hours after consuming it. Oft times, it was the attention she'd paid them, flattering their already overgrown egos and delighting them no end. Today, however, the talk was different. It was about how being in her company was akin to basking under a midday sun, or sliding cold toes next to a crackling hearth and feeling the life breathe back into them. Each tried to outdo the other as they sought to explain the effect she had upon them. It was evident they were deeply touched. Matthew was reminded anew how people—not only men—responded to Rosamund, and his heart filled.

Did she sense Aubrey was gone from her life?

Trying to be patient with the customer searching among dusty tomes for something he might gift the lord who had invited him to dinner that night, he willed him to make a decision so he might ascend to the chocolate house and sit among the patrons knowing that the woman who elicited such passions was the one he wished to spend the rest of his life with.

For that was the truth—a truth he'd denied acknowledging until yesterday. To think, Aubrey Blithman had proposed to her. The gall of the man knew no bounds.

With Aubrey's capitulation, everything changed. He could put the past behind him. He was done with it, done with it all. Time to live.

Swiftly wrapping the man's purchase and scraping the coins into a tin, he propped a "closed" sign on the counter, hung another near the door and took the steps two at a time, almost bowling over Sam in his enthusiasm.

"Whoa," said Sam, flinging himself against the wall, palms up in mock surrender. "Why the hurry, Lovelace? There's plenty of chocolate for everyone now our ships have been permitted to dock."

Matthew halted abruptly. "Sam, forgive me, I didn't see you."

"That much was evident." He squinted at Matthew, trying to make him out in the dark stairwell. "Are you all right, sir?"

"Fine, thank you."

"You seem . . ." He looked him up and down. "Altered somehow, and not merely because you've abandoned that satchel you're always carrying." Sam propped his chin on his fingers as he studied him further. "You seem . . . focused, but also damnably happy."

Matthew smiled. "That's because I am, Sam. I am. Now, if you'll forgive me, I have a drink to request and a lady to address."

"Ah." Sam smiled knowingly. "Well, be prepared for a wait, my friend. I don't know what it is about Rosamund today, but she's shining like King Midas on a dull day. Everything she touches is turning to gold—gold dipped in diamonds and sprinkled with sunshine." He chuckled at his own fancy. "Why, the queue for her services hasn't diminished since I entered. Everyone wants to luxuriate in her radiance. Something's happened—you mark my words." He tapped the side of his nose. With a tilt of his hat and a good day, he went on his way.

Matthew's grin broadened as he entered the chocolate house and saw Sam's apt description confirmed. A line insinuated itself from the bar and around the booths as men waited impatiently for their drinks. Thomas and Solomon kept offering to mix them, but the men preferred to wait for Rosamund's touch, as if she were His Majesty and they had scrofula. To think they once eschewed this woman's service. He buried his laughter and bypassed the line to stand before Solomon, who immediately began preparing a drink.

Rosamund glanced over from where she was serving a customer and gave him a smile that took his breath away.

Taking his bowl, he found a position from where he could watch her working. He'd denied himself the pleasure for months, aside from surreptitious glances, and relished the view—and he was not alone.

Seeing her now, so comfortable with the men, able to control them with a raised brow, a curved lip or a twinkling glance, it was funny to think of how he first encountered her. Fighting like the harridan he christened her, she'd laid into those two lads like a street urchin. Determined to defend herself, she'd been so caught up in the fight she'd failed to hear him come to her aid.

For a fleeting second, he'd thought her Helene returned from the dead, but as he swiftly drank in her features, watched the way the anger left her eyes but not the passion that fueled it, and then saw her offer compassion and justice to the two rogues, he knew this was no Helene reincarnated but a wondrous woman who, already, drew him the way shrines did pilgrims.

Loath to part from her, guessing who she might be yet reluctant to acknowledge it, he was determined to learn more about her. Were all women like Helene, capable of donning vizards that hid their true identities? That question had dominated his mind for weeks.

Meeting her in Will's bookshop had been an unexpected boon as he maintained his vigil over the chocolate house and fulfilled his plans for revenge upon Sir Everard. That she was a Blithman he could barely reconcile, yet, when he learned she possessed no knowledge of what was going on, he knew he would shield her from the fallout, whatever happened.

When Sir Everard died, he felt responsible not only for his untimely death, but for the widow left behind. Offering her a stake in the chocolate house was easy—leaving her was the difficult part. Yet he'd felt he had to. If he was to mend the rent the Blithmans had torn not just in his heart, but in his life, he had to face the truth and confront the last of his nemeses.

His quest was over. Like Odysseus, his work at last was done. He could come home.

Stretching his long legs out, swaying to the melody of a lute and pipe, he nodded toward John Evelyn and Sir Henry Bennet, sipping his drink slowly, savoring it as he inhaled the fragrance. As he did, he imagined a pair of cinnamon-chocolate eyes gazing into his own, the laugh he knew would bubble from those rose-tinted lips and the embrace they'd share when he finally expressed his constant and deep affections. Quashing the tiny flicker of doubt that tried to flare in the wake of Aubrey's parting words, he reassured himself that the look he often saw in her eyes, the touch of her hand upon his arm, suggested something more than simply a friend or a business partner, something deep and lasting.

At closing time a combination of starlight and candles turned the empty chocolate house into a fantastical space of shadowy nooks and lambent planes. From the kitchen came the faint sounds of Grace washing the dirty bowls and the boys cleaning the equipment, as did their incessant teasing. Mr. Nick sat by a far window, wreathed in pipe smoke, gazing upon the street below. Bianca was at the bar, polishing the wood and bringing it up to the sheen she insisted was imperative before they could offer service again on the morrow.

Shooing Rosamund away when she offered to help, she nodded in Matthew's direction. "Close the door and join him. You've worked so hard today, *signora*, and while I know why, he's been inordinately patient. I've taken the liberty of pouring you both a jug of canary."

Grateful to Bianca because her feet were aching and she was weary—and not merely because they were busy but because she'd worked so hard to suppress emotions that kept batting away at her all day like moths at a lit window. The patrons had been joyous in their drinking, lavish in their praise of the chocolate and the Phoenix.

Matthew should be pleased.

When he'd first appeared, the rush of warmth that flowered in her belly and traveled to her cheeks found release in the smile she bestowed upon him before, once more, Aubrey's face appeared and banished her joy. She forced his image away—after all, he was no longer a pressing concern, having quite unexpectedly withdrawn his suit and offered her the use of Blithe Manor for the foreseeable future. Memory of the utter relief his note brought filled her again, and she relegated him to the recesses of her mind.

Only, she suspected the reason for Aubrey's actions. It was no coincidence, surely, that his hastily penned note and its generous offer arrived a few hours after Matthew would have seen him. What had passed between them? If she read him aright, Aubrey was not a man whose pride would allow him to easily relinquish what he had set his heart upon. She chose not to dwell on the cause, but to be grateful for the effect. The effect and the man who made it possible.

All afternoon she was aware of Matthew sitting only a few booths away, observing the bar. It was hard not to think he was also watching her. No matter how often her glance wandered in his direction, it continued to find his. Why would he choose today of all days to indulge in such things, especially when her own flights of fancy had taken wing?

Finally she was free of Aubrey and the multiple pressures he'd placed upon her from the moment he stepped into Blithe Manor. He'd become a disease eating away at her contentment—no more.

Ever since she left Bearwoode Manor there'd been people dictating what she should do, think, feel—how she should behave. Why, even her grandmother had, but to good purpose. Now for the first time in her life it was as if, like a reptile, she'd shed her skin, abandoned an old version of herself and was ready to strike out anew, every day becoming more resistant to the expectations of others—of men.

Part of her longed to fly free, not to escape the chocolate house or Blithe Manor, but to relish what these places gave her—freedom and safety, and within those bounds, the liberties they bestowed.

Sliding along the seat, she took in the sight Matthew presented, his face half shadowed in the flickering candlelight, his eyes mysterious, beckoning pools. He had given her opportunities—first by asking her to lease the chocolate house and manage it in his absence, and now by helping to remove the impediment Aubrey had become.

Who would've thought the day she was knocked down by horses on that dusty road in Gravesend she would one day run a London chocolate house and share ownership of a bookstore, let alone bear a title and have a manor to dwell in? Who would have thought her best friends in the world would be a blackamoor and a correspondent whose favorite pastime was to needle the conscience of the King and court? Who would have thought that she, little Rosamund Tomkins, the abandoned babe, would have the courage to help him?

"Shall I?" she asked, picking up the jug and, without waiting for Matthew to respond, pouring them both a glass of the sweet yellow wine.

"A good day, my lady," he said softly.

"It *was* a good day—a fine one," said Rosamund, gazing around the room.

"Ah"—Matthew smiled—"I think the best is yet to come."

"Do you now?" said Rosamund, picking up her glass and holding it out ready to toast. The liquid sparkled like molten gold. Tiny bubbles climbed to the surface before dissolving. Mesmerized, she gazed at the glass, turning it, only becoming aware that once more, Matthew was transfixed by her face. "What is it, Matthew?"

For the first time since she'd met him, he appeared awkward. He sat up straight and stared at his glass, his gloved fingers wrapped around the stem. Rainbows of light shot over the table. Lowering her own, she could see he was struggling for words.

"Matthew?" she asked quietly, placing her hand over his, stilling his movements. Had something else happened when he visited Aubrey? Dare she ask?

"I . . . I'm not sure how to say this, Rosamund." Matthew looked at their joined hands. "I've wanted to do this for so long, dreamed of a time when I might be able to, and now that I can, that the moment has arrived, I find that even though I make a living from words, I can't seem to find the right ones."

Rosamund sat very still. She could feel his breath on her cheek as he spoke, leaning so far across the table their mouths were but a sigh apart.

"What I'm trying so very badly to say is—" His voice was suddenly deep, strong and certain. "I wonder, if you would honor me, Rosamund Blithman, by becoming my wife?"

Rosamund caught the words, inhaled the scent of them and him and all the chocolatey-vanilla promises they contained. She clutched them to her heart. She thought of how he'd come back to her after so long away, how they'd suffered so much since then, lost too many loved ones. How death compressed time but also bestowed a clarity that life oft lacked.

Matthew was asking for her hand. Rosamund Blithman. Aye, that's who she was now. From Tomkins to Ballister to Blithman—a series of names, like masks she wore for others, adopting a costume and being whatever and whomever they wanted her to be. He was asking her to forgo all those and become Rosamund Lovelace. It was what she'd long hoped for, without really acknowledging it—in the way we don't admit our most secret desires lest we risk losing them. Except she had to ask, why? Why was he asking her? And now of all times, when Aubrey's relentless suit was withdrawn?

Sir Everard had married her to serve a purpose; Aubrey proposed because he was trying to hurt Matthew, of that she was in no doubt. What other reason could he have for suggesting such an outrageous match? But

Matthew? What was she but a widowed chocolate maker with an empty title—a title that had no lands or wealth attached to it? A woman who bore an uncanny resemblance to his former wife. Or was he asking her in order to secure complete victory over Aubrey? Succeed where his former brother-in-law failed?

The little shard of self-doubt that lived in her heart dislodged itself, as it sometimes did, only to reinsert itself with cruel precision. The voice she tried so hard to ignore began to whisper, fueling her uncertainty.

It's not really you he loves, is it, Rosamund? It's the woman who looks like his Helene, only you're unencumbered by lovers and a babe that is not his. This is about triumphing over the Blithmans once again—whereas once it was Sir Everard, now it's Aubrey he seeks to vanquish. The voice went on and on in Paul's tone, as it always did, undermining her joy.

That was the other reason Aubrey had wanted to marry her—to replace his lost sister with a wife; it mattered not to him that she'd been wedded to his father. On the contrary, that made her the perfect choice.

For the first time in her life, as a widow and businesswoman, she could choose. For the first time she could be herself, in her own image, not Paul's, Helene's, Sir Everard's, Aubrey's or anyone else's.

Was she so ready to surrender herself again? Even to this man?

In the seconds it took for these thoughts to whirl through her head, the distance between them remained as it was. He was waiting for her to close the gap, seal his declaration with a kiss.

Freeing her hands from his, she tipped her head and looked at him, really looked at him, in the candlelight. His dark unruly hair. Those midnight eyes that contained galaxies within them, galaxies and a fire that tonight burned just for her. No question, he was a fine man. Maybe not handsome in the conventional sense, but to her, he was beautiful. His heart shone in his expression and that was enough—or would have been, once upon a time.

"Matthew." She sighed. "You have no idea how much I have longed to hear those words from you."

His eyes explored her face, moving from her nose to her cheeks and lips before lingering on her chin. He raised a hand and cupped it gently.

"And?" he prompted.

"And," she hesitated, "I'm afraid my answer is no."

His hand fell.

"I cannot marry you, Matthew. I cannot."

FORTY-THREE
In which an adjournment is requested

The hurt in his eyes was a dagger that skewered her innards again and again. She had to remain resolute.

"At least, not yet," she added, almost wincing at how calculating it sounded, when she felt anything but.

"Not *yet*? What does that mean?" Matthew flung himself back in the seat.

"It means . . . well, it means not yet. Do you understand?"

"No, not really." He picked up the glass of wine and drained it.

Rosamund supposed that at this point many men would stride off in a huff, vowing never to see the woman again. But not this man. Not Matthew. He would stay, understand too, if he could.

Aye, he was a man worthy of her love. So why was she rejecting it?

She wasn't. She was simply asking for an adjournment. "If you could see it in your heart to ask me again sometime in the future, that is, if you don't meet anyone else worthy of your affection in the meantime . . ." The idea he might was a sword in her ribs. "Then I would indeed agree to be your wife."

"You would?"

She nodded.

"May I ask why not now?" he asked.

Rosamund sighed. "Of course, though I'm not sure I can explain it sufficiently—even to myself." She opened her hands, stared at the palms as if they were pages containing the words she needed. "I simply need time to be me. To not be beholden to anyone—not even you. No, *especially* not you. I want to enjoy my hard-won liberty, for which I know you're partly responsible. Does that make sense?"

Matthew nodded slowly, considering. He unhurriedly poured himself another drink. "Do you have any idea how much time you might require?"

Rosamund buried a smile. "I'm afraid not. But if you could be patient, I would be very grateful."

"Ah, madam." He sighed, putting the decanter down carefully. "You have been so patient with me and

I didn't do you the courtesy of asking first." He rested his head on the back of the seat and began to chuckle.

"What's so funny?" she asked.

"Never before have I been given such a rejection."

Rosamund arched a brow. "I see. You make a habit of asking women to be your wife?"

He ceased to laugh. "No. I do not. As you well know, there has been one other, and that didn't go well."

Rosamund could've kicked herself for being so tactless. "Forgive me, Matthew. I . . . I—"

"Forgive you? Pray, what for? For not deceiving me? For not leading me on with falsehoods and duplicity? Madam"—he reclaimed her hands and held them as one might a fragile butterfly—"your honesty both refreshes and pains me. It assures me I have given my heart well and that yours is more than worth waiting for . . . Lest my intentions not be clear, I want you to know, I love you, Rosamund."

Their eyes locked. The moon waxed and waned for eons as they made unspoken promises, quenched their desires in a chaste silence.

Letting her go reluctantly, Matthew slid out of the booth, picked up his glass and held it out. When she had gathered her own, he tapped his against hers—crystal lips sharing the kiss they denied themselves.

"Here's to the future. Our future—whatever form it may take."

"Ours," said Rosamund and drank.

She set down her glass and turned to thank him, but before she could utter a word, he leaned toward her and drew her into his arms.

The embers of her passion, burning steadily since she had sat down, leaped to sear her insides; armies of tiny sparks scattered over her body, igniting little fires.

His mouth descended toward hers, and a groan that was matched by her breathless one escaped him before, placing her hands against his chest, she prevented him from coming any closer.

"I cannot, Matthew. As much as I want to, I must not . . . not yet. I'm . . . . I'm afraid, if I do, I won't be able to stop."

Tilting his head until his forehead rested against hers, he sighed. "On that score, you're not alone."

She forgot to breathe.

Cradling his cheek with her palm, she leaned back in his arms and gazed into his eyes. "Thank you."

Releasing her, he took her hand from his face, planted a long kiss upon it. "You're a cruel mistress, Lady Harridan, but you are *my* cruel mistress. Don't forget that."

Unable to speak, she shook her head.

Bowing to her, then Bianca, who was pretending not to watch, and touching his hat to Mr. Nick, he left.

Rosamund fell back into her seat. Dear God, but that had been difficult. Her senses reeled, unable to settle as ribbons of pleasure traveled along her veins. And what was that delicious, hot nudging in her lower regions? Placing a hand over her stomach, she pressed. Dear God, there was a thirst she needed to quench.

Laughter began to build within her—a joyous, unforced, uninvited release. Leaving the confines of the booth, she began to twirl about the room, exchanging smiles and laughs with Bianca, with Mr. Nick—who pulled his pipe from his mouth and gave a crooked grin. When Grace came out to see what all the fuss was about, Rosamund swung her around, the little bouquet of flowers Grace had taken to pinning to her neckline scattering petals about the floor. Dancing now, with a smile, Rosamund invited Filip and the boys to join her, and together they clapped, stomped and laughed with abandon. Not once did she strike a table or bench, but magically avoided contact with anything but her wild and naughty imagination and her full but tortured heart.

FORTY-FOUR
In which revenge is served warm

If anyone had ever dared to suggest to Rosamund that Matthew Lovelace and Aubrey Blithman had anything in common, she would have dismissed them with sharp words for having the temerity to compare chocolate to bilge water. But as the weeks rolled by, she was forced to admit that both men did indeed seem able to keep their word—albeit for very different reasons.

Surprised she'd not heard from Aubrey despite his claim he would no longer contact her, and the coincidence that his notes ceased the day after Matthew paid him a visit, she finally confronted Matthew, who admitted he had extracted an agreement from the man, but how he had accomplished this, he refused to reveal. Rosamund chose not to pry further lest she upset what was a very pleasing outcome. Rumor had it Aubrey had gone to Portsmouth to lick his wounds and employ a new agent to deal with shipping, the last one having defected to the Dutch. Contradicting this was gossip that he'd been sighted at court, spending time with Joseph Williamson. Williamson was renowned as a ruthless and efficient spy, uncovering plots both real and imagined in order to keep His Majesty safe and his own role at court secure.

While most men who'd had their marriage proposals spurned might have become bitter, bellicose or persistent, Matthew did none of those things. If anything, he was more respectful of her and was oft seen propped in the chocolate house writing, content to share her with the customers. Likewise, Rosamund felt no discomfort in taking him a drink in the bookshop and lingering to discuss something in a current news sheet or receiving copies of his latest anonymous tract for the drawers to covertly distribute.

One day upon returning from dropping pamphlets at Charing Cross and St. Paul's, Adam, Kit and Hugh—all of them adept at disguising themselves and staying clear of anyone who looked like they might be from the government—asked to speak to Rosamund.

Leaving the bar in Filip's capable hands, Rosamund found the boys changed back into their uniforms and waiting near the table at the rear of the kitchen. They looked worried, which immediately put Rosamund on alert.

"What is it?" she asked. "Were you seen?"

"No, my lady. Not delivering the pamphlets," said Adam.

Hugh and Kit nodded, and Rosamund relaxed.

"But," Adam began, "the last few times we've gone out, we noticed a man watching the chocolate house."

"Either here or the bookshop . . ." corrected Hugh.

Pulling the boys further away from the kitchen, Rosamund lowered her voice. "Explain what you mean."

"It might be nothing," said Adam. "But there's this fella been hovering around the lane the last few days. He thinks we don't notice, but because you asked us to be extra vigilant, we seen him."

"Never in 'ere, mind," said Hugh. "Only out there." He jerked his thumb in the direction of the windows.

Rosamund was thoughtful. What if this man was watching the bookshop? The dissenting tracts being left about the city were causing a great deal of talk, especially the one about the behavior of the court while at Oxford, detailing how the courtiers drank themselves senseless, shat in fireplaces and corners, had their way with the ladies of the city—willing and unwilling—all while their fellow citizens suffered and died. It had done nothing to enhance the King's already precarious reputation, nor those of his hangers-on who were named, including Aubrey. Members of the Nonsuch Club in particular, a group of well-known republicans who plotted to seize the gates of the city and restore the Commonwealth, had made much of Matthew's words, using them to recruit people to their cause and attracting the authorities' attention. While not a republican (he came from a family of loyal royalists), Matthew wasn't alone in disapproving of what the court had become. The intention of the pamphlets was to rouse the conscience of courtiers, not rebellion; it was a call for sense and discretion. Not that L'Estrange or Joseph Williamson would see it that way with the Nonsuch Club using his words to inspire seditious action. Rosamund feared that government spies were after the author of the piece.

Or was it the Quakers they were seeking? For the past few weeks Bianca and the Friends had been meeting every Sunday evening in the bookshop, entering through the rear gate so it appeared as if they were going to church. They sat quietly around the counter, offering their mostly silent prayers and communion, leaving one at a time so as not to attract attention. Not even Filip and the boys knew of their presence. Could they have been seen?

"Can you show this gentleman to me?" she asked the boys.

They nodded eagerly.

"Not in an obvious way, mind. We must make it look casual. Return to your duties as I will mine. Shortly, I want you to come to the bar, Adam, and whisper something in my ear. We will both go to the table near the east window and from there you can show me this man you speak of."

The boys nodded again.

Fifteen minutes later, having shared this news with Matthew, causing his brow to furrow, Adam approached her. Rising, both Rosamund and Matthew made their way to the table near the easternmost window, gently pushing past the patrons who were keen to engage them in conversation. While Matthew distracted the men, Rosamund sidled close to the window with Adam, a tray balanced against his hip, by her side.

It was a moment before he casually rubbed his nose, his finger pointing toward a man of medium height. Dressed in the ordinary clothes of a worker, he leaned against the old stationer's store directly opposite. Now a lacemaker's, it wasn't a good spot for surveillance for a man; it was evident he had no interest in the goods in the shop.

Adam returned to service while Rosamund remained and watched for a few minutes. Matthew finally broke away from the men and joined her. She simply smiled, nodded down at the street and left him, her heart thumping, her former confidence flowing into her boots with every step. If that man was a spy, then they were in trouble.

She caught Filip's concerned look and donned a smile. Working around her, the drawers attended to the patrons as if nothing was amiss.

Dear God, she thought, thinking of what she asked Adam, Kit and Hugh to do, the risks they took on her behalf.

They could all be in trouble.

The months flew past and as the premises continued to be watched they took extra precautions. Matthew ceased to print his anonymous pieces, sticking to authorized material only. The Quakers terminated their meetings. They were neither raided nor arrested.

Still the surveillance continued.

From Matthew, Rosamund learned there were two men watching them: Peter Crabb and Samuel Wilcox, who took it in turns to observe the building throughout the day. The two had done work for Sir Edward Nichols, King Charles's Secretary of State, but had transferred their services to Sir Henry Bennet.

Sir Henry . . . His Majesty's spymaster. And Matthew's occasional employer. Suddenly, Sir Henry's interest in Rosamund, his desire to engage her in conversation every time he entered the chocolate house, took on a sinister cast. Rosamund always ensured she had a ready smile and a store of safe conversations with which to regale him. She began to wonder if she'd ever inadvertently mentioned anything to him from Matthew's illegal pamphlets. Praying she hadn't been so foolish, she worked hard so as not to appear wary and made sure she expressed appreciation for his continued patronage.

Aware Matthew watched her interactions with Sir Henry, she also noted how the man followed Matthew down to the bookshop on a number of occasions. When she asked Matthew if Sir Henry questioned him about his writings, he reassured her their conversations were safe. She was safe. Sir Henry had their interests as well as those of the King at heart. Crabb and Wilcox, while Sir Henry's men, oft acted of their own volition, but as far as Sir Henry knew, they were not investigating Matthew or the chocolate house.

Matthew admitted it was also possible someone else was paying the two watchers—they were hands for hire, after all. For the moment, whomever that might be, and for what purpose, remained a mystery. Matthew assured her he would get to the bottom of it. She wondered who had hired the men and what their motivation might be, tormenting herself with terrible possibilities.

Spring arrived, bringing with it another bout of hot, stormy weather. Hail as big as the tennis balls the King loved striking rained upon the capital, breaking windows, damaging barrows and carts and even killing a couple of unfortunate souls. Lightning split the sky in jagged spears and flashes at once haunting and ethereal. Reading them as portents of divine displeasure, prognosticators reveled in making dire predictions almost as much as preachers in the pulpit.

The *London Gazette* and the trade publications that contained information about shipping, horses and forthcoming auctions were also filled with news from foreign shores, much of it about the war preparations the Dutch and French were making.

Regardless of the never-ending war, disillusionment with the King was so rife, it was rumored even those closest to him were growing tired of his selfish ways. Matthew learned that John Wilmot, the Earl of Rochester, was working on a satire about him.

"This is what he's penned thus far," said Matthew one quiet evening after closing. "Make sure no one else reads this."

Rosamund scanned the few lines, swallowing hard to still her laughter, more than a little shocked at the tone. "How did you manage to get this?" she asked.

Matthew's eyes sparkled. "I have my ways."

"If the King ever sees this—" She stopped.

"Aye, Wilmot will be for the Tower. It's not intended for His Majesty's eyes." Matthew folded it carefully. "God knows what else he'll compose."

Rosamund nodded. "The King gives him so much material. To think, that's how his own courtiers regard him."

"Not all," said Matthew. "Not those who find great advantage in encouraging His Majesty's vices." He sighed. "What's of greatest concern is the common folk are far more likely to put angry words into foolish actions. When I first started writing about the court's foibles, I didn't understand the resentment bubbling below the surface. It's just as well I'm forced to stop at present." He gazed toward the windows. "We must keep our ears and eyes open, Rosamund—and not just for spies. The last thing we need with the Hollanders and French breathing down our necks is another civil war."

Matthew was right. But if this was what a courtier was prepared to write—one of the King's own, a noble—it was hardly surprising plots to overthrow the monarch abounded.

Nor was it surprising that one of the greatest of these was hatched at the Phoenix.

FORTY-FIVE
In which a plot thickens

It was late April before the sea battles that were supposed to end the Anglo–Dutch War were waged. The chocolate house was relatively quiet, the day was warm and many had taken to the river to enjoy the spring sunshine. The fighting was far away, akin to a bedtime story. As she cleaned one of the booths, Rosamund took the opportunity to rest awhile, flicking through the *London Gazette,* wondering if she could persuade Bianca and Matthew to accompany her to the latest production at the King's Theater, *The Duchess of Malfi.* According to the bill, it was a bloody play of revenge and murder. While she read, a group of men arrived and settled themselves in the booth next to her. They called over the drawers and placed an order, then began to whisper in urgent voices.

At first, Rosamund didn't pay them heed. Men were always gossiping like fishwives, persuading themselves that their discussions of Frances Stewart's beauty, or whether or not the King had fathered Lady Castlemaine's latest brat, or which lord was fucking which courtier's wife, were worthy of consideration merely because they came from a man's mouth, whereas if a female pondered the same subjects she would be dismissed as a mindless blatherer. Rosamund put down the bill and scanned the contents of a new pamphlet. It was yet another piece on what the number 1666 signified and how they were all doomed. Then she heard something that made her skin goose and her heart seize.

"It's not that difficult," said a low, hoarse voice. "It may be a fortress, but if you take it from the water, cross the bleedin' moat, no one will know. I'm telling ye, the walls aren't defended."

Rosamund sat very still. The voices were unfamiliar.

"He speaks true. And after we enter the Tower with weapons aplenty"—the accent was northern; the harsh words had a pleasing burr—"we seek out Governor Robinson and General Browne and put an end to them once and for all."

There was heavy silence.

"And you say the others are ready?" asked a recognizable voice finally.

"I have it on good authority they merely await our word. Once given, there'll be uprisings all over the country—Scotland especially. They're as sick of this Stuart bastard, his roaming cock and spendthrift ways, as the rest of us."

There were more names mentioned, and Rosamund did her best to consign them to her memory. A date was given. Her blood froze.

She needed to move, to see who was talking and try to ascertain if this was something to be taken seriously and not merely a fantasy borne of discontent, but she had to do it without giving away that she'd been eavesdropping. At that moment Hugh approached the men with a laden tray, and she pleaded with him with her eyes not to acknowledge her.

Confused by the faces she was pulling, he shrugged and served the men, who ceased to talk the moment he appeared.

Taking advantage of the interruption, she slid out of her booth and went to the bar, approaching it from the kitchen as if that were where she had been all along. It was easy to see the men. She knew one quite well—the familiar voice belonged to John Rathbone. According to Mr. Nick, he'd been a colonel in the old Parliamentary army. Ever since the plague, he'd been a regular who kept to himself, preferring to take his pipe and news sheet and sit at the end of a table. This time, there were two others with him. She couldn't see the man sitting opposite, but the one next to him was of Sir Everard's vintage and possessed of a very untidy periwig and dirty clothes, as if he'd ridden a fair distance.

This was information she couldn't keep to herself, no matter how much she respected the privacy of her patrons and their right to converse about all manner of topics. This wasn't merely dissent—it was treachery.

Furthermore, if she reported it, it might satisfy whoever sent men to watch them to call them off once and for all. Surely if she or Matthew plotted to overthrow the government, they wouldn't betray those attempting to do it.

Rosamund excused herself and asked Bianca to supervise the bar, then she immediately went downstairs to Matthew and told him everything.

Matthew agreed this could be just what they needed to deflect any unwanted attention. Bidding her mind the shop and to write down all the details she could recall, he went upstairs to investigate.

A few minutes later he returned, looking grim.

"This information must be passed to Bennet and Williamson at once. I'm all for poking people's conscience, for keeping the government accountable, but not violence. Not treason. It brings nothing but misery—to all."

"You know Mr. Williamson well enough to reveal this to him?"

Matthew became distracted, straightening a stack of bills on the counter. "He helped establish the *London Gazette*, publishes my writing. He's also given me . . . other work in the past."

"Other work? You mean, the work that took you to the Continent? Occupied you in the New World?"

He grinned. "I didn't spend all that time away chasing my former wife's lover. Bennet and Williamson gave me a second chance—the opportunity to prove my worth after the Blithman debacle. I wasn't going to forfeit that. Bennet trusts me now. Listens to me."

Which explained why Matthew believed him when he said they weren't being watched by his command. Rosamund regarded him quizzically. "There's so much about you I don't know."

"I'm a real conundrum. The Sphinx of London." He winked as she laughed. "I pray you'll have years to uncover all my secrets," he said, taking the list of names from her. "Just as I will yours."

Suddenly shy, Rosamund was the first to look away. Her finger trailed across the counter. "You think it's genuine, then? These men pose a real threat?"

"Anyone who discusses a coup and setting fire to the city on a day that's dear to all Cromwellians, September the third—the anniversary of the Lord Protector's death—must be taken very seriously," said Matthew.

He looked at what she'd written and let out a long whistle. "This goes far indeed. Thomas Flint. John Cole. My." He folded the paper carefully and placed it in a pocket. "Can I ask you now, my lady, to entrust this knowledge to my keeping? I will see to it the information gets to the right people. Hopefully, this will prove my—our—loyalty."

Rosamund was glad to wash her hands of it. Men who were so disloyal they would plot a coup and set fire to the city—and dared to do so under her roof—should be severely punished. Rosamund returned upstairs and it took all her skills to pretend nothing was amiss and to treat the conspirators as she did all her customers—with a smile, a laugh and offers of more drinks.

It was only later that night, as she related what she'd overheard to Bianca, that it occurred to her these men might lose their lives. The price for uttering the wrong words in the wrong place was very, very high. Furthermore, these men were known Parliamentarians. The King tolerated them about as much as he did those with dissenting faiths—as Bianca well knew.

Just as words could do so much good, they could also destroy and change lives in an instant. Did the men understand the power they held in their mouths? She feared they didn't. It was why she respected Matthew so much: he knew both the good and the evil words could bring.

As if carried in on her thoughts, Matthew appeared at the door, ushered in by Ashe. Matthew thanked the housekeeper and waited until she left before speaking.

"Well, Rosamund"—he threw himself into a chair and accepted a glass of wine—"it looks like you may have uncovered a veritable nest of snakes."

"Are the men to be seized?" she asked.

Matthew shook his head.

"Not immediately. Bennet says they'll be watched and followed. He intends to see how far this stretches, who else is involved. As yet, there is time."

"Until September the third. Unless they succeed, after which, London will be no more."

"Yes." Matthew laughed. "And the world as we know it will end. You've been reading too many almanacs, Rosamund."

"That's what I told her." Bianca chuckled. "And listening to the prognosticators."

Rosamund smiled good-naturedly at their teasing. "I believe a group of plotting men far more than I do those who foresee the end of the world, however it comes. Mind you, those who claim to see the future have been wrong so far. They said floods would destroy us, pestilence too—and neither did."

"What does that leave in their arsenal of predictions?" asked Matthew, holding up his glass for Bianca to refill.

"Fire." Rosamund grinned. "All that's left is fire."

FORTY-SIX
In which a baker
burns pudding on the
2nd of September, 1666

As it turned out, the only good to come of the plotters being uncovered—apart from a deadly plan being foiled—was that the surveillance of the Phoenix and the bookshop ceased. Either whoever had hired them was also seeking proof of the Rathbone plot (as it came to be called), or, Rosamund thought, the men they'd sent learned to avoid detection. Whatever the reason, Rosamund's days continued much as they had before, until one hot day in early September.

Standing in the yard at the chocolate house picking flowers, Rosamund paused and sniffed the air. "Can you smell that?" she asked Grace. After church that morning, Rosamund and Bianca, along with Grace, had walked to Birchin Lane carrying a basket of food so they could share a meal with Filip, Mr. Nick and the boys. It was also a convenient excuse to see Matthew, who was busy stocktaking in the bookshop. Looking for something to decorate the luncheon table, she and Grace had snuck downstairs.

Grace swept her hair off her face—the sultry wind took braids as a challenge and sought to untangle carefully styled plaits—tilted her little chin and inhaled. "Aye, my lady. I can. Strong like, too."

Summer had struck the city with blazing vengeance. The rains had ceased to fall, the river receded until its muddy banks were nothing but cracked earth displaying the rotting carcasses of stranded fish and eels. Boats couldn't pass the locks. Mighty thunderstorms continued to growl above the city, and lightning punctuated the sky, all without the relief of rain. Though the heat and the hot, desiccated air had grown uncomfortably familiar, this was different.

Rosamund handed the last of the little bell-shaped flowers to Grace. "Take a few for your neckline and put the rest in water, will you? Tell Bianca I'll be there shortly. I might go and have a word with Mr. Lovelace. Thank you, Grace."

Rosamund navigated the maze of corridors at the back of the bookshop and found Matthew staring out the front window, hands folded behind his back. Pausing to drink in the sight he presented in his Sunday best blue jacket and crisp white shirt, Rosamund noted how his hair shone where the sun struck it. Grateful to be out of the heat, she quickly tidied herself, then came around the counter to join him.

There was no sign of smoke on the street, just the cloudless heavens, but she could see people pointing in the direction of the river. Some looked skyward, but at what she couldn't tell. There were frowns, hurried words and then people turned and scurried away as if pursued by bandits. All the while, their skirts and jackets blew around their bodies. Hats flew off and carriage blinds bellied in and out like devil's bellows.

"There's a fire," said Matthew, turning toward her. "It was all they could talk about at St. Michael's this morning. It started in the wee hours in Pudding Lane. Baker Farriner's place."

"Aye, well, if that's the case, it's not been contained there," said Rosamund. "You can smell it on the wind."

Matthew looked at her. "Hmmm. I noticed it when I arrived as well."

"Should we be worried?" asked Rosamund. "The reverend at St. Helen's made no mention, nor any in our congregation."

Matthew gave a slight shrug. "I'm not certain. I think I might go and see what I can find out. Prop the door to the chocolate house open. Our regulars will see and, if they're passing, pop in." He glanced at the ceiling. "They'll keep you informed."

Rosamund nodded. "True. Your best source is Sam—if anyone knows what's going on, it will be him."

"I'll go to the Navy Office immediately. Promise me you won't do anything rash. Remain here until I get back. I can't imagine the flames traveling this far."

"To Birchin Lane?" Rosamund scoffed. "If it started down in Pudding, we'd be very unlucky if it came anywhere near."

"I don't believe in luck—not in the way most mean it," said Matthew. "Good or bad. We make our own."

"Or God makes it for us," said Rosamund softly. "That's what the reverend said this morning." She gazed at a woman outside who grabbed her young child with one hand and held on to her hat with the other and raced by the shop, turning into Exchange Alley and narrowly avoiding a courier on horseback. "He'd be a cruel God to inflict fire upon us so soon after pestilence, would he not?"

Matthew rocked back on his heels. "In my experience, God is cruel."

Rosamund reached for his hand and squeezed it. "Mine too." They exchanged a long look.

"Find out what you can. I will do the same. I will return as soon as possible."

Even with the door open, hardly anyone came by the chocolate house that day, and those who did spoke of nothing but the fire raging down by the river. Their tales added to the growing tally of disaster and the sense the blaze was creeping closer, street by street, lane by lane, house by house. It had already consumed the Fishmongers' Hall and the old church of St. Magnus the Martyr. By midday, it had skipped a few streets and started to burn northwest. Whoever came in sat by the windows while Filip, Solomon, Thomas and Grace found excuses to linger beside them and peer outside.

It wasn't long before any pretense of eating luncheon was abandoned and they all stood, shoulder to shoulder, gazing out upon a sky roiling with thick black plumes. People flocked onto the rooftops opposite, pointing and crying out in alarm.

While she tried to remain calm, Rosamund nonetheless felt a sense of urgency, and concern for Matthew. The few patrons who stumbled in after the bells chimed noon were dismissive, saying it would be out by nightfall, while others merely stopped by to gossip. Some entered to down a drink before going home to consider whether it was worth gathering their belongings and hiring a coach or wherry to take them out of the city. Then there were those determined to find a Frenchman or Dutchman to hold accountable. As the afternoon wore on, it was evident that, despite all the reassurances, London was burning.

Rosamund could see Lombard Street was already thick with vehicles and people heading north, out of the city.

Dear God, it was like the plague all over again.

By midafternoon, there were no more visitors and the light was dimmed by choking clouds of Stygian smoke. Scintillas of ash and molten sparks pirouetted in the hot wind, landing on eaves, cobbles, people's clothing, threatening to spark. Birds had long taken wing, dogs ran barking up the street, chasing those fleeing, while cats slinked into dark voids.

Instead of rushing to help put out the flames raging by the river, people were intent on looking to their own well-being—and, Rosamund noted wryly as cart after cart bumped down the road, their material goods as well.

When three of the clock sounded and there was still no sign of Matthew and it was evident the fire was worsening, Rosamund quickly helped clear away their uneaten meals and, along with Bianca, Filip, Thomas, Grace, Solomon and Mr. Nick, sat vigil by the window.

The sky grew unnaturally dark. What had been an opaque dome lowered to become a thick, suffocating curtain. Filip ordered Thomas and Solomon to douse the fires in the kitchen by pouring the great pots of water on them, while he began to clean and pack as much of their equipment as he could. Rosamund and Mr. Nick worked silently beside him. Unable to say what drove her to do such a thing, Rosamund knew Filip's instincts were right and they had to do all they could to preserve their equipment. If there was one thing the plague had taught her, it was that people needed the familiar in times of crisis. To cling to hope, they needed to know all was not lost—"all" being even the simplest things. And what was chocolate if not the most complex of simple things? If God preserved them, she would offer solace in whatever way she could. Serve chocolate from Bishopsgate Street if that was required—if God saw fit to leave the manor standing.

When Matthew staggered through the door just before four of the clock, his face and clothes blackened with soot, his hair damp with sweat, he was met by a room piled with crates of bowls, pots, *molinillos*, *metates*, sacks of chocolate cakes, spices, cacao beans, coffee beans, piles of ledgers and whatever else they'd managed to pack.

Pails of water and milk stood at the ready in case an errant spark or flame should kindle a conflagration.

"I see you've been busy," he said, flashing a look of approval even as he reached for the water Rosamund gave him, drinking greedily. Some he splashed over his face and hands, staring at the streaks of brownish gray in disgust as he wiped them on a cloth. He slapped Filip's shoulder in greeting.

"Well?" asked Rosamund.

"Listen," he said, collapsing on a bench. They gathered around. "I found Sam. I also went to the offices of the *London Gazette*. I figured between them, Sam and the staff there would know what was going on." He swallowed more water. "Almost a quarter of the city within the walls has burned."

Rosamund gasped. Bianca sat down heavily. Filip's eyes flicked from Matthew to Rosamund. Matthew had knocked away the last bit of hope to which she'd been clinging. She sank down beside Bianca and stared at him. This was worse than she'd anticipated.

Matthew nodded toward the windows. There was no sky anymore, just tumbling clouds of catastrophe. "The mayor is all but useless, and rumor has it the King or his brother will take over and try to put this conflagration out."

"Are we safe here?" asked Filip.

Matthew lifted heavy eyes to him. "If the wind keeps blowing in this direction, I fear not. It's time to do what so many others have already done and prepare for the worst. I see you've packed the equipment.

I suggest we take it to Bishopsgate Street." He glanced at Rosamund.

"Of course. We can decide what to do once there," she said.

"You're not remaining with us, are you?" asked Filip of Matthew.

Matthew shook his head. "I'll help you get this to Blithe Manor, then I must do my duty by my sovereign and my city."

"I'll come with you," said Filip. Mr. Nick swiftly volunteered as well. Matthew gave them a flicker of a smile.

A lump formed in Rosamund's throat. It was hard to push the words through, but she managed. "You intend to fight the fire." Her eyes were locked on Matthew.

He flexed his fingers in his gloves. "I do, my lady. I do."

Rosamund didn't know when she'd been prouder of him—or more afraid.

FORTY-SEVEN
In which London burns

Miraculously, Mr. Nick managed to find a carter happy to carry their goods to Blithe Manor in exchange for some cakes of chocolate. As they followed the cart, arms filled with sacks and linens, and more than a few books Rosamund rescued from the chocolate house and bookshop, they passed pale and tear-streaked men, women and children laden with their own belongings, all coming from the direction of the river. Some were covered in soot and ash, their eyes betraying what they'd lost.

The sky was a furious tempest, as if demons writhed in an eternal struggle, raining glowing embers and ash upon the city, indifferent to the frightened mortals below. The world had been turned upside down, and hell was now above—where heaven existed, God only knew.

Among the evacuees were messengers and couriers running between the authorities in London and Whitehall. Rumor had it the King was upon the river, and sure enough, when they managed to waylay a messenger they discovered not only that the King was, indeed, abroad and taking matters into his own hands, but that the fire was moving swiftly west along Thames Street. It had destroyed nine churches, and the warehouses lining the river were all but blackened powder. Their escape from the chocolate house was timely as the fire surged toward the Royal Exchange and Cornhill, threatening even St. Paul's and the Inns of Court.

Releasing the messenger, who was wild-eyed with exhaustion, Matthew urged them on. They needed no prompting.

At Blithe Manor, the goods tumbled from their arms as footmen and maids ran out to help unload the cart. Ashe brought them water. Barely waiting for them to quench their thirst, she begged news and added her own.

There was a call for workmen to help the Duke of York, who'd been placed in charge. The footmen longed to be excused so they might offer their services. Before Rosamund could release them, Sam arrived.

"Come, come," he said. "You can't stay here. You're in the path of the flames. You must come to my place. Bury what you can and then let's get you to Seething Lane. We've a fine view of the fire, and what's more, a command post has been set up nearby, so we can keep abreast of the news."

He sounded invigorated.

Instead of burying the equipment, at Rosamund's suggestion they lowered everything into the well in a corner of the courtyard. Ashe included some of the household silver as well as other valuables.

Rosamund sent the maids to fetch anything they might have need of, then stood outside, reluctant to go to her room and retrieve any of her own belongings. It seemed pointless when what she most feared to lose was about to face the fierceness of the fire.

Matthew called the footmen to him, along with Filip, Mr. Nick, Thomas and Solomon, who swore their services as well. Then he turned to Sam. "I'm placing her in your care, Sam—look to her."

"You've no need for concern, Matthew. Rosamund is family and I always take care of my own."

Thinking how he barely had time for his wife, Elizabeth, Rosamund nevertheless forgave him the hyperbole and was grateful for his confident presence and his offer of safety. With a bow, Sam went to supervise the carter, who was prepared to carry whatever Rosamund deemed worthy of saving to his house. Co-opting a couple of the maids, with whom he flirted outrageously, together Sam and Ashe began supervising the loading of the cart.

Content all was under control, Matthew paused only to take Rosamund in his arms and hold her tight. Shocked and painfully aware of the eyes upon them, at first she froze before melting into his embrace. He smelled worse than burned coffee, like the fires that crackled on the streets during the plague.

Filip cleared his throat. Thomas and Solomon nudged each other and Grace gave her a knowing look, while Mr. Nick grinned. Pulling away from Matthew, she rested her hands upon his chest. Beneath her palm, she could feel his heart pulsing—for her. All for her.

"Look to yourself, Matthew, please. I'll not forgive you if you don't return this time."

"You admit you'll miss me, then?" Even as death drew closer, he could make a joke.

"Just a little," she conceded.

With a laugh that was half cry, she pulled his face toward her and pressed her soft lips into his firm ones. All at once, the slow roar of the fire that had under-pinned their entire journey dulled. The faces of those nearby disappeared as she stared at the man whose mouth captured hers. Leaning into him, she felt a heat that had nothing to do with the approaching conflagration rise, and she melded her body to his, found the crevices and planes into which her own flesh fitted so perfectly.

With a deep, urgent moan, it was Matthew who pushed her away this time, his eyes molten with desire. "Do that again and I may burn where we stand," he said hoarsely.

"I'd rather that than risk you in the fire," said Rosamund, nodding toward where a spire of orange rose above the rooftops. It was the first actual flame she'd seen, and it filled her with dread.

Matthew took her face in his hands and kissed her three times in quick succession before finally pushing her away so hard, she stumbled and would have fallen if Bianca hadn't caught her.

"Go," he cried, waving first at the young men waiting for him, then, running backward, gave the same direction to Rosamund. "Go, and God be with you."

"And with you—" whispered Rosamund. "Look after one another," she said, throwing her arms around first Mr. Nick, then Filip, and kissing him soundly as well.

She stood a moment longer, watching Matthew and Filip lead the group of nine lads and men through the gate before they disappeared, their cries mingling with those on the streets.

"Come," said Bianca. "Let's quickly retrieve some clothes and leave."

Reluctantly, Rosamund did as she was bidden, aware of Bianca's droll gaze as they all but ran through the corridors.

"What?" she asked, panting.

"And you refused to marry him?" She shook her head. "Are you mad?"

Rosamund paused on the stairs, staring past the open door toward the street. "Aye, I think I might be . . ."

Rosamund didn't have much time to appreciate either Sam's house or the warm welcome Elizabeth extended. Before dawn the following morning, the household was on the move. The fire had surged closer, and only the direction of the wind marked the difference between safety and threat. It was too great a risk.

Bundling Elizabeth, Jane and his other servants into a cart he'd borrowed from Lady Elizabeth Batten, Sam, still dressed in his nightgown, rode them to safety at Bethnal Green, while Rosamund and Bianca stayed behind with Ashe and Grace, supervising the packing of the other belongings he wanted transported, which he intended to return and collect as soon as he could. Sam rode into the shadows, constantly looking over his shoulder and gauging the distance between holocaust and home. Feeling no such attachment to Blithe Manor, Rosamund pitied Elizabeth, who'd been in tears at the thought of losing her much-loved house. For years the Pepyses had been renovating, adding new flooring, reupholstering furniture, hanging paintings and tapestries they'd acquired, making it theirs. As she observed the two remaining servants unhook a particularly grand arras and roll it ready for transport, Rosamund wondered if she'd ever feel the wrench Elizabeth and Sam evidently did.

Before midday, Sam returned and joined Rosamund, Bianca, Ashe and little Grace for a quick dinner. Bursting with news, he told them how outside the walls the roads were filled with farmers, porters and coachmen from outlying villages and towns, eager to make coin transporting people's goods.

"Their rates are exorbitant," he grumbled.

"I'm sure the wealthy can afford it," said Rosamund. She'd seen the poor struggling with their meager belongings, and being all but trampled by those with the money and carriages to leave swiftly. She could hardly feel sorry if a few porters exploited those with the wherewithal to hire them.

"What of those fighting the fire?" asked Rosamund, thinking only of one. "How do they fare?"

Sam drained his coffee. "There are firefighters at every command station across the city. Even so, the fire destroyed the waterwheel on the Bridge, which was a blow from which I doubt the city can recover." He sighed. "The Duke of York has a band, the Dean of Westminster and many others are leading men and boys to fight the flames. There's been a concerted effort to prevent it reaching the Tower." Drifting to the window, he looked out upon the city. Screeds of blue sky could be seen in the distance, where the smoke was thinner, but closer than any of them liked were undulating banks of fierce orange.

"Overall," he said, his usual optimism fading, "it doesn't seem to matter what's done—the fire spreads. Even houses far away are being torched as burning ash lands on rooftops and dry eaves. The flames leap from one building to another like Bedlam inmates. The post office has been consumed, so any chance of news has now given way to alarm. People are blaming arsonists. There's talk that Dutchmen and Frenchmen are being set upon, accused and felled where they stand."

"*Mio Dio,*" said Bianca.

Rosamund thought of Filip. Englishmen often couldn't distinguish between a Spaniard, a Frenchman or a Dutchman. They were all foreigners and worthy of suspicion.

Bianca continued. "This is no act of war or vengeance—none except God's. We heard that it started at a bakery in Pudding Lane."

Sam nodded. "That's what I heard, and from many sources. I've no doubt it's true. I was upon the river many times yesterday and it's evident where it commenced. But when people are afraid, they look to blame those who are different from them." His eyes alighted upon Bianca. "I would advise you not to wander alone in the streets, my dear. Stay close to Rosamund."

"But you will be with us, won't you, Sam?" asked Rosamund.

"Shortly. I still have to see to the removal of my household items. I also have to maintain contact with Whitehall—the King, you see. It was I who alerted him to the seriousness of the blaze. He's relying on me." His chest expanded. He slapped his hands against his breeches. "You're welcome to come with me or remain here. At least here you can see how the city is faring. I've also asked Captain William Lark from the local command station to notify you at once should the fire change direction. I will return this evening and we can assess whether we remain or flee."

Happy to stay at Seething Lane in case news arrived of Matthew and Filip, Rosamund and Bianca went with Ashe and Grace to the rooftop to watch the city burn.

It wasn't until Sam returned at seven that evening, his clothes streaked with ash, carrying the scars of falling cinders, and his face gray, that Rosamund realized more than exhaustion dragged his feet and made him unable to meet her eyes. He had come straight up to the roof, where he found her transfixed by the sight of the conflagration.

Her heart went into her mouth.

"What is it, Sam?" she asked, tearing her gaze away from the golden arcs of fire. "Is it Matthew?"

Sam blinked, resembling a confused owl. "Matthew? No. No. I do not know what has become of him. I am sure he is fine. Señor de la Faya and that giant, Mr. Nick, as well."

Relief made Rosamund turn away lest the tears banking behind her eyes fall. She sat back on the stool she'd brought to the rooftop. Bianca found her hand and gave it a reassuring squeeze. Ashe drew closer.

"What is it, then?" she asked, trying to make her voice heard above the fury of the flames.

"I'm afraid I do bear grave tidings, Rosamund." He came and kneeled by her side.

Bewildered, Rosamund beckoned Grace, who'd ceased to arrange the flowers she'd managed to pick from Sam's garden, and the young girl leaned against her.

"Dear Lord," said Rosamund, sitting upright, her arm creeping around Grace's waist. "Please, tell me it's not Solomon or Thomas?" Sam shook his head. "Adam, Hugh, Kit, Art or Timothy?"

"No, no, no, no. As far as I'm aware they're still fighting that." He waved a tired arm toward the west. "No, Rosamund, this is about Birchin Lane."

Rosamund's throat grew dry. "What?"

"I'm afraid the fire jumped the breaks and consumed most of Lombard Street before traveling through all those little alleys and snickets that wend their way toward the Royal Exchange . . ." Sam paused. There was such sympathy in his round eyes. The glow of the city was reflected in them and made his chubby cheeks into shiny planes. "Pasqua Rosée's Turk's Head is no more. Rosamund . . ."

Her hand flew to her mouth. For all she declared no affinity with those who saw their houses as more than just buildings, a wave of nausea rose within; nausea and despair.

"The Phoenix—" She gasped.

Bianca made a strangled noise.

"The Phoenix?" Her eyes swam. She felt suddenly cold. Grace touched her hair.

Sam shook his head sorrowfully. "It and the book-shop. They're ashes, my dear. There will be no rising from them—not this time. I'm sorry to tell you, they're nothing but a charred ruin."

Rosamund felt the world spin. "Poor Matthew . . ." she said, as if her losses were not as great—greater. They were all she had.

A lead weight settled on her shoulders, dropped to her middle and welded her legs to the ground. She sat immobile, a solid lump of aching sadness. The chocolate house—gone. The bookshop—gone. Why, the very idea was preposterous. How could something that contained so much hope, so much joy, so much of herself and her ambitions, vanish like this? She glanced up at the molten border limning the horizon. It marked the great golden crack in her world.

How could the hopes and livelihoods of those dependent upon her be wiped out so unthinkingly? Were they not good boys and lasses who worked there? Good men? Hadn't they struggled to survive so much already? And what of those who had died? No longer would her success be a monument to their memories—to Robin, Harry, Cara, Owen, Wolstan, dear Mr. Henderson . . . Jacopo . . .

How, having failed to understand the misery of others, could she feel this way about a place? Yet the Phoenix was so much more than just a place. It was her business; it was her investment. It was, like the bookshop, a great gift that gave her life purpose and through which she gave to others. It was what united her and Matthew when nothing else did.

Without it, what was she? What did she have?

Nothing.

Not even Matthew.

What did any of them have?

Like the blackened ruins she saw around her, the smoking hulls of buildings, homes, churches, businesses, she too was reduced to nothing. She might be Lady Blithman, but she was nobody. She was *nessuno*.

Ever so slowly, aware of Bianca's hand rubbing her back, of Sam's resting gently on her knee, Ashe's fingers upon her shoulder and Grace tucking one of her flowers behind her ear, she buried her face in her hands and wept.

FORTY-EIGHT

In which what starts in Pudding ends in Pye

Rosamund never left Sam's house. There was no need. It was there she learned that Matthew and the others were alive, and that by Tuesday morning the fire had swept through the Royal Exchange, melting the iron-lace framework and leaving the great bell an igneous puddle. The statues of the kings and queens of England fell face-first to the ground, many losing their heads as their subjects had in life. Only the statue of Sir Thomas Gresham, the man who built the Exchange, survived. Even Baynard's Castle was taken, its glorious facade tumbling into the river, swamping boats and overturning rafts. A central tower remained, a last post to history.

The odor of spices drifted about the city as the great storehouses in the cellars of the Exchange owned by the

East India Company were destroyed as well. Many believed it to be incense lit by Papists, and the idea that the fire was a Catholic plot spread as swiftly as the flames.

When the fire leaped the River Fleet, the King finally gave orders to remove valuables from Whitehall. That was the signal the nobles had been waiting for, and as they abandoned their grand mansions in the Strand, the Thames was filled with craft stacked to the brim with the goods of the rich, all moving west as fast as they could.

In Seething Lane, Rosamund learned these things piecemeal. When explosions rang out throughout the city, it was only later she discovered that they were efforts to create a firebreak ordered by the King himself, who, instead of remaining detached, as he had during the plague, was in the thick of it, unrecognizable, according to Captain Lark, as he rolled up his sleeves, pitched in beside commoners and did whatever had to be done.

To no avail.

While the King's involvement might not have changed the outcome, it did make a huge difference to the way people regarded him. Hailed as heroes, he and his brother were cheered wherever they went. Money was given to those who manned the command stations, and bread and beer were handed out.

Beer. Rosamund's mouth watered as the captain told his story. Since Sunday, they'd been surviving on Sam's leftovers, and his pantry was now practically bare, especially as another man had joined their sorry band—Tom Hater, who had lost all he owned when Fish Street Hill burned.

Hungry, tired beyond reckoning—for how could anyone sleep when so much was at stake?—they waited on the roof, dozing when exhaustion overcame them, stirring when something exploded or a building nearby collapsed, or when coughing fits overcame them. The stifling heat didn't subside despite the strong winds; they tried to remain vigilant. They owed it to the men risking their lives to survive, even if the city didn't.

Sam's friend Sir William Penn came and joined them, the two men retiring to the garden to discuss prospects. Neither believed their offices or their homes had much chance of survival. They rescued reams of Navy papers, books and reports, intending to bury them like the wine Sam had already dug into the ground with his huge wheel of Parmesan cheese.

Returning to the men some time later, bringing a flask of sack she'd found stashed at the back of a kitchen cupboard, Rosamund surprised herself by scolding them.

"Listen to you both. You haven't ceased with your dour predictions since I left. So what if the buildings don't survive? So what if Seething Lane is reduced to rubble? Surely it's far more important that we live—that people survive. We can rebuild. We can re-create what is lost. Not exactly, but something even better."

There was a moment of silence. Beyond the walls of the garden flames roared, and they could hear the shouts of men and cries of women and the never-ending grind of drays and carts. Another explosion resounded; no one even flinched, they'd become so common.

"It's not the buildings, so much, Rosamund," said Sam in a condescending manner, turning a meaningful glance upon Sir William. "As a woman, you wouldn't understand. It's the fact that such a loss will undermine the King's business."

"Will it?" said Rosamund, looking from one to the other. "Surely, Sam, losing you and Sir William here, let alone all the clever men he has working for him and the country, would hinder it a good deal more?"

As she left, she couldn't help but notice Sam's chest swell and Sir William's eyes brighten at her words. All this value placed on possessions, when the greatest prizes were those who breathed life into them.

Unexpectedly, she found herself comforted by the thought. Back on the rooftop, she gazed out over London. Night had fallen, and before her lay an unrecognizable expanse of blackened, smoking and burning buildings. Instead of forests of spires piercing the sky, dancing arches of tangerine, titian and blazing gold bordered what was left of London. It might have been beautiful if it weren't so dreadful, so utterly devastating it made her chest tighten.

Started by humans, it was beyond anyone to contain it, and yet . . . She pondered what she'd said.

No longer did she worry as the fire crept closer to the White Tower and its stores of gun powder—for they'd be long gone before that was a danger. No longer did she dwell with a heavy heart upon the destruction of the Bridewell, Newgate and Ludgate prisons, instead thanking the dear Lord that those confined within had made good their escape. When St. Paul's finally erupted in flames at nine of the clock—all the books stored in its cellars providing marvelous fuel for the hungry fire, ruining all but a few booksellers in the city, and the lead on its roof raining down into a river of mellifluent marvel through the streets—she watched without shifting, even when the stones erupted like cannon, shooting up into the air and landing with loud cracks.

No longer did she see the wreckage of a once-glorious, if grimy, city filled with spirals of burning paper, silk and God knew what else, but endless possibilities. Aye, there would be hardship, there would be despair—but there would be opportunity as well.

What were buildings but the work of man? And what were buildings if there were no men, women or children to fill them? To make the walls echo with conversation, arguments, joy, grief, laughter, tears and, above all, love?

The buildings were empty shells that she—all of them—must, when this was over, rebuild and fill.

She stared into the distance. And what of her building? They'd saved (at least, she hoped they had) the equipment from the chocolate house. The chocolate maker, the apprentices and all those who worked with them were, she prayed, safe as well. What was the Phoenix in the end but a roof and walls? Much had happened beneath and within them—happiness, discovery, death and love. But it was the people—both in the kitchen and those they served—who made the chocolate house what it was.

Be damned if they couldn't re-create that again. Maybe not at once, but over time . . .

She stood and went to the edge of the roof, trying to discern how far the fire had spread, how much more damage it would wreak. The wind whipped her hair, and cinders floated about her like crazed insects, stinging her eyes. She blinked them away with a curse.

The streets glowed red. People were everywhere, dark shadows flitting between blazes of shocking light and bursts of sparks, geysers of fiery flames.

On the street below, she saw that Elizabeth and her maid had returned. Despite all the danger, the threat coming up the hill toward them, Elizabeth chose to be with her husband . . .

That man was busy rescuing stone and wood, silver and gold, other precious objects—but also cherished memories, prized possessions; like others, the sum total of his livelihood, his entire wealth. She must remember that while she could see their value was mutable, not everyone could. While she could rebuild a future for some, she couldn't for all.

At that moment, she made a promise to the Almighty. *Please*, she asked, *let Matthew Lovelace live, and if you do, I will not mourn the loss of a mere building, of one or even many futures. I will, I promise, make a new one—for myself, for all of us.*

The Phoenix might no longer stand, but Sam was wrong. *I will rise from its ashes. London will. Please just let Matthew Lovelace live so I may rise with him.*

FORTY-NINE
In which truth rises
from the ashes

After four long days, the fire was quelled. As soon as she learned from Matthew that Blithe Manor was, against all odds, untouched, and that he would meet her there as soon as he was able, Rosamund could no longer presume upon Sam and Elizabeth's hospitality. Thanking Sam for his generosity at such a time, she once more packed the cart belonging to Sam's friend Lady Elizabeth and set off with Bianca, Ashe, Grace and the maids to return to Bishopsgate Street.

Refusing to admit to herself that Matthew was the real reason for her haste, she picked her way through the streets, feeling the heat of the cobbles through the soles of her shoes. Thin beams of sunlight penetrated the pall of gray, striking the smoking ruins through which, even now, scavengers picked. Passage was slow and difficult. The wind had dropped, but rubbish, flakes of burned paper, parchment and clothing whirled through the air in a macabre dance. They often had to stop to hoist crumbling beams or shattered pieces of stone out of the way, or simply to wade their way over hot hillocks of debris, the detritus of lives ground beneath their scalded feet.

Ashes to ashes, dust to dust.

Aye, this was a burial, their journey akin to a cortege; the city had died. But they lived. They lived and they would resurrect it too.

Rosamund couldn't yet rejoice, but the hope that bloomed in her heart on Sam's rooftop had not been crushed to cinders. On the contrary, she gathered it close so it could be rekindled when it was most needed.

Blithe Manor was a relief she could not have foreseen; as she entered, it overcame her. The rooms were awash with the odor of smoke, but it was fresh air compared to the streets. For the first time since she had come to this place, she felt a sense of ownership and pride. Aye, Blithe Manor was hers—for the time being—and never before had she relished its welcome embrace as she did now.

She supervised the unpacking of the cart and found coin to pay the grateful carter, who, after downing an ale, lumbered out the gate and back to Sam's. He'd decided to head north and skirt the city, anything to avoid negotiating the wretched streets again.

Rosamund understood.

Ashe wasted no time getting things out of the well— including the precious chocolate-making equipment— and setting the house to rights. Seeing the crates of bowls, pots, *molinillos* and sacks of spices around them, relieved beyond measure they were unscathed, only then did Rosamund allow herself to relax.

Somehow, Ashe found water for her and Bianca to wash. Not wanting to see another naked flame, they both relished its coolness. Finding clean clothes was easy, but not ones free of the reek of smoke.

Once they were bathed, clothed and fed, Bianca begged leave to see how the Quakers fared. Careful not to reveal where she was going in front of Grace or Ashe, Rosamund agreed, realizing how selfish she'd been. Of course, Bianca was part of an entire community outside Blithe Manor. She prayed they managed better than they had during the plague. Remembering Sam's warning to Bianca about the suspicion of foreigners on the streets, Rosamund urged her to be careful. Bianca flashed her a smile.

"I will be among Friends," she said, using their informal title. "You've no need for concern, *bella*." She kissed her on the cheek and left.

With Bianca gone and Grace put to bed, the poor child having hardly slept for the last four days, Ashe and some of the maids went out to find what victuals might be for sale. Rosamund found the tiredness she expected to overcome her swept aside in the joy of being back—of knowing all was not lost. Truth be told, she also didn't wish to sleep lest she miss Matthew's return.

Instead, she went to her closet. It had been a while since she'd spent time within her cave, reading, learning, allowing her imagination to be filled with the treasures she hoarded.

Bringing her bowl of chocolate with her, she sipped it slowly, sinking into the chair by the window. Outside, the alley looked much as she'd last seen it, except that it was empty. Beyond the line of houses to the west, smoke still billowed in great coughing plumes. North, past the walls, she could see rows and rows of tents, blankets, boxes, carts, drays, horses, sheep, dogs, chickens and people. So many people. The carter said there were thousands upon thousands of homeless people spread out across Moorfields, Parliament Hill, areas around Islington—wherever a clear patch of ground was available. Looting was rife, and there'd been more than a few scuffles, especially when rumors spread that the Hollanders and Frenchies were coming to attack and rape the women. People were starving, afraid, and so very, very despondent. Most had lost everything.

If there was room left at Blithe Manor once Matthew and the others returned, Rosamund was determined to offer shelter to whoever might need it—even Bianca's Quakers. This was not a time to worry about difference but to cleave to what united them.

Losing an appetite for chocolate, guilty she could so indulge when there were people over there—just over there—who suffered, Rosamund turned away from the window and sought comfort from her books and papers. Humans were remarkable, really, she thought as she scanned some titles. Had not the Trojans continued after the Greeks and their armies all but wiped them out? Had not the Roman Empire survived in the Italian people, as diverse and complicated as they were with their city-states and dialects, producing great works of art and literature, wise philosophers and magnificent inventions? And look at Bianca's Quakers (funny that she thought of them belonging to Bianca)—did they not continue despite the efforts of the King and Council? Well, London would as well.

Running her finger along the mantel, she found a small ruby and cerulean brooch she'd kept that had belonged to Lady Margery. She thought of the Blithmans. Against all odds, they'd endured—not only Aubrey, but she too carried their name, even if Bianca could not. As she put the brooch down, it rolled behind a pile of books. She pushed them aside to reach for the brooch only to strike a box.

How peculiar. Just as she was thinking of Lady Margery, what should she find but the box she'd discovered years ago. Good Lord, she'd forgotten all about it. She retrieved the brooch and set it carefully aside, then picked up the box and blew the dust from the top, coughing as it struck her in the face. It took a while for her coughs to subside, a legacy the fire had left them all.

Sinking back into her seat, the box on the table in front of her, she first wiped her eyes, took sips of chocolate and then, with a strangely beating heart, lifted the lid.

When she'd last opened it, she'd found a collection of pretty beads and a sheaf of tightly folded papers beneath them. Covered in neat handwriting, they appeared to be torn from a book. She'd always intended to examine the contents but had never done so. Now she could read, she no longer had to rely on anyone else to tell her what they said.

Carefully she pulled out the pages, and as she did so, she recognized the beads for what they were—the remnants of many broken rosaries. Had Lady Margery been a secret Catholic? She wouldn't be the first to hide her faith. But why destroy the rosaries?

Rosamund unfolded the pages and smoothed them out. The writing was untidy, and blots stained the paper. On the final page was a signature: Margery Blithman. Dear God . . . these must be from one of Lady Margery's diaries, the diaries Sir Everard had been so keen to destroy. Above her name, in a shaky hand, were the words, *May God forgive me*.

Forgive her what?

Though the room wasn't dark, Rosamund found a candle and lit it. She brought her chair closer to the table and began to read.

FIFTY
In which
Lady Margery speaks

2nd February, 1660

Dear God,

I can barely hold the quill for the shaking in my hands, but I must needs set down what I've just witnessed; the moments that led to my discovery.

Lord, give me strength . . .

I had come from Everard's study. There, he revealed to me that Aubrey's so-called friend Matthew Lovelace was investigating our son because he was suspected of transporting weapons to England's enemies. He'd been asked by the government to look into these base accusations. Everard has bought *Lovelace's* silence by promising him *Helene's* hand—the man is besotted with her—and bringing him into the family fold. One can hardly accuse a person of treason when their name is aligned with yours, not without grave injury to your reputation.

In return for the betrothal, *Lovelace* has promised to cease delving and report to his superiors that *Aubrey* is innocent.

Knowing *Helene* would be disconsolate at such a match, having oft expressed no desire to be courted, let alone wed, and to a poet's son with few prospects, I thought to comfort her and explain the real reason for her father's acceptance of *Lovelace's* unwelcome suit.

I'd no doubt *Aubrey* would console his sister, so I made haste to *Helene's* bedroom to add my sympathy to her brother's and to defend *Everard's* decision. *It's our only choice if we're to protect our name and Aubrey's. Once Helene understands this, she will comply. She is a Blithman, after all, and knows that necessity must govern our choices.*

As I approached her room, noises came from behind the door—strange noises. At first, I thought the siblings were arguing, so grotesque were the *sounds. Opening the door silently, I peered in the gap . . .*

The ground beneath me opened, and all the fires of hell and its screaming demons rose up to pull me into their depths.

Helene was lying on her bed, naked, groaning like a trull, her legs wrapped around Aubrey's back while he groped her breasts and thrust into her again and again. Aye, my children, my son and daughter fornicated like a pair of dogs in heat.

Rosamund stopped reading. Tiny blades of ice sank into her flesh. A terrible metallic taste filled her mouth. She peered out the window. Aye, the world was still there. She took a deep breath, then returned to the page trembling in her hand. She reread words that could not possibly be true.

But there they were, in all their stark, awful ugliness: Aubrey was his sister's lover.

It was Aubrey whom Matthew chased across the globe to return his correspondence; Aubrey with whom Matthew sought to find an end.

Aubrey and Helene.

This was not love; this was sickness. Afraid what else she might discover, nevertheless Rosamund had to continue reading.

I wanted to pluck out my eyes, rend my hair, reach into my breast and tear my heart from my body, only I felt it had already been taken and crushed.

I covered my mouth with my hand, capturing both my disgust and the bile that followed. The air grew close, tight; the world spun. And still I could not move. How could this be? The love between my two children be perverted into this incestuous coupling? Was it the loss of Gregory that prompted such unnatural closeness? Was it Everard's announcement of Helene's betrothal that drove them to . . . to this? Or had this been happening for years?

In my secret soul, I knew the truth.

The fondness Aubrey and Helene bore each other ever since they were small and which had grown as they matured was cast in the most unpalatable and ungodly of lights.

I forced myself to watch.

Was not their sin also mine?

Sated, Aubrey lay beside his sister, stroking her face, and, adopting a tone I'd never heard him use before, made a vow to love her for eternity, no matter whom she wed. With devotion in her eyes, Helene took his hand and brought it to her stomach, covering it with her own. She reminded him that the babe growing in her womb would be their promise to each other made flesh, no matter what.

3rd February, 1660

Incest. Incest beneath my roof, Everard's roof. My children are going to hell. We are all going to hell. And it's my fault. I'd refused to see what was before my eyes. I should have insisted Aubrey go to Oxford as his father wished instead of allowing him to remain in London with me and Helene; I should have hardened my heart when he refused to accompany his father on his journeys, forced his compliance. But how could I? Dear Lord. I'd nurtured this, just as I had the babes who even now were suckling each other's breasts.

Whether or not Lovelace was right and Aubrey betrayed his country is a moot point. What he and his sister are doing is betraying us all—under God's laws and those of the kingdom. If a whisper of this should ever escape . . . . we would be ruined. We would be better off dead.

I have to tell Everard. But I cannot. This burden, this shame, this terrible sin is mine to harbor alone, but it must end now. Getting Helene and Lovelace married has taken on a fresh urgency.

A babe. A babe is to be born.

13th February, 1660

I can scarce look at my children, yet I have to keep up the pretense. I fear what Everard will do if he ever finds out. I pray he will not see the changes in his daughter that are so obvious to me—the swollen breasts, the radiance in her face, the dark confidence in her eyes. Not to mention Aubrey's solicitous attention to her, their stolen looks.

I, who once disapproved of Lovelace, am now his greatest champion. Today I asked Everard that the marriage be brought forward; after all, what's the point of waiting?

Everard has refused. Having lost one child, he will not surrender Helene to another man so soon.

Dear God in heaven. What do I do? I fear I've no choice but to confess to Everard all I know . . .

14th February, 1660

The deed is done. I have told him. Waiting until he was alone, I begged his attention. After I completed my sordid tale he did not speak. When he finally did, he was crude and vulgar and asked me to clarify what he could scarce believe: Are Helene and Aubrey fucking?

God help me, I tried to defend them, to turn it into something other than the immoral, perverted act it is.

He proceeded to blame me for everything: Aubrey's unnatural desires, his sister's. This was all my fault, and God would punish me evermore for what I'd done.

Not once did he raise his voice. "All I worked so hard for is at risk. My name. My reputation."

"What of mine?" I wailed, but he closed his ears.

He sank into himself. To my horror, he began to weep. "If word of this should escape, if anyone finds out, we are destroyed. We would be pariahs—on earth and in heaven. We are damned."

His weakness gave me strength. "Then we must ensure we are not." I reiterated my plan for Lovelace and Helene to marry immediately so the truth of the baby's conception might be hidden.

Much to my surprise, Everard was outraged I could contemplate deceiving Lovelace in such a manner, making him party to this mortal sin.

I spat rage at his hypocrisy. I reminded him he'd been prepared to use our daughter to buy his silence when he believed Aubrey guilty of treason. How was this different?

I thought Everard would strike me then—for my defiance, for the truth I insisted he see. He claimed they were very different things. He allowed Lovelace a choice—I did not. The fool said he refused to be involved in such a deception. But I was relentless. I am doing this for the children, for his children, for us. What is the honor of one man if it means saving us all? Saving Helene . . .

God in His mercy understands . . .

Knowing how to force his surrender, I kept referring to what would be best for our daughter. After all, was she not the sun on his horizon, the fragrant flower in his garden? It worked. Everard agreed to a date. Without another word—only an expression I pray never to see again—he left the room, leaving me alone with my hollow triumph.

17th February, 1660

Everard spoke to Helene and Aubrey today. Helene is to be married within the fortnight. Aubrey will leave for the colonies forthwith. They've both been threatened with disinheritance should they fail to comply with their father's wishes.

Aubrey left the house; I know not where he has gone. Helene is in her bedroom. I can hear her wails from my closet—whether she cries because her secret is now family knowledge, for the shame of her deeds or because Aubrey is soon to depart, I know not. I cannot comfort her. I cannot care. We do this to protect the Blithman name, to protect her and Aubrey as well as the babe.

24th February, 1660

Aubrey has left for Virginia, and Lovelace and Helene are wed.

Do I feel guilty about using Lovelace in such an ill manner? I do not. Lovelace is a virtuous vizard that my daughter and the rest of us don to conceal our transgressions.

God knows, I feel such relief. It is visceral, a lightening that enables me to look my daughter in the face once more. Lovelace's evident joy in his wife goes some way to assuaging my guilt. The child no doubt will do the same. May he never learn the manner of its conception.

20th March, 1660

    Aubrey must die.

    Today I told Everard that if he wants the marriage between his daughter and Matthew to survive, then Aubrey must cease to exist. His death will free Helene from her unnatural longings, her refusal to embrace Lovelace as a wife should, and force her to cleave to the man she calls husband.

    At first Everard refused to countenance such a notion. Death is not to be trifled with, he said, no matter the reason. He scarce spoke to me but brooded.

21st March, 1660

    Everard announced today that he is taking Matthew to Spain to research a venture they are to embark upon together. I believe the trip is to escape me and the thoughts I put into my husband's head.

19th June, 1660

    I do not know what occurred while he was away, but upon his return, Everard wasted no time but conceded to my desires. He wrote at once to Au-

brey outlining what he wished him to do—how he wanted him to die.

There was no more on that page. Rosamund flicked to the next one, her heart a stone in her chest. The diary continued weeks later.

3rd August, 1660

Today we told Helene her brother was dead. I thought she would lose the babe, she was so distraught. I have never seen the like. Blaming her father for Aubrey's death, for sending him away, and me for encouraging his departure, she ordered us out of her house and declared she never wanted to see us again. For now she is hurting. She does not understand we do this to ensure her future, the child's. She will welcome us back in time . . . please God.

15th August, 1660

The babe is born. A son whom Helene has named Everard. I was wrong to assume forgiveness on our daughter's part. We learned of the child's birth from my cousin Sam Pepys, who blurted it without realizing we knew nothing of his entry into the world. As Sam left, a note arrived from Mat-

thew informing us of the boy's arrival. Full of apologies, he explains Helene still doesn't wish to see us. He assures us he will do all in his power to alter her mind but asks for our patience.

Little does he know.

Denying us access to baby Everard is her way of punishing us. What a cruel blow—to name her son after her father while keeping him away, punishing Everard in particular, whom she believes the architect of her separation from her brother, his death and her false marriage, in one fell swoop.

I am heartsick and soul sore. I pray to God that He will see fit to forgive me, forgive Helene and Aubrey. I do pray night and day. I cannot eat; I can scarce drink. My rosary is worn, my knees chafed. My clothes hang loose upon me. I care not. I remain in my rooms—in my closet, writing, or in bed. Only Bianca tends me. Even Everard ignores me. Sleep eludes me. Every time I close my eyes, I see nothing but my children fucking . . .

5th September, 1660

This will be my final entry. I must record these last hours and my encounter with Helene and, at long last, my grandson.

Upon learning I was abed and very ill, Lovelace insisted Helene bring the babe to me. Propped against pillows, I did not wish to see this evidence of my children's sins. His innocence could never compensate for their guilt or my complicity in it. Yet, I must look upon him and face my part.

Lord in heaven up above. I can still see his tiny features as if they were seared upon my soul. To an inexperienced eye, he was merely an ill-formed newborn who might outgrow a poor start. To me, his too-large skull, his swollen, misshapen mouth and his pale gold hair, the finest down that crept from his scalp to envelop his limbs, indicated something corrupt. In this poor little babe, God has seen fit to announce Aubrey and Helene's sin.

My mind was in havoc. Helene, mistaking my expression, shot me a look of pride filled with resentment and daring.

"Oh, Helene." I drew the babe's swaddling tighter; I lifted him to my breast, inhaled his sweet scent and kissed his furry brow. "What have you done?" I asked quietly. My tears soaked his blanket.

"What all mothers do" was her ice-cold reply as she snatched her child from me and departed without another word. With a sorry bow, Lovelace followed. What else could he do?

I was not blaming her, but myself. What have I done but allowed this tiny being to be birthed? Aye, she's done what all mothers do, and what I'd demanded: married an unsuitable, blameless man in order to give the child a name and a family—and to hide her shame. Our shame.

Seeing the baby today, I wonder if it was worth it.

My son and daughter, as wrong and grossly sinful as their actions have been, are still mine, and, God help me, I love them even as the very sight of them disgusts me. I pray now Aubrey is "dead" that Everard will continue to do whatever it takes to protect the family. All too soon, I will be unable to do so. As for the babe born of such an unholy union, I can only pray for his salvation.

God may have abandoned me, but I hope He has not yet seen fit to turn His back upon the rest of my family.

Earlier, I called for Bianca and Jacopo and commanded them to look to my husband, their father, though they know not why. May he find comfort in the dark seeds he has sown. God knows, those we've sprouted have brought none. Ignorant until such time as I revealed his children's sin, Everard, for all his faults, had no choice but to aid me in my plans to spare Aubrey and Helene punishment, de-

ceive Lovelace and bestow a legitimate name upon Helene's child, one that disguises the worst of sins. Everard was never a willing accomplice, but a suborned one.

   I would do anything to secure my children's future and preserve their good name. Ours. Anything. I do not regret one thing. Not even what I am about to do.

May God forgive me.

Margery Blithman.

With a long sigh, Rosamund put the letter down. Her hands shook. She was sweating. Uncertain what she expected when she began to read, it was not this . . . this . . . unholy confession.

No wonder Sir Everard had consigned what he could find of his wife's diaries to the flames. No wonder he feared Rosamund learning to read lest she discover the awful truth. No wonder he'd acceded to Matthew's demands—the threat of those love letters between Aubrey and Helene being exposed was so great he'd do anything to keep them secret. Even kill.

Sir Everard had no choice but to aid his children, his wife. Even after she died (When had that happened? How?) he had no alternative but to protect the lies she'd set in place.

Matthew believed Sir Everard had orchestrated the whole ghastly deception and sought to destroy him.

In so many ways, they had both been trapped in each other's web of lies and betrayal; both wanted revenge for acts committed against them. Sir Everard had sought to permanently remove the last person who could reveal the truth. And to use her as his instrument to do it.

How would Matthew feel when he learned all this? Should she tell him? She brushed a hand across her brow. Aye, she must.

It also explained why Matthew had never revealed the lover's name . . . it wasn't to protect the Blithman family; it was to protect her. Rosamund Blithman. The name was bitter on her tongue.

Wiping away tears she didn't even know she'd begun to shed, Rosamund marshaled the pages carefully.

So many victims. And what of Bianca and Jacopo? Their presence aroused jealousy, ensured they were treated with—how had Bianca once put it?—"cold contempt." They hadn't deserved this. What had they seen, heard, guessed? She shuddered. Dear Lord. Putting down the pages, she rubbed her temples. She needed to think, to ponder these revelations, but first, she needed some wine.

Feelings of disgust, sorrow and confusion warred

within her as she collected the papers, left the closet and went to her bedside table, where a decanter waited. As she was about to pour, there was a knock on the door.

No doubt Matthew had arrived. What would she say? He would surely sense the terrible knowledge writ on her face. If anyone deserved to see the remnants of this last diary, it was him.

Before she could even summon a word, the door opened and who should be standing there but none other than the monster himself: Aubrey Blithman.

FIFTY-ONE
In which a
long-worn vizard slips

Trying to keep her voice neutral and summon a smile, Rosamund moved toward him. She'd no intention of admitting this man to her Aladdin's Cave, the same place his mother had likely poured out her soul. Shaken by what she'd read, she was unprepared for the effect his presence would have on her. Revulsion swept her body, followed by a driving need to get him away—from her, from the room, from the house if she could.

Deciding assertiveness would be better than pleading, she folded her arms. Only then did she become aware she still held the pages in her hand. She tried to curl them into a smaller shape without him noticing. It didn't work, so she made a point of folding them brazenly before him.

"What are you doing here, Aubrey? You made a promise to Mr. Lovelace, or have you already forgotten?"

"What do you know about my agreement with Lovelace?" he asked swiftly, jittering from foot to foot. Glancing at what she held, Aubrey's gaze went back to her face.

He looked thinner than she remembered, and mauve crescents sat in unflattering pouches under his eyes, eyes that regarded her slightly warily. She tried hard not to let her repugnance show.

"Only that you made one and, up until this moment, adhered to it."

Aubrey made a noise of disparagement. "Circumstances change, my dear—so do people. You know that better than most." Any rebuke was softened with a smile. "I need to talk to you," he said. His cheeks were red. His hat and hair were littered with small pieces of ash. Streaks of gray ran the length of his jacket. He'd made an effort to tidy himself and failed.

Rosamund's heart plummeted. "Shall we retire downstairs? We would be more comfortable there." Before he could protest she pushed past him.

Subdued, Aubrey followed her down the stairs and into the withdrawing room. Musty from being closed up for the last few days, the room was filled with tiny motes that spiraled in the sunbeams. Rosamund pushed the pages into a pocket, crossed to the windows and opened them. The air outside was warm, infused with ash, dreck and stinking of smoke; smoke and whiffs of burned metal, straw and other things Rosamund didn't wish to identify. All the same, she needed to let the outside in.

Silently counting to ten, Rosamund turned to face Aubrey.

"What is it you wish to say to me? I've only just returned from Sam's place, and I have much to do . . ." Her gesture encompassed the whole house.

"This is more important." Without waiting to be invited, he sat down, gesturing for her to take the chair opposite.

Instead, she found a decanter and some glasses and poured them both a drink, taking the chance to shove the pages further into her pocket. They still protruded slightly, but it was the best she could do. She handed Aubrey a glass and sat down.

"What is it you want?" she asked, taking a sip of the wine. It was warm and too sweet.

Aubrey settled, regarding the room with a proprietary air. "You know," he began, "I never imagined I could set foot in here again after Helene died. I thought the place would echo with memories of her. And it does.

Memories that not even your redecorating has managed to bury." His eyes settled upon her. "I wondered about that at first. How a place that's altered, even slightly, can still evoke the same feelings. How, even with her gone, I can still be happy when I'm here. Then I worked it out. It's because of you. You suit this place, Rosamund, and it suits you. You belong here."

Rosamund didn't like where this was going. "*That's* what you wished to tell me?"

"Partly." He took a long swallow of his drink and pulled a face. "What I also wanted to do," he continued, reaching across to deposit his glass on the table, "is offer my condolences on your losses. I heard about the chocolate house, the bookshop."

Rosamund bowed her head.

"They were your . . . How do I put it? Assets. If I recall, once the will was executed, they were the sum total of your wealth, if I'm not mistaken? Unless you count your slave, Bianca."

Rosamund snapped, "Bianca is not an asset except in the way that a good friend always is." She met his gaze steadily, wishing Bianca were here now.

"Ouch," said Aubrey, then laughed. It was shrill, discordant and more than a little unnatural. "I assume from that you neither value nor trust me." He placed his hand over his heart. "A pity. You've no reason not to."

Rosamund could barely countenance what she was hearing. But then, he didn't know what she now knew.

He rose and began to walk about the room, touching objects, lifting curios and putting them down again.

"You see, when I learned of the destruction of the Phoenix and the bookshop, and knowing the value you placed on them, how essential they were to maintaining your—how do I put it?—your means of living and maintaining a household, well, once I learned they were gone up in a puff of smoke"—he made a motion with his fingers—"I began to wonder and, I admit, to reevaluate my promise to Lovelace. Before the fire, you were an independent widow, a woman of small means, but means nonetheless. You had shares in a bookshop, in the chocolate house too. Now you have nothing. You don't even have a roof over your head, except through my munificence."

Rosamund stared at Aubrey. What was he playing at? "I thought you a man of your word."

As she slowly rose, unaware of the pages falling out of her pocket, Rosamund made an effort not to let her perturbation show.

Aubrey gave a bark of laughter. "What you need to understand is my word was given under duress, when I was in no position to bargain. Therefore, it does not count. Things have changed. The fire caused a great alteration not only to this city, but to your circumstances. Lovelace's as well. As far as I am concerned, this voids any prior agreement."

Rosamund narrowed her eyes. "I'm afraid I don't see how . . ."

"Don't see? Come on, Rosamund, you're being deliberately obtuse. Lovelace threatened me. If I didn't leave you alone, desist in my wooing, allow you to live here with no obligation, he would injure my person or worse. I'd no choice but to obey, especially since you appeared determined to refuse my advances." He leaned toward her. "Truth is, while you had the chocolate house and the bookshop, you had alternatives. I would have to be patient. Now my patience can come to an end."

"Ah, I see." So much for his word—it was as empty as the wind. "You wish me to leave." She made to pass him. He grabbed her arm, forcing her to stop. She looked at his fingers wrapped around her sleeve, then up at his face. His eyes were so different to the deep, dark azure of Matthew's . . .

"On the contrary, I insist you stay." He released her. "You will stay here. With me." His finger stabbed his chest.

Needles pricked the back of Rosamund's neck. "No, Aubrey. I won't."

Aubrey threw back his head and let loose a merry burble. "Is that so? Where will you go? I tell you now, if you do not remain here, with me, then I will tell the government what I know to be true about you."

Rosamund went cold. "What do you know?"

"Not only do your chocolate drawers disperse dissident material written by Matthew Lovelace about the streets, but you harbor Quakers beneath your roof. You even welcomed them into the bookshop." He gave a coarse laugh at her expression. "I've known for a long time about Bianca's religious disposition. If you care about her as you claim, then you will do all in your power to protect her . . . and those boys you dote on at the Phoenix. If you care about Matthew Lovelace, you won't want the authorities knowing what else he writes—those delightful little pieces to which he doesn't put his name." He laughed. "Doesn't matter the place no longer exists; proof of what he was doing, they were doing—what you were facilitating—does. All it takes is one word from me and the men I paid to watch you all will run straight to the Secretary of State. They work for him, and, it turns out, anyone else for the right fee. Very convenient. And don't think for a moment of turning to Lovelace. Once he knows the information I have, the witnesses I can produce, the damage I can do to you, to those you harbor affection for and, indeed, to him, his threats to me are rendered neutral. Choose carefully, Rosamund—you can either live here with me as my lawful wife or you can languish in prison after you've been thoroughly questioned. I hear Henry Bennet is a master at extracting confessions, he and Mr. Williamson . . . Ah! I know what you're thinking, but ponder this: when one is proved a traitor, friendship counts for nothing; I know. Just ask Lovelace. As for Bianca, well, she'll be bundled on a ship and sent to a plantation somewhere—if she survives. And while I know you employed a boy without a hand, how will the other drawers find employ with none?"

Rosamund's mind galloped.

When she didn't answer, he smiled. "As of this moment, I'm taking possession of my home, and, my dear, sweet Rosamund, my little chocolate maker, I'm taking possession of *you*."

He whipped an arm around her waist. When she pushed him away, his hand closed over hers, holding it captive. She could feel the thud of his heart through his jacket.

Stroking the hair that fell down her back, he bent toward her.

"Rosamund, Rosamund. Don't you understand? This is how it should be. You and me. We can live beneath this roof. If not as husband and wife, then just together. It's all I want. It's all I've ever wanted . . ." His voice was a furnace in her ear. "Just you and me . . . always. Not one word of what I know will ever escape my lips. I will keep you safe—and those you lavish your affections on—with my silence. I'll give you everything you ever wanted—another chocolate house if need be, as many slaves as your heart desires, a babe to love. Just say the word."

He caught her lobe in his lips and nibbled it.

Disgust made her pull away. His mouth made a popping sound as her ear escaped.

"The word is 'no,' Aubrey. It's always been 'no.'"

Suddenly, he released her. Staggering back to a chair, she saw the pages crumpled beside it.

"Without a chocolate house, without a place to call your own, where will you go? You can't go back to Gravesend. As for Lovelace, you think he'd take you? The woman who looks like the wife he despised? Whom he killed? He didn't deserve her. He doesn't deserve you."

Rosamund could not tear her eyes away from the pages.

"But *I* want you. I want to take care of you. Love you. I do. We are Blithmans. Together, we can live here, run the business. Don't you see? It's perfect. God brought you into my life so I might atone . . ." He stopped.

Sweeping up the torn pages, Rosamund was left with no choice. She had to stop this lunacy before it went any further. "Atone for what, Aubrey? What were you about to say?"

His eyes flicked to what she held and back to her face. He frowned. "What's that you have there?"

She shook them. "The truth, Aubrey. I hold the truth."

At first she thought he was going to snatch the pages from her. Instead, he strode to the table and scooped up his drink and downed it.

"Truth? What are you talking about?"

Making sure the table remained between them, Rosamund held up the remnants of his mother's diary. "I know about you and Helene, Aubrey. I know *everything*. About your obscene sins, about the baby."

His face paled. His expression became guarded. "What nonsense is this?"

"Your mother . . ." Rosamund stopped. She was about to betray a woman's last attempt to admit to all the wrongs she'd done. While she was unrepentant, Aubrey could at least own his actions, admit his wickedness. "Your mother blamed herself for what you and Helene did . . . She took responsibility for everything, including hiding the truth, and it killed her."

Aubrey's glass dropped from his hand. The sound as it struck the floor was stark. It rolled under the chair. "You don't know what you're talking about," he said. "Killed her? What nonsense is this? Helene and I did nothing wrong. My mother was ill, unwell . . ."

"Lady Margery pulled strings, made decisions, manipulated people, all to protect you and your sister, concealing your foul sin. She knew everything; she wrote it all down in her diary, confessed to God that it sickened her just as it sickens me."

"Sickens?" exclaimed Aubrey. "There's nothing sickening about love."

"Love? You call *that* love?" Rosamund stared at him aghast. "Because of your *love*, innocent people died—Robin, the baby, your mother. Even your father declared you dead. Matthew Lovelace nearly died because of you."

His face contorted. "He should have."

Rosamund shook the pages in his face. "Matthew? He was innocent, deceived. Your father was willing to become a murderer to protect your secret, to turn me into one."

Aubrey's face changed. "But don't you see?" His voice was wheedling. "This is why you must stay. This is why we have to be together. We can make all that right. We can undo all those terrible things—the baby's death. Father's actions, Mother's . . ." He frowned. Shaking himself, he scooped up her hand and held it tight. "Helene and I were foolish, misguided—I know that now. But you, you're not my sister, you only look like her. You were my father's wife in name only. With you, I can love openly, out of the shadows. Even God Himself would bless our union. Why else would you have come into our lives if it isn't God's will?"

Rosamund stared at him in disbelief. The man was deranged. He wanted to replace his dead sister with her. She bit back a laugh. They all did. Everard. Aubrey. She once thought Lady Margery was the dead woman whose shoes she walked in. But all along it was Helene's shoes they'd wished her to wear.

No more.

"God would never bless something so, so wrong." She snatched her hand away. "I don't love you, Aubrey. I never could. Don't you see? Your so-called love for me is iniquitous as well." She lowered her voice, infused it with empathy. "I am not Helene. I never will be. You're sick, Aubrey. Your mother saw you and your sister for what—"

There was a loud crack. Rosamund's head flew back and the pages scattered as she fell against the chair. Her cheek burned. Flashes of yellow and crimson arced across the horizon of her sight.

There was a rattling sound: Aubrey locked the door.

Rosamund blinked. Nausea rose. She was being tossed on a wild sea.

"Sick, am I?" snarled Aubrey. All pretense of civility and persuasion was gone. His eyes were wild, sweat dotted his forehead and ran in rivulets down his face.

He grabbed her by the throat and shook her. "Dear God, it would be so easy to stop those vile words coming from those lovely lips." Bending, he pressed his mouth against hers. When she tried to push him off, he tightened his hold. She couldn't breathe. Forcing her lips apart, his tongue scraped her mouth. Planting his knee between her legs, he pulled her against him as she fought the darkness at the edges of her vision.

As quickly as he bundled her to him, he flung her away. She tumbled into the chair. Drawing lungfuls of air, it was a moment before she became aware of him standing over her. He was reading his mother's words. His face was blotched with patches of carmine and a spiderweb of veins. He finished one page and tossed it aside, his shoulders slumping as if by reading it, he had taken the weight of the contents upon himself.

Rosamund surreptitiously wiped her sleeve across her mouth and searched for something to arm herself with. Anything to prevent him hurting her again. Her neck was tender; it was difficult to swallow. Blood was in her mouth. There were candlesticks, but they were too far away.

A tortured sound escaped him and he fell to his knees. As she watched, moment to moment his expression changed from calmness to storms and back again. Her heart swelled. How could she feel so sorry for such a man? Yet she did. Like Fear-God and Glory, like Ben and Jed, like her, children are the choices their parents make. Aubrey was the result of the choices his mother and father made. He was not absolved. But at the same time he never understood the price others paid for his lustful sins—and Helene's. Now he confronted his mother's anguish.

Tears rolled down his cheeks. He dug the heel of his hand into one eye then the other before continuing. He looked at Rosamund at one stage.

The room finally stopped spinning and Rosamund was able to sit up. On the table by the window was a statuette of Venus. If only she could reach it, she could use it to deter Aubrey if he struck again.

Finally, he let the last page drop. Rosamund lurched out of the chair in an attempt to get to the table by the window. He caught at her skirts, tripping her. Her head struck the floor.

He dragged her toward him, uncaring that the dress tore, and gathered her into his arms. "I'm sorry," he sobbed into her breast. "I'm so sorry. I only ever loved you. With all my heart and soul. I felt good, right, when I was with you. Only you. How can God not bless such feelings?" He raised his head, searched her face, then burrowed into her neck. "Father said what we did was the worst of transgressions, that we would go to hell for them. When you died, I thought he was right—this was God punishing me. I wanted to die too. But then you came back. He brought you back to me. Our love was never wrong . . . But that—" His arm flailed toward the pages. "Mother . . . How could she . . . how could she say those things? How could Father? Lovelace was never good enough for Helene. She was meant to be with me. With *me*." Sobs strangled his words.

Vacillating between believing she was his sister and understanding she was not, his mind was torn asunder. Almost every instinct in Rosamund screamed at her to crawl from beneath him and escape. All except one. She listened to it.

Putting her arm about him, she drew him closer, swallowing her abhorrence, gritting her teeth as she stroked the back of his head. "Hush, there, Aubrey. Hush. It will be all right, it will be all right."

How long they sat like that, Rosamund didn't know. Her head ached, and her body began to protest at the peculiar position she was in. Staring at the wall, she watched the light change as the afternoon sped on through a smoke-filled haze: from golden to white-hot to lucent. Still Aubrey didn't move. His weeping quietened. The rancid, wine-soaked, sweaty smell of him grew. She wanted to put her head back and close her eyes and sleep until the world righted itself. She wished Bianca were home, that Matthew would come in search of her, that someone would understand the door was locked and release her. But she knew that couldn't happen just yet.

If she came through this, she would leave Blithe Manor. She had no real rights here—nor did she want them. It was Aubrey's house. His house, his memories, and he was welcome to them. What a sad, terrible place. What a sad, terrible family.

Aubrey ceased crying. He lifted his head and stared at her. Mucus ran from his nose to the top of his lips. His cheeks were smeared with wet saltiness. More than anything he resembled a naughty little boy. A boy who committed the sin of loving his sister too much.

As he continued to stare, his mouth worked itself into strange shapes, as if trying out words and discarding them. She reached out to brush away a stray hair that had fallen on his forehead. He slapped her fingers away and, without warning, stood up.

Rosamund toppled from his knees.

"You're right. You're not Helene, you ungrateful cunt." He spat and kicked her. "Helene wouldn't make me cry. She would never cause me such pain. She crafted beautiful letters to buoy my spirits, to remind me of her constancy. She did everything she could to be with me, risking her life and the babe's. We always promised we'd find each other, sail to the ends of the earth. That's what she tried to do . . . not like you." His foot flew out and connected with her ribs.

She gasped and tried to protect her side with her hand, but he kicked her again, her fingers bearing the brunt this time.

"Please, Aubrey." She tried to roll away.

"There's no pleasing you." He followed and kicked her in the head. There was a burst of agony, followed by darkness. She could still hear his voice.

"I offer you marriage, a life together, but all you say is no. I offer you my house, my name. You say no."

She heard footsteps crossing back and forth, back and forth over the floor.

"Helene *loved me*. She understood me. You're just like the rest. You tell me it's wrong. Lovelace used our letters to bribe me, to manipulate me. You're just like him, using those awful words Mother wrote to make me behave the way you want. Father threatened me too. What about me? What about Helene? Why couldn't you all just let us be? We never hurt anyone."

Rosamund had the presence of mind not to mention the baby . . . or Matthew.

"You had to interfere; you had to try to keep us apart. It wasn't our love that killed Helene. It was you. All of you. You never should have been given to Lovelace. Never. Mother deserved to die. Father too."

Through a veil of agony, she watched as he scrunched the pages together. As he threw them on the chair, she saw there were other things stacked there. Books, a news sheet, some pamphlets he found, a shawl. Searching his pocket, he added his pouch of tobacco, his pipe, before pulling out a flint. She heard him strike it a few times before it finally caught. Why was he doing that? Surely if he wanted to burn the remnants of the diary, it was much safer to do so in the hearth.

With growing horror, she saw him lower the flame to the pages.

"No—" she croaked.

"No?" cried Aubrey, without bothering to turn. "Is that all you can say to me? Why not? Just as fire cleansed London, I'm going to have my own little ritual and cleanse the past. Burn these foul musings and all their untruths." The corner of a page caught, blackening and folding as a thin ribbon of orange rippled across it. "May as well keep going." He lifted the flaming page and held it against the other papers stacked on the chair. "If you don't want to live here, well, neither do I. In fact," he said, moving back as the objects began to smoke, "no one will. It will be my monument to Helene . . . . to our love."

He turned, a ghoulish grin upon his face.

Behind him, flames leaped. The paper was old, the chair too. The other bits he'd found to feed his fire crackled to life. The time-worn pillows, the shawl, the upholstery covered in fine specks of ash and soot from days of blazes, became hungry kindling. The flickering grew and danced, rising higher, catching the edge of the curtains.

Rosamund tried to move, to cry out, but she couldn't. Before her, Aubrey leaped from foot to foot like a pagan. He added more fuel, other news sheets, more books from which he tore the pages. He threw them on the chair, which had become a torch. The heat was furious.

Hand over hand, she hauled herself away, barely able to breathe. Her ribs were blistering bands of bruises; blood trickled down the side of her head. The curtains were aflame. The windows she'd opened to admit air now fanned the fire. It jumped across the windows, crawled across the walls. Paint peeled, plaster charred and dropped. Artworks became scorched, the faces stern and unmoving as they melted.

Smoke rolled around the ceiling, falling to descend upon them both and choke them in its thick, cloying grasp.

Shouts followed by screams issued from outside.

"God!" she cried, before a volley of coughs interrupted. "Help me." Dragging herself along the floor, the distance to the door was so vast, it was another country.

A hand fastened around her ankle.

"Don't leave me, Helene. Please, not again." Ignoring her limp kicks, her pleas, her hoarse screams, Aubrey threw himself on top of her. She tried to thrust him away, but he was too heavy. She had no energy; she couldn't breathe. Above her she was aware of his face as it swam in her vision; he was saying something, but the roar of the fire was too loud, the way it undulated across the ceiling in a blur of gold and orange seared her vision, she couldn't look away.

That was how she saw what happened next. There was an almighty crack and the ancient beam above began to sag before, with a great groan of protest, it fell.

Rosamund watched it coming toward her over Aubrey's shoulder. She tried to warn him, tell him to move, but the words wouldn't come.

At the last moment she cowered in the shelter of his chest before something struck with a flash of white-hot torment and blessed oblivion claimed her.

PART FIVE

September 1666 to March 1667

Though Seas and Land betwixt us both,
Our Faith and Troth,
Like Separated soules
All time and space controules:
Above the highest sphere wee meet
Unseene, unknown, and greet as Angels greet.

—To Lucasta, *Going Beyond the Seas,*
Richard Lovelace, 1618–1657

FIFTY-TWO
In which truth rises out of the ash of lies

Matthew yawned and straightened his cramped legs, trying to shake off the leaden sleep that had overcome him as he sat vigil by Rosamund's bed. For five days he'd barely moved except to talk to the doctor and to Filip, Bianca, Sam and the boys. All that time she'd drifted in and out of sleep, her head bandaged, her hand too. Her face was bruised. Her skin had been so very red when they first brought her to Seething Lane, but at least that had faded, unlike the memories that shrieked from her mouth and caused her to thrash about the bed.

Dear God.

If he hadn't arrived at the house when he did, if Filip and Mr. Nick and the women hadn't already started to fight the fire with pails of water, he might never have been able to enter the manor. He shuddered; it didn't bear thinking about. The additional burns he'd received when he kicked in the door, heaved the beam out of the way and threw Aubrey off her, they would heal.

So would Rosamund—at least, her physical self would. But what of the scars those moments with Aubrey would sear into her soul? And, as he'd learned these last days and nights, there were other, older scars, upon which these would now be grafted.

Alarmed by what spilled from her mouth as she drifted between consciousness and nightmares, he was helpless to soothe her. With Bianca's aid, between them they settled her—if you could call the frown that puckered that sweet brow, the tremulous hands and mouth, "settled."

Able to piece together what haunted her nightmares, not wanting to acknowledge what must be true, Matthew slumped into despondency. How could anyone commit such terrible crimes against her? He'd thought he'd been dealt an unkind blow by fate when he encountered the Blithmans, but it was nothing compared to what Rosamund had been forced to endure before she ever met them. To think he'd once suspected her of knowingly being in league with Sir Everard to defeat him.

He was ashamed.

If Bianca hadn't coaxed out of him what he'd heard and how he felt, and in turn offered what Jacopo had told her about Sir Everard and his intentions toward Rosamund, he might have done something hasty. When Bianca admitted she too had at first suspected Rosamund of having questionable morals, and how it wasn't until she saw the marks upon her flesh that first night she began to doubt her initial impression, he felt somewhat mollified.

Later, Bianca explained, she saw in Rosamund what everyone did who bothered to look beneath the large eyes, the quick smile, the joyous laugh and natural ebullience—not only a genuinely good-natured person who refused to allow outrageous misfortune to keep her down, but also a reflective and clever woman who was quick to read in others what they often didn't recognize in themselves.

Matthew thought on Bianca's words as he studied Rosamund's face in repose. He knew every hair in the arch of her brows, every fine vein atop her eyelids. The bow of her mouth, the sweep of those long eyelashes against the curve of her cheek. An artist could not have captured her the way Matthew could merely by closing his eyes.

After Helene, he'd never have believed he could admit a woman into his heart again and allow her to take

it into her keeping. For that's what this woman of endless surprises, resilience and kindness had done—this
fine chocolate maker had taken the raw and bitter ingredients that made up who he was and remixed them
until he was altogether more palatable.

He smiled at his own musings and wondered, for the
umpteenth time, what Rosamund would make of them.
If only she would wake . . .

He rose and opened the curtains to admit the gray
light. Outside, rain was falling. Blessed rain after all
this time. Hopefully it would be enough to quench the
last of the fires. He watched it flow in shuddering bands
down the glass. Perhaps he could yet hope for a miracle.

Almost afraid to look, he turned to the bed to see
what changes a new morning wrought, if any.

What he didn't expect was a pair of chocolate-deep
eyes gazing back at him.

He fell to his knees beside the bed and searched for
her hand.

"Rosamund," he whispered.

She tried to talk, but nothing came.

He poured her a glass of small ale, then tucked an
arm behind her and gently pulled her upright. Lifting
the drink to her lips, he could only stare as she winced
when the cool fluid hit her dry, sore throat. A peculiar
itch threatened the back of his eyes.

When she signaled she'd had enough, he put the glass down and eased her back among the pillows.

"How long?" she asked, finally. Her voice was little more than a susurration and the effort clearly cost her. She began to cough, and he held her while she barked and wheezed, relieved the doctor had warned them to expect that as her lungs cleared themselves of all the smoke she'd inhaled while she was unconscious in the burning room.

Slowly, he retracted his arm and watched her sink into the pillows. She looked so young with her hair cascading over her shoulders, hair that had been singed and even now bore a bright orange streak at the front, like a flame. A reminder of what she had survived. It would grow out. If she hadn't been wearing a cap, if Aubrey's body hadn't borne the brunt of that beam and protected her from the flames, well . . .

Never believing he could be grateful to Aubrey for anything, he was for that. He could forgive him much for saving Rosamund's life.

He fought back the tears. God damn, but they were perilously close to his eyelids these days. He blamed lack of sleep at the same time as he almost crushed her fingers.

Her dark eyes flashed and recorded everything around her. The flowers Grace picked each day and refreshed in a glass of water. The books Bianca brought and read to her. The news sheets Sam had collected so Matthew might also keep abreast of tidings, even if it was old news and much of it written by him. The bowls of chocolate lovingly prepared by Filip and the boys. In those chestnut eyes he saw a deep suffering he couldn't recall seeing before, as if she'd caught a glimpse of hell and been forever altered. The very notion ate at him. He would take all that away if he could.

"How long?" repeated Matthew lightly, waiting until her last coughs subsided, summoning a small smile. "A mere five days. You've been asleep"—*near death*—"or close to it for five days." An eternity by any other measure. "But look, we have rain."

They both gazed toward the window, the shower now a heavy, steady thrumming that cast a silver light over the room and drowned the sounds of the street. Above them, footsteps resounded. A door slammed shut. He didn't know what to say. No, he didn't know how to say it.

"Where am I?" she asked.

Matthew gave a half laugh. "Sam's. We all are. For now." Then, seeing the questions in those extraordinary eyes, he told her everything—well, almost everything. He focused on how he'd carried her out of the room and down the stairs, Filip running to his aid, just before the ceiling collapsed and the entire roof caved in.

"If it hadn't, there was a risk the other houses might have ignited, but it meant the flames were contained within the walls. But I'm afraid Blithe Manor is no more."

Rosamund took the news well considering the last of her sanctuaries was now but rubble and ash. The rain became heavier. Sodden ash.

He went to stroke her face but held back. Once he'd learned what had happened to her at the hands of her stepfather and brothers, how they'd made free with her, touching and more, the Satan-spawned bastards, the caresses he'd stolen, of her face, arms and fingers, ceased. If he couldn't touch her with permission, he'd deny himself the pleasure. It was the least this precious woman was owed.

Understanding she wanted the entire story, he told her how Sam once more offered his house—not only to her, but to any of her maids and the drawers who could not return home, to Filip, Thomas, Solomon, Ashe, Grace and Bianca—Mr. Nick as well. Even to him, as Mr. Henderson's house was nothing more than a scorched husk. Soon, he would tell her how he and Sam had grown quite close, the naval clerk enjoying having another set of ears into which to pour his accomplishments.

Sam would join Matthew's vigil by Rosamund's bed and share his daily adventures with him, a responsibility Elizabeth was more than content to relinquish. Thus Matthew learned that in the days since he had brought Rosamund here and the doctor had treated her, the King had not only addressed the thousands of homeless spread across Moorfields and beyond, he'd been greeted like a hero. Fighting the fire side by side with commoners, on horseback for over thirty hours, he'd earned the respect none of his other actions had since taking the throne. Matthew had seen the King for himself, and his brother, the Duke, both covered in filth, bone-weary, not only using hooks to pull down roofs, wielding shovels to help make firebreaks and laying explosives, but shoring up flagging spirits with praise and bonhomie and sharing the basic rations that were distributed. He and Sam agreed they hoped His Majesty would take advantage of the people's goodwill to shore up his position and do more good. Somehow, knowing the fickleness of the people and the propensities of the pleasure-loving King, they confided that they doubted it.

He wondered if he should mention Wat. How the curmudgeonly man, shocked by Aubrey's death and what had led to it, and at a loss what to do with himself, had remained in the vicinity of Seething Lane and set about making himself useful. Every day he would inquire after the young mistress's health—seemingly not out of duty as much as a genuine desire to know. One could almost believe he was relieved to be free of any obligation to Aubrey.

Rosamund lay quietly, her hand limp against the bedclothes.

"Aubrey?" she asked finally; his name a wound upon her lips.

Matthew shook his head. "I . . . I was too late." How did he explain that as soon as he saw her, crushed not only beneath a great burning piece of wood, but Aubrey as well, his only care was for her? With a strength he didn't know he possessed, he'd heaved the beam aside, then pushed Aubrey off. What the poltroon was doing there, having sworn to keep away, he would yet discover. Out of the corner of his eye he'd seen the man was unconscious, that his legs were already burning. Even so, he'd intended to come back for him, and would've too, had the house not fallen.

That was his intention . . .

"He's dead?" she asked.

"Yes." Matthew would never tell her about his animal screams, the way they echoed as he fled down the stairs with her in his arms, how Aubrey's pleas to save him haunted his nightmares.

"Perhaps"—she began to cough again—"it's better that way," she said.

Matthew didn't dare speak for a moment. It was better. Most of all, for Aubrey. "When you're able," he said, clearing his throat, "I want you to tell me what Aubrey was doing there. How the fire started."

A pained expression furrowed her brow.

"Only if you wish, my lady," he added quickly. "If it causes you too much—"

"I want to," said Rosamund hoarsely. "I must. There's something you need to know . . ." Her voice died away, and her eyelids grew heavy.

Matthew stared at her, willing her to be with him once more. Learning what had befallen them had been too much. She fell back into the blessed release of slumber.

Three nights later, knowing everyone else in the crowded house was occupied, Rosamund sent for Matthew and Bianca. It was time to tell them what had happened before the fire at Blithe Manor, and about the pages from Lady Margery's diary.

Sam, with help from a subdued Wat and a jovial Mr. Nick, had spent the entire day transferring all the household goods he'd stowed away because of the fire back into the house. After enjoying luncheon at the Globe, he was off to Deptford to fetch his wife, who'd been away again. Apart from Filip, Solomon, Thomas, Grace, Adam and Hugh, who were enjoying a game of Primo in the kitchen with Sam's servants, Jane and Will, and Mr. Nick, who had found a nearby alehouse, they were quite alone.

Rosamund felt so much better. Bianca had been solicitous in her attentions, feeding her soup and bread dipped in warm milk, while Filip prepared special bowls of chocolate. Sam had ensured the chocolate and the chocolate-making equipment were salvaged from the wreckage of Blithe Manor. Most of it suffered only some singeing and the indignity of soot.

Each day, the boys and Grace had spent time with Rosamund, mostly to reassure themselves she was really on the mend, but also to boast of their bravery during the London fire. Able to crawl out of bed, she'd sat on the chair Matthew usually occupied and listened as they spoke over the top of one another, trying to earn her admiration. Draped over the back of Thomas's chair, Grace hung on his every word.

Hardly boys anymore. Thomas was broadening across the shoulders and his voice had deepened. Solomon, who was looking more and more like Filip each day, appeared to have grown inches since she last saw him. Perhaps the water with which they'd fought the flames had, as it did plants, helped them grow. The thought made her smile.

It was from them she learned that Wat was also staying in Seething Lane, albeit bunking down in the stables with some other homeless people. Bianca explained that by making himself useful, he wanted to make amends. Rosamund wasn't sure she was ready for that and was grateful to learn Mr. Nick was keeping a close eye on him. What she was ready to learn was that Adam, Hugh, Kit, Art and Timothy had found work at one of the few surviving coffee houses.

Prowling the streets each day, looking to help where he could while also collecting stories for the *London Gazette*, which returned to publication on the 10th of September via an open-air printing press, Matthew had come across a coffee maker who was desperate for more boys. Provided with excellent references, and demonstrating these were not mere hyperbole, the boys had been welcomed. Their work came with accommodation. Spilling into her room, awkward and grateful, the boys bade Rosamund farewell and let her know that when she opened again, they would return to her faster than she could twirl a *molinillo*.

With a heavy heart she watched them leave. She would hold them to that. When she reopened.

When? Who was she fooling? The question was *if* she reopened.

Ever since she'd regained her faculties, it preoccupied her every waking moment. Aubrey's reminders of her financial situation had struck a chord. He was right that without an income from either the chocolate house or the bookstore, she'd be forced to rely on the generosity of others. "Others" meaning men.

With Blithe Manor gone, the situation was even more dire. And what of those dependent on her? It was grand the boys had found work, but apart from rebuilding and cleaning, the sort of skills Filip, Thomas, Solomon and even she herself possessed needed not only demand, but a place in which they could be utilized. That required money, time. And what of Ashe and young Grace?

Losing the chocolate house and bookstore, not to mention three-quarters of the city, while very inconvenient (she almost laughed hysterically at how inadequate that word was)—as long as they'd had a roof over their heads, their circumstances were not completely grim.

Losing Blithe Manor changed everything. All she'd owned had been contained within those four walls.

While the chocolate-making equipment had survived, what good was it to her now?

While it was fine to presume on Sam for a few days, this arrangement couldn't last forever. How could she remain in London when it was little more than charred rubble? How could she open another business without a cent to her name? Without any material goods to barter with? As a woman? Well, there was one way, and she wasn't even going to consider that.

The fact was, she had nothing. She was a nobody with a title, and that wouldn't pay the rent or put food on the table.

She could hear Sam now: *What you need, my dear, is a husband.*

Matthew's face rose before her. A face that was so dear to her and yet, what happened back at Blithe Manor, learning the truth about the whole sordid mess, the way in which Matthew had been manipulated, the lengths to which Aubrey, Helene, Lady Margery and Sir Everard would go to protect the family name no matter the cost, left her feeling scraped out and hollow.

Everything was now tainted. She'd known almost from the outset that she resembled Helene Blithman. It was the reason Sir Everard married her; he depended on the similarity to make his vengeance complete. Aubrey had regarded her as not only a reincarnation of Helene but God's approval of their incest made flesh.

The thought made her skin crawl.

What of Matthew? Did he see Rosamund as a second chance at love? Or a second chance at his first marriage, minus the incest and cuckolding? Was that why he brought her into his business so willingly? Why he had been so delighted that Mr. Henderson left the bookstore to both of them? It had bound her to him in other ways.

Thoughts whirled in her head, mixed with flames and ashes. Her dreams were nothing but charred ruins. She didn't even know if she wanted to rise like a phoenix anymore. After all, didn't the damn bird just burn again? She would have to make up her mind soon; it wasn't fair to keep Matthew close under a false pretext, to offer hope where there was none. If she did, then she was no better than those she despised.

Before she could make those kinds of decisions, she owed Matthew and Bianca the truth. They needed to know what Lady Margery had written.

Bianca lit some candles and stoked the coals in the hearth while Matthew mixed them all bowls of chocolate. The rain was light now, so light they heard the distant bells of one of the remaining churches chime the hour. Seven of the clock. Rosamund prepared what she would say.

Matthew and Bianca settled in neighboring chairs, steaming bowls of chocolate in their hands, their eyes upon her. Slowly, interrupted by the occasional cough, she relayed the contents of the remnants of Lady Margery's diary. Then she briefly told them what Aubrey had done and said. How he'd threatened her and, through her, those she cared about. Her voice was still husky, scorched by the smoke.

When she finished, Matthew's eyes fixed on her face for a long moment. He let out a protracted whistle.

"His threats . . . to expose me, you, they were empty, you know. Said to frighten you, force you to capitulate to his whims. He'd no proof. I made sure of that once I realized Sir Henry wasn't paying the men to watch us. I had him call them off and order them never to work for Aubrey again. I told Sir Henry their time was being wasted over a matter of the heart when it would be better spent ferreting out real traitors. But you weren't to know that." He sighed, his eyes downcast. "As for Lady Margery . . . I never knew . . . never suspected." He placed his bowl on the floor and raked his hair with his hands, as if turning over the topsoil of his mind. "She was so quiet, remained so much in the background. I'd never have guessed the level of her involvement." He shook his head. "It always appeared she was obeying Sir Everard's whim." He looked to Bianca for confirmation.

"I believe that was the impression both of them wanted to give. She was a very strong and able woman for all she appeared . . . demure."

"Like Helene," he whispered. He looked at Bianca. "Did you know about them . . . Aubrey . . . Helene?"

Bianca bit her lip. "I had . . . suspicions. Jacopo and I both, but we dared not speak about them, lest they . . . be made manifest. But," continued Bianca hesitantly, "it does explain why Lady Margery took her own life."

"She *what?*" Matthew sat forward.

Rosamund drew in a sharp breath. She had wondered how Lady Margery died, but never suspected she'd killed herself. She recalled the words in the diary:

> . . . *I would do anything to secure my children's future and preserve their good name. Ours. Anything. I do not regret one thing. Not even what I am about to do. May God forgive me.*

"How?" asked Rosamund softly. She leaned back and closed her eyes for a moment.

"She hanged herself from the bedpost. Plaited a sheet and looped it about her neck and . . ." Bianca took a deep breath. "I found her the next morning. I woke Sir Everard immediately. Together we . . . we took her down, untangled the sheet, placed her back in the bed and the master ordered me to tie a scarf about her neck so when the doctor came, he would not see the dreadful bruising. We told him she died in her sleep."

Rosamund's hands crept to her own throat. "It explains so much." Not only the words in the diary, but why Sir Everard was so guarded when he spoke of his wife. Suicide. Incest and suicide. May God forgive her, forgive them.

"He ordered us to never speak of it again," said Bianca softly. "Of her. I oft wondered why she did it. I prayed for her soul, at Meetings." Her hands fluttered. "As for the baby . . ." She shook her head. "Again, I wondered but I never saw, only heard rumors. Helene was careful as few as possible laid eyes upon him."

She flashed an apologetic look at Matthew.

"She kept him heavily swaddled." He paused. "I scarce saw him myself. I never suspected what I learned later. I believed God had sent us a flawed child to love and nurture. I would have, too, you know." His eyes took on a faraway look before they snapped back to the present. "In many ways, I should be grateful to them, I suppose—to Aubrey and Helene."

"Grateful?" Bianca spat. "How can you, of all people, say that?"

Rosamund knew what he meant, or thought she did.

"Had Aubrey not defied his father's orders and written to Helene from the colonies, had she not kept the letters and copies of those she sent to him, I might never have known the truth. I would have believed my wife and my baby drowned at sea and continued to blame myself. I would have spent my life grieving and being held to account for deaths in which I played no part." He released a long, sad sigh. "Knowing about Aubrey and Helene, their unnatural love, I've had years to reconcile her death and the babe's, but even so, it has been difficult. Now to learn of Lady Margery's part in all this, when I thought it could not become more sordid, has, I confess, quite flummoxed me. I always thought . . . I believed it was Sir Everard alone who set out to deceive and then punish me for learning the truth. I used it to bring him to his knees, force him to compensate me for the humiliations and deception I suffered." He gave a contemptuous snort. "But it was never the whole truth, was it?"

"It never is," said Rosamund softly. She was thinking back to Bearwoode and what Master Dunstan used to say whenever she asked him why her mother had abandoned her. *There are always three sides to every story: yours, theirs and God's.* She wondered what God would say about this one. Wash his hands of it and pass it to the devil?

Now she understood why Matthew never revealed the name of Helene's lover. What was it he'd said when she asked why Sir Everard didn't force his daughter to marry the man who got her with child? There was an impediment to their union. *Impediment.* Aye, incest. No wonder Sir Everard was desperate to have the letters returned; no wonder Matthew was able to use them to force first Sir Everard and then Aubrey to do his bidding . . . for a time, anyhow.

Once more, the terrible power of words was laid bare. The ways in which they could be both used and abused . . .

"And Aubrey thought to find redemption by taking you to wife," said Matthew sourly, interrupting her thoughts. "His reasoning beggars belief."

"He said"—Rosamund tried to recall the exact words—" 'we can undo all those terrible things—the baby's death. Father's actions.' " She paused. "He said to me, 'But you, you're not my sister, you only look like her . . . With you, I can love openly, out of the shadows. Even God Himself would bless our union.' "

Her eyes dropped to her hands twisted together on her lap.

"*Mio Dio*," whispered Bianca.

"He was deluded," said Matthew, shaking his head. "Not even God could forgive what he did. What Helene did too."

"What they all did," finished Bianca.

There was silence.

"Bianca," began Rosamund, "do you think Sir Everard suspected there were pages missing from one of Lady Margery's diaries? From her last one?"

"He would have turned the house upside down if he'd known they existed. He simply didn't want anyone to read any of her diaries—he destroyed whatever he found."

"Were there many?"

"*Si*. Written over years. She would oft be found in her closet writing the day's events." Bianca frowned, her voice thoughtful. "I came across Sir Everard in there once, not long after you"—she nodded toward Matthew—"married Helene, reading them. The following day, they were all gone. After that, Lady Margery took to hiding them. He remonstrated with her for being so foolish as to record everything. I did wonder what she wrote that so perturbed him."

"Do you think tearing out those pages, the ones where she reveals everything, was her vengeance upon him? For destroying her words, silencing her?" asked Rosamund.

They all exchanged a long look.

Bianca nodded slowly. "In more ways than one. Sir Everard never tolerated her Papist sympathies either. Forbade her its rituals, the solace of the confessional. She must have kept the beads after he broke her rosaries and covered her confession with them. It was also her way of undermining him and of adhering to her faith."

Matthew stared at the ceiling, exhaling loudly. "I don't know whether that makes me feel worse or better. All that time, I dedicated myself to revenge—but I was punishing the wrong person."

"Not entirely," said Rosamund. "Sir Everard chose to take up the mantel. Remember, he *did* try to kill you."

"He tried to get *you* to kill me."

Rosamund went quiet. Imagine if she had succeeded. Imagine life without that man sitting opposite her now. Imagine if she were still married to Sir Everard and had the weight of Matthew's death on her conscience. She shuddered.

Bianca moved to cover her.

"Are you cold, my lady?" asked Matthew.

"Not really." She waited until Bianca finished tucking the blanket in, and thanked her. "I was just thinking what a wasted emotion revenge is. It fills the soul with nothing but darkness."

Matthew gave a sardonic laugh. "The important thing is not to get swallowed by the darkness. To remember, even when the shadows grow long and you fear they will consume you, there's still light in the world." He glanced at her before turning to face the fire. "You just need to find it."

And love, thought Rosamund. *And love. You just have to be brave enough to acknowledge it.*

FIFTY-THREE
In which Rosamund walks in her own shoes

The three of them were interrupted by Sam and Elizabeth returning home. Bursting into the room, Elizabeth threw herself upon Rosamund and declared herself delighted to see her cousin in such remarkable health considering Sam had painted such a grim picture of her condition.

Before Rosamund could respond, Sam also charged toward her, lifting her from the chair, pressing her to his chest and smothering her with kisses, much to Elizabeth's chagrin, and declaring her recovery nothing short of a miracle. Rosamund refrained from reminding him he'd seen her that very morning before he'd set out for Tower Wharf and Deptford.

When he finally let go of her, she slid back into the chair, rearranging the rug. Elizabeth wasted no time bidding them good night and all but dragged Sam back to their chamber, from which a sound scolding was heard followed by noises that had little do with anger and a great deal to do with a husband and wife having a long-awaited reunion.

As any attempts to talk above the din failed dismally, Matthew and Bianca made their excuses and left; Matthew to the room he shared with Filip and Will, Sam's clerk, and Bianca upstairs to the maid Jane's room to share a bed with Grace.

Unable to consider sleep while Sam and Elizabeth frolicked, Rosamund reflected upon Matthew and Bianca's reactions to her news. Altogether, it was what she expected. Bianca stoic and unsurprised; Matthew horrified to learn the extent of Lady Margery's role, and remembering how his drive for vengeance against Sir Everard had led to him becoming a blackmailer.

As far as Rosamund was concerned, Sir Everard could have made different choices. He had been as determined as his wife in his own way. Margery had used him and Matthew, and he had been prepared to use Matthew and Rosamund.

It was a sorry, sad affair. Thank God it was over. They could put it behind them.

Or could they?

Echoes of the Blithmans survived in the derisive,

doubt-filled voices whispering to Rosamund that Matthew didn't really love her, that the only reason he remained was because she looked so much like Helene . . . That with her, he could recapture a version of what he had once desired so much. In that regard, Matthew was no different from Aubrey . . .

It was becoming harder to defend Matthew. How was she to think differently when, ever since the fire, he'd been so distant? There was a time when he would welcome her with a gentle caress. Her cheek or hand would burn for hours after, and all she had to do was recall his touch for her center to melt like a cake of chocolate. Sometimes he would reach for her hand and wrap his gloved fingers around it. And there were those looks he would bestow, the ones that set her heart racing. They were as incendiary as the sparks that had flown around London during the fire. But since they'd been at Sam's house, he had treated her like a fine porcelain bowl that would chip if he touched it. Retreating like a wounded soldier, he'd become almost maudlin in her presence. What battle was Matthew fighting? What had she done to suddenly become the enemy?

Was it because he wanted nothing to do with the Blithman name? Listen to her. There *was* a battle, and it was raging within her. She knew how she felt about Matthew. She had for a long time now. Together they'd survived the plague and now the fire. There'd been so much loss, so much death. So much sorrow. She didn't want to waste another moment without him. Not anymore. So why was she churning over old ground?

Blithman ground.

Flinging herself on the bed, Rosamund rested her chin in the cup of her hands, rubbing her flesh against the bandaged one, and gazed at the glowing hearth, marveling at how such a dazzling thing could become all-consuming and deadly. Just like revenge. It too needed to be contained lest it spread and run unchecked.

Her mind raced. Every time she attributed to Matthew thoughts that the Blithmans had put in her head, she was allowing their corruption to pollute her feelings. Not once had Matthew done or said anything to make her believe he didn't care for her—*her*, Rosamund, not the woman who resembled Helene. Even his recent coolness was probably more to do with her being hurt than any change of heart.

If she continued to convince herself their relationship was based on what happened in the past, then she was as bad as the Blithmans. No—worse, because she was allowing their poison to kill any hope she and Matthew had.

Was that why Matthew had withdrawn from her? Because he sensed *her* ambivalence?

She sat up suddenly and kneeled on the bed. But her ambivalence was born of what she'd persuaded herself *he* felt. She was going around and around like a waterwheel. If she didn't tell him how she felt and allow fate, destiny, whatever, to take its course, then the Blithmans would win, the Blithmans and their sinful, sour history; their revenge upon Matthew would be complete and she would be the instrument because he would never know her love—her *love*.

Her hands flew to her head, her breast. She loved him. A delicious bubbling began in her very center, filling her up with tremulous joy, with wonder as she tasted the notion. *Rosamund Blithman loves Matthew Lovelace.*

What was it Matthew had said? *The important thing is not to get swallowed by the darkness. To remember, even when the shadows grow long and you fear they will consume you, there's still light in the world. You just need to find it.*

She would offer him a way out of the Blithmans' never-ending midnight. It was up to him if he followed. She climbed off the bed, threw a shawl over her gown and opened the door carefully, shutting her ears to the sounds still emanating from the Pepyses' bedroom. And went up the stairs to where she knew Matthew's room lay.

She was beyond caring about the impropriety of what she intended to do. Her newly won courage would light her way. She was on a quest. To find love. She prayed with all her aching, pounding heart that it wanted to be found.

FIFTY-FOUR
In which love finds the way

The last person Matthew expected to see at this hour was Rosamund. As if conjured from his fevered thoughts, she stood on the threshold, that cloud of pale hair shining in the candlelight, her eyes luminous pools of promise.

When he remained silent, drinking her in, staring like an urchin offered a guinea, she flashed one of her luscious smiles with those dimples that appeared just for him.

Standing on tiptoe and peering over his shoulder, she whispered, "Are Filip and Will here?"

He tried not to show his disappointment that she was after Filip or Sam's servant and not him. He opened the door a fraction wider so she could see the candle on the small table, his quill, ink and paper. As he struggled to answer, she slipped in and stood in the center of the small room, looking about like a visitor at St. Paul's. Clearly, neither man was present.

"Filip's with Solomon and Thomas. Will's playing cards with Wat in the stables." Matthew looked at her, puzzled. "What do you want with them?"

"Nothing. I wanted to make certain you were on your own."

Flopping on one of the beds as if for all the world this was her room and he the intruder, she gestured for him to shut the door.

He knew this was most improper, but he wanted to know why she'd come, especially when he thought they'd said as much as they could about the diary. A frisson of hope and need had begun to burn in his center, but he resolved to remain calm. To not touch her though his body and mind were daring him to do just that. How could he not? Here was Rosamund, in his room—well, Sam's attic—alone with him. He could hear his heart in his ears. He wanted to draw her into his arms, inhale the fragrance that was hers alone, and yet he dare not touch her.

Instead he stayed by the door, folded his arms and, praying he sounded rational, asked, "And why is that?"

Leaning forward gingerly on her bandaged palm, swinging her legs a few times, Rosamund suddenly ceased moving and locked eyes with him. "Because I've something to both ask and tell you—though not necessarily in that order."

Matthew hardly dared to look at her. "Go on, then."

As he spoke, the space between them contracted, and the invisible thread connecting them wound tighter. Waiting as patiently as he could, aware of her with every fiber of his being, he raised his head when she didn't speak. What he saw almost broke him.

Those great, wondrous eyes were aswim with tears.

"Rosamund—" he began, before she held up a hand to stop him coming closer.

"Please, I beg you—" She made a strange choking sound. "If you come closer I may not be able to say what I must."

Matthew dreaded what she had to say lest it confirm the doubts and anxieties he'd been harboring. He stepped back to his position by the door.

"I need to tell you," she began softly, "that ever since you made your offer of marriage to me, some time ago now, I've been giving it very serious consideration."

Dear God, but he wanted to kiss the little furrow between her brows away. "Of that, I am glad."

"Shush, Matthew, I cannot do this if you interrupt."

"Forgive me," he said quickly, trying to look serious though his eyes twinkled.

"But, before I give you an answer, I need to ask you some things and I want you to be entirely truthful with me, even if you fear what you say might hurt me."

Matthew said not a word.

"When you leased the chocolate house to me, why did you do that?"

Caught unawares, Matthew blinked. "Because, because . . . you were an astute businesswoman; Filip and Jacopo sang your praises, and . . . and . . ."

She'd tilted her head to one side, studying him. "And?"

"It made sense."

"Sense! I think there are many men who would argue the contrary."

He sighed. "Very well: the truth. I wanted to keep you close."

"Why? Because of Aubrey? Because even though he'd not yet returned, you knew he lived and what had happened between him and Helene?"

"Partly. I didn't trust the scoundrel and, it turns out, with good cause. After Sir Everard died, I thought if I gave Aubrey the letters that would put an end to it all. I would be able to excise him from my past, and he would leave me alone. I also hoped it would mean he would leave you alone. I admit, I was concerned what he might do should he set eyes upon you." He gave a wistful sigh. "As you now know, by the time I arrived in the colonies, he'd left. It wasn't until I returned to London, understood he was here and intending to insert himself into your life, that I used them to extract from him a promise to leave *you* alone. Fearing exposure, like his father, he didn't dare refuse me."

They stared at each other.

"But," said Matthew, taking one step closer to her, "I also leased the chocolate house to you for entirely selfish reasons. Just as I kept returning to the bookshop all those times in the hope I would see you, get to know you better, listen to you, look at you. Bask in the glow of your laugh, talk to you. I shared my business to ensure I could see you every day. It was the smallest of sacrifices. Forget profit, I was never a canny businessman anyway. I hoped to turn your head and win your heart."

"I see."

"But," he went on, "my plan didn't work very well, did it? You refused my offer of marriage."

"Refused? No. Adjourned, yes." She regarded him seriously. "Which brings me to my next question. A harder one, perhaps." She took a deep breath, lifted her chin, straightened her back and, gesturing to herself, asked, "Am I like Helene?"

If Matthew had been astonished before, his capacity for surprise increased tenfold. "Are you like Helene?"

Rosamund frowned. " 'Tis not a difficult question, sir. All I've heard since I became a Blithman was how much I resemble her. I have seen her portrait and can admit to a likeness. Before he . . . died, Aubrey went so far as to confuse me with his sister. I want to know do *you* think I am like Helene? Because, over the last few days, I've noticed a . . . can I say, a cooling of your evident interest, and I'm wondering if, in light of all that has happened, my similarity to your former wife is too much for you to . . . to . . . contemplate." She lowered her gaze.

All of a sudden, Matthew understood the pain he might cause her if he did not answer this both carefully and truthfully.

"Madam." He held his hands out like a supplicant. "When I first laid eyes on you, yes, I thought you did resemble Helene."

Her face crumpled.

"Your hair, your brows—your coloring is most unusual. Your skin, the fine nose. But, within moments an understanding arose in me that my later meetings with you confirmed over and over. You are nothing like her except in the sense that a person in possession of cropped black hair and of the same sex may be like another with the same coloring and style. In the manner that one green gown with silver piping may be considered similar to another, but all it needs is two different people to wear it and they are nothing alike; just as one pair of brown leather shoes might be said to resemble another—all it requires is for one to sink into mud and there the likeness ends. It's all superficial and meaningless except to those who are shallow and store weight by these things."

With each example, he drew closer to her, until he was standing in front of her. "To me," he said ever so softly, "you are as unique as each star in the sky and just as dazzling. Whether it be your wondrous dark eyes that draw me into your orbit, or the kindness of your spirit, which radiates from you with each and every word and action." Kneeling suddenly, he took her hands in his and willed her to look at him. When she finally did, he drew in his breath.

"It took me no time at all to learn you were nothing like Helene, not to me; in fact, I forgot I ever considered it for a second. One had only to look beyond your obvious physical beauty and see the strong, courageous, sweet heart that beats beneath the apron, look into your soulful eyes and exchange words, ideas with you, to know that below those unruly locks is a clever, considered mind. Helene . . . well, while I do not want to speak ill of the dead, she was in possession of none of those attributes. Moreover," he said, untangling her hands from each other and putting first one then the other on each of his shoulders, being very careful with the bandaged one, before sliding his own warm hands around her waist, "you are someone entirely different. I would be lying if I didn't say I found Helene comely—I did. But I was young, swept off my feet by the gilded frame as much as I was by the picture it contained. What I failed to do, until it was too late, was understand its composition."

He rested his forehead against hers and whispered, "To me, you have never been Helene." He chuckled at such a preposterous notion. "You have always been Rosamund, my Rosamund, *my* Lady Harridan. From the first moment I saw you, I knew what you were. I knew what you could be. I just prayed that one day, you might be mine as well."

There was a gasp.

All he wanted to do was to kiss those soft, soft lips, but he could not. He kept his forehead against hers, his arms about her waist. He felt her tremble. There was an intake of breath, a tremor of shoulders and then they fell. Huge glistening jewels slid down her cheeks. It was almost more than he could bear—but he had to.

"Rosamund," he said, his voice hardly audible. "Please, don't cry. You see, it's my turn to ask you a question."

Unable to speak, she just sniffed in a loud and most unbecoming manner and nodded her head.

"When you were struck down by the fire . . . by Aubrey's attack, and you were in and out of consciousness for a few days, you spoke of—nay, you relived, much of your past."

Rosamund began to cry more freely. She tried to pull away. He wouldn't let her.

"No, no, my love, I don't tell you this to upset you, or make you ashamed. I tell you this to ask you something. Now, dry those tears. Here, allow me." He used his thumbs to whisk them away. "It's evident to me that for many years"—the words were faint, but the violence he wished upon the subject of them was anything but—"you were touched against your will, coerced into a giving of yourself that no one, least of all a man you called father, has any right to force. Bianca told me about your first night at Blithe Manor—the bruises upon your body. When I heard your screams and cries, saw you reliving those times, I understood why, even though I see you smile, hear you laugh, I had also sensed a troubling shadow deep within. Now I know what placed it there. Something within me broke. I thought of the moments I'd stolen a kiss from you, touched you, all the hours I desired you." His voice was hoarse. "I understood that in doing those things, I was no better than the men who compelled you—under whose attention you suffered more than anyone should. I swore I would never again lay a finger upon you unless you gave me the right."

Rosamund began to cry again. As he held her at arm's length, Matthew could barely see her as his own eyes filled.

But he wasn't finished yet.

"I love you, Rosamund. Whether you allow me the honor I request or deny me, it does not change the way I feel. I love you. I always will."

"You still love me?" she asked, her eyes growing wider, unshed tears glimmering like diamonds as the light he feared extinguished began to shine forth. Her radiant wonder at his pronouncement encompassed them both.

"I never stopped. And, before I seal my love with the kiss I long for, I would ask again: Rosamund Blithman, would you do me the honor of becoming my wife?"

Rosamund gave a deep and delicious laugh, throwing her head back, letting it strike the roof and bounce about the room before coming back to reside in her sparkling eyes.

"No, Matthew Lovelace—I would not."

The smile that had been growing on Matthew's face disappeared so suddenly, it was if a candle had been snuffed. "But," he began, as pain seized his chest and made his heart turn over beneath his ribs, "I don't under—"

"Because that's the last question I have for you."

He shook his head in puzzlement. "What?"

Taking his hands in hers, she began to pluck at his gloves. She pulled off first one, then the other, and threw them aside. As she held his hands, she ran her fingers along the ridges, caressed the melted skin before kissing one desecrated palm, then the other. He inhaled sharply, his flesh goosing. He could not credit it.

Then she replaced his scarred hands about her waist, and wriggled so they sat just above her hips, and her knees rested either side of his middle. Having believed all sensation in his fingers was dead, he was astonished to find he could feel her—he could sense her through the fabric, as if she were a musical instrument and he the musician; her body was humming. He longed to pull the material away, touch her flesh.

Leaning in until her lips almost touched his, she took in his breath, his life force, allowing the scents of musk and cinnamon and the heady spiciness of chocolate she always associated with him to capture and hold her, as it always had—as he always had.

"You see, you were chosen for Helene Blithman to mask a terrible sin. I want to undo that by choosing you for myself. So I wanted to ask if you, Matthew Lovelace, would do *me* the honor of becoming my husband."

Matthew made a choking sound.

"Will you promise to always touch me, hold me, love me?"

Matthew's face was like a lanthorn, so richly it glowed. His smile matched hers for warmth, for joy.

"I will," he growled.

Drawn by their words, their lips slowly joined, mouths melting as they sealed their vows. Years of pent-up desire, longing and fear were released in that one moment.

With trembling hands, Matthew twined his fingers through her hair.

As Rosamund fell back on the covers, her hair a shawl of pale gold upon which they both collapsed, laughter burst forth from her, unbridled, exuberant. It rose to the ceiling and cascaded about them until he had no choice but to join her merriment. Resting on his elbows above her, he melded the rest of his body against her, almost shutting his eyes as she rose to meet him.

Allowing her euphoria to wash over him, he watched the way it transformed her face, lifted his soul. He'd never heard anything quite like it. He felt as if he'd touched the heavens and been blessed by all that was holy and pure, so jubilant was her gladness. It lodged in his heart, and he knew the memory of that laugh, of real happiness, would never leave him. Warmed from within, he laughed with her before one kind of ecstasy was replaced with the desire for another.

Her eyes locked onto his, darkened, and her beautiful, perfect lips opened in a different sort of smile.

"Love me now, Matthew," she whispered, and helped him unlace her gown as her fingers, some peeping from the tops of bandages, busied themselves with his clothes.

Matthew's shirt slipped to the floor, his breeches following as his Lady Harridan, still laughing in a devilish, naughty way as her excitement grew, was liberated from the shackles that bound her to an old identity. Cut free, she became what he always knew in his heart she was—his.

Having given her soul to him, her body was surrendered. A gesture of love that took his breath away. Releasing her breasts, those bountiful, beautiful breasts, he did what he'd always longed to do, touched them, touched her. Gently at first, until her groans of pleasure were the permission he'd also been waiting for, emboldened him. Soon, her gown was but a memory, her body, her sweet, luscious body, was his for the taking—and, he thought, as he stared at the beauty being revealed, he'd never known such willingness, such passion, both borne of love.

Their lips joined and parted, reunited and followed the paths trailed first by eager fingers. Silken thighs opened and, as he stroked her, he once more felt that glorious humming, as if he'd immersed his hands in music and, in doing so, brought them, brought himself, back to life. He gave a burst of laughter, pulled her mouth to his as they explored each other with scorching, liquid tongues.

Their simmering flesh grew even hotter, their legs entwined, matching the conjoining of their souls. The world shrank to a tiny attic room as they searched and found, searched and found, as the bud of excitement extended into long ribbons of utter pleasure, before exploding outward in tiny stars of wicked shrieks, giggles and unbridled laughter. Effervescent bubbles of bliss and delight.

The narrow bed with its mussed sheets and blankets became a meadow of sweet flowers, showering them with perfume. The small fire transformed into a burning sun shedding light and warmth just for them as the hours slipped by and their ardor, far from being extinguished, grew and grew, expanding into a universe where only they existed.

Uncertain what he'd done to deserve such a woman, such a soul mate, Matthew sent silent prayers to God and the ancient ones that this coupling might endure.

It wasn't until the embers in the fireplace were a distant mountain whose caldera offered a blaze to the pagan gods and the moonlight streamed through the window offering a road along which they might escape, that they lay beneath the covers, Rosamund's head pillowed on Matthew's chest. Their legs were a plait of flesh, their hearts beat together, but all Matthew could hear was, *She's mine, she's mine and I am hers, hers.*

A noise below brought them to their senses and another bout of laughter as they became aware of how exposed they were—Filip or Will could have walked in on them at any moment. Perhaps, whispered Rosamund in a faux-shocked voice, they already had.

Matthew wouldn't have cared. Nothing and nobody could take away what they had, what they shared and would share again.

Nothing and Nobody. He began to laugh.

"What's so funny?" Rosamund purred, her voice deep with satiation.

Matthew found it very arousing. He could feel her nipples pressed against his flesh, the soft curls of hair between her thighs nuzzling him, and he found it hard to concentrate.

"I was just thinking, remember when you said you were nothing, nobody? You could have been talking about me."

Rosamund rested her palm against his heart. "Ah, but you're Nobody with a capital *N*, which is a synonym for 'Somebody.' All who read your words fear them for the truth they tell and lest they become a target. I am nobody with a small *n* and therefore nothing."

Matthew smiled. Her faith in him was only surpassed by his in her. "Have you never heard the expression, madam, nobody's perfect?"

Much to his delight, Rosamund laughed, a clear, sonorous bell to which his very soul responded. "Truth is," he added, "for a gentleman, I've nothing of real worth to offer you. You at least have a title. I have meager rents from some land, income from my penmanship; you deserve so much more, my lady. In that regard, I am Nobody with Nothing."

"Then we are a fine pair, are we not? Lady Nothing and Mr. Nobody. Let us live on love and dine on passion—that can be what succors us."

"Us perhaps, but what of Bianca? Ashe? Filip, Solomon, Thomas, Mr. Nick and Grace? The others who depend upon us for a living? What will they live upon? For I swear by all that is holy and unholy, I'll not share you."

The happiness that had encircled them briefly dimmed.

"Aye," said Rosamund. "And there's the rub." She sighed. "What will we do, Matthew? We cannot impose upon Sam forever. I mean, I can find some work, I guess. Maybe I can find employ in one of the coffee houses still standing? I can sell the chocolate equipment, that will provide a small sum to tide us over for a while. You have your writing. There is much to record with the rebuilding of London. And didn't you mention that the builders and all those looking to make a profit from the fire will have to be watched closely lest they exploit the needy? There will be a great deal for you to do." She thought. "As for Bianca, well, she is unable to secure any work . . ." She didn't need to tell him that. Because Bianca was deemed a slave, she had no rights; she could be purchased, but never paid.

"There won't be enough to keep us, let alone those who need us," said Matthew. He folded his arms behind his head and stared at the ceiling, at the play of light across it. "If only we had enough to start again, to leave this place, this city, and make a fresh beginning."

Images of the wreckage London had become replaced the lunar glow above. Not even the King's grand plans for a new city could offer them a solution.

"It will be years before London returns to normal," said Matthew.

"I hope it never does," said Rosamund.

Matthew rolled over and looked at her in surprise.

She smiled. "I hope it's reborn. I mean, isn't that what it should be doing? Looking to improve? I said as much to Sam and his friend. Maybe that's what we should do as well. Go somewhere we can have a better life. Where there aren't so many memories." So many shadows.

Matthew's mind began to work fast. Stroking Rosamund's face, running his fingers over her cheeks, marveling that the love he felt for her was not only returned and reflected in her eyes and her touch, but that it magnified his. He began to consider his options . . . their options.

"I do have shares in a ship," he began. "Minor ones, but if I also work for passage, we could leave London . . ."

Rosamund put her hand over his, staying his fingers. "Leave? Where would we go?" she asked, her voice small but filled with possibility.

"Wherever we want," he said, knowing that wasn't entirely true, but wanting the romance.

"France is out of the question," she said. "Holland, too. I don't think I'd like Spain, for while I love Filip, I doubt I could settle in a Papist country, one as strict about faith as we are." She ran her fingers up and down the line of hair from his navel to where the sheet rested just above his groin. If he didn't stop her soon, the sheet would fall off. "What about a place where there is toleration?"

"Toleration?"

"Aye, for faith, for skin color," she said. Her fingers became bolder. "Where women also have opportunities."

"I'm afraid Camelot is too far."

Rosamund laughed again before her face became thoughtful. "Did you like the New World, the colonies?" she asked, kissing his fingers one by one. "I heard there's much can be done there, if one only has the ambition, the desire."

Finding it hard to think, he chuckled. "Well, I'm not short on the latter, and if you keep doing what you're doing, this conversation will be over. But ambition is all well and good—"

"We have that aplenty. Do you think we could start afresh there? Open a chocolate house?"

"I don't see why not. My uncle oft writes there is much of merit there, especially for those prepared to work hard. The only thing stopping us is exactly what's stopping us here—"

"Money," they said in unison.

"We are officially the Nobodies with Nothing," said Matthew.

"Oh, to be somebodies." Rosamund sighed. "Imagine what we could do, Matthew. Sail into a new life along with Bianca, give anyone else who wanted to come with us a chance and give those who wanted to remain behind enough to build their futures upon." She took his hand and placed it over her breast. "Till then, all we can do is hold our vision in our hearts."

Stroking her breast gently, loving how she pressed her body into his hand, arched her back, he bent over her. "I can think of something else we can do as well," he murmured and, once more, turned his long-held dream into a sensual reality.

FIFTY-FIVE
In which Nobody becomes Somebody

When she wasn't recalling her nights with Matthew, shivering with scorching anticipation and remembrance, marveling that a man could be both so gentle and yet so . . . so . . . firm (she blushed), that being touched by a man, by love, could feel so right, so heavenly and so wondrously, deliciously joyous, Rosamund was trying to solve the problem of what the future held.

Sam had generously offered a loan to help them secure rooms so they might have their own place to live, but a chocolate house was beyond his means and her expectations. This was something she had to do for herself—something she and Matthew had to resolve. Matthew spent each day pacing the streets, talking to Mr. Newcombe, the publisher of the *London Ga-*

zette, seeking out stories and, in the evenings, writing them—that was, until he joined her. The money he earned was not much, but if they bided their time, the rents on his land would be due, and if he sold his shares in the ship, in a few months they would have earned enough to secure passage for them all.

Bianca was uncertain whether Filip, Solomon and Thomas would want to come. And if Thomas didn't go, it was unlikely Grace would, so Rosamund asked Sam if he could try to find them work in Whitehall's kitchens. The King and so many courtiers had frequented the Phoenix and praised its chocolate as the best in town. If they really meant it, then who better to make it exclusively for the court than the Phoenix's very own chocolate makers? Especially one who had the cachet of having worked for the King of Spain?

Sam promised he would see what he could do. If that didn't work, Rosamund tried to think of other options but, as Bianca said, they were, like time, fast running out.

Hoping to find some answers in the capital, Rosamund was shocked when she finally walked the streets and was reminded of the devastation. Despite the heavy rains that had fallen, many of the ruins still smoldered, the fires having burned long and hard, melting lead, precious metals and so many books and papers. Word was that deeds, wills and leases had gone up in smoke, causing no end of friction among landholders, business owners and private households. Not that any of that was relevant to Rosamund. When one owned nothing, a missing deed was neither currency nor credit.

Entire streets contained only the blackened bones of what had once stood—shops, houses, taverns, guildhalls and churches. Homeless people, their faces etched by despair and hardship, picked over the ruins. Fights were frequent, theft moreso as families returned and set up camp in what remained of their houses, bringing with them the few things they'd rescued from the flames. Food ran short; people were starving.

Farmers from outside London were encouraged to bring in their goods. The more unscrupulous charged extra, attempting to profit from the city's misery. Some were stoned and run out of town when tempers flared. Others sold their goods at reasonable prices and were welcomed. Workers came from everywhere to help with the rebuilding. Not for altruistic reasons, but because there was coin. It didn't matter—London needed them and they needed the city. It was an uneasy symbiotic relationship.

Rumors still abounded that the fire had been a Papist plot. Dutchmen, Frenchmen, Spaniards and even Italians were hunted down and hauled onto the street;

some were killed in a brutal form of misplaced justice. Even though Parliament and the news sheets swore the fire was an accident, an act of God, no one wanted to believe that God could be so cruel.

Rosamund believed it. She'd witnessed the depths to which He could stoop. But she'd also seen the heights to which He could ascend. Problem was, His benevolence and judgment were so arbitrary and, she quietly thought, patently unfair. Still, she was grateful for Matthew. And for Bianca, Filip, Ashe, Sam and all the others around whom they clustered in these trying days.

The King, so grand and noble while the fire raged, now focused on rebuilding the physical structures of his city—not on the people who had lost so much. Rosamund's heart broke every time she stepped out. If only there was something she could do . . . but how could she hope to help others when she couldn't even offer succor to those who relied on her the most?

One morning an unexpected visitor arrived at Seething Lane. Rosamund received him in Sam's parlor, dressed in a black gown with one subtle piece of ruby embroidery that Elizabeth had kindly loaned her. She looked pale, and there was a fragility about her that disguised a determination honed by the steel of experience—something those enchanted by her smile overlooked to their detriment.

A flaw the lawyer Mr. Bender did not possess.

Bianca was also in a borrowed gown; plainer than Rosamund's, it nonetheless showed the household was in mourning.

"Lady Rosamund," said Mr. Bender, giving her a bow. "Mistress Abbandonato," he said, offering the same to Bianca.

Returning the compliment, Rosamund gestured for him to join her by the window. Bianca took another chair while the Pepyses' maid, Jane, poured some coffee. Filip, Thomas and Solomon had gone with Sam to the palace, so enjoying their chocolate drinks was out of the question, and Rosamund didn't feel comfortable enough in the kitchen to search out ingredients and mix her own. Elizabeth, who was very aware of social rank, would not hear of it anyway. Rosamund respected her hostess's wishes, even as a wayward part of her longed to challenge them. Fortunately, Elizabeth and Sam remained unaware of her and Matthew's nocturnal activities—if they'd known, then chocolate making wouldn't have even rated a mention. The thought made her smile.

"What a lovely surprise, Mr. Bender," she said. "To what do we owe the pleasure?"

Putting down his bowl of coffee, believing the smile on her face was for him and enjoying the way it made him feel, Mr. Bender returned a wide smile to both ladies.

"May I say how glad I am to see you both looking so well. When I first heard what happened at Blithe Manor, how you, Lady Rosamund, were trapped upstairs . . ."

Rosamund had no desire to taste the coffee, but in order to consider her response, bought some time by lifting the bowl and swirling the contents. Screwing up her nose at the bitter smell, she quickly put it back down. No matter what Elizabeth said, she would make a trip to the kitchen after this and make some chocolate.

"If it hadn't been for Mr. Lovelace," she said, "it might be quite a different story. I would have met the same fate as Mr. Blithman."

Bianca gave a discreet cough.

"Ah, yes, Aubrey," said Mr. Bender. "He's the reason I'm here."

Anxiety plucked at her spine.

"Well, not *him* exactly," continued Mr. Bender. "But his holdings."

Rosamund glanced in Bianca's direction, brows raised. As the lawyer drew some papers out of a satchel, she thought yet again about the inferno at Blithe Manor and the losses it entailed. Whereas the London fire had, to date, only four casualties, Blithe Manor had one. Fortunately, apart from Aubrey and, of course, Rosamund, not a single other person was injured. The same couldn't be said for the contents. Not only was every piece of furniture and all her clothes, most of the household goods and the belongings of just about every maidservant and footman destroyed, but also Sir Everard's library and her Aladdin's Cave. All the books and news sheets, pamphlets, booklets and bills reduced to fodder for Aubrey's demented ambitions. All those words of history and poetry and every one of Matthew's letters and pamphlets that she'd savored, transformed into cinders.

That had been the hardest loss to bear. Aubrey's death was beyond awful, no doubt, but she'd be telling falsehoods if she didn't admit—at least to herself—she was relieved he was gone.

The fact he saved her was a bitter pill to swallow. She didn't want to feel a debt of gratitude to him, yet she did. She sent a silent prayer for his soul, wherever it resided.

"You see, my lady," said Mr. Bender, moving the coffeepot and sugar bowl to one side and laying out some papers. "While the fire consumed many legal documents, some lawyers being slow to remove their records to safer places, I was not so remiss. Which, it turns out, is very good news indeed."

"Is it?" asked Rosamund, failing to understand what this had to do with her.

"You see, in light of Aubrey's death, and in the absence of a direct heir, the entire Blithman estate goes to you."

At first Rosamund didn't quite catch what he was saying, she was busy admiring the secretary hand on the pages before her. She only realized he'd said something else when he cleared his throat and she saw Bianca staring at her, eyes wide.

"Beg pardon, my lady," said Mr. Bender, daring to touch her hand where it rested on the arm of her chair. "But do you understand what this means?"

"What *what* means, Mr. Bender?"

Passing her a thick document, Mr. Bender pointed to a list on the first page. "You may have lost the manor house, but that was just the spire on the church, the nib on the quill. The Blithman holdings sustained some losses due to the embargoes in place during the plague and the forfeiture of perishable stock, but they've recouped hefty profits since. Furthermore, the lands Aubrey acquired in Virginia, along with his existing cotton and tobacco plantations, are doing very well, as are the estates Gregory acquired and managed in Guinea up until his untimely death. Even once the Chancery Court takes their percentage, you're a very wealthy woman, Lady Rosamund. Very wealthy indeed." Rosamund saw the figure at the bottom of the third page.

This couldn't be happening. Dazed, her mind whirled. What of the letter that Aubrey had threatened to use and thus render her less than a widow? The one that would have annulled her marriage to Sir Everard?

"Forgive me, Mr. Bender. But did . . .did Aubrey ever give you or make mention of a letter from his father? A report from a doctor?"

Mr. Bender gave her a long, steady look. "No, madam," he said in an expressionless voice. "I do not recall such a letter or report. I do not recall that at all. Now, if I may continue?" He turned a page and went on explaining.

Rosamund continued to stare at him when she heard a word that unsettled her deeply. "Did you say 'slaves,' Mr. Bender?"

"I did indeed. You see, some of your greatest profits are derived from the trade Sir Everard set up when he signed a contract with the Royal Adventurers into Africa. Currently, he has three dedicated slave ships, but with Aubrey's additional two ships—"

Rosamund didn't hear any more. She saw the light go out of Bianca's eyes, her full lips draw back in what was almost a rictus. Without being told, she knew where Bianca's thoughts had traveled. To her long-dead mother, to Jacopo. To those years with the Blithmans. No matter how loyal or clever she was, no matter her paternity, there would always be those who would never let Bianca forget her birth.

"Mr. Bender," said Rosamund, a tad more sharply than she intended.

The lawyer waited expectantly.

Any doubts she had about being in receipt of such beneficence fled. "I want to thank you for bringing me such unexpected news. I think it will take me some time to digest this." Her hands swept the table. "Is it possible to keep these papers so my . . . friend . . . Mr. Lovelace, and my cousin Sam might examine them with me? So Bianca and I might pore over them?"

"Certainly," said Mr. Bender, arranging them in a stack. "I have the originals in my office." He paused. "If I may be so bold, my lady. With such wealth at your disposal, you'll have suitors knocking down your door. I shouldn't be at all surprised if the court approaches you for a loan, what with the privy purse being so . . . tight."

Rosamund inclined her head.

"If I may also proffer a word of advice," he said gently. "From an old father with a lovely daughter to someone of her age and also possessed of great beauty?"

"You may," said Rosamund, a rush of warmth for him blossoming in her smile.

"Regarding the suitors I've no doubt will come in droves once word of this gets out." He held up a finger to halt her protests. "No matter how guarded you might be, my lady, mark my words, it will get out. If there's one thing all Londoners talk about, it's tragedy and money. They can't get enough of either. Except maybe scandal. The news sheets are full of rubbish. If they're not alarming us, they're depressing us or turning us into some kind of moral constables standing in judgment of one another . . ." He took a deep breath. "Forgive me, my lady. Once I get onto the subject, I'm like a preacher at the Cross. What I'm trying to say is, keep your powder dry."

"I beg your pardon?" Rosamund bit back a laugh.

"That is, don't be hasty. If there's one thing money does buy, it's the leisure of time—to make decisions. Better still, to make the right ones."

Rosamund rose. "I thank you, Mr. Bender." Moving around to his side of the table, she dropped a kiss on his cheek, delighting him. "From the bottom of my heart." She returned to her seat. "You know, advice is a funny thing—it's too often given by those least equipped to provide it. But in this case, you're the perfect person and offer the best of its kind. Now, if I may ask some more of you?"

"By all means," he said.

"These slave ships you say I've inherited. I confess, this disturbs me deeply. Part of me always suspected it might be how Sir Everard made his fortune. I've been derelict in not discovering the truth. If only I'd asked Jacopo . . . Dear God. After Sir Everard died, he kept the business going . . ." She flashed an apologetic look at Bianca. "Forgive me that, Bianca. Forgive me."

Bianca gave her a small smile. "There's nothing for you to forgive. Even if you'd known, you had no rights over the business then."

"She's quite right, Lady Rosamund. There was nothing you could have done. No difference you could have made . . . then."

Rosamund stared first at Bianca, then Mr. Bender. "No. Not then." At that moment, Rosamund made up her mind that she would do whatever it took to free Bianca, to rid her of the invisible shackles that bound them to each other and allow her beloved friend to know the joy of liberty and, wherever possible, choice. Taking a deep breath, she gestured to the documents. "What I wish to know: Is it possible to change the purpose of these ships now?"

Out of the corner of her eye, Rosamund saw Bianca's chin rise.

"You mean, from transporting slaves? Of course. It would take time, some money." He chuckled. "But it can be done. Only, if you're interested in making considerable profit"—he avoided looking at Bianca—"then slavery is the way to go. The demand in the New World and the territories being opened up there is—"

"You said yourself, Mr. Bender," interrupted Rosamund. "I'm a wealthy woman. Surely if I wish to change the focus of my shipping business"—the personal pronoun gave her an intense flash of pleasure—"I am now well within my rights to switch from human cargo to something else more . . . palatable." She looked meaningfully at Bianca.

"Ah, er. Quite. Forgive me. Both of you."

With dignity that made a royal wave appear the coarsest of actions, Bianca bowed her head.

They spoke for a further hour as Mr. Bender outlined her immediate obligations. He asked her to sign a few papers and then arranged for her to come to his offices in a week. In the meantime, he left her with a generous purse of coins and advised her to hire a capable man as soon as possible to attend to her interests. Someone she could trust. Possibly an assistant as well, as the holdings were really quite vast.

Barely able to withhold her excitement, she grabbed Bianca's hands and spun her around as soon as Mr. Bender was escorted from the room.

"Can you credit this? Why, Bianca, this is preposterous. This is bloody marvelous!" She danced in circles, her hair coming loose. "I thought I was a nobody, that I had nothing. I've been so worried about what we'll do, but now all my problems are solved. *Our* problems are solved. I am somebody."

Tolerating her mistress's ebullience for a little longer, laughing at her evident delight, Bianca finally shook off her grip and sat down. "Aren't you forgetting something?"

"What's that?" said Rosamund, panting and falling back into her chair.

"You didn't want to be beholden to the Blithmans for anything, and now you are."

"True," conceded Rosamund. "But I also have to be realistic. And the facts are, Bianca, with this kind of money at my disposal, estates, houses, ships and so much more, not only can I make amends—you heard what he said about the slave ships"—Bianca reached for her hands and held them tight—"I can make a difference. A *real* difference."

"To what?" Bianca stared at her mistress, hope radiating from her.

Rosamund leaned forward, her eyes sparkling. "Everything."

FIFTY-SIX

In which a new world beckons on the 4th of March, 1667

The last of the ropes were untied, the anchor weighed and the sails slowly unfurled. Gulls swooped and cawed overhead, their cries competing with those of the sailors clambering up ropes, scurrying across the deck and up and down the stairs between the decks. To stand on the high poop deck of the *Odyssey*, the two-masted ship of which Matthew was now proud sole owner, brought with it a new appreciation of the water and the crowded banks that dissolved into the distance. The wind brought with it the pungent smells of tar, pitch, brine and the pervasive bouquet of human habitation—Deptford was a large port and carried the sins and graces of all such places. From their position on board, Rosamund could see the long line of houses and businesses, the dry dock where Navy ships were repaired, as well as the numerous berths, many of them empty due to the outbreak of more hostilities. Behind her lay the Isle of Dogs; before them the hill that loomed over Greenwich and, at its foot, Greenwich Palace.

They had feared they wouldn't be granted leave to travel because of Dutch aggression and the King's desire to press every man and every ship into service. However, Sam had managed to use his connections in the Navy Office and at court to get them the necessary documents, his job made easier when the gentlemen responsible found out they were for the lovely Lady Rosamund, who'd presided over their favorite chocolate house. Nothing was too much trouble.

Rosamund could just make out Sam, Elizabeth, Solomon, Thomas, Grace and Mr. Bender standing on the dock, waving their hands and their hats, and shouting out final messages of farewell that carried across the water despite all the wherries, barges and fishing boats using this part of the river.

They'd made a jolly group as they traveled down to Deptford by barge the day before to meet the ship, which had been refitted over the last few weeks, and proved a demanding party at the lodge where they stayed overnight, almost draining the cellar dry and eating a season's worth of coneys, eels and mutton, or so the landlady protested. But there'd also been the underlying sadness of imminent farewells.

Rising early to meet the tide, they'd been subdued, especially Sam, whose cheeks were a little green and his eyes bloodshot. Already on board was another group of folk who'd paid a minimum fare for their passage. What they lacked in coin, they made up for in gratitude and willingness to work, both on the journey and once they made landfall.

When Rosamund and Matthew learned that Bianca's Quakers were being hounded by the authorities, who intended to arrest and transport them, they worked tirelessly to squirrel them out of the city and find safe houses where they could wait until such time as the ship was ready to sail.

After the port authorities had done their final sweep of the ship to ensure the cargo was as stated on the documents and excise had been paid on goods leaving the shores, the passenger manifest scrutinized and matched with those already there, only then were the Quakers smuggled on board under cover of darkness. The Great Fire (as it was now called, though in Rosamund's mind there would always be two of those) had meant there were also a number of merchants and their families ready to quit the capital for good and seek their fortune elsewhere. Learning a ship was leaving for the colonies in March, they'd sought out Matthew and begged passage. All those applying were questioned closely, and in the end two families, four couples and three merchants came with them.

The passengers were told to be on board two days before sailing, and had stowed their goods and found their bunks, hammocks and, for the wealthier ones, cabins. When they discovered they were sharing the ship with thirty Quaker families as well, Rosamund and Matthew noted their quiet approval for what they were risking to ensure the Quakers' freedom. It was a pity their tolerance didn't extend to Bianca as well. As they stood on the deck, Rosamund could sense appraising eyes upon her friend, looks Bianca was all too familiar with and was able to ignore, even if she could not. She would never understand how one could be judged so superficially by the color of their skin. Perhaps it was her own experiences that made her peculiarly sensitive to it, but she preferred to think not. She liked to imagine a world where things like that no longer mattered. She prayed the New World might be that place, even though Matthew had reminded her it was no Utopia, merely another version of what they were leaving behind but without many of the social constraints. In other words, a place where opportunities weren't so contingent on birth. For the men, at least. For the women, there was still a long way to go.

It wasn't enough, but it was a start.

The fine mizzle they'd awoken to had long been pushed aside by a cold wind, and a curtain of cerulean was drawn across the heavens as the sun beamed down its warmth, touching their heads and blessing their voyage. The bends in the river obscured most of the city, but the pall of smoke hanging over London from newly erected chimneys and furnaces pinpointed its position as clearly as if God Himself had extended a long, dirty finger. Rosamund wondered if she would miss it very much and decided she wouldn't. It was the people who cried out their farewells on the dock who would carry a little piece of her heart with them for the rest of their lives. For the rest of hers. She wished she didn't have to leave them but, just as she saw her future across the seas, theirs was very much here.

Standing taller than Sam now, Solomon and Thomas stood side by side—Solomon, a grave young man with glorious gray eyes and such dedication and talent, had been given a position in the King's kitchen. Thomas, too, had earned his place. Both of them were to work with chocolate and Sam, who'd helped secure their new roles and promised to watch over them, believed that in time they would rise to become the King's special chocolate makers. If not for this current regime, he'd whispered, then maybe for the monarchs who followed. Rosamund prayed it was true. It was what Filip hoped for them. It's what she wished as well.

Dear Filip. Standing beside her, shedding tears without shame or care, he cried out to his son. Unable to secure a position at court due to his Papist ways and a souring of relations with the Spanish court, he'd no choice but to leave lest he be arrested as a spy. Desiring his son avail himself of such a grand opportunity at the court, he insisted Solomon and Thomas remain. There were objections in some quarters at first, but after Matthew had a word with Sir Henry Bennet and raised Rosamund's name, they magically disappeared. The son would not be punished for the perceived sins of the father.

Rosamund placed an arm around Filip and brought her lips to his ear. "He'll be fine, you know. They both will be."

"I know," Filip wept through his smile. "I know." She kissed him on the cheek and waved back to those on the shore.

She knew he wasn't thinking only of his son and the young apprentice who was now a master, but of Jacopo as well. Her thoughts turned in the same direction, and her heart swelled. Jacopo, Mr. Henderson, Robin, Harry, Owen, Cara and all the others who'd meant so much to her and were now with God. It must be hard for Bianca, leaving the place where Jacopo rested eternally. She found her friend's hand and gave it a squeeze; her own was held tightly in return. Whether it was the wind or her thoughts, Bianca's eyes were suspiciously dewy.

Before she could whisper something to reassure her, Grace raced to the very edge of the dock, cupped her mouth and shouted across the water. "Thank you for the chocolate and stuff!"

Filip shook his head. "The *señorita* will be a *molinillo's* worth of trouble."

He was not wrong.

A month earlier, Grace had moved in with Mrs. Tosier, Thomas's aunt, who determined to teach the girl both manners and her letters, much to the young one's objection. All Grace wanted was to be with Thomas and, if she had to satisfy herself with seeing him on his half days off for the time being, it would suffice. But that girl would carve her own path in life—and Thomas's, thought Rosamund with a smile. Obsessed with chocolate, Grace was also fixated on Thomas. Rosamund had given her a silver chocolate pot, a *molinillo* and a lovely porcelain bowl along with some chocolate cakes. Wide-eyed and uncertain how to thank her, having never been given such a glorious gift, Grace threw her arms around Rosamund and wept a storm. As her cries subsided Rosamund had peeled her away and kissed her tearstained face.

"I . . . I'm . . . I'm going to be just like you . . . I am . . . Lady Rosamund. A chocolate maker. Just you wait and see . . ."

Rosamund did not doubt it.

She'd also tried to gift Solomon and Thomas the chocolate-making equipment, but they'd declined.

"The King's kitchen is well appointed," said Thomas. "We've no need."

"You and Papa will need it more than us, *señora*," said Solomon shyly. "You must take it with you, and thus a part of us, over the seas—take our chocolate to the settlers there."

This time, it was Rosamund's turn to cry. She did, however, insist they take a silver chocolate pot and *molinillo* each.

Unbeknownst to them yet, Rosamund had arranged with Mr. Bender to settle a tidy sum upon all three, enough to secure them a comfortable future—as royal chocolatiers, business owners, or whatever else they might choose to be. A generous dowry ensured Grace could select her own husband and not be subject to what she'd endured, treated as a chattel for men to own, control or dispose of at will. Whatever their hearts desired, they would one day be able to realize, though she suspected, when it came to Thomas, it would be whatever Grace desired. Bless her.

As the wind filled the sails, the distance between them grew and her stomach lurched. She could just see Grace's quirky hat and the little bunch of mauve and ivory flowers she persistently shoved down the front of her dress. Rosamund wore a matching bunch against her décolletage. Touching it lightly, she knew these tiny white and purple flowers would always make her think of Grace, just as chocolate would always make her think of Jacopo and the young men who'd trained beside her, who along with Filip had helped her through so many setbacks to rise and become a success. She hoped that the wave that had lifted her would keep them all buoyant for a long, long time.

Among those she was leaving behind, it was Sam who stood out. He'd come to join Grace and was standing with her, his hand shielding his eyes. Dear Sam. What an odd and wonderful relation he'd turned out to be. Irrepressible, oft times inappropriate but with a bundle of goodwill, he'd proved the staunchest of friends. All he required was to be listened to and admired. It hadn't been a difficult exchange. For all his faults and peccadilloes, he was what he was, her cousin, her little naval clerk who, the moment he set eyes upon her, ensured their faint familial connection was made real. She'd miss him.

As the sails snapped she waved madly. The ship was carried forward, around a bend and toward the open sea and their new home. She glanced up at Matthew. He stood behind her, one hand upon her waist, and smiled down at her. Aye, wherever they went, wherever they settled, she'd found home. It wasn't a place—it was a person. It was Matthew.

Was it justice or irony that those who sought to use her to destroy Matthew were also responsible for this? For them finding each other? Maybe, in the end, God was laughing. The Blithmans were now, in death, recompensing for their mighty, terrible transgressions—each and every one of them.

From the day Mr. Bender revealed her change of fortune, Rosamund decided it was justice of the heavenly kind and didn't question it further. Satisfied Aubrey's proof—if it had ever existed—that her marriage to Sir Everard was invalid had burned along with him, she accepted God's and the Blithmans' gift gracefully. She would use it to make life better for all those she loved. She'd done what she could for those remaining in London; she would do the same for Matthew, Bianca,

Filip, Ashe and Mr. Nick in their new home. She was aware of Bianca soothing Ashe, who looked so nervous being on a ship but would not consider remaining behind. She bestowed a warm smile and silently thanked God for both of them.

Of all the extraordinary things that had happened, and of all the people who'd come into her orbit, it was Wat Smithyman who proved to be strangest. Understanding he'd unwittingly aided and abetted the Blithmans in the most heinous of crimes, now the man could not do enough for her. Like Rosamund, he wanted to shed the skin of his old life, grow a new one—not only in the New World but at the side of the woman and man he'd once mistakenly thought a social-climbing trull and a murderer and despised. Appointed Matthew's assistant along with Mr. Nick, he'd proved his worth over and over in the weeks leading up to their departure. Before Christmastide, he'd gone ahead to Boston to find a house and premises in which they could start their new venture, and he'd sent word he'd found the most perfect of sites and was even now, as they sailed, preparing them for their arrival. Could Rosamund trust him? Not yet, but knowing Mr. Nick was over there with him did much to soothe her concerns. She would give Wat time. As Mr. Bender said, she now had the luxury of buying as much of it as she wished.

With the exception of one thing . . .

There was one count of time that no one could delay. It was a period God decided and no man or woman could tear asunder. Resting a hand on her stomach, she felt a rush of heat fill her body. Though the child within didn't show yet, she would be born in a new world, a world where she had both a mother and a father and a ready-made unconventional family to cherish her, give her strength, love, protection and tell her oh-so-many marvelous stories. She would one day know pain—one could not live and grow without it—but not abuse. She would never be abandoned, except to the sunshiny blessedness of wonderment. In her world, curiosity would be her breakfast, imagination her dinner and the dreamy silkiness of chocolate and words her supper.

As she looped her arm through Matthew's, Rosamund saw the captain approaching. With him was a man in plain garb, a book tucked under his arm.

"Are you ready?" she asked Matthew, the stiff breeze trying desperately to lift off her hat and unravel her hair.

Matthew's smile broadened. "I've been ready since the moment I knew who you really were. My heart." He bent and captured her lips with his own, withdrawing slowly. She would never grow tired of those eyes, those twilight eyes with their touches of violet. Dazzling, they were filled with a pulsing light and what she knew was love and a healthy respect—all reserved just for her. She felt the familiar bubbling starting deep inside her chest. Dear God, ever since she'd admitted her love for Matthew, that reservoir she'd kept locked away inside her for so many years was refilled day after day. Being with him brought nothing but joy. Forget the wealth, the opportunities the Blithmans had bestowed upon her; the greatest gift they had given her was this man.

God bless the Blithmans, she thought, and with it, the last of the shadows that had haunted her for so many years fled.

Never before had she so many reasons to smile, to laugh with the springtime abandon of her childhood. What would her grandmother say? Master Dunstan? She decided they'd be happy for her—though her grandmother would remind her to maintain her dignity. *Oh, fuck dignity,* she thought, *it's my wedding day. My day,* and she wanted to laugh even more. Even better, she knew this wasn't the most glorious of days, it was simply one of many that had already been and were yet to come.

To think, Paul Ballister, his thuggish, brutal twins and her uncaring mother had tried to make her see the world through their blighted eyes, as a dark, dismal place where trust was broken, hearts were cruel and bodies and lies were currency. Being married to Sir Everard, learning the extent of his deceits, his family's sins and their legacy, had almost confirmed it.

Matthew had taught her to see the good in the world again. What was just and true. So had Bianca, by teaching her to read. Oh, she knew there was darkness and horror—dear God, not only had she survived so much of it, but all she had to do was think of Bianca and she was given a staunch and clear reminder of humanity's capacity for cruelty—and foolishness. Nevertheless, wherever possible, she would try to choose mercy and allow others to see, by her example, the wonder it created.

This was what she'd establish with her new chocolate house. A place where people could come to forget and remember. To forget their troubles and to remember what makes them laugh: companionship, good food, music, poetry, stories, news, gossip; being reminded that for all you might think your life is woeful, there are those who fared far worse.

Matthew had also, through his words, taught her to search for reasons and find answers—and to seek the good even through the evil. Wade through wrong to find right and stand by it. He did that as a correspondent; he did it as Matthew Lovelace, too, making sense of the world, acknowledging that honesty and corruption coexisted, and in the end it's all down to individual choices. The important thing was to make the right ones.

Matthew was her choice, and she was his. Love had risen from the ashes because, when she was given the chance, she chose well. She almost hadn't, and that thought terrified her.

"My lady, sir, I believe you know Mr. Hershey," said Captain Browning, pulling off his hat and introducing a tall man who kept his on. One of the Quakers Bianca knew, Mr. Hershey often acted as spokesperson for the other Friends, and had been instrumental in helping Matthew and Rosamund rescue many beyond Bianca's group.

"Hope you don't mind," said the captain, "but he tells me there are others who wish to bear witness to the ceremony. I said it would be fine, especially now we're away from Deptford. After all, it's not every day we have a marriage on board."

Not only had the other passengers come forward to watch, but as many sailors as possible ceased their tasks. Best of all, coming up from the belowdecks were the rest of the Quakers, blinking in the light and inhaling the fresh river air. They looked toward where Rosamund, Matthew, Filip and Bianca stood, Ashe clutching another bunch of flowers that Grace had thrust into her hands, smiles breaking out on their faces.

Thus it was, as they sailed along the Thames and the sun reached its peak before sliding toward the horizon, that the captain of the *Odyssey*, watched by his crew, a Spanish chocolate maker, a former slave, rescued Quakers and paying passengers, performed his first marriage.

Rosamund Blithman became Rosamund Lovelace.

Busy exchanging vows with Matthew, she never noticed as they sailed past Gravesend. Her heart and mind were fixed on the man holding her hands and gazing into her eyes with such devotion, a world of sacred promises radiating from his face—and on controlling the laughter that threatened to overcome her and interrupt the ceremony. It was the laughter that comes when hearts' desires are realized, when the future is sunrises, rainbows, fresh falls of soundless snow and shared burdens.

Unable to hold it back any longer, as they sealed their promises to each other with a long and not-so-chaste kiss, and a cheer rose from all those who'd witnessed the union, Rosamund let it ring out. Uninhibited, otherworldly, it was a clarion. For a moment, silence fell upon the ship before, as one, everybody—even the usually reticent Quakers—threw back their heads and laughed as well. Powerless to resist Rosamund's joy, the passengers threw their arms around one another, women and girls were swung in wide arcs, their skirts flying up. Children stamped; men cried out in glee. From somewhere came the music of pipes, and dancing commenced. Ashe was swept into the fray before Bianca and then Filip were taken too.

Eyes sparkled, mouths were filled with mirth, hearts and souls soared. The captain guffawed the loudest at the laughing siren on the poop and the bell-like sound she emitted, which announced a God-blessed union like no other.

It was the same laughter a newborn child gave the day she came into the world, not knowing the misery and misfortune that would take her down a sometimes-dark path toward damnation, but understanding in the deep instinctive way that only those who have recently left the abode of angels do, that one day, God willing, all would be set aright.

A devil and an angel would see the beauty in each other and joy would be reborn, tenfold, a hundredfold; joy with all its bittersweet promise.

And love. One could not forget love.

Or a bowl of sweet, dark chocolate.

Author's Note

Little did I know as I began my research on chocolate, England in the 1660s and the Restoration, an era about which I knew a little, that by the time I was ready to write almost two years later, I would be completely besotted and challenged by the period.

It was a naughty, violent, politically and religiously fraught, dangerous, cruel, exhilarating and incredibly sensual time. Poverty and wealth existed side by side; resentments, racism and xenophobia ran deep, and so did plots. Increasingly literate people stretched their religious and other rights and sought to be free of the constraints the King imposed on them in a variety of ways. Arts and theater flourished, as did the sciences. But war was omnipresent, and fear of a return to the chaos of the Civil War dominated many people's minds and motivations. Women began to make their presence felt in science, literature, arts and business—so much so, as Antonia Fraser writes in *King Charles II,* "the position of women in the second half of the seventeenth century was in many ways preferable to their position in the nineteenth."

It was so easy to lose myself in this era, and it is a testament to the splendid academics, historians, journalists, diarists and novelists, as well as artists and musicians and their work, that it's been such a fascinating delight and provocation. While I won't mention them all (there's no room), I do wholeheartedly thank those people I read, listened to, studied, watched, devoured and, mostly, learned from.

I also did some on-the-ground research, going to London in 2017 and traveling around the UK and parts of Europe. Before leaving Australia, I contacted David Gottlier of Bowler and Hatte tours and spent the most marvelous time in London with him, walking the streets of my characters, visiting monuments, churches and important buildings, most of which appear in the novel, as well as many of the sites where chocolate houses and some coffee houses (including Pasqua Rosée's Turk's Head—purportedly the first—Garraway's, Lloyd's, etc.) had stood. David was a tireless and knowledgeable companion who tailored his time to my specifications (and then embellished), and I'm grateful to him for sharing his wisdom and tolerating my endless questions.

But before I go into where fiction interweaves, diverges from or collides with fact in the novel, I should explain how I came upon the idea of writing about a chocolate house/maker. I'd heard about coffee houses, but the idea of a chocolate one was completely new to me. I was in the UK in 2014, fine-tuning research for my earlier novel, *The Brewer's Tale*, and researching the subsequent one, *The Locksmith's Daughter*, and traveled out to Hampton Court one day with my dear friend Dr. Lesley Roberts. We saw a sign directing us to a chocolate room. Unable to help ourselves, we trotted along the cloisters to find it, only to be greeted by a very long queue. Having a natural aversion to queues, we sighed, continued past and struck gold. Further along, uninhabited by people, was a small room, blocked by a rope, filled with an assortment of shiny utensils, mortars and pestles, pretty bowls and saucers and an array of interesting objects. The sign above declared it was a chocolate kitchen, and it was where a man named Thomas Tosier, the King's chocolate maker, would prepare King William's favorite drink. If that didn't tweak my imagination, then the picture hanging on the wall certainly did. It was of a homely woman of middling age, dressed in an ordinary gown with a large hat and a bunch of flowers shoved into her décolletage. Her name was Grace Tosier, wife of Thomas, who, the information beneath announced, had a famous chocolate house in Greenwich and was renowned for both the chocolate drinks she made and what went on behind its doors.

That was it. One look at Grace and the chocolate kitchen and my imagination went into overdrive. There and then I said to Lesley, I am going to write a book and it's going to be called *The Chocolate Maker's Wife*. Initially, I thought it would be about Grace, but as I began my research, I found I was more interested in how chocolate first came to England, how it was received and those early places that built a business out of it, borrowing ideas from the fast-growing coffee houses and what they learned from Spain and other parts of Europe. Grace does appear in the novel, as a young apprentice/helper in Rosamund's kitchen, where she shows not only her devotion to the apprentice Thomas Tosier (yes, poetic license allowed me to ensure he made a start there too), but her general quirkiness and penchant for flowers.

So, Thomas and Grace existed. So too did Solomon de la Faya, as a chocolate maker (first, to King Charles II and later, his brother James), though his father, Filip, and their beginnings, are my invention. Of the main characters in the book, the only other *major* one to have lived and breathed the period was Samuel Pepys. It must be very difficult to write about the 1660s without reference to his amazing, funny, detailed, shameless and chatty diary. After reading a few biographies of Pepys—to set a context and get to know the fellow better (and I thoroughly recommend Claire Tomalin's *Samuel Pepys: The Unequalled Self* and Robert Latham's *The Shorter Pepys*, as well as Stephen Porter's *Pepys's London*, which also sets a terrific framework), I resorted to his diaries. They were originally written in code (probably so his wife didn't find out about all his masturbatory fantasies and peccadilloes—he even coded in French!), and it wasn't until they were eventually "found," put aside, "discovered" again and, in a series of fortunate events (or what Tomalin calls a "tragi-comedy"), translated, that the world was able to read Pepys's observations about everything from comets to naval matters, people, major and minor events, personal triumphs and tragedies and even his bowel movements. Available online as well, these diaries, which span ten years, are a fantastic resource, and I confess to quite falling in love with the funny little man with the sharp mind, dedication to duty and awareness of his growing social rank. I couldn't *not* include him in my novel, adding more inventive flesh to the meaty bones he left us.

Every time Sam appears in the novel (with the exception of his interactions with Rosamund et al.) and mentions what he's been doing, whom he's seen, where he's gone and why, what he's accomplished (or not), the references to his house (for example, the renovations it undergoes), his wife and his duties, it is accurate according to his diary. From Pepys, I was able to gauge the weather, the whereabouts of other historic figures on particular days—including the salacious deeds of Buckingham, Sedley and co., various duels, theatrical performances and so much more—the condition of the roads and other little gems that I've tried, where appropriate, to incorporate, including the sighting of the two comets.

Sam lived through the plague and the Great Fire. The former he relished and often referred to the plague year as one of the happiest and most fulfilling of his life. The scenes with Sam and the Great Fire, where he went and whom he spoke to and who stayed at his house (apart from Rosamund) are also precise according to his diary.

I have occasionally taken liberties with Sam—mainly in his scenes with Rosamund or at the chocolate house and Blithe Manor. I like to think he would forgive me for that and, hopefully, enjoy his role in the story.

Sam also underwent the surgery he describes to Rosamund early in the book. Suffering from kidney stones his entire life, Sam's bravery and the pain he must have been enduring to even contemplate such a risky procedure is mind-boggling. He was the first patient on the surgeon's list that day. Apparently, most of the other patients who also had surgery that day died—probably from being operated on with unclean instruments. It's no wonder that every year Sam had an annual dinner to celebrate his survival, exhibiting his stone, which he kept in a jar.

There are many real historical figures populating the book and the chocolate house, from King Charles II and his chief mistress, Lady Barbara Castlemaine, to Sir Henry Bennet (who really did wear a plaster on his nose), Joseph Williamson, the Earl of Clarendon, the Earl of Rochester, the Duke of Buckingham, Sam's servants, relations and acquaintances, Charles Sedley, Robert Boyle, John Evelyn (another famous diarist whose works were also invaluable) and Lord and Lady Sandwich. A full list of historical figures and fictional ones is included for the curious. Just as an aside, I should also add that Matthew Lovelace is the fictitious son of a famous poet of the times, Richard Lovelace. There is no record of Richard ever having had a son, so it was easy to create Matthew. The poetry of Lovelace is both political and of the heart, and I tried to imagine what kind of son a man who could produce such lovely language and thoughtful verses might have. Matthew is the result. Matthew's uncle Francis also existed and was later appointed the governor of the colony of New York—though he ended his life in ignominy in an English jail.

Apart from the ships of the Blithman fleet and Matthew's *Odyssey*, every ship mentioned was real, including the doomed *London*, which really did blow up and kill three hundred women and children. Even the *Black Eagle*, which Fear-God and Glory were press-ganged to serve upon, was real, and not only was the captain arrested, but it did indeed have a hull full of infected Quakers, causing the crew to abandon ship and thus spread the pestilence.

The information about the transmission of the plague, including the figures in the Bills of Mortality, the crowded church services, the awful slaughter of dogs, cats and other animals, the evacuation of London, the removal of the court to Oxford and their subsequent appalling behavior, the heat and swarms of flies, all really happened. People were shut up in houses once infection was discovered—even the uninfected—for forty days and guards were posted and crosses painted. Bells tolled relentlessly, burial pits were dug as the churches' graveyards filled. The women who visited the infected really did garner a bad reputation for killing them and stealing—some deserved—though there were also those who showed remarkable compassion, bravery and dedication. Descriptions of people running naked, spitting, dying where they fell, etc., are all documented. It's heartbreaking to read.

Some terrific books I read which covered the plague were Stephen Porter's *London's Plague Year* and *The Great Plague*; *The Plague and the Fire* by James Leasor; Daniel DeFoe's *A Journal of the Plague Year*; and Rebecca Rideal's *1666: Plague, War and Hellfire*—a wonderful addition to the plague (and Great Fire) canon. Of course, many books about Stuart London have chapters dedicated to the plague as well.

Then there is fantastic fiction: Geraldine Brooks's (no relation, sadly) marvelous *Year of Wonders* remains one of my favorites. *The Darling Strumpet* by Gillian Bagwell was terrific; Charlotte Betts's *The Apothecary's Daughter*, *Plague* by C. C. Humphreys and the wonderful *The Vizard Mask* by Diana Norman were also superb reads.

The movements of Sam and the royals during the

Great Fire are accurate, as is the description of the flames' devastating path, what burned and what happened to the dispossessed. According to official records, only four people died. This has since been contested as the homeless, the very poor, Quakers, Jews and other "dissenters" would not have been accounted for—similarly with the plague figures.

The Great Fire was a catastrophe of biblical proportions. Coming on the back of war and plague and considering approximately three-quarters of the city burned, London's recovery (which took decades—not the three years contemporaries claimed) was remarkable. Starting in Thomas Farriner's bakery in Pudding Lane, it swiftly spread. Allegedly it was finally stopped in Pye Corner, where, according to historians, it continued to burn and smolder for weeks after. But there's something neat and poetic in the notion that what started in Pudding ended in Pye, hence the chapter title. There are various monuments erected in remembrance of what happened, the most famous being the huge Doric column at the junction of Monument Street and Fish Street Hill. At one stage, the plaque at the base of the monument blamed Catholics for starting the fire. This was later removed. Sadly, Robert Hubert, a native of Rouen and a watchmaker who'd worked in London, maintained he started the fire, throwing fireballs into

Farriner's window (there was no window where he said). While the authorities knew he didn't do it (and that he was mentally ill, though they wouldn't have described it that way then), due to his own testimony, he was hanged on the 29th of October, 1666.

Really useful books covering the Great Fire were Walter George Bell's *The Great Fire of London in 1666*, Stephen Porter's *The Great Fire of London*, Neil Hanson's *The Dreadful Judgement*, Adrian Tinniswood's *The Great Fire of London: The Essential Guide, 1666* and Rebecca Rideal's book above, and again, many other general books or those focusing on Charles II also dealt with both the plague and the fire, each one revealing different aspects and details.

For general books on the era, including those on Charles II as well as about his father and the Civil War led by Oliver Cromwell, I found Geoffrey Robertson's *The Tyrannicide Brief* so informative and helpful; likewise, Jenny Uglow's *A Gambling Man: Charles II's Restoration Game* was invaluable. As always, Antonia Fraser's *King Charles II* and her magnificent *The Weaker Vessel* were essential reading. Peter Ackroyd's *Rebellion* and *The King's Bed: Sex, Power and the Court of Charles II* by Don Jordan and Michael Walsh were great reads, as was Jordan and Walsh's *The King's Revenge*. Julian Whitehead's *Rebellion in the Reign of*

Charles II, which I purchased last minute in Glasgow on my research trip, was a complete gem of a book. Gosh, this list is growing, but there is more: so many fabulous works of fiction, including *Girl on the Golden Coin* by Marci Jefferson, *Royal Escape* by Georgette Heyer, Jean Plaidy's *The Loves of Charles II,* Andrew Taylor's *The Ashes of London,* Susanna Gregory's Thomas Chaloner series and Edward Marston's Christopher Redmayne series. My absolute favorite, if I have to pick one, would be *Restoration* by Rose Tremain and the sequel, *Merivel: A Man of His Times.* Wait! I also cannot go past Iain Pears's *An Instance of the Fingerpost.* What a book. This is just a sampling of some of the books I read to help me understand and immerse myself in this period. I have reviewed many on my website and on Goodreads.

One of the first books on chocolate I read (and reread) was Sophie D. Coe and Michael D. Coe's *The True History of Chocolate.* A sublime, erudite and wonderful read, it takes the reader right back through time and to cacao's origins, its introduction to the world and how it became, basically, an economic tour de force as well as a taste sensation, imbued with all sorts of connotations, many sexual. It doesn't steer away from chocolate's dark and shocking relationship to humans—specifically, slavery and the exploitation of local populations in Africa, South America and other colonized outposts so the Western world might indulge in "sin in a bowl."

I also want to recommend Dr. Kate Loveman's fabulous work on the history of chocolate and acknowledge her enthusiastic response to an early email I sent her outlining my project. Among the many other books on chocolate and its history that were very useful were: *Chocolate: History, Culture, and Heritage* edited by Louis Evan Grivetti and Howard-Yana Shapiro; James M. Bugbee's *Cocoa and Chocolate: A Short History of Their Production and Use* (1886); *A Curious Treatise of the Nature and Quality of Chocolate* by Antonio Colmenero de Ledesma, translated by Don Diego de Vades-forte (1640)—the treatise Rosamund tries to read and finally masters did exist and is very readable, if dry in parts; *The Indian Nectar, or, a Discourse Concerning Chocolata* by Henry Stubbe (1662); *Chocolate: A Global History* by Sarah Moss and Alexander Badenoch; *Taste: The Story of Britain Through Its Cooking* by Kate Colquhoun; *Chocolate, Women and Empire* by Emma Robertson; *The Chocolate Plant: Theobroma Cacao and Its Products* by Ellen H. Richards; and *Sacred Gifts, Profane Pleasures: A History of Tobacco and Chocolate in the Atlantic World* by Marcy Norton.

Chocolate and its relationship to slavery must be acknowledged, and I only really brush on it in this novel. Immediately after this period, human rights abuses and terrible injustices occurred. They are arguably still occurring. I think it's really important to be aware of this. In writing this book, I found it a struggle to accept that the production of something so delicious could also be such a damning indictment on humanity.

During the period in which the book is set and afterward, slavery was growing, and the brutal, inhumane treatment of African people was wrenching to research, as was that of the South and North American natives during what was regarded in Europe as a time of conquest and discovery—something that involved so much bloodshed, trampling of human dignity and gross mistreatment in the name of kings, queens, power, faith and country. I don't delve too deeply into this except tangentially with Matthew Lovelace's observations and, of course, the way Bianca and Jacopo are generally treated. But it's important to know that there were people, even back then, who were appalled by slavery and the vicious and cold-hearted justification for abuse on the basis of skin color. Not that it prevented slavery continuing for a long time afterward. People like Rosamund and Matthew did exist, just as those arguing for religious and other tolerations did as well. Some of the books I read in order to understand this better include: *The Logbooks: Connecticut's Slave Ships and Human Memory* by Anne Farrow; *Classic Slave Narratives* by Frederick Douglass; and *African Voices on Slavery and the Slave Trade*, edited by Alice Bellagamba, Sandra E. Greene and Martin A. Klein.

The other specific group to have a long and complicated relationship with chocolate was the Quakers, or Friends. This really developed after the time the book ends, though I do hint at it—first, by including two main Quaker characters but also by having persecuted Quakers (and they really were treated terribly by Charles's government) aboard the ship Rosamund and Matthew sail to the New World at the end. The presence of Mr. Hershey (of chocolate fame) is no accident and, as Quakers were regarded as exceptional businessmen (because they were considered honest and fair), you can imagine the conversations that might have occurred en route to Boston.

Many of the well-known major chocolate companies have their origins with Quakers: e.g., Cadbury, Rowntrees, Fry's. Quakers also introduced very fair working conditions—for white men and women (while, sadly, exploiting black workers)—education programs and

health care, and they were among the first abolition-
ists as well. Researching the Friends' incredible history
was enlightening to say the least, and I owe a huge debt
of gratitude to the wise and wonderful Mark Nicholson for a conversation on my stoop about Quakers and
chocolate. Because of him, the book took a particular
direction, and I learned so much. Also, his lovely wife,
Robin McLean, a Friend and my friend, furthered my
relationship with the Friends and took me to a Meeting
in Hobart, where I experienced their fellowship and
was so very warmly welcomed. Mark and Robin also
hosted a lunch so I could further expand my knowledge
and ask a thousand questions of the patient and knowledgeable Dr. Peter Jones, a scholar of Quakerism and
much more besides. It was from him and the academic
articles he subsequently sent me that I learned there
could indeed be "Quakers of color" such as Bianca and
Jacopo.

I also read the writings of George Fox and James
Nayler, the "founding fathers" of Quakerism, as well
as more recent writings such as Rosemary Moore's
*The Light in Their Consciences: The Early Quakers
in Britain, 1646–1666*, H. Larry Ingle's *First Among
Friends: George Fox & the Creation of Quakerism* and
the marvelously named Pink Dandelion's very useful
The Quakers: A Very Short Introduction.

The time in which the novel was set is also regarded as the birth of journalism as we know it (for better and worse). Roger L'Estrange and Henry Muddiman and their news sheets, news books and handwritten pamphlets all existed. Correspondents wrote both under their own names and anonymously. L'Estrange and Muddiman had "sources" planted everywhere to report to them various goings-on, and people clamored for the type of news and gossip they printed. The clamp-down on the presses really happened, as did the punishments mentioned. The men who died for their craft and a stubborn belief in what we call the "freedom of the press" were all real people. I found the whole history of journalism and publishing fascinating, especially when I discovered the words "false news" were often leveled at antigovernment stories—an echo of how the term "fake news" is used to discredit journalists and newspapers today. In the seventeenth century, there was a concerted effort to control the dissemination of information and ensure that only "good" things were written about the King and his government—of course, it failed. I always say this, but the more I learn and write about the past, the more resonances I find in the present. It's scary.

Some fabulous books that explored the complex and volatile history of newspapers and journalism were *The*

Restoration Newspaper and Its Development, by James Sutherland, and *Read All About It!: A History of the British Newspaper* by Kevin Williams.

It was in London's coffee and chocolate houses that news was shared, and dissent in many forms was born—you really cannot explore one without reference to the other. Chocolate and coffee houses were quite democratic in that anyone (male) could enter, providing he could pay for his drink. Nobles literally drank with people of lower social ranks and communicated with them. A sober pastime, drinking chocolate and coffee became associated with the distribution of information up and down the social scale. Because literacy was increasing and people had access to news in a way that was unprecedented, it was natural they sought to challenge, if not overturn, the status quo, which was very threatening for the powers that be. So much so that in 1675 Charles II tried to close the coffee and chocolate houses, believing they posed such a threat. There was an outcry, and he was forced to back down.

Almost immediately after the book ends, around 1680, newspapers as we recognize them were born, and the coffee houses of Garraway's (which existed during Rosamund's time) and Lloyd's (which came soon after and metamorphosed into the famous Lloyd's of London) were host to the kind of debates, auctions—including candle auctions—and gossip that occur at the Phoenix. The political parties of Whigs and Tories have their origins in these houses, and many, many plots against the government and/or their opponents were hatched beneath their smoky roofs. Chocolate houses that encouraged this kind of discourse and political affiliations sprang up, such as Ozinda's and White's in St. James's Street and the Cocoa Tree in Pall Mall—but these were established well after the book finishes. The relationship between the printed word, politics, dissension and chocolate and coffee was very real.

Some of the fascinating books I used that explore the history of the coffee houses are Brian Cowan's *The Social Life of Coffee: The Emergence of the British Coffee House*; Markman Ellis's *The Coffee House: A Cultural History*; Anthony Clayton's *London's Coffee Houses: A stimulating story*. Again, all references to coffee houses in the novel and their owners and locations, with a couple of exceptions, are factual.

For general information on the era, including language, clothes, fabrics, houses, etiquette, politics, major and minor events, social customs, etc., I used Liza Picard's thoroughly entertaining and wonderfully detailed *Restoration London* as well as *Daily Life in Stuart England* by Jeffrey Forgeng and *The Growth of Stuart London* by Norman G. Brett-James. Ian Mortimer's marvelous *The Time Traveller's Guide to Restoration Britain*, which I only found as I began the official edit, was terrific. One book I found so helpful and amusing was *The Canting Academy, or, The Devil's Cabinet Opened Wherein Is Shewn the Mysterious and Villainous Practices of That Wicked Crew, Commonly Known By the Names of Hectors, Trapanners, Gilts* by Richard Head (is that his real name? I wonder), written in 1673. It explores the patois of the day and helped make some of the language my characters deploy more colorful and accurate to the era.

All books and other publications mentioned in the novel existed at the time as did their authors.

I have been asked numerous times if I ate or drank much chocolate while writing this book . . . Of course I did! How often can a person down drinks of dark chocolate or stuff their mouth with seventy percent cacao and liquor-filled treats, and claim it's for research? I tasted good, bad, rich, decadent, watery, powdery, ghastly, scrumptious, moreish and irresistible drinks and food. Before you ask, the best drinks I had were in Pittenweem in Scotland (an amazing place with a dark history which will feature in my next novel), and Venice—in Venice, my spoon quite literally stood up in the drink, it was so thick and luscious. Nutpatch in Hobart, Tasmania, makes divine chocolates—try to stop at one—but I also enjoy Lindt and Cadbury. Understanding cacao's history better meant I felt guilty the entire time I was eating or drinking. It truly became a guilty pleasure, which I think sums up the relationship we have with chocolate—for all sorts of reasons—perfectly.

While I take great care to make my story as historically accurate as possible, it is primarily a work of fiction, written from my crowded head and full heart. Every accurate fact is due to the diligence and hard work of all the wonderful writers I have mentioned (and many more I didn't), and I thank them profusely. Any mistakes are happy accidents of creativity or, let's face it, "whoops" moments (I cringe and pray they're not held against me), and I do humbly beg your pardon and take full responsibility.

Mostly, I hope you enjoyed reading *The Chocolate Maker's Wife* as much as I loved writing it.

—Karen Brooks
Hobart, 2018

List of Characters

Real and Imagined (in no particular order)
The ones marked ★ are actual historical figures.

Jacopo Abbandonato

Bianca Abbandonato

Adam

★Duke of Albemarle

★John Allin

★Henriette-Anne,
  Charles II's sister

Art

Widow Ashe

Avery

Fear-God Ballister

Glory Ballister

Paul Ballister

Tilly Ballister

Sissy Barnes

★Lady Elizabeth Batten

★Sir William Batten

★Earl of Bedford

★Mr. Stephen Bender (real
  and imagined)

★Sir Henry Bennet

★Matron Margaret Blague

Sir Everard Blithman

Gregory Blithman

Helene Blithman

Aubrey Blithman

Lady Margery Blithman

Farmer Blount

*Thomas Bloodworth,
  Lord Mayor of London
  late 1665–1666

Mr. Brogan

*William Boghurst

*Christopher Bowman

*Elizabeth Bowman

*Robert Boyle

*John Bradshaw

*Anne Brewster

*Thomas Brewster

Widow Cecily Brickstowe

*Alexander Brome

*General Browne

Captain Jake Browning

*Dr. Alexander Burnet

*Elizabeth Calvert

*Giles Calvert

Cara

*Sir George Carteret

*Lady Barbara
  Castlemaine

*Queen Catherine of
  Braganza

*Sir Robert Catesby

*Margaret Cavendish,
  Duchess of Newcastle
  upon Tyne

*King Charles I

*King Charles II

*William Chiffinch

*Earl of Clarendon

*John Cole

Conrad

Harry Cooper

*Peter Crabb

*Lord Craven

*Mr. Creed

Barbara Crew

*Reginald Crew

*James Croft

*Oliver Cromwell

Davey

Filip de la Faya

*Solomon de la Faya

*Antonio Colmenero de
  Ledema

Master Denis

Dorcas

Simon Dover

*Sir George Downing

*John Dryden

Master Dunstan

*John Evelyn

*Thomas Farriner

*Thomas Flint

Frances

*George Fox

*Jane, Samuel Pepys's
    maid

Jed Franklin

Jerome

*Thomas Gage

Robert Gilligan

Peter Goddard

*Grace

*Sir Thomas Gresham

*Charles Hart

*Thomas Hater

William Henderson

Mr. Hershey

Hilary

*Thomas Hobbes

Hodge

*Dr. Nathaniel Hodges

*Thomas Hollier, Samuel
    Pepys's surgeon

Hugh

*Anne Hyde, Duchess of
    York

*James, the Duke of York

*Edward Hyde, Lord
    Chancellor

*Henry Ireton

Kit

*Betty Lane

Captain William Lark

*Dean of Westminster

*Sir John Lawrence, Lord
    Mayor of London
    1664–1665

*Roger L'Estrange

Lewis

*William Lilly

Matthew Lovelace

*Richard Lovelace

Grant McSearle

Lucy

Reverend Madoc

Ben Miller

*John Milton

*General George Monck

*Morat the Great

*Richard Mortimer,
  chocolate maker

*Henry Muddiman

*James Nayler

Mr. Nessuno

*Thomas Newcombe

*Sir Edward Nichols

Mr. Nick

*Sir Thomas Ogle

Otway

Owen

*Sir William Penn

*Elizabeth Pepys

*Samuel Pepys

*King Philip of Spain

*Francis Potter

Ralph

Mr. Remney

Isaac Roberts

Robin

*Governor Robinson

Clementine Rochford

Mister Rohan

*Pasqua Rosée

Rosie

*Prince Rupert

*Lord Sandwich

*Countess of Sandwich

*William Scott

*Sir Charles Sedley

*Mr. Shepley

Silvester

Wat Smithyman

*John Starkey MP

*Frances Stewart

*Henry Stubbe

Timothy

Tolerance

Rosamund Tomkins

Lady Ellinor Tomkins

Sir Jon Tomkins

*Thomas Tosier

*John Twyn

*Mr. Unthank, Elizabeth
  Pepys's tailor

*George Villiers, Duke of
  Buckingham

*Captain Wadsworth
The Wellses (tailors)
*Samuel Wilcox
*Will, Sam's servant
Isaac Roberts

*Joseph Williamson
*John Wilmot, second Earl
  of Rochester
Wolstan
Zeal

Acknowledgments

O nce more, I come to one of my favorite parts of writing a book. This is where I get to acknowledge the people who have supported, inspired, championed, been there for (or politely avoided) me while I write. I've said this before, and I will say it again: while there is usually one author, a book is a collaboration in so many unforeseen ways, and now I get to thank each and every one of those who either wittingly or unwittingly helped me while I wrote this one.

First and foremost, I have to thank my dazzling, funny, stylish, kind and oh-so-insightful agent and beloved friend, Selwa Anthony. An advocate of this book from the moment I explained my idea, she not only vanquished my crippling doubts as I wrote (and wrote, deleted, wrote and deleted), but when it was complete and she read it, advised me on where it might be tweaked/altered and thus strengthened. Bolstering me with calls through long, lonely stretches of writing, giving me confidence and inspiration, she was a complete marvel, over and beyond any call of duty. I owe her such a debt of gratitude and love, moreso because she also did this during what's been an intense and seriously unpleasant time for her. One of my writer friends described Selwa as a fairy godmother. That's so apt. I don't know what I did to deserve you in my life, Selwa—and Linda, Brian and the sweet furbies—but you are there spreading your love and fairy dust, and I (and many others) am so thankful.

I also want to take this opportunity to thank the entire team at Mira/Harlequin/HarperCollins. Not only did I luck out with my agent, but with my publisher as well—what fantastic people and such a pleasure to work with. From the lovely Michelle LaForest, who, from the moment I told her the title of my book, expressed such enthusiasm and positivity for the project, to the beautiful Sue Brockhoff, who has always been such a rock and support, as well as one of the hardest-working and kindest people I know, and whom I'm proud to call friend. Then there's Jo Mackay, another fabulous support and literary advocate; James Kellow; Adam van Rooijen; and Annabel Blay, who is as clever and creative as she is kind and understanding. I also want to thank Natika Palka, campaign manager at Harlequin.

To my U.S. agent, Jim Frenkel, thank you—for your wonderful, chatty emails, your enthusiasm for my work and your unstinting consideration. Thanks as well to the terrific Catherine Pfeifer. The superb team at William Morrow in the US, from my editor Rachel Kahan, another great champion of my work, to Rachel's assistant, Alivia Lopez; Julia Meltzer, the production editor; publicist Libby Collins; Alicia Tatone and Mumtaz Mustafa, the art directors who created the beautiful package in which this story comes; Amelia Wood for marketing; and Jennifer Hart, the paperback publisher, who was responsible for so much, as well all deserve a huge thanks for their encouragement and support.

My Australian editor, Linda Funnell, is a gift that keeps on giving and I'm blessed she's been given to me. She understands how to make a story stronger, tighter and so much better, and, having worked with me on my last three novels, she understands what I'm trying to accomplish. I thank her for all the effort she's put into this book.

I also want to wholeheartedly thank my proofreader, Sarah J. H. Fletcher. Having had the great pleasure and fortune to work with Sarah before (on my the Curse of the Bond Rider series), I know what a sharp eye and keen sense of story she has and was so damn lucky to have her work on this book. I hope I get to work with you again, Sarah. It's been an utter joy.

I also want to thank my beloved and dearest friend, Kerry Doyle. Kerry is one of the few "test" readers to whom I pass an early complete draft of my novels and who feeds back to me, honestly, what she thinks. This is a terrible burden to place upon a friend, who must put aside fears of bruising an ego and undertake the task at hand. Kerry always does it with such grace, thoughtfulness and veracity. Her acumen and suggestions are always insightful.

Furthermore, Kerry and her gorgeous husband (and my darling friend as well), Peter Goddard, traveled with me and Stephen around the U.K. and Europe in the second half of 2017 for almost six weeks where, if we weren't dragging them to breweries and distilleries (for my husband Stephen's work-related stuff), they were being pulled into an endless stream of museums, churches, ruins, bookshops and strange byways for my research. They stood by while I sometimes asked embarrassing (endless) questions or threw in their own and made the most stupendous recommendations about places I might want to go and things we might want to see as I fact-checked and story hunted. Over many, many kilometers, through all kinds of weather, drinks, food, and in and out of more bars than I care to (or can) remember and interactions with incredibly knowledgeable and generous people, we had the best of times. Their goodwill, humor and friendship mean the world to me. A person cannot ask for better or more loving friends—they're incomparable, as is the love I bear them both. Thank you, my lovelies. Thank you.

While I am over the other side of the world, I want to again thank David Gottlier from Bowler and Hatte, my intrepid and fabulous guide who wandered all over Restoration London with me and patiently answered my questions and added his own erudite observations.

I want to say another thank you to Dr. Peter Jones, a Tasmanian scholar whose work, guidance and conversations were invaluable.

And thanks to Drew Keys for reading the manuscript and for his kindness, support when I was down and consistent belief.

To Mark Nicholson (Mr. Nick) and Robin—you are such treasures—thank you both so very much. I outline in the Author's Note just what a boon you both were. And Mr. Nick, a quiet little shout-out to you for planting the seed (or should that be preparing the bait?) for my next novel . . .

Gav Jaeger and Jason Greatbatch, two dear friends, thank you for your support, and Gav (who was a paramedic for many years) for sharing your vast medical knowledge with me, particularly about strokes and heart attacks—something about which I wish you personally knew less.

I also must thank Dr. Elizabeth Griffin for giving me the idea and information around Sir Everard's ailment.

I also want to thank some more friends who weren't always aware how much their earnest and enthusiastic inquiries about how my writing was going and invitations to coffee, drinks, dinners and getaways (accepted and refused) were so very much appreciated, who showed nothing but compassion and/or understanding when I declined or was withdrawn or depressed about my writing prowess. You are all the very best of people and I love you dearly. Thank you, my beautiful neighbors, friends and all-around magical people, Bill, Lyn, David and Jack Lark, who have supported me and all my books from the get-go; so blessed to have you in my life. My gorgeous friends, Christina Schultness, Mike Crew, Clinton and Rosie Steele, Simon Thomson and Lucinda Wilkins (Lucy), the lovely Emma, Robbie and Harvey Gilligan, Dr. Kiarna, Chris, Jake and Samuel Brown, Dr. Frances Thiele, Dr. Lisa Hill, Professor Jim McKay,

Dr. Helen Johnson, Dr. Liz Ferrier, Professor David Rowe, Dr. Janine Mikosa, Bentley Deegan, Tim and Jess Byrne, Mimi McIntyre and Hamish, Mark Woodland, the friends of Captain Bligh's (our) Brewery—so many of whom, when I'm pouring them drinks at our monthly bar, astonish me by leaning over and whispering, "How's the book coming along?" much to my delight and chagrin. I also have to thank Jenny Farrell for being the best sister ever, my stepmother, Moira Adams, and my former editor at the newspaper where I'm a weekly columnist, Margaret Wenham.

Sheryl Gwyther; Dannielle Miller; Dr. Kim Wilkins; Terry and Rebecca Moles; Wendy Moles; Mick and Katri Dubois; Fiona Inch; the staff at the IASH at the University of Queensland, where I am an Honorary Senior Research Fellow; Karalynne Redknapp; my loyal, smart and encouraging Facebook friends on my author page—thank you. To those whom I'm terrified I'm inadvertently excluding—but only from these pages, not from my heart—forgive me. I do thank you as well.

I also want to thank my still very much missed soul sister and inspiration, Sara Douglass.

And thank you too, my big-hearted, patient readers. Without you, there'd be no purpose to what I do. And thank you to the bookshops and libraries, bloggers and book clubs, who foster writers, books and lovers of reading. You are the gatekeepers of stories and culture, and I'm so grateful. Where would any of us be without you?

As crazy as it sounds, I also want to give a shout-out to my four-legged companions. Day after day, my beautiful, loving and beloved dogs sit with me as I write—thank you, Dante, Tallow and Bounty. My furry muses.

Which leads me to the last thank-yous. First, I want to thank the man to whom this book is dedicated, Stephen Bender. You may note he is a character in the book. I hope Stephen understands this is my way of paying tribute to him and what he means to our family. Stephen first wandered into our brewery looking for something to do in retirement a few years ago, and basically he never left—and thank goodness for that. A former career Army officer and then a criminal prosecutor for many years, Stephen has always fought the good fight. He brought not only love and friendship into our lives, but many great conversations, unwavering support, loyalty and an acumen borne of years of incredible experiences. While some of these would have broken many a person, they've simply made this man not only stronger, but kinder, more compassionate, less tolerant of fools and just an all-around beaut bloke whose integrity shines in everything he does. We often butt political heads, have the most frank and meandering conversations about anything and everything, grump to each other, tease, but most of all, laugh. I love this man like a big brother. Dedicating this book to him is a very small token of the deep affection I bear for him and a public acknowledgment of the important part he plays in mine and my Stephen's lives.

Thank you, Lieutenant-Colonel Bender—love you dearly, sir.

If it wasn't for the unwavering faith, humor, intelligence and challenges posed—and often—by my fantastic adult children, Adam and Caragh, none of my novels would ever see the light of day. They keep me grounded, elevated, frustrated, anxious and proud in equal measure, and I adore them. It's hard to have a writer as a parent because in many ways, they've not always there, but divided between their lexical children, the inventions of their mind, and their real flesh-and-blood ones, who aren't anywhere near so demanding. Thank you, my best creations—for supporting this exasperating and yet wonderfully fulfilling thing I cannot help but do.

Which leads me to the other person without whom, not only would I not be able to write a word, but my life would be utterly incomplete. Stephen Brooks, my love, my heart, my life. The man who knows me better sometimes than I know myself and who is there for all the triumphs and disappointments. Who picks me up when self-doubt paralyzes me, brushes me off, dries my eyes, gives me pep and other kinds of important talks, makes cups of coffee and hot chocolate, pours glasses of wine or whisky and pushes me back toward my desk. Together, we laugh, cry, despair, celebrate, make and pour beers and other beverages and dream. Always there, he also understands why I sometimes don't hear him, wander away to my computer midsentence, stay awake into the wee hours writing, reading or thinking, gaze dreamily out the window or toward the sky, look at him without seeing him. He's never jealous of the Matthews, Leanders, Nathaniels and other men and beautiful women who take me away from him but embraces them and the myriad other children of my imagination who share our crazy, loving and fantastic world.

I love you, Stephen Brooks—thank you from the bottom of my very full heart. Like all my books, my so-very-sweet man, *The Chocolate Maker's Wife* is for you.

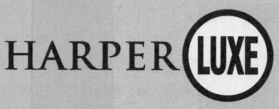

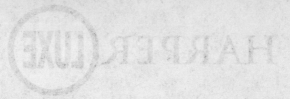